Jane Eyre's Husband
The Life of Edward Rochester

Tara Bradley

Based on Charlotte Brontë's Classic Novel

Copyright © 2007 Tara Bradley

All rights reserved. No part of this book may be reproduced or transmitted without the written permission of the author, except where permitted by law.

ISBN-13: 978-1463670191

ISBN-10: 1463670192

Cover Layout by Ray Radigan

www.facebook.com/janeeyreshusband
http://sites.google.com/site/janeeyreshusband/

Contents

Part One

Prologue 1
Chapter 1 - Another Boy 3
Chapter 2 - Elizabeth's Son 11
Chapter 3 - Losing Elizabeth 15
Chapter 4 - Edward and Grace 22
Chapter 5 - Grace Poole 28
Chapter 6 - Edward Returns 37
Chapter 7 - Jamaica 52
Chapter 8 - Mr. and Mrs. Rochester 66
Chapter 9 - Four Years 75
Chapter 10 - A Nurse for Bertha 84
Chapter 11 - Céline 93
Chapter 12 - In Love 99
Chapter 13 - Pregnancy 105
Chapter 14 - The Fillette 111
Chapter 15 - Betrayal 116
Chapter 16 - Leaving Paris 125
Chapter 17 - Pilot 129
Chapter 18 - Letters and Visits 135
Chapter 19 - Will-o'-the-wisp 142
Chapter 20 - Giacinta 148
Chapter 21 - The Message 154
Chapter 22 - Back to Paris 160
Chapter 23 - Taking Adèle to Thornfield 164
Chapter 24 - Vienna 170
Chapter 25 - Clara 176
Chapter 26 - Heart-Weary and Soul-Withered 183

Part Two

Chapter 27 - The Governess 193
Chapter 28 - Jane 199
Chapter 29 - At the Leas 206
Chapter 30 - The House Party 212
Chapter 31 - Gypsies and Uninvited Guests 219
Chapter 32 - Mason 231
Chapter 33 - A Month Without Jane 239

Chapter 34 - Marry Me 245
Chapter 35 - Confiding in Mr. Carter 251
Chapter 36 - Before the Wedding 262
Chapter 37 - The Wedding 272
Chapter 38 - After the Wedding 277
Chapter 39 - What Will I Do, Jane, If You Leave Me? 282
Chapter 40 - All Happiness Torn Away 289
Chapter 41 - Fire at Thornfield Hall 300
Chapter 42 - Alive, but Sadly Hurt 307
Chapter 43 - Better to Be Dead 315
Chapter 44 - Tenacious of Life 327
Chapter 45 - The Road to Ferndean 334
Chapter 46 - Phantom Pain 341
Chapter 47 - Voices in the Night 346
Chapter 48 - Sweet Madness 349
Chapter 49 - I Am Come Back to You 353
Chapter 50 - Jane, Will You Marry Me? 360
Chapter 51 - Reader, She Married Me 364
Chapter 52 - With My Body, I Thee Worship... 369

Part Three

Chapter 53 - Lost Without You 381
Chapter 54 - Sight Restored 395
Chapter 55 - His Father's Eyes 417
Chapter 56 - The Rochesters 432
Chapter 57 - Grace Restored 445
Chapter 58 - Adèle Demands the Truth 457
Chapter 59 - Adèle's Engagement 471
Chapter 60 - Nothing Without You 476
Chapter 61 - Through the Valley of the Shadow 484
Chapter 62 - From Mrs. Rochester to Mrs. Fitzjames 496
Chapter 63 - The Rochester Children 501
Chapter 64 - Off to School 508
Chapter 65 - Letters to Loved Ones 515
Chapter 66 - A Wedding in the Family 522
Chapter 67 - The Rochester Line Goes On 530
Chapter 68 - I Shall But Love Thee Better After Death 535
Epilogue 548

Author's Note 559
Acknowledgements 560

Jane Eyre's Husband

Prologue

January, 1836

Evening had come and dusk spread its lengthening shadows over the English countryside as the three travellers made their way home.

Two of them – one a large black and white dog, and the other, a huge black horse – did not know that they were headed for home. For years they had journeyed with the man who now rode on the horse's back. Often they had all run together as they did tonight; sometimes they travelled by ship, and occasionally the horse ran alongside a carriage while the man and the dog rode inside. But they always ended in a different place and it was all the same to them.

The man was headed to his home, but had none of the eager anticipation usually found in one who has come to the end of a trip to rest in a beloved place.

Thornfield Hall had been the home of his family since long before he had come to own it. He had been born in one of the manor's many bedchambers, as had nearly everyone in the family before him. But Edward Rochester felt nothing except the heavy hand of dread upon him as he pulled on the reins and spurred Mesrour in the right direction. He recognized the borders of his land through the gloom, glimpsed the hedgerows that separated his rich fields, and saw his tenants' homes, where cheerful plumes of smoke rose from stone chimneys.

He had not notified his servants that he would be arriving. It did not matter, for whether he was present or absent his home was run as though he might appear at any time. All his life, he had had only to say, "Do this," and it was done. He wore his arrogance as he wore his own skin, so naturally that no thought was given to his right to it.

His servants were at his home but he gave them little thought unless they failed to meet his needs. His housekeeper, a relative by marriage of his late mother's, meant little to him until her chatter began to wear on his nerves. An eight-year-old girl watched and hoped every day for his return, but he gave her little conscious thought either. She was not his child, only another obligation that he had to meet.

Rochester was thirty-seven years old, a fairly young man still, and yet he no longer believed that life had anything fresh and new to give him. He was headed home only because his business demanded it. He had left nothing he cared about behind him and he travelled towards nothing that mattered.

He flicked his whip lightly against his horse's flank and gripped its sides with his thighs, the muscles rock-hard from over thirty years of almost daily riding. He was a man of average height, but when seated appeared much larger, with his broad shoulders and powerful chest. He was an athlete, restless and active, with an equally active mind.

He was not a particularly handsome man. He was black-haired, dark-eyed and stern, when the fashion of the day was for the fair, the graceful, and the light-hearted. No one would look at Edward Rochester and think of him as light-hearted. An observer would have been surprised by the humour and the sweetness of manner that had once been his, and still was, though now it was hidden deep beneath his sardonic exterior. Only someone discerning would see past his glowering appearance and his sarcasm, and in recent years he had not moved in circles known for their attention to internal things. That he was wealthy, accomplished, and possessed of a fine old name was enough to satisfy the requirements of those with whom he associated. There had been no need for anyone to take the time to discover whatever beauty lay within him.

Externally, Edward Rochester had only two beautiful characteristics – one was on constant display, but the other was something he rarely showed. The first was his eyes: they were large and brilliant, such a deep brown that the pupils could not be discerned from the irises. Framed by thick black lashes, his eyes flashed and snapped with life and expression, yet were capable of warmth and tenderness and depth of feeling.

The other beauty he possessed was in his smile, and he hardly ever let it be seen. Oh, he had a social smile, quick and cold, that never extended to his eyes. It was just a momentary change in the shape of his firm mouth; in repose, his face was serious, with an expression that could even be mistaken for ill-temper. But when one of his rare genuine smiles touched him, his entire face altered. It lit up from within, making his rock-like features almost handsome. One who happened to see the transformation could warm instantly to him, even if a moment previously they had dismissed him as a dark-humoured martinet.

His appearance was the last thing on his mind as he headed down the road near his home. He thought only of how he could accelerate the expected ceremony that would accompany his return so that he could retire to a light meal, a glass of port before a roaring fire, and his warm, comfortable bed.

He barely had time to register the sight of a child standing by the side of the road when he felt Mesrour falter and stumble, then begin to slide as his iron-shod hooves hit an unexpected patch of ice in the road. The horse fell heavily to one side, causing Edward's foot to slip in the stirrup and wrench as his leg was caught between the animal and the frozen earth of the causeway.

Mesrour attempted to right himself, requiring Edward to move quickly to extricate his foot from the stirrup before it was further strained by the weight of his nervous mount. Furious, he released a torrent of curses as he worked himself free from his horse.

He leaned over and gingerly tested the extent of his injury and as he did so, he became aware that the child standing nearby had come over to him and was asking him if he was hurt. He looked up at her – no, not a child, a young woman, so small he could understand his initial impression. He doubted that she was a full five feet tall, but her shape, though slender, was that of a woman, not a child. She wore a black merino cloak and a black bonnet, and the slightness of her figure was at variance with the maturity and gravity of her face.

She reached out to him, her eyes large and filled with concern, "If you are hurt, sir," she said, "I will be glad to fetch you some help, from Hay or from where I live."

He frowned at her, trying to place her among those he remembered in this area, "And where might that be?"

She gestured with her outstretched hand, "At Thornfield Hall."

Chapter 1 - Another Boy

When the lusty cry of the healthy male infant sounded through the second level of Thornfield Hall that cold evening in January 1799, one would have expected it to be an occasion of great happiness in the Rochester family. But for all the excitement and exclamations among the staff at the birth, the family members themselves looked on the event with little real joy.

For the baby's exhausted mother, her relief at having given birth was overshadowed by her disappointment that she had delivered another son instead of the daughter she had wanted. She looked at the red, screaming, black-haired child the midwife held up and could barely manage a smile before she closed her eyes and fell into sleep. The infant's father, summoned later, looked without expression upon his second son, giving a nod and a grunt of acknowledgement before he moved over to confer with the surgeon regarding his wife's condition.

John Rochester was the owner of Thornfield Hall, and now the father of two sons, Rowland, and the as-yet-unnamed infant now receiving his first bath at the hands of his wife's maid. He cared about only two things in life: Thornfield Hall and the fortune that accompanied it. He feared only those things which threatened either one.

He had an affection for his older son, the heir to his beloved Thornfield. The sole thought in his mind now as he looked at his second son was that the newborn would be a drain on the family fortune, which would ultimately have to be apportioned to provide for both sons. This unavoidable diminution of his cherished estate was an event far in the future, but the mere contemplation of it bothered John Rochester greatly.

For eight-year-old Rowland Rochester, the idea of a sister had not been an unpleasant one. He imagined an adorable baby – a small pet to lavish attention on as he desired – and this was an appealing thought. It would not matter that a sister would occupy his mother's time, as Rowland had given his mother little thought since early childhood, preferring the riding and outdoor pursuits so favoured by his father. But the idea of another boy in the family, someone whose mere existence would take attention away from him, disturbed Rowland, and it was with little grace that he took this news, stomping angrily to his room and slamming the door.

Less than an hour after the difficult birth, the baby's mother suffered a hemorrhage that nearly resulted in her death. The surgeon was hastily summoned back, and the midwife used her every skill in the meantime to preserve the mother's life. Her life was spared, but Elizabeth Rochester was very ill and would remain so for weeks to come.

The newborn was separated from his family and turned over to the wet nurse who had been engaged some time before, for even a healthy gentleman's wife would not nurse her own infant. Thus, the second son of the Rochester family began his life.

John Rowland Rochester was himself the only surviving child of his generation of the Rochester family, and the undisputed heir to Thornfield Hall, all the farms and fields surrounding it, and the wealth and prestige that accompanied it. He gave no thought to what it must have meant to his own mother to have all but one child die, the others lost to stillbirth, infant death, or childhood illness.

John Rochester believed that God in His infinite wisdom had ordained him as the rightful owner of Thornfield Hall, and that all was as it should be. He presided over his small kingdom – not royal, not noble – just gentry; but John Rochester believed that he had been rightfully born to his position of wealth and class. He would go to his death feeling that he and God had an understanding: that the Almighty would look with approval upon whatever assured the continued prosperity and position of the Rochester family of Thornfield Hall.

John Rochester made a formidable master. He was not a tall man, but powerfully built. His brown hair had a touch of red in the sunlight, and his brown eyes were of a russet shade as well. Until his later years, when intemperate living gave him a high colour that spoke of impending apoplexy, he was considered a rather handsome man.

He lacked grace on the dance floor, but made up for it when he swung into the saddle to lead a neighbourhood hunt. He lived for the hunt, for riding and shooting, for the outdoor life so prized by gentlemen of his day. He had an excellent estate manager and conferred with him when necessary, but did not like anything that kept him too long indoors.

In his late twenties, John Rochester realized that it was time he choose a wife and beget an heir to his flourishing estate. He had grown up with the Dents, the Eshtons, and the Ingrams of the neighbouring estates, and although among these fine families there were several ladies he could have considered, none of them appealed to him.

If the truth were told, he appealed to none of the ladies either. They had long known his arrogance, his high-handed ways, and none were willing to put up with what was required, not even to be the mistress of Thornfield Hall.

It is not to be thought that John Rochester lacked for feminine companionship. In his late teens, with the help of his own father, he engaged the first of many mistresses. He was careful also not to risk squandering any of his wealth paying for the care and upkeep of illegitimate children. Along with the service his father had provided in taking him to see one of his cast-off mistresses to introduce his son to the pleasures of the flesh, he had pulled him aside to tell him in the frankest terms how to avoid impregnating any of his women.

"It may be difficult, son, to pull it out, but it's even more painful to pull out your pocketbook every month and give over your money to pay for your bastard brats." Putting it in financial terms brought to John Rochester the seriousness of the issue, and whether through luck or careful thought, he could say that he had never been embarrassed with having to account for a by-blow. He was not sure that his own father could say the same.

He was discreet, generous – and quick to release himself from any woman who appeared to be growing too domestically inclined. Most of his liaisons were with older women – some married, some widowed and living comfortably. He saved his inclination for younger women for his search for a wife, and at the age of eight-and-twenty, his patience was rewarded.

The Reverend Fairfax and his wife Alice had come to Hày to minister to the small congregation of the village church. They were a young couple who had not been blessed with children, and they missed their large extended family when they moved to take the parish which included Thornfield Hall.

The Reverend Fairfax was the third son of a fine family, and he had been obliged to embrace the church when his oldest brother had inherited the family estate and the second brother joined the Army. There was very little money, but they were a happy couple, and they were pleased to have their niece, Elizabeth, the daughter of Reverend Fairfax's oldest brother, pay them a visit a few months after their arrival in Hay.

Elizabeth Fairfax was seventeen, a tall, dreamy girl with a mass of black curls and large, deep, almost black eyes. She was pretty in a somewhat Spanish way, although there was no Spanish blood in her that she knew of. She was an intelligent girl, a reader, and her parents despaired of marrying her off. With her shy and scholarly nature, her parents expected to have her in their home the rest of her life.

She loved stories of knights and chivalry, of Arthur's Round Table, of Guinevere and Lancelot; of the majesty of the court of King Edward III, with its Order of the Garter, its pageantry and feasts. She was a romantic, having no desire to marry until she too could find a knight to strive for her hand.

But practicality intruded, and she knew that, with several younger siblings, at least one of them had to marry well. Her father had inherited an estate, but there was some financial imprudence there, and with other children to provide for, the Fairfaxes could not claim to be rich. And so when her Uncle Fairfax extended his invitation, and casually mentioned the single owner of the nearby manor, Miss Fairfax was not entirely reluctant to go.

John Rochester made the acquaintance of Miss Elizabeth Fairfax one Sunday morning shortly after she had come to stay with her aunt and uncle. He was immediately attracted to what he considered her dark, mysterious beauty. Her extreme youth was also a point in her favour, as was her quiet nature, which he mistook for submission to male authority.

For her part, she found Rochester appealing as he galloped across the green fields that surrounded beautiful Thornfield Hall. She could almost imagine him in a suit of armor, her scarf flying on his lance as he smiled gallantly at her before heading down the lists.

For John Rochester, eager to find an accommodating wife of childbearing age, the quiet Miss Fairfax seemed perfect. For Elizabeth, romantic and unworldly, the rich, athletic, dashing John Rochester seemed matchless as well.

Rochester appreciated the fine old name of Fairfax and the accomplishments of the family, although compared to him, the Fairfaxes were relatively impoverished. Despite his avaricious nature, he did not mind that his intended bride could bring only a thousand pounds to the marriage. He was wealthy and felt that her youth and beauty were compensation enough.

He travelled to her home to meet her parents and ask for her hand, and while he travelled, took notice of a small estate in the area which he thought would do for a hunting lodge. It was called Ferndean, and it was nestled deep in a wood, an excellent game cover for the dedicated sportsman. He negotiated for both the girl and the estate in the same time period, and as his life went on, he would be hard pressed to decide which had been the better investment.

John Rochester married the young Elizabeth Fairfax in the village church at Hay, two months after they were introduced. She was delivered of a son, as her husband boasted loudly, "Nine months and twenty minutes later." Overhearing the remark, his appalled wife still had to chuckle bitterly to herself at the notion of an entire twenty minutes (although privately, she was glad that none of his coarse and sweaty fumblings lasted anywhere near that long).

Elizabeth Rochester lost her romantic notions soon after the wedding, but she carried a deep vein of loving passion which she would later pass on to her second son. In the hands of a patient and affectionate husband, that passion could have been fully expressed. But John Rochester approached the marriage bed the way he approached the hunt, with an eye only towards speed and victory. He knew no better – the mistresses who were financially dependent upon him were loath to correct him, and his young bride was completely innocent. Ultimately her potential gave way to the bitterness of passion denied, and by the time their first son was born, all pretence of love had disappeared.

She had actually been relieved to find herself with child so soon, knowing it would bring an end to what she had at first found unspeakably disgusting. All her dreamings of love, all her romantic reading, had not prepared her for the shock of the actual physical side of marriage.

Her husband was glad of her pregnancy, pleased to accomplish so soon what had been his goal. He returned to his mistress, hoping for the best for his young wife, but giving her very little thought in the course of his day. Her virgin shyness, so appealing on their wedding night, soon bored him, and first her revulsion, and then her indifference, every time he entered her bedchamber made him relieved that he was able to impregnate her quickly, and so have done with the business.

Mrs. Rochester safely delivered a boy, who was named John Rowland after his father, but thereafter called by his middle name. She held the baby before turning him over to his wet nurse for his first feeding, but she felt completely unconnected to the child, who was a miniature of his father – the same light brown hair and eyes.

She tried to be a loving mother, visiting the nursery daily, taking her child for walks, and reading to him, but young Rowland seemed only to want his father. As he grew, he was fascinated with the trappings of his father's life: the dogs, the horses, the guns. From the time he could toddle, he followed his father, refusing to sit still for his mother's stories and quiet games. At the age of three, he received his first pony and riding lessons, and soon wanted to gallop everywhere his father went, eventually protesting bitterly when he was made to come in and attend to his schoolwork.

The life Rowland's parents led was similar to the lives of the other members of the gentry. Externally, both appeared fairly satisfied. John Rochester spent his time managing his estate and engaging in his outdoor athletics and pursuits, while Elizabeth Rochester occupied herself with social visits, with service on behalf of the poor of the parish, and especially with her books, which she ordered by the box from London. Another woman unfulfilled by her husband might have taken a lover but Elizabeth Rochester could not think of any possible reason to do so. She had no physical desire to do so, nor did she want to risk the only things that gave her any purpose in life – her social position and her husband's wealth.

John Rochester took occasional trips to Ferndean to hunt, accompanied by his current mistress, and later his son. Elizabeth Rochester never accompanied him. Shut off from his life, and the life of her son, who seemed a stranger to her at any rate, she settled into her life as mistress of Thornfield. John Rochester knew he had failed his wife, but he did not care enough about her to determine why, nor what she wished him to do about it. He knew she was repelled by him in her bed, and was glad to stay in his separate bedroom and pursue his separate interests for the most part, although he still reserved the right to come to her if he wished. He was discreet in his visits to his lady friends, not wishing to humiliate his wife, and Elizabeth was appreciative of his consideration in that respect.

Elizabeth was an obedient wife, and therefore acquiesced to John's occasional exercise of his marital rights, generally when he was between mistresses. She knew that it was part of the bargain she had made back when she married, and while she never grew to enjoy it, she was able to tolerate the infrequent occasions when her husband made his visits to her bedchamber. It was as a result of one of these visits that she realized she was once again with child, in the early summer of 1798. Having not conceived again for so many years after Rowland was born, Elizabeth was extremely surprised at first, and not totally happy about it at the beginning, although she grew used to the idea.

Rowland Rochester was by now about seven years old, and he had long ceased to want to spend much time with her. Once his mother realized that her second pregnancy was a reality, she began to think that perhaps another child would make her empty life more enjoyable. She thought of how nice it would be to have a daughter, a little girl to take care of. A child who would love her, remain with her, talk to her and allow herself to be read to. By the time she went to her husband to tell him that they would be having another child in mid-winter, she was beginning to look forward to a new baby in the home.

If John Rochester was not pleased by her news, neither was he upset. Every parent lived with the unhappy awareness of childhood mortality. Having another child would at least help ensure that the Rochester lineage would continue.

His only concern was that if the child should happen to be a boy, it would present problems of inheritance later on. Rochester did not like the idea of dividing his wealth between two sons, diluting the power of Thornfield, even if he would be dead when it happened. But both Rochesters felt that they would have a girl – Elizabeth because she felt God would take pity on her miserable life and grant her desire, and John because he felt God could surely see how much better it would be for the Rochesters if there were only one son to claim the inheritance.

As Elizabeth had the first time, she carried the child with a minimum of bother, feeling quite well and eager to have her daughter. She planned to name the child after herself, calling her Beth, or Betsy, names she wished she had been called instead of the more serious and formal "Elizabeth".

When she was pressed for a name for a boy, she brushed off the idea. Her son was named after his father, as he should be, and as the time for the birth grew closer, her husband urged her to consider her father's name, or the name of the uncle who introduced them. She did not like those ideas. Neither of those men had cared for anything but marrying her off, never mind the unhappiness that would follow, and she did not want to honour them by naming a child after them.

Her husband insisted the name should be chosen by her. So she thought of the old stories she had always liked, the romantic stories of heroes and chivalry. She no longer believed in romance, was not even sure she believed in love anymore, but those stories had once brought her great happiness.

She rejected her first choice – there were just too many "R's" in Arthur Rochester. So she thought of her next favourite heroes – the brave and heroic Edward III, and his son Edward, the Black Prince. *Edward Rochester*. She let her husband know. That name would suit just fine, and if all went as she hoped, it would not be needed.

Elizabeth Rochester entered her confinement in the second week of January, which in truth she rather enjoyed for then she could lie in bed and catch up on her reading. Other than her servants, she saw no one in the course of her day but her husband and son, who paid her an awkward visit each morning to inquire after her health.

It was January nineteenth, a cold, bleak afternoon, when she felt the first mild contractions, and before long her labour had begun. It progressed fairly quickly and the midwife assured her that she would be holding her daughter in her arms before it was full dark.

It was only after she had been pushing for over an hour that the midwife realized that things were not going as well as she had hoped. She turned her patient in several positions, checking the infant's lie from several angles on the outside of the abdomen, before she realized with a sinking heart that the child was not in an optimum placement for delivery. The surgeon was hastily summoned, and he too, realized that the patient could go on straining in vain without succeeding in delivering the baby.

He did not confer with Mrs. Rochester, but instead went into the hall to speak with her husband. The surgeon felt that no labouring woman was in a condition to decide her own treatment, that the husband and father should be the one to decide what course to follow. He and John Rochester conferred in low and serious tones before he re-entered the room, having been told to do whatever was needed to save the life of Mrs. Rochester, at the expense of the child if need be.

He informed the tiring and terrified patient that the baby was not turned properly, that he would need to perform a series of internal manipulations to attempt delivery. Elizabeth nodded, her black eyes huge with fear. She knew only too well, as did every pregnant woman, what the surgeon's bag contained – the crochets, the small knives and saws, and to what ghastly use they would be put if he could not succeed in turning the infant and delivering it normally.

What neither her husband nor the surgeon knew was that Elizabeth had no intention of letting him do anything beyond the norm to deliver this child, that she had no wish to live if her child had to be sacrificed for her to do so. She was prepared to get up and leave the bed if need be rather than let the doctor reach into his bag for so much as one instrument.

She lay back, submitting to his manipulations with a white-faced silence that the midwife and servants found more frightening than the situation itself. Fortunately, once the surgeon had done some reaching and turning, he realized that the situation was not hopeless, and the stoicism of his patient made his work easier. He was able to grasp the infant's feet and pull them down, enabling the rest of the body to be delivered. It still took some work on the part of the mother, but she was able to finish the delivery.

Partway through the delivery, with the child coming feet first, it was Elizabeth Rochester's maid who first realized that the coming infant was a boy rather than the girl her mistress had wanted. She whispered intently to the midwife, who cut in loudly as the doctor began to announce the sex of the baby before the child was fully delivered. She was afraid that it would strip the exhausted patient of all remaining energy if she was disappointed now, so she broke in cheerfully, talking some nonsense to distract them all, with an aside frown to the surgeon. The surgeon shook his head in puzzlement over the actions of women, but by then was too absorbed in finishing the delivery.

"This child is almost here now," he told the mother. "Do not strain further; let me do the rest, for it is a delicate business."

Elizabeth Rochester was only too glad to close her eyes and fall back, nearly unconscious with pain and fatigue. She could feel the doctor as he worked, hear the excited voices around her, but she had gone to a far place in her mind, away from what was going on about her. It was through a fog that she heard the first cry of her child, now safely delivered. It was also then that she heard the doctor tell her that she had another son.

It did not seem possible that she had worked so hard, and been prepared to die for her daughter, only to find out that she had another boy. Another male in her life who would neglect her, who would find her so boring and annoying that he would not want to be around her.

The midwife took over from the surgeon, cutting the cord, bringing the crying baby to her side so she could see the results of her hard labours. "Mrs. Rochester, look at this child," the midwife told her intently. She had seen many women like her, usually women who had delivered daughter after daughter while desperately wanting a son. It was rare for a woman to be disappointed in the birth of a boy, and she felt that if this woman could but see her son, feel empathy for his cries, she would instantly love him and her disappointment would end.

Elizabeth Rochester turned her head weakly, noting the large, fine form of the child the midwife held before her. He was black-haired, as she was, and screamed loudly, squirming in the woman's hands. She tried to smile, to assure the midwife that she saw him, but she was too tired. She closed her eyes, and drifted off.

The midwife shook her head, taking the baby over to the waiting maid and to Mrs. Rochester's Aunt Alice Fairfax, both waiting to bathe and wrap the screaming newborn. She and her assistant bathed the patient and covered her after the surgeon had finished and then they fetched the husband to inform him of the safe delivery. She let the surgeon tell John Rochester all that had transpired.

The midwife looked with anxiety at Mrs. Rochester's white face, and palpated her abdomen with worry. She had a nervous feeling about the woman's condition, a worry that was borne out when suddenly the white sheets that covered her were red with gushes of blood. It took all the skill she possessed to stem the flow, calling anxiously for the surgeon to be fetched again from the road on which he had just headed for home.

Elizabeth was in poor condition for days following the delivery, and the household feared for her life even after the terrifying blood flow was staunched. She lay, white and still, occasionally opening her eyes and closing them again without responding to what was around her. The midwife and surgeon came daily until she was pronounced out of danger, then a nurse was engaged to tend to her physical needs as she lay there, too weak to even move herself in the bed.

John Rochester took over the situation. The child was being cared for by the wet nurse and her family, but his father wanted to have him baptized, and was not willing to wait until his wife could recover sufficiently to go to the church.

Rochester was somewhat superstitious, and felt that it would not do to tempt fate by not christening the child. He remembered that his wife had chosen the name Edward, to which he had no objection, although he could not imagine where it came from. There were no Edwards in the family that he knew of. He went along with his wife's choice, giving the boy his wife's maiden name as a second name, as fit the fashion of the day.

"Name this child," Rev. Fairfax intoned. John Rochester responded in a clear voice, "Edward Fairfax Rochester." As it was early February, and frigid in the church, Reverend Fairfax did not immerse the infant as was sometimes still done, but instead applied the water from the font onto the child's black hair. A few drops trickled down the baby's head, and he shivered and blinked his huge dark eyes, already so like his mother's even at the age of two weeks. The minister traced the sign of the cross on the child's wet forehead before leading the small group in the prayers for baptism.

Baby Edward fell back to sleep in the arms of the godmother who had been chosen by his father, and after the ceremony Edward was handed back to the wet nurse, who took him back to her home. There was no celebration at Thornfield afterwards, as there had been after the baptism of his brother Rowland. Elizabeth Rochester still lay in her bed upstairs, no longer near death, but too weak to participate.

The newly-baptized Edward Fairfax Rochester, of course, was unaware of any of this. He cared only for the milk that he was fed on a regular basis. Nestled in the wet nurse's arms as she nursed him along with her own six-week-old daughter, he did not know that this woman was paid, and paid well, for feeding him; nor that his real family did not occupy this small farmhouse, but instead the grand manor down the road.

He lay in his cradle near the fire, looking around with his great dark eyes, fussing only when his stomach grew empty again. And so, contented and healthy, he began his life.

Chapter 2 - Elizabeth's Son

It was two months before Elizabeth Rochester was able to get out of bed and move weakly about her bedroom. A pale March sunshine was beginning to slant across the floor, turning the diamond shaped glass sections of the casement windows to prisms and sending small rainbows across the carpet beneath her feet.

The thin, pale woman wrapped herself in a shawl and huddled on a chaise near the fire. Today the wet nurse was to bring the baby to her for the first time, her son Edward, who had represented the last of her dreams.

Elizabeth did not know if her low spirits were due to her illness and lack of activity, or to the realization that nothing in her life had turned out as she had hoped. She was nearly twenty-seven years old, too young to be living a life devoid of hope and passion, yet she felt that was her lot. She was not generally given to depression, but her natural thoughtfulness, added to the life-threatening complications she suffered following Edward's birth, had left her in a state that would have frightened her had she had the energy for fear.

A knock on the door heralded the arrival of the young wet nurse, who carried the Rochester infant in one arm and her own child on the other. Elizabeth did not even know her name; the wet nurse had been interviewed and hired by the estate manager. The woman looked overwhelmed by the richness of the surroundings, dropping an awkward curtsy before handing the baby boy to Elizabeth, who thanked her with a smile.

Elizabeth instructed her maid to take the wet nurse to the kitchen and feed her well, then she turned her attention to her son, who looked pink and well-fed. She was relieved. Their previous wet nurse, she suspected, had fed her own child before she fed Rowland, and he had always seemed fretful and fussy. But Edward looked fat and placid, his plump pink fists balled up near his face as he slept.

She settled him into the crook of her arm and leaned back against the chaise, watching him. She unwrapped the blanket, looking at him, his chubby legs under the lacy linen dress that all infants, male and female, wore until they were over two years old. His thighs were chubby also, although they looked small in proportion to the several huge bulky diapers that were tied around him. He looked well cared for – he was clean, his nails trimmed, his black hair sleek and free of cradle cap. She leaned her cheek against his silky head, feeling his warmth and softness.

Just then, the baby opened his eyes, and she looked into them, large and black just like hers. He blinked several times in the light, and as his face focused on hers, his rosebud mouth opened wide in a large, toothless smile.

As she had not since the last days of her pregnancy, Elizabeth Rochester felt a lightness in her heart, and she bent and kissed her baby son for the first time.

As spring moved slowly into summer, Elizabeth grew stronger, slowly regaining her health. The surgeon had warned her that another pregnancy could kill her, not realizing that she had no intention of ever having another child, no intention of ever getting close enough to her husband that another pregnancy could be a possibility.

The wet nurse, Nellie Carey, brought the baby to Thornfield daily, and it had become the one happy time of Elizabeth's day. Baby Edward thrived, and it soothed his mother's lonely heart to see him so healthy. When he was brought to her, he smiled and eventually began to hold his arms out to her. She would clasp him to her, kissing him, nuzzling his neck to make him laugh out loud. His large dark eyes followed her as she sat him on her lap, played little games with him, and sang to him.

When he was six months old, she brought up the idea of bringing him back home to the large sunny nursery down the hall from her bedroom. John Rochester objected, however, saying it would disrupt the household, disturb her still frail health, confuse the infant. He stated that it would be too difficult for the wet nurse to travel up and down the road each time the baby needed to be fed, and that his crying would throw into disorder the peaceful atmosphere of Thornfield. Many members of the gentry sent their infants away for their early years, he argued, and it never hurt the child. When he was weaned, and could be depended upon to behave, then he could be brought back to live with the family.

Elizabeth was not happy with the arrangement, but could not dispute the logic. Only the thought that it would confuse and upset the baby kept her from marching down to Nellie's home herself and demanding her child. She was willing to walk him back and forth for his feedings herself, but she was still too weak, too easily tired by even the slightest exertion. So she reluctantly acquiesced to the situation and looked forward to his daily visits.

Edward grew strong and vigorous under Nellie's careful nursing and care. She had only the one child, a girl slightly older than Edward, and the two children grew up side by side, playing, squabbling between themselves, crawling up to nurse side by side on Nellie's lap, their hands reaching out to each other as they fed.

Nellie's life was not an easy one. Her husband was one of John Rochester's tenants, but he spent more time drinking and brawling than actually farming, and the money Nellie was paid to nurse baby Edward was more often than not the means of feeding and clothing the family.

Nellie's husband resented his wife for making money, but his feelings did not prevent him from trying to get his hands on the few shillings she made every week and spending it on drink. It took quite a bit of Nellie's ingenuity to keep it away from him long enough to buy a bolt of cloth, or a pound of flour.

Elizabeth Rochester and Nellie Carey were close in age, and equally dissatisfied with their marital situations. As Nellie brought Edward daily to his mother's bedroom, it became natural for the two women to exchange a few words at the beginning and end of each visit. They gradually became more comfortable with each other, and their conversations began to grow more equal, finding a common point in their two children.

Elizabeth began to ring for tea in her room, and the two women would visit, sipping their hot drinks, chatting and laughing until Nellie, sensitive to the limited time Elizabeth had with young Edward, would pick up her daughter and slip from the room to go visit downstairs in the servants' area. Edward would watch after them as they left the room, fussing a little, until his mother distracted him with a game or a little song.

As the months passed, Elizabeth gradually resumed her activities in the parish, although she felt constantly tired. Her once-olive complexion was now sickly pale, and she was quite thin. The other women of their circle noticed it, but were afraid to mention it, as Mrs. Rochester's pride seemed at times to surpass her husband's. She went about her business, with her well-coiffed head held high. If she paused at times to sit, or stopped to fan herself after a sudden dizziness struck her, she made no reference to it, and others learned not to risk her displeasure by acting concerned.

John Rochester and his son Rowland also went about their lives. They sat at dinner, mostly in silence when Elizabeth was present. They would tend to talk loudly about riding, or whether a good season was expected for hunting this year, but Elizabeth's presence at the table seemed to inhibit the natural camaraderie the two shared. She cared nothing for anything the two talked about and no longer pretended to.

Rowland was now ten years old, and a tutor came to the house every day to teach him his lessons. Eventually he would have a live-in tutor, and would someday go away to school, like the sons of all gentlemen. He was a poor scholar, wanting only for his lessons to be done so he could go ride, or fish in the pond on the estate, or walk for miles on the sprawling grounds.

His father, who was no scholar himself, did not mind that his son did not care for learning. Neither did his mother, who had in her mind turned him over to his father for raising. She spoke politely to her older son, even brushed his hair in an occasional caress as she passed him, but she felt like she did not know him. Had she not remembered his birth, she would forget he even came from her. He did not resemble her in the least but was a miniature of John Rochester.

Edward Rochester would grow to be very much like both his parents. He had his mother's dark skin, her black hair and eyes, her serious and intense mien, although he also had a ready smile and his mother's kind nature. In adulthood, he would stand two inches above his father in height, although he would have his father's muscular build, heavier and more powerful than the thin and elegant fashion of his day allowed. He would also have passed down to him his father's athletic inclinations, and his excellence in sport would be one of the only things that would make his father look with favour upon him as he grew to manhood.

Unfortunately, he had also inherited his father's tendency towards arrogance and his total inability to be patient with those who annoyed him. It was perhaps inevitable that he would inherit the pride of both his parents. But Nature, as it is wont to do, endows every human with certain leanings, and Nature meant to make Edward Rochester a good man. No matter how later events would bend and twist his soul, that basic goodness would endure still, and it was that which would someday save him from total ruin.

Edward walked early, holding onto the furniture in his mother's bedroom, letting go to toddle a few steps by himself before falling on his diapered bottom. He took his first real walk one October morning, stepping between the outstretched arms of Nellie and his mother, walking unsteadily past Nellie's daughter, who paused in her play to watch him with her sombre hazel eyes. Older than he, she was still creeping slowly across the floor, content to sit and bang objects together while Edward moved intently from chair to table to sofa.

Once he had mastered walking, he began to run, and there was no stopping him. He was constantly on the move, running, falling, getting back up again. He played hard from the time he woke up until the time he went to bed, leaving Nellie's little girl toddling quickly as she tried in vain to keep up with her active playmate. But at night they fell asleep together in the little cot beside Nellie's bed, quiet for those hours as they slept, hours that seemed all too brief to Nellie as she tried to get the rest she needed to cope with two very active toddlers.

Although Edward was very energetic, he loved to be read to, and would sit for a long time on his mother's lap listening to her read to him. His black eyes would follow her finger as she traced the words of a nursery rhyme across the page, would grow large as she told him fairy tales. It was on his mother's knee that he would learn his ABC's and his numbers, ticking off his counting on each chubby finger. As he grew older, he loved to sit at Elizabeth's writing table, drawing on a sheet of discarded paper, painstakingly learning to trace the letters that spelled his name.

He became more active, his vocabulary more advanced, and when Edward was nearly two years old, there came the day Elizabeth had been living for and Nellie had been dreading. He was finally completely weaned, and Nellie could postpone it no longer: she packed the child's clothes and belongings and took him up the long road to live in his parents' house for good. Nellie had sat him upon her knee and told him that he would be going to live with his mother and father now that he was such a big boy. She felt he did not fully understand, but he watched her solemnly with his big dark eyes as she explained to him that he would no longer sleep in her house at night.

Nellie cried, but only a little, for Elizabeth Rochester had offered her a position as a part-time nurse to little Edward. It would only be for part of the day, with one of the housemaids taking over the job the remainder of the time, but it meant that she and her daughter would not be deprived of Edward, nor he of them. This cheered Nellie somewhat, for she had grown to love the little boy, and knew her daughter did also. They had few enough pleasures in life, and their love for the master's younger son was one of them.

Edward did well the day he was brought back home to Thornfield, but as the afternoon wore on and Nellie did not come to take him back to her house, he became quieter. He picked at the small supper he was served in the nursery that was now his room, and grew so fussy that the housemaid decided he was over-tired and needed to be put to bed early. He was placed in the unfamiliar bed, alone in the big room, and it was then that he began to cry. He had not slept alone since his birth, when he had gone to live in the Carey household; always he had slept with Nellie's child.

He cried loudly and more frantically, until John Rochester burst into the nursery, demanding loudly that the brat be made quiet. This caused little Edward to scream harder, which frightened the young housemaid and greatly upset Elizabeth, who glared at her angry husband across the black head of her sobbing little boy. John left the room, slamming the door.

Elizabeth rocked her child, crooning to him as he lay against her. He was hiccupping softly after his frantic crying. His mother held him for a while, helpless against his continued distress. She tried to lie down with him, which quieted him somewhat, but he still whimpered, and tears still fell from his eyes. Finally Elizabeth kissed him and slipped quietly from his bed, secretly relieved to be able to escape to her room. She felt guilty, but knew that to remain with him was to do him no favours; his father would expect him to sleep alone and be quiet about it.

So it was only the housemaid, sleeping on a narrow bed in the dressing room off the nursery, who heard the little boy. He had given up his crying and now just lay quietly, saying the name of Nellie's little girl as if the repetition would bring her there to sleep beside him.

"Grace," he whimpered, clutching his blanket against his wet face, "Grace."

Chapter 3 - Losing Elizabeth

Gradually Edward became accustomed to life at Thornfield Hall. He stopped crying at night when he learned that it would not do him any good, and since he still saw Nellie and Grace every day, he did not miss them too much.

Nellie arrived at seven every morning to dress and feed Edward, and to allow him to play in the nursery with Grace. She remained until three every afternoon, when Elizabeth would come in to have an early tea with her younger son. Then one of the housemaids took over, getting Edward ready for bed and seeing to his night time needs until the next morning when Nellie would come again.

The routine of the young boy's life varied little for the first two years at Thornfield. With Nellie, Grace, and his mother, he had all the companionship he seemed to need.

His father, occupied with the estate, his outside interests, and Rowland, paid him little attention. When his brother noticed him at all, it was to tease him in some way, but since Edward was usually accompanied by someone else, Rowland could not do much to torment his younger brother. Edward's life was spent mostly indoors, except for his daily walks outside with Nellie or with his mother.

It was on these walks that he first noticed his father and brother riding out on their magnificent horses. Edward watched, his dark eyes wide, as his brother would tear past, beating his horse with his crop to get it to gallop faster. He watched his father jump over fences and hedgerows, and gradually his childish drawings began to involve horses.

Elizabeth was not an enthusiastic rider, but she recognized the need for every English gentleman to be able to ride well, so she had no objection when John insisted that Edward start riding soon after his fourth birthday.

For a child who seemed to love the indoor pursuits of reading and music, he was also active and naturally athletic, and John's private fear – that his second son would be feminized by the constant attentions of his mother – did not come to pass. Edward showed an even greater natural talent for riding than had his older brother, and it was not long before his pony was traded in for a larger horse, and the young boy began to train in jumping as well as ordinary riding. John, who thus far had found little to draw him to his younger son, was pleased that the boy did not seem to be afraid of outdoor sports.

John always found himself annoyed at the sight of Edward, although he tried his best to hide it. In his younger son's dark and thoughtful gaze, he saw too clearly the accusing eyes of his wife, and he always felt he was being judged by them both. He had never felt any real love for Elizabeth, but he had to admit that she was a faithful wife and a good mistress of Thornfield.

She had given him two sons, which caused some envy among some of his contemporaries, and the house ran smoothly under her supervision. She spent very little of his money, except on her infernal books, and was well-respected in the surrounding area for her charity and good work. Besides her obvious disdain for the physical aspects of marriage, John could truly find little fault in her, but it annoyed him to witness her obvious love for Edward when she seemed unmoved by himself or Rowland.

But to everyone, even her usually oblivious husband, it was obvious that Elizabeth Rochester was not well. She had never fully regained the strength she had lost after the difficult birth of Edward, and as the years went on, she grew weaker. Her once dark skin became so pale that it was hard to remember the "Spanish" appearance that had first attracted her husband. Her figure had once been quite womanly, but she grew thinner.

Grey began to appear in her thick curly black hair, and her eyes, always large and dark, grew enormous in her white face, with dark shadows beneath them. When she was thirty-two years old, she appeared the same age as her husband, who was her senior by eleven years. John Rochester began to summon doctors, who came, examined her, and prescribed various remedies and concoctions, none of which helped for very long.

When Edward was six years old, several things happened to shake his fairly secure world. His brother Rowland, now fourteen years old, left for school, and his father's focus, so long on his elder brother, now fell upon him.

It was decided that Elizabeth was too frail to continue with her son's lessons, and so a private tutor was hired for him. Elizabeth protested that she felt fine, but her objections were overruled, and soon a Mr. Thurman was hired. He was a tall, thin, bespectacled man, with a seemingly permanent frown on his face.

John Rochester took one look at him and decided that he was exactly what Edward needed to counter-balance his mother's indulgence, and so Mr. Thurman became part of the staff. He had been a village school master, but had been so stern and unyielding that his students' childish pranks had turned vicious, so angry did he make them; and he had been forced to leave after he had struck one pupil so hard that he had fractured his nose.

Mr. Thurman knew that he could not strike a gentleman's son, but he nodded in agreement as John confided to him how spoiled his younger son had become under his mother's teaching, and assured him that there would be no coddling of the boy from now on.

The tutor examined the child's skills, and was surprised to see that he read out loud as well as a child twice his age, that he knew a surprising amount of history, and wrote his letters with a neat, careful hand. He did not give Elizabeth's patient and loving tutelage any credit for the boy's love of learning, instead, was amazed that young Edward was able to learn under such an atmosphere of dangerous indulgence. He was even more eager to be strict; confident that he could teach the boy twice as much as any doting mother could.

For two years, Edward laboured under the teaching of Mr. Thurman. He did well in his studies, although he would never again enjoy learning as he had with his mother. She had been enthusiastic about everything her son learned, and he was as much encouraged by her attitude as he was by the words she spoke. Mr. Thurman gave no indication of being intrigued by mathematics, of being enthralled by the mysteries of science, of being entranced by the stories he read. In stark contrast, the knowledge Mr. Thurman had acquired was drilled into his young pupil by rote learning and unending recitation. Edward learned readily but unhappily under this new regimen, because Mr. Thurman's methods drained the joy of learning from nearly every subject.

When Edward was eight years old, the happiness he knew was cruelly shattered by his mother's death, and the innocence he had known through her love was gone. He learned that the world was a cruel and random place and that joy could never be fully trusted.

Elizabeth had grown steadily weaker in the last two years of her life, but tried to maintain a calm demeanour and continue her normal activities. She began to spend more time reading her Bible and talking to the Reverend Fairfax, as though knowing her time was growing short and that she needed to make her peace with God.

She talked to Edward of the goodness of God, of the heavenly home that awaited her. But he could not fathom what she was talking about. When he sat in church, even under the benign preaching of the kind Reverend Fairfax, God seemed to Edward a Being too vast and frightening to approach. Perhaps if he had had a loving father of his own to compare God to, he might have understood his mother's hope. But God seemed to be nothing but a larger and more terrifying version of John Rochester: stern, remote, ever-judging, and certainly not loving and kind.

When Elizabeth took to her bed for the final time, no one but Nellie noticed the white, frightened face of her younger son, watching from the shadows as the doctor visited daily and the servants moved quietly through the grim silence that had settled over Thornfield. Mrs. Rochester was loved and respected by her household staff, and many prayers went up for her well-being, and when those prayers failed, for her very soul.

No one knew how her husband felt. He went about his business as he always had, stern and silent, expecting rapid and unquestioning obedience from the staff. If he retired to his room to sink to his knees and pray for his wife, no one ever knew it.

He refrained from hunting and riding, from visiting his current mistress (he was growing tired of her and welcomed the chance to be free of her for a time), and stayed at Thornfield, conferring with the doctor in a low voice, but sharing none of his feelings. He made a daily visit to his wife, where he spoke to her in forced cheerful tones of the days when she would be out of her bed to resume her normal activities.

Rowland was sent for from school, to be at his mother's deathbed, and he waited in silence for events to play themselves out. He rarely came across his younger brother, but when he did, he had few kind words for him. Stress and tension permeated the household, and Edward was kept to his room, watched over by Nellie, his lessons with Mr. Thurman suspended for the time being. Nellie usually only came during the day, but John, knowing his wife's end was drawing near, showed a rare sensitivity by engaging Nellie's services at night for these last days. He was smart enough to recognize that Edward, the person who loved Elizabeth the most, would perhaps be hard to handle once his mother was gone.

John Rochester had no intention of keeping Nellie on after his wife's death. He welcomed the chance to remove the constant feminine influences from his son's life. But he knew that for this brief time, Nellie's services were needed. He paid her extra, installed her in the dressing room off Edward's room, and allowed Grace to come to the house as well following her mornings at the village school.

As long as he didn't have to watch his daughter, Josiah Carey was happy to let his wife go to the Hall for a few days, thinking of the extra money her services would bring in. Grace followed her mother around the nursery, frightened of the stern and quiet atmosphere of the Hall, but two eight-year-olds cannot remain solemn for long, and her presence gave Edward his only respite from the fear and sorrow that now filled his home.

The night finally came when Elizabeth sank into unconsciousness for the last time. She had had a restless day, tossing and turning. Her husband and eldest son came to her, but she had no words for them. Nellie brought Edward to her, and only then did Elizabeth's composure break. She wept bitterly, her thin white hand reaching up to caress her younger son, but falling short. In a weak, breathless voice, she told him she loved him, and to remember that God loved him too, before Nellie took him out of the room.

Nellie and Edward knelt by his bedside to pray for his mother, before she sent him to the dressing room to clean his teeth, wash his face, and use the chamber pot before bed. She left him lying quietly in his darkened room, but when she had departed, he rolled over in the darkness to beg God to spare his mother's life. He felt guilty for not getting out of bed to kneel by the side, but he was cold and he hoped God would understand. He was still praying for his mother when sleep stole over him.

Nellie pushed the door open, wincing at the high metallic creak of the iron hinges. She peered into the darkened interior of the room, but could see nothing.

"Master Edward," she whispered hoarsely, pushing the words past the obstruction in her throat. There was no reply. She moved hesitantly into the room, towards the bed, again attempting to rouse the child. She lifted the candle high over the bed and noticed that Edward had pulled the covers high over his head, covering himself completely.

Nellie raised her hand and brushed quickly at the tears that fell upon her cheeks, before reaching down and laying her hand upon the blanket-wrapped boy. She bent towards him.

"Neddie," she whispered, "are you awake, love? It's Nellie." Still no answer. She began to pull gently at the covers, but felt immediate resistance as Edward held on to them tightly, not allowing their removal. She sighed, leaning over to set the candle on the table beside the bed, before she sat down next to him.

"Master Edward," she said in a normal tone. "I know you're awake, love. Your father sent me here to fetch you. Come out now."

Slowly the covers began to move and the little boy sat up, his face tear-stained. His lips trembled as he looked up at her.

"Is my Mama dead?" he asked her, his dark eyes fixed steadily upon her face. She looked back at him for a moment, before nodding, "Yes." A shudder ran through the length of his small body, and he blinked rapidly.

Nellie held her hand out to him. "Come with me, love. Your father wants me to bring you to him. You must be brave now."

She helped him out from under the covers, reaching down to get his slippers, reaching to get his robe from the foot of the bed. He was shivering, but she could not tell if he was feeling the chill from the room or if he was overcome by his own emotions. He stood for a moment, as if not sure where to go.

"Where is Mama now?" he asked.

"She is in her room," Nellie said gently. "I am to take you there now."

"No," Edward shook his head, "I mean, is she in Heaven now?"

Nellie felt the lump in her throat grow, threatening to turn into the tears that she was trying to suppress for the boy's sake.

"Yes, I have no doubt she is with God. She was so good, she loved God and his son Jesus Christ. She is not in pain now."

Still Edward did not move. Nellie reached over to stroke his black curls. "Do you need to use the pot before we go?"

He shook his head, then looked up at her. "Where is Grace?" he asked.

"Grace?" Nellie brushed her hand over his hair again. "She is with Cook, who was watching her in the kitchen. I believe she is sleeping down there with her tonight. You will see her tomorrow. But no playing. The house must be kept quiet." She nearly said, "as your mother lies here", but she stopped herself in time.

She could not bear to think of this motherless child, of this boy who had lost the only person in his family who appeared to love him. She hated to bring him to see his mother, wished he could have been allowed to sleep until morning, but Mr. Rochester had insisted.

She reached for his hand and they left the room, heading down the hall towards Elizabeth's room. Small groups of servants stood in the corridor, some crying openly, others standing in silence. All went quiet as Nellie approached with Edward's hand held tightly in hers.

She approached the bedroom door and looked in. Candles were lit around the room, throwing ghostly shadows over the furnishings and over the people who stood around, looking at the silent figure lying in the large bed. John Rochester stood near the head of his wife's bed, Rowland beside him. Rowland's face was sullen and he never looked up as his brother approached.

The Reverend Fairfax and his wife stood near the bed. Alice Fairfax looked stricken, her eyes red and swollen, and her tears began anew as she saw Edward enter the room.

"Oh, there he is, the poor lamb," she choked out, raising a lace handkerchief to her face. "He was his mother's darling, her pet..." She could not go on.

At her words, John turned to see his younger son approaching, frowning to see him holding Nellie's hand.

"Come here, Edward," he said impatiently. "Thank you for bringing him, Nellie. You may go now."

Nellie tried to lead Edward forward, but his grip on her hand tightened convulsively. She tried to pull her hand away gently, but Edward clutched her hand in both of his and as she attempted to push him towards the bed, he suddenly turned and grasped her firmly around the waist. She felt his small body tremble against her and her heart ached for him.

She started to bend down, to speak to him gently, but just then Rowland reached over. Grasping Edward's arm roughly, he jerked him away from Nellie. "Stop clinging to your nurse like a baby," he taunted. He shoved Edward towards their father. Edward gasped, reaching out to steady himself, and a sob escaped his throat.

"Rowland," John Rochester's deep voice cut through the quiet room.

He reached down to his younger son, but instead of a steadying hand or a gentle caress, he grasped the boy's shoulder with a slight shake. "Come now, Edward," he told him. "I expected better of you. You must try to act like a man now."

Edward looked up and Nellie wanted to cry at the desolation on his face. But he looked from his father to his brother, and with an audible swallow, he took a deep breath and stood up straight. He squared his small shoulders and looked up at his father steadily. Only Nellie saw his fists, clenching and unclenching. John waved her away impatiently, and the last thing she saw was her charge being led to the bedside, ordered by his father to kiss his mother goodbye.

Nellie left the room, the tears spilling over as she departed. She walked quickly down the stairs, towards the kitchen that was left open and lit for now, to provide tea for the groups of people who were not sleeping this long sad night. Nellie wanted only to see her daughter, to hold Grace to her and feel her warm little body against hers. She wished she could leave this house for good, this house which, unbeknownst to some, had just lost its heart. She did not want to be here now that Thornfield's mistress was gone. She would like to leave it forever, leave it to its stern and heartless owner. The only thing that kept her there was the thought of the grieving child that Elizabeth had left behind.

Edward stood looking at his mother, but she did not look like his Mama. This thin, white creature was not his smiling mother, who had laughed and kissed him, played with him and read to him. He had bent and kissed her cold, waxy cheek, touched her still, frigid hand, and pulled away suddenly, thinking that her skin felt like one of the candles that was even now burning around her bed. He wiped at his lips, wondering if he would ever get the feel of her cold skin to leave him. He felt the cold, at that moment and in the days that followed.

When Nellie came the next day, assisting him to dress in the newly-dyed black clothing he would wear for weeks, when he sat quietly, thinking of his mother instead of praying for her soul as he was supposed to be doing, when he walked behind the casket with his father and brother, the memory of her cold hand and cheek rested its chill upon him.

He stood watching as his mother's casket was lowered into the ground, threw in a clod of earth that felt as cold and hard as his mother's skin. He watched the dirt cover her casket, his mind blank and his heart empty, feeling nothing but the relentless, waxy cold closing around him.

When Nellie came to help him to bed the night of his mother's funeral, he at last gave way to some tears. Nellie held him tightly, and his head rested on her shoulder as he cried the only tears he would be able to shed for Elizabeth.

"Nellie," he asked, when the tears had spent themselves somewhat, "why didn't God let Mama live? I asked Him and asked Him."

She shook her head, still holding him closely. "I don't know, Master Edward. God wanted your Mama with Him; we don't know such things. But someday you will see her again."

"I want to see her now," he whispered. "I wish God would take me too." He sniffled loudly, swiping his hand across his nose.

"God will take you in His own time," Nellie whispered to him. "But your Mama will watch from Heaven, and she will see her boy grow up to be a fine man.

You will marry – marry a good woman like your Mama, and have children of your own, and your Mama will see you all from Heaven."

"Rowland told me that it was my fault," Edward whispered, the words catching in his throat as he forced them out. "He said Mama was never sick until I was born, and if I hadn't been born she would still be alive."

Nellie could have willingly strangled Rowland Rochester with her bare hands had he been standing before her at that moment. She nearly burst into tears as she felt Edward standing motionless, his head still on her shoulder, waiting for her words. She prayed for the right words to say to him.

"No, Neddie, you must not listen to Rowland. He is hurting in his heart too; people sometimes say cruel things without meaning to." Nellie doubted that Rowland had given a thought to his own mother or was very affected by her death, but she did not want to give Edward cause to harbor any more anger towards his brother. It was not for her to come between brothers. Edward would see in time what an ass Rowland Rochester was.

"Your Mama got sick, that happens sometimes. It was not your fault. You were not to blame and I won't have you thinking you were. Your birth brought your mother great happiness; she loved you very much. Promise Nellie you won't believe what Rowland has said about this." For a moment Edward did nothing, then she felt him nod against her shoulder, sniffing loudly. He reached up to rub his hand against his nose again, then put his arms around her, remaining in her comforting embrace.

Edward was silent, resting his head upon her shoulder. He had stopped feeling the cold waxy feel of his mother's skin all around him, but a hard little sliver of ice had slipped inside him, into his heart. He would feel it inside him, even in times of great passion and high emotion. He would feel that coldness in his soul for the next thirty years.

Chapter 4 - Edward and Grace

May, 1812

Edward walked back and forth beside the creek bed, watching the rush of the water as the usually small and stagnant trickle rushed by. The heavy spring rains of the previous week had filled the nearby waterways and cisterns, and there was even talk of flooding in outlying areas. He had heard the farmers talking about moving the flocks to higher ground, and had noticed the bustle of activity in the fields as the sheep were rounded up and moved into fenced areas in preparation for possible herding elsewhere.

He wondered if that was why Grace was so late today. Usually she met him every afternoon at two o'clock, after his lessons were finished, and she was done with her chores. That gave them several hours in which to walk, talk and play together. He had occasionally gone by her cottage and had even helped her at times to feed the chickens, to gather the eggs, and to carry the water to the hen houses. But on the last few occasions he had been aware of Josiah Carey's cold eyes on him as he had lingered in the yard, had watched as the burly man had stood in the doorway, his blue eyes under the bushy brows never leaving Edward's face as he raised the jug to his mouth, drank deeply of the foul-smelling brew and wiped his mouth with the back of his hand.

Finally, Grace had whispered to him, "I don't think you ought to come help me any more. Father doesn't like it."

He had responded indignantly to her, "Why should he care, as long as the work gets done? I'm done with my lessons, and I've nothing to do until time for tea. Why should I not help you?"

She had shrugged, "He thinks I'm slacking. And he thinks if you help me, you'll expect payment of some sort."

Edward had laughed, "Payment! With what? You have less money than I have, and I have... well, nothing!"

She had looked down at the ground, scraping her toe in the soft dirt of the yard. "He says you're the master's son and I'm just a servant's daughter, and you'll take liberties with me."

He had shaken his head, laughing again. "Liberties! As if I could. You'd knock me into the dirt." He reached up and squeezed the muscular part of her upper arm.

She had laughed then also, and shook his hand from her arm. "Yes, I would. And don't you forget it, Neddie." She grabbed his hand and twisted her wiry body quickly before he had realized what she was doing. He found himself with his arm behind his back, her skinny frame plastering it up against him so that he could not get free no matter which way he turned. They were laughing by the time he had wriggled around and freed his arm, and then he had chased her around the farmyard, trying to yank the ties of her apron.

He thought back to that day, last summer. It seemed a long time ago. This past winter, he and Grace had both turned thirteen, she in early December, and he in mid-January, and it seemed just those few months had wrought a change in them both. She was quiet and more serious than previously, somewhat snappish with him at times, and he could not understand it. He had not changed in his feelings for her, except that he found himself looking at her strangely at times, noticing things about her that he had not noticed before.

He had always been taller than she, but now they were eye to eye, and last week he had found himself looking into her eyes and thinking how warm and pretty they looked. They were brown, like his, but where his were so dark and deep, hers had lovely flashes of green and gold in them. He had found himself watching the sunlight gleam through her red-gold hair, and wanting to reach up and touch it. He had reached up, but instead of stroking it as he wanted to, letting it slip through his fingers, he had yanked a loose curl as it escaped from beneath her cap. She had knocked his hand away with a glare and a toss of her head. He had felt embarrassed, for he had annoyed her, and that was certainly not what he had set out to do.

He found himself at times growing annoyed himself as he looked at her. Their friendship had seemed so simple just last year, and now he found himself thinking of her at odd times, waking up in a sweat in the middle of the night with strange aches and longings in his body and head, her face in his mind. It confused him, and he wished he could talk to her about it. But she seemed as far from him in mind as her body was close.

Now he again looked at his watch. Nearly half past two. He sighed with impatience, leaning over to pick up several stones so he could toss them into the creek. As he did, he spied her standing in the shadows of the trees off to the side.

"You sly thing," he shouted to her. "Here I've been thinking evil of you for abandoning me, and you've been here all the time. Quick, catch that." He lobbed one of the small stones to her, knowing how quick she was, how much sharper her eyes were than even his. But instead of reaching out to catch the rock and crowing about her prowess, she dodged the stone, and continued to stand quietly among the trees.

He stopped, looking at her keenly. Even the shadows couldn't hide the sight of her red-rimmed, swollen eyes. "Grace?" He moved towards her. She backed away, swiping at her face with her hand, leaving a smear of dirt across one pink cheek. He dropped the remaining rocks and moved towards her more quickly. She turned away as he approached, and he came up behind her, touching her shoulder. She pulled away, not vehemently, but with an air of weariness.

"Grace," he said again, and turned her towards him more forcefully. She once again pulled away, but not before he saw the livid bruise across her cheek, the red handprint clearly visible on her face. He sucked in his breath and his hand dropped from her shoulder.

"Gracie, look at me." His voice was quiet, but with an air of firm authority that Grace had not heard from him before. It was his father's voice. She looked up at him, the cursed tears starting to flow again. She had tried to force them back, down inside where she always tried to keep them, but they welled up. She could only express herself with two people, always, her mother and Edward Rochester, and now with her mother sick, she tried so hard to maintain a cheerful countenance around her. And with Edward, she tried not to show too much either. She could still hear her father's taunting voice, the words that cut through her more sharply than a slap.

"Aye, girl, thinking you're high and mighty because the master's boy drank at the same well as you, and you're his friend these years." he had laughed a nasty laugh, teetering towards her, leaning close to her, his rank beery breath hot in her face.

She had wrinkled her nose and turned away, but that had just made her father more angry. "Look at me when I talk to you, you little hoor, you. I've seed you, out there giving young Rochester the glad eye, thinking he likes you. And like you he will, what's under your skirts, and when he's done won't he be off, leaving us with you and likely another mouth to feed."

She used to fight back against her father's taunts, but he had just become more angry, and when he would turn his anger against her mother, she had stopped. Now she just stood, stony-faced and silent, but that made him angry too. But angry as he had always been, he had never struck her, until today.

"Did your father do that to you?" Edward asked angrily, reaching up to touch his fingers to her throbbing cheek. She pulled away again, before he could touch her, and glared at him, not sure why she was angry at him, too, except he was a man, like her father, or almost a man. He looked so fierce and angry. She was so used to his sweetness of temper, his patience. She had not known he could look so furious, so stern.

"I'll kill him," he said through his clenched teeth, and she looked up in alarm at the vicious tone of his voice.

"Stop it!" she said. "You're not making this any easier for me. I just came to tell you why I was late and that I wouldn't be able to be with you today. I've got to get back home."

He shook his head, reaching out and grabbing her hand, "Just come with me first."

He led her to the mossy creek bed and made her sit down. She protested, but he insisted, and surprised by his new attitude, she sat, looking up at him with wide eyes. He crouched down, reaching into his pocket for his handkerchief, which he dipped into the cold water. Squeezing the water out, he reached up and gently wiped at her other cheek, the uninjured one. He bathed it, wiping it clear of the dirt smudge and the tear tracks.

Then he rinsed it again, and folded it into a compress, wringing it out and laying it against the darkening bruise on the other cheek. She didn't know what she had expected, but this tenderness, after her father's harsh treatment, broke down her fragile defences, and the tears came again, sobs tearing at her. She held the handkerchief against her face as she wept harder than she could ever remember weeping.

Then she was suddenly aware of Edward's arms around her, his hand pulling her face down against his shoulder. He did not tell her to be quiet, as her mother did when Grace cried around her. He just held her, rocking her slightly in his arms until her sobs began to ebb. She looked up at him, just wanting to tell him thank you, and as she raised her eyes, she saw he was looking at her intently.

His whole heart was in his face, his concern, and love, and something else she could not put a name to. Before she could speak, he leaned over and kissed her lips. She didn't have time to pull away before his arms came around her, and without thinking, she put her arms around his neck and was kissing him back. Gripping the handkerchief in one hand, she held tightly to him as his lips pressed hard against hers.

For a long time they clutched each other, two frightened, lonely, half-grown children trapped in a world they couldn't control, a world that had already mapped out their respective destinies. He pulled away, but she still held him tightly, and he kissed her again and again. Her hands were in his thick black hair, and he reached up with his hands, pulling off her cap and running his fingers through her fine, soft hair as well. They touched each other's cheeks, he ran his fingers along her jawline, and still they kissed, over and over.

Finally they pulled away, looking at each other, each of them seeing something they had never seen before. They were breathing hard, faces flushed, sensations sweeping through them that they had never felt. Grace reached trembling fingers up to her mouth, tracing them against her lips, which felt as bruised and swollen as her cheek.

Edward reached up and grasped her shoulders tightly. "Grace, I won't let him hurt you again, I promise."

She shook her head, "And how will you stop him? He listens to no one, he would never listen to you."

"My father, then. I'll talk to my father." He was thinking desperately, shaking his head as well. "My father can tell him he'll throw him off the land if he does it again."

She laughed at him then, laughed in spite of herself. "That shows how much you know. No one meddles in a man's family, that's his own affair. He could kill me and no one will say a word to him. And why should your father care? My father works the fields, pays his rent. Your father only cares for that. Why should he notice me? He doesn't even care about you."

The words hit Edward hard, and Grace saw him flinch. She was seized with a sharp remorse to have hurt him, but Lord above, had he not said those same words himself many times?

She reached for his hand, her face gentle. "I'm sorry, Neddie, but it's the truth. You said yourself your father cares only for money. He'll not care what my father does to me behind his own door."

"I'll take you away," Edward said fiercely, squeezing her hand. "We'll leave, and go somewhere where they'll never find us."

"Where?" she asked him, shaking her head. "There's no such place on earth."

"I don't know," he took a deep breath, trying to think of a place. "London? Or, I know, Jamaica! My father talks about it, he has friends there. It's supposed to be a paradise! We'll sleep under the stars and eat exotic fruits. We'll bathe in the ocean."

"I don't believe such a place exists!" she laughed at him. "And I don't want to try any exotic fruits – they would likely kill you instead."

"I'm serious, Grace, I will take you there," he insisted. "I'll keep you safe." He took a deep breath, "You're my best friend, Gracie, my only friend. Don't you know that?" He reached for her again.

She let him take her into his arms. It was foolish, silly talk. He couldn't take care of her, any more than she could take care of herself. But as she moved towards him, leaned her head against his shoulder again, she thought of how much she loved him and always had, and how nice it was to pretend, just for a little while, that he could protect her.

"I love you, Neddie" she told him softly.

He hugged her to him, resting his cheek on top of her head for a moment. Then he pulled away from her, turned away, staring down at the rushing water of the creek. He had to tell her. He didn't want to, but it was time.

"I'm going away," he told her quietly.

She shook her head, not certain she had heard him correctly. "What?"

"My father is sending me away," he said, folding his arms over his chest. He stared at the water as if mesmerized. He tucked his hands under his arms, feeling suddenly cold all over. "I'm thirteen, long past time for me to go to school, my father says, and next week he's sending me away."

Grace felt the tears well up again, "Where?"

Edward shrugged, hunching over, not looking at her. "Eton." He swallowed hard. "Near Windsor." He finally dared to look at her, saw her staring at him with tears in her eyes. "It's time now, it is. I can't believe he hasn't sent me away before this. I don't know why he's sending me so far; a school nearer home was good enough for Rowland."

He laughed suddenly, a short, mirthless laugh. "Well, I do know. Rowland's an idiot. He was lucky to finish where he did. He's no scholar. He's barely making it through college; I think Father's paying someone to ensure he finishes, even at that inferior school he's going to now. But Mr. Thurman says I should go somewhere better. My marks are high, I've learned all he can teach me, the ass. It looks good for him too, that I could get into Eton. He can brag about that, brag to the next family with some poor misfortunate that gets him for a tutor."

"Why didn't you tell me straightaway?" Grace burst out angrily. "You sat here and talked of us leaving, sat here and kissed me, for God's sake, and said you'd take me away from this, and all the time, you knew you were going away." Her lips trembled and she bit down, forcing them to be still. "Take care of me. You won't even be here!"

Edward reached for her, touched her sleeve, but she pulled away from him, averted her face. His shoulders sagged, and he looked away from her. Neither of them spoke for some moments.

"I'm sorry, Gracie," he said quietly. "I don't want to go. Don't want to leave you. But Father is insisting. He says the Rochesters have to make their mark; that we have wealth and it's time we took our place. Rowland is going to inherit the estate, so it really doesn't matter that he's not smart. But I've got to make my way, I'm going to have to support myself. I can't believe Father's parting with the money, but it makes him look good, to have a son away at a school like this. It is done, I have no choice."

Grace sniffed, swiped at her cheek. She did not look at him.

"I'll be back," he told her. "Back for holidays. I'll come to see you. You and your mother. Nothing will change."

"Yes, it will," she whispered. "You'll be off, you'll see things you've never seen, do things you've never done. You'll have no time for me when you come back."

"I will," he insisted. "You're all that matters to me here." He grinned, reaching over to poke her arm, "You and Arrow."

"Your horse?" She whipped her head around to face him, saw him smiling at her. She reached up to punch his arm. "You know what you have to say now, something nice to me."

He laughed, "That your teeth are not so yellow and you don't fart when you eat oats?" He dodged her as she went to punch him again, jumping up and moving away from her. She advanced on him, fists clenched, and he backed away, laughing so hard he didn't see a huge tree root, and tripped, falling backwards. "Ow, damn it!"

Grace pounced, pinning him to the ground as he lay, digging her fingers into his armpits. He heaved, trying to throw her off of him, still laughing. He grabbed for her hands, wrenching them away from him.

He held her fists tightly, feeling her pull hard to get away from him. But he had grown stronger since the last time they had wrestled, and he held her easily. She was laughing, feeling a brief respite from the pain in her heart. "Say it, Neddie, say it!"

"What?" he asked her, still holding her fists tightly, still pinned to the ground as she sat on him.

"Something sweet, you dolt!" she said, giving a huge heave as she tried again to pull her hands free. "Something that tells me that you like me more than your horse."

He grinned up into her face, "Oh, is that all?" He laughed, "Well, your backside is not nearly as big as Arrow's." He burst into laughter again, dodging quickly as she gave a quick stab of her arm downward, trying to dig her elbow into his ribs.

"No!" she told him. "You have to do better than that, or I will sit on you all day."

Edward gave a quick tug, pulling her arms apart so she fell forward, her face suddenly inches from his. He reached up, kissed her quickly. "You are far more beautiful than any horse." He let go of her arms, reached up to push back her brilliant hair. "And your mane is prettier too." He smiled then, and for a moment she was still, looking into his eyes. "Wait for me, Grace, I'll be back to see you whenever I can," he whispered to her.

She smiled back at him, then sprang up quickly, digging her toe into his ribs. "I can run faster than that old horse of yours too," she cried, darting away from him. He jumped up too, and gave chase, their laughter ringing through the trees, shade and sunshine alternately dappling the grassy bank of the creek as the two of them ran alongside.

Chapter 5 - Grace Poole

January, 1814

Grace tossed the remainder of the chicken feed to the ground and picked her way carefully among the birds that had gathered around to peck excitedly at the dirt. She shook the basket upside down to dislodge any remaining feed and made her way back into the cottage.

Shutting the door, she stood with her back against it and surveyed the small main room, silent but for the quiet crackling of the fire in the hearth. Grace was not yet accustomed to being alone during the day and she quickly moved to find some task to do to keep her mind occupied so she would not think of her mother.

It had been nearly a month since Nellie had died, growing steadily thinner, paler, and weaker until she was a mere ghost in the cottage's bedroom, dying slowly day by day. Grace had nursed her faithfully, as Nellie had for so long nursed others in the areas around the Thornfield estate. Doing all the cooking, cleaning, and care of the chickens, seeing to her mother's needs by day and by night, had filled Grace's time so that she had no need to think or to feel.

Her father had been no help to her or to his wife. Working in the fields by day, drinking in the pub with his friends all evening, Josiah Carey would stagger home after dark to weave drunkenly to the table, eat quickly the meal that Grace kept warm for him, and drop down on the small pallet bed by the fire, the bed that Grace herself had once slept upon.

During Nellie's final illness, Grace had begun to sleep in the one bedroom with her, and after her death, Josiah seemed to have no inclination to take back the bed he had shared with his wife, so Grace remained there. Only once had Josiah re-entered the bedroom, one night in the past week, and Grace, sweeping the stone floor in front of the fireplace, frowned now to think of it.

She had awakened with the hairs rising up on the back of her neck, to find her father, a small stub of candle in his hand, standing near the bed, swaying drunkenly, staring down at her.

Grace had sat up, pulling the neck of her nightdress closed where it gaped open slightly, and where his bleary eyes seemed to be fixed.

"Father?" she asked.

Josiah attempted to stand straight, his unfocused eyes watching her. He smiled a sloppy smile, stepped towards her.

"What are you doing, Father?" she whispered, reaching for her shawl and getting out of bed. He held the candle up, stumbling as she came towards him.

"Ya look like yer mother, girl," he slurred, reaching a hand to her. Grace dodged his grasp, frowning in irritation. She did not care of the intoxicated fool fell over and spent the night on the stone floor, but she wanted to get the candle out of his hand. Her life was a misery to her at present, but she did not relish the thought of burning to death. She had seen cottage fires before, knew how quickly flames, deadly and dangerous, could rage through the small thatched-roof homes.

Josiah had mumbled and stumbled, but had let her lead him back to his pallet, surrendering the candle without protest. He had fallen onto the pallet, legs off to the side, snoring loudly before Grace had even hidden the candle stub and gone back to bed herself.

Her father had said nothing in the morning, dousing his head and upper body under the pump in the yard as he did every morning, winter or summer, before dressing and gulping his breakfast of tea and bread. He had put on his cap, grunted at Grace and left for the day, his lunch tucked in the cloth bag he wore slung over his shoulder. He did not meet her eyes.

They barely spoke, Grace and her father. She had no idea how he felt when sober. At night he sometimes sobbed in a maudlin manner over his dead wife, but when not inebriated, he never mentioned her name or gave any indication that he knew she was gone.

Grace missed her mother with all her heart. She did not understand why God could not have taken her father if He had had to take a parent from her. Her father had never struck her again after the time when she was thirteen, but he had stayed away from her, only speaking to her when he had to.

Grace felt tears prickle behind her eyes, and she blinked rapidly, pulling her shawl around her as she moved to the window to look out at the cold winter day. Her heart felt heavy and dark within her breast.

In the back of her mind she knew what day it was. She had gone to sleep the previous night thinking of it and woke at the first grey light of dawn with this date fixed on her mind.

January nineteenth.

It was Edward Rochester's fifteenth birthday. He was now the same age she was. How she had teased him and laughed, those six weeks each year when she was older than he. And how he had teased her in return when his birthday arrived and once again they were the same age. She wondered about him, how he was spending his birthday. Was there anyone there to celebrate it, to celebrate him?

They had always spent their birthdays together, by arrangement when Mrs. Rochester was alive, and by their own choice once they were older. They never had a gift for each other; neither could afford it – Grace because she had no money, and Edward because he could not use his money to buy a gift for a servant. But spending time together, each acknowledging the value of the other in their lives – that had been the true gift. Other than their mothers, each was the only one glad the other had been born. But that was before.

Grace missed him. She had not seen him since the day, nearly two years earlier, when he had come to say goodbye to her mother and her. He was leaving for Eton the next morning, and had come that evening to bid them both farewell.

Josiah Carey had been home, as he often seemed to be when the master's son had come to call. He had no liking for the Rochesters, any of them. They stood in too vivid contrast to what he did not have. And he had been rebuked more than once by the estate steward employed by Mr. Rochester, for his drinking and fighting. The Rochesters, father and sons, were at the top of the list of those he blamed for all that had gone wrong in his life.

Josiah had stood, arms folded, as Edward had embraced Nellie and received her tearful kiss. Edward had turned to Grace, who had begged him with her eyes not to single her out for any special attention. She knew her father would be angered if he did. Had they been alone, she would have thrown herself into his arms, but now she merely folded her arms in front of her and said, "Goodbye, Master Edward, I wish you the best."

"And I you, Grace," he replied, inclining his head towards her in a greatly formal manner that would have had her hooting with laughter at him if they were alone. As he moved to depart, Edward deliberately walked too close to her and bumped his shoulder against hers. "Excuse me, Grace," he had said with a solemn nod. She remained in her spot, eyes to the ground, but a smile tried to force itself through her sombre look even as a lump the size of a hen's egg rose in her throat. She turned then, to look after him as he walked away, and when she turned back, tears swimming in her eyes, she caught her father looking at her as though he'd like to kill her.

Grace had not seen Edward since. As far as she knew, he had not been home since he left. She had heard bits of information from the other servants when she was brought to the Hall to help as an extra maid for a house party or a hunt ball; or when she chatted with Mrs. Fairfax after church.

"Master Edward made top marks in school," Mrs. Fairfax told her. Or on another occasion, "The funniest thing, Master Edward had his nose broken with a cricket bat, and the Master wrote and told him to stop playing it or he'd cut his allowance. Master Edward was furious, but you know the Master... "

"Master Edward has gone to Brighton this holiday with a friend from school," the cook was heard to tell her assistant as Grace folded linen napkins nearby. No one who spoke of him could know how she listened for any mention of his name, or how her heart rose and plunged again to hear him spoken of so casually. Or how in her bed at night, she hugged herself tightly and remembered his arms around her, and his lips upon hers.

But he did not return to Thornfield. Nellie sickened, languished, and died without ever again seeing the boy she had nursed at her breast and loved like a son.

And now Grace was alone. The other girls in her age group – the ones who had gone to the village school with her, where they had all attended only long enough to learn to read and write – were working as hard as she was. They worked their parents' allotted plots of land, or were in service to the surrounding estates, or were even beginning to marry and raise families themselves.

Grace peered out the window as she saw someone approaching, pausing to unlock the gate before stepping in and closing it behind him. Grace groaned inwardly, but moved to the door to greet Abel Poole as he came up to knock.

Seeing her in the doorway, Poole snatched off his cap and smiled, revealing his greatest defect – a mouthful of missing, broken, or rotted teeth. He was not the most handsome of men when he wasn't smiling, but when he did smile, Grace could scarcely bear to look at him.

This made her feel guilty, as always, for Abel Poole was the kindest and gentlest of men, and she knew he liked her very much. He always had a friendly word for her and he did not drink to excess, which made him quite unique among her father's friends. But he was forty years old and had a daughter older than Grace, already married with a family of her own.

Abel was balding, with greasy hair combed across a shiny skull, and his clothing hung upon his scrawny frame as though he were a scarecrow in a field.

"Gracie Carey, ye're a sight to warm me heart," Poole told her now. Grace wasn't sure where Poole hailed from, but his accent was different from that of most of the people in this area.

"Good morning, Mr. Poole," she answered, her guilt for her hidden feelings making her speak more warmly towards him than she might have otherwise. "How are you?"

"Oh, fine, fine, thanks to ye for asking." Abel Poole had a dreadful cough at times and Grace prayed he wouldn't start now. But he was a hard worker, and though frail and plagued with poor health, he was much in demand as a labourer, because he would give a full day's work and could be trusted to supervise others as well.

"I wondered, Gracie, how yer father does this morning? A group of us are up at Rochester's stables, doin' some work, and Joe was expected to be among us, but no sign of him, and the steward is askin'."

Grace sighed. Her father's work was erratic at best, and in the winter when little farming could be done, he often did not come through when hired for an extra job. It was difficult enough to get any money from him for the household, but as the winter went on it might be well nigh impossible.

"I don't know, Mr. Poole," Grace said with an angry shrug. "He doesn't tell me where he goes and I only know if he's been working or not by the money I get or don't get. Half the time he's at my egg money and I have to put it in hidey holes all over the place. If you're looking for him, try the pub – you know that as well as I do."

Poole shook his head, "Ah, that man. He were there yesterday, but it rained and we couldn't do the roof so we knocked off early. I saw him standing his round at the pub, as if he had all the king's money, hoisting his pint with the rest, but then I went home. Rachel had me supper. But today, no sign of Joe."

Grace shrugged again. For all she knew he had fallen into a well on the way to work. One could hope.

Poole turned his cap nervously in his hands, "And ye, lass. Are ye all right yerself?"

"I'm fine, Mr. Poole, thank you." She swallowed. "Missing my mother."

Poole patted her arm awkwardly. His hand was callused and grimy and he dropped it after one or two pats, as though knowing she wouldn't welcome his touch. She thought he would leave then, but he continued to stand awkwardly at the door. Grace clutched her shawl around her.

Abel Poole started to speak, then stopped. He scratched his head awkwardly, then opened his mouth again.

"Gracie, I know I've no right to ask ye. Ye're a fine lass, lovely and all, with plenty of boys yer own age, I think. But I like ye. I've been noticing these few months as ye've cared for yer Mam, what a good girl ye are. And I'm lonely. Since me Ruth died, more'n two years on now, I've been alone. I've got Rachel and her man and their children, but they've their own lives. I'm not a young man, but I'm not old. And I'd like a wife to care for. And one to care for me."

It was a long speech for Poole, and his awkwardness touched Grace, even as she shrank away from the very thought of marriage to this man.

"Mr. Poole," Grace began. Her voice was shaking, "I'm sorry, I truly am. But I cannot marry you, I am not marrying anyone. Not now. I'm not ready, and my mother has just died... "

She felt the words pouring out and she clamped her mouth shut. She swallowed, not meeting his gaze. He was silent for some moments, then put his cap back on.

"Aye," he said, his voice quiet, "aye, I know I shouldn't have asked ye. But I had to try." He turned away, skinny shoulders sagging.

"Mr. Poole," Grace stopped, then took a breath. "Thank you. I do appreciate it."

He nodded, then left. As he left the yard and headed down the road, Grace heard him coughing.

For a long time afterwards, Grace would think back to that night and wonder if there had been a point at which she could have said something different or done something else, to change how she and her father ended their life together and went in separate directions. But had they not always been separate? Had he ever thought of her as anything but a nuisance? Had he ever cared about her at all?

The evening of Abel Poole's proposal, Josiah came home early. It was not quite dark and he was not quite drunk when he came into the house, slamming the door behind him. He was walking nearly straight tonight, and came right to the table where Grace sat, taking in the seams of a blouse of her mother's so that she could wear it herself.

Grace looked at her father, surprised that he was home already, and that he was already angry before he had been in the house a minute.

"So," her father breathed, his face hostile, "Abel Poole is not good enough for you, Miss High-and-Mighty."

"What?" Grace had not been thinking of Poole at all, had tried not to think of him, and it had taken her a moment to remember the events of earlier in the day.

"He told me," her father continued. "He came by the pub, said that you'd told him I might be there. He was looking for me, to tell me I was off the job. And he told me he had made an offer to you and you turned him down. I could've told him you would. Little bitch. Got a taste of life up at the Hall and nothing down here where we are is good enough for you now!"

Grace shook her head. She knew it was the job – he was upset about losing the job. She needed to stay silent, to not talk back to him. Maybe he would go back to the pub, drink himself to a stupor, and leave her be. Her mother had always told her not to backtalk him when he was like this.

Her head bent to her work. In two strides, he was at her side, ripping the fabric from her hands, tearing it in two and throwing it down.

"Look at me!" he hissed, advancing towards her. "What makes you think you're too good for the likes of Abel Poole?"

"I don't... " she started, but he shouted her down.

"Don't what?" His eyes were narrowed, his face red.

Grace cleared her throat, licked her lips. Her eyes darted from side to side, looking for an escape. Josiah's hand reached out and grasped her jaw, forcing her face to turn up to his.

"I don't think I'm too good for Mr. Poole," she whispered. "I just don't want to get married. He's older than you are, Father."

"Poole's a hard worker, and he'd take you off my hands," Josiah shouted, letting go of her face roughly, making her flinch. "I'd sign tomorrow to have you go to him; how long will I have to support you? And who else is going to marry you? Your friend, young Rochester? He's got what he wanted off you, and there's an end to it."

Something snapped in Grace, and the words she was hiding behind her clenched teeth came pouring out.

"You, support me?" she cried out. "Mother made every cent that took care of me, and I've been working since I was a child. If I've gotten money it's likely from myself. And I don't know why you hate Edward. He's never touched me, not that way. He would not, you drunken fool!"

Josiah Carey slapped her then, first with one hand, then the other. He was angry beyond reason, humiliated before his cronies by being fired yet again, and just drunk enough to lose control without the alcohol relaxing him. Grace was a convenient scapegoat and all his rage came pouring out at her.

She leaped up to get away, and this time he went to slap her again but got her nose instead. Blood began to run from one of her nostrils and a hot, white rage washed over her. Raising her hand to fend him off, she accidentally scratched him and he lost control completely. Raining blows down upon her, he knocked her backwards until she tripped and fell back upon the pallet bed, hitting her head against the wall.

Her father came after her and suddenly he was on her, his hands holding her shoulders to the bed.

"You little hoor," he breathed, his whiskey breath hot in her face. Through a daze she heard his words, "Everybody knows about you and young Rochester, knows he's had his way with you. That's why his father sent him away, why he's never come back."

"No!" she cried out, as she felt his hands drop to her breasts, squeezing painfully. She twisted beneath him, trying to break his grip on upon her. "He's been here, hasn't he, the little sod." He squeezed her again, harder, making her cry out again. His breathing was fast and hard and she felt his knee force itself between her thighs, trying to shove them apart, "And he's been down here too, hasn't he?" His body lay heavily upon hers, pinning her down, and she writhed beneath him like a wild thing. She felt one hand leave her breast, move down to her skirt, which he yanked up. She felt his rough hand sliding up her thigh, trying to push her legs apart with his hand as well as with his knees.

Grace shrieked like she'd never before known she could, fighting with all her might. Luckily for her, a neighbour down the road was walking in the twilight with his wife and the two of them heard her screams.

Bucking frantically, she had nearly succeeded in getting out from under her father but she sobbed with relief as the passing couple came to her aid. The man pulled Josiah Carey off her, and the woman helped Grace up, noting her bloody nose, bruised cheeks and disheveled clothing. By the next morning, Grace was staying at the parsonage under the watchful eye of Mrs. Fairfax.

John Rochester, who for years had been aware of Josiah Carey's disruptive behaviour, had listened to the pleadings of the vicar and his wife, and had cancelled Carey's tenancy, giving him but a few days to be off the land and on his way. But Carey had countered this threat by demanding that Grace come with him.

She could have testified against him before the magistrate, but would have had to repeat his shameful words to her, would have had to show to someone the livid bruises on her breasts and at her upper thighs. She did not think she could bear that. She knew her father did not want her, that he was only demanding she come with him because he knew it would be a punishment for her. Mrs. Fairfax had offered to keep her until a situation could be found for her, but she was only fifteen years of age, and not yet a legal adult. Josiah Carey was her father, and could demand she come with him.

John Rochester, tired of the whole business, refused to get involved further and Grace found herself in the position of having to leave all that was familiar to her to go with the man who had beat her and attempted to assault her. Deep in her heart, she did not believe that he would have carried his attack to the fullest extent, but who really knew what was in his heart? She knew she could not live with him ever again, and frantically contemplated running away.

Grace could not wait until the marks on her face had faded completely. Her father was due to be off the land in two days' time, and unless she could find an alternative, she would have to go with him.

She asked to see him in the parsonage with the Fairfaxes in the next room. The Careys, father and daughter, spoke a few short words to each other, and then Josiah departed, slamming the door with a curse on the entire house.

"Are you sure, my dear?" Mrs. Fairfax asked Grace, her face a picture of distress.

"Yes," Grace said quietly. "My father has agreed to give his consent. I won't go to the magistrate and he won't force me to go with him, if I do this."

"But your face, what he's done there, surely that will be enough... " Mrs. Fairfax, said, taking her hand.

Grace reached up to touch the bruises on one cheek, "He's my father, he's allowed to discipline me for talking back. No one will interfere. He just wants to make me do something I don't want to do, just because he can. This way I'll be safe. Abel Poole is a good man. And I must marry someone."

Mrs. Fairfax was still shaking her head when Grace left the house, to tell Abel Poole that she had changed her mind and that she would indeed marry him.

Mr. Poole was happy, pleased that her father would consent and that she would take him. He reached up to touch her bruised face.

"I heard what he done to ye, lass. I'll never lay a hand on ye that way, ye know. Ye can be sure of that."

Several days later, Josiah Carey left the area and his daughter never saw him again.

Abel Poole moved out of the house he had lived in with his daughter and her family and moved into the house the Careys had rented for so many years. After the small wedding in the parsonage parlour, with the Fairfaxes and Abel's family in attendance, Grace moved back to her old home with the man who was now her husband.

That night, before he took her to bed for the first time, Abel told Grace, "Yer father told me, ye know. About young Edward Rochester."

"What about him?" Grace asked wearily, her shoulders sagging beneath the white nightgown she was wearing.

"That ye had, ye know, been with him." Abel put his hand over hers. "He wanted to warn me. But I don't care, lass. It don't matter to me. It's not yer fault. He's the master's son, he can take what he likes. Ye couldn't help it and I'll not hold it against ye."

Grace shook her head wearily. "No, Mr. Poole," Grace whispered, "I swear, nothing like that ever happened. My father never stopped thinking it did, but I promise you, we did not. Master Edward was my friend, all our lives. But he'd not have done that."

Abel led her gently to the bed, "Call me Abel now, Grace. Anyway, I wanted ye to know, that it's all right. I love ye the same, no matter what's been done to ye."

The next morning, Poole stood next to the bed, in his work clothes, watching his young bride as she gathered the bedclothes together to change them. Looking down, he saw the small reddish stain on the sheet, and looked over at Grace, running his fingers through his hair. Her face was very red.

"I told you," she said quietly.

Poole nodded, "I am sorry, lass. I should have known yer father was just havering away, speaking nonsense. And I'm sorry, if I, ye know, hurt ye. It gets better, I promise."

Grace looked down, "No, Abel, you were gentle. You were kind to me."

Her husband touched her arm, "It's too early to be up, Gracie. Go back to bed. Surely ye're allowed to, today. Don't worry about nothing, the house will keep, for today."

Abel Poole left then, to go to work. Grace waited till he was gone, then crept over to a cupboard where she knew her father had kept some jugs of whiskey. Shaking each one, she found some that still had some drink left in them. She sat down next to the cupboard, tilting her head back to drink deeply.

The whiskey burned going down, inflamed her throat and made her stomach churn. She gagged and choked, but it stayed down. She sat for a while, willing the drink to take away the thoughts in her mind.

Her brain kept replaying the previous night in her head. Her new husband had tried to be gentle with her. She thought of how he had laid her down, kissing her, his sour breath in her face. She had finally turned her head aside and buried her face in his neck, just to keep his mouth away from her face.

This had aroused him, and he had proceeded, no doubt still believing she was more practiced than she was. He had fondled her breasts, still tender from her mistreatment by her father. She was glad it was dark, but he was not looking at her anyway, merely lifting her gown and his to attend to his business.

His hand moved between her legs, his rough callused fingers hurting her tender flesh. She stifled a cry of distress as he pushed inside her, the sharp pain shocking her. He thrust into her again and again, his breathing as rough and jagged as her father's had been when he was attacking her. Abel had no control, could not wait, and Grace could only clench her fists against the pain and pray he was finished soon.

"Ye're so nice and tight," he breathed in her ear, and she turned her head away, tears slipping down her cheeks, "Ye're so good, lass, so good... " He stopped for a moment, reaching down to lift her legs around his hips, before he resumed, faster and faster until he ended with a grunt and one last hard thrust.

Grace drank again, forcing the thoughts from her mind, beginning to feel the whiskey's warmth spread through her aching body, and numb her hurting mind. She waited until all her thoughts were a distant buzz that could no longer upset her. Then she stood up unsteadily and went back to bed.

Chapter 6 - Edward Returns

February, 1814

Grace Poole spent the first day of her married life in bed, sleeping until nearly three in the afternoon. When the weak sun of midwinter shone across her rumpled bed, she sprang up, feeling suddenly guilty. Trained from earliest childhood to be up and busy at day's first light, she was unused to being in bed during the day, even on days when she was sick.

Standing up, still in her nightgown, she felt as wretched as she had ever felt. Her head pounded and waves of nausea flooded over her. Her mouth felt as dry and fuzzy as the balls of dust she swept off the stone floor every day. For the first time in her life, Grace felt the tiniest pinprick of understanding for her father. If the drink had made him wake up every morning feeling so dreadful, no wonder he was such a hateful and bitter man.

Grace hesitated for a moment, unsure of what to do first. She felt a stinging rawness between her legs, felt so sticky and filthy she could not stand herself. Despite her throbbing head and queasy stomach, she fetched her clothing and went behind the screen to wash. The water was nearly gone but she was not ready to go to the pump to get more.

She washed herself in the cold water, grimacing at the dried blood on her thighs, and as she scrubbed at it, the nausea overwhelmed her and she had to lean over the basin where she gagged and retched until her eyes streamed with tears. There was nothing in her stomach and her throat burned agonizingly from her vain attempts to vomit. Exhausted, she slumped to the floor, sobbing weakly.

"Mama," she wept, "I miss you so. Why are you not here?"

By the time she had cried out her grief and pain, slumped naked on the cold stone floor, the hour was growing late and she had to rush to dress and make the cottage presentable. She hurried to feed the chickens, to bring in fresh water for the kettle and jugs.

She stripped the bed, putting on the only other clean sheet, and balled the other up, setting it aside until she could scrub it and hang it to dry later that night. By the time Abel had returned, she had time to make only a meager meal of bread, potted cheese, and some baked apples.

"It's a poor meal I have for you tonight, Abel," she said, her eyes downcast. "I'm sorry, but I will do better after today."

"Ah, it's all right, Gracie. Simple food suits me just fine. Did ye have a little rest for yerself today?"

Grace nodded, shamefaced, "Yes. But I'll not do that again, I am very far behind in my work."

"It doesn't hurt, just one day," her husband said. He leaned back and lit his pipe, smiling as Grace poured him another cup of tea. She sat quietly with hands folded, surprised at the pleasant feeling of sitting at the table sharing a meal with someone else, even Abel Poole. She was so accustomed to the mounting stress of this time of day, waiting with stomach knotted for Josiah's return, never sure of what mood he would be in. She had to remind herself that this home was hers now, hers and Abel's, and that Josiah was out of her life forever.

Abel broke into her reverie, leaning over to touch her wrist lightly, "I'll not take ye tonight, lass, if that worries ye. I know ye're... " He swallowed. "Well, I know ye're bound to be a little, sore, like, from last night."

Grace nodded, feeling her face grow hot, "Thank you," she whispered.

"But it was nice, and all," he told her. "And ye'll tell me when ye're, ye know, feeling better?"

Grace nodded, and stood to clear the dishes from the table, feeling a sudden lightness of spirits from sheer relief.

Grace settled into life as mistress of her own home very quickly. She was so used to hard work and caring for both her mother and her father, that seeing to just two people was amazingly easy for her.

She kept a clean house, as was her habit, and cooked a good meal every night, finding an appreciative recipient of her labours in her new husband. He turned nearly all his wages over to her, apparently having done that for years with his first wife. He kept just enough to buy tobacco for his pipe, and the rest went to Grace.

At first she was overwhelmed to have enough money to fund the household, but her careful nature soon took over and she was budgeting carefully and saving the rest. Abel did not ask for an accounting of the few shillings she brought in from her hens, and Grace began to see how satisfying it was to watch a small amount of savings grow.

Their second morning together, she had left him a clean shirt, a towel, and a cake of rough soap, as she had always done for her father. Abel was surprised, but when she stammered that it was a habit for her, he appeared touched and went out to wash. With his normally greasy hair washed, wearing a new shirt, he was easier to look upon this morning and his gratitude warmed her heart.

"I'm not used to someone doing for me anymore, Gracie," he told her. "My Rachel tried, but with her man and the children, it was all I could do to get a cup of tea and some clean clothes of a week. My Ruth took care of me before, but she was sick for so long, and I've gotten used to doing for meself."

Grace did not love her husband, and his physical appearance still revolted her, but she had to admit that he was kind and patient with her. And he tried to please her. He would bring her a flower that he had picked from the roadside, or a new ribbon for her hair.

Now that her mother was gone, she missed having someone to tend to, and she in turn tried to care for Abel, even brewing a special herb tea to loosen his chest and give him some relief from his terrible cough. So even though the love in the Poole marriage was entirely one-sided, there was kindness there, and Grace was more content than she would otherwise have expected.

For a man who appeared scrawny and wracked by ill health, Abel Poole had strong needs, needs that he had not been able to fulfill for a long time, first with a sick wife and then as a widower. With a new young bride, he was eager for the pleasures of the marriage bed, and Grace soon realized that if she wanted to repay Abel's compassion towards her, tolerating his frequent desire for her was one of the ways to do it.

After their first night together, Abel gave her several days to heal, every night asking her hopefully, "Are ye all right, lass?" Each time she shrugged and did not answer, but the third night she felt guilty and met his eyes, "Yes, Abel, I am fine tonight." This time it did not hurt so much. He rose over her, reaching down and opening her legs with a gentle palm to her thighs before he pushed himself inside her. There was just a little pain as he thrust and panted on her. She lay quietly, not moving until he asked wistfully, "Will ye put yer arms around me, love?" and she did so.

She thought of how she had waited until he had gone out to the privy before bedtime, and had rushed to the cabinet to take several long drinks from one of the whiskey jugs. She had rinsed her mouth out with cold, leftover tea before going back to bed, taking a rag with her. Now she felt the lovely, heavy warmth of the liquor make her limp and relaxed and uncaring as her husband moved within her, stopping with a cry of pleasure before he rolled off of her. Grace pushed the rag between her legs to catch the disgusting wetness he left in her, and rolled over, pulling her nightgown back down and waiting for the whiskey to carry her off to sleep.

Soon it did not hurt at all, what Abel did to her at night, but she felt no pleasure either. She was aware that he was enjoying it very much, but she felt nothing that he did. She knew a little of how she was supposed to feel. She remembered the warm, wet, melting that she had felt low inside her when Edward had kissed her, how she had wanted him to touch her, and thought that that must be why people wanted to do this thing, but she did not feel anything like that with Abel. It was the opposite – she felt tight and dry when he looked at her, and her skin crawled when he touched her. The whiskey she sneaked every night made those feelings go away, made her relax and able to tolerate it. But the liquid in the jugs was diminishing quickly and she knew she would need to get more.

She was not afraid she would end up like her father. She only needed the drink to get her through Abel's attentions, that was all. She finally asked Abel to bring her something to drink, telling him that her monthly cycle was so painful, giving her such terrible cramps that she needed the relief. She blushed red to mention the curse to him, but he had been married before, he reminded her, and took the subject with a matter of fact attitude that mollified her.

Truthfully, she had only had her first cycle the month before she was married, and it had been light and nearly painless. But she almost looked forward to having it again, knowing that at least Abel would not touch her for those few days.

Abel brought her a bottle, not of whiskey, but of gin, the drink he favoured on the rare occasions he drank alcohol. Grace found that she liked it very much and it did not leave her sick in the mornings. Every night she would drink a little, in case her husband should want her, as he so often did. And every night, the gin would carry her away.

With the exception of Abel's frequent attentions, the marriage was better than she had expected. Grace got on well with his daughter Rachel, who visited often with her three children. There would soon be four children and Grace often helped with the others as Rachel grew larger and more uncomfortable.

Rachel did not resent Grace's marriage to her father; in fact, she welcomed someone who would take her father off her hands, leaving her own family more room in their house and more food for their table. Rachel was older than Grace, twenty-one years old, but the two girls became friends.

Grace watched and listened to her stepdaughter's experience with pregnancy and was present at the birth of Rachel's child later that spring, but in the autumn of 1814, when Grace began to vomit in the mornings, it was Abel who noticed and asked her if she thought she might be with child. He was so happy with the idea that Grace felt guilty for praying frantically that she was not.

But the nausea continued, her monthly cycles stopped, and eventually she could not deny that she was pregnant. Abel was very pleased. He had been disappointed that his wife had only given birth to one child, and had always wished for a son.

He was now even kinder to Grace, urging her to rest, bringing her little tidbits to tempt her appetite, not even minding that she did not want to share his bed as she grew larger. He had timidly tried to introduce other ways that Grace could satisfy him, but she flatly refused, and not wanting to upset her at this time, he dropped the idea and resigned himself to waiting.

As the child grew in her belly and began to move, Grace grew more used to the idea, and eventually began to look forward to the baby's birth. She sewed small clothes, and knitted throughout the winter. She felt good physically once the nausea had passed. Her small breasts grew lush, her flat hips bloomed with sudden roundness, her hair was thick and shiny. She would look back on this period of her life as the only time she had ever felt beautiful.

Spring, 1815

Grace had just let go of the pump handle, reaching down to pick up the bucket, when she heard his voice.

"Good day, Mrs. Poole."

She turned and saw him. "Neddie!" she gasped, and the bucket fell from her suddenly numb fingers. It hit the ground and water splashed everywhere.

"Oh, no!" Grace cried out. She was so large and ungainly that she could not move to avoid a good dousing, and so tired that the thought of drawing another bucket was discouraging. She stood up straight, one hand held to her aching back, and surveyed her wet dress. She sighed, and turned to her visitor.

"I'm sorry, Grace," Edward Rochester said, "or Mrs. Poole. I'm not sure what to call you now." He rubbed his forehead, frowning at her, and moved to pick up the bucket, taking it to the pump and reaching for the handle.

"Give me that!" Grace said, reaching for the bucket handle.

Edward dodged her hands, "You don't need to be carrying heavy water pails right now."

Grace snorted, "I carry them every day, morning and night. If I give birth in the morning, I'll be back carrying pails again the next."

Edward shook his head, looking over at her as he began to pump the handle. He jerked his chin at her. "When?" he asked.

Grace shrugged, "Any day now, the midwife says." She stood, hands to her back, stretching. It felt good.

She took a deep breath, "I hardly know what to say to you."

Edward glanced at her, then back down at the bucket, which was rapidly filling with water. "'Hello, Edward' would be a good start."

Grace smiled then, pushing a stray lock of hair back and tucking it up into the scarf that tied up her red gold hair. "Hello," she said. "When did you get home?'

"Yesterday." Edward pulled the bucket away from the pump, letting the last bit of water gush over the ground.

"I can tell you don't do this too often," Grace sighed. "If you did you'd know not to waste the water."

"They don't offer water-pumping classes at Eton," Edward retorted. "Don't be ungrateful. Where do you want this?"

Over your head, Grace thought.

She pointed to the cottage door, "There by the door is fine." They walked over to the bench next to the door, and Edward set the brimming pail down. "Thank you," Grace said, indicating the bench, "Will you sit for a moment?"

They sat down side by side, both of them silent. Grace leaned back, hands on her belly. "You're taller," she observed.

"Thank God," Edward said wryly. "Tall as my father now. I hope to pass him up but we shall see. I'm taller than Rowland. Bigger too."

"So why are you home?" Grace asked. "We've not seen you for so long, I was wondering if you remembered you had a home."

"End of term," Edward said. "I haven't been home in a long time, and my friend was wanting to meet my family, such as it is. I've availed myself of his hospitality for so long. His family enjoys seeing me. I cannot say the same for my father and Rowland."

Grace sat back, watching him. He was taller, but thinner than she remembered, not yet having developed the muscles of early manhood. There was a dark down visible on his upper lip and his hair was shorter than it had been when she had least seen him.

"I talked to Mrs. Fairfax," Edward continued. "She told me of your marriage and that you expected a child. I was... surprised."

"Why?" Grace asked.

He shrugged, "I suppose I thought I would return to Thornfield and find all the same as when I left it. That you and I would meet after my lessons to walk in the wood and picnic next to the stream."

"Nothing is the same," Grace said shortly, standing up. She paced back and forth along the flagstone path that led to the cottage.

Edward watched her. It seemed strange to see her, her belly huge with child, her face full. She was a woman now, years beyond him. He was still just a boy. It embarrassed him now that he had acted so strong around her, had talked about taking care of her. What an idiot he must have seemed.

"I was sorry to hear of Nellie," he said quietly.

"Yes," Grace said quietly, "It's too bad you could not have come to see her while she was ill. She would have loved to have seen you one last time. She spoke of you the very day she died." She could hear the hard edge in her own voice.

Edward looked surprised, "I am sorry. It just seemed easier to stay away."

He stretched his legs out, leaned back. "A whole new world opened for me at Eton. I was learning, taught by people who enjoyed teaching, meeting new people. The teachers approved of me, of my hard work. Unlike my father who never approves of me."

"What did you expect?" Grace said, "He never did."

"No, but one always hopes," Edward said, bitterly. "Wait, I take it back," he said as he held up a finger, "I do well in sports, and for some reason that pleases him. I work my ass end off at school, get high marks, never a word; I help row a boat down the Thames, we beat another boat, and he approves."

"He got rid of my father," Grace said, "For that reason alone I have a better opinion of him than I once did."

"I heard about that," Edward said.

"What did you hear?" Grace said, swallowing.

"That he'd lost a job, beaten you. I was amazed my father stepped in; usually he won't lift a finger or inconvenience himself."

"I believe the Fairfaxes spoke up for me," Grace told him, resuming her pacing. The baby was squirming inside her, its head pressing painfully against the bones of her pelvis. Every time it moved, something ached down low.

"Yes, I heard about that too," Edward said grimly. "Mrs. Fairfax is still angry with my father for not doing more to help you. She said it's his fault you had to marry Abel Poole."

Grace frowned, "That's none of her business. I chose to marry Abel Poole."

"Are you happy, Grace?" Edward's dark eyes caught hers, held them.

"Happy?" She was still frowning, made an impatient gesture, "What's happy?"

Edward sighed, looked down at his hands.

"Abel's a kind man," Grace said. "He cares for me."

"And do you care for him?" Edward asked her.

"He's my husband, I'm having his child. We are happy about that. Why are you asking me all this? This is my life, you have yours. Are you happy?"

"Yes," Edward said, "I love school. I love being out in the world, away from Thornfield."

"That's nice," said Grace, bitterness in her voice. "Some of us have to be here."

Edward went on as if she had not spoken, "And other times, I long for Thornfield. The house, the gardens… the fields, riding a horse over the grounds, playing in the woods. Being with you. I long for it all. I want it all back." He swallowed, looked away.

"It's all gone now," Grace said, "All changed." She was looking away, and when she turned back to him, he saw the tears on her cheeks. "Gracie… " Edward stood, came towards her, reached out his hand to her.

"Don't," she said, batting away his hand. "You need to go. You should not be here. If anyone sees you here," She blew her breath out. "Everyone thinks we have been together. As lovers. My father told everyone that you had had me. Even Abel thought so. Until I proved otherwise."

"We were children," Edward said.

"We were old enough," Grace said. "Old enough for people to believe it." Tears ran slowly down her cheeks. "I wish we had." She wiped savagely at her face with both palms, "I wish I'd had that with you, just once."

"I'm sorry, Grace," Edward said. "I wish I could give you more. I wish I could fix it for you, as I once thought I could."

"Yes, so do I," Grace said.

John Rochester caught his son as he was starting up the stairs to his room.

"Edward," he said, "I have been looking for you. Where have you been?"

"Out," Edward said shortly. "Visiting in the neighbourhood."

John beckoned him towards his study, "Can we have a word?"

"Hugh's waiting for me," Edward said, pointing towards the front door. "I told him to meet me at the stables; we're going to have a long ride this afternoon. He's waiting there now."

"He will wait for you," his father said. "There's plenty to see down at the stables. We have had to expand twice. I trust you found Arrow in good shape since you saw him last?"

He ushered his son into the study, moving to the liquor cabinet to pour two glasses of brandy. He handed one to Edward, who was relieved that for once Rowland was not around, poking into his business. He had heard that Rowland was poking into a Hay shopkeeper's daughter, which could account for his absence. The less he saw of his brother, the better off he would be.

"Arrow is well," Edward said, taking the glass. Unlike some of his classmates when they were on holiday, he had not yet developed much of a taste for drink. He sipped at it, trying not to grimace at the taste, "I'm not sure he knows me anymore." He smiled, but his smile faded when his father did not respond.

Rochester held his own glass and sat down, taking a large swallow.

"This friend you've brought home with you, this Hugh Lathrop – he seems a pleasant enough fellow. You get on well together?"

"We've shared a room for over two years. I've gone to his home on holidays. We fight a little on the playing field, compete on test grades, but I think that helps us do better. We do get on well."

"He lives on Grosvenor Street in London?" his father asked. "His father is a barrister, is he not? They don't make much money, from what I hear."

"Hugh's mother has money," Edward said. "It's not a secret; they speak of it openly in the home. It was quite a love match, apparently, and she and her parents were willing for it to take place, despite his lack of wealth. But he has done well on his own."

Edward had never seen a couple like his friend's parents. Robert and Charlotte Lathrop had a love that permeated everything around them, took in everyone who entered the house. It was the warmest home he had ever seen. He had decided upon his first visit that he would marry for love and have a home like Hugh's.

Rochester snorted, "Nice if you can get it. It's easy enough, I suppose, to love a woman with all that money."

Edward felt a flash of irritation, thinking of the kindness of Hugh's mother, who had been so good to him from their first meeting. He said nothing.

"So," his father said, taking another large drink of his brandy. Edward had barely touched his. "Have you given any thought as to what you will do with yourself in future? When you're eighteen, you're off to Oxford, so you say, and when you are done there, then what?"

Edward was silent. As always, it took only a few moments with John Rochester to make him begin to envy orphans. He grinned, trying to think of a way to best annoy his father.

"I'm hoping to find someone who'll pay me to play cricket for a living."

Rochester was not amused, "I am serious, Edward."

Edward shrugged, "So am I. It is what I like to do. Or what I did like to do, before you made me stop."

"I'm sure Hugh's parents would not approve of him running around, getting his nose broken, knocking balls about."

Edward smiled, "Well, Father, Hugh is the one who broke my nose to begin with. It was an accident. And we did get our balls knocked about also." He shrugged. "All in the game."

Rochester was frowning, "Your sense of humour in this case is far from appropriate. I am trying to discuss a serious matter. At any rate, rowing is a better sport. It is more dignified, and I'm sure you meet a better group of people. People who might be valuable to know, in the future."

Edward, who knew his fellow rowers very well, doubted that any of them would be good to know in the future, but he stayed silent.

His father gestured to his son's barely touched drink. "Not a drinker?"

"Not much," Edward told him. "No doubt I'll develop a taste for it as time goes by."

"Been with a woman?" his father asked.

"Sir?" Edward asked. He had heard him the first time, but was debating whether or not he should lie, as he had to all his friends. And they to him, he suspected.

"Have you had a woman? Bedded her?" Rochester asked.

"No," Edward admitted. "No doubt that will come in time as well."

"What are you waiting for?" his father asked sharply.

Edward sighed. This was it. He hoped his father would not injure himself laughing.

"I had rather hoped to be in love, Father," Edward said, with dignity, "not just bed a woman because I can."

As he predicted, his father spent some moments laughing, having to stop to cough before he settled down, shaking his head.

"You are just like your mother," Rochester said, suddenly scornful.

"I very much hope so," Edward said in a low voice. His dark eyes were suddenly piercing and narrowed, and he fixed them on his father.

"Josiah Carey told the whole town that you'd bedded his daughter. Carried on about it in great detail."

"Josiah Carey is a drunken animal not worth shooting for loss of the bullet," Edward said, angrily. "I never slept with Grace. We were children. She was my friend."

"I never believed it, mind," his father said. "What would you want with that skinny, homely little scullery maid anyway?" Edward felt a flash of anger and was silent for a moment. *It's not worth it,* he told himself.

"Grace was my friend," Edward repeated. "I will always remember that. She is the truest friend a boy could have had."

"Rowland had at least one woman by your age, perhaps more," Rochester said, apparently bored with the subject of Grace.

"I do not doubt it," Edward said in reply.

"I saw to it myself, as my father did for me once," his father said. "A clean girl, pretty. I can make an arrangement for you, should you want it."

"No, thank you," Edward said, decisively. "I would not consider myself much of a man if I could not see to my own... arrangements."

His father's eyes narrowed, hearing the insult there. He chose to pass it over.

"So, I repeat, what are you going to do?" his father asked again. "You'll not get a penny of the estate; it's all tied up in Thornfield. You'll need to make your own way."

"I know that," Edward said, impatiently. "You and Rowland have both made it a point to remind me of that fact. Actually, I found Hugh's father's work rather exciting. He took us to court on several occasions."

"A barrister?" his father said. "No money, toiling away, hoping to eventually make good, please the right people, and so be given cases?"

"It won't be easy, but then what would be, in my case?" Edward said. "The army? The navy? The church? The law at least interests me."

"Oh, that is important, that you are interested," his father said sarcastically.

"You asked," Edward said coldly.

"Yes, and I have a reason to ask, as you'll see." His father picked up a letter, "I have here a letter from an old school fellow of mine, a Jonas Mason. He came to visit here, years ago, but you were a small child; you won't have remembered.

"He's a second son, like you, sent out to Jamaica to inherit a relative's plantation. He has built it up to quite a business, growing and exporting sugar. He has a son, about your age. He will be teaching him the business, which grows busier and more demanding. He asked if I might send you also, to learn the export business with his son."

"Jamaica?" Edward asked, "In the West Indies?"

"Where else?" his father replied with irritation. "After college, when you are twenty-one years of age and can conduct business legally, you will go to Jamaica and learn the export business. I have investments there, in sugar. You can look to them for me, and learn about exporting goods back home."

"Hugh and I had talked about making the Grand Tour after college," Edward said. "France, Italy, Spain."

"On my money," his father said.

"All the young gentlemen go," Edward said.

His father made a dismissive gesture, "You have a chance to go somewhere exciting, exotic. The other men will probably never leave Europe. You'll be on the other side of the world."

Edward shrugged, "It sounds as though I have little choice."

"It is a good opportunity," Rochester said, "and there is something else."

"Mason has a daughter, a young girl of... well, your age. She will be seeking a husband and as they are wealthy, she is prey to fortune hunters, which are in abundance in Jamaica. She is said to be very beautiful. Mason would love an alliance with an Englishman of a good family."

Edward frowned, looking down at the well-worn rug of his father's study.

"It's four or five years yet," Rochester said. "Think about it, it is your choice."

"The marriage or the export business?"

"The marriage, of course," his father said. "It's a good opportunity, that's all. No one is forcing you to do anything. If you do not want Miss Mason, I'm sure plenty of other young men will."

Edward leaned over the ship's rail, peering down at the blue waves that reflected the dancing rays of sunshine. There was nothing but water as far as his eyes could see, and he took a deep breath, feeling his chest expand with the intake of tangy salt sea air. He felt well, had suffered no sickness, but then it had been a smooth voyage so far. His spirits were high – he felt almost giddy with the excitement of being on his own in this lovely place. He had never seen a sky so clear, nor water so blue.

Since the ship had raised anchor in Madeira three weeks earlier, Edward had felt a sense of autonomy that was new to him. Long years under his father's control had cramped his soul, made him feel trapped and helpless, leaving him unsure of how to break away from the iron will of John Rochester. Now, with every mile that stretched out behind him, he felt his world expand. At times he would wake in the night and creep from his cabin, moving to the ship's rail to gaze out into the unending darkness around him. Had he not been afraid of looking like a crazy man, he would have thrown his arms into the air and laughed aloud for the joy of freedom.

Now he bent lower, his attention caught by quick flashes of white and grey that appeared on the water's surface and just as quickly disappeared. He squinted his eyes at these glints of light that glittered on the top of the water.

"Dolphins," he heard a voice beside him say. He turned quickly at the sound, and saw a thin sailor, one who seemed close to Edward in age, standing next to him. The young man smiled and gestured to the swimming creatures.

"Quite large fish," Edward replied, somewhat at a loss. He was accustomed to being treated deferentially because of his wealth and position; this casual familiarity was a startling departure from his usual social interactions. The sailors had ignored him, moving around him as though he were invisible. Their rough accents and curses had seemed foreign to his ears and yet he had observed them with a feeling of envy that was new to him. They seemed so at home as they scurried about on deck, climbing the riggings and maneuvering the sails of the huge vessel. Edward wondered what it would be like to have a set job to do every day, to know his place in life and what he was supposed to do. To work with his two hands and be paid a wage.

"Well, sir, they a'nt fish exactly," the sailor said. He thought for a moment, "Not sure what kind of animal, rightly. Sort of very small whales." He smiled again.

"I've never seen a whale either," Edward admitted. "Have never really seen fish, except on a platter just before I eat them. And those fish came from a river, not the sea, caught with a line and a hook."

"You've never seen the sea, sir?" the sailor asked.

Edward shrugged, "Just the seashore, at Brighton, some years back. And then the harbor when we set sail in Southampton, five weeks ago."

"It's nothing like this," the sailor said. "That's grey and cold. This is warm and blue. I wait every voyage for this part of it, then I know why I stay on the sea."

Edward asked him, "You sail to Jamaica often?"

The sailor nodded, "Several times a year. Back and forth, carrying rum and tobacco, passengers and cargo. I been on the sea since I was a lad, just seven. Your first time to Jamaica, then?"

"Yes." Edward did not know what to add to that. What could he say? *"I'm going to meet the daughter of my father's business acquaintance, and if we like each other, we shall be married."* So he said nothing, and continued to look at the dolphins as they continued their playful leapings alongside the ship. He turned, the words, "What is Jamaica like?" forming on his lips as he did so. But the sailor was already stepping back.

"Well, sir, good luck then," the sailor said. He touched the brim of his cap and moved away from the rail.

A week later a different picture was before him as he stood at the rail, watching the sailors scurrying to ready the ship for its arrival at the dock in Kingston, where Richard Mason would be meeting him. It was still morning, but already the sun was beating down hard upon the travellers as they waited on the ship for the tender that would convey them to shore.

The Masons had a villa near the sea, an hour by carriage from their main house in Spanish Town and a day's journey from their holiday retreat in the hills. Mason's final letter of instruction several months ago had indicated that it was to the seaside home that his son would take Edward after meeting his ship. Thinking of this, Edward smiled at the thought that this mysterious friend of his father's had one more house than John Rochester, who fancied himself far more successful.

Edward could see the land, the white sand and strangely shaped trees, with the distant forms of oddly square buildings beyond, their roofs not as high and peaked as he was used to seeing in England. The constant sun beat down upon him, burning his head in spite of the hat he wore. Now that they were not surrounded by water, the warm yellow sunlight seemed suddenly oppressive, no longer the novelty it had been at first, compared to the often cloudy skies of England.

His head ached in a steady throb now, the sunlight harsh in his eyes despite the nearly constant squint he maintained to protect his gaze. His stomach felt ill, rolling in time with the steady beat of the pain in his head. His entire body felt damp, the sweat rolling off his skin beneath his clothing: heavy cotton drawers, shirt, breeches and coat. He wiped his wet brow with a slightly unsteady hand as he used it to shield his eyes as he scanned the harbor.

He could see groups of sailors as they maneuvered long rowboats to the ladder beside the ship. And for the first time, among the now-familiar faces, he saw a sight he had been expecting, yet could hardly believe: black faces, dozens and dozens of them, all shades from just slightly darker than his own olive complexion to the darkest ebony.

He was no stranger to dark skin, having seen black men and women in London and in Oxford, and several on the very ship that had carried him here. But here in Jamaica, they were the majority. He had been expecting to see slaves; he knew it was rude to stare and yet he could not stop his gaze from following them.

His trunks had been unloaded hours before, along with the rest of the cargo bound for various towns and cities all over Jamaica. The luggage stood on the end of the gangplank awaiting the arrival of the carriage that would bear him to the

Masons' home. Jonas Mason had written his father that his son, Richard, and some servants would meet the ship and convey Edward safely to their home.

When the boats were in place, the few passengers began to disembark, moving to the side of the ship and climbing down the heavy rope ladder with the assistance of the crew members waiting in the boats. Edward closed his eyes as he began to climb down, not wanting to look at what seemed a huge drop to the boat below and not wanting to look up and let the sun hit his throbbing eyes. It seemed hours later that he felt a steadying hand upon his arm, and opened his eyes to see the damp wood of the boat inches below his boot. He exhaled with relief and sat shakily down on one of the empty benches. His heart was racing and he felt such tension that it was several moments before he realized that they had shoved off and the boat was being rowed rapidly away from the ship, the sailors' bodies rising and falling in rhythm as they laboured together over the long oars.

For one crazy moment Edward longed to jump up and call for them to take him back so he would not have to face the mysteries and fears of his unknown new life in this alien place. Euphoric with the excitement and freedom of his passage over the sea, he had not really considered what lay ahead when he finally reached Jamaica, and a momentary panic seized him, making his stomach clench painfully.

The boat reached the wharf, and it was pulled alongside by the sailors, who deftly laid down their oars and moved to assist the passengers to leave the boat. Once again Edward had to climb a small rope ladder, this time upwards to the wharf. The wooden boards beneath his feet lurched and rolled and he swayed as he stood there.

"Whoa, mate!" One of the sailors seized his arm. "It'll take you some time to get your legs under you again." Edward felt embarrassed and that added to the turmoil he felt.

It seemed as though he were in a dream, moving slowly, dizzy with the continued headache and with the sun relentlessly beating down upon him. His ears were buzzing and he was suddenly cold in spite of the incredible heat around him. His vision began to blur and he felt his knees buckle. The voices that surrounded him came from far away and he was only dimly aware of arms supporting him, guiding him to a place where he could sit down.

He heard his name and he tried to respond but it was too much effort to raise his head. He was terribly afraid he would vomit and add even more humiliation to what he already felt, add to the contempt he knew these seasoned seamen felt for him, despite their seeming kindness in his weakened state.

Edward felt something cold placed against his forehead and a glass was shoved against his lips. He gulped, expecting water, but gagged and sputtered at the taste of the rum he was given instead. He heard laughter around him and was in enough control of his faculties to wish not to appear weak and more foolish than he seemed already. When the glass was offered again, he took another drink and this time the unfamiliar taste did not seem to difficult to swallow. It took a long time, but gradually the buzzing voices grew clearer, the darkness that invaded his field of vision cleared, and he came back to himself.

He found that he was sitting with his back to a pile of trunks, his own trunks. His knees were bent and his head was resting on them. He raised his head slowly, and looked up. A man of about his age stood above him, smiling down upon him nervously.

"Edward Rochester, they tell me?" He nodded slowly and the man reached down, giving Edward his hand to assist him to stand. Edward took the proffered hand and stood unsteadily. The man's hand was small and soft, like a woman's, and clammy besides. Edward resisted the impulse to wipe his hand off on his trousers.

"I am Richard Mason," the young man continued. "My father sent me to fetch you to our home." Mason had an odd rhythm to his voice, a nervousness, as though he had had a childhood stammer and had been carefully coached out of it. He was about Edward's height but lacked his sturdy muscular build. He was slight, his shoulders somewhat rounded, and with a strange habit of drawing back after each phrase, as though cowering.

Mason had brown hair, combed back from a low forehead, and wide-set brown eyes. He was handsome in a weak, almost effeminate way, with slightly pursed lips that detracted from his otherwise even features. Edward found himself discomfited by Mason's failure to make eye contact.

"Don't be ashamed, Mr. Rochester," young Mason continued in his soft voice. "It must be hot and miserable, accustomed as you are to the cool weather and rain of England." There was no mockery in Mason's face, and Edward's acute embarrassment melted away at the obvious concern he showed. He did not care for the appearance of Richard Mason, but he appreciated the kindness.

He was suddenly seized with a rush of homesickness – not for England, but for the solid masculine companionship of his best friend Hugh. How he wished Hugh could be here with him now. Hugh would have teased him unmercifully, as he in turn would have done to Hugh had he been the one to show weakness. But his friend was probably even now roaming the streets of Paris, tasting all the delights of the Continent. What on earth was Edward doing here, alone in this hot and distant land?

Mason was waiting for him to speak. Edward took a deep breath, "Yes, it's true that this is very different from what I am accustomed to. Very hot." He swallowed, aware of his exhaustion and unable to speak further.

Mason gestured down the gangplank towards a waiting carriage, and said "Shall we go?" Mason made a move as though to take Edward's arm, then thought better of it and pulled his hand back, motioning Edward to precede him. Then he changed his mind and went ahead of him. Edward found the man's nervousness irritating and was relieved to finally be installed inside the conveyance, sinking in relief against the soft cushions. Mason remained outside and Edward saw him gesturing and speaking to two dark-skinned men, pointing to the trunks that remained behind. Craning his neck, he looked past the men, seeing a crude wagon behind the carriage.

Mason entered the carriage and knocked on the roof to get the driver's attention. The carriage lurched to a start and rolled away. Edward would have liked quiet, would rather have been allowed to lean his head back and close his burning eyes, but Mason felt compelled to be a host, and Edward found himself having to turn his still-aching head this way and that as Mason pointed out various attractions and landmarks.

When Richard Mason was talking about the history of the area, his nervousness disappeared and he grew animated. It was then that Edward could see how Mason could be considered handsome. He wondered if he was engaged or had a young woman to whom he was attached.

While he was on the ship, he had thought about Miss Mason and wondered if she would come to the dock to meet him, but since his spell of sickness he was glad that she had not. He felt a strange anticipation at the thought of making her acquaintance soon. He supposed it would not have been considered appropriate for a young lady of fortune to come to the docks to meet a ship, even if the ship was bringing her prospective bridegroom. He thought of his father's words during their last dinner together.

"Miss Mason is said to be a beauty, indeed, the boast of all Spanish Town." John Rochester had winked at him. "You could do worse than to have a woman such as that on your arm, eh, Edward?" He turned to Rowland, "And in his bed."

Rowland had smirked, "Edward wouldn't know what to do with a beauty if he found her in his bed, Father. Don't frighten him!" The two had laughed, hoisting their glasses, and Edward had felt a pull deep in his belly at the thought of a woman in his bed. Rowland had not ceased to make light of what he called Edward's "damnable innocence," and had even made doubtful remarks about his younger brother's manhood, laughing at his notions of romance and his refusal to bed a woman just for the sake of it.

Now, far across the ocean and away from his father and his brother, Edward was glad he had not listened to his brother's hateful teasing, had resisted his brother's and father's efforts to help him lose his innocence. He was glad he had held out for something greater. He wanted love and respect to accompany his physical efforts.

He knew that his young bride would be untouched also, and so would not notice if her new husband was somewhat unschooled. He knew the theory of the marriage bed, and was excited at the thought of them learning together. He thought again of Miss Mason, wondered if she was looking forward to his arrival and if she was frightened as well. He felt a strange tenderness towards this unknown girl.

The carriage had barely left Kingston when Edward dozed off, and it was far later in the day when he awoke, embarrassed to see that they had travelled a long way as he had slept. Richard Mason said nothing when his guest sat up with a start, and Edward, trying to appear as nonchalant as though he had been awake all along, noticed that they were advancing down a short dirt road that led to a large white house surrounded by walled gardens. Still drowsy and feeling ashamed of himself for his weakness, Edward saw only glimpses of large airy rooms and dark-skinned servants before he was shown to a small guest room that looked out onto a patio surrounded by lush greenery. His legs felt heavy and it was all he could do to put one foot in front of the other as he was led to the room. A young girl, whom Richard addressed as Evangeline, brought in a ewer filled with cool water, her deep brown eyes raking Edward up and down before she left the room.

Richard Mason had told him that his father was still in Spanish Town but that he would arrive at six and they would eat dinner at seven. He offered to call for something for Edward to eat in the meantime, but with his stomach still unsteady and exhaustion overtaking him, he refused with thanks. Richard told him he would fetch him just before seven to show him to the dining room.

Edward could wait no longer before he asked, "Will I be making the acquaintance of Miss Mason this evening?"

Richard hesitated, then said, "My sister is at our house in Spanish Town, and I do not know if my father will bring her with him today. If not, she will arrive soon and you will meet her then." He seemed eager to leave, and he nodded at Edward and left the room, shutting the door behind him.

Edward laid down his hat and removed his coat, untied his cravat and took off his shoes and stockings. His whole body felt damp, and after a moment's hesitation, he removed his breeches and shirt as well, sighing at the feel of the air from the open window as it finally cooled his skin somewhat. He bathed his face in the cool water that Evangeline had left and then dipped a rag in the water, moving it over his arms and chest, wiping away the sweat and grime of the journey. Moving slowly, as if in a dream, he went over to the bed. He intended only to rest his aching eyes, but exhaustion overtook him and he fell asleep almost before his eyes were fully shut.

Chapter 7 - Jamaica

I never loved, I never esteemed, I did not even know her. I was not sure of the existence of one virtue in her nature: I had marked neither modesty, nor benevolence, nor candour, nor refinement in her mind or manners—and, I married her:—gross, grovelling, mole-eyed blockhead that I was! With less sin I might have—but let me remember to whom I am speaking.
Edward Rochester - Jane Eyre

He should have known.

At the small, airy house in the hills to which they had been taken for their honeymoon, Edward stood on the verandah and looked over the path back to Spanish Town, the way back to the sea and to home.

He should have realized. *How could I have been so stupid?* He gripped the railing of the verandah, feeling the rough wood beneath his hands, the hands that had spent the night caressing Bertha's body, the same hands that had fended off her frantic, scratching nails as well.

It had all gone so quickly, once he'd agreed to the marriage, feeling only the pulsating of his blood, the hot insistent pressure of his body, listening only to the warm ocean breezes over his skin and the soft whispers of her voice in his ear, smelling only the salt air and the sweet perfume of her warm skin.

Back in England, he had been calm and smart and sensible. He had done his studies, carefully managed the small allowance his father grudgingly gave him, was prudent and mindful in all his dealings. He had looked forward to learning a business, to being trusted with important legal and financial arrangements. And he had anticipated a quiet courting of Miss Mason as a pleasant aside to his labours, as a possible blossoming of friendship and like minds.

But he had not been prepared. The enthusiasm displayed towards him by Jonas Mason and his son, Richard, before they even knew what he was about. Night after night of parties, of seeing Bertha across the room, beautifully dressed, smiling, following him with her eyes. Seeing the other men as they watched and whispered, their eyes following her.

Evening after evening he dressed up, ate rich foods, drank a variety of exotic brews, and danced beneath a canopy of stars while the ocean pounded in his ears. And all the time, the heat. The heat and the damp. Pushing at his skin, making it hard to breathe. Not the cool damp of England that made the roses grow lush and filled the lungs with a cool vigour. This humidity drained him, made him feel as though he were wading through water.

Staying up late into the night, falling naked on top of the cotton sheets of his large bed, sleeping until the relentless heat of the August morning would not allow him to sleep any longer. He woke to wash and dress in the light clothing favoured by the men here, just breeches and a white shirt, eschewing the coat and cravat a gentleman would otherwise not be without. He followed the family mindlessly from their villa on the outskirts of Spanish Town, where Mr. Mason conducted the majority of his business, to the equally large ocean home where Richard spent the majority of his time.

Richard Mason showed no interest in his father's business. He was an indolent man, moving slowly, his expression dreamy and his words coming slowly to him. He would rise late, taking his time over a lazy brunch, and spend his afternoons in lounging on the verandah, reading, visiting. He seemed puzzled when Edward had mentioned to him their learning of the business, waving his hand and murmuring something about the steward seeing to all that.

Finally, when Edward had asked several times, the elder Mason had taken the young men into the hills, to see the fields of sugar cane, to see the rows and rows of field labourers, naked to the waist, bending and cutting, their voices raised in mournful dirge-like songs that would echo in Edward's head for years to come.

Mason had taken Edward to the factory, spending two days showing him how the raw cane was eventually made into crystalline sugar that was put into bags that were then loaded onto vessels at the docks, to be shipped overseas. It was interesting, Edward admitted, but it was obvious from the first day that the business was well run, that no extra management was needed, and that the promise of his learning an occupation had been a somewhat empty one. Mason had told him he'd be glad to teach him the ropes, but it had been a quick and automatic agreement, a fast promise given to someone to keep them temporarily satisfied.

That, Edward realized now, would have been the time to leave – those days at the factory and the shipyard, when he had begun to realize that there was more, or less, to his being sent to Jamaica than met the eye. While his head was still somewhat clear, before she had begun to fill his days and nights with her looks and her whispers and her hot, searching fingers.

Night after night, he was given little time alone with Miss Mason. If he managed to maneuver her to a quiet corner, managed to start a whispered conversation with her, he was soon interrupted – sometimes by Richard, coming over to stand with his sister and his new friend, or by Mari, Bertha's childhood nursemaid and nearly constant companion, coming to see if her mistress was too warm, or required a drink, or a rest. Or by a young man, coming to see if he could claim the next dance from Miss Mason.

Only a few quick conversations had passed between himself and Bertha. One about music, in which they both expressed a liking for Mozart and Bach and an unfamiliarity with Beethoven. That had seemed promising, with Bertha giggling as she lifted her gloved hands to imitate herself playing the piano before a group of her father's friends. They had laughed together, their eyes meeting as they broke off and lifted their drinks to their lips. They had agreed that sometime soon they would sit and play together, looking forward to hearing each other sing.

Then, they had had a conversation about the ocean. Bertha had told him that she loved the sea, loved the pounding and receding of the waves that was a much a part of her as her own heartbeat. And indeed, from the verandah, on more than one occasion, Edward had spied her, accompanied by Mari, wading into the ocean, her dark hair unbound and flowing behind her, her face turned up to the West Indian sun, dressed in a simple white dress that clung to her curves when wet. Watching her, Edward had felt a strange tenderness, and he had smiled and waved to her as she turned to see him looking.

But that was all. Only those brief meetings, and those two short conversations. The rest of the time it was a whirl and a bustle of activity. Meals, at which she was seated too far from him for easy conversation. Passing in the gardens of the villa, he with Richard, she with Mari or another servant. And at night… always at night. The parties, the dinners, the constant press of people – all strangers to him, all wanting to talk to him about the England that was a far away memory to most of them.

It was not just Bertha with whom he was put in company. There were other women too – women in bright silks and satins, all colours of hair in elaborate uplifts that displayed slender necks and smooth shoulders. There was the sight of their lush bosoms above their bright dresses, the feel of their arms around him briefly as he danced with them.

Far from the relatively male-dominated world of Oxford, where he had bent diligently to his studies and gathered with groups of classmates to drink and to debate, he stood now in a new reality made of high, feminine laughter and flirty conversation. He had been careful in college. It was amusing to some of his friends, his avoidance of female entanglements. Hugh knew how he felt; they had spent many hours in their room talking of poetry and the nature of love and attachment. Hugh knew how taken Edward had been with the loving warmth of his family, and he agreed that it was something he himself wanted. But it hadn't even stopped Hugh from going out and meeting up with this shop-girl and that young doxy, enjoying his youth, he said, before he was tied to home and hearth.

Edward shied away from this, not even sure why himself. Oh, he wanted it. When he would wake in the morning, hard and eager, he would have liked nothing better than to roll over into a woman's loving arms to take his relief. But in the cold light of day...

He had known what it was to have a woman love him. Not romantically, not yet. But the strong love of his mother, of Nellie. He had felt its warmth, its safety. And Grace... he winced when he thought of her. He still felt he'd failed her. He still wished he could do more for her. And he still remembered what it was like to feel that love and longing for the first time, and to know that a girl had loved and looked up to him. It was impossible, he knew. There was no place for the two of them, nowhere on earth where a gentleman's son and the daughter of a tenant farmer could have a life together. And he lacked the burning ardor for her that would have made him find a way. He loved her with the quiet warmth he would have felt for a sister. She had been a source of such security for him when he was a boy, and for that he would always think of her fondly, even while he felt that, had he been a real man, he could have done more for her. He felt guilty when he thought of her. He knew she had loved him, loved him with a woman's love, one that was far more intense than the brotherly affection he had for her.

So he knew a little of what it was to have a woman's love, how it was a bulwark and a shield against the rest of this world. And he knew that he wanted that for his future. His heart was eager for it, more eager even than his body. He had thought of the faraway promise of Mason's daughter, waiting in Jamaica for him to come and court her. And he felt that he should save himself for her, as she was no doubt saving herself for him.

"I am as good as engaged," he would murmur, to the college friends around him when the subject of women came up, "I cannot dishonour her." He always made sure the wistful tone came into his voice when he said the word "her". Made his eyes shine with loving light. They were not to know that he had never seen her, and that the engagement was a mere wisp of possibility.

He had always come away from those pub table encounters laughing within himself at the respect the men had suddenly shown for his fidelity to his "betrothed". How they had quickly raised their glasses to his future, before moving on to another subject. He did not realize he had such a talent for acting. What a pity the stage was not a possibility for a gentleman's son. He was almost sorry he had not brought up that idea to his father. That would certainly have gotten an enjoyable response...

But now he was here, here in Jamaica, and the woman in question was with him. With him and yet not with him. But the conversations at the table, swirling around him, grew more and more certain of his union with her. All around seemed to expect it; he saw it on all sides. In Mason's casual use of the word "son" when speaking to him. In Richard Mason's dog-like friendliness. In Bertha's fathomless dark eyes, searching for his across the room.

He and Richard went to the ocean every day to escape the heat. Hurricane season was threatening, with its dark horizons and hot winds that made everyone edgy. In a week, perhaps two, the household might have to pack up and head farther inland, to the Masons' holiday lodge in the mountains. But for now, the ocean was safe as long as they avoided swimming in the riptides that could come up without warning.

In the afternoons, the two men would go to the water's edge and wade into the rushing greenish-blue water, the hot white sand between their bare toes. Their clothing would come off and into the surf they would rush. The first time Edward had seen Richard divest himself of all his garments he had stopped, a shocked look on his face. Richard had laughed, one of the first true laughs Edward had heard from him.

"This is the West Indies, brother," he had told him. "It's our private shore; no one here but us." At Edward's hesitant glance towards the house, Richard had laughed again. "No one can see you. No one but a few kitchen maids, and who cares about them? My sister can't see you. Although nice if she could; she'd know what she is getting."

Edward had grown used to it, to tearing off his clothes and diving into the cool, salty water that rushed up over him and threatened to engulf him completely. It was then that he would feel some sanity steal over him with the cooling of his body. The rushing waves of the ocean seemed a perfect counterpart to the rest of his life, his future washing towards him and breaking over his head. This all seemed natural, seemed the way his life was supposed to go.

I am in too deeply now...

The first time she had stolen into his room, he had been shocked into silence. He had felt rather than seen her, opening his eyes to sense someone else in the room. He had grabbed for the sheet, made sure it was pulled up completely over his nakedness. He had seen her come from the shadows, seen her come towards the bed.

"What are you doing?" he'd asked in a hoarse whisper. "Where is Mari?"

She had laughed, a slow laugh that sent a shiver to the base of his spine. "I have managed to sneak away from her. She sleeps very soundly after these parties."

He had swallowed, his throat suddenly dry, and he looked over to his table, to the carafe of water. Bertha came forward quickly, her silk dressing gown whispering. She poured him a glass of water and handed it to him, their fingers meeting. She moved closer, reached behind him to hold his head up, warm hand on his neck, helping him drink. She smiled at the gulping sound he made, took the glass from his hand. But her hand stayed behind his neck, and when she put the glass down, she reached down and kissed him.

Oh, God... Her lips were so warm on his, her breath like cinnamon. Her hands were behind his neck, cupping him as her mouth opened to his. Their tongues danced together, came apart, their lips moving gently against each other's. It was his first kiss since he and Grace had kissed so long ago. But with Grace, it had never felt so hot, so dangerous.

He broke the kiss, hardly able to breathe. Her hands came up, and slowly slid the dressing gown off her shoulders. His heart gave a lurch, and he was almost relieved to see that beneath the gown she wore a lacy white camisole and a pair of... well, they were drawers, like the ones he wore, only white and lacy like the camisole, and clinging to her lush and rounded curves.

He had been excited, even before the kiss, even before she shed her gown. From the moment she came out of the shadows, she had aroused him, but now he was rock hard, his shallow rapid breaths audible in the room. Bertha heard him, and he saw her slow, seductive smile.

She moved the sheet away, and looked down at him, a soft chuckle low in her voice. He would have been embarrassed, but he was too excited, too stimulated. He waited for her to touch him, but she didn't. She just looked at him for a moment and then climbed slowly onto the bed, throwing her leg over him and straddling him.

He groaned to feel it, the pressure of her cotton clad warmth pushed completely against him. Her thighs were on either side of him, and the hot, sweet softness between her legs was up against him, pressed against his aching hardness. Only a thin layer of fabric separated them, and as she began to move herself against him, he was shocked by how good it felt.

She leaned forward, her warm breasts under their thin layer of cotton resting on his bare chest, and he reached up as in a dream, placing his palms on her back and pressing her to him. She moved, steadily and rhythmically against him, again and again and again, and her breath grew faster. He felt his breathing quicken also, and he was longing for the release that seemed just out of his reach.

She was moaning softly as she supported herself on her arms over him, rubbing against him. He slid his hands down her back, cupping her backside, pushing her against him right where he needed it. He felt his own hips rise up against hers, his own groans deep in his throat. He heard her moans go higher, a soft *yes, yes* from her lips as she pressed herself fully against him and he felt her body jerk gently. But he was not there yet, and his need was relentless. He increased his pressure against her, needing only a moment or so more to be where he sensed she had already been.

She was still as his hips rocked up into hers, but then leaned over, his lips against his ear. "Do you think you could love me, Edward?" she whispered.

The tide was washing over him, higher and higher, the heat building in him. So close, so close, and he pushed her down onto him, grinding his hips into hers.

Do you think you could love me, Edward?

"Yes!" he choked out, his voice nearly a whimper, as the pleasure peaked, and then a blessed relief came over him, pumping through him with an intensity he'd never felt on his own.

"Do you?" Bertha asked, insistently, still pressed against him, her clothing damp from the wetness that had shot out onto his belly.

"Yes," he whispered, still in a hot fog of pleasure. He felt her fall forward on him, her lips came over his again. He felt her mouth on his cheeks, his neck, his chest. A film of perspiration covered him, and he felt her over him, smothering him with her heat. He wished she would go, for now he felt embarrassed by his reactions, by his lack of control, by the hot fluid that he had stained her with, undeniable evidence of what had happened between them. He lay quietly, letting the relaxation wash over him, and to his relief, when he didn't talk further and his breathing grew more quiet and even, she quietly got off him and took her leave, throwing her gown over her shoulders and dropping one last kiss on his unresisting mouth.

When he was sure she was gone, he reached up, wiping himself off with the edge of the sheet and turning over, his heart suddenly pounding with the realization of what he had done. He knew that if Mason, or Richard, caught wind of this, he was in trouble. He had not resisted her, had not behaved in any way like the gentleman he was supposed to be.

In the morning, he would get up earlier than usual, go down to the ocean wrapped in the stained sheet and wade in, letting the water cleanse him. But for now he drifted off, troubled thoughts poking in and out of his dreams all night, sleeping, but not rested.

Edward rested more easily after his early morning dip in the ocean. He hung the wet sheet over a chair to dry, put on his drawers, and slipped back into bed for a few more hours sleep. But he could not get the picture of Bertha out of his head, lush and beautiful in her lace undergarments, the thick black braid over one breast showing up against the white of her camisole. Remembering the feel of her atop him, her soft lips upon his.

Edward was on fire.

She was all he could think of. Every time he closed his eyes her face was what he saw in his mind. All other thoughts – the export business, worries over what his father had been thinking, even his growing discomfort at the thought of the slaves working Mason's fields – all were a faraway buzz in his mind with Bertha in the forefront.

It wasn't a courtship – how could he call it that when they had hardly exchanged ten words in private? But all around him, all seemed to expect him to marry her. Everywhere he looked he saw approving faces, and the envious looks of the other men his age.

That morning he could barely meet her eye. He felt that everyone in the estate knew what had happened between him and Bertha. But Richard seemed no different towards him than otherwise, Mr. Mason was his usual friendly self, and when he slipped into his chair at dinner that night, Bertha, who was always very quiet and subdued at the table, looked over at him slowly and dreamily with a slight smile playing on her lovely red lips. She did not look as though she felt she was being taken advantage of.

A few days later, Jonas Mason finally came out and addressed the idea of his taking Bertha as his wife. Edward did not know if he brought it up because he simply felt it was time, or because word had gotten back to him about his daughter's foray from the room and her stained undergarments when she returned. But he was immediately stricken with a guilty conscience as he remembered what he had done with this man's daughter under his very roof, and so he listened seriously and respectfully to what Mason had to say.

"Er, Rochester, it cannot have escaped your notice that my daughter Bertha is quite taken with you," he said, as they walked around the gardens at Mason's request.

Quite, Edward thought, his mind suddenly flashing to Bertha's hips moving against his, her head thrown back, her face rapt with pleasure. He took a deep breath.

"Miss Mason is a lovely woman," Edward said, clasping his hands behind his back to still their sudden trembling.

"Yes, she is, and quite intelligent and accomplished," Mason continued. "I have striven to provide the best education for her, and have had hopes of a union with someone of fine family. Here in Jamaica there is not much to choose from, many newly rich Johnny-come-latelies, anyone who could afford the price of passage here from any other country. I know your father well, know from what fine stock the Rochesters descend."

I feel rather like a stallion being sized up for his stud potential. Edward did not know what to say, just nodded, "Yes, sir."

"No doubt, before you arrived, your father mentioned Bertha and the possibility of a union between our two families," Mason said, turning to face him.

"Yes, sir," Edward said. "Although he mainly mentioned my being shown the workings of the export business and the sugar plantation."

Mason frowned, "I had not realized. No wonder you were so interested. I thought you were just being polite."

"I was interested," Edward said "I am interested. I'm sure you know that my father will give me nothing. I can bring nothing to a marriage with your daughter except, as you say, my good stock as a Rochester. But I am the younger son, and my brother will inherit all. I wonder that you did not approach my father regarding Rowland as a suitor for Miss Mason. He will get the estate. I must make my own way."

Mason was silent for a moment, his mouth working. Then he regained his composure. "Bertha is my only daughter. I lost her mother some years back. I lost a younger son also. I do not wish for my daughter to go away from me. To marry her to your brother would be to send her to England for life. Here she can stay with me. I will settle thirty thousand pounds upon her, and I own some property. There is a house on this same road, also with its private beach. It's a small house, only a few bedrooms, not a large villa like this one. But good enough for a pair of newlyweds. There will be servants aplenty, and if you like I can teach you my business. My son shows no interest, and his health is not the best. Perhaps my worries of having someone to take over the running of the businesses will be alleviated by your help. Will you consider my daughter's hand, Rochester?"

Edward's instincts told him all was wrong. Should he not be taking control, asking Bertha to marry him when he felt they knew each other better, speaking to her father about it himself?

"Should I not ask Miss Mason myself?" Edward asked him.

Mason replied hastily, "She is shy, she fears that you will not want her, that you will feel pressured. I assured her that I would speak to you, and for her. She welcomes your attentions. She is not a worldly girl, she has been gently reared. She has been raised to look to the men in her life for her guidance in all things, as she will to you when you are married.

"Will you think about this union, Edward? There are many advantages on both sides."

"Yes, sir," Edward answered, "I will think about it."

That night, Bertha came to his room again. He heard the click of the latch of the door leading to his small patio. He had been sure he had locked it, but she opened it easily and slipped inside. He was not asleep yet, but lying on his back thinking of all that Mason had said to him today. He was uneasy. His father had been so adamant about the export business, only talking about Mason's daughter in an abstract way. But clearly, here in Spanish Town, a union was expected.

So he was not sleeping; rather his mind was racing. After Bertha had made her previous visit to him, he had taken to again wearing his underwear to bed, so as not to be caught unaware. When she came into the door, again wearing her red silk dressing gown, he was at least covered and not at such a loss.

"You should not be here," he whispered, rolling over to face her where she stood next to the bed. She smiled at him, reached down to stroke his cheek with her hand.

That sweet, unexpected caress caught him off guard, and he lay very still, feeling her stroking hand upon him. She bent to kiss him, sat down on the edge of the bed, reaching up to pull something out of her hair. Her hair fell from its chignon, tumbled around her shoulders. The air filled with the smell of perfume, flowers and musk and sunlit air. His breath felt suddenly shaky as he let it out slowly.

She stood, took off her dressing gown.

Underneath, she wore nothing. His sharp intake of breath made her smile.

He had seen pictures of unclothed women before. Classical paintings, and ribald pencil sketches both. But to see her in the flesh...

His wide eyes took in the soft slope of her shoulders, the full, heavy breasts with their pink tips, the soft curve of her belly, and down lower, a darkness where her legs met. He had seen pictures too, crude drawings of what was within that darkness, and the glimpses of those pictures had sent such desire through him that he had had to look away, only to remember them later when he was in his darkened room, aching to possess that mysterious pleasure for himself.

Bertha lay down next to him, and turned to take him in her arms.

He wanted to resist. She was not his, and he was not hers, and if he was a decent man he would leap from the bed and refuse to be in the room with her. But he lay as if paralyzed, feeling her lips search for his. He longed to pull away from her, to refuse to lie here with her, to go away and sort out the jumble of thoughts and worries in his brain, but the only thing he was aware of was the painful throb in his loins and a longing to feel the softness of her skin.

Mindlessly, as though someone were controlling him from outside, he turned to her and wrapped his arms around her, his lips finding hers hungrily. He rolled over to feel her warm, soft body beneath his, and it drove him wild. His hands were out of his control, moving over her, touching her everywhere. And she was not trying to avoid him, she was responding, and allowing every touch.

Finally she reached up and stilled his frantic movements with a hand, whispering, "Shhh." She lay him down on his back, and gently worked his drawers down his legs. She lay down next to him, reaching for his hand, and moving it up to her breasts, showing him how to stroke her and touch her, then leaned over to let him take them in his mouth. His ears were roaring and his breath was coming fast as he moved from one breast to the other, his mouth filled with the taste of her.

He felt her hand on his belly, stroking, going lower, before she ran her hand over him, over the spot where he wanted it. She stroked down lower, back, deep between his thighs and then back up again. He opened his legs to allow her access and he clenched his teeth, feeling his breath hiss between them. He lay back, not able to concentrate on anything but her fingertips, stroking him over and over until her hand closed around him, moving with a firm grasp and an expert rhythm.

She's done this before, the certainty came into his mind.

She was kissing him, and he felt her mouth against his ear, as she whispered, "I see you, down at the ocean. I stand and watch you as you swim."

"I thought you couldn't see us," he gasped, wanting her to be quiet, so he could concentrate on what her hand was doing to him.

"I see you," she whispered, "I watch you, and all I can think of is you, here in my arms, in my hands. All I want is you inside me."

He gasped suddenly as he finished abruptly, hard and strong and powerful. He didn't know if it was her words or her hand or both together but it was intense, leaving him lightheaded and nearly unable to catch his breath.

She smiled at him, getting up to fetch a cloth from the washstand, washing him off, rinsing the rag out and hanging it up. She pulled the sheet up over him, and leaned to kiss him with a light, demure kiss.

"I had better get back," she whispered, "my darling Englishman."

The next morning, he awoke with her words echoing inside his mind, "All I want is you inside me." As soon as he dressed, he went to speak to her father.

And now, six weeks later, he stood on the wood verandah of the honeymoon home Mason had rented for them near his own mountain retreat. This was a paradise, and they should be so happy. A mountain stream clean enough to drink from, horses sent up with them and stabled for riding, servants here to attend to their every need, the lovely weather of early November with its relief from the heat.

But it was not as he had thought. Somewhere along the way, he realized he had been duped. He should have known, he should have realized.

Was it when he overheard two of the servants talking a few mornings after the wedding, and realized Bertha's mother was not dead as he had been told, but locked away in a mental asylum for life?

Was it the first time he witnessed Bertha's hateful demanding behaviour to the servants, speaking to them as if they were less than human, ordering them to do one thing, and then later, the opposite? Was it when he heard her break down and weep for hours, wailing and crying, refusing to be comforted and refusing to tell him what was wrong?

Or was it the first time she lifted her hand to him, giving him a stinging slap to his wrist because he had said something she disagreed with? He had gasped and pulled his hand back, and she had put her hand to her mouth, apologizing profusely.

He did not know when all these fears and doubts coalesced in his mind, and came down to this shadow that hung over him, filling him with foreboding as to his future. He wondered how he could finish this honeymoon, which was to last another week, and take his bride home. He wondered what the time ahead would hold.

At the start, it had gone promisingly enough. He had spoken to her father, formally asking for her hand, and soon a date was set for three weeks hence, October 20, 1820, barring any major interruptions from bad weather. But the season was uneventful. The weeks went by quickly, but with the servants at their disposal, the preparations went smoothly.

Before he knew it, almost before his head had stopped spinning with the swiftness of it all, Bertha was coming down the aisle on her father's arm, coming towards him, smiling into his eyes. She wore her mother's wedding dress, and a white veil with orange blossoms in her thick black hair. Edward tried to keep down the voice that was nagging inside him, telling him to turn and run now, while he still could. This was his only recourse.

He thought of the thirty thousand pounds that had been transferred to a bank account in his name, to be given to him after the wedding. He thought of his uncertain future without his tie to the Masons. Wondered where he would go, what he would do.

And he looked at her in her white dress. White meant purity, virginity. But she wasn't pure, and neither was he.

They had been together, lain together. He had done as she said she wanted, he had been inside her. He had to marry her; he owed it to her, as a gentleman.

He had not meant to. He had meant to wait, meant to go to his marriage bed having waited for her. It was only three weeks, and then they would be together.

I will talk to her, get to know her, and my fears will be relieved. It will be all right. It has to be all right.

One day during those three weeks, as he had been getting dressed, a maid came in to clean. She had seemed surprised to find him there, and had begged his pardon, but he told her to go ahead, he was just leaving.

He had noticed her before. She told him her name was Evangeline, but he had heard Richard call her "Evie". She was young and very beautiful. Her skin was the colour of the cinnamon sticks that were placed around in vases to scent the house, and her hair was a dark curly cloud around her head. He needed to go, but he remained, for some reason not wanting to stop watching her. She chatted to him as she worked. And he learned from her that Bertha's younger brother, the one whose death Mason had spoken of, was a pitiful child, twisted and disfigured from birth: dumb, deaf, unable to care for himself or to do even the simplest tasks.

"They say it runs in the family, Master," Evangeline said in her soft musical voice. "I be careful if I was you. Your babies might be like that too, not too late to change your mind."

Edward pulled Richard aside, asked him. Richard tried to allay his fears, put aside his questions.

"A quirk," Richard told him. "These things happen. Unhealthy children, death in childhood. Unfortunate, but merely chance. It's got nothing to do with my mother's death, or her illness beforehand. She was broken-hearted over losing her son; that could have led to her death. But his death and hers were just chance happenings."

Edward had never said anything about the mother, and the fact that Richard brought it up added one more layer to the deceit he felt piling up around him.

He went to bed with a pounding head and a sense of foreboding. He tossed and turned, and finally got up to pour himself a brandy, drinking it down quickly and then drinking another. He was beginning to drift off when he heard her, heard Bertha coming in through the door. She came straight to him, straight to his arms, and he felt her shaking with sobs.

"Edward, please don't leave me," she cried. "I'm sorry you had to find out about my brother, but it is true, what Richard said. It's just chance, just fate. We will have no such problems, I promise. Please don't go away from me, I love you and don't want to be without you."

He held her then, whispering to her, reassuring her of his constancy. His head felt distant, and his limbs felt heavy, everything far away. When she pushed him back, kissing him, he let her. She took off her dressing gown and once again stood before him naked. He felt as though he were sitting across the room, watching the man in the bed as the woman leaned over and unfastened his drawers, tugging them down to mid-thigh.

She straddled him again as she had the first night, and reached for his hands, moving them over her body. He stroked her breasts, reached down between her legs. He didn't know what to do, so just moved his hand over her, for the first time finding what a woman felt like there. She was wet, and for some reason that made him want her unbearably. He grabbed for her, pulling her down on him, kissing her hard and long.

He was barely aware of her wiggling on top of him, maneuvering herself, grasping him and guiding him into her, and by the time he realized what she was doing, it was too late. There was no resistance to his entrance, no hint of pain on her part, just an easy sliding up into her, into a delicious sheath of wet, soft heat. He yelped with surprise and pleasure, and she clamped a hand roughly over his mouth.

"Shhh," she hissed at him, holding her hand there as she began to move on him, a slow up and down motion that made him gasp and go rigid, a tight whimper escaping from his throat. All his senses seemed to shut down, his sight and hearing and certainly any sense of honour and decorum. All feeling was now concentrated to one spot, to the rapture and delight taking place between them.

Her hand slid from his mouth, and she leaned over to kiss him as he reached down to grasp her hips, holding her tightly as he drove his body up into hers. She was gasping, moving against him too, and for several minutes Edward felt nothing but incredible surges of pleasure, and then a quick hard release, spilling his heat deep into her.

Two days later, he held her hand and automatically repeated the words that bound him to her and her to him.

And three weeks after that, he stood on his verandah, holding tightly to the rail and wondering how he had gotten there and what he should do.

Surely, he thought, when we get back to Spanish Town, things will get better.

It had not started off badly, he thought. Their wedding night was nearly perfect. Bertha had emerged from the dressing room in a lovely white nightgown, which had been hand-embroidered by Mari herself, in preparation for the day when her Little Miss would take a husband. Edward admired it, and her within it, for she did look lovely. With her hair unbound, her dark eyes shining, she looked for a few minutes like all he had dreamed of, all his hopes and wishes for the future.

She had come to his arms, and they had embraced lovingly, falling together, rolling over on the big white canopied bed. Their clothes came off, they caressed and embraced each other, and finally he had moved over her, into her, looking deeply into her eyes as they moved together. He tried to wait for her, moved slowly, tried to pour into her all the hope for the future and his desire for a love to grow between them.

"Bertha, beautiful Bertha," he whispered to her, "I will try to make you happy."

It had been lovely, some of it. He thought of the picnic they had taken beside the stream, eating fruit and bread, the juice dripping off their fingers, sweet on their lips as they kissed. Bertha did not like to ride, but one day Edward had gotten onto one of the horses, let her step up on to his boot tip, and lifted her up in front of him. They had ridden up higher into the hills, where they had found a waterfall, and a lovely pool. They had stripped off their clothing and swum together, their naked bodies looking white and translucent in the strange light that filtered down through the water from the mountain sunshine. They had caressed each other in the cool stream, and then he had floated on his back, watching her as she danced for him in the shallow area by the waterfall, the water sluicing down her body. He had gotten up then, pinning her against a rock, and lifting her onto him, making love to her slowly as they stood together.

Such beauty, such happy moments.

But such anguish, such pain as well... His realization that they had nothing to say to each other. That he had known nothing about her and she nothing about him. Her mind could no more stay on one track to have an intelligent discussion than he was able to fly. She lost her train of thought, one thought reminded her of something else, and he learned not to get into a discussion, for it would soon end in her speaking of something nonsensical and totally off the original subject.

One day, bored in the house, Bertha refusing to go for a swim or a picnic, Edward had, for lack of anything better to do, attempted to take her to bed. She exploded in a furious temper over his brutishness, his insistence on constant sex, his total inability to satisfy her. She worked herself into a fury, and he stared in horror as she suddenly reached up and scratched her own face. When he tried to stop her, she turned on him, her nails digging into his outstretched hands, and he dodged her with mounting shock in his voice.

"Stop it, Bertha!" he cried, ducking to avoid her hands, grasping her wrists, holding them tightly. As always, these outbursts didn't last long, and then she collapsed into herself, sobbing, begging his forgiveness.

"I can't stand this," he cried out, and went to the verandah, staring at the sun as it sank into the western horizon. How could he make this marriage work if they could not get through the honeymoon without scene after scene of unpleasantness?

He was determined to make it work. He would try everything. That night, he crept into bed next to her, reaching out to hold her, and told her he was sorry for not satisfying her.

"I didn't know," he told her. "You have been my only one, I've been only with you. You should have told me. I will do anything to please you."

"If you love me, you would know," she wept. "I should not have to tell you."

He laughed, kissing her gently, "I cannot read your mind, my darling." He reached a hand up, stroked her face. "Show me now. Show me what you need."

He had coaxed her, and she had taken his hand then. Pulling up her nightgown, she had placed his finger where she needed it, guiding him to the spot where he needed to touch her. He had lain next to her, kissing her cheeks and lips and neck, as his finger slowly rubbed her just the way she showed him. It took a long time, as he gently and deliberately moved against her wet, tender flesh. He moved down to rest his head on her stomach, watching his hand move on her, feeling her grow more and more excited, hearing her cries, and finally feeling her arch up and give a tiny scream, which trailed off into a long low moan. It had excited him too, and when she moved under him, welcoming him, they had moved together sweetly, the tension between them temporarily eased.

He had pleased her, and for a day all was right with them, but soon things changed again. Her moods grew more mercurial, and were marked by little slaps, tiny painful pinches, quick hard scratches. Each day he grew a little more resistant to her; now when she reached between his legs, he remembered other spots on his body where she had inflicted mild pain, and he turned from her, protecting his delicate flesh, wincing at the thought of what she could do. She in turn became more angry and resentful. After less than a month, the delicate fabric of the Rochester marriage was unravelling quickly.

Hacienda Del Sol
Spanish Town, Jamaica

Mr. John R. Rochester
Thornfield Hall
Hay, Derbyshire
England
15 November, 1820

Father-
I trust this letter finds you in good health.
I am recently back from my honeymoon, having secured you such a daughter-in-law, I scarce know how to describe her.
I will not ask you what you knew. I do not want to know. I can only guess at the motives, the thoughts, the discussions between you and my brother that led me to this. It is too late to change, so to find out the extent of complicity between the Masons and the Rochesters must not be dwelt upon, for the sake of my own mind.
I ask one thing, and I hope that you will agree that you owe me this one favour. I ask that you not make known to our general acquaintance the situation of my marriage. It has been less than a month, and already I know that no good can come of such a union. In the future, steps will need to be taken, one way or another, to make this life a bearable one, but in the meantime, I ask to be granted one small gift from the one who saw fit to place me under such a burden.
If there is inquiry, say that I was sent here to learn a business, as indeed, you presented it to me in the first place. It is not altogether a lie. Mr. Mason feels some remorse, I believe, over his part in my situation, and has agreed to teach me what he

can about the business of exporting, and about other investment opportunities available. It shall keep me busy and give me perhaps some reason to move forward in this wretched life in which I have been placed.
Your obedient son,
Edward F. Rochester

Chapter 8 - Mr. and Mrs. Rochester

Jane, I will not trouble you with abominable details: some strong words shall express what I have to say. I lived with that woman upstairs four years, and before that time she had tried me indeed: her character ripened and developed with frightful rapidity; her vices sprang up fast and rank: they were so strong, only cruelty could check them; and I would not use cruelty. What a pigmy intellect she had—and what giant propensities! How fearful were the curses those propensities entailed on me! Bertha Mason ... dragged me through all the hideous and degrading agonies which must attend a man bound to a wife at once intemperate and unchaste.
Edward Rochester - Jane Eyre

June, 1825
Sometimes he thought he was in Hell.

Certainly, Edward reflected, the demons in the pit could make no more fearsome noises than the ones he heard coming from the room several doors down from his own. He heard Bertha now, the shrieks and groans that sometimes became recognizable as words. Words of abuse, often directed at her nursemaids but more usually directed at her husband.

Bertha's room was on the ocean side of the house, where once Edward had thought perhaps she might be comforted by the sound of the sea she loved so much. It was difficult to tell. Little helped her and at times something that had once brought her comfort and quiet only served to set her off and make her rage and storm without cessation. As she was doing now.

Edward would have loved to have been outside, himself, listening to the sound of the ocean, but the long verandah on the side of the house, the side that faced the sea, was right next to his wife's bedroom. *Bedroom, hell, her prison.* Where she was locked up day and night, to prevent the havoc she was capable of wreaking.

Edward rolled to his side, pulling the pillow over his head to drown out the sounds. It was the middle of the night but there was no sleep to be had for the inmates of the house this long night. Bertha had been hysterical and raging for nearly twenty-four hours now, set off by God-knows-what in the wee hours of the previous morning. The doctor had been called and had come with a medication to try, but there had been no lull in her frantic outbursts.

Since being pronounced officially mad by more than one independent physician, and proving repeatedly that she was a danger both to herself and to others, she had been confined to this room with Mari in attendance and always at least one maid to assist. Mari was getting old, but she remained fiercely devoted to Bertha. She and Rochester did not get along, for a number of reasons, but he had earned her loyalty for refusing to consign Bertha to an asylum as had been done to her mother before her.

Why did he not put her away?

He did not know himself. He had investigated two asylums, one in Kingston and one in Montego Bay, where he often had to go on business, as it was Jamaica's main sugar port. The asylum there was where Bertha's mother was housed, but he did not ask to see her. He did not want to see his wife's future laid out before his eyes. Did not want to imagine her in such a horrible place.

He could not cast her away. He had married Bertha, eyes wide open, although it could be argued that he was not in his right mind at the time. From the clearer vantage point of later months and years, he wondered what in the name of God had possessed him. He had been insane himself. But he had married her, had stood in front of the vicar and pronounced the vows. There was nothing left in his heart of those first tiny hopeful seeds of love that he had once thought might take root back at the very beginning, but he could not deny that he had married her of his own free will.

He hated her. He could not deny that he hated her. But he would not lock her away, at the mercy of others. He had seen the degradation, smelled the filth, seen the mocking looks on the faces of the asylum-keepers. He could only imagine what went on there when no visitors were present. He would not see an animal locked within those walls.

He knew now, as he'd slowly absorbed the information as he was able to, that she had begun to show the signs of insanity when she was in her teens. And she was thirty-one years old now. Five years older than he. They had even lied to him about her age. But she had been sick for so very long. *She cannot help it,* he had told himself a million times.

He rolled over on his back, groaning with exhaustion and frustration. Outside, far over the ocean, a spring storm brewed and thunder rumbled. It seemed the world itself was at fever pitch, at the height of tension – awaiting the sudden drop in pressure when the rains poured down. Maybe that was why Bertha was in such a state, he thought. Perhaps the very pressure Edward felt squeezing his aching chest, setting him on the edge of panic, was doing the same thing to his wife's head.

His wife. He lay, staring into the darkness above his head. And thought back...

In the last week of their honeymoon, Bertha's menstrual flow arrived. They were not sleeping in their large white nuptial bed together, for another fight had sent him out onto the verandah in despair, where he had fallen asleep in a chair. He awakened to her shrieks and screams, and had rushed into the bedroom. He saw her there in the bed, naked and sobbing. He saw the blood.

Frantic, he called for Mari, who rushed in to see to her mistress. Mari took in the scene with disgust, before turning to Edward.

"You so stupid, why they send you across the world all alone?" she asked him. He looked, dumbfounded, from Bertha to her nursemaid.

"It's just the curse, same as always. It always hit her hard. I ask Mister Jonas if he let me bring the medicine for her just for that time, but he say she don't need it. She fine in her body, Master; it just mean no babies for you this month. She always cry and cry when the curse come, it mess with her head." She waved him away, and turned to care for her mistress.

Later, Mari came to him on the verandah.

"She fine now, we get her cleaned up and I give her a little something I have hid away." She came towards him, fixing her eyes upon him, eyes that were even darker than his, hooded and ancient.

"I'm sure you see, Master, that if you smart you make sure you put no babies in her. You lucky this time. She always been pretty lucky... just that one time, and she lose that baby, bleed it right out."

She caught his look of shock, the sudden whiteness of his face. "You think you the only one? They do wrong to you, Master. She can't help it, what her head tell her to do, but they do wrong not to tell you."

His mind whirled with pain and confusion as she continued, "You best get her home and back on her medicine. She pretty calm when you first came, but I see now she losing control and I tell Mr. Jonas, you better tell that boy before he find it out himself. And I tell them not to be sending her here with no medicine, but they say she be all right here with you, now that she married.

"I tell them she don't need to be married, but Mr. Jonas worry what happen to her when he gone. And Mr. Richard, he not good for killing spiders, someone have to care for him some day too. Mr. Jonas just think Miss need a husband and babies. Fool! I take care of her. I take care of her from the moment I take her out of her Mama."

It was an additional shock to Edward to realize that the entire two months of his stay before the wedding plans, Bertha had been heavily medicated. He thought back to their dinners together, her calm demeanour, her dark eyes, cutting dreamily to his from her end of the table, saying nothing.

Edward felt like he had been doused from head to toe with icy water. How could he have been so stupid and heedless? For a month they had come together, for a month he had gone into her, rutting with her like an animal, spilling his seed into her without hesitation. What if he had gotten her with child? His breath caught, his heart pounded hard as he thought of his narrow escape. His life lay before him in a hideous landscape, but how much worse would it have been had he brought a child into it? Even a healthy child, let alone one who would end up like Bertha and her mother and her brother?

A dark veil of shock descended upon him and he felt a cold sweat begin to dry over his entire body. That darkness hovered over him as the honeymoon concluded, as the couple left the mountain retreat and returned to Jonas Mason's home briefly, and as they made preparations to move down the winding ocean side road into the home Mason had promised them.

When the honeymooners returned to his home in Spanish Town, Jonas Mason had only needed one look at his daughter and her husband to see the truth. He saw the wildness in Bertha's eyes, the shock and numbness in Edward's.

Jonas was not an evil man. He was a sad and frightened one. Devastated by the plague that had fallen upon his house, horrified by the demons that had wracked his wife and children, he had acted only to attempt to save his daughter.

Jonas Mason had not known Edward Rochester. He had known the father, a cold and greedy man if there ever was one. The sin was on John Rochester's head, being willing to sell his son into slavery. Jonas had justified his actions, saying that for all he knew, the son was just like his father.

From the start, he had seen that he was not. Under the formal English manners, the slight air of entitlement and arrogance, he had seen the kindness, the basic decency. He had seen a man who would try to do the right thing if he could. Mason's conscience had smote him.

But not enough to warn him. Not enough to prevent the wedding.

Oddly enough, as Edward spent the next four years trying to come to terms with his plight, trying to reconcile the darkness in the souls of others, trying to figure out what he had done to make his father hate him so, he could not really hate Jonas and Richard Mason as much as he wanted to. He recognized desperation. He recognized fear and weakness.

He recognized it because he saw it in himself.

The Masons could not do enough for him when he returned. Servants were provided, money was freely given, help of all sorts was offered. Richard was devoted to his poor sister, spending many long hours with her while Mason took Edward to the factory and the shipyard, teaching him what he had learned in nearly forty years in business.

Edward faced his father-in-law and his brother-in-law with a cold, hard demeanour, one that was new to him, and mostly the result of shock and confusion. One that kept him from falling apart completely. They understood. He did not confront them, did not ask, "Why?" He knew why. They all knew what was unsaid. He saved his hatred. Saved it for the ones who really deserved it.

His father and his brother.

Someday, he would repay them for what they had done to him. But not now. He had no power, no tangible wealth compared to his father's, unless he considered the money from Bertha's dowry, which at times he forgot was really his. But mere money was not enough. He would bide his time, learn business dealings, plan a revenge that would be harsh and complete.

Bertha resumed her heavy medications when they returned to Spanish Town, where they stayed while their seaside home was prepared. It had been proven that she could not do without medication. Watched over by Mari and several maids, including Evangeline, who had been sent to work in their new home, Bertha spent most of her time in a daze, wandering the rooms of their house.

Each day someone would take her to the ocean, let her wade in. Edward never watched her there now. He could not bear to.

He did not touch her. They took up separate bedrooms by unspoken agreement. He stayed away from hers. One night, a few days after moving in, she left her own bed, slipped past Mari who lay snoring on her pallet, and came to his room.

Edward lay numbly as again she removed her gown to reveal her nakedness. What he had once loved to see now made him feel ill. She leaned over and kissed his unresponsive mouth, ran her hand over his body. Her long black hair fell like a veil on either side of them as she leaned over him. He lay like a dead man.

From far away, he felt her untie his drawers, reach inside and take him in her hand. She caressed him in a way that had once driven him wild and brought him to a climax in minutes. Now he remained limp and flaccid in her hand, and as she grew more and more frustrated, rougher in her movements, he wrenched her hand from his pants and flung it from him with a sharp curse.

Bertha became upset and then hysterical. If only to shut her up, he sat up and reached between her legs. With lifeless, mechanical movements, his body held stiffly away from her, he began to touch her. If he could pleasure her and be done with her, perhaps she would leave. But she sensed his feelings, and left his bed, crying wildly and cursing him.

As she left, he heard her outside his bedroom door, shrieking. He heard the tinkling of broken glass as she shattered ornaments and decorations all the way back to her bedroom. He lay, staring dully at the ceiling, his drawers gaping, exposed.

Finally he roused himself, gathered his energy enough to cover himself and tie his garment closed.

They never touched each other that way again. They had been married for six weeks.

Bertha told everyone, of course. Every maid, every gardener, eventually every doctor who treated her. For the next fifteen years, everyone from Spanish Town to Thornfield would learn that Edward Rochester could not get it up. It would become one of her favourite themes.

Edward's life went on, he grew older. Twenty-two, twenty-three, twenty-four. He was not sure when the word "insane" first crossed his mind; surely it had been on his honeymoon? He began to consult doctors, although he knew Jonas Mason had already done so from the time Bertha first began to exhibit symptoms.

One doctor said she had the nervous complaints of the childbearing female and advised him to get and keep her pregnant. One said she was merely high strung and delicate. One pulled him aside and said that he should have frequent coitus with his wife, but to avoid her orgasm at all costs, lest they stir her passions uncontrollably. Another told him to have frequent coitus with his wife and to always ensure her orgasm, to give her an outlet for her passions. None could offer a solution.

Eventually, more than one doctor agreed: she was insane. Incurably.

He then consulted lawyers, but found he had no legal recourse to end the marriage, because she was insane. Incurably.

Something inside him – some softness, some hope – died that day, when he realized there was nothing he could do legally.

But Bertha's insanity was only part of it. For some reason she was given to fits of unbelievable passion and decadence, going after other men even from the early days of the marriage. Somehow she had been kept under control during the time before their wedding, but once they were married, her true self came forth.

Shortly after they returned to Spanish Town, they had attended a party. An hour or so into the affair, Edward had noted her absence. He had gone looking for her, and found her in a darkened room, pinned against the wall by a man who was known to him only by sight. She was jerking with the force of his thrusts, her legs wrapped around his waist. The man did not see him, but Bertha did, and she looked at him with a slow, crooked smile. Edward knew he should make a scene, call the man out and challenge him, redeem his manhood. But he did not; he did not care enough. He turned on his heel and walked out of the room.

In the carriage on the way home, he had turned to her and, with a savagery he had not known he possessed, grabbed her jaw and threatened to kill her if she ever made a fool of him in public that way again. She was intimidated enough to say she would not. But it mattered little, for the Rochesters stopped going to parties. Edward thought back to the glances of the other men during his courtship. He had thought it was envy. Now he knew it was pity.

Bertha was not always out of control. Part of the time she seemed nearly normal. She would sit quietly, hands folded, looking lovely and serene. She would speak calmly and politely to those around her, and venture a comment that seemed appropriate. It smote Edward's heart at times – it was a too-vivid reminder of what could have been. But these quiet times could not be trusted, and all too soon she would lose control again.

In the second year of their union, Jonas Mason suddenly died. He had been out in the field, plotting out which land to sow and which to lay fallow, and he collapsed. He was dead before he could be carried to one of the outbuildings.

Bertha was in a quiet period, but she was not especially lucid, and they did not know if she understood that her father was gone forever. She was kept from the funeral, and her life went on in much the same way, although several times she was seen crying. But she cried often anyway.

Richard Mason was now the owner of his father's holdings, the fields and the factory, but it was Edward who talked him through the decisions that needed to be made in the weeks after Mason's death. Mason trusted him completely, followed him blindly, which led Edward to ponder how easily he could cheat the poor fool out of everything he had. But he was scrupulously honest in his dealings and even consulted legal means to further protect his brother-in-law's holdings, including placing them in a trust should Richard Mason become incapacitated, should he follow his sister into madness.

Shortly after her father's death, Bertha began to disappear from the house. Mari seemed unconcerned. "You try to keep her locked up, Master," she told him, contempt on her face. "Why you can't just let her be free?"

"Because she cannot be trusted to care for herself, do you not understand that?" Edward said with frustration. But it was no use; she did not listen to him.

Mari had been in Jonas Mason's household for years. She had come as part of the dowry of his wife, whom she had seen born and had raised, as she had then reared Bertha. She held the other slaves in an iron fist and they worked without complaint for her. But towards Edward they were reluctant and disrespectful. He thought of the servants at Thornfield, who would never drag their feet at the smallest order by their employer. But trying to run a household here, under these conditions… it was one more frustration in an already endless number.

One night, when Bertha had been missing for two days, Edward received a message from the owner of a seedy waterfront bar near the shipyard, a place he would have been afraid to enter otherwise. The message said to come and fetch his wife.

He had gone, his heart filled with cold, heavy dread. He had taken with him a burly yard servant whom he trusted somewhat, as well as a loaded pistol. He was pointed to a small back room, where he found his wife in the company of several men. Through a haze of red, his head roaring, Edward saw her.

Bent over, her skirts up around her waist, a man behind her.

Her face bent to another man who stood in front of her, her head held tightly in his grip.

Edward did not recognize his own voice as he thundered, advancing on the group. He was aware that he had drawn his pistol and dimly heard the shots he fired into the air. There was screaming, cursing. Bertha was cursing most of all, because she had not finished and therefore did not get the money she had been promised. Edward grabbed her by her upper arm and dragged her out. She fought so hard that eventually he had hold of only her hair as the man he had brought with him lifted her into the waiting carriage.

Later, he would wonder why he had bothered. He thought of the shots he had fired, of his wild frenzy. People could have been killed. He could have been killed, and for what? She would not stop.

Part of him wished he had been killed.

Bertha continued to leave the house despite his best efforts to keep her inside. She would return in a day or two, disheveled, smelling of drink and body odour and other men. Edward continued to get an occasional message to come and get her. Most of the time it was just for bothering people for money for drink. But at least once, he had found her in another dreadful situation. Once again he was horrified by what he saw her doing. Once again, she got angry at him for coming to get her.

One day a letter arrived from his father. Periodically, letters arrived and he would read them and toss them in the fire. He never wrote back. He only remembered one line from an early missive:

"We have become aware of the infamous conduct of your wife. Be assured there has been no intelligence here that would connect our name with hers."

Good, good...

This current letter authorized a sum to be sent to Edward, to be put into investments and managed by him for his father. Edward took it as a challenge – his father taunting him, waiting to see him fail.

He put the money away for a time. He was tempted to take it to Kingston, gamble it away. He even briefly considered taking a few days to himself, going to a town on another island and spending it on whores. God knows he had had no satisfaction from a woman in years. He deserved a little, he thought.

But thinking of whores made him think of Bertha, in the back rooms of those saloons. And the thought made him feel sick, physically ill.

In the end he had done what was expected with the money. He let it gather a little interest while he researched the market. Then he invested it. His father was already heavily invested in sugar. But he took this money and diversified. He put a little in rum, a little in indigo grown in America and fetching a tidy sum. He invested in American rice and Caribbean-grown cotton.

And all of it dependent upon slave labour, the thought of which would smite his conscience in the dead of night. He tried not to think about it, about his part now in the vast machinery of the slave trade. He knew about it, the so-called Triangular Trade. How ships left Bristol and Liverpool loaded with trade goods which were then exchanged on the West African coast for slaves bound for the Caribbean. How the slaves were sold there at considerable profit for labour on plantations, and later the ships were loaded with the products of slave labour, such as sugar or rum, for their export back to England.

He tried to keep down the inner voice that told him he should have no part in the trafficking and ownership of humans, even the tiniest, most peripheral role – but in his mind, his list of sins grew. He tried to justify it all by telling himself that the slaves who saw to his every need were owned by the Mason estate and not by him. He told himself the slaves were well-fed, well-kept, and not abused. Mason himself had bragged that he had never beaten a worker in all the years he had owned slaves. But Edward knew that was not for the sake of the people themselves, but to preserve their value. Mason had made sure he treated his animals well too, from the finest brood mare to the smallest chicken.

Edward tried not to feel guilty; he tried to treat the servants with quiet authority and courtesy, as he would have back home. But the servants saw him as weak, and their insolence made him angry. Deep down he felt as much a slave to the Masons as they were, and felt that everyone knew it.

But all the investments he made prospered, and the Rochester wealth increased.

His father was pleased, God rot his soul. *The Devil take him.*

One day Bertha left and did not reappear for five days. Edward and Richard had made discreet inquiries at the local infirmary and the constabulary. No sign had been seen of Bertha. The men then asked at some of the bars she frequented, Richard showing great shock at how low his sister had fallen. Edward had tried to protect him, but it was now time for him to see how Bertha really lived.

One bar owner had told him of seeing Bertha several nights ago. There had been an altercation, and she had taken a small knife and stabbed a man in the hand when he had angered her. The owner had seen her being taken out in the company of several men. But he had not thought to intervene, had not thought to notify anyone in authority.

Edward thought surely she must be dead. He didn't know whether to be worried for her or hopeful for himself.

The next morning, a stable hand, out exercising one of the horses, came upon her, lying in a field near the house. She had either been taken there and dumped, or had been turned loose and walked back home. Edward couldn't imagine how; by all rights she should be dead.

She was brought in and laid upon her bed, the female servants weeping all around. Richard, summoned from his home, sobbed as though his heart was broken. The doctor had been sent for, and when he came, Edward had locked everyone out – only he and the doctor and Mari were there to see the full extent of the savagery that had been inflicted upon Bertha.

Her clothing was tattered around her, shredded and bloody. It was stripped off her and thrown in the fire. They surveyed her naked body, Mari bathing her in warm water as they examined her. Her hair was tangled and sticky, matted with blood and probably other fluids as well. Her face was nearly unrecognizable. Her eyes were blackened, her nose swollen and misshapen. Her mouth was split and her lips cut and bruised. Bruises were evident around her neck and upper arms, overlapping finger marks plainly visible.

Edward felt tears in his eyes as he followed the doctor's pointing finger. She may have stabbed a man, but nothing was worth this horrendous abuse. How could any human do this to another? It was obvious to all that Bertha was not stable. How could anyone have done such a thing to someone so vulnerable?

There were bloody rope marks around her wrists and ankles, and what looked like cigar burns in several areas. Bruises covered her breasts and there was a bite mark clearly visible on the right one. There were bite marks on her belly, and as the doctor pulled her legs apart, they could see the overlapping bruises at her inner thighs.

"Different colours," the doctor said. "This was done to her over several days." Edward closed his eyes in horror, turning away as he realized the doctor was leaning down to examine her more intimately.

"She's badly torn, front and back," the doctor told him, straightening up. "She'll be awhile healing from this. A single man cannot inflict such damage as this. It was more than one man, and more than one occurrence."

Bertha was bathed tenderly and covered with a sheet, Mari weeping quietly as she vowed to take care of her, and calling down curses from above and below upon whoever had done this thing.

Edward was numb, his heart heavy. He looked at Mari, his face as bitter and ruthless as any she'd ever seen.

"I wanted to keep her locked up and you fought me on it," he said in a low strangled voice. "From now on, she will never leave this room. It will be locked up securely and she will be watched at all times. And if you are ever tempted to be lax in your supervision, remember what she looks like tonight."

Edward left the room, stopping to talk to Richard. "She will recover, but things will change. I am still her husband. She will be confined. She may be committed, should I so choose. I don't know yet; but I am taking control, and from now on I will act as I feel are in her best interests, instead of listening to others."

No one challenged him. They were afraid of the look on his face. Edward walked out of his house, and over the beach towards the ocean. He kicked his shoes off at the edge of the sand, but remained fully clothed as he walked into the surf. The water was black, the moon reflecting off it in a wavering yellow ball. Edward walked, walked, walked, until the water was up to his chest, and then he stopped, feeling the waves break over him. He turned his face up, let the water slap him over and over and over. He doubted if he could ever feel clean again, even should he stand there forever. He wished he had the courage to keep walking, to let the water close over his head and carry him away.

Chapter 9 - Four Years

'This life,' said I at last, 'is hell! this is the air—those are the sounds of the bottomless pit! I have a right to deliver myself from it if I can. The sufferings of this mortal state will leave me with the heavy flesh that now cumbers my soul. Of the fanatic's burning eternity I have no fear: there is not a future state worse than this present one—let me break away and go home to God!'
Edward Rochester - Jane Eyre

When Bertha returned to consciousness, several days after she had been brought back to her home, it was to find that she was now a prisoner in her own bedroom.

While her wounds healed, she was given powerful medications to keep her asleep, and was watched over by Mari. Several times a maid was brought in to sit by her while Mari left the house. Once, Edward had watched Bertha's nurse from his bedroom window, seeing her walk around the house by the light of the moon, holding aloft a headless chicken, whose blood she scattered in seemingly random motions as she muttered words that he could not make out.

He had long tried to suppress the heathen rituals and superstitions that were practiced by the servants of the household, but all to no avail. He did not attempt to stop Mari now. This house was already permeated with such darkness, he felt, what was the harm in a little more? And it might help Mari. She was heartbroken and guilty over what had happened to Bertha and if it comforted her to curse those responsible, Edward was not going to stop her.

As Bertha slept on, a carpenter was brought in to put a new door on her bedroom, one that was locked from the outside and could be further secured from the outside as well. The high windows of her room that ran along the verandah were covered over with boards, leaving narrow openings through which Bertha could see but could not escape.

When Bertha woke, she showed no signs of remembering her ordeal. She was often not lucid and Edward fervently hoped that the period of her abduction and assault was one of those times. He knew that a healthy woman might well have been driven mad by such an experience, and he hoped that a madwoman may have had some degree of protection in her mind from what had been done to her. As much as Edward now hated and resented his wife, he did not want such harm to befall her again.

I am not a murderer. I will try to keep her safe. When God takes her, He must do it in His own time.

And he tried to forget how part of him had wished to hear of her death...

Bertha fought and raged against her confinement in the bedroom but her husband was unmoved. He had been filled with a fresh resolve and the household knew it. Richard Mason saw it as well and deferred even more to Edward's judgment and decisions. For a time, his household responded well to his new authority. None of them ever wanted to see such a grim and bitter look upon his face again.

By the summer of 1824, Edward was twenty-five years old and had been married nearly four years. His life was occupied with assisting his brother-in-law,

Richard, in running the late Jonas Mason's business, as well as helping manage the estate. The business was thriving. Thousands of tons of sugar were exported from the West Indies every year, and the Masons exported a respectable amount of it.

Edward was becoming known to the men of Spanish Town as an intelligent and thoughtful young businessman, and he was respected for his honest dealings with his brother-in-law, who was recognized to be weak and ineffectual. With Bertha locked away, it became easy to forget that she was the reason Edward Rochester was associated with the Masons.

One night he had attended a dinner with some men of business, and a wealthy older matron had chattered for some ten minutes about how Edward needed to find a good woman and settle down in marriage. She did not notice the sudden silence that fell around the table, or Edward's face, which at first went stark white and then a deep red. As soon as possible, the subject had been changed, but the humiliation of it remained in his heart.

Certainly, Edward felt the lack of female companionship in his life. At one time he had hoped by now to be happily married, perhaps with a growing family. Something deep in his heart – some softness and capacity for love – had been choked off while still young and green, and the thought of what he had been cheated out of was more than he could bear. It was best to leave such feelings in a box, the lid securely fastened. His physical ardor had also been securely tamped down and put into a similar box. He tried to keep busy, tried not to dwell on what he did not have.

One day he had gone to Mason's to oversee the mating of one of Mason's fine mares. A stud had been brought in, a magnificent animal. Rochester's expertise in horses had been called upon and he came to assist the grooms. It could be a risky business, dealing with the mating of a nervous mare and a fully mature stallion. Enough people were needed to control the situation without having so many that the animals were made anxious, and Edward assumed the job of holding the mare's bridle securely, keeping her still while the stallion was brought in behind her.

The mare's nostril's flared and she side-stepped nervously, but Edward clucked and crooned to her, holding his head close to hers as the stallion covered her and the mating was completed. He was so calm and soothing that the mare was reassured and she stood still, letting the stallion proceed. But Edward was only calm outwardly. He was aware of a hot flush that came over him. The sounds and the sights of the mating brought home to him just how long he had been alone and deprived of the pleasures that should be natural and available to a married man in his mid-twenties.

The day brought forth feelings he had long thought to have mastery over, and that night he tossed and turned with dreams that awakened him early, his drawers wet and sticky, his body bathed in sweat, nearly in tears with longing and loneliness. His disturbed mood lasted for days and was noticed by everyone in his household.

Evangeline, the young girl who had served as maid in Jonas Mason's house, and who now helped to care for Bertha, took particular note of her Master's moods. She had watched him carefully over the years and was fascinated by his strong personality and dark-featured looks. She did not think him a handsome man, but he was not ugly, and he stirred something in the pretty young servant. She was no virgin, although her experience was limited. She was a passionate young woman, and she recognized a similar passion in the master of the house.

One sultry afternoon, Edward sat on his verandah reading a book. It was a week after the horses had mated, a week in which he had slept poorly and had been disturbed by his turbulent thoughts. The heat was oppressive, smothering, and the slightest movement brought sweaty discomfort. He was absorbed in his book, with a pitcher of water beside him, trying not to think, either of his life or of the heat that was threatening to drive him mad.

He looked up to see Evangeline standing near him. She wore a colourful skirt and a white low necked blouse. Her hair was tied up into a red head scarf, tendrils escaping. Her dark skin was shiny with perspiration. She approached his chair, holding a tray in her hands. He noted her white blouse, full breasts straining against it. Her nipples were dark and hard, plainly visible through the white cotton.

"What?" he asked sharply. She smiled enigmatically and set the tray down on the table next to him.

"I bring you some dinner, Master," she said in her soft voice.

"I didn't ask for anything to eat," Edward told her, his voice low and angry.

"I bring you some anyway," she told him. "You young, you got a lot in your head, you got to keep your strength up."

She bent to arrange the plates on the table and Edward could clearly see down the front of her blouse. Her full breasts hung down uncovered and the sight of them sent such a flush of heat over his body that he nearly gasped aloud. Evangeline straightened up and looked down at him with amusement.

He became aware of his reaction, the sudden tenting of his trousers where his legs met as he sat. He moved his book over his lap, his face burning. He knew she saw it and he was aware of a roaring in his ears. He could not make out what she was saying to him except for the last line, trailing in the air as she left the verandah, her voice sing-song and mocking:

"Yes, you got to keep your strength up, Master."

After that, Edward took greater notice of Evangeline and she of him. He had always thought her beautiful, but considered her too young, still thinking of her as the sixteen-year-old she had been when he was first married. The fact that she was a slave to the Masons also had struck him, and he had been careful to pay little attention to her. But now he could see nothing but her as she moved soundlessly through his house, going about her business. While most of the female servants looked down, not meeting his eyes, Evangeline looked squarely at him, her bold glance bringing repeated flushes to his dark face.

One July night he was awake, unable to sleep with the heat. He left his bed and went to the verandah, waiting in vain for the slightest breeze to waft over the ocean. He listened carefully but could hear no sound from Bertha's room. There was no noise around him except for the faraway cacophony of frogs and the long accustomed sounds of the millions of night insects.

He paced restlessly, bare feet making no sound on the wood. He had been lying on his bed naked, but when he got up he had pulled on his trousers. As he walked, he felt the fabric hot and rough against his legs. He turned at a sound behind him and saw Evangeline, standing at the corner of the house, staring at him.

"What are you doing here?" he whispered, annoyed to find her watching him. "Who is with my wife?"

She moved towards him quietly, dark eyes fixed on his face. She wore the same colourful skirt as before, the same white blouse, but her curly dark hair fell around her shoulders.

"Mari is asleep in Miss Bertha's room, and Jenny watching her now," she said softly. "I come to be with you, Master. It's not good to be walking alone with trouble on your mind."

"I'm fine," he said shortly, turning away from her. "It's this god-damned heat. How does anyone live in this heat?"

She said nothing, and he heard only the rustle of cloth behind him. For a moment he stood still, then turned to look at her.

She had taken off her blouse, and he stared at her for a moment, his breath caught in his throat.

Her breasts were perfect. He inhaled sharply, unable to stop staring at them. They were full, beautifully shaped and upright, a lighter brown than the skin that was usually exposed. Their tips were a dark brown, standing out. He took a step towards her, his mouth dry. She stood quietly, her blouse in her hand. Somehow he gathered the strength to speak.

"You need to get dressed and go to bed," he told her, not recognizing his own voice.

She was silent for a moment, and then she reached over and dropped her blouse over a chair. Her breasts swayed gently with her movements.

"It's all right, Master," she whispered. "You can have me and I won't get with baby. We know how to keep that from happening." She held her arms out to him, "Come here to me. I see you watching me, I know you need me."

He moved towards her, no longer having control over his legs. His hands moved up, held in front of him like a blind man's, and he groped towards her. They found her breasts, driving her up against the wall, and before he knew it he was kissing her savagely.

He was mad; he had no control. His hands squeezed her breasts, her beautiful, luscious breasts, his fingers sliding down to gently tug at her nipples before he moved his hands up to cup her breasts again. Over and over he did this as his mouth devoured hers. She was breathing quickly, tiny moans in her throat and he was aware of a growling sound deep in his chest. His desire was raging, and his hips moved against hers. She spread her legs to allow him to push himself against her.

His hands left her breasts and he grabbed for her backside, sliding the skirt up her legs. She wore nothing underneath, and he jammed a hand between her thighs, his fingers sliding into her slick heat as she cried out against his mouth.

He was ashamed of his lack of control, but not ashamed enough to stop, and he reached down with his other hand and began to unbutton his trousers. He was frantically working on the last button when Evangeline gave a soft cry of frustration and shoved them down around his legs, as he thrust forward. In just a movement or two, he was inside her, lifting her onto him. He slammed her against the wood wall, a satisfied grunt in his throat as he moved against her, driving his fullness up into her.

It took only moments, and he finished with a huge roar of relief. For a few minutes he leaned against her, her back still against the rough wood of the outside wall. His face was buried in her neck and he felt her arms around him, heard her crooning words he could not understand. He let her slide down his body, and he leaned over, resting his shaking arms against the wall. She leaned back also, eyes closed, sweat standing out on her face and bare chest.

"I'm sorry," he whispered, as his breathing slowed. He straightened up, reaching down to pull his pants up. She opened her eyes and smiled, reaching up to his cheek.

"You like that, Master?"

He didn't answer, just turned his head to kiss her palm.

"You go to your bed now, and I come to you later," she whispered.

He swallowed, caught her arm gently, "You said earlier, you wouldn't get with child. Tell me, how... ?" He broke off, aware as he did so that it was a fine time to be asking for clarification of such a subject, after the fact.

She smiled, "A little sponge, soaked in lemon juice. Or vinegar. Our mamas tell us. We put it up there and then all be fine."

His eyes grew wide for a moment, and he shook his head. "So, you have that in you, now?" She nodded, running her tongue over her full bottom lip.

"So you planned on this," Edward said, looking up at her, "You knew... "

She reached up to touch his cheek again, "I hoped. Now go, Master. Go to your bed."

Edward had gone back to his room, shame and satisfaction fighting for control in his breast. He stripped off his trousers, and washed himself with water from the basin, the moonlight his only illumination.

He went back to his bed and lay down, naked, still hot but more relaxed than he had been in a long time. He rested, drowsiness slowly overtaking him, but at the sound of his door opening, he was wide awake. Evangeline moved to the bedside, shedding her clothing and sliding in next to him. In seconds they were in each other's arms.

This time, their lovemaking was sweet and gentle and languid. Edward was sated from their first encounter and his desire was slow to return but it grew steadily within him. He felt no urgency, just a calm sweet passion and he took his time, wanting to savor it all. He kissed her for a long time, kissed her all over her upper body. She moaned, reaching up to hold his head, stroking her fingers through his thick hair. He moved his mouth to her breasts, gently sucking her nipples, first one, then the other, while his fingers explored her below, dipping slowly into her soft slick folds, marveling at the differences between her and Bertha, even while he felt guilty for comparing.

Bertha was nearly as tall as he, full-bodied, while Evangeline was small, her bones more delicate. Bertha had been forceful, taking control, while Evangeline was more timid, letting him set the pace. It was very arousing, and made him even more gentle with her.

His fingers worked gently in her wet, secret places. Bertha's hair had been so soft and silky as he caressed her there, but Evangeline's was wiry and coarse under his stroking hand, exciting him with the difference. She responded to his touch, her hips moving slowly as his fingers rubbed gently and rhythmically; and when she moaned and pulled at him, moving him over her and taking him in, he was thrilled to feel how much she wanted him.

The previous time he had been thinking only of quick relief from the pressure that had tormented him, but now he wanted to feel the pleasure. He went slowly, sliding into her a little at a time, until he could go no further. For a moment he stopped, trying to get control. It felt so wonderful, he could hardly bear it.

He was still, his breathing a roar in his ears, feeling the fabulous heat as she surrounded him fully, enveloping him in her softness. She reached down, hands on his buttocks and pulled him even closer, her legs coming up around him.

"Evangeline," he groaned, savouring her name on his tongue. "Evie." He began to move.

The pleasure was indescribable, and he moved slowly, trying to hold onto it for as long as he could. He could hear the high little sounds in her throat, and he held his breath, listening to her. She seemed to be in her own world, concentrating, and as she moaned louder and arched up against him, he could feel the tiny spasms of her climax, surrounding him, tugging at him and pulling him deeper into her.

He could no longer control his groans, and he gave himself up to what he was feeling, following his needs. The friction, the heat, built until he felt he might die with the glory of it, and then he gave way in a great rush that he felt down to his toes.

For a long time they lay together, wrapped around each other. He kissed her again, and he felt her cheeks, wet against his. He heard her speak softly to him, but this time she was not mocking. This time there was nothing but sorrow.

"Yes, Master, I know you need me."

Edward's thrill and euphoria, the tiny bit of joy that his time with Evangeline had given him, had lasted only until the afternoon, when one of the young servants had run to him, whispering to him that Mari was in the yard beating Evangeline. He had run to the verandah and down the steps, shouting at Mari to leave her alone.

Evangeline cowered in the yard, Mari holding her by the hair with one hand as she repeatedly slapped her with the other.

Edward rushed towards the two women, but Mari whirled towards him, holding up her hand.

"I talk to you in a minute, Master, but for now I deal with this whore." She turned back to Evangeline, slapping her again, first on one side of the face then the other before shoving her aside roughly. Evangeline dropped to her knees, face in her hands, sobbing.

Edward started towards her, but Mari advanced upon him, making him step back.

"What you think, Master, lying with this woman?" she asked, her face a mask of fury.

Edward felt the blood drain from his face and he stopped with a quick intake of breath.

"And you not even lying down the first time," Mari went on, "You take her up against the wall like a whore in an alley." She walked up to him, shoving him in the chest. He staggered backwards.

"You put your cock in her, up against the wall outside your wife's room, doing that thing together, and both of you rub her face in it," Mari continued. "You think my Miss have no feelings, but she lie there listening to the two of you banging on the wall and making such sounds. She cry and cry to hear you."

A mixture of shame and fury swept over Edward. He looked over at Evangeline, who was huddled on the ground, her eyes fixed on his face.

"It's never bothered your charge to take another man before my eyes, or have you forgotten that?" Edward asked Mari.

"She can't help what she do," Mari answered him. "You got no excuse. You don't lie with your maids in your wife's house, not while I'm watching you. Now that whore going back to Mr. Richard and you will let her go. You got to do what you need for yourself, but you do it away from this house."

Edward was ashamed, ashamed enough to stand by and do nothing as Mari jerked the younger servant to her feet and shoved her to her room to pack her things. He sat miserably on the verandah as Evangeline, her face bruised and flushed with humiliation, set off for Richard's home, casting one last furious glance at him as she walked down the stairs to leave.

He knew he had broken one of the unwritten rules of the house. Had he been at home, he would never have slept with a member of his household. It was folly, insane. Some did, he knew, but it was something his father would never tolerate.

Once again, Edward was aware of the anger and contempt of the servants and the increasing hostility of his wife's nurse towards him. But their hatred did not trouble him, for no matter how much they despised him, it paled in comparison to how he despised himself.

In April of 1825, a letter arrived from England. It was from John Rochester but this letter was written on the black-bordered paper used by those in mourning. Edward slit the letter open and read it to find that his brother Rowland was dead. He had died in February, breaking his neck when thrown by his horse. Edward stood for a long time with the letter in his hand, trying to figure out how he felt.

I am now my father's only son, he thought. And he knew without a doubt that in his father's mind, the wrong son had been taken.

Edward did not answer the letter. He had nothing to say to his father.

Only a day or so after his father's letter, another letter arrived from England. It was from Hugh's mother, Charlotte Lathrop, telling him that Hugh had been seized with a fever while travelling down the Nile and had died. He had died far from home – but happy, enjoying his life. He had so enjoyed his travels on his Grand Tour that he had continued to roam, eventually accompanying some naturalists who were travelling throughout Africa. He had written enthusiastically to his parents and they took comfort in knowing he had died pursuing what he loved.

Charlotte Lathrop expressed her best wishes to Edward and her hope that he would come to see them when he finally returned to England.

Edward, who had shed no tears for his older brother and had written no letter to his bereaved father, wrote at once to the Lathrops, weeping over the death of his dear friend, now lost to him forever. The mourning suits he had purchased upon his father-in-law's death were taken out and aired, and Edward wore them now, wearing them not for Rowland, as his household thought, but for Hugh.

Now, more than four years into his nightmarish marriage, Edward lay on top of his rumpled bed, fully dressed, listening to the shrieks and foul language of his insane wife.

The air was hot and close, bearing down on him, smothering him as though someone had wrapped him in a down comforter. He felt he could scarcely draw a breath and his body felt damp all over. When he moved he could smell his own sour sweat.

He felt he could go on no longer, and thought back to that evening when he had walked out into the sea, desperate for relief and cleansing. With all his heart he wished he had just kept walking, walking into oblivion.

Moving slowly, as though he were years beyond his age of twenty-six, he left the bed and crossed the room to the chest that had carried his belongings across the ocean, back when he was young, back when he had had hope. Kneeling before it, he released the clasp and opened the lid to stare at the contents. Some books, some maps, his mother's Bible.

And a brace of loaded pistols.

He reached down, raised one, lifting its heft, its cold metal feeling like a burning against his hot skin. Slowly, slowly, he brought it up to his head and pressed its icy hardness against his right temple. His eyes were closed, his index finger trembled, playing along the edge of the trigger. For a long moment he sat like that, then it was as though an unseen hand jerked his arm away and down. His hand dropped, still holding the pistol and a frigid wave rushed over him, making him shake with sudden horror. Tears sprang to his eyes.

Oh, God, what am I brought to?

How had it come to this? He thrust the pistol back into the chest and slammed the lid down, shaking all over. He leaned on the chest with both arms held rigid, as frantic sobs forced their way up from his very core.

For a few minutes his cries drowned out all sound, then he became aware of a roaring in the air. He raised his head and heard the rain pouring from the sky, drumming upon the metal roof of his house.

The windows were already open as he had tried in vain to catch any stray breeze that came from the ocean, and through them he felt it now: the softest, coolest breeze he had ever felt. It felt like England... it felt like home. His flesh cooled, his brain cleared and for the first time in what felt like years, a soft glimmer of hope entered his desperate soul.

"I can leave this place," he thought. "I have tried, I have tried to honour my commitments, but I can no longer live like this. I will go again to live in Europe, leave this cursed place, and that woman."

When the rain had passed, dawn was beginning to break over the horizon. Edward left his house and walked in the garden, under the trees heavy with fruit and dripping with water. The air smelled clean and light. Bertha's howls had ceased – whether the storm had calmed her or she had merely collapsed from sheer exhaustion, she was quiet. And he felt alive for the first time since his honeymoon. For the first time in years, he felt he could finally think clearly. He wondered, at what point did honouring his commitments and facing life's burdens turn into walking through life with an dead heart and an empty soul? No more. He was going to live.

For several days, hope buoyed him onwards as he quietly began to make plans. He inquired about passage to England. He remembered his previous trip. He had finished college in May, and left England in June, sailing from Liverpool to

Funchal, Madeira, a very pleasant trip of two weeks. From there it had been onwards to Jamaica, five weeks on board a ship.

He still remembered being met at the dock by Richard Mason – how benign and gentle, almost effeminate, Richard had seemed, so harmless. He shied away from remembering what had followed. This was to be his rebirth, his new beginning, far away from this cursed place. He would return to Thornfield, back to his rightful place as the Rochester heir. He would demand what was rightfully his. And by God, his father would help him with the frightful burden he had placed upon him four years before.

He was not comfortable with the idea of transporting Bertha back to England, six or seven weeks with her in a ship's cabin, but he did not want to leave her in an asylum in the West Indies. And Richard could not take her. Edward had completed legal proceedings for any eventuality involving Richard's health and future, making himself a trustee of the company with Richard's full permission, but he could not burden his brother-in-law with his sister's care. He pondered what he should do with Bertha. He was fairly sure that any asylum in England would be the same as the ones in Jamaica. But that decision was for the future; he would decide what was right to do. He was filled with excitement, with new resolve.

Then, in the midst of his plans, a letter arrived from Thornfield. It was not from his father; it was from his father's steward.

John Rochester was dead.

Edward's first thought was that he had been robbed of all hope of eventual revenge, robbed of the satisfaction of bringing pain and suffering to those who had so betrayed him. But they were gone, and all that they had had was now his.

He was now the master of Thornfield Hall.

Chapter 10 - A Nurse for Bertha

To England, then, I conveyed her; a fearful voyage I had with such a monster in the vessel. Glad was I when I at last got her to Thornfield, and saw her safely lodged in that third-storey room, of whose secret inner cabinet she has now for ten years made a wild beast's den—a goblin's cell. I had some trouble in finding an attendant for her; as it was necessary to select one on whose fidelity dependence could be placed; for her ravings would inevitably betray my secret: besides, she had lucid intervals of days—sometimes weeks—which she filled up with abuse of me. At last I hired Grace Poole ... she and the surgeon, Carter ... are the only two I have ever admitted to my confidence.
Edward Rochester - Jane Eyre

November, 1825

Grace sat quietly, her hazel eyes appearing to look straight ahead, but in reality missing nothing in the room around her. It appeared to be a room in transition, boxes about, stacks of books in one corner or another, as though someone was coming or going.

When Grace had received the short message from Mrs. Fairfax asking her to come to Thornfield regarding a position, she had expected to be interviewed by the estate's steward, or by Mrs. Fairfax herself, and she was still shocked to have been ushered into the library by John, the butler, and to have been told that Mr. Rochester would be with her directly.

Grace had heard, of course, of the death of Mr. Rowland, who had broken his neck upon being thrown from his horse while travelling to Thornfield in the middle of a Saturday night. She had heard the gossip, that he had been returning from a visit to his mistress in Millcote. Grace had also heard that old Mr. Rochester had been seized with a fit some four months after his son's death, and had lain in his bed for five days without speech or movement before another fit had ended his life at the age of sixty-four.

Grace had not thought of the implications of all these changes at Thornfield Hall. Her adult life had been one of unremitting work and hardship thus far, and her laughing and innocent childhood days romping in the woods and fields with the master's son seemed like a faraway dream, something that had happened to another, more fortunate girl. She had not stopped to think that the master's younger son, her long-ago playmate, was now the sole owner of Thornfield Hall.

She heard the click of the door and stood to her feet as the dark-haired young man entered the room with a strong and decisive step. He stopped a few feet from her, and for a few moments the former nurse mates stared in surprise at one another.

Edward Rochester would not have known Grace had he not been told to expect her. She still had the red-gold hair and hazel eyes of her childhood, but both had dulled. Her white skin had grown dry and ruddy, her hands chapped and red. The last time he had seen her, her form and face had been softened with the curves of advanced pregnancy; now her face was thin, her body spare and gaunt. He knew her to be his age, twenty-six, and yet she seemed ten years older.

Grace looked at Rochester and no longer saw her old friend. She saw a man now, a man far above her in station and in situation. He looked the same, and yet different. He was of middle height, having grown in both stature and breadth since she had last seen him. He looked muscular, powerful.

He was dressed in deep black, wore all the trappings of mourning, and they suited him. His skin was dark, his naturally olive complexion browned by nearly five years in the Caribbean sunshine. His hair, wavy, curling over his brow and down over his collar, was a true black, so dark that it reflected blue tints in the sunlight that streamed into the window. His eyes were black as well, and fathomless as he stared at her.

But his face, Edward's face... it was so changed. It had once been clear and open, his eyes by turns serious and mischievous, his intense and thoughtful look changing in an instant to a ready smile as he teased and joked with her. Once upon a time his voice had rung with carefree laughter. Now his face was closed and dark, his eyes narrowed and watchful, his mouth a grim, set line. His entire countenance spoke of anger and bitterness.

Oh, Neddie, what's happened to you?

He spoke first. "Mrs. Poole," he said formally, indicating the chair in which she had been sitting before he had come in.

Grace nodded in return, sitting back down. She folded her hands in her lap, not sure what to say to him. From her infancy, she had called him Neddie in private, Master Edward when they were with other people. Now for the first time, she gave him his rightful title.

"Hello, Mr. Rochester," she said awkwardly. The name felt strange on her lips. He gave her a small smile, watching her closely.

"It has been a long time, Grace," he said.

"Ten years, sir," she replied. The "sir" came from her mouth automatically, and it was only later that she reflected how strange it felt to address him thus. "You were preparing to go back to school."

He nodded, "And you were... " he broke off, not sure of how to continue. "You have a child?" he asked.

Her smile was genuine. "A son," she told him. On this subject she was comfortable, could speak freely. "He is just turned ten."

"What is his name?" Rochester watched her, his eyes fixed on her face. She felt he could not possibly be interested, and yet he focused his attention on her. He had always made her feel important; when they were together, she had always felt he truly saw and heard her.

"Abe," she told him. "Abel, after his father."

Rochester leaned back in his chair, "Mr. Carter, by whom you were recommended, tells me that your husband has died, that you do nursing jobs in various locations to support your son, who makes his home elsewhere, and that you send money for his care."

Grace raised her eyebrows, surprised that he knew so much about her. "Yes, sir. My husband had a daughter, older than myself. She is married, with five children, and my son lives with her family. I thought it best."

"I am sorry about your husband," Rochester told her. He leaned forward again, his face concerned. "That must have been very difficult."

Grace nodded. A small frown crossed her face as she thought of Abel. "It was. He was a good man. We had a few good years, and then he became so ill. He suffered greatly, and there was nothing I could do for him." For a few minutes the two sat quietly, both thinking thoughts the other could not possibly fathom.

Rochester asked her, "Do you often do nursing for Mr. Carter's patients?"

Grace was not sure how to answer his question. She shrugged, "He recommends me occasionally. Most patients are cared for by their own families. Mr. Carter had just come to this area at the end of my husband's life, cared for him in his last days, and said he was impressed by my care of him. My husband had grown quite difficult in the last year of his illness, hard to control – but he was calm for me. After his death, when my son was about six, Mr. Carter would at times send me to those who needed an extra hand. And it was through his good word that I got my job at the Grimsby Retreat, helping to nurse those who came for rest and care."

Rochester stood, motioned for her to stand also. "Come, Grace, walk outside with me. I have much to say to you, and do not wish to be overheard." He left the room and Grace followed him, puzzled, but asking no questions.

He said nothing until they were outside, walking in the gardens, away from prying eyes and ears. He walked, eyes bent to the ground, hands clasped behind his back, not speaking, and Grace walked along beside him, her curiosity growing stronger.

He sighed several times, finally spoke, "Tell me, Grace, you have remained in these parts long enough – what have you heard of me since last we saw each other?"

Grace thought for a moment. "Not too much, sir. I heard you were away at college, then heard you had been sent to the West Indies to represent your father's interests there."

He looked at her, "And nothing else?"

She shrugged again, unsure of what to say. "Well, there were rumours of a possible marriage at first, but then those of us in the area heard nothing else, and when you returned, we heard you were unmarried still. All those here knew of the death of your father and brother, of course, and that you would be returning, and that is all I heard until Mr. Carter came to me and said there was need of a nurse at Thornfield, and would I be interested. He said he would speak to someone here, and that was all, until I received a message from Mrs. Fairfax asking me to come for an interview. In truth, I expected to speak with her. I'd heard her husband had been poorly for some time, and expected to be called here to care for him. It was only when I arrived here that I heard he had passed away, and then I could not imagine why my services would be needed."

Rochester nodded, "The Reverend Fairfax died shortly before my arrival home from Jamaica, as a matter of fact. I instructed that Mrs. Fairfax be sent to stay with relatives right afterwards, to rest from her long months of caring for her husband. She has only just returned, and while she acts as my secretary at times, she knows very little of what I am about to tell you. I wanted to settle in at Thornfield in privacy, and had much arranging to do, to get the servants away from the place until I accomplished what I needed to do. I had them lodged elsewhere, on the pretence that work needed to be done to the Hall. It did need to be done, although it was not pressing. As the workmen accomplished their tasks, I was able to settle in without much notice from prying eyes."

Rochester paused beside a stone bench in the garden, and offered Grace a seat. "Grace, I am about to share something with you that I want no one else to know. Mr. Carter knows, of necessity, and I am about to tell you. If you choose not to work for me, I am asking you, in deference to our long years of knowing each other, to keep your silence about my circumstances. Can I depend upon you to do that?"

Grace looked at him, suddenly aware that she was about to learn of the secret behind her old friend's altered appearance and manner. Her heart was suddenly uneasy, but she nodded, her eyes fixed on his face. "Of course, Mr. Rochester. You have my word."

He took a deep breath, and began, "Grace, I was sent to represent my father's interests in Jamaica. He had long had investments there, and I was able to oversee them. I did well with them, and increased his fortune."

He gave a small bitter laugh, "One of the few times my father found something to approve of in me. It seems I have a head for business. It was quite unflattering, to see how surprised my father was to find I actually possessed some useful talents."

He continued, "But I also increased his fortunes in another way, a way no one here knows of. You are right in saying there was to be a marriage. It had been arranged long before. The last time you and I met, as I prepared for my last year of school, the plans were probably already being laid out by my father and my brother.

"I was sent to Jamaica to marry the daughter of my father's investment partner, and marry her I did, giving me a substantial income, in addition to my being there to oversee the rest of the investments of the Rochester family."

Grace could hardly speak for her surprise, "So you are married?"

"I am, and my wife lives here now, at Thornfield Hall." He spoke bitterly, eyes fixed on the ground. "But no one knows she is my wife. If anyone knows of her at all, they believe her to be a former mistress, or my bastard half-sister." He gave a small smile. "Granted, the existence of a bastard half-sister is a possibility, I am told, based on my father's behaviour, but I have never heard of such a woman." He sighed. "It is in my interest, however, not to deny a sister's existence, for I have reason to need an excuse for the presence of a woman in my upper rooms."

He continued, as Grace watched him intently. "My wife is insane, Grace, completely mad. I brought her back with me because I had married her and I am a man of my word, and I cannot divorce her. I spent large sums of money on lawyers only to be told it was impossible. Had I left her behind, she would have been dead in weeks – she cannot be trusted to care for herself. Or, worse, she would have killed someone else." He took off his coat, laid it across his lap, removed the cuff link from the right cuff of his shirt, and rolled up the sleeve. He turned towards her, showing her his right arm.

There was a large wound on the underside, repaired with a crooked line of black sutures. "Carter told me that even if you don't take the job, I should ask if you would remove these sutures for me, before you leave."

Grace eyed the wound, and nodded, "Of course I will." She reached towards his arm, remembered herself, and dropped her hand. "What happened?"

Rochester sighed, rolling his sleeve back down and refastening it at his wrist. He smoothed the coat over his lap, shook his head. "I hired several local women who were suggested by the servants as possible caretakers. Two only lasted for a matter of days; one could not bear the boredom of my wife's being quiet, the other could not tolerate the stress when my wife stopped being quiet. The last nurse appeared to be a woman of some sense, and she was told not to bring sharp objects into the room with her, but she insisted upon bringing a knife in with her to cut up their food.

"My wife feigned a fit, and when the woman bent over her, she knocked her down and in the confusion, seized the knife. She secreted it, and when I went up on one of my visits, to check on her and the nurse, she produced the knife, and greeted me with the wound you see here. It was deep enough that I knew it needed to be treated, and so I made the acquaintance of Carter, who now knows all, and has been most helpful."

Rochester stood, his coat slung over his shoulder, and began to walk back towards the house.

He continued to speak to Grace, offering her a salary of one hundred pounds a year, which stunned her, as she had never made half of that in any one year. Rochester cautioned her to think about it, and to wait until she had met his wife.

He took her into his study, produced scissors and a disinfectant, and Grace listened to him continue as she cut the sutures, pulled each out of his flesh, and cleaned the wound with the stinging solution. He sat quietly, his breath hissing between his teeth once or twice as she pulled at a particularly stubborn knot, but he remained stoic and impassive, his thoughts seemingly elsewhere.

"She is by turns quiet, and then extremely violent. I have some medicine that calms her, but when she is in the worst of her moods, it does not affect her." He sighed. "She is physically ill also; her excesses early in our marriage have produced some of her symptoms as well."

She looked at him without speaking, and he elaborated, "She has the pox." Grace must have looked startled, for Rochester frowned at her. "She didn't get it from me!" he told her.

"Her nursemaid in Jamaica showed me what she had found on my wife's body. She had lesions, a widespread rash. The nurse had seen them before on others. This was shortly before we left to return to England, and my panicked thought was that I would also be affected, but of course, she must have acquired it later in our marriage."

Grace looked down at the ground, embarrassed at the implications of her old friend's confidences, at what this told her about his marriage.

"I consulted doctors, who told me her disease would progress, and might affect both her mind and her internal organs, or she might live for years with few ill effects at all. There are no signs yet, other than a rash that periodically breaks out over her body, but when this rash appears you must be careful when handling her linens and food items."

Grace was silent, thoughtful, as she straightened the area and put the cover back on the disinfectant. Rochester sat, refastening his sleeve and putting his coat back on. He thanked her, and she nodded, still thinking. "So no one knows of your marriage? No one else, other than Mr. Carter and I, knows that this woman is your wife?"

Rochester shook his head, "No. It did not take me long to discover what my wife was about, and I hastily wrote to my father to tell him to keep the marriage a secret, which he was happy to do, once he knew the truth. He got me into the situation, and was unable to get me out of it, but at least he kept it quiet on this end." He stood, and looked at her. "Would you like to see her, Grace, or have you already decided that this job is not for you?"

Grace nodded at him, "You may take me to her, Mr. Rochester."

Grace followed Rochester as he led the way to the third floor. She had never been up to this floor; as the children had grown older, her mother Nellie had come less frequently, and so they had only been able to play together outside. John Rochester had had strong opinions about his sons mixing with those inferior to themselves, and so it would never have done to see his son playing in his house with the daughter of a tenant and a servant, once Master Edward no longer needed a nursemaid.

Elizabeth Rochester had been less strict in her feelings. While her husband's interests were those of an upper class gentleman, she had pursued charitable concerns that had thrown her often into the company of farmers and the surrounding townspeople, and she had come to know many of them on a more intimate basis.

She liked and respected Nellie Carey, and saw nothing wrong in her younger son playing with Nellie's child, with whom he had spent the first two years of his life. Mrs. Rochester had always been kind to Grace, and Grace remembered her well as a gentlewoman, someone who had always made her feel comfortable.

She thought now, glancing sidelong at Edward Rochester as she walked beside him, that he not only had the look of his mother, but made her feel the same way as well, somewhat comfortable in his presence despite the vast difference in their stations in life. But perhaps that was only because she remembered him so well as a child.

She put all these thoughts from her mind as they entered a small room hung with draperies, and furnished with a small bed and several large, ornate pieces of furniture. Grace watched as Rochester pushed aside a curtain to reveal a heavy door, which he unlocked with a key he removed from his coat pocket.

They entered another, larger room, which featured a large fireplace securely covered with a heavy iron grate. Several large chairs sat around the fireplace area, and there were a table and chairs against one wall. A woman sat in one of the chairs, a book in her hand that might be a Bible. The woman nodded at Grace, who recognized her as the wife of the church clerk. She stood to her feet as Rochester entered behind Grace, and dropped a small curtsy.

"She is sleeping, sir," the woman whispered, closing her book. Edward nodded, and inclined his head towards the form in the bed. He touched Grace's elbow, led her across the room.

Grace quietly approached the bed, looking at the woman who lay there, eyes closed, breathing quietly. She was dressed in a long white nightgown, her hair in a neat braid across her shoulder.

Grace could see that the woman was very beautiful. Her delicate brow, high cheekbones, full red lips, all spoke of a loveliness that was evident even in sleep. Her hair was as black as Mr. Rochester's, her skin a golden colour despite the pallor that being constantly indoors must produce. Her hands were folded innocently over her midsection as she lay on her back, full breasts rising and falling as she rested.

She looked over at Rochester, but his closed, still face revealed nothing as he looked at his sleeping wife. She expected to see a warmth, some sort of tenderness as he watched her, but there was nothing in his features to indicate that he felt in any way connected to the woman in the bed.

He turned towards the woman who sat at the table, motioned for her to accompany them into the anteroom outside. He closed the door, locked it securely from the outside.

"How has she been today?" he asked her keeper, sitting himself down at the table in the centre of the room.

"Very well, sir; quiet and calm," the woman answered. "She ate a good meal at mid-morning, and let me help her bathe and change her linen. We washed her hair – that took up a deal of the early afternoon – and she let me comb it out, and then she sat quietly at the table and spent several hours combing her hair and braiding it, combing it out and re-braiding it. She seemed to think there was a mirror there, and she was preparing to go to a party. She has seemed very tired to me, slept late this morning, and slept again this afternoon. I gave her the drops as usual with her meal, but if you ask me she didn't need them; I've not seen her nervous or out of sorts at all."

"You are fortunate, then," Rochester said shortly. He pulled his pocketbook out of his coat, and removed a coin, which he handed to the woman. "You may go, Mrs. Nash, and I thank you. Will you be back tomorrow?"

"I have a meeting of the ladies of the parish tomorrow, but Mrs. Carter is to come and sit with your sister in the morning, I am told, until I can be there. I can come at about eleven o'clock, but must be gone by four in the afternoon to make tea for my husband when he returns."

Rochester nodded, "I will see that you are relieved." The woman nodded her thanks, and gathered her book and outer wraps, which Grace now saw on a chair by the door. She gave a reproachful look at the locked inner door, and let herself out.

Edward motioned for Grace to sit at the table with him, but said nothing for several minutes as they listened to the sound of Mrs. Nash's footsteps walking away, back down to the second floor as she made her way out. He looked fatigued, his normal energy and vitality suddenly drained. Grace watched him, noticing, as she had not before, the dark circles beneath his eyes, the lines of exhaustion in his face.

He sat for a while, saying nothing, staring into space, and then seemed to come to himself, looked over at Grace.

"Mrs. Nash seems to think there is nothing amiss with the woman inside," he said. He gave a small snort, his lips twisting in a bitter little smile.

Grace asked him, "So Mrs. Nash is her nurse at present?"

Rochester shook his head. "When I felt the need to let the last nurse go, after she allowed me to have my arm slashed from forearm to elbow, Mr. Carter talked to his wife, who made a few discreet inquiries among the ladies of her acquaintance. She and one or two others are happy to come in during the day and earn a few shillings here and there sitting with my "sister", for whom my devotion is seen as heroic, as I have heard it said." He shook his head.

"Bertha, for that is her name," he said, nodding in the direction of the inner door, "is thought, I know, to be sad and harmless by the good ladies of the parish who sit with her day by day. She is quiet now, since her attack on me two weeks ago, as she often is following a violent outburst. I've seen her nearly kill herself in a wild frenzy, beating her head against the wall until she bleeds, and then be silent and docile for a month.

"But sooner or later, she will begin to grow agitated again. She will begin to talk, and when she does, will sit and spill her venom by the hour to whoever will be nearby to listen. She will reveal herself to be my wife, and will begin to enumerate my many faults and shortcomings, as a husband and as a human being. She will spill out her hatred of me in great detail.

"I hope, if these ladies are still here, that they will believe her to be raving in her insanity, but no doubt there will be some who will believe her when she says she is married to me. I need to find someone to stay with her, someone I can trust, for I need to go away for a time. I cannot be tied to Thornfield Hall; I have business elsewhere, and must have a nurse who can be relied upon."

"Why does she hate you so, when it seems to me that you have tried to care for her as best you can?" Grace asked him.

Rochester shook his head. "Who can fathom why the mind forms such antipathy for another person? Most of her family is dead, only a brother remains, and so I am the closest to her now, and we always seem to vent ourselves on those we are close to. I suppose she hates me most because I am the one who was supposed to love her, and yet I do not. I wanted to, I intended to, yet scarcely had our marriage been solemnized when I realized that we were worlds apart in our thinking, even if she had not been insane. I rejected her, body and soul, and that alone is reason enough for her to hate me.

"And so, Grace, I will tell you what is required. She will be quiet, as you see her, for some days, perhaps even weeks. Eventually she will grow more agitated, will begin to talk without pause, perhaps in foul and disgusting terms. She may begin to display behaviour that is no doubt revolting to a woman who has been reared with notions of decency, as I know your mother reared you. She will be unclean in her bodily habits, will not allow you to get near her to comb her hair or help her bathe, and at those times you must just allow her to do as she pleases, no matter how it might disturb you.

"She will move about the room, upset items that are placed there. She may attempt to get at the fire – I have placed a locking metal grate over the fireplace, but she tries to get at it just the same. You cannot leave a candle burning when she is alone, you will not be able to knit as you sit with her, for fear she will take the needles and use them as weapons against you. Thankfully, her violent impulses appear to come and go in a matter of a few days, and then she will enter another cycle of relative quiet. At those times, she is harmless, and can even appear to be appealing.

"She will smile at you, compliment you as though you are a guest at a party at which she is hostess. She was raised to be a great lady; her father was very wealthy, and so she was taught to be charming and gracious. She is book learned, and can recite poetry and sing lovely songs, and most of the time will be little trouble to you. It is just the times in which she loses control that she cannot be unattended."

Grace nodded at him, and he continued, rubbing his eyes with his hand. "When she is quiet, you can lock her in the room there, and come out here for some peace and some sleep and time to yourself. I don't expect you to be with her every single minute; that would be most unreasonable. For instance, with her being quiet as she is, I will remain out here for the night, read a book, enter the room occasionally to see how she is. I might even be able to sleep for a few hours as she keeps to her own pursuits inside." He sighed deeply, rested his face in his hands for a moment, pressing the heels of his hands to his eyes as though exhausted.

"You, Mr. Rochester?" Grace asked in surprise. "You are the one watching her during the times someone else can't be with her?"

"Yes, whom else would I get?" he asked her, raising his head to look at her. "I cannot ask the servants to watch her; that would be far above what anyone should have to expect. At any rate, there may come a time when I am in dire need of someone to watch her temporarily for me, and so I must spare anyone else in anticipation of those times.

"John would watch her for me, if needed, but I don't like to ask him. It is too much to expect from him also, and besides, the lunatic doesn't do well with men, in her agitation she tends to... " He broke off, not sure how to go on. "Well, let me just say she is not appropriate, she cannot be trusted to act decently, and John would be distressed by it."

He sighed. "I cannot ask Mrs. Fairfax, as she is elderly and would be easily overpowered by that woman. And I want to spare her as well. She believes the woman to be a discarded mistress, and as such does not approve of my caring for her here, but she doesn't need to hear Bertha shrieking about me as her husband, telling her all manner of revolting details.

"Anyway, Grace, the job would be difficult, I don't lie to you there, which is why the pay is higher than other members of my household are paid." Rochester drummed his fingers on the table, his eyes focused on them as his spoke.

"If the job works out, there would be pay raises, and you may take the occasional holiday with pay; I am not unreasonable. I know you want to see your son, in fact, you are welcome to bring him here for a few days' visit here and there. A child around the place would not be a hardship. I know you would keep him off this floor, and a room could be found for him, a place where you could visit him during breaks from your work up here."

Grace nodded, "Thank you, sir." She didn't need to think about it, she had decided early on in the interview that the job sounded to her liking. Having just one patient instead of several, having a set place to stay, making that much income... it was not difficult to decide to try the position.

"I will take the position, Mr. Rochester. I thank you for offering it to me. When would you like me to begin?"

Edward nodded, not able to keep relief from showing in his face. "As soon as you can. I will be making preparations to leave for France as soon as we can reach some agreement, but it will take me a week or so to be ready, time when I can be here to help you make the adjustment."

They talked for a few more minutes, deciding on a day a week hence for her to begin, which would give her enough time to go for a short visit to her stepdaughter's house to see Abel before she began her job. Rochester insisted upon giving her an advance on her salary, which he said she deserved for having him as a patient during his suture removal.

He smiled at her, and for a second she saw her old playmate reflected in his mischievous grin. It made her feel sad, but she smiled back at him. She was no longer used to smiling, except at her son, and it felt strange to do so now.

Edward stood, and told her, "I had better stay behind and check on the patient. I look forward to seeing you again, Grace, and I thank you. Can you see yourself out?"

Grace nodded, and moved towards the door, turning back for a moment. "Mr. Rochester, what should I call her?"

He thought for a moment, his momentary light-heartedness completely vanished, and shook his head. "I don't know. Madame, Miss, anything that seems comfortable to you." He frowned, his face suddenly twisted with bitterness.

"Anything but Mrs. Rochester."

Chapter 11 - Céline

And, Miss Eyre, so much was I flattered by this preference of the Gallic sylph for her British gnome, that I installed her in an hotel; gave her a complete establishment of servants, a carriage, cashmeres, diamonds, dentelles etc. In short, I began the process of ruining myself in the received style, like any other spoony. I had not, it seems, the originality to chalk out a new road to shame and destruction, but trode the old track with stupid exactness not to deviate an inch from the beaten centre.

You never felt jealousy, did you, Miss Eyre? Of course not: I need not ask you; because you never felt love.

Edward Rochester - Jane Eyre

Paris, February 1826

Edward stood, hands in pockets, watching Céline flit about the room, pausing to pick up one ornament or another, exclaiming over the ornate furnishings and the plush upholsteries and tapestried rugs. He had expected her to like it; it was certainly extravagant and richly appointed. Too richly appointed for his tastes, if the truth were told. He frowned, thinking of the heavy dark wood and stone of Thornfield, and then of the light, exotic teaks and bamboos, the airy fabrics of his home back in Jamaica. This was all gilt and cherubs, silks and satins, with a heady perfume anointing the air, but clearly it was to Céline's tastes and that was the deciding factor in this case. She floated over to him, her face ecstatic. He reached for her, and she came to his arms, taking his hands, reaching up to kiss him lightly on the lips.

"So, do you like it, my dear?" he asked her, picking up her hands and kissing them. "If you do not, we can ask to see something else, but this is a wonderful part of the city, and look at the view." He drew her to the balcony, still holding her hands in his, and opened the door, leading her out to the wrought iron balcony overlooking one of the most fashionable and exciting parts of the city. She exclaimed over it all, leaning over the railing, and looking up and down the street. From below, a man catcalled to her, raising his hat, and she posed and laughed lightly, blowing him a kiss. Then she spun around, back to Edward, kissing him again and laughing at the frown that had started to form on his face.

"Oh, such a look, my Englishman!" she said, with mock seriousness. "You know it is you and only you who has my eye." She laughed again, and took Edward's hand, pulling him inside. "This is a lovely place, I think we will be very happy here." She stopped, and pulled him to her, kissing him harder this time. Her tongue snaked out unexpectedly, the tip flicking across his lower lip, and his breath caught suddenly.

Edward had returned to England almost exactly five years after he had left. He and Bertha had boarded a ship in Kingston, making the six-week voyage back to England. He was determined not to dwell on the horrible trip back to England with Bertha locked up in her cabin, assisted by a sailor to whom he had paid an enormous sum. They had landed in Bristol in July, hiring a carriage to take them the long miles to Thornfield. He could still feel the relief of finally arriving at Thornfield to install her in a safe and private place, but then there had been a period of several months of searching for a proper nurse to care for his mad wife.

It was December before he finally was able to leave and go to Paris. He had always wanted to see France; that had been the first place he and Hugh had planned to go on their aborted grand tour, and it was with real envy that he had read Hugh's letters describing the beauties of Paris.

For the first two weeks, he had been so relieved at being free of the burden of his marriage, he had whirled through Paris in a euphoric state, sleeping as long as he wanted, eating and drinking whatever and whenever he cared to, answering to no one but himself. It wasn't until he had made the rounds of the tourist areas and had seen the sights that reality set in.

He was alone. No matter how happy he was to be free of his burden, to finally have a chance at a normal life, it didn't change the fact that, essentially, he had no one.

Parents dead, brother dead, best friend dead. Other school acquaintances scattered throughout the empire; his only real ties to England were a large, well-managed estate and an insane wife.

Loneliness and desolation settled upon Edward. For a day or so he was truly depressed, but then he pulled out the cards of address given to him by Lady Ingram and Mr. Eshton, two of his neighbours from Derbyshire. They contained the names of some of their social contacts in Paris. Edward made visits to them, and in a few short weeks had all the invitations he could handle.

It was one of those contacts who invited him to accompany their party to the famed Opéra Fantaisie de Paris. There he was mesmerized by the sight of the principal dancer, one Mademoiselle Céline Varens. And after the show, he was taken backstage to meet her in person.

He had been keeping company with Céline for two weeks now, two weeks during which he had seen her in show after show, picking her up afterwards to take her for carriage drives in the city, for dinners at fashionable restaurants. He had an eye towards making her his mistress, of that he had no doubt, and she seemed equally agreeable to that prospect.

But in their conversations, her light flirtations and sweet chatter, she had let him know that it would not do to meet in the home she shared with her friend and mentor, Madame de Simone. And she would not go to his hotel like a common prostitute. He would need to set her up in a fine establishment before he could reasonably expect her favours to be freely granted.

The kisses she had bestowed upon him, the delicious caresses that grew more and more bold as they rode along in the carriage together, or dined in a private dining room of a fine restaurant, had inflamed him to the point where he could think of nothing else, and it was to that end that he had leased this fine suite of rooms in a fashionable and expensive part of Paris.

He hoped that she would see his intention to take care of her, and that she would come to share the passion that he could not hide. He had presented her with gifts of clothing and fine perfume, and recently a lovely and expensive necklace that now rested just above her breasts. He reached up to run his finger along the bauble, where it circled her slender white neck.

"You look lovely in this necklace, my Céline," he breathed. "You make the ornament look even more beautiful, rather than it enhancing you."

She smiled, picking up the hand that touched the necklace, and kissing his fingers one by one. Edward stood, scarcely able to breathe. And definitely barely able to walk, so strong was the desire that pulsed through him at the touch of her fingers.

For two weeks, he had been consumed by this fire, walking around Paris in a daze, able to think only of her and of the relentless, pounding craving that was a permanent part of him since the first time she had taken his hand and smiled up into his face. He walked through his days constantly aroused, spent his evenings with her in a sort of sweet torture, and collapsed into his bed at the hotel exhausted with his longing, to dream of her all night. He could relieve his physical passions temporarily, but it only made him long for her all the more, for the relief that only her body could give him.

He was glad that the bedroom was only a few short steps away from where they stood, and he took her hand and led her there. "You have not seen this room yet," he whispered to her hoarsely, and she gave him her dimpled smile and let him lead her to the room. This fussy lady's boudoir had made his eyes open wide with amazement when he first entered it with the agent the day before, but he had had to admit that this room would probably suit Céline greatly. And he was happy to see that she seemed quite thrilled with it, spinning around with an exclamation of joy.

The furnishings and rugs were even more plush and exotic than in the sitting room – all red velvets and pink satins, with fringe and flowers everywhere. There was an enormous fireplace in which a fire was already blazing, with a chaise longue and several oversized chairs grouped around it. Against one wall was an imposing canopied bed in red velvet, with great numbers of lace and satin pillows strewn about. There was a dressing table with mirror, a large wardrobe, and across the room, velvet curtains were drawn across another door which led to a balcony next to the one they had just visited.

"Oh, Edward, it is lovely indeed!" Céline clapped her hands, and turned to him again, "We are going to be so happy here, I can feel it."

She came to his arms then, and he felt a thrill as her own arms reached up and circled his neck, and her body pressed firmly against his. He kissed her, slowly at first and then with a passion that grew stronger and stronger. He ran his hands down her back, over her little rounded bottom, which he squeezed in his hands, pulling her hard against him. He pressed himself against her, wanting her to feel him, to feel how she inflamed him.

"Do you feel that?" he whispered against her ear. "Can you feel what you do to me?" He had never spoken to her so boldly, all had been light and flirtatious up to now, if no less serious. But he felt her stiffen in his arms, felt her pull away from him a little.

He looked down at her. Her face was flushed, surely from passion, he thought, not embarrassment. Her face was stony for a moment, but she quickly smiled and tossed her head.

"Oh, you go so quickly, Monsieur!" she told him lightly, fluttering her eyelashes. "I hardly have time to catch my breath."

"I'm sorry," he said, taking a deep breath, "I didn't mean to startle you. But you must know how you make me feel."

"Yes, yes, I do," she said, seriously now. She reached for him again, "But we must go slowly, you know. We have all the time in the world." She came to his arms again, and this time their kisses were softer, sweeter. He took his time, kissing her face lightly, her cheeks, her forehead, before his lips moved to her neck, and down the slope of her breasts.

He kept his hands at her waist, her back, but finally could not resist bringing them around to the front, sliding his hands up to gently cup her breasts. Her breathing was faster, and she was moving her head lightly, eyes closed, to allow him greater access to her neck and shoulders.

He let out a shaking breath, his lips against her ear, his hands still gently caressing her breasts, running his fingertips over the hard little nipples that he could feel through the silky material of her gown. He had kept from pressing his pelvis against her, not wanting to upset her again, but he couldn't resist rocking his hips slightly towards her, needing that warm pressure of her body on his.

"Please, Céline, my love," he whispered, "I can wait no longer. Let me take you to bed. I will make you happy, please."

She pulled away lightly, reaching up to touch his burning cheek. "I am so sorry, my dear Edward. I did not know of a way to tell you, but this is not a good time for me." She ducked her head a little, a small embarrassed smile playing across her face. "I am sorry; I had hoped to... make this night a wonderful one for you."

He felt his entire body sag with disappointment, but before he could open his mouth to speak, she whispered, "Come, I will take care of you in another way," and led him over to the chaise longue, pushing him down gently until he was sitting upon it, looking up at her.

She smiled, and went over to the crystal decanter, pouring two glasses of wine. She handed him one, and he noticed how quickly she drank from hers.

As if she needs courage... the thought came unbidden to his mind, watching her as she drained her glass, then refilled it.

She smiled at him, holding the glass up, and he drank slowly, his eyes fixed on her. She set the glass down on the table next to the chaise, and then slowly came over to him. She took the glass from his hand, and pushed at his shoulders until he was lying back on the chaise. He brought his legs up, stretched out, and she raised one slender leg, sliding it up over his thighs and coming to rest there, straddling him, her skirts demurely raised just enough to allow her legs to part as she moved over him.

She leaned over him, kissing him, her pink tongue gliding over his lips. He could taste the wine on her tongue, on her lips. He closed his eyes, feeling her mouth on his, her slender body leaning over him. The wine was going to his head. He had not had much, not as much as she had, but he felt dizzy and suddenly out of focus.

Céline was moving down his body, kissing his neck, her hands caressing his arms, his chest. His coat and cravat were already off, but she slowly unbuttoned his waistcoat and helped him remove it, leaving him in his formal white shirt.

She stopped. "Give me your handkerchief," she said, holding out her hand. He frowned, puzzled, but reached into his pocket, pulling out the cotton square and putting it into her hand. She tucked it into the front of her dress, and moved her hands to him again, smiling down at him.

He felt her hands at his waist, working at the fastenings of his trousers, pulling his shirt free. Her slender fingers moved, unbuttoning his shirt, opening it from the bottom and running her hands up his chest. He felt her fingertips caressing his nipples as she leaned over him, and her hands moved back down, slowly, slowly. She moved her mouth to his chest, her tongue moving in a slow circle over first one nipple, then the other. He gasped with the feel of it, shivers snaking themselves down his back, a hot bolt of sensation going directly between his legs. Her mouth moved down then and he let out a ragged, shaky breath.

He felt her breath on his belly, felt her lips moving down, tracing the line of black hair that disappeared into his unfastened trousers. He felt a moan deep in his throat as she pulled the tie that fastened his drawers. She was breathing little puffs of warm air on his already hot skin, and he felt he was going mad. He could not stop his hips from moving, his hands from reaching for her, but she eluded him, and slid her hands into the waists of his garments, tugging them down. "Lift up," she whispered to him, and in a dream, he obeyed her, raising his hips.

He felt the deliciousness of cool air on his skin as she pulled down on his trousers, and he settled himself back onto the velvet softness of the chaise. So soft beneath him, but not as soft as her lips moving over him, not as soft as her hands which stroked upward on the insides of his thigh. A muted cry came from him as her nails slid up gently against him, caressing him, stroking the aching length of hard fullness between his legs. He felt her lips pressing against him, kissing him where he had never felt anyone's lips before, felt her face against him, her fingers brushing through his thick black pubic hair.

His head fell back, and he moaned again, cried out her name as her mouth moved downward, gently taking him in, just a little at first, then deeper and still deeper. His fingers spasmed, clutching the velvet of the chaise, his nails scraping against the fabric as she moved, her mouth, her sweet, hot mouth taking him to places he had never known.

Never, never in his life, had he felt anything like this. Never with Bertha, never with Evangeline... the pleasure built and built with every stroke, her slow, rhythmic movements making him crazy, making him moan and whip his head back and forth. He raised his head for a moment, wanting to see what she was doing. The sight of her head bent over him, combined with the wondrous pull of her mouth, nearly sent him over the brink, until she raised her head and their eyes met.

Her eyes were hard, her face blank. He watched her for the briefest moment. *She despises this,* he thought, *she despises me.* It was only the shortest of seconds, and her head went back down, scarcely a pause in her efforts, but for a moment his pleasure was swept away in the coldness that washed over him.

He pushed the thoughts away, closed his eyes, and lay his head back, trying to return to where he had been, back to the rapture, to the sweet warmth of her. Back to the heat pulsating through him as her mouth took him in again and again, her fingers caressing him, stroking his hips and thighs, other exquisitely sensitive places. He brought his hands up, grasping her head, his fingers twining in her hair, his hips moving involuntarily in rhythm with her mouth.

He feared he might be hurting her, but he could not let go, could not make his hands let go of her head as the coming release swept over him. He felt the hot pleasure move through him, gathering in one spot, building into a rush of the most delicious response he had ever felt. He climaxed in pulsation after pulsation, his voice crying out hoarsely as the exquisite sensations emptied him, wrung him dry. Her mouth slowed, then stopped, and he felt her move away from him as his hands dropped limply to his sides.

Edward opened his eyes. She sat next to him, his handkerchief held up to her mouth as she spat into it. He watched her, his breathing harsh, his chest heaving. She wiped her mouth, balled the handkerchief up in her hand as she reached over for her wine glass. She took a huge drink, swishing the wine around in her mouth before she swallowed with a grimace.

He moved, his limbs heavy, his hands shaking. He reached down for his trousers and drawers, lifting his hips as he pulled them up and fastened them with his unsteady fingers. Céline sat unmoving, her hazel eyes fixed upon nothing. He reached a hand to her, and she seemed to come back to herself, smiling at him. He sat up slowly, took the handkerchief from her clenched fist.

"Thank you for that," he said. He leaned over and kissed her cheek, holding her head against his for a moment. He thought of himself a few moments before, his hands gripping her head in a fevered grip. Her honey coloured hair was still in disarray from his clutching fingers, and he reached up and gently stroked the spots where he had held her so tightly. "I have never felt anything like that before, it was... " He stopped, shook his head.

He stood up, unsteady on his feet for a second, reaching for the back of a chair to regain his footing. He moved a few steps and tossed the handkerchief into the fire. He stared at the flames as they briefly rose around the crumpled white cotton, and then sank down again. He was thinking of that quick glimpse of her face, of her set and sullen look. He turned to look at her. No sign of that hardness now in her face; she was smiling at him with her usual gaiety.

He did not want to think of anything negative, didn't want to think that just a few minutes ago he had been certain of her hatred for him. He wanted to think of the magic of her, of the delight she brought to his soul, and tonight, to his body. He wanted things to be good and lovely in his life, wanted to feel he was important to her. Wanted to believe she could love him.

"I know you will be tired now, my Edward," she told him, standing up and taking his hand. "It is late, shall we try this large lovely bed?" They prepared for bed, she singing softly to herself, and Edward trying only to remember how wonderful she had made him feel. They lay under the covers together, her fragrant hair unbound, her head against his chest. Edward held her tightly in his arms, trying to sink into a sleep, an oblivion, in which he did not have to either think or remember.

Chapter 12 - In Love

Summer, 1826

"Non, ne te couvre pas," Céline wheedled, rolling over and sitting up next to Edward as he reached down to pull the sheet up to his waist. "J'aime te regarder. Tu es si beau."

"Handsome. For a man, you say 'handsome'," Edward corrected her. "Elegant." Céline had begun to learn English, and had asked him to let her know when one word would be more correct than another.

"Besides, I am not. You can take me out in public and I will not frighten anyone, but handsome I am not, let alone beautiful." He reached behind him to shove another pillow under his neck, and lay back with his arms behind his head.

Céline crept closer, ran a hand over his chest. She moved her hand up, fingers brushing over the black hair under his arm, reaching up to squeeze his bicep teasingly.

"You have a 'beauté mâle'," she told him, leaning over to kiss his forehead. She squeezed his arm again, "How did you get such big muscles?"

Edward closed his eyes, enjoying the feel of Céline's fingertips on his skin. "Rowing," he told her. "Four years at Eton, four years at Oxford. I was a great oarsman. My team members loved me. I was big anyway, broad shoulders, and I put on muscle easily. I could have rowed across the Atlantic."

Truthfully, Edward was proud of his strength, his athletic appearance. Even though he had not touched a pair of oars since leaving Oxford, the muscles he had developed in his back and upper arms had remained – less bulky, but still strong and impressive. He had a fairly narrow waist, strong, taut abdomen, and well-muscled thighs from all his riding. His facial contours were a bit too harsh for him to be considered handsome. The only way to lessen the severity of his features was to smile a large delighted smile, and he refused to walk about with a huge grin on his face like some great idiot. Although if anything could put a smile on his countenance, it was a day like today.

He and Céline had spent most of the day in bed together. They had made love twice, which, he had to admit, appeared to be his limit now at the age of twenty-seven. He had managed more when he was younger, but he thought, with regret, that those days were over.

Twenty-one years old. On his honeymoon. Over and over, he and Bertha together on their large white bed, white lace curtains fluttering at the windows...

His eyes flew open, meeting Céline's. She was still stroking his arm. She raised her eyebrows questioningly.

"Sorry," he shook his head. "Drifting off. What were you saying?"

"You have the 'taille d'athlète'," she told him. He reached up and kissed her, his hand at the back of her neck.

He had acquitted himself well that day, he thought with satisfaction. He had made love to her, and before, in between, and after, he had repeatedly pleasured her with gentle fingers and warm probing tongue. He had nothing to be ashamed of, certainly.

He and Céline had been together for six months. He was in love. For the first time in his life, he was in love. She had burned like a fever in his brain, on his skin, and even though the initial fire had stopped its out-of-control raging, it still smouldered within him. He went about his business, mixing with Paris society at night as was expected of a rich Englishman. But he lived for the days when he could be in her presence.

She would not see him every day. "You will tire of me, Edward," she would say. "And I have friends I must see, things I must do." She had her shows, three or four nights a week, with two shows on Saturdays.

He still went occasionally to see her shows. To watch her singing, dancing, gliding elegantly across the stage. He would lean forward intently, watching her there, in her lavish costumes, his eyes following her every graceful movement; knowing what was beneath those costumes: her small upright breasts with their pale rose nipples. Her tiny waist, her concave stomach. The light brown curls between her slender legs, opening to such moist warmth. It used to drive him wild to sit there and think of it. To think that all that beauty was there for him and for him alone.

Him alone.

But of that he was not certain. It had made him insane, at first, until he had simply decided not to think of it. He put the ideas into those boxes in his head, where he locked away the things he could not face. Things he could do nothing about.

She allured men, certainly. When they were out together, the eyes of men followed her and she often did not discourage them. There is a certain look to a woman who has resolved to belong to only one man.

Céline did not have that look. There were always things to bedevil Edward. A glance. An expression of the face. A sheet of paper hastily folded and put into a desk drawer as he entered the room. Flowers that had not been sent by him.

But there was nothing he could prove. And he did not want to prove it. He loved her. She said she loved him. And so he closed his eyes.

He bought her gifts. Clothing, jewelry, perfume. A carriage. Servants attended her in the hotel suite that he had rented for her. The same agent who had arranged the rental of Céline's hotel suite had notified Edward of a chance to lease a small villa in the south of France. He had eagerly arranged to take possession of the place, thinking that he and Céline could have a quiet place for a lovely holiday. But when he surprised her with the news, he found that she refused to go. She did not want to leave Paris. She did not want to leave her dancing, or her friends from the theatre.

"There is always someone who would love to move in and take my place, Edward," she would say. "Dancing is my life! I cannot be away for long."

He allowed her that. He understood her need for independence. She was talented, deserved the adulation she received from the audience, the money she made. But he longed to possess her, to know that she belonged to him alone. And the more he tried to hold her, the more distant she became.

So rather than risk losing her, he had retreated. He made few demands. Did not question her, did not ask for more of her time. He learned to be content with what she gave him. And she was usually sweet, charming, generous. She said all the correct words.

Yet Céline was not an easy mistress. There were difficulties. She had a foster mother, Madame de Simone – a sharp-tongued, bitter woman of faded beauty. She had rescued Céline from the streets, had raised her, had managed her career. Céline was devoted to her. Madame de Simone and Edward did not like each other. He did not trust her. He suspected that some of the gifts and money he gave to Céline made their way to her foster mother instead.

Céline was moody. Not in the wild and hysterical way Bertha had been. But Edward never knew how he would find her. Sometimes she was gay and lighthearted, teasing him, doting upon him and making him sure that she returned his affections. Other times she was quiet, her answers terse. Sometimes she was tearful. Questioning her made it worse. He had learned to be quiet, to stay away and let her come to him.

She had requirements for their intimate times together. She would not make love on a Sunday. He had laughed at her, teasingly saying that he had not realized she was the religious type. That had made her so angry she had refused to speak to him or let him touch her for several days. He had learned that lesson.

He was not allowed to climax inside her. She was terrified of pregnancy. It would end her life, she said, ruin her career. He had told her about Evangeline, about the little sponge she had mentioned, but Céline had wrinkled her nose in distaste. She had produced a sheath for him to wear, something called a "French letter". He had heard them spoken of when he was in Oxford, but he had never seen one. They were greatly in demand, not so much for prevention of pregnancy, but for prevention of the pox. They were made of sheep's intestine. Durable. Thick.

He had hated it. It had felt terrible, distracted him, robbed him of his pleasure. And it had to be washed and re-rolled afterwards. He supposed, given the arrogance of the upper class, that there might be men who would leave the chore to their valets. But he was damned if he would. So he had seen to it himself, feeling like a fool.

He had worn it to please Céline, but after a few times had refused. So she insisted he would have to withdraw from her, which was unpleasant as well. When they began, she was nervous, visibly uncomfortable as he learned the technique. Mindful of her worry, he had interrupted his thrusts far too early, having to finish by her hand or his own.

Eventually he became quite skilled. He could go nearly to the last second and then pull out with perfect timing, spilling himself across her flat pink belly. All men had talents, and Edward supposed, with a sly grin, that that was one of his. Not one that could be bragged about, he thought ruefully.

He developed other talents as well. Céline loved, preferred in fact, the feel of his mouth upon her. This was the only time she could really relax, could really receive full enjoyment. The first time he had been kissing her breasts and she had pushed his head forcefully downward, he had stopped, not quite sure of what to do. He was not entirely ignorant of the practice, but had never done it himself. But he realized how much it pleased her, and under her careful tutelage, became quite skilled. It fueled his desire, feeling her fingers twined through his thick black hair, holding his head as she urged him onwards. The sound of her voice was nearly as intoxicating as what he was doing to her.

Oui, Edward, oui. Oh, Dieu, n'arrête pas. Un peu plus haut. Maintenant juste le bout de ta langue, doucement. Oui, ah oui.

Yes, he tried to please her. And for the most part, he was happy with the results, happy in his life with her. As his mistress, he could not take her into the more genteel society that included his English friends, but as an opera dancer, she was popular and sought after and he could be seen with her in many fashionable places. At times he would mingle with her friends from the theatre, allow her to drag him to fashionable salons and parties where actors, singers, dancers all mingled. Some of them were outrageous in their behaviour and attitudes and he felt out of place with his foreign ways. He learned to pretend to be enjoying himself, because he knew it made Céline angry if she felt that he was looking down upon her friends.

He imagined taking her to Thornfield, seeing her mix with the Ingrams and the Eshtons. No, that would never do, never in English society. But sometimes he wished he could marry her, live with her here in Paris and never have to leave here. Perhaps if he could marry her, she would then truly belong to him. But he knew he was dreaming foolish dreams.

One place he could not take her, he thought, as he tried to rouse himself to get ready for his evening, was to his upcoming meeting with Richard Mason. He maintained a regular, if not frequent, correspondence with his brother-in-law, and had received a message that Mason would be in Madeira on business. Then Mason had sent word that he would come to Paris, to see the sights and to visit with his sister's husband. They had arranged to meet at a fashionable restaurant. Edward knew he could not bring Céline with him, but she had a show that night, and so would be otherwise occupied.

Edward got up, washed, and dressed for his meeting with Mason. He had kissed Céline good-bye, wished her a good performance, and told her that he would most likely be late, that she should not wait up for him.

When he arrived at the restaurant, he found Mason already seated and waiting for him. Edward sat down, surveying his brother-in-law across the table.

"Fairfax," Richard said, lifting his glass to him, "you look well. Paris agrees with you. Pale though. You have quite lost your Caribbean colour."

"You're looking well too," Edward said tersely. He felt tense and uncomfortable sitting across from Bertha's brother. It brought up too many unpleasant memories, called to mind too many things he had tried hard to forget. He raised a finger towards the waiter, who hurried towards him to take his drinks order. He frowned, leaning back in his chair. "Cold, Mason?"

Richard Mason still had his coat thrown across his shoulders, despite the rather warm spring night. "I have been cold since setting foot in Europe," he said. "How does one stand it?"

"I find it quite comfortable," Edward said, as the waiter brought his drink. His stomach was in a knot and he could not think of eating. Mason had already ordered a small meal, and it was partly eaten. He had always been a delicate eater, picking like a bird over his food. It had once driven Edward mad to watch him.

"Certainly the cool of the Continent is preferable to the damnable heat and wet of the Caribbean," Edward said, taking a long swallow of his drink.

"How is she, Edward?" Richard asked in a low voice. "Is she well?"

"She is well," Edward told him shortly. "In good health. I have engaged a nurse for her, and she seems content." He set his glass down with a resounding thump.

"You have told me where you are keeping her," Richard said. "It is so much better than an asylum, I know, but it grieves me so to think of her locked away, not able to feel the sun."

"She is fine. Better there than any other place she could be. You must not worry, Richard. I do not know why you even concern yourself with her. You could wash your hands of her, leave her to be my problem now. You give yourself anxiety of mind for nothing."

"It is not nothing," Richard said, his face hard and his voice unusually forceful for him. "She is all I have left of my family. I will never have my own children, our line will die with her and with myself. I will never stop worrying for her, never stop wishing things could be different."

Edward turned his face aside, as a flush of anger ran through him. The nerve, the gall. To talk as though he carried this burden, when he had been part of placing the onus and responsibility for Bertha on Edward. He wondered how he could stay there in his seat, could remain cordial.

He raised his head, looked at Richard, "Yes, I know all about wishing things could be different."

Richard had the good grace to blush. He bent his head to his plate, ate a few more bites while Edward lit a cigar and smoked it, eyes narrowed, watching Bertha's brother.

Richard said, "I trust you have received the financial statements I've sent."

Edward answered him, "My steward has. He keeps me apprised. I have no complaints."

Richard cast about for a topic. "Mari still has not forgiven you for taking my sister from Jamaica."

Edward laughed bitterly. "Dear God, is she still alive? No doubt you have hardly a chicken left, the way she must be cursing me."

Richard did not smile. "You must take her seriously, Edward. It is not something to laugh about. Do you remember when my sister was so badly... wounded?"

"Of course I do," Edward told him, his voice hard. "Do you think I could ever forget that? That's why she is in the place she is and not roaming about freely today."

Richard leaned forward, his voice low, "A few months after you left for England, three men were found in a gambling den. All were bound, their throats cut. A fourth man was arrested for the murder. He was hanged. Mari told me that they were the men responsible for Bertha's... injuries. She told me she had cursed them and that God had told her he would let her know when the men were dead. She said it came to her in a dream, that they were the men and that her curse had worked."

Edward felt a sudden chill, but forced it away. "That is utter bollocks, Richard. You have lived in the Caribbean far too long. You need a good strong dose of English sense."

Richard shrugged, "It gives me comfort to think that she is right, and that those men have paid for what they did."

"Well, think that, if it makes you feel better," Edward said. "I prefer to deal in what I can see and touch."

"Speaking of what you can touch," Richard said with an unpleasant smirk, "Evangeline sends her regards to you."

Edward's breath caught. Nothing further about Evangeline had been mentioned once she had left to go back to Mason's estate. He had barely seen her except from a distance when visiting Richard, but he still felt uneasy about her, did not like to remember their brief liaison.

"How is Evie?" he asked, assuming a casual tone, deliberately using the nickname that he had heard Richard call her back in Jamaica.

"Oh, she is fine," Richard told him. "Lovely as ever. A skillful lover. I suppose I have you to thank for some of that."

Edward's eyes narrowed, "Oh, I think she had picked up a great deal of that long before she ever dealt with me."

"But she loves me," Richard said. "I will never marry, never bring an heir into the world, but Evangeline and I are happy together."

"I'm glad for you," Edward said, finishing his drink in one swallow.

The evening ended as cordially as the two men could manage, and Edward left, glad to get away from Richard's irritating manner and mocking smile. He glanced at his pocket watch, heartened to see that it was earlier than he'd thought. He decided not to go back to his hotel, but instead to return to the suite and surprise Céline. She should be arriving home from the theatre right about this time, and would be happy to see him, he hoped.

The rooms were dark when he arrived, and the sleeping maid acted confused to find him there. She said that her mistress had not come home from the theatre; she appeared so tired and befuddled that Edward waved her off to bed. He went into the bedroom, and lit a lamp, looking around the empty room.

He knew that Madame de Simone was nearly always at the theatre. She supervised some of the younger girls in the corps de ballet, and attended every performance. Most likely, knowing he would not be with her that night, Céline had gone home with her, back to the flat where she had once lived with her foster mother.

Edward sat for a while in front of the fireplace, looking into the ashes of the fire that had completely gone out. Then he got up and went slowly to the large empty bed. Taking off his shoes, he laid down on top of the bed, his eyes fixed on the canopy above him.

Then, as he had so many times before, he simply closed his eyes.

Chapter 13 - Pregnancy

Paris, April 1827

"Bloody hell, Edward!" Céline exclaimed angrily. "Can you not knock before you enter the room?"

Edward had often found amusement in Céline's use of some of his English phrases, as her knowledge of the language grew, but in this case, there was nothing amusing about it. She was very annoyed at him. They had always gone freely into and out of the large dressing room off the bedroom, knowing that anything truly personal would be done behind the screens that were set up in the corners of the large room.

The couple were dressing for dinner, and Edward had wandered absently into the room in search of his cuff links. Céline had been standing naked in front of the full length mirror, and had quickly pulled her dressing gown in front of her, but not before Edward had caught a glimpse of her staring at herself intently.

He moved towards her. "Céline... " he murmured, reaching out to touch her shoulder. She pulled away, not meeting his eyes.

"We need to hurry," she said. "Now, go! I need to dress and so do you." She turned her back on him and put her dressing gown on.

He sighed, and went over to the dresser to get his cuff links, before going back out to the bedroom to give her some privacy.

Things had not been going well between Edward and Céline for several months. All during the winter, Céline had been distracted and distant, and although Edward had tried everything to bridge the gap, she still seemed maddeningly far from him. There were times he would talk and know that she was not even listening to him, and their physical encounters were less frequent and less enjoyable.

Céline was tense and snappish with him. He had called several nights to find her not at home, and nothing he did seemed to please her. Through the months of December and January things were strained between them, and by the time they had been together a year, Edward was despairing of their relationship.

Added to this stress was the fact that he had recently had to make a visit to Thornfield. He had received a message from Mr. Carter saying that Bertha was ill, as well as several messages from the steward asking about repairs that needed to be made. So in March he had gone to England for nearly three weeks, to see to estate business as well as personal concerns.

By the time he had arrived, Bertha was nearly recovered. Edward was told she had suffered a high fever, and for a few days Grace and Carter had believed she might not survive. But recover she did, and Edward, who had not been able to avoid the fleeting hope that freedom was within his reach, looked down at her sleeping form with nothing but bitterness in his heart.

He stayed long enough to authorize a few repairs and to make a day trip to Ferndean to check with the man who acted as caretaker for that estate. He had stopped briefly at the London home of Robert and Charlotte Lathrop, to find that they were on holiday, and he left a message wishing them well and telling them he would call again the next time he was in England. Then he returned to Paris, anxious to get back to Céline; privately afraid of what she might have been up to in his absence.

He had come back to Paris to find little changed between him and Céline. She was still tense and distracted, and they rarely touched each other. She turned away from him, and in his frustration, he had blurted out that since he supported her, the least he could expect was for her to do her duty by him. She had sobbed and then gone silent, and he had slammed out and stayed away for several days.

When he came back, it was to find her in her bed, ill with nausea and fatigue. He had come over to her, finding her red-eyed and weeping. He sat on the side of the bed. "Céline, what on earth is wrong?"

She had rolled over and cried into her satin pillows. Her voice was muffled, "I thought that you had left me and would not be back."

"Oh, no," he told her, gathering her in his arms. "I was angry, my love, but I am fine now, and I am so sorry. You should have sent me a message, I would have come back at once. Now, what is this about your being ill?" He stroked her hair, wiped away her tears with his thumbs.

"I have just been very tired and can keep down no food," Céline whispered. "Some of the other girls have been ill, but I cannot dance like this and the girl who is replacing me is terrible. She would love to have my position, but she is no good."

"I must fetch the doctor for you, and you will soon be set to rights," Edward said, getting up from the bed.

"No!" Céline caught his arm. "All will be well. Now that you are back again, all will be well."

That had been two weeks ago, and although Céline was back dancing, she was still not herself. Pale, thinner than ever, still having occasional bouts of sickness. Edward was worried.

But tonight he had seen her in the dressing room, and was reassured. She was usually so frail looking, with her slender arms and legs and knobby knees and elbows, like a child. She had collar bones that stood out above the necklines of her dresses, and her ribs were visible in her back. However, tonight he had seen her breasts, looking fuller than they had the last time he had seen them. And her belly, usually concave and far too thin, had a soft curve to it. He supposed she was able to eat and keep down food after all. He had always fretted about how little she ate, trying to keep her figure and make her light on her feet for dancing.

Soon she came out of the dressing room looking lovely, although still pale. She had applied some rouge to her cheeks and swept out to him in a cloud of perfume. Her posture was straight and she glided over to him and took his arm.

"You must forgive me, Edward, mon amour," she smiled, pressing her cheek against his arm. "I am in a bad temper, I realize. Things are not good at the theatre, and I am letting myself bring my fears home to you. I will try to do better, chéri."

They went to the restaurant, and he, at least, had a wonderful time. They had a very nice meal, although Céline just picked at hers, nibbling the chicken and a few of the vegetables, and leaving the rest.

Edward wiped his mouth with his napkin and leaned back, "Was your dinner not to your liking, darling?"

"It was fine, just perfect." Céline said. "I'm just not very hungry tonight. I would like some more wine though."

"Would you like to tell me about the troubles at the theatre?" Edward asked her. "I know nothing about the workings of an opera, but it might help to talk about it." He raised his hand for the garçon, and ordered a new bottle of wine for their table. Céline waited until it was poured, taking up her glass and drinking from it before she answered.

She waved her hand, "Oh, no, I am having such a lovely time this evening and I do not want to talk of that troublesome subject. You have been home from England for several weeks and you said nothing of what you did there. Why do you not tell me about your trip?"

There was nothing exciting to tell, unless she wanted to hear about drainage ditches, but he told her a bit about the local gentry. He had been obliged to attend a couple of parties, and had held a small dinner party to return the favour before he came back to Paris, so he told her a little about the guests, embellishing a bit to make them sound far more entertaining than they actually were.

She had eagerly pounced upon the name of Blanche Ingram, and Edward had assured her that there was nothing there to take note of.

"She is but sixteen years old, Céline, perhaps seventeen. She is newly out in society, and came to the party with her parents. She is a charming young lady, and sings beautifully. We were persuaded to sing a few duets and all seemed pleased with them, but it was she who was the attraction, and rightly so. Someday she will be a match for a man, but I assure you, she appeals little to me; she's like a pretty child."

Céline pouted and acted quite jealous, and by the time they left the restaurant, her arm firmly in his, he felt more light-hearted than he had in some time. She was like the old Céline, full of gaiety and high spirits and he felt that perhaps they had passed their rough patch of the winter. They had both had a good portion of wine, and the friendly atmosphere of the dinner lingered over them both as they waited for their carriage to be brought to the front.

The April night was still a bit chilly, with only the sweet promise of a warm spring in the air. Céline, wrapped in an expensive Indian shawl he had bought her, huddled close to Edward in the carriage on the way home, clinging to his arm. When the carriage stopped in front of Céline's building, she turned to him with a dazzling smile.

"My darling, you will come in tonight?" she whispered. "I know that we have not been close the past few months, with your travels and my little worries, but I have missed you and I hope that we may have a lovely night tonight."

She squeezed his arm and looked into his eyes. His heart skipped a beat, and he felt a pull in his groin. It had been a long time, and he needed no further persuasion to follow her out of the carriage and up to the suite.

The candlelight cast a soft yellow glow over the room as they lay together in bed. Edward kissed Céline for a long time, stroking her hair and moving his lips over her face. He kissed her ears and ran his lips down her neck, moving the sheet down to bare her breasts to his searching mouth.

"You look different," he whispered, his lips brushing over the soft flesh at her bosom.

She stiffened in his arms, "What do you mean?"

He moved his mouth down, and reached his hand to cup her breast.

"Your breasts are fuller, and here… " He brushed his fingertips across her nipple, "They used to be the palest pink, and now they are darker, nearly brown."

She twitched irritably, her hand coming up to brush his away. She turned from him, frowning, "That is ridiculous."

"No, I mean it." He bent his head. "There's nothing wrong with them, they are quite lovely." He took her nipple in his mouth, sucking gently.

"Ow!" She moved away sharply. "Stop it!"

He raised his head and looked at her. "What is wrong?"

She covered her breasts with her hands. "Leave them alone, they are very sore," she snapped.

He leaned up on one elbow, "We always do this, Céline; you never minded it before. I was not trying to make you angry, I was just making an observation." He looked away. "Good God," he muttered, rolling onto his back and staring up at the canopy over them.

Céline sighed and lay back with her hands still covering her breasts. "I'm sorry. I guess I'm still a little nervous. I have a lot on my mind; you must not pay attention to my little tempers." She moved her hands away, looking down at her breasts. "They don't look different to me. But my time of the month is coming, probably this week, that is why they might look different and are tender."

She leaned up over him. "I am sorry, darling."

He said nothing. She moved over to him, and began kissing him, moving her hand lightly over his chest and down his stomach. At first he was barely responsive, but it had been a long time, after all, and as she continued to kiss and caress him, he warmed up to her, reaching up to kiss her in return.

At last he moved over on top of her, and began to kiss down her abdomen, to pleasure her the way he knew she liked. For a long time he touched her, with mouth and tongue and fingers, her moans the only sounds in the dim room, before she arched her back and gave a sharp cry. Usually this was his signal to move up and cover her body with his own, but this time she sat up and pushed him back, crawling up over him.

He knew she did not really enjoy other positions, and he was surprised to feel her moving over him, taking him in and sinking down on him, kissing his neck fiercely.

"Céline... " he whispered, reaching up to take her face in his hands, but she said, "Shhh," her body beginning a slow rise and fall over his. He tried to catch her eyes, but hers were closed, her face serious and still. He finally let his head fall back upon the pillow, letting the glorious heat and friction of her take him in. His hands moved over her body, and rested on her waist, as he arched up to thrust into her.

It did not take long to realize that he was perilously close to losing control, and he used every ounce of will inside him to stop, and tightened his hands upon her waist.

"Céline," he whispered hoarsely. She did not pause in her movements, and he squeezed her waist again, gently. "Céline," he said, louder this time.

He moved his hands down to her hips, stopping her movements, "Céline!"

She opened her eyes and looked down at him, frowning.

He gritted his teeth, still deeply inside her. "I... we have to stop now." His voice was rough, "I cannot hold on much longer, we need to stop now." She looked down at him for a moment, her face immobile, then she shook her head, closed her eyes again, and again began to move. She bent over him, pressing her hips firmly against him, head down against his shoulder, her movements quick and firm. She was not pausing, not stopping, and her breathing was fast, hissing in between her clenched teeth, echoing in his ear.

He felt himself losing control, and he groaned, "Céline". It became a cry, and he moved his hands to her hips again, trying in vain to keep her still.

"Shhh!" she hissed sharply at him, and pressed herself more tightly against him, tightening around him. The heat was sweeping over him, and he could hear himself moaning as the climax overtook him. He had tried to resist her, tried manfully to pull away, but as the end came he gave up. He thrust his hips up towards her, filling her, coming inside her, and she was freely allowing it as she had never done before.

For a long time they lay together, their harsh breaths the only sound in the room. He felt himself slipping from her, and she shifted slightly, moving to his side and laying her head on his chest.

"Why didn't you let me stop?" he whispered to her. "I tried to stop, and you wouldn't let me. I was inside you; what if you get pregnant?"

She was silent, breathing softly against him. "Would you be upset?" she asked him.

He said nothing, then replied, "I don't know how I would feel. How I feel is not the point right now. For a year now, I've never been able to... do that, and now you let me – I don't understand."

Céline shrugged. "It felt too good to stop," she finally said. She sat up, blowing out the candles nearby. She lay back down, and he eventually felt her go slack against him, her breathing slow and regular. But he lay awake, his eyes looking up into the darkness.

Late May, 1827

"You're pregnant," he repeated, his dark eyes fixed on hers. "How do you know this?"

Céline sat next to him, her voice soft as she told him the news. He had just come in, looking forward to a pleasant afternoon with her, and had found her lying on the chaise by the fire, one arm up over her eyes. When he came in he could see she had been crying, and he moved towards her, concerned. She had gotten up and bade him sit beside her, his hands held tightly in hers, and it was then that she had told him, her eyes fastened to their linked hands.

"My courses have stopped," she told him. "And I went to the doctor, the one who treats the dancers. He examined me and told me I am pregnant."

He was silent. He opened his mouth, but he could not ask the question that was foremost in his mind. He closed his lips firmly, afraid the words "Is it mine?" would come bursting out. He took a deep breath.

"When?"

"I think that night that we... in April. When you... you know, inside me... "

"No," Edward said, sounding calmer than he felt. "When is the baby coming?" *Baby*... the word sounded strange and alien on his lips.

"Oh," she said, "sometime in January, perhaps even early February." She shrugged, "I have never been too regular, so it is hard to be sure."

She swallowed, "How do you feel about it, Edward?"

He looked over at her. She was watching him, a tiny line between her eyes, her gaze dark and intense upon him. She did not tell him about the measures she had tried, the hours of hot baths, the foul potions Madame de Simone had obtained and forced upon her. Nothing had worked, the pregnancy stubbornly refused to come to an end.

"I don't know," he said, shaking his head. "I will have to get used to the idea."

"I had never planned to have children," Céline told him. "It is not what I wanted, but now I must make the best of it. I'm sure you had planned on a family someday, with someone... "

"I have always assumed it was in my future," Edward said quietly. "I had thought of it, in a distant way, in the setting of an established home."

"We can provide this child with a home," Céline said. "I will try to be a good mother, if you will help me."

Edward said nothing.

"Edward, I need to know. I'm sorry." The momentary brightness was out of her voice, "I know that you are a good man. But are you going to stand by me? I have to know if I will be doing this alone." The tears sprang to her eyes again, and her lips trembled.

Edward shook his head. He did not know how he felt. His brain felt on fire with the thoughts that were going through his head. He knew that, if he could be sure the child was his, he would probably be happier about the idea. But he did not know. And he did not know how he could be sure.

He shook his head again. "No, you won't go through this alone. I will be here."

Chapter 14 - The Fillette

... the Varens, six months before, had given me this fillette Adèle; who she affirmed was my daughter, and perhaps she may be, though I see no proofs of such grim paternity written in her countenance. ... I acknowledged no natural claim on Adèle's part to be supported by me; nor do I now acknowledge any, for I am not her father ...

Edward Rochester - Jane Eyre

December, 1827
Céline kept dancing until August, when she could no longer hide the small bulge of her abdomen under her elaborate costumes. She had wept piteously when she had come home from her last performance, although the theatre managers had kissed her hands, wishing her well and promising that her place at the Opéra would be there when she returned.

Edward had tried to be understanding of her moods and her unhappiness. He understood how difficult it was for her to give up the dancing that she had been doing ever since she was a child, but it upset him that she did not seem content to relax and allow him to care for her. At last, he had her where he had wanted her, belonging to him, depending upon him, but instead of the happiness he thought it would bring him, he had to put up with her tears and her obvious displeasure at being beholden to him and dependent upon his support.

She rarely mentioned the baby, although she kept her appointments with the accoucheur that Edward had insisted she see. He was a perfumed and pomaded man with annoying mannerisms, and he appeared rather snide and sarcastic about Céline's unmarried state, but Edward had heard he was the best obstetric expert in the city, and that all the women of quality were attended by him.

The man examined Céline and recommended tonics and drinks to build up her strength. He also insisted she eat and put on some weight, but it was hard to break the habits of a lifetime, and when Edward tried to tempt her with food she became irritated and resistant.

She slept more than usual, complaining of constant fatigue, and to Edward's dismay, Madame de Simone was a frequent visitor to the hotel. Her foster daughter's pregnancy seemed to delight her, no doubt for the financial advantages it might bring, and no visit was complete without her bringing another tiny and overly-elaborate baby costume with her.

One positive result had occurred as a result of Céline's pregnancy. Once her initial fatigue and illness had passed, she grew more agreeable to Edward's advances, and now that she was pregnant, she had no restrictions upon him. At times she even appeared to enjoy it, something he had never been entirely sure of before.

For the first time, the physical side of their relationship was natural and spontaneous, although there were times when he felt that she was only initiating contact with him to keep him happy. She was embarrassed about her changing body, but he found it lovely, enjoying the feel of her rounded belly against his as they moved, loving the sight and feel of her growing breasts. He loved to push deep inside her as he finished, to feel her pleasure as well, to hear her cries and feel her body tighten and relax around him. There was tension and uneasiness in the rest of their life together, but for once their time in the bedroom was frequent and pleasant enough, and he was anxious to keep that bond between them.

Out of the bedroom, Edward was tense and worried. He had not wanted a child, not under these conditions, and he was afraid of the responsibilities, of how he would be a real father to a child born to his mistress. He was sorry that this baby would be illegitimate; he had never intended that fate to befall a child of his. He realized that this would tie him to Céline for life, and while he loved her, he was aware that the relationship was fraught with problems. This upset him, and he wished for assurance that her love for him was equal to his for her.

His doubts were still present. He had not asked her about the baby's paternity when he should have asked it, and so it became harder and harder to imagine asking now. But he thought of it constantly. He thought of how things had been in the winter. How distracted Céline had been, how she had obviously had more on her mind and in her life than just him.

He thought of how they had not come together very often, how he had been away from Paris, and of her illness when he had returned. He remembered the subtle changes of her body, the fuller breasts and belly, her darkened nipples. He did not know much about the female body when it came to childbearing, but he knew enough to be suspicious.

And most of all, he remembered her pinning him down, refusing to let him stop, letting him climax deep within her when it had once been her biggest worry.

But all these questions, once so close to the surface, remained unasked, were buried deeper, and were finally impossible to put into words.

Once Céline was no longer dancing, her time was her own, and Edward persuaded her to leave Paris and go to the villa down south. She agreed, to his surprise, and to Madame de Simone's dismay. Edward felt that she had been hoping for an invitation to accompany them, but he was damned if that was going to happen. The accoucheur examined Céline and said she would be fine to travel, but had to come back a month before the expected delivery day.

"So," Edward calculated, counting on his fingers, "We must return in early January."

"Oh no!" Céline exclaimed, "We must return in… late November or early December!"

Edward looked at her questioningly.

"I don't know," she said, shrugging. "I will miss Paris, and all my friends. I do not want to be gone too long. And we must get ready for the baby, it will need a room to sleep in, and we must hire a suitable nurse, as well as someone to feed the baby." Taking note of Edward's sharp glance at her breasts, she said, "You cannot expect me to feed the child myself; I must get back into shape and begin dancing again. And feeding the baby will ruin my figure."

Edward agreed. And wondered.

The time at the villa was very nice, he had to admit. They slept late into the morning, and got up to bathe in the ocean in the hot sunshine. Later in the afternoon, they would retire to their room, sleeping away the warmest part of the day. They would awaken to eat a delicious meal made by the woman who was their only servant. She would make delicacies native to the area, standing over Céline and making her eat them, telling her that they would make the baby strong. Or make the baby beautiful. Or intelligent.

In the cool of the evening, they would stroll along the lane in front of the villa, mindful of the fact that the doctor had told Céline to take regular exercise. When they returned to the villa, they would again go to the beach, sitting in the sand with the water lapping up over their feet.

Until Céline grew so large that she was no longer interested, they would often wait until it was dark and then make love in the sand, the soft evening tides washing up over them.

Sometimes, when he had climaxed and they were still lying together, she would turn her face away and cry. She would not tell Edward what was wrong, and those times his heart would freeze within him, knowing that she had slipped away and he did not possess her, neither her heart nor her mind – only her body, and that only temporarily.

At night, he would hold her in their large bed while the moonlight streamed over them. He lay with his arm across her, feeling the baby inside her twist and turn.

"A dancer, like its mother," he would say, rubbing his hand over her abdomen. Céline would smile, and say nothing, her eyes sad and far away.

One night, they had both drunk a little too much wine with dinner. Céline was now so large, her belly so taut and uncomfortable, her back so sore, that they had stopped making love. They had had a tense and unhappy day, with an argument precipitated by Céline's moodiness and tears.

Edward had lost patience and gone for a long walk alone, returning to a silent dinner, in which there was not much to do but drink. They had both gone to bed early, silently, turning away from each other, but later they had awakened to find themselves facing each other in the moonlight. Céline had moved closer to him, and he put his arm around her. She turned her back to him, spooning against him as he laid a palm on her belly. For a long time they lay like that, and finally the words pushed at his lips, forcing themselves out.

"Céline," he whispered into her ear.

"What?" she murmured drowsily.

"Is the baby mine?" He let out a long, shaky breath, relief flooding over him at being able to ask at last.

She said nothing. She lay quietly under his arm. She did not react, she did not ask why he wondered. For a long time she lay silent.

Then one word, whispered into the night.

"Yes."

They returned to Paris in early December, as the cold of winter was beginning to overtake the city, requiring warm wraps and hot blazing fires in the fireplaces.

Céline was exhausted, her belly impossibly large, her every movement uncomfortable. She was snappish, constantly irritable, and Edward could hardly bear to be around her.

Edward had hired a painter to make ready the guest room as a nursery for the baby, and as Céline spent most of her time now sleeping, it was he who had consulted the accoucheur and hired a baby nurse and a wet nurse.

One day, in the week between Christmas and the New Year, Edward was invited to join a shooting party with some acquaintances. They had company from England, and were eager to have Edward join them for a day of masculine companionship. Had Céline been in any way happy to have him around, he would never have gone, but she seemed so eager for him to be away most of the time that he agreed without hesitation to join the men.

Céline had been restless all night, tossing and turning and once even getting up to vomit into the commode in the dressing room. But she sometimes had bouts of sickness even still, and Edward was not unduly alarmed. She shushed off his concern and told him to go back to sleep, but he was exhausted and bleary-eyed when he got up before dawn to go with the shooting party. Céline was sleeping, finally, a light sheen of sweat across her brow, and he did not kiss her, afraid of waking her.

The men spent all day tramping through the woods of a huge estate on the outskirts of Paris, doing their best to rid the surrounding area of whatever birds and small animals could still be flushed out of the brush. A dinner followed, and after that brandy and cigars. Many of the men were spending the night, but Edward thought he had better return to Céline. He did not tell the men assembled that he had a pregnant mistress to return to, but made his departure as soon as he decently could.

The carriage let Edward off in front of the hotel, and he looked up to see every window of the suite blazing with light. He had expected to find the suite darkened, a single lamp burning to guide his way, and he was concerned. He took the stairs two at a time, and burst through the door.

The sitting room was empty, and he was taking off his hat and coat, when the door to the bedroom opened and the maid came out, accompanied by the accoucheur.

Edward looked from one to the other, "What... ?" His heart began to pound. "What are you doing here? Where is my... where is Mademoiselle Varens?"

The accoucheur came over to him, a wide smile on his face. "Now is a fine time to arrive, when we have done all the work."

Edward's heart was thudding in his chest. He reached over and grasped the man's arm, "What? Tell me, what is going on?"

"A healthy girl, and she and her mother are doing fine." The man put on his hat, "In fact, you may go in. All is finished, all is normal. I will call tomorrow to check on mother and child." He moved to go.

"Wait!" Edward stopped him, still grasping his arm. "The baby, it is too early. It is too soon, it is not supposed to be here until late January, perhaps even the beginning of February. How can she be healthy; she is too early?" He heard himself sounding like a babbling fool, and he forced himself to be quiet.

The accoucheur was silent a moment, looking at Edward and then glancing towards the closed door of the bedroom. His mouth tightened to a grim line.

"You cannot always be sure of dates and times," he finally said. "Babies come when they are going to come. No way to make them come later, no way to make them come sooner. But the child is healthy. That is all you need to remember." He nodded and left the suite.

Edward moved with trepidation towards the closed door. Finally he turned the knob and went in.

Céline was lying under the covers, on her side, facing the small cradle that they had purchased and set up next to the bed. The small guest room had been prepared as a nursery, and the baby would be moved into it when the wet nurse arrived.

He approached the side of the bed, and Céline looked over at him without speaking. She smiled, and reached her hand towards the cradle.

He looked down at the sleeping baby. She was a tiny bundle, wrapped in blankets up to her little chin. Her head was a little misshapen, but they had been warned to expect that. A soft layer of pale brown hair covered it, and Edward could see sparse light brown eyelashes resting on her pink cheeks. He reached out and rubbed a finger over her tiny head, his hands suddenly unsteady.

"Are you well?" he asked Céline, his voice not quite steady either. She nodded.

"I am fine now," she said, her voice husky. Her face was very pale, a light covering of what looked like freckles over her skin, from straining so hard, she told him later. Dark circles shadowed her eyes.

"It hurt badly," she whispered. "I thought she would never get here. I am never going to do this again."

He smiled at her, and leaned over the bed to kiss her forehead, before turning to look at the baby once again.

Chapter 15 - Betrayal

Opening the window, I walked in upon them; liberated Céline from my protection; gave her notice to vacate her hotel; offered her a purse for immediate exigencies; disregarded screams, hysterics, prayers, protestations, convulsions; made an appointment with the vicomte for a meeting at the Bois de Boulogne. ... then thought I had done with the whole crew.
Edward Rochester - Jane Eyre

Paris, June 1828
Edward used his key to open the door to Céline's suite, quietly entering the sitting room, where a single lamp was burning on the table. He listened for any sounds from the bedroom, but could hear nothing, and he began to move quietly towards the nursery.

He had met some people for dinner, acquaintances of his English friends here in Paris. He had expected to make a night of it, but upon learning that they had plans to attend a musical revue after dinner, he had begged off, saying he had an early day. He was glad to have the chance of a free evening, and was anxious to return to Céline and to Adèle. He had not seen them for nearly three days, occupied as he had been with some business matters and the out of town guests.

Céline did not expect him to call until the next day; indeed, they had made plans to take Adèle out for an airing in the park in the afternoon and then to have a quiet dinner at the hotel afterwards. Céline did not have any idea he was free this evening, or that he was planning to surprise her.

It was a lovely, warm June evening, and rather than take a cab to Céline's suite, he decided he would walk the two miles. It was early yet, and he'd had no chance to take any exercise recently. He strolled briskly along the busy streets of Paris, enjoying the fragrant air of early evening and tipping his hat to an acquaintance or two he met as he walked.

Now he was back, but it appeared Céline was out. He decided he would wait for her in her boudoir, but first he wanted to look in on Adèle. He knew she had probably been put to bed, but thought he would tiptoe in and look at her. He tapped on the nursery door and opened it a crack to peek in. The young wet nurse, Manon, was rocking in the chair by the window, doing some mending by the light of the day that remained. She looked surprised to see him, but set down her sewing and stood to her feet, motioning him in.

Because Adèle had been born more than a month before she was expected, the wet nurse Edward had hired was not available, since she had not yet delivered her own baby. Therefore, the doctor had recommended this young woman, whose own child had died shortly after being delivered only a day or so before Adèle's birth. Manon was a sad-eyed girl of only sixteen or seventeen, but she was experienced with infants and had been very helpful, moving in with Céline and feeding Adèle, then taking over the baby's care after the temporary nurse had moved on to other families.

Edward moved quietly over to the cot and looked down at the sleeping baby. At six months old, Adèle was quite active and vocal when awake, but as ever, Edward was struck by her sweet appearance when asleep. He felt most tender towards her then, and leaned over to listen to her quiet, even breathing. She lay on her back, her plump hands thrown up over her head, fingers curled. Her light brown ringlets lay across her forehead, slightly damp from sweat, her cheeks pink. As Edward watched, she turned her head slightly, her fingers curling and releasing, her full lips making tiny sucking motions before she again quieted and lay still.

There was nothing of himself in Adèle's appearance, even though he watched her for any emerging similarities every time he saw her. She was Céline made over, the same soft curly hair, and though Adèle's hair was showing signs of growing darker than her mother's, it was nowhere near Edward's raven black. Her eyes had started off blue, but were now forming different shades within her irises, giving promise of the hazel eyes of her mother. She was a petite baby, although slightly plump, with good health, and her facial features showed every sign of being just like her mother's.

Edward was still unsure of Adèle's paternity, and while it bothered him, the rest of his life was so good that he was able to set it aside and attempt to enjoy the feeling of family that his mistress and her child gave him. Céline was a loving mother when she was with Adèle, although she was quick to leave her with the nurse to go out in the evenings. But he could not fault her care when they were all together. She did very little of the feeding, bathing, and dressing of her child, but she was affectionate and attentive, holding Adèle up to make her tiny feet dance across her lap, singing her gay songs and reciting poems, rhymes, and amusing lines from operas she had starred in. Adèle was always happy to be in her mother's arms, her wide eyes following her, and her mouth breaking into a wide smile when Céline entered the room.

Adèle appeared happy to be with Edward too, smiling at him and being equally content in his arms, and at those times he was able to quell his doubts and enjoy her. He had reveled in six months of happiness in his little household, for since Céline had recovered and gone back to dancing, she had not been able to do enough for him. She would meet him at the door when he arrived, hugging and kissing him, asking about his day, guiding him to a chair by the fire and making sure he had a drink in his hand and that he always had access to the chocolate candies that he had grown fond of. She would make sure a bath had been drawn for him, and that his dressing gown was placed by the fire to be warmed. She would stand behind him, rubbing his shoulders while he relaxed.

It had taken awhile for her to welcome him back to her bed after Adèle's birth, but he was understanding, knowing how uncomfortable she was following her ordeal. He made no requests of her, assuring her he could wait until she was recovered. She was quiet and moody after the birth, although her spirits improved when she was back in rehearsals for the next opera. She had forced herself to be ready, quickly losing the small amount of weight she had gained with the baby, and returning to the theatre within three weeks of the birth, pushing herself. She had practiced and rehearsed for a month, and a mere two months after delivering Adèle, she returned to the stage.

She also returned to Edward's arms, and although she professed herself not quite ready to make love, she saw to his needs in other ways, and he was quite satisfied. As long as he had her affection and the assurance of her love, he could wait for the rest to happen naturally, and she finally allowed him into her bed when Adèle was three months old. It was lovely for him, although they of course had to return to their earlier precautions. Céline was most anxious to avoid pregnancy again. She loved her baby, she said, but would never have another one, and Edward was only too happy to do his best to prevent it also.

So despite his private worries that he had not been the one to father Adèle, he was quite happy in his life now. Had he known that having a baby would make Céline fall so in love with him, he would not have worried so much. His early love for her had returned full-fold under her loving attentions, and he felt that she loved him completely. Indeed, when he told her of his passion for her, she assured him that hers for him was even greater.

Looking forward to an unexpected night with his lover, he smiled at the young wet nurse and motioned her to be seated again, leaving the room with one last look at Adèle.

He went into Céline's bedroom, taking a seat and stretching out his legs, a bit sore and stiff from all his walking. It was dark; there was no light except the faint glow of embers in the fire place, the remains of a fire that had not even been needed that day. He leaned over and helped himself to a bonbon or two, and took out a cigar, lighting it up and relaxing. After a while he grew tired of the stuffy air in the room, which smelled strongly of flowers, Céline's perfume, and the smoke from his cigar. He rose and went out to the balcony, leaving the door slightly ajar to air out the room. He sat down on a chair in the dusk, breathing the fresh air, anticipating Céline's return. He was slightly aroused, hoping for a long night in her bed, and he leaned his head back, closing his eyes and imagining what the night would bring forth. He wondered if he could persuade Céline to massage his aching thighs, and then imagined her soft hands moving to other places upon his body. He smiled, thinking of the pleasures that surely lay ahead.

So absorbed was he in his lovely fantasy that it took him a moment to notice that one of the passing carriages on the street below had slowed and then stopped in front of the hotel. He leaned over, and instantly recognized the fine horses and elegant lines of the carriage he had given Céline. His heart began to pound, the black wrought iron rail of the balcony hard and cold against his palms. He watched as the door opened and a small slippered foot emerged.

"My angel," he whispered.

Céline stepped delicately out of the carriage, and he nearly called to her from the balcony, but something stopped him. He noticed that she was wrapped in a cape, a light cape, but one that was still unnecessary in the soft warm air of early summer. He watched as she stepped away from the equipage, and then his dark eyes widened when he noticed that someone had gotten out of the carriage after her.

A man. Those were spurred boots he heard on the pavement, that was a man's hat he saw, pulled low over a face he could not yet see.

His heart, beating with anticipation, seemed to catch in his chest for a moment, and briefly, he could not catch his breath. He swallowed against a sudden obstruction in his throat.

He stood up, and came over to the partially open balcony door. Hardly aware of conscious thought, he reached through the crack and pulled the curtain partially over the open area of the door, leaving only a small area through which he could look.

For they would come to her bedroom. Of course they would.

He stood there, his heart once again beating wildly in his chest, but this time not from arousal or anticipation. He was aware of a feeling of being trapped – of having to stand here and see what he did not want to see, to know what he did not want to know.

He wished he could turn time back in its flight, to be able to return to the early evening, and change the course of the path his life would now follow. His eyes darted rapidly back and forth, looking for an escape, but knew that, of course, he was stuck there, on the balcony. He felt as though his entire life with Céline was replaying before his eyes, coming down to this final act in their time together.

It was too late for anything to change. He heard voices, and then he saw the door open and the maid enter to light the lamps in the room. Céline entered, the man following closely behind her. The maid finished lighting the lamps and exited the room, and he watched as Céline took off her cape, to reveal an elaborate dress, low-cut, fashioned of the most brilliant scarlet satin. It displayed her white bosom, which was draped with jewels. All his gifts to her.

The man removed his hat and his cape, and Edward finally saw his face. It was someone he knew. Not well, but a face he was familiar with from the salons he had attended with Céline. He was a young vicomte, the son of wealthy parents, who had bought him his rank of officer despite his young age. He was a mere twenty or twenty-one to Céline's twenty-six.

Edward had disliked him on sight. He knew the type: an arrogant youth, one who had never known a moment's work or hardship, one whose casual cruelty to others seemed as natural as his own breaths. He had reminded Edward of his brother Rowland. The young man was known to be a flirt, fancied himself a temptation to all the ladies, and although he had paid lavish attentions to Céline, she had appeared not to notice him. And Edward had never been jealous, had never viewed him as a threat, because he had been so contemptuous of him.

He felt his breath hiss between his teeth, a hiss like that of a snake, as a pain so sharp and so hard struck him in the heart that it took his breath away. The jealousy came full force, hitting him in the mid-section, as hard as an actual blow. It was all he could do to stand upright, and keep his eye to the aperture of the balcony door. He forced himself to be silent, for the couple had begun to speak.

For a while they moved about the room, laughing and talking about people they both knew, people they had seen at a party they had apparently been to that evening. Neither of them had much good to say about anyone, not their hostess, nor the other guests at the party, nor the food and drink they had been served. They chatted about the love affairs of some of the people present, names that meant nothing to Edward. His legs were tired, his body stiff from bending over to look through the crack in the door. He was nearly glassy-eyed with boredom and for a few minutes he wondered if he was crazy to be so suspicious. Perhaps the young man had just escorted Céline home. Perhaps the vicomte would put his cloak and hat back on and leave, having done nothing more than kiss her hand in parting.

Céline waved her hand in the air, turning to smile at the young man. "No matter what, I still smell the cigars in the air; I will never get that smell from my nose."

The vicomte returned her smile, "So I should not smoke around you, my lovely Céline?"

"No, not if you want me to kiss you!" She moved towards him, reaching up to kiss his mouth, trailing a finger along his cheek, which was barely whiskered. Edward doubted he had been shaving a full year. He was tall and slender, but there did not appear to be a true muscle on his entire body. Edward gave a sharp intake of breath, seeing his lover kiss her young escort. His teeth clenched.

"So, where is the Englishman tonight?" he asked Céline, rolling his eyes and looking around the room.

"He had plans with some out of town visitors," Céline answered, "He is supposed to come tomorrow, but I have had a day or so of rest from his attentions."

"Oh, you do not like such attentions?" the vicomte asked in a seductive voice. He had come up behind her and put his arms around her waist. She reached up behind her, wrapping her slender arms around his neck.

"Umm, I like these attentions," she said, moving her hips back against his. Edward watched as the man's hands left her waist, coming up to cup her small breasts. Edward ground his teeth, and he swallowed audibly. He pressed a hand against his chest. Surely his heart was stopping. Surely he could not continue to breathe and to live with the pain that had lodged there.

The man spoke, still cradling Céline in his skinny arms, "I don't know how you can let that man touch you. He is so ugly – all that dark hair and those black eyes and those glowering looks. If I were a woman, I would not let such a man lay a finger on me."

Céline smiled, "Well, when you close your eyes, a man can be whoever you wish him to be." She chuckled, "And when you think of all that money, a man becomes quite bearable to look upon, in spite of his deformities."

Edward's mind conjured up picture after picture of Céline, lying in his arms, eyes closed, soft moans sounding in her throat as he moved inside her, as he kissed and touched her, as he put his mouth on her. He wished he could die. He wished his life would cease, right there on that balcony, before he had to hear another word.

"So whom do you picture, when you have to be in his arms?" the vicomte asked her in a wheedling tone. "And surely you gain no pleasure while he is with you?"

Céline turned to face him, giving him a small playful slap. "You ask such personal questions, my darling. But I'm sure you can guess whom I am thinking of when I am with him. And any pleasure? Never! But I can pretend. I'm good at that – I can make all the sounds and say and do everything he expects. I am an actress, remember!"

The vicomte frowned, "But you do not pretend with me?"

Céline laughed, "Of course not. I do not have to pretend with you. You excite me."

"And the Englishman does not?" the man persisted.

"No, he does not!" Céline said in mock exasperation. "He is so short and so big, with those large disgusting muscles. Sometimes I feel I am going to suffocate beneath him. And he is so hairy!" She shuddered. "That moustache, those hairy arms around me, that hairy chest. And those legs. I cannot stand all that fur, it is like sleeping with a monkey."

"He does not have hair on his back, does he?" the vicomte asked, laughing.

Céline grimaced, "No, thank God. I truly could not bear it then; the rest is bad enough."

"So you like my smooth chest and face?" the vicomte wheedled. "I please you?"

"Of course you do," Céline said. For a few moments there was no sound but the sounds of their kissing. They stood in each other's arms, their kisses growing more passionate and more forceful. The vicomte took off his coat, his belt, kicked off his boots, and grabbed Céline again, pulling her against him, his hands on her buttocks. He growled deep in his throat and she gave a high giggle.

"There, what do you think of that?" he asked, "I'll bet your Englishman has nothing like what I have. I think Englishmen are probably very small. They are all so arrogant, they must be making up for a lack... "

Céline giggled again, trailing her fingers across his chest. "Now that, I will never tell!" she said, turning away with a flirty batting of her long lashes.

"Come now, you have my curiosity aroused!" the young man persisted. "What about the Englishman's ... ?" He said a word, a French word Edward was not familiar with, but he could guess its meaning. His face grew hot to hear himself spoken of that way. "You said he is so big and muscular, does it include that? I must know, is he bigger than me?"

He came up behind Céline again, pulling her against him and pawing her eagerly. Edward knew she would never have tolerated such actions from him, but instead of growing angry, she just giggled.

"No, if you must show such vulgar curiosity, he is not bigger than you are," she said with a toss of her head, "If you lined up every man in Paris to compare them, Rochester would be right in the middle. Nothing remarkable at all in that area. You are without compare in every way."

The vicomte smiled with a satisfaction that made Edward want to charge through the door and wipe the smirk right off his face. He heard himself give a low moan. His eyes prickled with frustrated tears, and he did not want to go in right then, did not want to risk crying in front of the two of them. But he did not want to have to stand there and see what he knew was coming either.

He stood still, like a statue, wondering if the rest of him had turned to stone as his heart had surely done. But no... if his heart was a stone, it would not hurt like this.

He listened. The vicomte had taken Céline in his arms again, and was kissing her neck. He murmured against her as he kissed her, "But my darling, how much longer are you going to make me wait? I have to think about you being in that man's arms, yet I can only see you a few nights a week and for few stolen hours during the day. How much more time must I linger, waiting for you to be mine?"

Céline leaned her head back, eyes closed as she enjoyed the caresses of this idiotic youth. He was not handsome. He was tall, slender, light-haired, blue-eyed. But his face was not a particularly good-looking one, and he even had traces of youth's erupting skin pustules every time Edward saw him. What could someone like Céline see in him? What did they talk about? How could this ignorant youth please her?

Céline spoke, so softly that Edward had to lean forward to hear her. "Be patient, my love," she said, "I am saving my money. I have sold some of my jewelry, and when he gives me money, I keep some of it back, for the time when we can be together. Someday soon I can tell Rochester to go away and leave me be, and then you and I can live together, be together always."

They stopped talking then, and Edward stood still, eyes fixed on the couple as they moved to the bed, fell on it together, their moans and cries growing louder. He watched them, his dark eyes narrowed and motionless. He had felt close to tears earlier, but now his eyes were dry, although they burned in their sockets. He had nearly doubled over with the onslaught of unbearable jealousy and pain, but now he felt nothing.

His love for Céline had burned within him only an hour before. It had warmed him, given him life, filled him up and moved him forward. Now it was gone. Vanished in an instant as he watched her with this man, watched her with her lover. He had thought he had known her, had thought her love for him was as genuine as his was for her, and now he saw what kind of man she preferred. As a result, all feeling of love was gone, the fire in his heart extinguished by the man who was now making love to Céline before his eyes.

He should feel something, but he did not. He just stood, watching. He saw the kisses and caresses, heard the groans of their passion. They were so caught up in their ardor that they did not even remove their clothing.

He watched as Céline pulled up her skirt and yanked her underclothing free. He saw the vicomte unfasten his breeches, push them down, saw his scrawny white buttocks move between Céline's slender spread legs. He saw her arch up, heard her cry out as her lover pushed himself inside her. He watched, and saw, and listened.

And his heart slowed, stopped beating. It turned to ice, to rock. He felt nothing. Cared for nothing.

But he tasted iron in his mouth, a metallic tang on his tongue. He reached up, wiped his lips. There was a smear of blood on his hand, where he had bitten through his lip. For days afterwards it would pain him, making him grimace as it stung from salt, broke open when his lips moved. But for now he felt nothing, was aware of nothing but the hot taste of blood in his mouth.

Céline and her lover were moving faster, their cries drowning out all other sound. His ears roaring, Edward shoved the door open, moved the curtain aside and stepped into the room. He took soundless steps towards the bed, his dark eyes narrowed and tight and completely expressionless.

It was the vicomte who saw him first. He had lifted his head, arching his back in readiness for his climax, but Edward's movements drew his attention. Céline, her head thrown back and her eyes closed, noticed nothing until her lover's movements slowed and then stopped, and she opened her eyes in annoyance. It was then that she saw Edward.

Had he not been dead inside, he might have found the moment nearly comical. From far away, out of his body, he noticed the vicomte springing away, his arousal still evident and probably quite painful, Edward would think later. Céline screamed, and scrambled back, her hands moving hastily to her skirts to pull them down, as though she could cover herself and deny everything.

From then on, all was a blur of activity. The vicomte moved to the other side of the bed, stammering and pulling his pants up. Céline jumped up, reaching for Edward. Dimly, he heard her speaking to him.

Edward, my love, my darling, it is not what it looks like. I can explain...

"Both of you shut up, damn it!" he bellowed, his voice rising above both their babbled explanations. Out of the corner of his eye, he saw the chamber maid, in her white nightgown and lace cap, peeking around the door, her eyes wide. Edward glared at her, "Get the hell out, go back to bed!" She scurried away.

Céline and the vicomte fell silent, Céline bursting into tears.

Edward advanced upon the vicomte, who looked suddenly very young and not so arrogant now.

Edward spoke. He was surprised at the strength, the forcefulness of his voice.

"You will meet me at sunrise, at the Bois de Boulogne. Bring a second. I am challenging you here, now. If you do not show up, I will expose you for a coward before all Paris. And your lover here will know what you are if you are not man enough to face me."

The young man's face whitened, then reddened. His lips moved, like a fish suddenly thrown out of water and onto hot, dry sand. He swallowed.

"Sunrise," Edward repeated. He took a deep breath. "Now I suggest you go, before I decide not to be civilized about the matter and settle things here and now."

He did not see the man pull on his boots, gather his cape and hat. His eyes were fixed upon Céline. Upon his former lover. The woman who claimed to love him, who claimed he was the father of her child.

She was sobbing, her face red and tear-streaked. He saw her lips moving, heard her words from far away.

My darling Edward, it is not as it seems. He means nothing to me; it is you I love, you and you alone. Please believe me...

He said nothing, watching her from a distance. He reached into his coat, removed his pocketbook, counted out the money that was in there. A sufficient sum to keep her going and to care for Adèle, until he could make further arrangements.

She was still talking. *Oh, my God, I love you, Edward, my only love. Please do not hate me, do not leave me. It is you and only you I want, I have been a fool, please...*

She left the bed, moved towards him, went down on her knees before him, her hands reaching up to grasp at the front of his coat. Her voice rose, her hysteria mounting...

Please my darling, you cannot believe that he means anything, that silly boy. I do not know what I was thinking; I love you...

He finally spoke. His voice was quiet but cracked like a whip. "I heard you, Céline. I stood on the balcony when you entered, and I heard it all, everything you said. Why did you not tell me you find me so disgusting? I would have gone. But nothing you can say will move me now."

Her eyes widened as her mind went back over the things she and her lover had discussed. A look of horror crossed her lovely face. Her tears resumed, her pleading...

Oh, God, I meant none of that, you cannot think I meant it. What about Adèle? She needs her father, she needs you. I need you, please, Edward, please my darling...

He spoke again, through cold, numb lips, "She is not my daughter and you know she is not. We both know she is not." He took his pocketbook and threw it down on the floor beside her, "Here is enough money to care for you for the time being. I will have to think about what else to do."

He strode away, ignoring her renewed screams and pleading. She was lying on the floor, looking up at him, begging him, but he no longer heard her words.

At the doorway, he turned to look at her, on her hands and knees, sobbing.

"You have two days to get out of this hotel. I do not care where you go, but you must be out, or I will take steps to see you thrown out. You may keep everything I have given you – clothing, jewelry. I have not the energy to collect it."

She sat back on her heels, her face red, her fists balled on her thighs as she cried, rocking back and forth. Edward stood for a moment, his dark eyes taking in the sight of his former lover.

Then he left, slamming the door behind him. He went downstairs to the stables where the carriage that he had given to Céline was housed. He woke the stable hand, giving him a handful of the coins that were the only money he had left, and left an address where the carriage should be delivered in the morning, with a promise of the rest of the money to be paid upon delivery.

Then he left the hotel and headed back to his own, on foot. It took him an hour to walk to his own rooms, his heart empty and his feet heavy, his mind fixed on nothing until he got to the hotel, speaking for a while to the night concierge. He reached his rooms and fell upon his bed. And when it grew close to dawn, and he had to rise again, to keep his appointment with Céline's lover, his eyes had not once closed in sleep.

Chapter 16 - Leaving Paris

Nothing.
He felt nothing.

Edward lay on his back on the bed in the room of his own hotel, a room in which he had rarely stayed. From the time he had rented the suite for Céline, he had considered that his home. But he had kept this hotel room, for his business and for entertaining the contacts who did not need to meet his mistress. And it was to this room that he had fled after his last meeting with Céline.

He did not know where she had gone. He assumed she had taken Adèle and gone to Madame de Simone. He had given Céline notice to get out of the suite, but he had not been able to bear being in it for one moment afterwards. He would need to contact the landlord, arrange for the lease to be broken.

Edward was in his shirtsleeves, staring up at the ceiling, smoking. He was normally a cigar smoker, but found their heavy aroma too much for his uneasy stomach after a night of drinking. The small French cigarettes were lighter, more palatable. He blew the smoke out, watched it drift upward. From time to time he reached towards the ashtray lying at his side and flicked the ash away.

Surely, he should feel something?

Yesterday he had been raging, beside himself. He was furious, bent on revenge, wanting to lash out at anyone who came into his path.

He had kept his appointment with Céline's lover, arriving at the Bois de Boulogne by sunrise. He had his loaded pistols in a case. He had his second, and was also accompanied by the man who would oversee the duel, lay down the rules, and count out the paces.

Amazing, what services could be bought through the contacts of a good hotel concierge.

Edward had stood, stony-faced, staring at nothing as the rules for the duel were laid out before the participants. The vicomte looked suddenly very young, very nervous. Edward imagined him wetting himself. They did not meet each other's eyes, never spoke a word directly to each other. But Edward noticed the young man's shifting eyes, his squirming, his shaky hands. He nearly felt guilty. It would be like shooting fish in a barrel.

Edward had walked calmly as the paces were counted out, then turned towards his opponent. He heard the crack of the vicomte's pistol as he fired. Inches off the mark. He did not even feel the air disturbed around him as the bullet missed.

Edward aimed, head and arm as steady as if he were merely relaxing at home with a drink in his hand. His finger squeezed the trigger and the bullet hit its target.

He had not killed him, of course. He was not angry enough to kill, not brokenhearted enough to take the life of his mistress's lover. He was merely making a point. Defending his manhood. Letting the world know that he would do what he must do to reclaim the property that was rightfully his, bought and paid for by himself.

None of this meant he cared. At least, that was what he told himself. But this vicious, brainless youth might now think twice before helping himself to another man's possessions.

The vicomte's military career might be ended. But perhaps not; the young man had been bundled up, arm wrapped, and taken away. But he had walked away on his own two feet, white-faced and shaky, yet still moving under his own power.

Edward had calmly put away his pistols, gone back to his hotel and begun to drink. He was cleaning his guns at first, but as he steadily began to empty a bottle, he had enough sense left to realize that pistol maintenance was most likely better suited to a sober man. He had locked the guns away and devoted himself to the bottle before him. He had finished one bottle, and made good headway on another, but he still could not dim the sound of Céline's mocking voice in his ever-more-foggy head.

"If you lined up all the men in Paris, Rochester would be right in the middle... nothing remarkable there at all."

If you lined up all the men in Paris, Céline, you'd probably screw them all, one after the other... By this time he had stopped pouring the drinks into a glass and was drinking directly out of the bottle.

In the middle of the night he had found himself awake, face in the chamber pot, vomiting his guts out. And then he had wept, but not tears of grief. They were merely the easy tears of a sick and angry drunk.

He had fallen asleep on the floor next to the pot, reeking of liquor and vomit and sweat. He was somewhat amazed to awaken in the late morning and find he had managed not to piss himself. He had staggered up, voided his bladder a long time down in the privy, aware what he must look like to anyone he passed on the hotel grounds.

Then he had gone back to the hotel room, to collapse upon his bed with the slender French cigarettes he favoured while in Paris. And he proceeded to smoke his way through the entire case, fingers still unsteady from the effects of yesterday's drinking binge.

He was numb, exhausted, and unsure of what to do next. He had no particular plans. Go to Thornfield, he supposed. He had not been there since before Adèle had been born. It was hard to remember that far back. But he needed to go eventually, to speak with his steward. To check on Grace.

And Bertha.

Edward grimaced, putting the thought of her from his mind. If his drink-addled head did not ache enough from the previous day, the thought of his insane wife would surely set it pounding.

Edward crushed out his cigarette, brushing ashes from the front of his white shirt, which was now stained, rumpled, and, he was sure, stinking.

He got up and rang for the hotel valet to get some assistance. The young man who answered his summons had wrinkled his nose delicately at the smell of the chamber pot, the sight of Edward's two-day beard growth, his red-veined eyes, and his hung-over unsteadiness on his feet. But he said nothing, hoping to be well paid for his endeavours. The young Englishman was known to be a generous paymaster when pleased, so the valet set about meeting his every need.

He prepared a warm scented bath, fetched hot strong coffee, and laid out fresh clothing. He called for a hotel chambermaid to clean the room as his hotel guest soaked in the bath, dozing off occasionally, barely answering with more than a grunt when awake.

Too weak to do more than lie there in the hot water, Edward looked down at himself. He had never felt he was particularly handsome, but to hear himself referred to as ugly had smote him, even as he told himself that nothing that Céline and her lover said could be trusted. He washed himself, looking down at the body that Céline had referred to as hairy and, how had she described him? Deformities? There was nothing wrong with his looks. He was dark, stern. His brow was heavy, but he had lovely eyes, a finely shaped mouth, a straight nose. He was broad of shoulder, but his form was muscular, athletic, well defined. He had hair on his chest, on his arms and legs. But no more than anyone else he had seen as he had stripped down at college with the rest of his teammates. And far less than some. He could see nothing about himself worth the ridicule of his former lover and her paramour. But he kept the words in his heart, vowed to never forget them. Just in case he should miss her.

Just in case he should remember he had once loved her.

When the young valet had come to offer more assistance, Edward had asked him to help him shave. His hands were still so shaky he was afraid he might inadvertently cut his own throat. He told him to shave the moustache. He had grown it just to see how it looked. Céline had admired it, admired him. *Deceitful bitch.*

"Are you sure, Sir?" the valet had asked, straight razor poised above him.

"Yes," he said curtly, closing his eyes and leaning back. *Make me look completely different. Make me into someone else.*

A few hours after he had rung for the valet, he was bathed, shaved, massaged and dressed in clean clothes. But it would be a day or so before his hands steadied, before the red was gone from his dark eyes.

He had been making plans as he bathed and dressed. On to Thornfield, and from there, perhaps to Ireland. He had briefly thought of going to the villa. It was June and the south of France would be hot, while Ireland would be cooler. The villa was tempting – to go there and spend the summer in heat and solitude. But he quickly rejected that idea. A picture entered his mind: Céline, belly big with Adèle, turning to look at him as she waded knee-deep in the warm surf.

No. He would not go there.

Many in his circle had extolled the beauties of Ireland – its green hills, its mists. And its horses. Edward had been hiring horses to ride; he could do with a good handsome mount. He thought with grim satisfaction how he had reclaimed the carriage from Céline. He could travel in style back to Thornfield. Of course, it was a lady's equipage. He would have to sell it, to get another one more suited to a gentleman travelling alone.

Alone. For a time his resolve deserted him, and he slumped desolately at the room's writing desk, hands pressed flat to its top as he stared down at them. Strong, muscular hands, with long fingers, black hairs on the backs of them. Hands capable of caressing a woman's body, of bringing her the greatest pleasure. Of squeezing the trigger of a pistol and ruining a young man's life just for taking a woman who was unworthy of the effort. He looked down at his hands for a long time, his heart cold as a stone within him.

He did not want Céline. His love for her was gone, ended, flattened beneath the crushing weight of her betrayal. He was done with her, finished with her false flattery and her lies and her cold, empty beauty. Let her have her strutting rooster of a vicomte. Let her cluck in horror over his crippled, useless wing. He was done.

Adèle...

For a moment his heart squeezed painfully in his breast. He thought of her – her dimpled cheeks, her chubby arms and legs pumping eagerly as he lifted her into his arms, her four white teeth gleaming as she smiled widely at him.

His daughter. But no – not his daughter. He had never been sure, even on the best days after her birth. Now he was even more sure that she was not his. So why did he feel responsible for her?

After a long time of sitting quietly at the desk, Edward lit the lamp, drew a sheet of paper towards himself, and began to write.

Mademoiselle-

I have received your two messages, begging me to come speak with you and repeating your insistence that your child is my daughter. All stands as it was. You have been given a purse for your immediate needs and that should suffice. I will be leaving Paris as soon as I can make arrangements.

I do not recognize Adèle Varens as my natural daughter, nor do I acknowledge any claim on her part to be supported by me. Nevertheless I stand aware of my moral duty to the child who was born into my existing household, whatever her parentage. An amount sufficient to her needs will be provided to you. Details will be made known to you as they are finalized prior to my leaving the city.

I have no plans to see Adèle at present although I do reserve the right to visit her in future to see to her welfare. As a condition of my support I require that your whereabouts be provided to my legal agent at all times.

I plan to maintain my box at the postal office as I did while living here. Messages will be conveyed to my steward in England who will pass them on to me. I trust there will be no messages from you unless urgently necessary.

I remain-
E. F. Rochester

The letter was addressed and posted-
Mademoiselle Céline Varens
care of Madame Agnès de Simone
Rue Vivienne 54
Paris

By the time it reached the recipient, its writer was crossing the English channel, on his way back to England.

Chapter 17 - Pilot

London, June 1830

"Edward!"

Standing in the spacious foyer of the Lathrops' Grosvenor Square home, Edward turned at the sound of Charlotte Lathrop's voice.

Hugh's mother came towards him, a welcoming smile upon her lovely face. She kissed him once on each cheek, and he in turn kissed her hand, holding it in both of his.

"Robert and I were so thrilled to receive your message that you were planning to stop on your way back from your travels. He is held up in court, but will be home as soon as he can, and we will have a quiet dinner together, during which we can hear all about your adventures! St. Petersburg! Who would have imagined it?"

The last time Edward had seen Charlotte Lathrop was the December after Hugh died, when he had stopped in to visit as he travelled to Paris for the first time. She had been dressed head-to-toe in deepest mourning clothes, her face grave and her blue eyes red-rimmed. She had always seemed far younger than her years, but her grief had aged her. Edward had sat with her by the hour, holding her hands as she spoke of Hugh, feeling dangerously close to tears himself as he watched her weep.

Now she looked years younger again, dressed in elegant lilac grey silk, with a white lace cap on her still-bright golden hair. Hugh had been a few months older than Edward, so he would have now been thirty-one. Charlotte had to be in her early fifties, but no one would have been able to tell it. There was a sombre depth to her eyes, a shadow that had not been there before, but otherwise she looked just like the elegant London lady who had made him feel warmly welcome in her home so many years before.

"I have ordered tea out here on the terrace," Charlotte told him, leading the way through the large, beautifully appointed rooms. "It's such a lovely day and I'm in need of some fresh air."

When they were seated on the comfortable terrace chairs and the tea service arranged, Mrs. Lathrop had turned to him, placing her hand quite unselfconsciously upon Edward's arm.

"Now you must tell me about St. Petersburg. We were so shocked that you had gone all that way!" she exclaimed. "Whatever possessed you? It is in Russia!"

Edward took a sip of his tea, "It is quite a voyage, true, but it is a fabulous place. I quite recommend it. Beautiful architecture and art, lovely landscapes. It is very cosmopolitan. Peter the Great founded it, and you probably know he lived and studied in the Netherlands. He also spent three months in England and was very influenced by all things European."

Charlotte chuckled and rolled her eyes, "You are quite complimentary to me, my dear Edward; you know I know nothing of its history and little of Peter the Great either. It all seems quite exotic to me. But surely you do not speak Russian. However did you manage there for over a year?"

"It was not quite a year that I lived there. I travelled there and back slowly, seeing the sights as I went. And the upper classes in St. Petersburg speak French, not Russian, so I felt quite at home there, having recently left France. Even the royal family speaks French at court. Only the peasants speak Russian, and I of course saw little of them, other than when we would ride out in the countryside. There were times I could believe I had never left Paris. Although it was cold, of course – far too cold for me." He sipped his tea again, and reached for a sandwich.

For a few moments they ate in a comfortable silence, then Charlotte wiped her mouth with her napkin and folded her slender hands.

"You did not say how long you plan to be with us, Edward, but I hope it will be more than just a day or so. I know Alice would love to see you."

"How is Alice?" Edward asked, leaning back in his chair. Hugh's younger sister had delighted in bothering her brother and his friend in their school years, but the last time Edward had seen her, as he and Hugh were preparing to leave Oxford, she had grown into a poised and elegant woman.

"She is well, thank you," Charlotte answered. "Very busy with the children. She has two girls, Charlotte and little Alice, and a boy, whom she named for her brother."

Charlotte was suddenly silent and tears filled her eyes, "Forgive me, Edward, but seeing you here makes me think so much of Hugh." She stopped and collected herself. Edward reached for her hand and squeezed it gently. For a moment they sat, both of their minds thinking back to by-gone days. Then Charlotte gathered herself by sheer will and patted Edward's hand. "Forgive me," she said again. "Now, when will I hear such good news of you?" she asked brightly.

"When will I get the message that you have settled down with a nice young woman and started a family of your own? Alice was terribly enamored of you back when you and Hugh were fifteen and she was twelve. But she is settled nicely with her Captain, although if he mentions taking her and the children to India with him one more time I cannot promise to act like a lady!"

Edward smiled, "Now you tell me about Alice liking me. If only I'd known it back then." His smile vanished from his face and for a moment a shadow moved across it, his mind full of fleeting images of Bertha, of Céline and Adèle. He looked at Hugh's mother, her kind, sweet face, and for a moment he was seized with a sudden wish to spill everything to her sympathetic ears. He was saved from any such impulse by the arrival of an enormous black and white dog trotting across the yard towards the terrace.

"Butterfly!" Charlotte spoke firmly, and the huge animal stopped short of their two chairs, sitting down with its tail waving happily. A bark issued from her large chest. Charlotte held her hand out and the dog came over to her, snuffling and wagging, her hindquarters moving with joy at the sight of her mistress.

"The butler has sent her out while he feeds her puppies," she explained, petting the dog. "They are four weeks old and ready to begin weaning, but Butterfly gets anxious while they are being fed. She's a very good mother, but tends to get in the way of their progress."

Edward gawked at the massive dog, which was now standing with both front feet planted firmly in Charlotte's lap, trying to climb up onto her chair. Her tail was still wagging madly and she seemed determined to share the chair with her mistress.

Edward laughed out loud, one of the first real laughs he remembered uttering in a long time. "Who on earth named that great lumbering beast 'Butterfly'?"

"I did, if you must know," said Charlotte, using all her strength to push the dog's front feet back to the ground. Her lips twitched. "The name seemed like an excellent idea at the time, when she was a tiny puppy. Robert had just gotten her for me, and I took her out into the garden of the home where we were staying in Ireland. She exhausted her little self chasing a butterfly. It was the most adorable thing I had ever seen and it made me laugh, back at a time when I was doing very little laughing."

She leaned forward, stroking the dog's head with both hands. "Oh, I know, it is the most ridiculous name. Robert still teases me about it. I had seen Butterfly's parents, I knew how big they were, but when she was so little I didn't think that in just a few years she would be this enormous girl." She smiled affectionately, scratching the dog's ears and speaking to her sweetly. The dog responded eagerly, her eyes fixed on her mistress as though she understood every word.

"What kind of dog is it?" Edward asked with trepidation as the animal left her owner and came over to him. She sniffed him delicately, cocking her head as he hesitantly reached to scratch her as he had seen Mrs. Lathrop do.

"She's a Newfoundland," Charlotte told him. "They are fabulous water dogs. We first saw them in Ireland, where we went to visit friends just months after we lost Hugh. They had several, there on their estate, and we were taken with how friendly and intelligent they are. They are said to rescue people from drowning, have been found at the site of shipwrecks, pulling people from the water."

Mrs. Lathrop sat back in her chair, seeming to change the subject, "Have you ever been to Ireland, Edward?"

"Oh, yes," he answered, lifting his teacup, holding it away from Butterfly, who sniffed at his hands, curious as to what he was doing, "In '28, shortly after I left Paris, I went over to see the sights, to look at some horses."

He gave a mock shudder, "I did not like it. Endless mist and rain, strange religion. I was not unfamiliar with the Roman religion after being in France, but they practice a most bizarre version of it in Ireland. Very superstitious; and some hostile natives. It was like Jamaica without the heat."

Charlotte laughed, "We love it there. We have very good friends, Anglo-Irish, of course, with an estate. They do report a great deal of trouble with the Irish, much hostility and rebellion. They have no gratitude for what has been done for them there. Our friends have seen no end of their mischief."

Edward was silent. He had seen first-hand the workings of countries under English rule and he knew that what he might have to say might differ greatly from that of the Lathrops' Irish friends. Mrs. Lathrop had no malice in her, and was only quoting what she had heard from others; he had no desire to debate with her. He merely smiled and bent to pet Butterfly again.

"She likes you, Edward!" Charlotte told him. "You seem to have a way with her. Have you ever had a dog?"

"No, not as a pet," Edward answered. "My father hated the thought of animals in the house. He barely tolerated the presence of a cat who kept the mice out of the Hall, or at least kept them out of sight." He stroked the dog's head. Her huge tongue lolled and she looked over at her mistress with a satisfied air.

Edward continued, "My father had hunting dogs, but they lived outdoors in a kennel. I think one of the neighbours took them when my father grew unable to hunt in his last years. I had never thought to have a dog, but as I own the house now, I suppose I could, someday."

"Well, you've certainly made a friend in Butterfly," Charlotte laughed. "Mind you, she's a terrible flirt. Anyone in a pair of trousers is her dearest friend."

She clasped her hands together excitedly, "Edward! I have an idea. Why don't you take one of Butterfly's puppies?"

"A puppy?" Edward frowned. "Good Lord. What would I do with a puppy?"

"Butterfly had six puppies, and in a week or so they will be ready to go to new homes. The owners of their sire get pick of the litter; they will take a female to breed. But that leaves five – three more females and two males. Two friends want to buy one each, but that would leave three. I would love for you to take one, as a gift from Robert and me."

"But I travel!" Edward exclaimed. "One city to another, one hotel to another. How would I manage a dog?"

"Take it with you," Charlotte said, "as a companion for you. You cannot tell me you are not lonely, I see it in your face. They are lovely dogs, friendly, loyal, intelligent. And as for travelling, I had hoped you might stay settled in England. Do you not want to remain for a while at Thornfield, now you are the owner? Hugh told us how beautiful it was there, how he enjoyed country life."

"I am thirty-one years old, far too young to go rigid with boredom," Edward said, "I will spend a week or two at Thornfield, just to see to the place, but then I must move on. I am going to Italy… to Rome, perhaps, or Venice. I've always wanted to see it, and Italy was on the list of places Hugh and I were going to go together."

Charlotte smiled sadly, "So long ago." She sighed, pressed both hands firmly against her knees. "I believe Hugh would have wanted you to take one of the puppies. He loved dogs himself, but we only had spaniels when he was a boy. How he would have loved a great dog like this one. Butterfly was such a comfort to me, back when I was newly grieving for Hugh. She was a godsend – she needed me, and was something to focus upon. A dog always loves you, always thinks you are wonderful."

Edward smiled, "Well, that certainly sounds tempting, a creature who always thinks I'm wonderful."

Charlotte laughed, leaning over to pet Butterfly again, "Were you not a comfort to me, my big girl! I believe Hugh would want Edward to take one of your babies, and he would probably say, 'name it after me'." Edward laughed, giving the dog one last pat, but shaking his head at the thought of taking a dog home with him.

Two weeks later, Edward climbed into the coach that would take him the first leg of his trip back to Thornfield. He was not alone. A small black and white bundle was buttoned up into his coat, looking up at him with large brown eyes.

He sighed, shaking his head at himself as he had so often in the last two weeks. He could not believe his own insanity, taking a dog. He knew he would not stay long at Thornfield. He had already written to a distant acquaintance in Rome, asking him to be on the lookout for a place he could rent there. The last thing he needed was to be burdened with an animal.

His first mistake, he thought ruefully, had been to go with Hugh's mother to look at Butterfly's puppies. He had watched as the six black-and-white balls of fur had tumbled across the floor, playing together, rolling over each other as they growled and nipped in mock squabbling. His next mistake had been to hold one of them. He had taken one into his arms, marveling at the softness of its fur. He had expected the fur to be long and heavy, like Butterfly's, but the baby hair on this puppy had been so soft and delicate. He looked down at the sweet, soft eyes of the little dog, and had felt a strange tug at his heart.

He was lonely, very much so. When he travelled, he always had letters of introduction from acquaintances in other places, and soon met others like himself, members of the gentry from England and other countries. The Rochester name was known, and soon his status as a wealthy landowner was known too, and no doors were closed to him. He mingled with the finest members of society, and enjoyed rounds of parties, concerts, hunts and balls.

But they were filled with the meaningless social chatter of any large gathering, and he met few people who gave him any feeling of friendship. A creature that belonged to him, that was solely focused on him, was tempting.

Edward set the little dog down, but an idea had been planted in his head and he went back to it again and again in the two weeks he spent with the Lathrops.

He enjoyed his time with Hugh's parents. It felt strange to be there with them, to feel once again the same warmth and kindness he had enjoyed years ago as their son's guest. He talked easily with them, but his heart ached at the sight of Hugh's father, older and now grey-haired, sorrow evident in his deep-set dark eyes. They shared with him some of Hugh's old letters, which revealed a love of travel and a growing interest in the sciences.

Edward in turn spoke to them, but he did not tell them that he travelled for a different reason than their son had – not for love of the new things that he saw and for the adventures, but to get away from something. He did not tell them that he was running... running from Thornfield, its sad memories, and its insane tenant. Running from his disastrous liaison with Céline, and from a little girl who may or may not be his child.

He did not tell them that he was running from himself.

He did not tell them about Olga, the one woman he had slept with in St. Petersburg. Of all the entanglements he had had in his life, he was ashamed of this one.

Olga was the much younger wife of a wealthy St. Petersburg businessman, a man who had treated Edward with nothing but kindness and hospitality. The couple had entertained him at lavish parties at their city home, put him up richly when he came to several hunts at their country home. And he had repaid the husband by sleeping with his wife. Olga was beautiful, and unsatisfied. She had no children, and as their friendship grew, she confided that her husband had been unable to sleep with her since the second year of their marriage.

But Edward had. For several months, they had met – at her homes, at his hotel. They had gotten together for short, frantic sessions in which they had found their bodies temporarily relieved. But each of them felt guilty and the relationship soon ended. They had not loved each other. She loved her husband, and Edward had not been able to help but like the man. They had temporarily served a purpose for each other, but when the liaison was over, Edward felt worse than he had before. Guilty, empty. Ashamed of his lack of control. Ashamed of himself for doing to an innocent man what had been done to him. He had felt the pain of being a cuckold. He was not proud of himself for doing it to another.

He had felt no love for Céline after he left Paris, but his heart had been affected all the same. A heavy, dull ache had remained in his chest for months after he had broken with her, and when the pain ended, there had been only emptiness in its wake. Olga had satisfied nothing in his heart, only the burning of his body. And when it was over...

There had been no one since Paris, until Olga. And there had been no one after Olga. Edward felt very few sexual longings these days. An occasional desire, when he woke up in the morning after dreams he could not remember, but a desire not worth acting upon himself, an arousal not strong enough to need relieving. He wondered how long he would feel this way, how long he would carry this deadness around within him.

So he had told the Lathrops funny stories about things he had encountered on his travels. Amusing accounts of walking in the Irish hills, humorous stories of trying to make himself understood in Budapest, exaggerated tales of the interesting characters he had mingled with in St. Petersburg.

But the Lathrops knew nothing of his heart. Or what was left of his heart, for he was no longer sure he had one. Something was still beating in his breast, but it was only keeping his body alive; it had no connection to his soul, to the part of him that had once loved... or thought he had loved.

Several times he stood on the lawn and watched the puppies tumble and run on the grass, and soon he was crouching down to check them over individually. He was drawn to one of the males, the quieter one, who could run without tiring over the grass, but who tended to sit down and watch when the puppies began to play with each other. His tiny pink tongue hanging out, he would settle back on his haunches, head turning, watching his brother and sisters growl and roll over each other, chewing on each other with their little needle-sharp teeth.

Edward found himself asking Charlotte many questions about dogs. How one house-trained them, what they ate, how one went about training a dog as it grew. And before he knew it, he found himself agreeing to take the quiet little male.

"What will you call him?" Charlotte asked, watching Edward cradle the little ball of fur against his chest, smiling at him as the puppy wriggled and turned, trying to lick his face as he bent his head to look into its eyes.

"Well, I thought about what you said about naming him after Hugh," Edward said, lifting the dog away from his chest and deftly turning him to get a better grip on him. "But of course, I could not. Then I remembered a joke of ours. I had joined the crew team, in which Hugh had no interest. He said that in our travels down the Nile and the Amazon, that I could do all the rowing and heavy work, and he would use his intelligence to be the pilot." Edward gave a small chuckle. "Sometimes I would call him that, Pilot. So... " He held up the little dog, "Pilot is what he shall be, and I will never forget who forced me to take him."

Charlotte laughed, tears shining in her eyes as she thought of her son, "Someday you will thank me, Edward. He will grow to be your dearest friend, mark my words."

Edward smiled now, sitting in the carriage. He reached down into his coat and rubbed his finger across the top of the little dog's head. The puppy looked up at him and yawned, leaning against the warmth of his new master's chest.

Edward sighed, scratching behind the puppy's little ears. "We change coaches in about two hours. I wonder how much time I have before I can expect you to wet all over my trousers?"

Chapter 18 - Letters and Visits

Mr. and Mrs. Robert Lathrop
37 Grosvenor Square
London

E. F. Rochester
12 Via Verde del Giardino
Rome
10 December 1830

My dear Mr. and Mrs. Lathrop-
My sincere apologies to you both if this letter does not reach you by Christmas. It is meant to convey my wishes for the best that this season has to offer, and I hope that this finds you in good health and spirits.

Here in Rome I am happy to be able to inform you that success in house-training Pilot has at last been achieved. Of this great beast that was foisted upon me I may yet find a tolerable companion!

No, I jest, and must hasten to assure you that Pilot has been all I was told he would be. He is quite intelligent and while at first our whereabouts could have been easily tracked from London to Thornfield to the Continent by a steady trail of puppy leavings, I am happy to report that progress was quickly made in that regard.

Pilot cares greatly to please his master and was eager to do what he felt I wanted.

Indeed, no penitent sinner could have more abased himself before the Father than the way this dog cringed and cowered before me when I would enter the hotel suite to find yet another lapse in bodily control. The lowered head, the look of shame upon the canine countenance, the refusal to meet my gaze – all these alerted me to the need to hunt for that hour's indiscretion. As my funds were rapidly diminishing under the onslaught of gratuities to the chambermaids, I often found myself upon hands and knees scrubbing another spot on the carpet or wrapping another malodorous offering in newspaper to be furtively removed to the trash pit outside.

Never have I raised a hand to this animal, yet to see his consummate acting skill as he submits himself before me, one would think he receives a daily beating with a carriage whip. And a mild "try to do better tomorrow, old man," heralds a volley of wags and licks such as has never been seen before in the history of new dog ownership.

You will be happy to hear, dear Mrs. Lathrop, that your advice was heeded and that I never allowed the pup into my bed despite his piteous cries. He has always slept outside my bedroom door, and at Thornfield was confined to the kitchen for the night, as his puppy transgressions were more easily dealt with upon the stone floor. The cook will be hard pressed to forgive me, however…

But I digress. How my heart smote me to hear the heart-rending howls and vocalizations of the lonely animal, yet I am very glad that I followed your advice, for this huge and ever-growing dog would afford me no rest if I had even once let him into my bed. I have since purchased a foal, a lovely black horse that I plan to train *as he grows, and at this time it would be easier to ride the dog, who shows every sign of growing bigger than this infant stallion.*

I shake my head at my foolishness, my dear friends, to read back over this missive and find that I have spoken of little but dogs. But you must know you were right; he is indeed a friend and true companion to this weary traveller.

I will be remaining in Italy for this year's holiday, but I thank you for your kind invitation to join your family this season. Rest assured that at all times my thoughts drift back to your son, my dearest friend, whose memory I will ever treasure, and with fond greetings and wishes for a lovely Christmas time I remain-
Edward

Rome, 19 January 1831

The young priest moved down the aisle of the huge church in the heart of Rome. The air was cool in the stone building, and it was dark despite the light of the January day. The aroma of incense and unwashed bodies hung thick in the air. Small groups of black-clad woman performed the Stations of the Cross, lit candles, knelt at various spots around the church. The priest moved quietly, not wanting to disturb, but he could not help but notice the young man sitting at the back of the church. He did not kneel, he did not bow his head, but sat staring ahead with a look of sadness on his dark-featured face.

The priest approached him. He had seen him before, here in the church. He never bothered anyone or caused trouble. He would come in, sit down, and remain quiet for a number of minutes, before getting up to leave again.

This time the priest felt compelled to speak to him. He approached him, sat down in the pew ahead of him. The man looked up at him as he sat down.

"May I help you with something, my son?" he asked in Italian, and to his surprise, the man answered in English.

"I am not a Catholic," he said, his voice deep, but dull and lifeless. "Scusi, non Cattolico."

The priest was surprised to hear his English accent. The man was dark enough to be taken for an Italian. Or a Spaniard, or a Greek.

"It does not matter," he said in his heavily accented English, "our Lord would turn down no one who came to His church for comfort."

"You speak English," the man said, raising his heavy black brows.

"Yes," the priest said, "I will leave you, but if you would like to talk… "

The man shrugged, "There is little to talk about. I am thirty-two years old today. I have no one. I am alone, and my sins press heavily upon my heart at times."

The priest nodded, "All have sinned, my son; all save our Lord."

"There are times I cannot bear the darkness of my heart," the young man said, swallowing, tears standing out in his black eyes.

"You are not of the True Faith," the priest said, "but do you believe?"

"Yes," the man whispered, his voice hoarse, "But I fear God has long since given up on me."

The young priest shook his head, "God gives up on no man. You must think of the sufferings of our Lord, who died for you. You must be thankful for His sacrifice for us. And when you feel pain for your sins, you must think of good deeds to balance those sins. Sometimes a single good action has the power to change the future, for others and for yourself. You must look for such actions. At times, something good done for another can wash all the darkness away. And in doing so, you might find your own redemption. Not all at once. But some day."

The priest stood, nodded at the sombre young man who sat, hands clenched on the pew in front of him. He moved away, back to his tasks, and when he looked again, the young Englishman had left the church and gone on his way.

Mlle. Céline Varens
Rue Vivienne 54
Paris

Edward F. Rochester
12 Via Verde del Giardino
Rome
3 May 1832

Mademoiselle-
This letter is to notify you that I plan to make a visit to Adèle in June. Business takes me from my current home in Italy back to England, and then briefly to Paris. I should like to stop in at that time. I will send another message when I arrive in Paris to let you know the exact days, but I believe you may expect me sometime between the 15th and the 22nd of June.
Edward Fairfax Rochester

---

16 June 1832

She stood in front of him. She still looked the same; the last four years had not diminished her beauty. But Edward was glad to feel nothing in his heart. There was no longing for her. No pain either. He stood looking at her, taking in her honey-coloured hair, pinned up in a demure style. Her high-necked dress, no jewelry.

"You are looking well, Edward," she said softly.

"I'm afraid I am still dark-featured and as hairy as the last time you saw me," he said brusquely.

She dropped her eyes, a red blush coming to her cheeks. "I must have been mad that night, to say such things."

"We were both mad, Céline," Edward said, his eyes hard. "Fortunately, there can be recovery from some forms of madness."

She stood for a moment, unsure of what to say. Edward spoke again, "My legal agent tells me you live here alone with Adèle?"

Céline nodded, "Yes. The home is owned by Madame de Simone, but she does not live here with us. She has another home, on the outskirts of Paris. She would love for us to live there with her, but I thought it best if we did not."

"Uncommonly wise of you," Edward said coldly.

"I have not told Adèle you are coming," Céline said. "And as you specified to the agent, I have not mentioned you as her father."

"That is good, as I am not," Edward said, his eyes meeting hers squarely.

"You are her father, Edward," Céline said quietly.

"That is nonsense and as I have pledged to support her regardless, I should think you could drop the charade," Edward told her angrily. "I talked to others of our acquaintance after the rupture. I know about the man you were seeing. Not the vicomte, the one before Adèle's birth. They told me of the wealthy, married man you were dallying with in the autumn before Adèle's conception.

"They told me he had gone back to his wife, refused to continue with you, although you hoped for marriage from him. Why no one felt compelled to tell me this at the time I do not know, but I suspect him as Adèle's true father. He abandoned you, did he not, and so you turned to me as your child's father? Clever. Keep one wealthy man on the string until you are sure of another, for in issues of paternity, it may prove useful."

Céline shook her head, her face sad. "I do not know who told you all this, but if you are determined to believe it, there is nothing I can say that will convince you. You are the father of my daughter, but you will never admit it. All I can do is thank you for your mercy to us, thank you for your care of her, despite what you believe."

"It is a good deed, nothing more," Edward said with a bite in his tone. "Now, I would like to see her, if you please. I have many things I must do today, and not a great deal of time in which to do them."

Céline left the room and returned shortly afterwards, leading a small girl by the hand. Edward's breath caught at the sight of her. He had not seen her since she was six months old, sleeping in her cradle the night he had found Céline with her lover. He supposed that in the back of his mind, he still thought she would be that infant.

She now was four-and-a-half years old, but tiny. She was dressed in a frilly pink dress; her hair, darker than Céline's, fell about her shoulders in a riot of curls and was held back from her face with a large pink bow. Her eyes were wide as she fastened upon his face, but then she moved close to her mother, hiding her face against her skirts.

"Come, ma petite," Céline said, moving Adèle out towards Edward. "This is a friend of Maman's, Monsieur Edward Rochester. He has come to see you, and he tells me he has a lovely gift for you."

Adèle lifted her eyes, looking at him for a moment, and he moved forward, holding out a parcel. She took it from him, and held it against herself, dropping her gaze again.

Céline bent down, "Shall we open it, my love?" The two moved to a low sofa, and Céline placed the gift on Adèle's lap, her fingers moving over the elaborate gift wrap and large bow that the clerk at the toy store had arranged for Edward.

Adèle kept her head lowered but her tiny fingers pulled at the bow. Céline supported the present as Adèle's fingers tore at the wrappings, which came free to reveal a large wax doll, elaborately dressed, with hair the colour of Céline's and done in ringlets. Adèle's eyes grew wide and she gave an exclamation of pleasure, darting a look up at Edward, and then looking at the doll again.

"What do you say to Monsieur Rochester, ma petite?" Céline urged her quietly.

Adèle looked up at him again. "Merci, Monsieur Rochester," she whispered. Her tongue tripped over the unfamiliar English name.

"You are welcome, Adèle," he told her solemnly. Her turned to her mother, "I wonder if I might not take her for a walk. I have left my dog tethered to one of the chairs out in your small courtyard and as he is rather large and rambunctious, I hate to leave him for too long."

Céline said nothing, her eyes darting from Adèle to him.

"Oh, come now, Céline," he said irritably. "Surely you do not think that I mean to take her? That is the last thing I need, to be saddled with a brat. I mean only to walk her and the dog up and down the street. Perhaps take her to the park at the farthest."

Céline shook her head, with a small smile. "Forgive me, Edward, I am being silly. I am her mother, I worry for her, but I have no need to worry with you, I know. Go, please."

She turned to Adèle with a smile. "Monsieur Rochester is going to take you for a walk, and show you his dog. Maman will take your doll and put her upon your bed; we must be careful of her. And you go with Monsieur Rochester, you will have fun with him."

Edward started down the stairs from the flat, slowing his steps for Adèle as she held tightly to the rail and walked down the stairs as a child will, both feet on each step in turn, her eyes fixed on her progress. Her dark brown curls bounced on her shoulders as she walked. She stepped out into the courtyard, blinking in the sudden brightness of the sunshine.

From his spot in the courtyard, tied in a shady place under a tree, Pilot stood up with an excited WOOF at their approach. Adèle jumped at the sound and stepped behind Edward, instinctively grabbing his leg as her eyes fell on the huge dog. Her lip trembled as though she were going to burst into tears.

Edward crouched down beside her, looking up at her. "It's all right, Adèle. He is a big dog, but very friendly. He will not hurt you." He moved over to Pilot, untying his leather lead from the chair and wrapping it around his wrist to gain full control over the animal. With his other hand he reached for Adèle.

"Would you like to come with me while I walk him?"

She nodded, keeping her eyes on the dog lest he get too close to her. They began to walk, through the small gate to the courtyard and out onto the sidewalk. Edward asked her some questions, and gradually she began to lose her initial shyness.

She began to talk, telling him about a dog who lived in a home nearby, one she saw in the park every day when she went with her nurse. Edward learned that her nurse came daily to the house, and that it was she who did the majority of the work of caring for Adèle.

Adèle told him that her Maman was very busy, that she was still dancing, and that in the afternoons her mother's friends would come to the house to listen to songs and poems and stories. Sometimes her mother would sing and dance, and Adèle told him that even she would sing songs and dance in the way that her mother had taught her.

Edward was tempted to ask her about men who came to the house, but was not sure how much she would go home and tell her mother, so he remained silent on that subject. After she had chattered about what she and her mother did during the day, a silence fell as they walked along. Seeing a horse and carriage go by, Edward asked Adèle if she liked horses. He began to tell her about his horse, Mesrour.

"Mesrour is a young horse, still in training and I cannot ride him all the time. He is learning, and every day I go out to the farm where I keep him, and sit on his back and make him do what I tell him to do. Soon he will be old enough for me to ride him all over, and then he and Pilot and I will go many places. But for now Pilot and I have to ride in a carriage. Pilot sits on the seat next to me and looks out the window and wonders where we are going."

Adèle giggled, and soon grew comfortable enough with him to resume her chatter. By the time they had walked to the park, allowed Pilot to run across the grass and to fetch some sticks that Adèle threw for him, and then walked back, nearly an hour had passed and Edward's ears hurt with Adèle's endless prattle. He thought he preferred her when she was shy and afraid of him.

He returned her to her mother, who invited him to stay and meet "a few people" who would be coming to visit that afternoon, but he begged off, pleading business responsibilities. It was true, he did have a property that he had bought when he was living in Paris, and it did have to be seen to. It could wait, but it was a convenient way to beg off staying for any longer. He was unnerved by Céline's presence, and a combination of tenderness and anger confused him as he tried to deal with Adèle.

He promised to return in a day or so, which he did, and it was then that he saw Adèle singing and dancing for her mother's assembled guests. She was dressed elaborately, her cheeks were rouged, and she simpered and pirouetted and generally behaved so much like her mother that Edward was upset and disgusted. When he left the flat later, he did not care if he ever returned, but with a trapped feeling he realized that, like it or not, he was tied to this child for life.

Richard Mason
Hacienda del Sol
Spanish Town
Jamaica

E. F. Rochester
12 Via Verde del Giardino
Rome
4 September 1832

Mason-
It was good of you to write with your assurance that there was no loss of life or property in the late slave rebellion that those of us in Europe have only recently been made aware of. As it was centered primarily in Montego Bay, I would have been surprised had it spread as far as Spanish Town, but I am glad to hear that your property has been spared.
In June I was home on a visit to England and the newspapers carried accounts of the Jamaican Assembly summary report, detailing the property damage there in Jamaica. It is true that in England, stirrings of abolitionist dealings grow more insistent. It may be yet that in our lifetime we shall see an end to slavery in British-held colonies. Should that happen, conditions will indeed change. But you do

yourself no favours by worrying, as I see by the tone of your letters that you are experiencing great anxiety of mind. These situations must be faced as they arrive.

Please be assured that all at Thornfield is well. There is unhappily no change for the better, but I see no change for the worse either.

I am sorry to have missed your messages letting me know that you would be on the Continent this summer. I have been doing a great deal of travelling this spring and summer; although based in Rome I have stayed for several weeks at a time in Venice and in Florence, taking in the sights, before coming to Paris to oversee some business matters. I arrived back in Rome in August to find your messages. Perhaps we will meet each other some time in the future.

I trust you this finds you in good health, and as ever I remain-
Edward Fairfax Rochester

Edward posted the letter to Mason, feeling that he had accomplished a task that had been hanging over his head for some time. He had breathed a sigh of relief when he had found Mason's messages and realized that his brother-in-law had come and gone while he had been travelling; thus he had not been forced to see him. He put Richard Mason out of his mind as he strolled away from the post office, and headed in the direction of Giacinta's flat.

He smiled as he strolled in the warm sunshine of the mid-morning. Only last night at a party he had made the acquaintance of a young woman he had not seen before. He had noticed her immediately, as she had the buxom, dark good looks to which he had always been attracted.

Tall and slim, yet full-breasted; dark haired, dark-skinned, Giacinta had been introduced to him by a mutual acquaintance. They had stood talking, both of them shunning others in favour of getting to know each other. When the distractions had become too great, she had placed a warm hand on his wrist, her long fingernails grazing his skin as her dark eyes met his.

Her voice low, she had given him her address and a few quick directions on how to get there. He had felt a tingle of excitement as he nodded and bade her good-bye.

Now he approached the door of the home to which he had been directed. He rang the bell and removed his hat. He had expected a maid or a houseman, but it was Giacinta herself who came to the door, dressed in a simple day dress, her luxuriant hair spilling over her shoulders. She gazed at him solemnly, leaning her hip against the door frame.

He smiled at her, "Good morning, Signorina. I believe I was issued an invitation to visit this home anytime I was in the area."

Giacinta ran her eyes down the length of his body, and back up again, looking into his eyes. She smiled a long, slow smile, and lazily moved herself from the doorway, stepping back to allow him to come inside.

Chapter 19 - Will-o'-the-wisp

What did I do, Jane? I transformed myself into a Will-o'-the-wisp. Where did I go? I pursued wanderings as wild as those of the March-spirit. I sought the Continent, and went devious through all its lands. My fixed desire was to seek and find a good and intelligent woman, whom I could love: a contrast to the fury I left at Thornfield—
For ten long years I roved about, living first in one capital, then another: sometimes in St. Petersburg; oftener in Paris; occasionally in Rome, Naples, and Florence.
Disappointment made me reckless.
Edward Rochester - Jane Eyre

November, 1832

A few days after his encounter with Giacinta, Edward left on his travels once again. He had enjoyed Florence and Venice and did not feel he had been able to see enough of them. Both cities were filled with exciting sights and he was hungry to see them all. He also wanted to spend some time in Naples.

The few hours he had spent with Giacinta were intoxicating to him, deprived as he had been of the touch of a woman's soft hands upon his skin, the sound of a woman's voice whispering in his ear. She had invited him into her home, fed him, given him some wine; and he felt alive again with the sight of her flashing dark eyes and her lustrous dark brown hair. He could not take his eyes off her full red lips as she spoke, could not stop watching the way she would occasionally run her tongue over her bottom lip as she listened to him speak.

For a while they had only talked, first of Rome, and then of Florence, for Giacinta had grown up not far from there. She told him the story of her life before she had come to Rome, following a lover who had come there to work.

"I was the eldest of thirteen children. My father raised goats and picked olives and by the time I was fourteen there was talk of my being married. I did not want my mother's life – bearing children year after year to a man who smelled of goat, getting old before my time from working so hard. At fifteen I ran off to Florence where I became an artist's model."

Edward lifted the wine to his lips, his body already warm and relaxed from one glass of the ruby liquid. He watched her sitting across from him on the sofa, her low-cut dress exposing her full, white bosom, her hair spilling over her shoulders. Their arms were across the sofa back, their fingers nearly touching. He felt himself growing excited at the thought of her lying naked, her lush curves the perfect inspiration for the paintings of a Florentine artist.

She was a courtesan, and made no secret of it. She had moved up, from one wealthy man to another, and was now the mistress of an elderly businessman who spent half the week at his villa outside Rome and half the week with her.

"He is old, and he can no longer give me the pleasure I crave. He wants my company, says I make him feel young. He loves to talk about his business, and I rub his back when it aches from the rheumatism. But, oh, I miss the feel of a young man in my arms, and then at the party I see you. I look at you, a strong handsome young man and I think, 'I would like to meet him'." She smiled at him with undisguised admiration and longing.

Edward, so long deadened to the thought of being with a woman, and with the mocking words of Céline and her lover still coming forth to haunt him in those dark moments before sleep claimed him, felt warmed and flattered by her words. When she moved closer to him on the sofa, and leaned over to kiss him, he eagerly kissed her in return.

For a long time they sat together, sharing kisses at first gentle and then more insistent, tongues exploring, their breathing growing faster. She dipped her finger in the wine and rubbed it along his lips, kissing him again. Her mouth moved lower, kissing his neck and the line of his jaw, and he closed his eyes, a soft humming sound deep in his throat. He had forgotten how good that felt, a woman's lips on his skin, and he reached out to cup her face in his hands, kissing her harder. She set her wine glass down as his mouth moved down her neck, and over her breasts, half covered by the material of her dress. He stroked them through the fabric, and she reached up with a moan to squeeze his hands over them.

She lay back a little, her head tipped back on the sofa cushions as his hands travelled over her. He reached down for her skirts, which were pulled demurely over her knees as she had sat, feet tucked under her on the sofa. He pulled them free, slid off the sofa to the floor, his hands reaching up under her skirts.

What did he feel? Arousal, certainly. Gratitude to her for seeing him there, for noticing him, for desiring him. He suddenly longed to make her feel good, to give her pleasure for the happiness she had unexpectedly brought to him. He reached up, felt her petticoats, her stockings, and the garters that kept them held up. Higher, higher, his fingers brushing the soft skin of her thighs.

She wore no undergarments, and he moaned as he came in contact with her warm, damp flesh, with her soft hair. Inflamed, he shoved her skirts up over her legs, kneeling in front of her. He slid his palms along her thighs, pushing her legs apart. His head came down, searching… She did not pull away, but slid down farther to meet his mouth.

For a long time he kissed her there, his lips moving over her, breathless with her heat, aroused beyond reason with her scent and the sounds of her moans, which grew louder as he went on kissing the soft flesh of her thighs and between her legs. His hands went higher, pushing her legs farther apart, his fingers gently brushing one of his favourite parts of a woman's body – the impossibly silky, supple skin of the hollows of her thighs, where her legs met her body. All the time, his lips were stroking, caressing. Her hands had been running over his arms and shoulders, but now she reached up to grasp his head, urging him on.

When he opened her with gentle probing fingers, and put his tongue on her, she gave a short, high scream, digging her nails into his head, bringing her hips up to meet his mouth. He chuckled to hear her, and slipped his hands beneath her to pull her forward, reaching up to drape first one leg and then another over his shoulders. His tongue found her most sensitive places, moved slowly on her, guided by her cries and her rapid breathing.

He was so excited he could hardly bear it, and when she wrapped his hair around her fingers and her cries became louder, he thought he would lose all control right then. He kept up what he was doing until he felt her go rigid in his hands, her cries becoming little screams. Finally her body relaxed abruptly and she had to push him away, whimpering, "No, no more, no more."

She slumped back, her thighs open, arms loose at her sides. He wiped his mouth, leaned over to lay his cheek against the inside of one leg as she gradually slowed her breathing and lifted her head. She reached out again and stroked his hair, smiling down at him.

"You are very good at that," she said lazily. "Someone has taught you well. Was it someone you loved?"

He shrugged, thinking of Céline and the first time he had done that to her, how clumsy he was, how she had had to guide him until the end. He shook his head against her thigh, eyes closed. One hand stroked her leg.

"Ah, well, how you learned is not important," she gave a soft laugh, "but I have to say, the only one I know who ever did that better was another woman."

His eyes flew open at her words, his shocked gaze meeting hers. She laughed again, "Oh, surely you are not surprised at that?"

She stretched out, her whole body tightening and relaxing like a cat's. "I think whatever brings you pleasure, you should do, and that was very, very nice, both with you and with my female lover. Surely you have seen two women together?" He said nothing, but his face mirrored his thoughts, his surprise.

"Oh, I thought all men loved the idea of that," she said, reaching down to turn his face up to hers. "I must teach you sometime."

Before he could reply, she reached to take his hand, bringing it up and pressing it between her legs. He groaned to feel her, wet and slippery under his fingers. He stroked her, pressing his lips to her thigh.

"Come, Eduardo," she whispered, "Come up to me. We must not waste this time we have together." She pulled him up, working his breeches off and down his legs. She lay back, bringing her legs up around him and then he was deep within her. They both cried out with the feel of his entrance, and when they began to move together, it took no time at all. She cried out again, and he felt her, felt her finish around him, and it brought him there himself. So good, so good... How had he gone so long without this rapture? He clung to her, buried his face in her shoulder, let himself go, their voices mingling together as they came as one.

They lay there a while, entwined in each other's arms, their breathing slowing and the sweat drying on their bodies. When they separated, it was with reluctance, but she had to get ready for her businessman's arrival the next day, and he already had plans to go to the other cities he wanted to see. She kissed him at the door, and told him to look her up when he was next in Rome.

He went back to his house, to finish making preparations to move on, but his mind was filled with her. He did not know if he would ever see her again, but he would not forget her wildness, the way she had given herself completely over to her pleasure, and seemed to long for him. His body, so long dormant, seemed to wake up, every cell unfolding, his skin tingling. Even colours seemed brighter to his eyes. He felt alive again.

Edward was restless. His encounter with Giacinta had left him once again longing for the warmth and comfort of a woman's body. For days after being with her he could only think of her and what they had done. He felt like a young man again, just learning of the irresistible pull and urge of the flesh.

For a long time he had felt dead inside, dormant, old before his time. But now... when he laid himself down to sleep, the thoughts came to him.

He never before had imagined two women together, and in the light of day the idea unsettled and even disgusted him, but at night he let his thoughts roam free and the excitement would come quick and hard. More than once he let himself reach down and relieve the pressure and tension of his arousal, his mind filled with images of Giacinta and a mysterious woman, equally beautiful, their bare bodies entwined. He felt as though he'd been bewitched.

He was a little afraid of Giacinta. She was wild, reckless, dangerous, and she was involved with other men. And not just men, apparently. She made no secret of it. And Edward longed for something more. He longed for love, for a woman he could claim as his own, one who would love him with all the love and passion he had for her.

He had long ceased to think of Bertha as his wife. Legally married he might be, but morally he was not. Emotionally, physically... all the essential qualities of a wife were denied him and his longings burst forth anew.

He would soon be thirty-four years old. He had been married for twelve years. Over a decade of marriage to a woman whose mind had twisted him, within her memory, to her mortal enemy. Years of being tied to a sick, pathetic lunatic whose title of wife was a mockery of the word. Wife – such a small, simple word for everything that was missing in his life.

He felt nervous, longing for freedom, for a chance to search for what he wanted so badly. He could not find it at Thornfield. Too many people there knew him too well, too many had inclined their ears to the whispered rumours of the mysterious woman who lived at the Hall.

When he visited Thornfield, thrown again into its society, there was always Blanche Ingram. From the quiet young girl he remembered, she had blossomed into a tall, dark-haired beauty, but there was an arrogance about her that repelled him. He was aware that he was talked of as an eligible bachelor, but he was also aware that it was his fortune and his land-holdings that attracted any young women near his home.

And so, only days after sleeping with Giacinta, he left again. He liked Rome, had enjoyed his time there and had mingled well in society, but he had to leave. His restlessness was like an itch beneath his skin.

1833

A new year... when it dawned, he was back in Paris.

He attended parties that holiday season, one of them at Céline's with some theatre friends. No one he knew or remembered – the theatre crowd was always changing. But he mingled, smiled, acted happy to be there when all the time he was aware of Céline nearby. They avoided each other.

He had come to see Adèle. She had just turned five, but her mother had tutored her well. She danced and sang, batted her lashes and flirted, and Edward's skin crawled to see how much she resembled her mother. He gave Adèle the presents he had brought her, asked her some questions. She was excited by the glittering crowd, barely able to concentrate for her fascination with the splendor and gaiety of the guests and after she danced for the assembly, he departed with relief.

The year passed quickly as he careened through various cities. He quit Paris for Antwerp and Brussels but they bored him and he moved on to Amsterdam and Berlin. They were serious cities, bustling with commerce, and he went back to Paris after just a few weeks. Once again he saw Adèle, this time in the company of her nurse, Manon, with no sign of Céline at all.

Edward returned to Thornfield at the start of summer, staying only a few weeks. Carter came to examine Bertha and he regretfully informed her husband that while her mind was as flawed as ever, her body was healthy and robust. Edward noticed that Bertha grew bigger and heavier, and Grace told him that she had an enormous appetite. Grace's body was square, but gaunt, her breasts nearly gone, the bones standing out in her chest, while Bertha seemed to grow larger, seemed to take up so much space in the room that Edward felt suffocated. He had to get out of there while he could still breathe.

Long after the door was closed and locked behind him, he could still hear Bertha's mocking laughter.

After Carter's exam, he and Edward sat together in the parlour, Pilot stretched out contentedly at Edward's feet. The two men talked, sipping cognac that Edward had brought with him from the Continent. They talked about England, about politics and about history – topics both men enjoyed.

Afterwards, Edward would think about how much he had enjoyed the intelligent conversation of the doctor, and how nice it was to talk about his country, in his own language. The visit was in such stark contrast to the empty chatter he would indulge in at the assemblies of the rich in Europe's capitals, that for a moment, Edward's heart lurched at the thought of going back, and for a brief instant in time he was tempted to stay.

Edward stopped in London after his visit to Thornfield and spent a day visiting the Lathrops. They exclaimed over Pilot, his size and his good behaviour. Pilot's mother Butterfly was less impressed, especially when he sniffed her and followed her around, finally trying to mount her. She turned and snapped at Pilot, and the two dogs were separated. Pilot was showing every sign of wanting to mate which, large as he was, had caused no little embarrassment to his master. Mrs. Lathrop suggested he breed Pilot, but Edward demurred.

"I have no time for such things," he told his hostess. "I should geld him like a horse, but cannot bear to."

"He needs to sire offspring and so do you," Charlotte told him. She was pale, and appeared thin and frail to his eyes, but she waved off his concern and spoke with spirit. "If only you would settle down and raise a family, how happy that would make me!"

Edward wished for that also. "A normal life," he begged God, in the lonely hours when he took to his bed to sleep, alone. "What other men have… " he pleaded silently.

But it appeared to be in vain. Autumn saw him again in Italy, first in Florence and then in Naples. For all his searching, for all his travelling, he had found no one. There was dancing, there were flirtations and light conversation. There were games and hunts and dinners. But nowhere did he see what he was searching for.

He did not require beauty or vast intelligence or great wit. Just one woman whose heart and soul seemed to be in communion with his. One woman who would look into his heart and see who he really was. One woman who would truly love him.

He kept his eyes on this possibility wherever he went, and nowhere, it seemed, was the love that he longed for.

Nearly a year after he had left Rome with high hopes, he returned there, his heart heavy with need and loneliness.

And there, at a holiday party shortly after the start of 1834, he once again met Giacinta.

Chapter 20 - Giacinta

... I could not live alone; so I tried the companionship of mistresses. ... another of those steps which make a man spurn himself when he recalls them. [Céline] had two successors: an Italian, Giacinta, and a German, Clara; both considered singularly handsome. Where was their beauty to me in a few weeks? Giacinta was unprincipled and violent: I tired of her in three months.

It was a grovelling fashion of existence: I should never like to return to it. Hiring a mistress is the next worse thing to buying a slave: both are often by nature and always by position, inferior ...

I now hate the recollection of the time I passed with Céline, Giacinta, and Clara.
Edward Rochester - Jane Eyre

Rome, April 1834

There was still a slight chill in the air and Edward pulled his coat more tightly around himself as he walked up the stone steps and into the church on this early morning.

The first Mass of the day was being said at the main altar of the church. In the background Edward could hear the Latin being intoned, could hear the responses of the congregants who knelt in prayer before going out to the various places their day would bring them.

Edward slipped into one of the side chapels where he often came to meditate and to be alone with his thoughts. He could not call what he did praying; he did not feel worthy to do that. But he would go into the room, drop a few coins in the box and light a candle or two among the vast number that surrounded the statue of the Blessed Virgin.

He looked up at the unseeing eyes of the plaster Lady above him; she seemed to gaze at and beyond him with a benign loveliness that soothed him. Wrapped in her painted blue robes, with her yellow hair, blue eyes, and pink and white face, she looked down upon him with no judgment of him, no anger. The way he imagined his mother might look upon him if she were still alive. But no... even his mother, who had loved him, would hate how he was living, this half-life, this existence.

He bowed his head upon his folded hands and swallowed past the sudden tightness in his throat. His eyes ached with unshed tears. He pressed his thumbs into the inner corners of his eyes, forcing himself to breathe slowly and easily. It would not do to go home to Giacinta with signs of his weakness, with the evidence of tears upon his eyes.

She did not know he came here, of course. She thought he went out early to clear his head, to buy a paper and to bring home some of the breakfast breads or pastries they both enjoyed. How she would laugh if she knew he sometimes came to this church, to sit quietly and long for some relief, some cleansing for his soul.

Giacinta slept late in the mornings, worn out by their lovemaking, or enervated by whatever was in the small flasks she sipped from at night, or tired out by the frenzy of activity brought on by the draughts and philters she got from her physician, an ex-lover. At least Edward thought he was a former lover; he could not be sure that Giacinta was not still seeing him. And unlike the doubts he had had about Céline, the thought of his current mistress being with someone else did not plague him. He cared very little.

Lovemaking. A strange term for what went on between Giacinta and him, for there was nothing of love between them and no pretence of either of them hoping for it. For so long he had wanted love, wanted the reality of a strong and equal relationship. And for so long it had been denied him. The body, deprived of food, takes any morsel it can get to keep from starving to death. And the heart, deprived of love, deceives itself that the bodily satisfaction it receives is an adequate substitute for the emotion itself. The body eventually cannot remember what it was like to be healthy and satisfied with food. The heart will also close in upon itself, not able to remember what it felt like to be truly filled and nourished.

He and Giacinta had met up again after more than a year, their eyes catching sight of each other across the crowded room at a party. She had given him a long, hostile look before looking away again. He had turned away, time now dimming his memory of her so that he felt no more than a second's pinprick of regret. For a long time they had circled the room, avoiding each other, and then he looked up to see her coming towards him. Giacinta had a wry smile on her face, and moved to his side with a toss of her head.

"I was very angry at you, but I may just forgive you for never coming to see me again," she told him.

"But I have only just returned to Rome. And you told me you had a – what would I call him, a benefactor?" Edward replied, stopping a passing waiter to claim two glasses of some rather startling liqueur. He handed one glass to her, and he took a quick drink from his own, and began to cough and choke at the heavy flavour and the fiery feel of the alcohol in this throat. Giacinta pounded him on the back and laughed, seemingly ready to forget her earlier pique and begin their acquaintance anew.

They had stood for a long time talking, as he told her of his travels of the past year and she had made sure to tell him that she was currently unattached. The freely flowing liquor at the party had made them both more entertaining to the other than they might otherwise have been and soon Edward was fetching their wraps and they were in his carriage, on the way to his two-storey rented pensione.

On the floor in front of the fire, Edward raised himself up on his arms, head thrown back and eyes closed, concentrating on the feel of his hips grinding against hers as he pushed into her as deeply as he could go. She was lying under him, hands digging into his shoulders, her legs wrapped around the small of his back. They were both in a place far away, he trying to prolong his pleasure, gritting his teeth to hold back the climax that could come any second if he gave up his rigid control. She was concentrating on the feel of his body against hers, of his hard flesh filling her again and again, moving her towards the finish she craved. At last she felt it, felt herself go over the edge and she reached down to grab his hips, pulling him to her.

"Harder," she panted, "oh, God, harder." He increased his thrusts, the tiny wail in her throat pushing him beyond what he could control, and he felt her, felt her spasms all around him. He forced himself to hold off, to let her reach her full pleasure, then he pulled back and out, reaching down to help himself finish, his seed spilling over his hand and onto the floor. With a sharp gasp, he slumped down over her.

They had barely been able to contain themselves. They had begun to kiss in the carriage on the way home, and it had been all Edward could do not to take her right there. He had buried his face in her breast, she had reached down to rub the hardness that strained against the front of his trousers. He was sure the coachman could hear their moans, the sound of their breathing. But he had left them off in front of the house without comment and with only a tip of his hat, before he drove off to the stables.

They had nearly fallen into the front door, still kissing. Edward did not even think of his one servant, serving as both cook and maid, who slept in a bedroom off the kitchen, and would hear everything, as he kissed Giacinta, kissed her and kissed her, taking off his coat, his cravat, his waistcoat. It was only when Pilot came out, yawning and stretching, that he remembered it was not just him anymore, and he kissed Giacinta hard one last time.

His voice sounded hoarse, as he whispered, "Build up the fire and I will be back in a moment. I want you there, naked in front of it, when I come in."

He had gone outside, and was shifting from foot to foot, the hot, hard ache of desire still burning within him. Pilot ran around the yard, lifting his leg, first in one place, then another.

"Wretched dog, what insane impulse possessed me?" he muttered. He jammed his hands in his pockets to protect them from the chill of the night, having worn no coat. Against the side of his hand, he felt his erection, somewhat diminished but still throbbing and burning. He longed to be inside the house, with Giacinta. He imagined her there, waiting for him, ready for him.

At last, Pilot appeared to be finished, and Edward nearly dragged him into the house, urging him back into the kitchen and shutting the doors. He rushed back to the front room and there she was, as he had requested, naked in front of the fire. He had stood over her, looking down at her with her beautiful full breasts, the dark triangle between her legs. He tore his clothing off, his hands fumbling. He heard the *plink* of at least one button from his shirt hitting the floor, but he was crazed, unable to stop his frenzied longing. He stood naked for a moment, before he lay down on her, fully upon her, his mouth taking hers hungrily. She was ready for him, and he for her, and in no time he was inside her, and he was out of his head, beyond himself, out of all time and place.

That had been two months ago, and at times he still felt he was out of his mind. The days were a blur to him at times, caught up as he was in the frenzy of Giacinta's world.

She was beautiful, and sometimes to look at her was to feel instant desire, desire that left him weak and breathless. But she was volatile, hot-tempered and nearly insatiable at times. She wore him out, she exhausted him. But there was no tenderness, no real caring between them. At times he felt his sole purpose was to bring her satisfaction and the times he was away from her he had to blink, to try to come to himself and remember who he really was.

He sat there now, on the hard wooden bench in the church, thinking of his life. He did not want to think of the sins of the flesh here in the church, but his mind went back to the night before. They had both had a great deal to drink. For some reason since he had been with her, he seemed to be drinking more than he ever had. Not as much as she did, he could say, but enough that he felt he was never completely sober.

He had started off lying on his belly while she poured warm oil on his back and rubbed her hands over his muscles until he was limp and relaxed. Then she turned him over, and before he could work up the energy to move, she had taken first one hand, then the other and was tying them to each bedpost. He looked at her in alarm, roused from his lethargy, but she had just laughed softly and kissed him, whispering, "Don't worry." She took his legs, tied each of them to the bottom of the bed, and then took a soft silk scarf and wrapped it around his eyes, tying it firmly.

For the next hour she had moved over him with lips and hands and tips of fingers, even leaning over to rub her nipples slowly against his skin. Her hands and fingers moved over every inch of him, massaging, rubbing, probing, exploring, and by the time she moved between his legs he was nearly ready to beg for relief. Even then she tortured him, touching him for a long time without giving him any satisfaction. By the time she took him in her mouth, he was shaking and it took only seconds for her to finally finish with him, his whole body jerking and his cries echoing through the small house.

He felt he was losing his will. At the start of their relationship there were things she wanted to do that he refused to do, and before long he found himself doing them, and enjoying them. For reasons he could not fathom, she found him attractive, desired him, although not enough to refuse the money he gave her. Her admiration of him, the fact that she wanted him, was a heady feeling, made it difficult for him to resist her.

She liked to make love in the carriage and he had at first said no, but before too long he dreaded going out, because he knew that they would end up entwined along the seat. On one occasion they were at their destination and were not quite finished, and she refused to get out until they were done. They had climbed out, sweaty and disheveled, she with a satisfied smile on her face, he unable to meet the eye of the coachman.

Giacinta was irritated by Pilot, shooing him away at every chance, although she knew that to actually abuse him would push Edward beyond his endurance, for he loved his dog. She knew just how far to go, and was wise enough to go no further.

She laughed at him for his insistence on pulling out of her when they came together. She insisted that she knew the cycles of her body and did not need such precautions, but he would take no chances.

At the beginning of their relationship, she had told him how she had twice conceived, and twice had gone to have the baby taken out of her, first by an old woman who had hurt her dreadfully, making her bleed for weeks; and next by the doctor who, when she recovered, became her lover. He had given her something to drink that had made her go to sleep, and when she woke up she said, the baby was gone and only some mild cramping and bleeding had resulted. She had no objections to again having a child removed from her womb, and while Edward did not want a child, something inside him recoiled at the thought of what she had described. So he insisted on taking responsibility for making sure she did not conceive.

Often they did not even come together in ways that could create a child. Giacinta knew things to do that Edward had never dreamed of, and she insisted that they try them all. Some things he liked more than others, but he always came back for more. He hated himself for his weakness, for not being able to resist her, for not being able to resist his own body.

She liked to make love when she was menstruating, saying it felt wonderful and relieved her pain. Céline had never let Edward get near her at those times, and so he had rarely seen blood or known what was involved. Giacinta had no such compunctions. He did what he could to avoid a mess, but still cringed at what the maid must think.

The maid had said nothing when Giacinta moved into the house, but soon had soon become sullen and angry under Giacinta's demanding control, and after a month she had quit. Edward had been forced to hire a couple, Angela and Paolo, who cooked and cleaned and maintained the home. Edward's rare anger had surfaced when Giacinta had caused the maid to quit, and from then on, Giacinta had done nothing to interfere with his household help.

Edward knew Giacinta was moody and unreasonable, and the first time she had thrown something against the wall, breaking it, he had slammed a fist down on the table in front of her.

"Clean that up, damn you, and let me never see you do that again." She had complied, and for a while controlled her temper, but it flared up again. She broke things fairly regularly from then on, and Edward would slam into the bedroom without speaking. For a day or so he would avoid her, but he always gave in, always came back to her, to her red mouth and her beautiful lush breasts, and the tight, wet velvet warmth inside her, taking him in, making him forget everything but the feel of her all around him.

He felt he was in a pit, one he could not climb out of, one that was getting deeper the more he tried to scramble up the side to escape.

He sat for a few more minutes in the church, drinking in its peace and serenity. He wished he could believe in the Church. He believed in God, but his natural scepticism did not allow him to fully embrace an institution that had such wealth while its people scrabbled for a daily living. He did not feel that a mere man was the voice of God on earth, and he felt that if God were a loving and all-powerful Being, that a priest could not be the go-between, was not needed to speak between God and the people.

But he admired the beauty and the ceremony, wished it were that easy, that all he had to do was pay some money and be rescued from damnation; that all he needed was to say some words, eat a wafer and drink some wine to achieve Heaven. He wished he believed that it was truly as the young priest had told him, that good deeds could make up for a thousand little sins, could change the course of his life forever.

He got up and moved to leave the church. His heart was heavy and his steps felt dogged. He needed to go home, to face Giacinta, but he was not ready. She was often in a foul temper, and he did not know if he could tolerate it this early in the day.

She had begun to bring up trying something new, and he avoided the subject, knowing it would be a source of conflict. She wanted to bring in another woman, to bring someone else into their bed. She had told him how exciting it would be, how good it would feel for both of them. He refused and she sulked, but it was too much. He could not do it.

The idea disgusted him, but it also excited him, and at times he was afraid of what she could talk him into doing. He had to insist that there were some things he would not do. Some part of himself that he could say was strong. He knew he had let down his guard, had become dissipated. But he did not want to be debauched, to slide so far down from his ideals that there was no turning back again. He had already become someone he did not recognize. He did not want to lose himself completely.

He left the church, putting on his hat and heading towards home. Giacinta was waiting for him and he did not want to make her angry this early in the morning. Exhausted and numb, he turned his feet towards his house. It was the place he lived, but it was not a home.

Chapter 21 - The Message

Rome, September 1834

Edward rolled over in bed, groaning at the sudden pain that knifed through his head as he opened his eyes. The morning sunlight seemed far too bright and a wave of dizziness washed over him as he sat up. He leaned over and held his head in his hand, wondering what time it was.

He looked around, suddenly aware that he was naked, his clothing strewn over the floor around the bed. He closed his eyes, swallowing against his rising nausea. He lay back again, feeling as though someone had stuck a knife into his left temple.

"Knowing Giacinta, that might be possible," he thought to himself, pressing the heels of both hands to his eyes as the events of the night before began to come back to him. He certainly remembered drinking the wine, and his pounding head and queasy stomach testified to it as well.

They had had an argument, their most bitter and violent yet. It seemed that their relationship consisted of nothing but arguing and confrontation, followed by passionate encounters when they reconciled. Edward would never have imagined himself caught in such a union, but here he was.

He was beginning to be aware that Giacinta needed such drama; that she could not sustain such an association unless it was fraught with the highs and lows that she seemed to so enjoy. Edward was exhausted by it, and whatever relief of loneliness he had achieved was swept away by the constant conflict.

It had started innocently enough last night. They had been invited to yet another party, one of the constant whirl of social activities available to their circle. Giacinta had wanted to go, claiming that she was bored. Edward, who was tired, had declined but told her to go and enjoy herself.

That had started the fight, as she accused him, first of being boring, and then, when he offered to call the carriage so she could go, of not caring about her. Weary of the fights, he had repeatedly left the rooms, only to have her follow him. He had gone into the bedroom and locked the door, but she beat on it, screaming at him through the barrier.

He had stayed on the other side, not trusting himself not to go out, seize her by the shoulders and push her down the stairs. He had had enough. When she calmed down, he was going to throw her out. This time he meant it. No more.

At last she had tired herself, and he had eventually gone downstairs hoping to have a light meal in peace and quiet, only to find her in the kitchen, an open bottle of wine in front of her. She had started the argument up again. He sat quietly, letting her nagging wash over him, pretending to be far away as he poured himself some wine just to keep his hands busy and away from her throat. He had always believed a man should never strike a woman, but Giacinta might have the distinction of being his first.

He had drunk several glasses, and his calm demeanour only frustrated Giacinta more. He knew part of what was angering her – she still wanted to bring a woman into their bed, and his continued refusals frustrated her. Once again she brought this up.

Edward brought his hand down on the table, "Enough, for God's sake. I have told you – no! Are you so stupid that you do not understand? If you want a woman yourself, go. I am not stopping you. Have a woman. Have two women. Have three, and when you are all done you will have a foursome for cards. Just don't bring them here. I am sick to death of dealing with just one woman, I do not want more!"

Angered, Giacinta brought her wine glass down hard upon the table, shattering it. Edward stood up with a sharp curse as tiny shards of glass scattered across the table. Giacinta pointed the sharp stem of the glass towards his face.

"I could cut you with this, you make me so angry," she hissed at him, her eyes narrowed.

"Go ahead and try," Edward told her, his voice low and menacing. "It will be the last thing you ever do."

He grabbed the wine bottle and headed up the stairs, hearing the glass break behind him as she flung the stem of the wine goblet to the stone floor.

He had stripped off his clothes, and gotten into bed, finishing the rest of the bottle. He had fallen into a deep sleep, forgetting to lock the door, and the next thing he knew, he awoke to find Giacinta all over him – her hands and mouth and body, and before he realized what he was doing, he was rolling over so that he was on top of her. He would never have let her touch him again if he had not had so much wine.

He groaned again, feeling a sharp stinging across his back. He could vaguely recall her fingernails raking his skin as they rolled together across the bed, but drunk beyond reason and too far gone in his own pleasure as he thrust into her, it had made little impression upon him at the time.

Now, sitting there in the morning light, he felt a flash of anger at her, pushing aside the notion, a more frequent one these days, that his encounters with her often resulted in pain of some sort. He did not want to admit it. He was tired of searching in vain, tired of hoping for the kind of female companionship he wanted. Giacinta's hands and mouth and lush, warm body were usually enough to allow him to ignore her tempers and whims, and the fights that resulted. She demanded pleasure and satisfaction, but she gave it as well, and for months that had been enough to hold Edward in her thrall.

It had only taken three months for the newness to go out of their relationship, for him to grow weary of her company, but when he remembered her hands moving over him, her hot mouth wringing every last bit of pleasure out of his body, the feel of her breasts and belly against him, her legs wrapped around his hips, he forced down his doubts and his irritations and found himself coming back for more, no matter what his brain told him.

Now all that was coming to an end; he was exhausted – sick of keeping silent, worn out from holding his temper in check, weary of the constant conflict. The delicious physical sensations he had so enjoyed were bought at a price he was increasingly unwilling to pay. He did not recognize himself at times, could not believe some of the things he was doing, nor some of the things she was doing to him.

And when he saw her, sipping at her flasks, surreptitiously swallowing pills, dipping into her mysterious powders with her delicate fingers and her long, pointed nails, he felt frustrated and angry.

Once, early in their relationship, he had tried something she had given him, letting himself be talked into it by her descriptions of its harmless nature and wonderful power to increase physical sensation. The potion had made his mouth tingle and burn, then go numb. It had made him aroused, to be sure, a hardness at first thrilling and then painful, lasting longer than normal and unable to be relieved, forcing him to wait until the effects had worn off naturally. Giacinta had loved what it had done to him and had been angry at him when he refused to repeat the experience.

His appetite had disappeared, he ended up with a blinding headache, and for hours he felt restless and agitated, his skin crawling and itching. Not to mention the raw soreness between his legs, from where Giacinta had used him again and again, climaxing repeatedly, screaming with pleasure while ignoring his pain, furious at him when he had made her stop. It had taken days to feel normal again and he had vowed to never again take something that Giacinta offered him. He had suggested that she stop taking all these medications and potions as well, and after a furious tirade from her that lasted nearly an hour, he decided never to bring the subject up again. He ignored the fact that she rarely ate, that her nose bled for seemingly no reason, and that her bursts of temper seemed ever more frequent and more unreasonable.

Now Edward groaned, and again sat up, breathing deeply as he sat on the edge of the bed. He spotted his drawers on the floor and leaned over to retrieve them but was instantly sorry as pain sliced through his head again. He swore violently, holding his hand against his throbbing skull, the pain sharp behind his left eye.

No more wine. Never again. Ever.

He stretched his leg out, managing to hook his toe around the garment and draw it towards him. He lifted his foot and succeeded in grabbing his drawers without having to move too quickly. Moaning and cursing, he worked them over his legs, standing up as he pulled them over his hips and fastened the tie at the waist. He felt as if he'd done a day's labour and wondered if it was early enough to go back to bed for a while.

He stood up, dizzy and queasy, and moved slowly across the room to the basin. He looked in the mirror, groaning at the sight of himself. His eyes, their whites shot through with red, fascinated him, and he stood for some moments, staring at himself.

"You look like hell, Rochester," he said aloud to his reflection. Pilot, who had been sleeping on the rug across the room, looked over at him at the sound of his voice, before sitting up to yawn and stretch, and then pad across the room to stand by his leg.

"Oh, God, I suppose that now you want to go out," Edward said, standing up as straight as he was able to. He turned a little, angling himself as much as his pounding head would allow. He surveyed his back, grimacing at the sight of the deep scratches and drops of dried blood that marred his smooth dark skin.

"Miserable bitch," he muttered. Pilot lifted his ears and cocked his head at the words, and Edward had to chuckle. "She is a miserable bitch, isn't she? But she must have let you out this morning, or you would be making my life very unhappy right now." Pilot barked, making Edward wince.

"Oh, no, please don't do that," he mumbled. He poured water from the pitcher to the basin, splashing his face until it tingled. He dried off, rubbing his face repeatedly with the towel.

"Giacinta!" he called, listening for her. He doubted she was in, for if she were, she no doubt would have been in the room with him, bothering him in some way. He moved to the doorway of the bedroom. "Giacinta!" he called again.

Good, the woman seemed to be gone. He moved over towards the wardrobe to find his dressing gown, but as he did he heard the insistent ringing of the bell at the front door. He waited for Paolo or Angela to answer, but moments went by and the doorbell rang a second time. He swore again and headed downstairs for the door, each step towards the door reverberating in his pounding head. No doubt Giacinta had been out and had forgotten her key, as she seemed to do with annoying regularity.

He opened the door to find a messenger standing there, holding a letter in his hand.

It was directed especially to him and marked *Urgent*, and Edward looked at it for a moment, frowning at the return address on the envelope. The messenger stood patiently as Edward tore the letter open and read the message quickly, his eyes widening in alarm.

"Wait for a moment," Edward said, looking around frantically. He headed for his writing desk, suddenly aware that he was wearing nothing but his drawers and giving this stranger a full view of his scratched up back. He caught a smirk on the young man's face as he stood there, but for the moment his mind was on nothing but the message he had just received.

He grabbed a sheet of paper and a pen, not pausing to sharpen its point before he jabbed it into the ink and scrawled a short message:

Madame Frédéric,

Have received your message. Do nothing until I return to Paris. Hand the child over to no one. I am leaving as soon as I can, and will be there for her, at which time you will be compensated accordingly. I repeat, give the child over to no one.

Edward F. Rochester

Edward realized he had no money upon him, and went upstairs hastily to where his coat was thrown across the bed, and pulled out his pocketbook. He opened it, to find it emptied of all paper money.

"Goddamn it!" he bellowed in frustration, throwing the leather billfold down onto the bed. He looked around quickly, found his trousers and bent to pick them up, again wincing at the pain in his head. He quickly fumbled in his pockets for the few coins that he could find. He threw on his dressing gown and ran back downstairs to where the messenger waited in the foyer.

Snatching up the paper and blowing on it to dry it the rest of the way, he folded it hastily, turning it over to copy the return address from the back of the message. He moved quickly, lighting a match and melting wax to attach his seal to the other side of the paper. He waved it in the air impatiently to harden the seal, before walking back over to the man waiting by the door.

He thrust the paper into the messenger's hand, giving him the few coins he had been able to come up with.

"I know that that is not enough to pay both for the message and for your part in bringing it. Take the message regardless, tell me how to find you and I will bring more money to you. Do that and you'll be amply rewarded, I promise you."

The messenger rolled his eyes, but gave Edward the address where he could be found, bringing his fingers to his forehead and leaving, after shoving the letter into the bag he carried at his side.

Galvanized into action, Edward forgot his headache in his haste to dress and be on his way. He felt almost giddy with the chance to get away from here, away from

Giacinta. He had no thought of what he would do next. He just knew that he had been given the means for moving on, for breaking free of his inertia.

Moving quickly, he went back up to the bedroom. Dropping his underclothes, he hastily washed his body in the water that was in the basin, shivering with the touch of the cold liquid on his skin. He would have loved a full bath, but did not want to take the time. He dressed hastily, and once he was in his trousers and shirt he rang for Paolo to come up and pack his things for him, and sent him to carry a message to the stables to have Mesrour saddled and ready to go as soon as possible.

He cleaned his teeth, combed his hair, and was just putting on his coat when he heard Giacinta's light step downstairs. He sighed. He had been hoping to avoid seeing her, hoping to just leave her a note. Indeed, he had asked Paolo to secure his trunk and keep it from Giacinta's reach, knowing that if she could not deal with him she might take out her wrath upon his possessions. He could not take the time to hire a carriage, so the trunk would have to be sent on to him later.

Giacinta came into the bedroom, carrying several parcels in her hand and chattering excitedly. There was no sign on her face of the quarrel they had had the night before, and she brushed by him in a cloud of expensive perfume, kissing him quickly before setting the parcels on the bed.

It was then she noticed that he was fully dressed, and that there was a small travelling bag on the bed, ready to be strapped to the back of Mesrour's saddle.

"What... " she started to say, but Edward cut her off.

"I am leaving, Giacinta," he said quietly, "This is goodbye. I will settle the house until the end of the month, but then you will need to find some other place to live. I will not be back to Rome."

"Where are you going, Edward?" she asked him, moving towards him, "What do you mean you will not be back to Rome? This is your home now."

He shook his head, "No, it is not. I am no longer sure of where my home is, but it is not here. You may keep whatever I have given you already, but you will get no more from me. Now, I must go, I have no time to waste."

Tears started into her dark eyes, she stammered, she pleaded, but something new was in her lover's voice, something strong, and she suddenly knew there would be no changing his mind. She tried the tricks she had used with him before, speaking softly and seductively to him, tracing her fingernails down the front of his trousers. She reached for the buttons at his waistband, but he evaded her touch, picking up his bag and moving away from her.

With a sudden cry of fury, she reached up to rake her nails across his skin, but with a lightning fast movement, he grabbed her arm, grasping her wrist firmly. He pushed her hand down, and started to step away from her. Quickly she brought up her free hand, punching him hard in the mouth. He felt his lip split, felt a sudden sharp pain and a feeling of wetness, before he licked his lip and tasted the blood. He wiped his mouth, looking down at the smear of red on his hand.

For a long moment he looked at her, then he raised his bag to his shoulder and headed for the door.

"Come on, Pilot," he said, and walked down the stairs and out the front door. Giacinta followed him, staring at the door as Edward slammed it behind him.

He secured his bag to the straps behind his saddle, mounted Mesrour, and rode away, whistling for Pilot. After a brief stop at the postal office to make sure his message had been sent, and to leave some money for the messenger, he again mounted Mesrour and was on his way, headed to Paris.

Chapter 22 - Back to Paris

Paris, September 1834

Edward stood in the parlour of the large house on the outskirts of Paris. He had been ushered into the room by a uniformed maid, after having been kept waiting, standing in the foyer, for nearly fifteen minutes. He had walked back and forth, slapping his hat against his thigh as he paced restlessly. From time to time, children would pass through, staring at him with undisguised curiosity. Some of them had running noses and hacking coughs, and none seemed to possess a handkerchief.

The click of the parlour door made him turn to see a thin, severe-faced woman of about fifty enter. She inclined her head towards him.

"Monsieur Rochester," she said, her voice unusually deep for a woman, "I am Thérèse Frédéric. I thank you for coming."

"You received my message, Madame Frédéric?" Edward asked.

"Yes, Monsieur," she answered. "I have not told the child you are coming, but I will fetch her if you wish."

"Wait a moment," Edward held a hand out to stop her, "I don't understand. Where is her mother, Mademoiselle Varens? What is this place? An orphanage? A school?" He rubbed his forehead, frowning, looking about the austere parlour.

Madame Frédéric drew herself up as though offended by his questions, "We are a home for children. They board here and we are paid for their care, and we provide some basic schooling."

"But how did Adèle come to be here?" Edward asked, "I had not seen her since this past Christmas, and a week ago I received your message, saying she was here. I rushed here as soon as I could, to prevent her from being taken by someone else, but I still do not know the particulars."

Madame Frédéric lifted her head, seemed to be thinking.

"This past spring, a woman came to me, calling herself Madame Varens. She said her husband had died and she found herself unable to care for her child at this time. She paid me then for several months of care and promised to send more. Shortly afterwards, a nurse brought the child to us. I took the mother's address but when my husband paid a visit, he found no one there by that name. I also got the address of the nurse to contact her if needed. Madame Varens herself supplied your name and the information needed to contact you. You are the girl's father?"

There was a silence, then Edward shook his head, "No."

Another long silence followed, then Edward said, "But I am responsible for her; I have supported her since her birth."

Madame Frédéric could not hide her raised eyebrows, her look of regal disdain. She continued.

"It has been weeks since we had money left from what was given to us by her mother. My husband and I are not rich. We depend on what we are paid to feed and clothe the children. If no money is forthcoming, we must resort to what we can – the nuns, or relatives, or as I related to you in the letter, someone who comes forth to claim the child, as has been the case here.

"As the mother specifically named you as the only other person who could make decisions about the child, I felt duty-bound to contact you, to give you the choice…"

Edward was shaking his head before she finished, "Yes, you were right to contact me. I will see to it. I will take care of her."

Even as he said the words, he felt he must be insane. But he could see no other choice. The nuns? Madame de Simone? No, it had to be him.

Adèle looked at him silently, solemnly. She was taller than he remembered, dressed in a drab brown dress that looked far too big for her. Her hair, which had always been worn in curls around her shoulders, was pulled back severely from her face and secured in a tight braid. She was clasping her hands in front of her, her fingers working together nervously.

"Do you remember me, Adèle?" Edward asked her.

She nodded, her wide hazel eyes fixed upon his face, "But I forget your name."

"Monsieur Rochester," he told her. She said nothing for a moment, then pointed at him.

"What happened to your mouth, Monsieur?"

Edward put a finger to his lip, feeling the still swollen spot where Giacinta had struck him. He had nearly forgotten it, the blow that had temporarily loosened his tooth and given him quite a large split on the left side of his upper lip. The cut had nearly healed but it had left a bump, a spot that would take weeks before the full feeling would return to it.

"Oh, that," he told Adèle, "I ran into something that did not want to move. Very silly of me, but I shall not make that mistake again."

He sat down in the chair and motioned her to stand beside him.

"Adèle, do you know where your Maman has gone?"

Adèle frowned, looking down at her feet, "I do not know. One day she was gone, and Manon brought me here. She told me I must be a good girl and then she went away, and I have not seen my Maman or Manon in a long time."

Edward was at a loss. What to tell this child? And where on earth had Céline gone?

He blew his breath out with a frustrating feeling of helplessness. Once again he rubbed his forehead, nearly wishing he had not come.

"Adèle, run along now, back to what you were doing. I will speak to Madame Frédéric and we will decide what is to be done."

"Will you tell my Maman to come and get me?" she asked him, and now he saw tears swimming in her eyes.

Oh, God…

"I do not know, Adèle. I wish I could do that, but I do not know where she is either. Do not worry, though – we will watch over you."

Small comfort, he well knew, to a child who has lost her mother.

Edward stood at the window of his Paris hotel room, looking out at the lights of the city. He was in his shirtsleeves, smoking yet another cigarette. What was it about Paris that made him want to smoke? He had been planning to go to bed, but had only gotten as far as pulling his shirt out of his trousers and unbuttoning it. He inhaled deeply, and blew the smoke out, thinking wearily of the past two weeks.

He had spent a week trying to settle the situation with Adèle. He had paid the Frédérics for the amount that was in arrears, and then had gone in search of Manon, the young woman who had been Adèle's nurse since her birth. Fortunately she was right where she had said she would be, unlike Céline, who had given the Frédérics a false address. It was Manon who filled in the missing pieces of Adèle's story.

"There was a man, Monsieur," she told him in a whisper, as though Céline herself were listening outside the door, "Mademoiselle was greatly in love, spent all her time with him. Night after night I cared for Adèle while her mother went out. She was happy for a while, always smiling, always singing. Then the tears and the fighting started. He did not want a child. He was going away, to Italy, I think, and asked her to go but did not want Adèle."

"Mademoiselle cried and cried, she would not eat. I would find her, crying her heart out as she stood watching Adèle sleep. But in the end she chose her lover. She kissed Adèle goodbye one night and off she went. And when Adèle awoke, I took her to Madame Frédéric as I had been instructed. Mademoiselle told me that when she could, she would send for Adèle. But she will not. Her lover did not want the child then; he will not want her now. Then Madame de Simone appeared at my door, asking about Adèle. I do not trust that woman. I told her nothing."

Edward thought of his former lover and his fine mouth tightened to a grim line. Céline had been a liar, she had been faithless, but he had always believed that she loved her child. Never had he believed her capable of abandoning Adèle.

Edward thought of Adèle's tear-filled eyes, her thin little face looking up at his. He had always viewed with contempt those men who would abuse a woman, but at this moment, he felt that if Céline stood before him, he could slap her until his arms were worn out.

He was beginning to wonder – was there one woman on this earth who could be trusted?

After talking to the nurse, Edward had returned to talk to Mrs. Frédéric, telling her what he knew of the situation. The woman's eyes narrowed.

"I had suspected as much," she sniffed. "I had felt that the mother would not return for the child, but I did expect her to send money, at least."

"Do not worry about the money," Edward told her shortly. *Mercenary bitch.* "I will continue to pay you, for I am unable to take Adèle at this time. If you would allow her to remain here under your care, I would be grateful, and as to her schooling…"

Madame Frédéric broke in, "Adèle is in the first class, Monsieur, and shows progress. She knows her letters and soon will be ready to read. She knows her numbers also, although she dislikes them. Mostly she likes to sing and dance, although we try to confine that behaviour to her play times."

Edward nodded impatiently, "Yes, well, whatever you think best. I will leave and send a messenger with the money for her current time here. I will try to visit her when I can to check her progress."

He retrieved his hat and turned to leave.

Madame Frédéric stopped him, "Wait, Monsieur! The child's grandmother, Madame de Simone. If she returns, what shall I tell her?"

Edward stopped, turning back with a frown, "She is not Adèle's grandmother. And if she returns, say nothing to her. Throw her out and notify me immediately. I will take care of it."

Now he stood at the hotel window, once again finding himself in Paris. He did not seem to be able to break free of this city. He felt that he was back to the beginning, but this time he was not happy and excited to be here. How long ago that seemed, when he had first left Bertha in England and felt himself to be free, looking at Paris as the fulfillment of a dream. How old had he been? Twenty-six, twenty-seven? Life had seemed new and full of possibilities. Now he was thirty-five, and his life was a dull, dark, empty thing. He felt old, used-up, and tossed aside like a child's outgrown plaything.

He did not regret leaving Giacinta – that had been long overdue. He had only stayed out of his own inertia, and because it still afforded his body some pleasure, some sensation.

But his mind felt dull, his heart was a dried and desiccated thing. He felt that Giacinta had taken everything he had to give, and now that he was free of her, he marvelled that he had stayed so long, and fallen so low in his own eyes. He had not thought he could despise himself any more than he had, but now he could hardly bear the sight of himself.

1835 began, a cold winter that kept many indoors before warm fires.

Edward remained in Paris, not because he wanted to be there anymore, but because he was too exhausted and downhearted to go anywhere else. He had heard twice from his steward, asking him when he would be coming home to Thornfield. But he could not face the thought of packing up again and going somewhere else. Adèle was settled in the home of the Frédérics, and while she did not appear especially happy on the occasions when he visited her, she was not unhappy enough for Edward to notice.

He paid for her upkeep, and stopped there to see her every two or three weeks. It was not something he looked forward to. It was a duty, nothing more.

If he had been able to see Adèle safely to a permanent situation, one in which he knew she was safe, and thereby be done with her forever, he would have done it. But he felt he should watch over her, and also felt he could not fully trust the Frédérics, who seemed far too eager for money.

He knew he should look for a good boarding school for Adèle, but he had no idea how to go about it. He had nowhere to go, no one who particularly cared where he was or what he was doing. He stayed in Paris from lack of energy and because he could think of no acceptable alternatives.

He was taking care of Adèle. It was his good deed, the one that the Italian priest had said he should do. He did not know if his taking care of his former lover's bastard child was worthy of heavenly notice, but he hoped so. His many sins were great in his eyes, and his own goodness so small; he hoped when he drew his last breath on this earth, that God would see and bless his efforts on behalf of this one child. He hoped that caring for her, watching over her, would one day prove to be something worthwhile, one honourable act in a life that otherwise seemed empty and fruitless.

Chapter 23 - Taking Adèle to Thornfield

Sophie is my nurse; she came with me over the sea in a great ship with a chimney that smoked—how it did smoke!—and I was sick, and so was Sophie, and so was Mr. Rochester. Mr. Rochester lay down on a sofa in a pretty room called the salon, and Sophie and I had little beds in another place. I nearly fell out of mine; it was like a shelf.

... Mr. Rochester carried me in his arms over a plank to the land, and Sophie came after, and we all got into a coach, which took us to a beautiful large house ... called an hotel.

Adèle Varens - Jane Eyre

Edward Fairfax Rochester
Hotel de la Fleur
Paris

Alice Fairfax
Thornfield Hall
Hay, Derbyshire
England
1 March 1835

Mrs. Fairfax-
This message is to inform you that I will be arriving in England some time during the first half of April.
I will not be alone. I will be bringing a seven-year-old girl to live at Thornfield. She is the daughter of an acquaintance who is no longer able to care for her, and thus she has become my ward.
Please prepare the nursery and its adjoining chamber for the nurse who will be accompanying her.
E. F. Rochester

    Edward lay on the sofa in the salon on board the ship that would take them to England. Although he usually did well while travelling by sea, this voyage had been difficult. Tossed about by the waves of this late March passage across the channel, the ship was unsettling its passengers, most of whom had retired below deck to wait out the trip upon their bunks.

    Adèle was one of those below deck, in the tiny room she shared with her *"bonne"*, the nurse Edward had engaged while making preparations to go back to England. He had stopped in their room earlier to check on them. Sophie, the nurse, her moon face white and drawn, was fighting her own nausea as she struggled to care for Adèle.

    Edward's heart felt a pang as he saw Adèle – pale, looking tinier than ever, huddled in her narrow bunk. Her curly dark hair was stuck to her sweating head and there were dark circles under her eyes. Her usually talkative and exuberant personality was completely subdued by the misery she was feeling. As Edward stood there watching, she began to retch and Sophie moved quickly to put a basin under her chin. Adèle had nothing left in her stomach, but she heaved fruitlessly before falling back to her damp pillow, beginning to cry weakly.

Sophie dipped a cloth in the bucket of cold water that Edward had brought down for them and bathed Adèle's face, turning to Edward.

"Poor baby, she cries for her mother," she told him with an accusing tone to her voice, as though it were Edward who had ripped Adèle from her mother's arms. Watching Adèle's suffering, Edward was once again seized by the thought that he could easily strangle Céline if she stood before him. His frustration made him speak harshly.

"Of course she does, she is a child." He took a deep breath, holding on to the door frame of the tiny room, feeling his own stomach lurch frightfully. "Just keep her calm and keep trying to give her sips of water. It is not a long voyage. We will reach land and then we will all feel better."

He attempted to soften his tone. Sophie's mindless appearance irritated him but in the two weeks she had been under his employ, he could not fault her care of Adèle. And of course, her presence meant he did not have to care for Adèle himself as they made the trip from Paris to Thornfield.

May I bring you something?" he asked Sophie, "Some tea, or some bread to put something dry in your stomach?"

She grimaced and shook her head. Edward nodded with one last look at Adèle.

"Have me fetched from the salon if you feel I am needed." He turned and went back upstairs, where the air was a bit fresher, despite the faint smell of vomit that was beginning to permeate the ship. He found a sofa in the corner and lay down, careful to keep his boots off the satin upholstery. He put his arm over his face, taking deep breaths and struggling against his own nausea. He had crossed the sea before, back and forth to Jamaica, back and forth to Ireland, and had lost count of the times he had crossed the channel between France and England. But he could not remember a time when he had felt this wretched.

He worried for Pilot, crated below deck with the luggage, and for Mesrour, lodged in the ship's stable. They would all be better off when they reached land, and the sooner the better. He swallowed repeatedly, trying to put his mind on something besides his turning stomach.

It had been February when the message had come for Edward. Madame de Simone had again called at the Frédérics'. She was furious to find that Adèle was now under the protection of her supposed father, and claimed to have received a letter from Céline herself, asking her foster mother to take Adèle.

"She could not produce the letter, Monsieur, nor could she tell me where the child's mother was. But I wanted to inform you that she still wants Adèle."

Edward thanked her, imagining just why de Simone wanted Adèle. However reluctant he was to assume direct guardianship of Adèle, he was damned if he would let that woman have her.

He could not even imagine how de Simone had tracked Adèle to the Frédéric home to begin with, but it made him nervous to realize how well the woman knew Paris and the surrounding suburbs. De Simone had been born and raised in the city, and with her years of contacts from the theatre and from less savoury associations,

Edward felt there were few places in Paris where Adèle would be out of the reach of this woman.

It was then he decided to take Adèle to England. Thornfield was not an ideal place for a child, but it was wholesome, healthy, and far away from Paris.

He left his contact information with Madame Frédéric. If Céline did return or write, she would know that her child was safe. Not that the deceitful cow deserved such reassurance. And if she came back for Adèle… well, he would simply face that eventuality when it arose. He did not expect it to.

He stood in the same parlour at Madame Frédéric's where he had first seen Adèle, and spoke to her of coming to Thornfield. She had been happy to see him, chattering to him of her friends and what they had done that day, and as usual, not wanting to talk about her schoolwork. At last he had made her be quiet and had stood her in front of his chair, making her look at him.

"Now, Madame Frédéric has told me to come to get you. How would you like to come home with me?" he asked her.

"To your house?" she replied, a frown on her face as she tried to imagine where he lived.

"Yes," he told her. "I have a house in England. Do you know where that is?"

Adèle shook her head, looking puzzled.

He went on, "It is far from Paris, across land, and then across water, and across more land. We will have to take a carriage to the sea, then get in a boat, and then a carriage to my home. It is a big house and there is a lot of land where you can run and play."

"Are there children there?" she asked him.

"Uh… no," he said, momentarily halted in his efforts to make Thornfield sound appealing. He cast around in his mind for any of the area's gentry who had small children and could think of none. Not that any of them would consider Adèle a suitable companion for their brats. "But there is a very nice housekeeper, Mrs. Fairfax, and a cook and a butler and some maids, and they will all be very happy to meet you. We shall have to get a nurse to care for you."

He was thinking aloud as he went on and he was struck by what a huge undertaking this was. He wanted to find Madame Frédéric and tell her had had changed his mind, wanted to run as far from this place, and from Adèle, as possible. Life had seemed so easy when all he had to do was have his steward send Céline a check at the beginning of every year, when he only had to visit Adèle every so often, bearing pretty gifts and then going away again.

He drew a deep breath and continued, "In time, you shall go to school. Or we will get a governess to teach you." *Oh, God, he had forgotten about educating her. How on earth would he manage all this? He knew nothing about picking schools and governesses!*

Never had he wished so hard that he had kept his trousers securely buttoned all those years ago. And that at least one of Céline's lovers had as well.

He looked at Adèle. She was still frowning, and her full lower lip was quivering, her eyes shining with tears.

"Madame Frédéric told me Maman has gone to the Holy Virgin."

Magnificent. Lie to the child, tell her that her mother is dead. Then leave me to handle the situation.

He wondered how he would explain things to Adèle if Céline returned, if she tracked them down and wanted her daughter back.

Yes, Adèle, people do return from the Holy Virgin. Or at least from their lovers in Italy. Which got him thinking of another responsibility. He would have to see that Adèle went to church. He decided that could be the job of Mrs. Fairfax.

And inwardly he had to enjoy a small chuckle at the thought of Céline ever achieving the slightest proximity to the Holy Virgin.

It had been a busy few weeks leading to their departure. Madame Frédéric had recommended an agency where Edward had gone to attempt to hire a nurse for Adèle, but he had found no one willing to go live in England. In the end it was Manon, Adèle's former nurse, who found a friend who was willing to take the job.

Edward had offered Manon the position, but she was newly engaged to the man who had fathered her lost baby all those years ago, when she had been hired as Adèle's wet nurse. Now happy and looking forward to her new life, she would not leave France. But she introduced him to Sophie, who also had experience caring for children.

"Just between ourselves, Monsieur," Manon had confided, "Sophie is not, may I say, blessed with great intelligence. But I have known her all my life and you will not find one kinder or more caring. I would not suggest her for my Adèle if she was not a good nurse."

Edward had not been impressed with Sophie, a heavy, round-faced young woman of perhaps twenty or twenty-one. Her movements were slow and she had a vacant look about her. She apparently needed to think hard before answering a question even as simple as "how are you?" But she was willing to go to England, and Manon's recommendation left him as confident as he could be under the circumstances.

Once Sophie was hired and installed in the hotel room adjacent to Edward's own, he fetched Adèle from the Frédérics with his thanks and an extra payment for keeping Madame de Simone at bay.

"But I would give you even more if you hadn't told Adèle that her mother was dead," he told Madame Frédéric with a glowering look.

She sniffed with disdain. "I felt it was kinder than letting the child know that she had been deserted by her mother," she told Edward.

It was a hectic time, settling Adèle in with Sophie, booking passage to England for three people and two animals, and contacting Mrs. Fairfax. Ordinarily, Edward did not warn her when he was returning to Thornfield, but since he was bringing a new resident, he thought it was only fair.

On a cloudy, late March day that spoke alarmingly of turbulent dark waves and high cold wind, the group had boarded the ship that would carry Adèle away from the only home she had ever known.

Edward picked Adèle up, preparing to carry her over the gangplank onto land. She was weak from two days of little nourishment and vomiting, and she felt damp and limp in his arms. Her head dropped to his shoulder and he felt a protective tenderness as he cradled her against his chest. He wished he could always feel that way towards her, but she was quiet now. It was early on the morning of the fourth day of their trip, counting the two days they had spent travelling from Paris to Calais by carriage, and all were looking forward to their chance to rest in a bed that was not moving.

Sophie followed them, holding her bag with her pitifully few possessions. Edward spoke to some men at the dock, getting them to find him a carriage for hire, and he had left Adèle leaning against Sophie while he went to see to Pilot and Mesrour. Pilot was none the worse for wear, although he rapidly drank nearly all the water in the bowl that Edward found for him. It seemed hours before he had the luggage fastened to the carriage, everyone inside, and Mesrour securely tied to the back of the carriage to follow along behind. Edward did not feel up to riding him right now, as his stomach was none too steady.

It was early evening when they arrived at the hotel. Adèle had been able to nibble some bread and sip some soup when they had stopped at an inn for dinner, and she appeared a little stronger. But Edward still got the hotel's physician to look in on her and Sophie to make sure there would be no lasting effects from two days of seasickness. The doctor had given them both a mild tincture of opium well diluted in water and had said they would both be fine with good food and plenty of fresh air. He recommended that they not resume their journey for a few days.

Edward had refused the proffered medicine for himself, preferring to retire to his bed with a bottle of his own choosing. He drank a large brandy, which burned his nearly empty stomach and in the morning made him retch and gag as two days of crossing the Channel had not been able to do.

Their week in London passed quickly. Adèle and Sophie soon recovered their strength with good food and rest. Every day Sophie would take Adèle on a walk to a nearby park, where she delighted in feeding birds with a bag of bread crumbs begged from the waiter in the hotel's dining room. Adèle was a favourite of the hotel staff, with her big eyes and her chatter, and Edward found it amazing that she did not seem to annoy others as she annoyed him.

He was busy trying to shop for Adèle, for after a year at Madame Frédéric's, she had no ordinary clothing to speak of, and Adèle could not tell him what had become of her possessions from her life with Céline. Her dolls and stuffed toys had disappeared, and her few undergarments and petticoats were of a stiff, coarse material and were getting too short for her.

He had gotten a list from Sophie of the things Adèle needed, and he spent mornings taking her shopping, which exhausted his already dwindling patience to near non-existence. But by the time they got into the carriage for the trip to Thornfield, Adèle had a full trunk and clutched a doll in her arms, once again restored to her laughing and chattering self. The child and nurse rode in the coach that had their trunks strapped to the top, while Edward rode Mesrour and Pilot ran alongside him, barking with joy at being free to run.

When Pilot appeared to grow tired, Edward stopped the coach, opening the door and sending him inside with Adèle, who greeted him eagerly and spent several hours combing his fur. At the next stop, Pilot appeared relieved to once again be able to leave the carriage and run, out of reach of Adèle's loving ministrations.

They arrived at Thornfield in the afternoon, two days after leaving the hotel in London. Edward silently dismounted and handed Mesrour's reins over to John. He then lifted Adèle out of the carriage, glad to see that for once she was silent as her huge eyes took in the large stone house with its battlements. Mrs. Fairfax met them on the flagstone courtyard outside the front door, her usual bustling, cheerful self.

"So this is the child!" she exclaimed, looking her over, with many a glance at Mr. Rochester as well.

Edward set Adèle down on the ground and, in French, introduced her to "Madame Fairfax". The child curtsied prettily, sending Mrs. Fairfax into raptures.

He cut into her flow of words. "Madame, this is Miss Adèle Varens, my ward. Kindly show her to her room, and her nurse, Sophie, with her. We have had a long journey and we all need to rest. Please send John to me as soon as he is free."

He turned to Sophie and gave her rapid instructions in French, to see to Adèle's *"toilette"* and to make sure she had a long rest before dinner. He turned his back on the little group, whistling for Pilot and heading upstairs to his chamber.

For nearly a month, Edward remained in Derbyshire, seeing Adèle settled in, conferring with his steward, and visiting the neighbours. He did not take Adèle with him. He told himself that she needed to get settled without having to meet new people, but in reality, he did not know how to explain her presence, and knew that she would cause raised eyebrows and even more speculation than already existed.

He did take her to Ferndean with him, where she romped in the woods with Pilot and spent so much time climbing the fences and marveling over the sheep that his caretaker scowled, and eventually growled at her to stop frightening his animals. She had cried, and Edward had finally sent her back to the carriage, where she had fallen asleep, and not awakened until they were nearly back at Thornfield late that night. He had not even gotten her up to eat, knowing she could have a big breakfast in the morning.

It was less than a month before he started to feel his old restlessness, and he knew he could not stay at Thornfield much longer. He could feel Bertha upstairs – knew she sensed his presence, as he sensed hers. He had visited with Grace a little, and she reassured him that all was under control. But he could almost feel Bertha's eyes on him, could feel the malevolence that had seemed to hover over the whole estate from the moment he had installed her in that upper room.

In late April, he climbed upon Mesrour's back, whistled for Pilot and departed again. He was not sure where he was going, but it would not be Paris. Or anywhere in Italy. He had said good-bye to Adèle, promising to send her a present, and promising to return. He had ignored her tears, and looked over at Mrs. Fairfax, who stood in the doorway with Adèle, her lips crimped into a disapproving line.

"I will be in touch, Mrs. Fairfax," he told her, "with instructions about engaging a governess for her, or about a school, should I find one that can handle the language issue."

She nodded, saying nothing, but looking at Adèle with a sad shake of her white head.

Adèle, tears slipping from her eyes, ran inside to the window to watch her guardian as he galloped away on his big black horse. She had asked him to take her with him, but he had said no. She had asked where he was going, and he had said he did not know. She wondered if he was going to the Holy Virgin like her mother.

In her childish mind, she imagined Mr. Rochester, her Maman, and the Holy Virgin all living together in one big house. That night, after Sophie had made her wash herself and clean her teeth, and had dressed her in her long white nightgown, she had knelt by the bed and prayed that they would all send for her, so she could live with them too.

Chapter 24 - Vienna

June, 1835

Edward stopped in front of the small dress shop that had been recommended to him by a society matron.

While spending a Sunday afternoon at an art exhibition, he had encountered the woman who had been the hostess at a dinner he had attended when he had first arrived in Vienna, and they had recognized each other at the same time. "It is Mr. Guilford's friend, isn't it?" she had asked in perfect English. "He brought you to dinner one night, I recall. I am so sorry, I have forgotten your name."

"Edward Rochester," he replied, bending over her hand. "Madame. It is nice to see you again; I still remember the splendid capon."

He had forgotten her name also, but she did not seem to notice, launching at once into her opinion of the art they were viewing that day. Edward thought it was horrible. He had seen more interesting designs in the mud that Pilot tracked across his drawing room rug, but he smiled politely and listened to the woman rhapsodize over the brilliance of the artist's vision.

When she fell silent, he changed the subject by turning to acknowledge the child at her side, a young girl of perhaps ten. As they chatted about children, Edward found himself telling the woman of Adèle and how he needed to find a present to send her, as he had promised.

The woman had enthusiastically recommended a dress shop that included fine custom-made dresses for little girls.

"The owner of the shop has found a brilliant seamstress by the name of Clara Hoffmann, who designs and fashions one-of-a-kind dresses. She is quite talented! You should go see her to find a gift for your ward."

Now, Edward stood outside the shop. Feeling foolish, he removed his hat and entered. He knew nothing of little girls' dresses, but judging from the satins, velvets and laces he saw on display about the shop, the styles seemed perfect for Adèle, frivolous little flirt that she was.

A young woman behind the counter greeted him cheerfully and when he asked for Clara Hoffmann, she stepped behind a curtain and emerged to say Frau Hoffmann would be with him shortly.

He did not engage in his customary pacing, afraid he would appear too eager and impatient, so he stood feeling awkward and very out of place. He was relieved not to have to wait too long, for soon a woman stepped out of the back room.

"Frau Hoffmann?" he asked, pleasantly surprised to see how lovely the woman was. "I was told to ask for you by a Frau… " he stopped, aware that he had never learned the woman's name. He smiled shamefacedly. "I am afraid I was not using my best manners, because I could not remember her name and I was too embarrassed to ask her."

Frau Hoffmann smiled at his discomfiture. "It does not matter; I would not place her anyway. I have many women coming here to see me, and my memory is not good. You remembered my name, at least. How may I help you, sir?"

Edward listened carefully, translating in his head her German. She did not have an Austrian accent, but he had not been to Germany often enough to place where she was from.

"Do you speak English?" he asked her, "I am afraid my German is very rudimentary."

She switched to English, spoken with a very harsh accent. She knew a little of the language, she told him, learned from her late husband who was a man of business and had dealt with many Englishmen.

The dressmaker was not a very young woman; she was at least thirty. But she was very handsome indeed, slightly plump, with blonde hair, very blue eyes, and one of the most beautiful complexions Edward had ever seen. She had an angelic face with a small straight nose, pink cupid's bow lips, and lovely white teeth.

He was not ordinarily attracted to blondes, but only recently freed from the clutches of the dark, exotic Giacinta, Edward felt that looking at Clara Hoffmann was like stepping from darkness into the light. Her cheeks coloured becomingly under his frankly admiring gaze and he became aware he was staring.

It had been nine months since he had left Giacinta, and except for a quick, slightly drunken liaison in an empty room at a party in Paris one February night, he had not been with a woman in some time. He was so tired of society's empty niceties, the silly small talk and flirting. He had once been charming and attentive, interesting and even funny at times. Now the moment he walked into a gathering, he felt his face freezing, his eyes sweeping the assembly and seeing the same type of woman – elegant, monied, shallow.

He knew he was not being fair. Some of the women were probably very intelligent and kind. But at thirty-six, he was tired of the charade, worn out by disappointment and exhausted by the emptiness of the social dealings of his class.

He knew he was getting a reputation for being hard, cynical, even cold. But he could no longer arrange his face into the pleasant lines this superficial life required. He could no longer make his voice friendly, his tone light, could no longer find genial subjects for conversation. Most of the time at gatherings, he stood at the sidelines, a drink in his hand, trying to appear friendly or, at the very least, trying not to look as though he were scowling. It was all too much of an effort.

Watching Frau Hoffmann was the first pleasure a woman had given him in some time. It was amusing to him that he felt more at ease in the company of a dressmaker than he did with the women of his own class – the Austrian, French, and English ladies that he saw all the time at parties and assemblies. Here in the small dress shop, he felt no pressure to play the part of the sophisticated English gentleman he was thought to be.

Abashed to be caught watching her so frankly, he began to talk quickly, telling her of Adèle. Frau Hoffmann noticed his accent and asked him where he was from, although it meant nothing to her, as she had travelled very little.

He learned she was not Viennese, but German, from Berlin, having come to Vienna when she married her husband. He had died two years ago, and she had taken this job as a seamstress, then progressed to becoming a designer as the owner came to recognize her talent.

She had told him to please call her Clara, and had listened carefully as he talked of Adèle and the kinds of dresses she liked. She had produced several sketches with suggestions – one was simple, a dress that could be worn for everyday but still showed unique touches of individual design. She also showed him a design for a party dress, rich with lace and ruffles. Edward could easily imagine Adèle, dressed in this frock, dancing and singing for a collection of assembled guests. He chose that dress, and the simple day dress, and selected bright colours that he felt would please his ward.

When Clara had asked about Adèle's size he stopped, aware that he had absolutely no idea.

Clara smiled, "Very few fathers know the size of their children's clothing. She is a lucky little girl that you even come in here to select these dresses as a gift for her. Perhaps her mother can contact me later with the size."

"There is no mother, only me."

Clara's face softened in sympathy. Edward hastened to correct her impression, but he did not tell Clara that Adèle was the child of his former lover, instead saying she was the daughter of friends who could not care for her.

Clara smiled with amusement as he held his hand out, showing her Adèle's size in comparison with his own. She stepped nearer to him, holding a measuring stick against his side to record the approximate height. As she came close to him, Edward smelled her clean scent, a sort of light flowery essence that appealed to him.

He watched her bent head as she wrote out the measurements, getting caught staring at her when she lifted her head quickly. Once again her white cheeks flooded with a pretty pink colour.

"I will make the dresses a little big, so she might get more use of them," she explained.

He nodded, his black eyes meeting hers. She bent again, writing something on a piece of paper and handing it to him.

"It is a receipt, telling you what I will be making," she told him. "You can pay me a part now and the rest when you come to get them. Or you can pay now and I will send the finished dresses to your home."

"No," he said, still watching her closely, "I will return to pick them up." He removed his billfold and gave her some money, as she handed him the sheet of paper. Their fingers brushed and he felt a small tingle of excitement. Her fingers were slightly rough, callused from handling pencils and needles and lengths of fabric. He liked the feel of them, in such contrast to the soft, languid, useless hands of the society ladies he knew.

Clara's nails were short, filed down to keep them from catching on the soft materials she worked with. Edward compared them to Giacinta's long, pointed nails coming at him with predatory calculation, and this pleased him also.

He folded the receipt into his billfold and nodded his thanks, beginning to turn away. Seized by a sudden impulse, he turned back towards her. "Would you perhaps be free for a brief time, for a cup of coffee and a pastry?"

She had smiled again, raising her eyes to his boldly, and he knew then that she would be his next lover.

Edward had enjoyed that short time together with Clara. She had taken her lunch hour then and they had gone to a small café she knew of just a block away. They had drunk cups of strong Viennese coffee and eaten croissants.

Once out of the shop and in the sunlight, Edward had noticed the tiny lines around Clara's eyes, and once she drank her coffee he saw that her lips were pale; she obviously accented them with some sort of colour. As they talked, he found out that she was thirty-eight, two years older than he was. But she was still quite lovely, and could be mistaken for much younger, and Edward still found himself staring at her – at her lovely face, and the full round breasts under the bodice of her modest dress.

She was quiet; once out of the shop and not doing business, she had little to say, but she did tell him that she was saving her money and hoped to open a business of her own some day. "I have ladies who come to me to have special dresses made, but I have to sew into the night to finish them, and I have to work in the shop. Once I have money saved, I can sketch my own designs and hire some seamstresses to help me make my own dresses. And I can keep the money; as it is now, I have to give a percentage to the owner of the shop, even if it is my own design I make."

She said her husband had left her a nice little house in a quiet tree-lined neighbourhood, and it was paid for, but she had no other source of income. Other than her own modest needs, she had few expenses and so was able to save a great deal. She hoped to be able to quit the shop and open her own business within five years.

She had been quite a bit younger than her husband, and they had had no children. She said little about what kind of marriage she had had, but Edward felt she seemed very calm and unemotional about her husband's death. He wondered how things had been between them. He found himself watching couples, wondering how their marriages really were.

He told her about his life, the investments he had made in Paris and the West Indies and the ups and downs of the profits from those. He told her of Thornfield, and talked a little about Adèle. He did not tell her about Bertha, of course.

After a pleasant hour they had parted ways, and he left her with the name of his hotel so she could send him a message when the dresses were ready.

The next three weeks he had gone about his business, visiting, going to parties and meeting up with new acquaintances. But from time to time he thought of Clara. She was the first woman who had appealed to him since the early days with Giacinta. He did not fool himself that he could love her, but she appeared to be a pleasant companion and he had enjoyed his time with her.

Sometimes at night, lying in his lonely bed, he would think of her, her soft blonde hair and big blue eyes, the womanly curves he found very alluring. His hand would drift down and he would close his eyes, imagining her there with him as he worked at himself, taking his solitary pleasure as he had so often before. It was a temporary measure, but it would satisfy him and tire him so that he could rest.

He looked forward to seeing her again.

The message came to the desk of the hotel and the clerk handed it to him one day as he was leaving. He opened the note, pleased to see that the dresses were done and that Clara had let him know that he could come anytime to see them.

He had no particular place to go then, so he had put Pilot back up into the room and headed for the dress shop. Clara herself showed him the dresses. They were lovely, and Edward was sure that Adèle would like them. He arranged to have them sent to Adèle, and paid the rest of the money he owed, again asking her to come out for coffee with him. They had chatted again, and when he walked her back, she had invited him to her house for dinner that night. He had had an invitation to a small party that night, but did not mind missing it if it meant he could spend some time with Clara. She was a bit too quiet for him, but after Giacinta he was not going to complain. It was nice to sit down with someone and share a conversation, and perhaps she would grow more animated as she got to know him.

"I'm sorry," he told her, as they lay together in Clara's bed, "I don't feel you got much pleasure out of that." He reached up to push back her long blonde hair, slid his fingers down over one of her full breasts, stroking her nipple.

She was quiet, lying there for a moment, and then she rolled over on her back.

"It is not you," she said, with a sigh. "It is me. You tried very hard to… to make me happy, but I am afraid I feel very little during… that."

Edward was taken aback. "Why didn't you tell me?" he asked her, "We did not have to go to bed."

Actually, it had been at Clara's instigation that they had gone to her bed. After a delicious meal, they had shared some sort of sweet cordial with the dessert that Clara had made, and afterwards she had come over to him, taking his hand and bringing him to the bedroom. He was a little surprised, as she had given him no real indication of interest. She seemed to enjoy the fact that he found her attractive, but he had sensed no feelings of particular desire or arousal on her part.

She had gone behind the screen to undress, and had come out wearing a nightgown, but he had coaxed her into taking it off once they were under the covers. At first it was very nice. Her plump body was so warm and soft – he had never been with anyone quite like her before, and she felt so good he could hardly stop touching her. He was very aroused, and tried to pleasure her also, but she seemed tense, her mind far away. He had tried to caress her, but she seemed embarrassed, and when he began to kiss his way down her body, she made him stop. When he took her hand and put it on him, she had gone along with it, but he could tell she didn't enjoy it.

Confused, he had gone ahead and proceeded when she urged him to, but she was very dry at first, and it was not comfortable for the first few minutes. But finally he had begun to feel some excitement and he climaxed fairly soon, pulling out of her just in time.

Now she explained herself. "I have never gotten very much feeling when I have done this. My husband seemed to notice no problem; it was only when we did not have a child that I went to the doctor and he asked me about it. He asked if I 'came to satisfaction' when we came together and I did not know what he meant; he had to tell me. He said that was probably why I could not have a child. He gave me medications and various treatments, but I continued like this, never any real pleasure, and I never conceived. So you do not have to be concerned; I have never gotten pregnant and now I am too old, I believe."

She swallowed, looking at him for the first time since they had begun this conversation. "Of course, I will understand if you do not want to be with me again. I have had two other men since my husband, and neither of them wanted to be with me again when I told them of my troubles."

Edward protested that of course he wanted to be with her again, that he did not mind. He felt it was only right; he did not want her to think that that was why he was with her. Although, if he were to be perfectly honest, it was.

But when he thought about it, as he did, often over the next few days, he realized that he did not mind it as much as he thought. Had he loved Clara, or thought he could love her, the thought that they could not share this would upset him greatly. But he did not love her and did not plan in any way for this to be permanent, and he doubted that Clara did either.

Since he had first lain with a woman, he had often found himself with women who were aggressive, who wanted pleasure from him. Bertha, Giacinta, Olga, even Céline wanted him to provide satisfaction when they came together. And he had been glad to do so, finding his pleasure enhanced by theirs. But he was tired, and deep in his heart, he felt he had nothing left to give. He felt he'd been drained by women, by Bertha's insanity, by Céline's betrayal, by Giacinta's erratic behaviour, by the mutual sin he felt he had committed with Olga. The thought of a quiet, passive, non-demanding woman was now quite appealing.

"I do not dislike it," Clara told him, "I like the closeness, I like to be held in a man's arms. I even do not mind the feel of a man inside me. I just get no great pleasure from it."

Edward told himself he did not mind, and for a while he did not. She was willing enough; she would put her arms around him and move with him. She said nothing, and made no sounds, but he found that that did not matter. After Giacinta's wildness, and the years of frenzy that had sent him careening through Europe in search of peace after Bertha, in hopes of love, he found that some peace and quiet was not unwelcome.

After years of looking for the love that he had never been allowed to have, he was happy to have a mere physical outlet with no other expectations. His heart was weary, his soul felt dried and withered, and for now he was content to stay where he was, to let both heart and soul die quietly within him. He had tried to hope, and hope had failed him.

Chapter 25 - Clara

Clara was honest and quiet; but heavy, mindless, unimpressible; not one whit to my taste. I was glad to give her a sufficient sum to set her up in a good line of business, and so get decently rid of her. But, Jane, I see by your face you are not forming a very favourable opinion of me just now. You think me an unfeeling, loose-principled rake, don't you?
Edward Rochester - Jane Eyre

Edward Fairfax Rochester
Hotel Wilhelmstrasse
Vienna

Alice Fairfax
Thornfield Hall
Hay, Derbyshire
England
6 July 1835

Mrs. Fairfax-
Thank you for your messages regarding the progress of my ward. In light of what you tell me about her difficulty in making the transition from French to English, I do not feel that a school is the best place for her at present. I believe that private tutoring would be preferable for Adèle at this time.

With this in mind, I would be obliged if you would undertake to find a governess for her. I will leave it to you to use your best judgment; however I feel that Colonel Dent or Lady Ingram might perhaps be helpful to you as you go about this task, and my steward is always available to answer questions about the remuneration expected for such a position.

As always, I trust your decisions and know that you will select someone of good character, but I would require that the young woman chosen have a working knowledge of the French language so as to assist Adèle in learning English.

Please contact me at the above address if my help in this matter becomes necessary.
E. F. Rochester

Alice Fairfax
Thornfield Hall
Hay, Derbyshire
England

Mr. Edward Fairfax Rochester
Hotel Wilhelmstrasse

Vienna
26 September 1835

Mr. Rochester-

I trust this message finds you in good health and spirits and that you are finding Vienna to be all that you expected.

I am happy to be able to report that my search for a governess has gone well and that a Miss Eyre is expected to arrive in early October to fill the post as governess for Miss Adèle.

I consulted Mr. King as to the expected salary for this position and he tells me that thirty to thirty-five pounds per annum is customary for a new governess, along with room and board, of course. Miss Eyre has accepted thirty pounds.

This is her first post as governess, although she is not without teaching experience. She comes to Thornfield from a school in Yorkshire, where she has taught for two years.

I had intended to consult Colonel Dent regarding where to find a governess, because as you can imagine I was at quite a loss. However, the very week I received your letter, I had a friend come to visit me. Upon hearing of my project, she drew my attention to an advertisement in a copy of the Yorkshire Herald. I replied and was quite pleased to make the acquaintance of Miss Eyre via letter. She comes with the highest references and I hope that Miss Adèle will find in her a skillful teacher.

With all greetings and my very best wishes, I remain,
Mrs. Fairfax

Edward snorted and tossed his housekeeper's letter onto the desk in his hotel room. The woman seemed incapable of writing the sort of message he preferred, which would basically have said, "Mr. Rochester, I found a governess. Mrs. Fairfax." She always felt compelled to include every last detail.

He did not care how a governess was found or where she had come from. As long as she was capable of speaking enough French to teach Adèle English, and to turn her from the flighty little imbecile she was, into a sensible, literate child capable of being shipped off to boarding school, that was all he cared about.

Edward was in a foul temper. He was restless, not particularly enjoying Vienna but unable to think of anywhere else he wanted to go. He was feeling guilty for staying away from Thornfield for so long, especially since Mrs. Fairfax had kept him apprised of both Adèle's progress and of the child's continued distress over his absence. He was not sure how she knew that Adèle was distressed since she continued to repeat that she could not understand most of what the child said, but she insisted that Adèle was lost without him.

He was not happy with any aspect of his life here in Vienna. Although it had proved to be a lovely city, with a great deal of art, music and culture, there was only so much of that that could be absorbed. He was tiring of the parties and the superficial social life of a glittering capital such as this, and although he spent a good many hours riding Mesrour, walking the city, and exploring the countryside, he still could not fill all of his idle time.

It was for that reason that he had continued to see Clara. It was not for her company or her conversation, for she really gave him very little of either. She bored him, which made him feel guilty, as she was quiet, honest, and kind. But she had very little to say, very little interest in the outside world, and there was enough of a gap in their language abilities to make things even more difficult.

Edward, who was fluent in French and quite passable in Italian, found his tongue stiff and clumsy when it came to the German that Clara spoke. In higher society, those of his circle spoke French and some spoke English, and he conversed easily, but Clara's Berlin accent and rudimentary knowledge of English combined with his poor German meant that they passed a great deal of their time in silence. When they were getting to know each other, it had seemed easier, but now that they were more comfortable with each other, there seemed very little to say.

When Edward tried to sound her out as to her opinions of current events, he found that she paid little attention to them. She showed little enthusiasm for anything but her designs, her sewing, and her cooking. He read the papers, and was eager for someone with whom he could hold an intelligent conversation, but Clara was not interested, and society women cared only for chatter about current styles and love affairs. The men who gathered after dinner for brandy and cigars were a little more interesting, but even they spoke more of sport than of politics and of current affairs.

Out of sheer boredom, Edward had begun to pass some time at a tavern not too far from Clara's house, where he had stopped in one day on an impulse while prowling about the city. Although he would never speak German as well as he spoke French or Italian, he could understand more than he could reply to, and he would sit drinking a beer and picking up as much of the conversations as he could. Sometimes a tavern customer would get up to make a speech, and he enjoyed hearing what the men had to say.

His father never would have tolerated his son sitting down to drink among men whose coarse clothing, scuffed dirty shoes, and callused hands showed them to be workers, but he found he enjoyed sitting quietly among a crowd of strangers of an afternoon, listening to the men talk of history and politics. Some spoke of radical ideas, even advocating total overthrow of current systems, but Edward found their talk fascinating.

He knew he was viewed with suspicion, due to his fine clothing and the obvious lack of hard work and hardship on his face. He was as well-muscled as the men around him, but his were the muscles of riding and sport, not the well-earned muscle of labour. So he did not mingle with the men around him, but sitting there, listening to their talk, he found himself absorbing ideas he would never have heard in the fine drawing rooms of the gentry in England.

It did not change his style of living, but it did slightly alter his thinking in ways he did not even realize. In these few hours here and there of sitting among the working class, he found the only intellectual stimulation of his now-stagnant life. He became aware of his total inertia and inability to move forward. He was nearly thirty-seven years old, and was beginning to feel that his life was used up. He wondered when it was that he had ever felt as passionately as these men in the tavern did. He wondered if he ever had.

He did not tell all this to Clara. She did not appear interested in self-discovery of any kind, and the only thing he ever saw her passionate about was a new design idea or a particularly attractive bolt of fabric.

He was bored with Clara physically also. Due to her lack of enjoyment, for whatever reason, things had become stagnant in that respect as well. There was no mutuality to their union, no sharing of pleasure. She was merely a means, a warm place slightly more enjoyable than his own hand would have been. Sometimes he only shared her bed because he knew she expected it. Despite the fact that she did not find pleasure in what they did, he sensed she would be offended if he refused the offer of her body.

He was not sure what she wanted from him, even with the money he gave her. He had given Giacinta money, but he knew she was also stirred and aroused by him, and wanted his presence in her bed. At least he had the illusion of being more to her than a source of income.

With Céline he had maintained his own residence, and Giacinta had lived in his home, but he merely made visits to Clara several nights a week. Each week he let her know when to expect him, and she would have a hot delicious meal prepared for him, and some good wine. After dinner she would clean up while he smoked beside the fire, and then she would come and sit with him, sewing or sketching designs while he read the paper and they shared desultory conversation.

Later in the evening, she would bank the fire, and go to the bedroom to prepare for bed. At Edward's request she would leave her hair unbound and her nightgown off, getting under the covers to wait for him. He would come in, undress, and get under the covers as well. He had started off wanting the candles to remain lit, but now he did not care. In the darkness she could be anyone, and he found that more far exciting.

She would apply the oil that made his entrance easier, and would lie passively beneath him, legs open, as he entered her. Then she would lie quietly while he completed his task. Occasionally, he would request that she get on top of him, which she would obediently do, but other than allowing him free access to her soft full breasts, there was little advantage to a position he knew she did not enjoy, and when she was underneath him, he could control the pace and make the encounter all his own. She would put her hands on his shoulders or around his neck and move in rhythm with him if he asked her to, but that was as far as she would go in response, and he did not mind it, for he could let his mind wander.

In his fantasies, she was not his compliant, unresponsive mistress, but his beloved; someone with whom he shared love and respect, someone who adored and desired him. He would imagine how it would be, to lie in the bed entwined with a wife, someone who belonged to him.

And in his imagination, they would keep the candles lit, the better to see their shared pleasure. He would look into her eyes and she into his, and when they climaxed, at that moment of exquisite, spiraling rapture, they would see each other. He would caress and adore her body, and she his, and there would be no act they could not share – not out of mindless lust, but rather in mutual pleasure and excitement.

He imagined the kisses he would give her: the sweet caresses of love across the skin of her face, the soft feathery sweeps around her ears and down her neck, the deep passionate kisses he would press to her mouth. Their lips and tongues would join, deeper and longer, their breathing growing faster as their arousal increased. His lips would move over her body, and she would love it, love him, want more of him.

He imagined them holding each other tightly, wanting to be closer and ever closer; he imagined the delicious feeling of their joining, how he would slip into her with ease because of how ready he would make her and how much she desired him.

Lying above Clara, his eyes closed as he thrust into her still, pliant body, there was no sound in the room but his soft grunts and rapid breathing. And so he imagined what they would say to each other, he and his phantom love, this woman of his dreams. And the sounds of their coming together – there would be moans and cries, and words, such sweet words. He imagined holding her tightly, whispering to her, "I love you, my beautiful beloved darling." And he imagined her saying in return, "I love you, Edward."

I love you, Edward.

He had not heard that in so long. Not since Céline, and her words had been a lie, falling on his ears with bitter poisonous falsehood.

Now, getting closer to climax with the silent Clara, he imagined his beloved, rising up to meet him, soft cries of pleasure in his ear, her breaths as deep and quick as his own. He heard her words in his mind, crying out as she came, "I love you, I love you." He imagined himself saying the same in return, as he felt the pleasure build, the hard surges as he spurted deep into her. He bit his lip to keep him from saying them aloud, but in his heart he cried them out to his hidden sweetheart – the faraway lover he now felt he would never know.

I love you, my darling, oh, God, how I love you.

He stopped, and then collapsed upon Clara, damp with sweat, his breathing still rapid. He lay there until he felt himself softening, and then he withdrew, rolling over on his back, his eyes fixed upon the dark ceiling. He heard Clara moving, wiping herself off with the towel she brought to the bed with her. The bed moved as she got up and went behind the screen, and he could hear the splash of water, the rustle of cloth before she came back out.

She got back into bed, not touching him. He reached over and groped for her hand, some small gesture to keep a connection with her; it seemed only polite. She squeezed his hand in return, and for a while they lay there.

Finally he raised her hand to his lips, kissing it gently. "I need to leave now," he whispered.

"Yes," she whispered back. He debated kissing her, but did not want to expend the effort. He squeezed her hand again and got out of bed, moved to the chair to gather his clothes before he went behind the screen, relieved himself in the chamber pot, and dressed quickly.

He never spent the night. It would have seemed a mockery of the empty union of their bodies that they had just experienced, implying intimacy when there was none.

He thought of his other relationships. His first few nights of marriage when he and Bertha would drift off to sleep clutching each other, her long black hair all around them, like a silky coverlet.

He and Céline would lie spooned together, her back against his stomach, his hand reaching up to cup a breast or clasp her around the waist.

Even he and Giacinta would sometimes go to sleep in each other's arms. On one occasion, they had come together, she on top of him, and then they had drifted off to sleep, she still on top of him, covering him, his face pressed into her fragrant hair. Later they had awakened, and soon were ready again, repeating what they had done only an hour before.

But he could not spend the night with Clara, could not hold her in his arms all night long. He longed for solitude after they were together.

It was easier to be lonely alone, than lonely with someone else.

He let himself out, usually walking back towards the hotel. At that hour, only about nine or ten at night, he could usually find a cab once he left Clara's neighbourhood and reached the main thoroughfare. When he reached the hotel, he checked at the desk to see if there were any letters for him and then went to his room, where he quickly washed, and slipped naked between the sheets. His body, ready to relax after a large meal and sexual release, would feel warm and comfortable and ready to sleep. That was, in reality, the best part of his day, the content, drowsy moments of comfort before sleep gently overtook him.

But on nearly every one of these nights, he would grasp his pillow, wrapping it in his arms, thinking of the love he had fantasized of, the love that had existed only in his thoughts.

And he would drift off to sleep, wondering if he would ever find it.

Alice Fairfax
Thornfield Hall
Hay, Derbyshire
England

Mr. Edward Fairfax Rochester
Hotel Wilhelmstrasse
Vienna
17 November 1835

Mr. Rochester-
I trust this letter finds you in good health. I imagine that Vienna, like Thornfield, is feeling the approach of winter. We are building bigger fires and closing the curtains earlier in the evening to keep out the drafts that grow colder each day. Last week Leah, Grace Poole, and I got out the extra coverlets, aired them out and put them on all the beds and are now ready for whatever this winter will bring us in the way of long cold nights.
I am happy to report that Miss Eyre, the new governess, has settled in nicely and that already I see a change in our little Miss Adèle. She appears to like her teacher and Miss Eyre has excellent control over the somewhat frivolous aspects of her little French pupil.
Even Adèle's English has improved in just this very short six weeks of Miss Eyre's occupation.
I must say, I do not know how my friend happened to have just the newspaper that contained Miss Eyre's advertisement, or how I felt led to contact her, for, now I think on it, it is most unlike me, to contact a stranger sight unseen. But I bless the strange leadings of Providence, all the unknown factors and impulses that allowed me to hire her, for I feel that no one better could have come to Thornfield. A firm but kind teacher to your ward, a gentle and pleasant companion to your housekeeper, all in all an excellent addition to your household.
We look forward to a cozy winter and an enjoyable holiday season. John has promised a splendid goose and Mary will make a good meal, the preparations of

which are already being planned. Now that there are three young people here to share our solitude, we shall be a merry party at Christmas.

The only thing we lack here at Thornfield is your own presence. Mr. King will be contacting you shortly regarding some matters that require your attention, and two different gentlemen of the town have contacted him about how to reach you on matters of some importance regarding some boundary disputes that have arisen, so you should shortly be hearing from all of the above. I trust that soon we shall welcome you back to Thornfield, and with all my best wishes to you I remain-

Mrs. Fairfax

Chapter 26 - Heart-Weary and Soul-Withered

Last January, rid of all mistresses—in a harsh, bitter frame of mind, the result of a useless, roving, lonely life—corroded with disappointment, sourly disposed against all men, and especially against all womankind (for I began to regard the notion of an intellectual, faithful, loving woman as a mere dream), recalled by business, I came back to England.

Edward Rochester - Jane Eyre

Vienna, 30 December 1835

Charlotte Lathrop was dead. Edward held Robert Lathrop's letter in his hand, and turned to look out the window at the snow falling in the courtyard of the hotel. The letter had been written in late September and showed more than one address – it had apparently been misdirected before it finally reached him.

He clenched his teeth, pressed his lips together to control the tremble. It had been, oh, how long since he had seen the Lathrops... two years? Three years? He had thought Charlotte looked ill and weak when he was there last, but she had waved aside his concern and had acted no differently than ever on the day he was there.

Edward had sent them Christmas greetings, had written to them at the approximate anniversary of Hugh's death as he did every year, but he had thought of them very little, occupied as he was with his own life. He felt guilty for his selfishness, his self-absorption. He took a deep breath and looked again at the brief message.

27 September 1835

Dear Edward-

My dear Charlotte has been taken from me. I look at these words I have just written and I cannot believe them myself. Alice offered to write the letters for me, notifying friends who have no other way of knowing, but I choose to do it myself. Perhaps then I shall begin to believe it.

I know I should not mourn; she is with Hugh now and is out of all pain and suffering. But I am afraid I do not know how I shall live without her.

I hope you are well, Edward. And I wish you the love that I have known with my beloved wife. I know you always cared for her, as indeed everyone did, and I wanted you to know.

My best-

Robert J. Lathrop

Edward shook his head, turning once again to look out the window. He moved closer, resting his hot forehead against the frigid glass, watching the white flakes fall straight down. No two snowflakes are alike... he remembered someone at school saying that. Eton? Oxford? He did not remember.

The words repeated themselves over and over in his head. No two snowflakes are alike... no two snowflakes are alike. He closed his eyes. He knew he should just sit down and release the tears; the tears that he felt originating in his heart, moving into his throat, and now welling up painfully behind his eyes.

Was he crying for Charlotte or for himself? He shook his head again, annoyed at himself. Always, he ended up focused on himself. He did not like that about himself; he knew he had a tendency to dwell on his own problems, even when he should be thinking of others.

I wish you the love that I have known...

He looked out at the snow again. How did anyone know that each snowflake was different? No one had ever seen them all. Perhaps somewhere in that vast number of falling frozen drops were snowflakes who had one perfect partner, a flake that was exactly like itself. How would anyone know? No two alike. That made them special; unique.

In his mind, that just made them lonely.

He went over to the table, set the letter down. He looked at the open bottle of brandy on the table. He had already had some tonight. Too much, judging from the wandering of his thoughts. Far too much thought given to the damn snowflakes, of that he was sure. He leaned over and put the stopper back in the bottle.

He needed to go see Clara. He had not been to her house in nearly a week, since Christmas Eve, when she had cooked them a lovely meal and he had presented her with a bracelet as a Christmas gift. He did not miss her. While he was there, the crackling fire and the hot meal temporarily warmed him, and the softness of her body briefly took away the chill of loneliness from him, but the relief and the warmth did not last long. They had nothing in common, and he did not even know if she liked him.

She was kind, she was quiet. She was another human being and afforded him some small contact with the human race. But she was not what he needed, and it was not fair to her to continue as they were. He had had very little to give her at the start of their friendship; now he had nothing. He felt he had nothing to give anyone.

He could almost feel the chill of the winter outside, deep in his body. He remembered himself as a boy, eight or nine years old. He and Grace had gone out into the meadow in the snow, and had begun to throw snowballs at each other. He had forgotten his gloves and was too embarrassed to go back for them. He wanted to act strong, to impress her. They had played outside in the snow until his hands were bright red and numb, until he could hardly move them. She had offered him one of her mittens, but he had laughed at her, and kept on playing. They had finally gone in when he could no longer close his hands around the snowballs, and Nellie had scolded him soundly. She had made him hold his hands in a bucket of warm water, and he could still remember the pain when his feeling began to come back, an ache that still felt ice-cold even when warmed up.

That was what his heart felt like now, as though a sliver of ice was piercing his heart, stabbing deeply, freezing everything around it.

He stood in front of the fire, so close that the front of his body felt hot while the back of him felt cool. He held the mantle with both hands, his bent head bringing him close to the fire's burning heat, making his face flush.

And still he felt cold.

He did not have the nerve to tell Clara while they were sitting together after dinner. That would have been the logical time, but he said nothing, merely sipped his wine as he stared at the dancing shadows the fire cast upon the wall. Clara sat with a piece of sewing on her lap, a frown between her two eyebrows, turning the fabric this way and that as she stitched a design into it.

Edward swirled the wine in the glass, watching it. It looked like blood. He could almost imagine it, not cool and tart on his tongue, but hot and salty, with a taste of iron. He swallowed and put the glass down on the table. The click as he set it down made Clara look up, and she took that as a signal that he was ready for her. She put down her sewing, stood up and went to the fire, taking the poker and pushing it against the logs in the fireplace. She replaced the screen, leaned over and blew out the candle on the table beside her. The room grew gloomy.

Now, Edward. Tell her now. Surely you will not go into the bedroom with her.

He took a deep breath, opened his mouth. She turned to him, smiled a little and headed for the bedroom.

He got up slowly, followed her. He felt the words pushing at his lips. *Just open your mouth and say, "Clara...*

He did not say it. *Bloody coward.* He followed her, undressed, got into bed. He thought he would not be able to perform, thought that surely tonight of all nights he would stay soft, which would help him. He would say, "Clara, I'm sorry, but it's better this way, I have to tell you something... "

His treacherous body. His turncoat flesh. It grew hard, aroused, aching for relief. He felt the desire, wanted her against the better judgment of his brain.

He rolled over on her, kissed her. Kissed her cheeks, her forehead, pressed a gentle caress to her mouth. She kissed him back.

He buried his face in her neck. He did not want to proceed, but he did. She raised her legs around him, he pressed his hips against hers, positioned himself. He felt her take him in her hand, guide him into her. He brought his hands up, buried his fingers in her loosened hair. He pushed himself in as far as he could go, groaning with the sensation. There was a chill in the air of the room, but she was so warm inside. It felt good, very good, and he could not have stopped if he tried.

The last time. This is the last time. That thought brought him a curious mixture of relief and sorrow.

He felt her hands on his shoulders, felt her move a little with him. He knew she was not feeling any pleasure, she was only moving to help him along. It made him feel sad. He felt her cheek against his as he thrust, each movement into her increasing his pleasure. His breathing grew rapid, his head arched back. He moaned, deep in his throat.

She slid her hands down along his arms, grasped his wrists tightly. She had never done that before. Her eyes were closed, and she held his arms as they moved together.

It was building, building. He moved faster, deeper, his breath hissing between his clenched teeth. His fingers clenched and released, still holding handfuls of her soft, fragrant hair. A hot flooding pleasure gathered in his loins, making him gasp, then he felt the relief of the pulsations that emptied him into her. He was still, his breathing harsh in the silent room, and then he collapsed upon her. She still held his wrists in her strong, warm hands.

And before he could help himself, he was crying. He felt foolish, ridiculous. But he could not control the tears, burying his face in her soft blonde hair as he wept. She said nothing, lying still beneath him, and then she let go of his arms and he felt her hands in his hair, stroking, soothing.

"Shhh," she crooned, "It will be fine. Shhh."

Neither of them mentioned his tears. He was up, dressed, standing across the room when he told her. She had washed, put on her nightgown, pulled her golden hair back into a braid, then gotten back into the bed. Her large blue eyes went sharply to his face and narrowed, as he spoke the words that he had been needing to say for days.

"I am glad I have known you, Clara," he heard himself saying, "You are a wonderful woman. I wish I could give you what you need; you should have so much more."

She shook her head. "What are you saying?" she asked him, her voice flat.

He swallowed, "Clara… "

"You are going away," she said, looking down at her hands. "You are leaving me."

He nodded.

"I knew you would go," she said, shrugging her shoulders.

"I'm sorry… " he said quietly. Before the words were out of his mouth, she was shaking her head again.

"Do not say anything else."

He stood for a while, watching her. Then he reached into the inside pocket of his coat and pulled out a bankbook. He approached the bed.

"I have been to a bank," he began. "I spoke to a man there, whose name is written on the inside of this document. I have deposited a sum of money there, have spoken to this banker about what your needs will be. He thinks this is a sufficient sum with which to begin your business, and I have added a little extra, just to be sure."

Clara looked up at him. Her bland, sweet face was set and she looked into his eyes. She said nothing.

"You must go see this man – he is expecting you. There is some money set aside to be sent to you monthly, and another sum to be presented to you for the things you need to purchase for the business. With what you have saved already, you should be able to live comfortably while you begin your endeavours."

Edward held the bankbook out to her. She turned her face away.

Phrases ran through Edward's mind. Things he thought of saying. None of them, he knew, would do any good. He leaned over and set the bankbook on her lap, and turned and walked from the room.

He felt relieved. He hated himself, but he felt relieved.

He returned to his hotel room, and drained the rest of the brandy bottle. He was sick the next day and part of the day after that. When he felt better, he began to make preparations to leave Vienna.

He packed his trunk, made arrangements to ship it to Thornfield, and gathered the gifts he had bought for Adèle. He had not sent them in time for her birthday, but he arranged them now and packed them into a box. According to Mrs. Fairfax, she had been very excited to receive the first dresses he had sent her, and so, weeks ago, he had paid Clara to make an even more elaborate one.

There was a dark pink dress, made with Clara's special touches. He folded it carefully, covered it in tissue, and added the accessories Clara had suggested: silk stockings, white satin sandals, a petticoat to go under the dress, and for Adèle's dark brown hair, a circle of pink and white satin rosebuds. There were also some paper dolls, a doll made of china with delicate painted-on features, and a small silver brush and comb set. He wrapped and packed everything carefully, and the box went into his trunk, with the cards of address attached.

The letter from Mason had arrived the previous week, having been re-directed to several different places before arriving at Edward's Vienna hotel. Mason was in Madeira, planning to travel on the continent. He desired a meeting, and was willing to come wherever his brother-in-law wished.

Edward was tempted to throw it into the fire, but after leaving it on the table for several days, decided to answer it in a manner that would hopefully discourage further contact, at least on this trip. He was damned if he was in any mood to see his brother-in-law. Mason had never travelled to England to see him; he hoped that going there would discourage any thoughts Richard had of seeing him again.

Edward F. Rochester
Hotel Wilhelmstrasse
Vienna

Richard Mason
Vista Do Mar 8
Funchal, Madeira
2 January 1836

Richard-
I have only recently received your message of two months ago. I regret to inform you that if you are going to travel on the continent, I am afraid we will once again miss each other. I am about to leave Vienna; indeed this letter in answer to yours is one of the last tasks I will complete before departing.
I am recalled to Thornfield Hall on some matters of business regarding both my estate and events in the nearby town. I have no idea when I will resume my travels, but expect to be occupied in England for some weeks. I am dreading the thought of being there at this time of year, as the cold and damp will be uncomfortable.
I have continued to receive the financial reports sent by you, and must compliment you upon the continued successful business you are conducting.
With best wishes to you, I remain
E. F. Rochester

The second week of January, Edward landed in England, and proceeded to London. He had someone to see before he went on to Thornfield Hall.

---

20 January 1836

Edward sat across from Robert Lathrop, his intense black eyes fastened upon the man who had been his best friend's father.

Robert Lathrop was tall, with a slight stoop, as though he had been made to feel self-conscious about his height from an early age. He once-dark hair had gone quite grey now, and he had deep-set dark eyes, and a long aquiline nose. He had always had dark shadows under his eyes, and they were darker now, giving him a look of wisdom and weariness. He looked like an academic, as though he should be found in a university library, poring over an old tome with reading glass in hand.

Edward had seen him in court and knew that his mild, hangdog appearance belied his sharp tongue and even sharper mind. A felon standing in the dock might chuckle inwardly, initially thinking to himself that this barrister's quiet mien meant weakness and a tendency towards arguing before the judge for leniency. But by the time his sentence was handed down, he would realize that this man was not to be underestimated.

Lathrop did not look intimidating now. He looked like an old, tired man. When Edward had first arrived, Hugh's father had hugged him. Edward was surprised and a little embarrassed. Charlotte had always greeted him with an embrace, but Robert had always been kind but formal in his presence.

Lathrop had removed a handkerchief from his pocket and wiped his eyes, before ushering Edward into the drawing room, where candles were lit and a roaring fire burned in the hearth. Butterfly, Charlotte's old dog, slept soundly on the rug in front of the fire. When they entered, she cast her eyes over in their direction without lifting her head from her paws.

Pilot had been taken into the kitchen by the butler, to be kept there and fed after a day of running alongside Mesrour. Lathrop gestured over to Pilot's mother.

"Poor Butterfly. She is old now, and slow. Her hips bother her, in the mornings she can barely move, she is so stiff. If I were brave, I would have someone shoot her, put her out of her pain. But I cannot bear to. She hardly left Charlotte's side, especially towards the end. She still looks for her mistress." He smiled, "But then, so do I."

The house looked the same as Edward remembered it. Elegant, spotless. But there was something missing.

Lathrop commented on it, looking around once they were seated. "The house feels so empty," he said. "The heart is gone out of it."

Edward understood that feeling. In fact, it was all he knew, houses with no hearts in them. He nodded, concern for Hugh's father knitting his heavy brow.

Lathrop wanted to talk, and Edward let him. He was glad to listen, hoped his presence gave the man comfort. And he was relieved not to have to speak much, hoping that the despair and depression of his own situation did not show.

"I should not have been allowed to marry her," Lathrop said, staring into his glass of port. "Her father was wealthy and she was his only child. I had very little. A small bequest from my mother's side was all I could expect in the future. I had an uncle who had done well and had no children. He supported me as I trained for the law. But to a wealthy man with a beautiful daughter, I must have appeared a fortune hunter at the very least," he chuckled, his eyes far away.

"I first saw Charlotte at a ball. I was there with a friend, a wealthy young man who was keeping company with Charlotte's cousin… I was quite out of my league! But Charlotte and I danced, and fell into talking. And we knew. We both just knew." He sipped his drink, then continued.

"I was not wealthy. I did not consider myself especially handsome, nor did anyone else, that I could tell. But Charlotte fell in love with me."

Robert Lathrop's body was here in the drawing room in Grosvenor Square, but in his mind, he was at that long-ago ball.

"From the moment I saw her, Edward, there was never anyone else for me." He looked at Edward, smiled, "I was a normal young man. I had had a tussle or two with a willing lass. You were at Oxford, you know what was available."

Edward nodded. He knew. But he had never taken advantage, as Lathrop had. As Hugh had. He had saved himself. Should he have? Would it have changed his life's course? Would he have been smarter, seen Bertha for what she was had he, also, had a tussle or two?

No use thinking about that. The past could not be changed. If it could, he would have already done it.

Lathrop continued, "Those women, they were nice enough. I enjoyed them. But once I saw Charlotte, no one else would do. I never looked at anyone else that way again. I have been out in the world for forty years. You know what temptations face a man. There are often… opportunities. But I saw only Charlotte."

He leaned back in his chair, "She argued with her father, begged to be allowed to marry me. The old man gave in; he never could deny her a thing. And he lived to see me successful, and his daughter a happy woman. I was always glad he had lived to see his faith in me justified."

Edward spoke, "I can well believe that you made Mrs. Lathrop happy. I felt it when I was fifteen years old, when first I came to your home. The warmth of the home, of your family – it struck me. So different from my own family. I knew that I wanted that for myself. I wanted to have a woman look at me the way Mrs. Lathrop looked at you."

There was a long silence. Edward felt Lathrop's eyes on him, keen and piercing.

The older man spoke quietly, "And you have not found that, have you, Edward?"

Edward raised his eyes from his glass, looked at Hugh's father. "No," he said quietly.

Lathrop said, "Hugh would be thirty-seven now, had he lived. How old are you, as much as that?"

"I was thirty-seven yesterday."

"It's not too late," Lathrop said. "You are young yet. I know you do not feel it, but I am sixty-two and I tell you, thirty-seven is young."

For a moment Edward could not speak. He shook his head. "No," he finally said, "it is too late."

Lathrop watched him, his eyes sad. "You have given up. I see it in your face."

Edward hesitated, then nodded.

"Pity," Lathrop said. "Indeed, tragic. I do not say this to hurt you, Edward. Forgive a grieving old man's ramblings on his marriage. But I think of my wife. A woman, the right woman, can make you so much more than you would otherwise be."

"Well, that is my trouble," Edward said bitterly. He took a long swallow of his port. "I have consistently chosen the wrong woman. With maddening regularity, I have looked around at all the women available and seemingly deliberately have said, 'Now, how can I best commence to ruin my life?'." His low laugh held no mirth.

Lathrop breathed deeply, "All that I am, I owe to Charlotte." He smiled, remembering. "I always sought to make her proud. I would get up before the court and pretend that she was sitting in the gallery. And every word I spoke, rich with eloquence, was spoken to impress her."

He sighed, taking out his handkerchief again, "The funny thing was, her love for me was such that she was proud of me anyway. Just for being who I was. Her husband, her children's father. She just loved me... "

His voice broke, and he buried his face in his handkerchief for a long moment. Edward watched him, feeling a lump in his own throat.

His words burst forth, "Watching you, Mr. Lathrop, I am nearly glad not to have known true love. For who could bear to lose it? I may never have your joy, but neither will I have to know your pain."

Lathrop raised his head sharply; his eyes were wet, but he spoke decisively, "No, Edward, no." He shook his head.

"I would not have missed it, not for all the world. Yes, my heart is aching. I wake up each day missing her and I go to sleep each night wanting her, but to have had her those thirty-eight years... "

"It was worth every tear, every heartache." He smiled. "I would not have missed it," he repeated. He wiped his damp cheeks with the handkerchief he clutched in his hand.

He sat up straight, slapped his hands down on his thighs. "And my life is not so bad. I keep my hand in, over at court. And my Alice is nearby, she and her family. She hovers a bit, tends to annoy me, but thank God I have her."

Edward smiled a little, nodded. "Your grandchildren must be growing up by now."

"Yes, yes," Lathrop chuckled. "Young women, a young man. But they are kind to their old Grandpapa."

He looked over at his guest, "Now, young Rochester, what must we do with you?"

"Me?" Edward said. He drained his glass, shook his head at the offer of a refill. He tilted the glass at Hugh's father, "Excellent." He set the glass down and leaned back.

"No, Mr. Lathrop, I am afraid it is too late for me. I am going home to Thornfield, because my steward is threatening that if I do not make an appearance, my tenants will revolt and my walls will come tumbling down. There are no eligible ladies in the surrounding areas – well, none I can speak of favourably." He rolled his eyes, and Lathrop laughed.

"What do you want in a woman, Edward?" he asked.

Edward sighed, thought for a moment, "Well, up to now, a woman who is breathing and whose heart is beating has suited me just fine. Otherwise… " he threw his hands up, shrugged.

Lathrop laughed again. "When it comes right down to it, it is such a matter of chance. You meet woman after woman, and none of them suits you, and then you are thrown together with one who all of a sudden is what you were searching for and you did not even know it."

"It's just chance I went to the ball that night, you know," Lathrop told him. "I was such a serious boy, studying so hard. I did not want to waste my uncle's money, betray his faith in me. I had very little fun. The friend, well, acquaintance really, practically dressed me and carried me to his carriage. Said he was tired of my making everyone else look bad by always working diligently. And that night, Charlotte was there. I might never have met her otherwise."

"Now, Charlotte disagrees. She leaves that sort of thing not to chance but to Providence. She says God brought us together at the right time, and had I not gone to the ball that night, He would have brought us together another way. I do not know. Perhaps it is a little of both, what brings us together. Chance and God working as one."

"Had I not met her, no doubt I would have met someone else. Someone nice, someone suited to me. But my heart would never have been complete, and I would not have even known it."

He chuckled, again thinking back, "You are not to assume, Edward, that our life was perfect. We disagreed, we squabbled, we slammed doors and had our times of being piqued and annoyed. I was stubborn and had a temper. She was a little indulged and spoiled. She had a little adjustment to the physical side of marriage, and I'm afraid I was a little too eager for it at times."

"But we adjusted, we worked it out, we grew used to each other," he smiled mischievously, "In every way, I am happy to say."

He shook his head, looked over at his guest sadly, "Please, Edward, do not give up."

Edward lay in his large bed in one of Lathrop's guest rooms, thinking of their conversation.

Do not give up…

But he had. He had lost faith that he would ever find what he hungered for.

What do you want in a woman, Edward?

He lay there thinking. What did he want? When it came down to basics, what was he looking for? What had been lacking all those years?

He thought of Céline. He wanted fidelity, constancy, steadfastness, but Céline was lacking in all those things.

He thought of Clara. He wanted intelligence, a bright searching mind, someone who would talk to him.

He thought of Giacinta. He wanted love, affection, tenderness… not just mindless passion.

He smiled bitterly to himself. *Not asking too much, are you, Rochester?*

He did not think he had asked too much. Just an intelligent, faithful, loving woman. But God evidently thought he did not deserve one. And perhaps he did not – he had not done much to be worthy of love, of the love of a decent woman.

Years of wasted life, living for pleasure, making no mark on the world for good, indulging himself as though this life were all there was. Those were points against him, reasons he did not deserve love.

He had only done one good thing. Protected Adèle, taken her to Thornfield, set about raising her in a wholesome place. A lot of good that would do him. She was no comfort to him, no companion. And if Céline returned for Adèle tomorrow, knelt at his feet, professed her love for him, he would not take her back, tainted as she was with her other men.

As if he were any better...

He felt he would be punished; expected to be punished. He felt filthy inside, used up, wasted. He worried that he was diseased. He was surprised he was not. He had watched for it, worried about it, after Bertha. Now he worried again, here in his lonely, dark room. He deserved it. The pox. Some sort of pestilence, some sort of divine stroke to cleanse his soul forever.

He rolled over, squeezed his eyes shut. And waited for sleep to rescue him from his own thoughts and fears.

In the morning he was awake early. He bid a warm farewell to Hugh's father and thanked him for his hospitality. He took his riding cloak from the butler. He had gotten it years ago in St. Petersburg. It had a thick fur collar, and fastened up the front with steel clasps. He put on his gloves and his hat, took up his whip and mounted Mesrour.

And whistling for Pilot, he pulled the reins and headed away. Back to Thornfield Hall, where this wretched life of his had begun.

End of Part One

Chapter 27 - The Governess

On a frosty winter afternoon, I rode in sight of Thornfield Hall. Abhorred spot! I expected no peace—no pleasure there. On a stile in Hay Lane I saw a quiet little figure sitting by itself. I passed it as negligently as I did the pollard willow opposite to it: I had no presentiment of what it would be to me; no inward warning that the arbitress of my life—my genius for good or evil—waited there in humble guise.

When once I pressed the frail shoulder, something new—fresh sap and sense—stole into my frame. It was well I had learned that this elf must return to me—that it belonged to my house down below—or I could not have felt it pass away from under my hand, and seen it vanish behind the dim hedge, without singular regret.

Edward Rochester - Jane Eyre

January 1836

By the time he had dug his heel into Mesrour's side and cantered away, leaving the little governess behind him, Edward's ankle had already begun to throb inside his boot, and he fancied he could already feel it beginning to swell. It took an effort to keep his heel down in the stirrup and even the slight jostling of his horse's smooth gait made the pain worse.

It was the damnedest thing – one moment he had been galloping along, no thought in his mind but how he would soon be able to warm up in front of a fire and then... His mind flashed back to the sudden glimpse of the black-cloaked girl in the roadway, Mesrour rearing, Pilot barking, and the next thing he knew he was leaning on the girl, her arm about his waist, his arm across her shoulders.

He could still feel it, the thin bones of her shoulders under his arm, the fragility and the strength in one tiny frame, and most of all, the warmth of her. It had radiated up from her, through her cloak, the thickness of his coat, and all down the length of his arm.

Everywhere she had touched him, he could still feel her.

He pulled up on the reins as he approached the gates, walking Mesrour up to the front of the house. For a moment he sat in the saddle, contemplating how he should go about dismounting. Most of the time he got off his horse without a pause, either climbing off with one foot still in the stirrup, or sometimes even swinging around to the right and sliding off, landing with both feet on the ground. Either way, he was going to have to bear weight upon his sore ankle, and he dreaded it. He began to maneuver Mesrour closer to the mounting block.

Fortunately, as he had debated, John had looked out the window after hearing the barking of Pilot, who ran back and forth alerting the entire household to their arrival.

"Good luck approaching with stealth when you are around, Pilot," Edward grumbled, as John came out of the house and hurried towards him.

"Sir, we did not expect you so soon!" he called, "May I be the first to welcome you home!"

"No, you may not," Edward told him, "Some malevolent spirit was abroad in the lane and she was the first to greet me, by felling my horse."

"Sir?" John asked, his forehead knit in confusion.

"Never mind," Edward said, "I am afraid I have injured my ankle. Here, be so good as to help me down." John offered his arm and with some awkwardness he succeeded in assisting his master to the ground with a minimum of trauma, although Edward's foot was still jostled painfully, bringing forth from him a groan and a stifled curse.

John helped him into the house where a surprised Mrs. Fairfax went into a paroxysm of simultaneous greetings, exclamations of wonder, and summonses from all areas of the house. She called for assistance in taking the Master's outer garments, called for Mary to begin cooking, for the maids to prepare his bedroom, while at the same time lamenting his injury.

Edward felt that five minutes more in his housekeeper's presence and his head would be aching as much as his ankle. He waved aside offers of food and drink and consented to have Mr. Carter brought to see to his foot. Once John returned from fetching the groom to see to Mesrour, Edward allowed him to help him to his room, where he lay back on the bed, emitting a loud groan as John wrenched the boot off his throbbing foot.

The ankle had already swelled and was turning blue, and Edward sat on the bed examining it with fascination. John brought him cold water in which to immerse his foot, as well as a pair of clean stockings, before leaving to get Mr. Carter.

Left alone in his room, Edward soaked the foot until the cold became intolerable. He quickly washed the other, aware that after a full day of being encased in thick leather boots his feet might be rather unpleasant for Carter to examine. He grinned at the thought, as he dried his feet and put on the thick dry hose. He sighed with relief at having his feet warm, at least, then slid off the bed, stepping gingerly on to the sore leg. He could bear weight on the ball of his foot and he limped carefully over to the chair in front of the fireplace. One of the maids had evidently run upstairs to build up the fire, and Edward sat down in front of it, looking into the leaping flames.

He drew a deep breath and leaned his head back, closing his eyes. Unbidden, the governess came to his mind. He saw her face, a pale oval beneath her black bonnet, her eyes large and solemn, staring at him. He had been so convinced for just a moment that she was not real, that she had come from some far unearthly place. He had remembered all of Nellie's bedtime stories about fairies, both benign and evil, and briefly thought, in the advancing twilight, that he had finally come face to face with one.

Until he had leaned upon her, felt her warmth and substance against him. She had barely come to his shoulder. He smiled a little, thinking of her small hand resting against his waist.

He wondered if she had yet returned, had come back to his house. Her home now too, he supposed. That thought made him vaguely happy. He stood up, limping over to the bank of leaded glass windows overlooking the courtyard below. He leaned against the windowsill, weight balanced upon one foot, looking down on the empty expanse of stone, a lit lantern hanging by the front door. Was it lit for the governess' return? Or for John and Carter when they arrived? No matter, it illuminated the area of the front door and the steps leading up to it.

For some time he stood there, his thoughts wandering. He had dreaded coming home, but the low spirits that usually accompanied his return to Thornfield were surprisingly absent, supplanted now by his thoughts of the new inmate within.

Edward was looking out beyond the front of the house, wondering when John would be arriving with the surgeon, when a movement at the corner of his eye caught his attention. He turned and looked down at the courtyard again, noticing a small, dark-clad figure climbing the steps to the front door. He sighed to himself with a sudden feeling that was almost like relief, to think that the little governess had arrived safely back home.

"Well, it's not broken," Carter told him, looking up from where he had crouched down to examine and palpate his aching ankle.

"And I am obliged to pay you for coming to tell me that?" Edward retorted grumpily, "I knew that myself."

Carter laughed. He was a tall man, towering over Edward when they stood next to each other, with an erect carriage that spoke of many years in the Royal Navy. He was balding, and the firelight danced across his shiny scalp as he crouched before his patient, wrapping the ankle tightly with a length of cloth bandage.

"Well, now you have a professional opinion! Stay off the foot for a day or so, keep it elevated upon a hassock or stool, and if you have some ice in your icehouse, keep some of that at either side of the ankle. You will be right as rain in no time." He slapped Edward's knee and stood up, heading for the chair beside his host.

Edward gestured towards a corner cabinet, where a few bottles of liquor were kept, along with some glasses. "Help yourself to whatever you choose, and get me a glass while you are at it, if you would be so kind."

Carter crossed the room, moving his spectacles to the end of his nose and looking over the row of bottles, which were dusted as though someone drank from them every day. Selecting one, he poured a few fingers of amber liquid for himself and an equal amount for his patient.

Handing Edward the glass he asked, "Are you going to tell me what happened?"

Edward held the glass up, "My God, Carter, you are so stingy with the liquor you would think we were drinking yours instead of mine." He took a sip, "Ah, it was quite stupid, really. My horse got spooked, he reared, I slid from the saddle but my foot remained behind."

Carter stopped with the glass halfway to his lips, "The horse isn't hurt, is he? If he is, I would have gone to him first; your foot could have waited." His lips twitched with a suppressed smile.

Edward tried to give him a withering look but found himself chuckling, "No, Mesrour is fine, you will be happy to hear. Wretched beast."

Carter nodded his head before speaking again, "I feared, you see, that it was something to do with… " He broke off, raising his eyes to the ceiling.

"Oh, no, nothing like that," Edward reassured him. "I have only been back for two hours; I have not even been to the third storey yet. I assume all is well, or at least normal. I have not heard otherwise."

"And I have not been called here in some time," Carter told him, "You have a good enough nurse in Grace; she knows when a doctor is needed and when it is something she can do herself."

He took another sip of his drink, then asked his patient, "It is probably rude of me to ask while indulging in your liquor as I am, but have you ever known Mrs. Poole to... well... have a drink or two herself?"

Edward frowned, "No. I have never known her to drink, but then I see her so rarely. Why do you ask?"

"Well, it is probably nothing, but the last time I was summoned here, to see to a rash on my patient upstairs, I noticed Grace's eyes were somewhat red and she smelled of liquor. She seemed perfectly fine, and she was vigilant enough to catch the rash when it first appeared, allowing me to prescribe some ointment that took care of the problem. But to have a nurse who is fond of the drink... well, it could cause some... difficulties."

Edward shook his head, "Mrs. Fairfax has said nothing to me on the subject. I should perhaps ask her. I would be surprised... Grace's father was a drunk, a mean and cruel one, and she had her problems with him, before my father tossed him off the land. Before your time, but I would think Grace would avoid drink herself."

Carter shook his head, "One would think, but I have found that at times a child will, without meaning to, behave in exactly the way a parent has. Ah, perhaps I should not have said anything, but thought you should be aware."

Edward shrugged, "I will ask about it. I plan to go up to visit with Grace in the next day or so, see how her charge fares. I will see what I notice then."

For a few moments the men were silent, and then they began to talk about Edward's travels.

"I had to return; matters around Thornfield were too long left without its master's hand," Edward said, "But as soon as things are resolved, I plan to leave again. I am not sure where, so any suggestions are welcome." He smiled, but it was a grim one, and Carter wondered at the bitter edge in his patient's voice.

"I have always wished to visit India," Carter suggested. "I never made it there; I'm afraid in my travels with the Navy we never went anywhere so exotic. But if I could travel where I would like – if I did not have my household full of scamps – that is where I would go."

"Now that would truly be exotic, a wonder to behold," Edward replied, his smile larger and more genuine. "I cannot imagine, but then, I have not been anywhere but England and the Continent for years. Anything more might be too much for my cosmopolitan tastes. And you know you would not want to trade those boys of yours for all the travels in all the world."

"No, I would not," Carter replied. He stood up, "May I give you a refill?"

Later that night, knowing he could not endure Adèle's exultations at his return, or her disappointment that her gifts had not arrived at Thornfield with him, he had Mrs. Fairfax tell her that he would see her in the morning. He had allowed his housekeeper to send Leah up with a light meal to quiet the growling of his stomach, and had then prepared himself for bed. He would not see the governess again that night, of course, and was not sure if he was disappointed or not. He had planned to go to up to see Grace when he returned, but with his ankle paining him, he felt justified in putting off the encounter.

He was at last able to lie down to sleep, but his foot throbbed and true rest evaded him for a time. When he finally drifted off, his sleep was broken by vivid dreams of fairy rings and pale otherworldly girls with large searching eyes.

His first day back, unable to leave the house due to his injury and the snow that was now falling thickly on the ground outside, he had slept later than usual. He had been vaguely aware of John entering early to build up the fire and to lay out towels, water, and his clothes for the day. He had rolled over and gone back to sleep, tired from the tossing and turning he had done the night before.

He awoke at nine o'clock to limp painfully behind the screen, where he washed, grimacing at the vivid colours beginning to emblazon his swollen ankle. He replaced the wrappings Carter had applied the previous night and sat for a while with his foot elevated and surrounded by ice packs that Mary had fashioned and John had brought up to him. He had waved aside the offer of a meal served in his room and sat before the fire, thinking his own random thoughts.

From his position in the chair he could see into the long hall outside his door, and in mid-morning he was slightly surprised to hear the bright, high voice of Adèle chattering outside his door, followed by the quieter tones of the governess. The door was closed but for a crack, so he got up and limped across the floor. He opened the door a little wider allowing for better sound and an occasional glimpse of activity outside.

The snow fell steadily outside his window and Edward supposed that Adèle could not go outside to play that day. Had it been only she, he would have called for Sophie to take her to play elsewhere so he would not be disturbed. But the governess was with her and he wanted to see and hear more of her.

The governess. Miss Eyre. Miss Jane Eyre. He needed to think of her by her name rather than just "the governess."

He surprised himself. Why should he think of her at all? And yet he did think of her. Had been, he realized, since he had galloped away from her on the road to Hay.

"Miss Eyre," he whispered the name under his breath. A good English name. It sounded nice on his tongue after the years of pronouncing foreign names and speaking different languages.

He listened now to the gentle tones of Miss Eyre's voice. Hearing her, not being able to see her in front of him, he thought what a lovely voice she had. Quiet, low, calm. Even when she was correcting Adèle, she did not deviate from her controlled tones and yet there was a warmth in her voice that spoke of a natural kindness. He had certainly seen that yesterday. He knew that he had been cranky, surly. He had behaved badly to her and yet it did not seem to put her off, as he had put off many lately with his coldness and impatience. She had seemed so proper, so severe, until she had begun to talk and he saw her concern for a stranger, felt her steady support against him when he needed it.

He heard her kindness again, in her patience with Adèle. She responded gently to his ward's sometimes silly prattle, and played with her for an amount of time Edward would have found intolerable.

He sat listening, noting the slight accent he had not thought about when he heard her speak yesterday. There was a slight rolling of her tongue on certain letters that spoke of the Scots' influence on the north of England. Some vowels were pronounced with a very faint difference, some sounds held a little longer than one would hear in the clipped tones used in London. He could have listened to her all day and he was a little irritated when Sophie came along and Adèle went off with her.

Miss Eyre began to pace in the hall, and Edward could see her as she passed back and forth. She was quiet but not sulky, serious but not sullen. He enjoyed watching her thoughtful gaze as she passed by, and he was annoyed when Mrs. Fairfax's voice drifted up from downstairs, and he heard Miss Eyre make an offer of help. He willed his housekeeper to say no, that she needed no help, but Mrs. Fairfax said yes, that she would be obliged if Miss Eyre double-checked the figures of the household accounts before she had to turn them over the steward.

She left then, heading back to the first floor, and Edward was glad no one could read his mind, as he felt suddenly lonely and bereft just from Miss Eyre leaving the hall outside his room.

Chapter 28 - Jane

Very soon, you seemed to get used to me: I believe you felt the existence of sympathy between you and your grim and cross master, Jane; for it was astonishing to see how quickly a certain pleasant ease tranquillised your manner: snarl as I would, you showed no surprise, fear, annoyance, or displeasure at my moroseness; you watched me, and now and then smiled at me with a simple yet sagacious grace I cannot describe. I was at once content and stimulated with what I saw: I liked what I had seen and wished to see more.
Edward Rochester - Jane Eyre

February, 1836
He felt he was losing his mind, or what was left of it. How else to account for the fact that all he could think of was Miss Eyre?

Edward had always thought himself an intelligent enough man; one who sometimes made incredibly foolish decisions in the arena of love but was otherwise possessed of what Nellie would have called "good walking-about sense". But obviously that had failed him now, for his other senses were full of Adèle's ordinary little governess.

When he was anywhere in the house he was listening for her voice. He rarely heard it unless he called her to sit with him in the evenings, as he had on a few occasions. She was quiet and kept to her tasks, diligently teaching Adèle most of the day and the rest of the time going about her own business, helping the staff as she could or visiting with Mrs. Fairfax. She was an eager and willing worker – that, he could see – but not the type to put herself forward to make her Master notice her.

Yet when he closed his eyes at night, he could still hear her, could still recall the sweet tones of her voice, could remember her calm, well-thought-out answers to the subjects they discussed.

He did not often see her, for he was in and out of the house on business and she kept to the schoolroom or to the nursery. But occasionally they would meet each other on the stairs or in the hall and on those occasions, his heart would give a quick start. He was almost sure she would hear its uneven beat, see the quick leap of light in his eyes before he pushed such insane impulses back down within him, brushing past her with a brusque nod or a low muttered greeting to hide the feelings that her sudden appearance would ignite in his soul.

At times he would hear her before he saw her, talking to Adèle or to Mrs. Fairfax and when a few more steps brought them face to face he had already composed himself and was able to nod politely and bid her a "Good day, Miss Eyre," with a sober and dignified countenance.

There were a few times when he had been so busy, so occupied with business matters or with thoughts of Bertha that he had failed to notice her as they passed each other and it was a second or two before he would realize that he had inadvertently ignored her, never meaning to.

Whether he appeared rude, or preoccupied, or friendly, Miss Eyre's response was always the same – that of an employee to her employer. A small smile, a slight incline of the head, a murmured "Good day, Mr. Rochester." Always perfectly respectful, always completely correct. There was no sign that she gave him any thought beyond that of the master of the house, or indeed, no sign that she thought of him at all.

He was certain that she would be shocked if she realized how often he thought of her.

She fascinated him. He liked to watch people, to know how they thought and where they fit into the world. As he had gradually grown more disillusioned with the world and with its people, as he had started to withdraw into himself, he had gotten more skilled at observing the vast dichotomy between what people said and how they actually behaved.

Most of the time he could easily put people into categories, into the pigeonholes of his own thinking, as all people, perhaps, characterize others. All humans are seen through the prisms of another's experience and then treated accordingly. And Miss Eyre, or Jane, as he was increasingly thinking of her in his most private thoughts, was one who, by Edward's scope of experience, defied the easy labels he applied to others.

Her looks alone baffled him. Not even the most charitable could have called Miss Eyre beautiful, and only once or twice had Edward noted a turn of her features that could allow her to be called pretty. Had he passed her only once on the street, he would never have taken note of her. But after he had sat and talked to her, watched the play of the firelight across her pale features, or watched her eyes follow his face intently as he spoke, he found he did not want to stop looking at her.

The first time he had called her into his presence, his second night at Thornfield, she had talked to him with as sober and serious a mien as though she were sitting before a judge. But a few nights later, when she had watched Adèle open the gifts that had finally arrived with his trunk, and when they had talked together, she had smiled several times. Small, tentative smiles, but when they appeared, something had caught in Edward's chest – something tiny and fleeting, almost like a pain.

He did not seem to anger her, or annoy her, or discomfit her. At times he felt that she understood him, that she saw past his glowering face and into what was beneath his hardened shell.

But that was ridiculous and he knew it. He needed to stop thinking of Jane – Miss Eyre – and set about getting all his business at Thornfield and in Hay settled and done with. The sooner he resolved what he had come to resolve, the sooner he could leave Thornfield and could get back to his life, such as it was.

Late March 1836

Edward sat in his library, listening to the wind blowing outside. It was growing dark, with the chilling way nature has of hanging on to winter when spring wants to make its appearance. Sometimes the weather was showing signs of growing warmer, and when he walked out of doors in the bright March sunshine with Miss Eyre and Adèle, it was easy to believe that flowers and birds and warm weather were just a day or so away. But tonight, with the wind blowing fiercely and bursts of rain intermittently hitting the window, one could believe that winter would never leave them.

It had been beautiful earlier that day, when they had walked on the grounds. Adèle was beside herself with glee at having both her governess and her guardian outside with her, and she had run back and forth, chattering excitedly in the mixture of French and English to which she reverted when she was in any way stimulated and out of her routine. He had already impatiently shooed her away, and not very politely either, although he sensed that Miss Eyre did not approve when he was too harsh with Adèle. Easy for her to be patient – she was young. Wait until she was thirty-seven and had to put up with some chattering fool of a child.

He and Miss Eyre had strolled along the lifeless and gloomy site that in a month or so would show the splendor of the Thornfield gardens that John so lovingly tended with the help of an under-gardener. Edward had found himself talking, telling her about Céline. He had wanted to explain to her, as Adèle's governess, just how her pupil had come to live with him, how he had come to be responsible for her. Although he had meant to soften the story for her ears, before he realized it, he found himself telling her the entire tale – things he had never thought to tell to another... his love for Céline, her betrayal of him.

Miss Eyre had listened, and although Edward had glanced at her face for signs of disgust or repugnance, he saw none. Just the calm, steady pose she always adopted when she was listening to him, her face softening into compassion as he talked about Adèle. He had no doubt she understood his entire meaning as he told the story – the colour had come and gone in her delicate skin. But she did not indicate that she now found him hateful in her eyes.

She reminded him of a bird, when she sat listening to him. She would hold her head very still, her eyes fixed on his face, and when she was thinking, she would turn her head to the side, give a minute lift of her chin, a slight frown forming between her eyes. He had begun to notice she also did that when she did not entirely agree with him, and he had started to challenge her when he saw it, asking her to tell him how she felt. She would colour, and give a small laugh, and then she would quietly explain the way she saw the issue. He almost enjoyed seeing her make the gesture, for he knew it meant he had provoked discussion and thus prolonged her time with him.

But like a bird, she was quiet and alert, and at times he felt that at any moment she would suddenly spook and take flight. He supposed she had grown used to being extra vigilant at her school, fearful of the moment when she might do or say something forbidden. At those times, he wanted to clasp her to him, to hold her tightly, to stroke her hair and assure her that nothing she could do or say would lower her in his opinion, nor would ever make him want to hurt her.

Of course, he did no such thing. They had not touched except for that first day, when she had put her arm around his waist, allowed his arm about her shoulders, taken his weight upon her to help him when he had fallen. At times as they walked and talked, the uneven ground would make one of them step unsteadily, bumping them together by accident, but both were careful to right themselves and never touch unless they had to. At these times she was so close he could smell her scent, all soap and lavender sachet. It was so fresh, so totally clean, and at those moments he wanted to stand there and inhale deeply, although he knew that would make him look such a fool that she would surely know what he was doing.

He thought of all this as he sat behind his desk in the library that March evening. Thinking of her made his heart lurch, and yet he was overcome with a feeling of hopelessness about it all. He sighed, leaning back against the high leather chair behind the desk, where once his father had sat, questioning him about his life, his plans, his activities. He should burn the chair, and the desk too... but it was very good furniture, very expensive. He supposed if he were going to purge the Hall of his father's presence, he'd have to burn the whole damned place to the ground.

Mrs. Fairfax was bustling by, checking the rooms, and she glanced in to see him sitting there in the gloom.

"Why, Mr. Rochester, what are you doing sitting here in the dark?" she asked him, her hand to her heart as though he had jumped up and yelled "Boo." She came towards him, "I was wondering where you were; you barely ate dinner, and then you disappeared right afterwards and I did not know but whether you had gone out, although as I told Leah, surely he would not go out on such a night... "

For the love of God Almighty... Edward broke into her narrative, "Madame, if you are so worried for me, kindly show your concern in a tangible fashion by lighting a few lamps and telling Miss Eyre to come in to me. I would not mind hearing her read to me tonight, if she is not busy elsewhere. And a cup of tea would not go amiss."

Nothing made his housekeeper so happy as to have a task to please him, and she moved off to do his bidding, first lighting the lamps with great ceremony. He shook his head, casting his eyes to the ceiling. He sometimes felt guilty for how he felt about the old biddy, since she was his last real link with his mother, albeit by marriage. But at times she wearied him. No one had a better heart than she, but it was accompanied by such ado and such nervous mannerisms that she would try the patience of one more saintly than he. In other words, nearly everyone else on the earth.

When she was gone, he sighed, thinking again what a fool he was. Why call Miss Eyre to him, to what purpose? It did not matter how he enjoyed her company, how much hope and strength she seemed to give him when they were together, for sooner or later she must leave him, he to go to his lonely bed, she to go to hers.

There was no hope of her feeling as he did for her. She liked him, he was now sure, she enjoyed his company and conversation, she found him interesting. But the fondness he felt for her, the sympathy he felt between them... surely it was all on his part. He could be her father, nineteen years her senior and fathoms ahead of her in experience. Given her innocence, and his taint and corruption, surely there was no place that there could be a meeting?

He folded his arms upon the desk, dropped his head upon them. He was so tired, so lonely. His business here was completed, repairs were authorized for Thornfield and the funds released to Mr. King. The boundary disputes that had so bothered the village were now resolved to the best of the magistrates' abilities, and much more easily with the testimonies of all the landowners of the area. There was really no reason for him to be here, and yet he stayed. He could not bear the thought of leaving, in fact.

Not while she was here...

Worries pressed upon him. He had been several times to sit with Grace and to visit with her. He was afraid Mr. Carter had been correct. He had not smelled liquor upon Grace when they had sat together, but he had seen the signs. The roughness of her skin, the broken veins at the top of her cheeks, the hardened look of her face. She had had a pewter mug close by, half filled with the weak beer that Mary made and stored in the cellar. That wouldn't get Adèle tipsy, let alone Grace. But knowing her history, Edward was surprised she was drinking alcohol at all.

She had acted surprised and offended that he wanted to know about her drinking. She enjoyed a little porter, and when Madame was calm and sleeping, she was not above a drop of gin to quiet her and let her rest easy in her bed. Surely he did not begrudge her that? He had assured her he understood, and had complimented her upon her care of Bertha. He knew she did far more than many others could have done. And Mrs. Fairfax had frowned and shaken her head when he asked if there were any problems involving Grace. But he still worried.

A sound at the door made him look up with a scowl, but it was just Miss Eyre, standing in the doorway with a tea cup in her hand. She jumped a little when he sat up abruptly, but then smiled as his face softened to see her.

"You wanted me to come and read, sir?" she asked. She approached the desk, reaching out to hand him the cup, "Mrs. Fairfax asked me to bring this to you. She assured me that she had fixed it just as you like it."

He reached out to get the tea, and their fingers brushed as he took it. Just the touch of her fingers sent a tiny thrill of warmth through him, and he felt a weakness in his thighs. He was glad he was sitting down. And a moment later, he was glad he had his legs under the desk and his lap out of sight.

Miss Eyre stood there, and he saw the pink tinge to her cheeks. She looked around the library.

"What would you like me to read tonight, sir?" she asked, turning away from him.

He sipped the hot liquid, not trusting the steadiness of his voice. He wrapped his hands around the teacup, enjoying its warmth against his fingers. "You are not having any tea, Miss Eyre?"

"No, sir," she shook her head, still looking over his bookshelves, "I believe I have had enough tonight; I might never sleep as it is." She turned back to face him, her face composed.

He smiled, and then gestured towards a large black book that lay sideways on the shelf. "I would not mind the English history again, if it doesn't bore you into sleeping here and now."

She smiled again, and moved towards the book, hefting it with a slight intake of breath. Edward moved to set down his cup and help her, but she had already brought it over, laying it on the massive mahogany desk across from him and opening it, pulling up her chair and placing it close to the front of the desk. Edward sat down from the half-standing position he had assumed, glad that things in the vicinity of his lap had quieted somewhat in the interval since she had handed him his cup.

He was a little surprised and uncomfortable to have had such a reaction to her, but he supposed it was inevitable. It had been nearly three months since he had left Clara, and with his busy schedule, and his stress at being at Thornfield, there had been little chance to dwell upon his bodily impulses. He had not even laid a hand upon himself, something to which he had often resorted in times of feminine drought and famine. He smiled to himself at the thought, before hastily smothering it as Miss Eyre looked up at him briefly, and then looked back at the book and began to read. There had been times, he reflected, that he had resorted to that practice twice a day, just to kill the desire within him. But he had not even been bothered to make the effort since returning to Thornfield. He was just too tired, too worn out by loneliness and despair… too disheartened to even conjure up a fantasy lover.

He tried to leave such thoughts where they belonged, buried in their box deep within his heart. He concentrated on Miss Eyre's voice, so melodic and soothing. He watched her, watched her bent head over the book, the candlelight gleaming on her tidy hair. It was so smooth, it was as shiny as the top of his desk. He wished he could reach over and touch it, feel to see if it was as silky as it looked.

Her hands smoothed the pages of the book as she read, palms down. Her hands were pretty, very small and delicate, the fingers slim and surprisingly long for one so small. They looked boneless in the soft lamplight. Her fingernails were clean; small, white crescent moons on the tip of each finger, each one filed evenly as the one next to it.

He dreamed of those fingers stroking his cheek, delicately brushing over his lips. He thought of kissing the tip of each one, holding her warm palm against his cheek. *Jane, Jane,* he imagined himself whispering.

"That's enough, Jane," he said, rather more sharply than he intended. She looked up quickly, colour flooding her cheeks. "I beg your pardon, Miss Eyre."

Her face softened, her eyes meeting his. Her eyes appeared dark in the light of the lantern, although some times they looked as grey as the channel sea between England and the continent; other times as green as the English hills.

"I realize that I have never before called you by your Christian name," he said, taking a deep breath to steady his voice. "Do you mind it, such informality?"

She shook her head, "No, Mr. Rochester, I do not mind." She smoothed the pages of the book again, leaned back in her chair.

He was silent for a moment. "So, Jane, what do you think of our former monarch, throwing off the Church of Rome to marry his young lover? Do you feel he was justified in upturning all of history, all of morality and convention, for love?"

She paused, considering her words. "I have never desired to be separated from the Church of England. I was baptized there, my father was a clergyman there... "

"He was?" Edward asked. *Oh God, a parson's daughter... that is one you have not corrupted, Rochester, some small mercy up to now...* "I didn't know that."

"I was just a baby when he died; I did not know him." She sighed, "I comfort myself with the idea that he was most likely not like the Reverend Brocklehurst."

"Oh, surely not," Edward agreed. "Now, in your answer, which I rudely interrupted, I am sensing a 'but' to follow your words."

"But... if I think of the origin of the church, I find myself uncomfortable. So much liberty taken because of his position, so much... sin, with the excuse that he was avoiding sin by divorcing his first wife. Surely their marriage was legal, his actions just an excuse to be with his... illicit love." She shook her head, "I wonder how we can justify that, when we sit in our pews each Sunday."

"I wonder how we can justify everything," Edward answered. "For every good thing done in the name of God, surely there are countless sins and evils done as well?"

"Yes," Jane agreed. "And yet, when I get on my knees to pray, to speak to God, which He tells me I can come freely to do, I feel such comfort. I know He loves me, and feel that surely He does not condone such wrongs done in His name."

"Well, He certainly does not stop them," Edward retorted. "If He were bothered by the wrongs, why does He not come down and put a great and awe-inspiring end to them? Why does He not stop us, who are supposedly His children? When we are ready to do wrong, why does He not reach down a hand of love to curtail the wrongdoing? I would stop my child from doing wrong, were I to see it.

Does that mean that our wrongdoing is of little consequence to Him? It should be, in comparison to the great evil done all the time in His name."

She gave a soft laugh, "If you had a child, would you not want to see him decide for himself to avoid wrongdoing, based on what you had taught him? Or would you want to have to follow him around all his life, making the decisions for him?"

For a while they debated back and forth, about sin, about whether or not God could be trusted as a loving Father or merely worshipped in fear as a vengeful Deity. Both were smiling, refreshed by the dialogue, when the clock struck the hour of eleven, and Edward suddenly realized that he should perhaps allow her to retire to her room. He stood up to usher her out, smiling at her.

"I enjoyed our little debate," he said, gallantly holding his arm out as she left the library, "and now, good night, Jane."

"Good night, Mr. Rochester." She left the room.

He followed a few moments later, when he felt she had had time to get up the stairs and to her room. Once in his room, he stood for a long time, gazing at himself in the mirror, his smile suddenly gone, his customary scowl back in its place. He washed his face, cleaned his teeth, but could not resist pouring himself a brandy from the bottle over on the bookshelf across the room.

He finished his drink in a few gulps, pacing the floor. He unbuttoned his shirt, pulling it from his trousers, and lay down on the bed. He rubbed his eyes, staring up at the canopy over him. He felt strangely excited. He did not want to go to bed yet, just wanted to lie there and go over every word he and Jane had spoken to each other. He wanted to think of her eyes, her lovely smile. He felt the thrill of connection with her, the warmth of their communion.

Jane. He thought of her, her sweetness and compassion towards Adèle, her refusal to harshly judge his behaviour. Her humour, the depth of her thoughts... he closed his eyes, seeing her face in his mind, still thinking of her as he drifted off into the softest sleep.

Chapter 29 - At the Leas

He is gone to the Leas, Mr. Eshton's place, ten miles on the other side of Millcote. I believe there is quite a party assembled there; Lord Ingram, Sir George Lynn, Colonel Dent, and others.
...I should think he is very likely to stay a week or more: when these fine, fashionable people get together, they are so surrounded by elegance and gaiety, so well provided with all that can please and entertain, they are in no hurry to separate. Gentlemen especially are often in request on such occasions; and Mr. Rochester is so talented and so lively in society, that I believe he is a general favourite: the ladies are very fond of him...
Alice Fairfax - Jane Eyre

Edward paused at the bottom of the stairs to hastily button his shirt, tucking it into his trousers before once more picking up the candle and going up the steps. He entered the anteroom, his heart thumping, wondering what was hiding in every shadow. The room was dark but for a gleam of light through the door to the inner room which was, as he suspected, ajar.

A glow from the fireplace within cast a pale yellow light into the outer room, throwing a large, looming shadow of his shape onto the far wall.

Edward set the candle down on the table in the anteroom and went to the door, cautiously pushing it open, half expecting Bertha to be lurking behind it with some sort of weapon with which to fell him. He simultaneously registered the sights of both his wife and Grace Poole as he entered. Grace was slumped over the table by the fireplace, her head turned away from him. He could hear the sound of soft snoring. He ignored her for the present and looked over at Bertha, who was huddled in the far right corner of the room.

She was crouched down on all fours in her long white nightgown, her curtain of black hair hanging down over her face. He approached her, still remaining well back from her. He had not been this close to her in a long time. He stepped a little closer. The smell of smoke was thick in his nostrils, and he could not tell if it came from him or from her.

He stood for a moment, watching her. He could see faint grey strands threaded through her ebony hair, and against his will, pity flicked at his heart. He had come into the room filled with rage, but that strong emotion had faded away and now he felt only an empty sorrow.

Bertha was rocking back and forth, a tuneless hum sounding hoarsely in her throat. Edward spotted Grace's keys, the ring suspended from a short chain, on the floor near her.

He came slightly closer, never taking his eyes from her. He felt a stir of fear as he bent in a lightning-fast motion, snatching the keys from the floor and stepping back quickly. But whatever murderous rage had compelled Bertha to go on her fiery prowl had spent itself and she did not react to his presence.

He clutched the keys, feeling their cold metal bite into his hand. He stepped closer again. "Bertha," his voice was low, unsteady. She did not change her actions but continued to rock, still humming to herself.

"God damn it, Bertha, you could have killed me." She did not react. "Is that what you wanted? If I am killed, burned to death in my bed, do you know what will become of you? You will go to the asylum. Is that what you want, Bertha?"

Still no reaction, still she continued rocking and humming. His frustration grew. "Maybe they will not even bother with the asylum. Perhaps they will just hang you for a murderess." Bertha shifted for a moment, crouched down further, folding her arms around her knees, her head still down. In a moment she resumed her rocking.

Edward blew his breath out and turned on his heel, holding the keys in his clenched fist. He approached Grace, who was still slumped over at the table, her hands splayed out onto its surface. They were red, dry, and chapped, her fingers bony. He could still hear her, snoring lightly, air blown out between her lips each time she exhaled.

There was an earthenware mug in front of her and he picked it up and took a sniff. Gin. He wrinkled his nose, set the mug down with a thump, "Grace!" She murmured, turned her head.

"Grace!" He brought his fist down on the wood table. Grace jumped and sat up quickly, with a gasp. She looked around with a moment's confusion, then up at him, a stricken look passing over her face. Her eyes were swollen, a crease across one cheek from her sleeping position.

Edward picked up the mug, jerking his head in the direction of the outer room. "Come with me," he said harshly.

She followed him out of the room. He slammed the door, locking it with her keys. She looked down at herself, fingered the broken chain fastened to her belt. Her eyes met his, her look shamefaced. She sank into a chair by the table, rubbing her eyes with a shaky hand.

"Can you explain this?" Edward asked, once again thumping the mug down. Grace looked up at him, her eyes fearful. For a moment, Edward thought she looked like Pilot when he knew he had done something wrong.

"I was just awakened to find my bed hangings on fire!" he told her, his voice loud and steely with fresh anger, thinking again of what might have happened.

"Thank God Miss – thank God someone happened to be awake and heard the noise," he continued. "I could be dead right now, or wish I was. Is this why I pay you five times what I pay my other employees, so you can drink yourself into a stupor while my – while your patient prowls the house trying to murder people in their beds?" He stopped, out of breath, his chest heaving.

Grace swallowed audibly. Her voice was rough, "I am sorry, Mr. Rochester." She stopped, wiped her cheeks with her palms.

"How often does this happen?" Edward asked, his voice sounding desperate to his own ears. "How many times do you sleep while she roams freely?"

Grace was shaking her head. "This has never happened before, sir," she told him, her voice unsteady.

Edward pulled out the chair next to her, sank into it. He dropped his head into his hands, suddenly overwhelmed by his burden. For so long he had been able to nearly forget Bertha, knowing she was safe, knowing his household was safe from her.

Or rather, he could never forget her; she was always a tiny malignancy in the tissue of his entire life. He had been able to relegate her to the back of his mind, pretend he was free and had a possibility of a normal life. But at times, such as now, the realization came rushing over him, a fresh knowledge that it was not just Bertha who was locked away, trapped in Hell.

All his small, tentative hopes for the future, all the freshly awakened dreams he had dared to allow to touch his mind, were suddenly a mockery again. He wanted to break down and sob like a frustrated child. He would never be free of all this.

He lifted his head. "Grace, do you realize what could have happened? Not just to me – it is expected she would attack me. But to Mrs. Fairfax, to the servants? To my ward, Adèle? She is just eight years old. I plan to send her away to school, but she is not ready yet. She has to be here now. What becomes of her if that woman gets free again, burns the place down around us?"

He did not say it, but he thought it... Jane. He imagined her lying in her bed, her white nightgown showing up against a background of darkness, her shining hair spread out across her pillow. He imagined her surrounded by flames, stupefied by smoke, opening her eyes to a conflagration around her. She had come to him, saved his life. What if he could not keep her safe?

"I have been invited to a house party at the Eshtons," he told Grace. "How can I go? How can I leave, knowing you might be allowing your patient to get loose and wreak havoc in my household?"

Actually, Edward had not planned to go to the Leas. He said he could not be bothered, but in reality he did not want to leave Thornfield. For the first time in his life, he wanted to stay. Had found something here worth staying for.

Grace's eyes met his. Her face was red, her eyes tear-stained and bloodshot, but her face was rebellious.

"I have said I am sorry, sir," she told him. "It was an unfortunate mistake; it will not happen again."

Edward sighed. "Is the task too much for you?" he asked. "Do you need a rest, time off to see your son? Perhaps I expect too much from you. Just because you are free at times to mingle with the other inmates here, and do not have to spend every moment with Bertha, does not mean you do not need a larger society at times."

Grace's nostrils flared, "I have said I am fine, Mr. Rochester. I get out enough, here at the Hall, at church on Sunday. I have grown fond of my patient; I believe I understand her. She is tense, stirred up by the extra people in the house. She does not mean to harm anyone." Edward snorted.

Grace held out her hand, "Please give me the keys. I must return to Madame, she needs me." Edward's eyes searched hers for a moment. Hers were hard, betraying no emotion. He reached up and handed her the keys.

Grace turned away to head back into the inner chamber. Then she turned back. Her voice was flat. "Go to your house party, all will be well. But I hear things, *Master*. If you mean to bring a bride to Thornfield, you might perhaps think again."

Edward's breath caught. For a moment he could not think. "That is hardly your business," he finally said, his voice indignant. Grace did not reply, but turned her back on him and unlocked the door, slipping into the room without meeting his eyes again.

For a few minutes Edward stood outside the door to his room. He had put his dressing gown around Jane's shoulders, sat her down on one of his chairs by the fire and told her to stay there. He had been afraid Bertha was still at large in the house and had dreaded to think of Jane meeting her in the hall.

He did not know if Jane would be there in his room when he returned. He half hoped to see her, half dreaded it. What would he tell her? Surely she had picked up some whispered gossip in the nearly six months she had been resident here. What did she know? She would never stay here if she knew the truth.

He stood, hand on the doorknob, thinking of Jane as she had looked, standing in his room after saving his life. Her glossy brown hair had hung down, tumbling over her shoulders, hanging down her back. For a few minutes they had worked together to control the fire, and then he had led her over to the chair, feeling her tremble with cold and tension. Her eyes had been wide, staring up at his face, dropping down to stare at his body, rising back to his face again, a flush spreading over the flawless ivory skin of her cheeks. For the first time he remembered his shirt was gaping open, revealing his chest. He realized with a slight shock that she had never seen a man's naked chest before and a fresh sense of her innocence flooded over him, filled him with tenderness.

He took a deep breath and opened the door.

April, 1836

Edward stood in front of the mirror in the guest room at the Leas, where he had been for nearly a week now. His chin was lifted as he tied the cravat to his formal evening suit. He noticed a small nick on the underside of his jaw where he had cut himself shaving earlier, and he reached down to the dressing table for the handkerchief that was waiting to be tucked into his breast pocket. He dabbed at the small bloody spot, grimacing at the sting.

Most of the other men had brought their valets, but he had not. His only thought after he had sent Jane back to her room, and had himself spent the restless remainder of the night on the library sofa, had been to get away, to clear his head.

The Eshtons' home, the house party to which he had been invited, had been his spur-of-the-moment choice. Looking back, he wished he had thought to go instead to Ferndean, where he could have stayed in total peace and quiet, could have taken long walks in the woods with Pilot, and used the time to think and work out his dilemma.

He had risen that morning after the fire, hastily washing and dressing, and packing a small bag with necessities. He had found John, up early as he always was, and had instructed him to pack the smaller of his trunks, and to make sure he had several formal suits, to be shipped to the Leas later that day. He was eager to go, before he chanced to meet Jane. He was sure his heart would be written on his face, that she would just look at him and know his thoughts, that she would be able to tell what he had done, lying on the library sofa, thinking of her with passion and longing.

He was afraid she would look at him and know he loved her. He felt mad, out of control. He needed to get away from her, to think some rational thoughts. And so he had done the least rational thing of all, he had come to the Leas, where he would be expected to remain at least a fortnight, required to be a gay and gracious guest, adding laughter and entertainment to the activities of every day and night.

Now that he was here, he would rather have taken the straight razor and sliced off one of his fingers than go down to the assembled guests and play the charming bachelor. But like a fool he had galloped off the morning after the fire with little thought but to be away from Thornfield and the passion which he could no longer deny.

He finished tying the cravat, and straightened it, looking at himself full on in the mirror. He frowned at himself. There was not much he could do with himself, but he supposed he looked as acceptable as he could. His thick black hair curled over his forehead, and down onto his collar. He had been to the barber in Millcote two weeks before, but could have used another trip, as his hair grew so fast. He ran his fingers through it, trying to make it lie neatly. He reached down and picked up his pocket comb, straightening the part, smoothing his long sideburns. He tried to tame his thick dark brows. His eyes looked dark and glowering, his eyelashes cast shadows on his cheeks. Céline and Giacinta both had said they were envious of his thick black lashes.

He looked over at Pilot, fast asleep, lying on his back before the fire, all four paws in the air, reveling in the warmth. Edward smiled, "Look at you, you shameless thing. I have to get dressed up in this ridiculous suit while you lie there with your glory revealed to all." Pilot did not even wake up. His master made a mental note to himself to ask the butler to have someone go up and let the dog out in the course of the evening.

Edward reached over and picked up his jacket, putting it on. He folded the handkerchief, making sure the tiny blood drop didn't show, and put that in his breast pocket, putting the pocket comb away as well. He cupped his hands and breathed into them, checking his breath. He had cleaned his teeth with some of his tinned tooth powder, but wanted to be sure. He tucked a few anise drops into his pocket, the spicy candies a mask for the smell of liquor and cigars on his breath after dinner.

He wondered why he bothered. The only woman he wanted to impress was back at Thornfield, and God knows how his breath had smelled when he and Jane had stood so close together, that night after the fire. Probably like a distillery.

He was aware of the fact that he was being eyed by Lady Ingram and by her daughter Blanche as a prospective bridegroom. Since he had remained at Thornfield for over two months, and had mingled with the area's gentry, the rumours were growing that he was in the market for a bride. High time, the neighbours said, at thirty-five or thirty-six, or whatever age that young Rochester was now. All this time and never a bride brought home to the Hall. Even his father had been married younger than that. Edward could imagine their gossip.

Blanche had been standing in the foyer when he arrived at the Leas, dressed in her riding habit. The Ingrams had not been sure Rochester would attend, and when he was announced and entered to join the already-assembled guests in the drawing room that morning, Edward had caught the self-satisfied look on her face, had seen the triumphant glance she had exchanged with her mother. It had annoyed him right from the first and he was dreading the evenings ahead, but he had determinedly pushed Jane from his mind and had been as charming a guest as he could. He had ridden with Blanche during the day, played games in the drawing rooms in the afternoons, and joined in the conversations over the elaborate dinners each evening.

As he had suspected, he found himself thrown together with Blanche repeatedly, forced to partner with her at games, and dine by her at night. After brandy and cigars with the men in the dining room, the guests would all come together again and he and Miss Ingram were always prevailed upon to sing. He had not sung in such a long while that he felt totally inept each time, but no one was looking at him anyway. It was Blanche, with her elaborate costumes and loud theatrical trilling, that everyone was looking at. That she made sure of... he was just a backdrop, an accompaniment to her talent.

She was talented, and beautiful. No one could argue that. But just being near her irritated him and it was all he could do to smile, to respond in kind to her flirting, and to endure her tiresome discourses on subjects upon which she believed herself to be an expert.

He could not help comparing her with Jane. Edward could clearly see the two of them side-by-side in his mind, as if someone had painted a picture of each woman and had held the images up in front of him. He could see Blanche with her haughtiness and her pride, and what she believed were her sophisticated opinions. He could see Blanche's rudeness to her servants, her dismissive behaviour to the other guests now that she had focused on him, her disregard of even her mother's opinions.

She may have looked appealing, with her tall, voluptuous body, her lustrous black hair, her flashing black eyes, and her brilliant satins and velvets in all colours. But she left him as cold and unmoved as he could ever imagine being.

He then turned to the picture of Jane in his mind. He thought of her kindness to his servants, her affection for Mrs. Fairfax, her loving care of Adèle. He saw her sitting before him, quietly discussing whatever subject came up between them, listening by the hour as he talked, hungry as he was for someone intelligent to share ideas with. He was aware that sometimes he talked on and on, for the first time having someone worth talking to, but she always listened to him, smiling at him in her quiet way.

He thought of her simple grey dresses, so nondescript that they at first hid her looks and features, and eventually allowed them to stand out. He saw her clear white skin, her great, changeable eyes, her smooth shiny hair. All her inner beauty shone forth, and his breath caught in his chest when he thought of her. He longed to be with her again; he would have given anything for Blanche and everyone else to fade away, and for her to be there with him tonight. Just the two of them, talking into the night.

But Jane was at Thornfield, miles away from him. He wondered what she was doing that night. He wondered if she even thought of him, even paid much attention to the fact that he was gone.

And because of his stupidity, his hasty behaviour, he was stuck here at the Eshtons', dressed in his very best, prepared to go down and spend another stupefying evening as Blanche Ingram's prospective lackey-for-life. *What an appalling thought, a lifetime with that bitch.* He grimaced at himself in the mirror one last time, and squared his shoulders, heading out of the room for yet another elaborate dinner among the gentry.

Chapter 30 - The House Party

Edward F. Rochester
The Leas

Alice Fairfax
Thornfield Hall
12 April 1836

Mrs. Fairfax-
I have decided to host a house party at Thornfield. There will be a fairly large group of ladies and gentlemen, so sufficient accommodation for fifteen to twenty people will be needed, as well as rooms for their maids and valets. If you think you need more help at the Hall, please feel free to inquire at the taverns at Hay and in Millcote. I will leave it to your excellent planning skills to determine what is required. Please spare no expense in this endeavour, as I have not hosted any sort of party in years and feel a great need to repay any hospitality I have enjoyed from my neighbours.

I will be arriving, along with my guests, on the afternoon of 16 April, and we can confer then on the further needs of the Hall, as necessary to accommodate guests for at least a fortnight and perhaps longer.

E. F. Rochester

Edward felt a slight twinge of guilt as he waved the letter in the air to dry the ink. He knew that this would strain his housekeeper's strict routine and give her added stress. On the other hand, she had often said how long and lonely the months of his absence felt to the inhabitants of Thornfield. She might think again about expressing her feelings about desiring his presence at the Hall if this would be the result.

Ah, well, he reasoned, pulling his writing box towards him and selecting a stick of wax for the seal, he paid Mrs. Fairfax a decent amount for the job she did. Although she did it very well, most of the time the job consisted of bustling about giving directions to Leah and to the other maids, and planning menus for the cook to prepare. So while this would be increased work for her, it was merely what she did all the time, albeit on a larger scale. He was sure she could arrange everything, and she might even enjoy the added excitement.

Edward held the red wax stick over the candle flame and let a large drop of wax fall upon the folded paper that contained his message. He waited a moment and picked up the metal seal that bore a large "R". Pressing it to the half-dried wax, he affixed his initial, putting the seal back into its slot in the box and leaning back in his chair, waiting for the wax to harden completely.

He sighed, looking at the message, addressed and ready for one of Eshton's servants to carry to the Hall. Everyone had been quite excited to learn that he was thinking of hosting a party, Lady Ingram most of all. No doubt she believed he wished to impress Blanche by showing off Thornfield to its best advantage.

He shook his head, smiling to himself. If they only knew how far from the truth that was, those ladies would be furious. And they certainly would not attend his party.

He was not sure when he had formulated the idea of the party. He had spent his spare time thinking of Jane, of course, and at some point it had occurred to him that he wished she could see him surrounded by attractive ladies, being charming, making people laugh. It was a huge effort for him, taking all his patience, but he did it, and sometimes he wished Jane could see him in a different light than that of her dour, cranky, brooding employer.

At the time it did not occur to him to sit Jane down, to tell her honestly of his feelings, and to ask for hers. Accustomed as he was to the subtle maneuverings of society, the veiled truths hidden in a hundred tricks of social machination, he was not used to dealing in a straightforward manner with women, as he might have done with a man. He wasn't used to being honest with decent women, that is; God knows he had been frank enough with his mistresses.

Much later he would think of his actions towards Jane and would rue every blunder, every manipulation of Jane's emotions – and his own. The most honest of women, she would have reacted better had he dealt plainly with her. But she seemed so private, so guarded in her dealings with him, he simply was not sure how to proceed.

He had started off hiding the truth about Bertha from her – he knew he couldn't tell Jane about her, not if he wanted her to stay. The hiding of one fact led to the covering of other facts, and before he knew it, he was trapped in a web of his own dishonesty.

Speaking of dishonesty… every night he watched Blanche doing her level best to charm him, and couldn't help wondering how Jane would react if she could see it. Would it make her notice him? Would she be jealous, would it spur her on to a love for him, as jealousy had increased his love when he was first with Céline?

Would Jane even care? He had wished Jane could see Blanche's lavish attentions to him, then perhaps he could tell by the look on Jane's face how she felt about him. But he could not bring Blanche to Thornfield by herself, as that would be tantamount to a proposal of marriage. Thus the idea of the house party had evolved in his mind.

He owed his neighbours, certainly. For years during his short visits he had been treated to dinner after dinner at most of the homes of those present here. A large party, lasting weeks, would certainly repay all his social debts.

And if Jane noticed, if she grew jealous enough to raise her eyes to him, to perhaps want him a little for herself, so much the better. Certainly he wished to impress her, to show a little of the wealth that was his. He wanted her to be proud of him, proud to be part of his household. Proud that he was a man of means, of some standing in the area.

He did not know for certain that she cared a bit for him. He only wanted to increase her regard for him.

He had no idea that he would cause her quite so much pain.

Lady Ingram had gone into raptures when he made casual mention of his party idea, and as Eshton's was winding down, she began to focus upon his. In fact, she and Blanche told him so many times what he simply "must do", that one night he had turned to them with his best phony smile and said, "Perhaps the two of you should leave now and arrive at Thornfield ahead of the rest of the party, as I am sure my housekeeper could use your assistance in planning the affair."

Lady Ingram's brow had wrinkled with a fleeting look of annoyance at his sarcasm, but Blanche had let out a high peal of laughter.

One day when he had first taken notice of Jane, he had stood outside the schoolroom, sight unseen, watching her teach Adèle. She had accidentally scraped the chalk against the blackboard, resulting in a screeching sound that had made Adèle give a little shriek and clap her hands over her ears, and had made him cringe, feeling the sound clear down his spine.

That was what he felt every time he heard Blanche squeal with laughter.

"Mr. Rochester, you are such a tease!" she said loudly, making sure all eyes in the room were drawn to them. She snapped her fan shut and tapped him rather sharply on the arm, making him want to snatch it from her and use it to smack her on the side of her perfectly-coiffed head.

The mental picture amused him and he smiled. Blanche thought he was smiling at her and she drew closer to him, sliding her arm through his. He could feel her breast against his arm, could feel how she squeezed his arm to it, and more than once.

He felt a slight pull in his groin – well, he was only human. He let her pull him along to the side but was not really listening as she began to whisper something fairly rude about one of the other guests. He was feeling her as she rubbed her breast against his arm, and his mind was busy working.

He knew her sort, had seen enough of such women in his travels. She was the type to sidle up to a man, to rub herself against him, to cast lascivious glances, to promise a man all manner of delights until she had him where she wanted him, at which time she would withdraw all favours.

He knew what marriage would involve with someone like her. She might look lustily at him but he had no doubt that any husband of hers would have to beg for whatever bit of her body she cared to bestow. She would clamp her legs together, and when she opened them, all within would be tense and dry. She would probably time his performance, bringing the curtain down if it lasted too long.

She would measure the duration of their union with a clock, the frequency of their unions with a calendar. She would use her body as a reward, not letting him inside her unless he brought her a gift or otherwise earned the privilege. She would hate the feel of a man's cock, would not be able to look at it or touch it, and pity the poor delusional fool who thought he might ever get it into her mouth. She would probably like a man's mouth on her, though. Anything to feel powerful, to get a man on his knees.

She would allow him to beget heirs of her, because that would be part of her job, but when they were born, they would be hers. And when she had done her job, when she had provided an heir and perhaps a spare, and some daughters whom she would turn as spiteful and shallow as herself, she would cut him off and force him to either live without sexual union or seek comfort elsewhere.

Edward gently disengaged his arm from hers, using the excuse of a passing maid with drinks on a tray. He did not want one, but it provided an excuse to pull away from Blanche, who looked at him petulantly and tossed her black curls. She caught the eye of one of the Eshton girls, and moved away to speak to her.

Edward felt relief as he watched her go. He stood there, drink in hand. Thinking of the marriage bed, his thoughts turned to Jane. She would be passionate, she would not withhold anything from the man she loved.

He had felt her desire, standing there with her in his bedroom after the fire. He had seen her flushed cheeks, her trembling limbs, had felt that she was stirred and aroused by his nearness. He had seen more heart and more ardor from her in those few minutes than he had seen in Blanche in eight years.

When Jane loved someone, she would love him completely.

And with a pain that was almost physical, one that seized him at his heart, he realized how much he wanted to be that someone.

Three days later, Edward rode within sight of his home, Pilot running excitedly alongside him, barking like a maniac, and Blanche riding beside him in her elaborate habit and plumed hat. He had to admit that she was a good rider; in that alone they were well-matched. She could handle a horse well, and she apparently saved any softness and decent treatment she was capable of for her mount, for at least she was good to her horse.

Edward was in good spirits, but it was not because of the ride. He was surprisingly happy to be home, his heart pounding at the thought of seeing Jane again. He and Blanche rode up to the front entrance, where he quickly dismounted, handing the reins to the groom, who had evidently been watching, for he had hurried out before their horses had even stopped.

Edward turned to Blanche, to help her dismount. She held out her gloved hands imperiously, and before the groom could bring the mounting block to her, she had slid from her saddle, forcing Edward to catch her about the waist. He felt annoyed, but forced himself to smile at her, turning as he noticed Mrs. Fairfax coming out of the door, raising her voice in greetings.

The carriages had begun to arrive, and the courtyard grew noisy with horses' hooves and the crunch of wheels upon the stone. Edward cast a quick glance around, seeing John and Leah, seeing the faces of some of the maids at the window, but he saw no sign of Jane. A sudden flash of panic seized him. He had been gone for three weeks, and had had no word of her, sent no message to her. What if she had gone? Surely Mrs. Fairfax would have written to him, but what if she was saving the news? It would be ironic if he had set up this entire party, partly with her in mind, only to find that she had quit and left Thornfield Hall two weeks before.

He had seen Blanche into the house, played the gracious host and ushered the other guests into the foyer. He knew Mrs. Fairfax was anxious to direct the gentlemen and ladies to their rooms, so they could prepare for the dinner that he could smell even now, but he took a moment to pull her aside.

"How do you do, Mrs. Fairfax?" he greeted her. "I see that you have prepared the Hall in just the manner I expected, and I thank you."

"Oh, you are most welcome, Mr. Rochester. It was a bit of work, cleaning and preparing, for as you know we are not used to such gay society here. But the entire household pitched in admirably, and as you instructed, we were able to hire several additional hands from the George Inn at Millcote, and all was well."

Edward cast about in his mind for some way to mention Jane, but before he could fashion a decent excuse, Mrs. Fairfax herself provided the means.

"Oh, sir, Adèle has been beside herself with glee all day today, so excited for your return and so eager to see the ladies in their fine apparel. Miss Eyre has been as busy as the rest of us, preparing for the guests, and she has had some job keeping Adèle in check. The child has been granted a short holiday from her work, and my, if you could see her... "

The housekeeper's voice went on, but all Edward could concentrate on was a feeling of relief. Jane was still here. He would see her soon.

He broke into Mrs. Fairfax's raptures, "It is late tonight, and by the time we are finished with dinner, it will be Adèle's bedtime. But tomorrow we will eat earlier and we will gather in the drawing room. At that time she may come in to meet the ladies and to see them arrayed in all their finery. Miss Eyre may bring her, and stay there with her."

"Oh, Mr. Rochester, I do not know how Miss Eyre will feel about that; poor dear, she is quite unused to company, and has no great experience with fine society. I fear she will be made uncomfortable. Perhaps Adèle's nurse can bring her."

"No, I wish Miss Eyre to be there; whenever Adèle is present, I wish Miss Eyre to accompany her. And if she will not come, I will go to her chamber and fetch her myself."

That evening, Edward stood in his finery, holding a glass and surrounded by his guests. He could not see Jane, but he had heard the high pitched tones of Adèle, up in the gallery. He could hear urgent whispering along with Adèle's voice, and he knew it was Jane. He did not look up, never once did he see her, but he could feel her presence, could feel her eyes upon him. He knew she was there, and it made him feel complete.

The next day dawned clear and bright, the sky a lovely blue, fluffy white clouds scudding across the sky. The entire party set off for a high, flat spot a mile or so off, where there was a view of the entire valley. By carriage, and by horseback, they left for a picnic. Spirits were high and all was well with the guests.

Edward had slept poorly, knowing that for the first time in three weeks, he slept down the hall from Jane. He did not have the hot aching desire he had had after the fire, the strong wish that he could go to her, kiss her and touch her. This night, he merely thought of her with tenderness, imagining her in quiet slumber beneath her sheets. He saw her turn and stretch, imagined her sighs and the sweet repose of her face. He wished he could sneak into her bedroom, just to stand over her bed and watch her as she slept.

He endured the day, impatient for the evening, when he would see her. The picnic seemed to drag on; in spite of the beauty of the day, he wished it would be evening.

The party returned to Thornfield in the late afternoon; there was no sign of Jane or of Adèle, and Edward assumed they were in the schoolroom. Like the rest of his guests, Edward went to his room to rest. He wanted to be fresh that night. He lay on his bed and sank quickly into a sleep that lasted more than two hours. He was surprised to have slept so well, so dreamlessly, and he felt better when he awoke, felt better able to handle the evening ahead.

He took care with his appearance that night, his hair neatly combed, his face clean-shaven. He knew that evening wear suited him, and hoped Jane would agree.

His stomach was in a knot and he picked at his food, although it was all very good. He sent compliments in to Mary and to her helpers, and wished he could do it justice. Then the ladies left the room, to go to the drawing room while the men lingered, and smoked. The conversation rose and fell about him, but he sat silently, waiting, waiting.

And then they were rising, leaving the room. He would see her soon. He entered the drawing room in a group with several other men, all talking. He answered as was necessary, but his mind was not on them. He forced himself not to look around, his neck was almost sore with the effort not to turn and look for her.

He could hear the urgent tones of Adèle, and Jane's equally urgent whispered replies. He could see her now, out of the corner of his eye. She was looking around at the guests, her face composed, a book on her lap.

And then he saw her watching him. He was talking to the Eshton girls, and he wanted nothing more than to look over at her, but he did not. He forced himself to look at his companions, to smile. He could feel Jane's eyes on him. And it flooded his soul with warmth and gladness. How he wished it were just the two of them, alone in this room.

The evening wore on; there was lively conversation, laughter, and games were played in different areas of the room. Adèle mingled with the guests, who doted on her and asked questions. All except Blanche, who at first commented upon her, but when Adèle seemed to be getting too much notice, quickly revealed her resentment. She stepped forward, commanded his attention, and before he knew it, the conversation had turned to governesses.

He listened to the catty remarks of Blanche and her mother about the various governesses they had known. Their words were petty, vicious, and it was all he could do not to stand up and roar at the two harpies to shut their damned mouths unless they could speak civilly. But he did not. He did not look at how Jane was taking all this, but he was angry on her behalf.

He did not even reply when Lady Ingram singled Jane out personally, although he could have cheerfully shaken his guest by the shoulders until her teeth rattled in her brainless head. He forced himself to stand by, his expression bland, his posture casual. He could see Jane with his peripheral vision, and she was sitting, head down. She gave no indication she heard the mocking words of the so-called ladies, but Edward was sure she heard them; she was not deaf, after all.

Mercifully, the topic ended, and he and Blanche were called upon to sing. He did not even want to stand near the spiteful little bitch, but he made himself smile, take his place by the piano, sing the song that Blanche chose for them.

It was a love song, and no doubt Blanche felt that their voices blending in song would inspire him to heights of passion for her. The more fool she! Edward sang and did indeed raise his voice with spirit and feeling, but it was not Blanche he thought of.

He was singing to Jane.

Can you hear me? Listen to these words, can you tell I sing them to you? He glanced over at her, looked over her and on to something else, as though he were just casually perusing the room. She was watching him intently, her lips parted, her eyes wide. He wanted to look at her, sing directly to her.

But he did not, and when the song was done, he accepted the compliments, smiled graciously, and moved to join his other guests as the talk again rose around them.

It was then that he saw Jane get up and slip quietly from the room.

"Excuse me," he said to Dent and Eshton, to whom he had been listening as he stood near them. He followed Jane, came upon her in the corridor, as she bent to tie the lace on her shoe. She stood up quickly, facing him. Her face was flushed.

He was not sure his voice would be steady. "How do you do, Jane?"

"Very well, sir." Her voice was quiet, subdued. She did not smile.

He burst out, "Why did you not come up to greet me when I came in?"

She looked startled, and for a moment, a bit offended. His heart leaped at her spirit. "You seemed engaged with your guests; I did not want to disturb you."

He asked her what she had been doing, if she had fared well after the fire. She answered quietly, the momentary flash of indignation gone. He came closer to her, looking at her face. It may have been a trick of the flickering candlelight, but he could see moisture in her eyes.

"Come back to the drawing room, there is more to come, it is early."

She shook her head, her face lowered, "I am tired, sir."

"And depressed?" he asked her, hoping she would reveal herself to him. "Tell me, Jane, what is wrong?"

Head still lowered, she shook it again, "I am not depressed, sir."

Watching her intently, he saw it then. A tiny drop of moisture, dropping onto the stone floor beneath her feet. A flood of love and compassion rushed over him. He wanted to pull her to him, kiss her hair, her forehead, her lips. Lay her head against his heart. Feel her warmth against him, just as he had that first day they had met.

He spoke, forcing his voice to sound stern, "Well, I suppose I can excuse you tonight. If I had more time, I would make you stay, find out what all this is about, how you feel. Go to bed, but from now on, I want to see you in the drawing room each night; it is my wish."

She nodded, head still lowered.

"Get Sophie, send her back here for Adèle," he said, "And good night, my —" He caught himself, bit his lip; he had nearly slipped. He drew in a breath, was silent. She looked up at him quickly, then looked down again and turned away, swiping at her cheek with the edge of a finger. He stood completely still, watching her go.

Good night, my love.

Chapter 31 - Gypsies and Uninvited Guests

April, 1836

The days of the Thornfield house party dragged on, for Edward at least. All the guests seemed to be having a wonderful time, and there were plenty of activities for all to do. The food, prepared by Mary and her helpers, was delicious and compliments flowed freely, as did an abundance of fine liquor. Edward spared no expense on this gathering, his first real expression of hospitality in years. It was a shame that the only person who did not seem to be enjoying the party was the host himself.

Edward was tired of people, weary of having to play the genial host. He looked around at everyone and realized how little he had in common with most of them. He liked a few very much. Eshton had always been, if not a true friend, more than an acquaintance. He liked to discuss history and politics with Colonel Dent, for all that the old fellow had a tendency to be a bit pompous at times. Some of the older women were true ladies, gentle and kind. They were decent to his staff, showered attention upon Adèle.

Then there was Blanche, his supposed love interest. He had, since her late teens, noticed her tendency towards hauteur and self-importance. When he had thought about it at all, he had thought that perhaps she was just young, that a few years in society would make her more humble.

Now he was convinced that she was a mean and petty person, enjoying whatever small cruelties she could find to inflict. She was rude to those who waited upon her, both his employees and her own. She had already shown her utter contempt towards Jane, who was quickly becoming the most precious person in Edward's world, and it had not taken him long to see how she reacted to Adèle.

Her first brief flash of interest in his ward had been fleeting, designed to make her look kind and concerned. But Edward, who occupied his time watching both Jane and Blanche, mostly because the contrast so fascinated him, saw it all.

Adèle was so excited to be included among the fine ladies, and her guardian, who himself sometimes found her presence annoying, was nevertheless appreciative of those who would take notice of her and show her kindness. But Blanche could not be bothered, looking at her with irritation and shooing her away at every turn. Blanche took care not to do this in his presence, or so she thought. When they were together, she was as sweet as sugar to the small girl. But if she thought Edward was out of earshot or could not see, her latent cruelties came out.

She had not reckoned upon his powers of observation. She thought she had him where she wanted him, at her service, blinded with affection. Had she known how he really felt, it would have made her blood run cold within her.

She was not the only one who thought that his devotion to Blanche was secured and definite. It seemed all of those assembled assumed that her presence at his side was just the first step towards her becoming Mrs. Rochester, and the lady of Thornfield Hall.

Edward looked around at Blanche, and at the other assembled guests, who would have been surprised to know how he really felt about her.

Jane continued to come to the drawing room every evening, dressed in her grey silk dress, her hair neatly arranged, her face composed. It hurt Edward's heart to see her, so drab, so obviously wearing her best. The assembled ladies wore different gowns every night, their satins and velvets brilliantly coloured, a beautiful swirl of different shades and styles. He wished he could see Jane in some of these dresses, her shiny chestnut hair curled and arranged. She would put these women to shame.

She was sombre, hanging back, never bringing herself forward except to control Adèle. She was not sulky, and when spoken to she responded in a quiet, respectful manner. Edward thought she looked a little more pale every night, and although she moved with her usual quiet grace and upright posture, she seemed to be shrinking into herself a little every day.

He caught her at times, watching him, and the look on her face would have thrilled him a week or so ago. She felt something for him, he was sure of it. But she was still so calm, and while a fleeting glance of desperate longing might move across her features, they soon arranged themselves again into their usual composure. She did not approach him; they rarely spoke except for the most basic pleasantries. The walks, the frank, intimate talks of just a month ago, seemed never to have happened.

This party was causing her pain, he could tell. And he had never meant for that to happen.

He wished he could know exactly how she felt. He wished he could get some glimpse into her heart.

By the end of April, the weather was as beautiful as anyone could have wished. The party had been going on for a fortnight, and every day the activities involved more and more time outside.

One day the plans had been in place for the entire group to visit a gypsy camp nearby. The ladies were eager for their fortunes to be told, and to see how the gypsies lived. But the day of the planned excursion dawned cloudy and dark, and by breakfast time rain had begun to fall, casting a pall over the group and forcing the cancellation of their outing.

Edward had made light of their disappointment. "Now then, it is not the end of the world. If today and the next are rainy, surely the sun will be out soon and we can plan another trip then. We would not want to venture into the woods and to the camp until the ground is completely dry; we would not want to ruin the ladies' shoes. Rest in front of the fires, catch up on your reading, and think up some good ideas for another game of charades – I quite enjoyed that the other night."

He wiped his mouth with his napkin, and pushed back from the long dining room table. "I regret that today I must go out of town to handle some long-neglected business, but I trust that you can all entertain yourselves whilst I am away, and tonight I expect the ladies to have come up with some exciting activities to be played later." He bowed to his assembled guests and strode from the dining room.

He had John fetch his outer wraps, and whistled for Pilot, before going outside to mount Mesrour, who was saddled and standing outside, his reins held by a wet and miserable-looking stableboy.

Edward started towards the road, but once away from the sight of anyone watching from the house, took a quick detour and began to head across one of his fields. He was chuckling to himself. He had an elaborate plan, several days in the making, and he was looking forward to seeing it carried out.

Unbeknownst to his guests, Edward had already had some contact with the gypsies at the camp. They were gathered on Thornfield land, at the very outskirts. It was a heavy wood, relatively unused. Certainly Edward himself had no occasion to venture out there, and had not since he and Grace had played and explored there when they were children.

One of his tenants, who claimed to be merely taking a long walk through the forest, but was most likely poaching, Edward assumed, had come to him when he had first returned from Eshton's to tell him that a group of gypsies had made an encampment upon his property.

Edward, after all his travels around Europe, was not entirely unfamiliar with gypsies and their ways. He neither hated nor feared them, but neither did he want them walking off with his property. He had decided to pay them a visit and speak to them about their reasons for camping nearby.

He approached the camp on Mesrour, but dismounted as he came within sight of the people living there. He walked up to those assembled, gathered in knots of twos and threes. He could see by the hostile looks on their faces that they expected to be thrown out of their camp.

Edward looked around, smelling the smoke from several fires, hearing the cries of babies and small children. He glanced at the inhabitants, and then introduced himself, directing his remarks to the oldest woman there, as he would have been expected to do in eastern Europe. The woman had appeared amused, and had called over to a man standing nearby. He was a big, rough-looking man of about sixty, who looked Edward in the eyes, apparently uncowed.

"My name is Edward Rochester. I own these lands," Edward told him. "I have no objection to your stopping here, but thought I should come and determine your intentions."

"Intentions?" the burly man raised his eyebrows. "No intentions. Just a stop on our way, no mischief meant."

He had offered Edward a seat, and a mug of ale, and Edward's willingness to sit down and take the hospitality of the camp's inhabitants went a long way towards setting a more friendly tone to the visit.

"These woods are long unused," the land's owner told them. "Camp here, use the wood, hunt if you will. How many are you?"

"About twenty, not counting babes in arms," their leader said.

"Not enough to bother a thing in this wood," Edward told him. "But you know who will bear the blame if my neighbours find their homes disturbed or their possessions lost or stolen. And I will bear the blame as well, for allowing you to rest here."

"Aye," the leader nodded, "but we mean no harm. Just resting here, on our way back up north now that the winter's over. Just to sell a few trinkets, fix some things on our travels. We'll help harvest the hops, when the time comes. The ladies do a little fortune-telling at fairs and on Market Days."

"And pick a few pockets?" Edward asked dryly.

"If some of the children lift a coin or two from those who should be paying closer attention, I never hear about it," the leader told him.

He gestured to a woman standing nearby, stirring something in a pot over a fire, "My lady here will tell your fortune, if you'd like. She has the Gift, the sight." The woman nodded, smiling at him.

Edward had demurred with a laugh, "Thank you kindly, Madame, but I think it's best that I do not know what the future brings for me."

They had parted on friendly terms, and several days ago Edward had ridden over to speak to the woman again and ask if she would be interested in coming to Thornfield to tell the fortunes of the assembled guests.

"I will give you a purse myself, and then you can ask a coin or two from those whose fortunes you tell. I believe they will enjoy themselves; they are talking of coming to visit your encampment themselves."

The woman was named Bridie Lovell, and it was her husband Mike who was the leader of their small band. They planned to join their larger group in Manchester, before heading back down south to work some of the farms.

"I will pretend to have some business out of town, and will come to get you on the appointed day," Edward had told her. "I have prepared the room outside the library for you to set up your operation. We will sneak in another way, you can sit in front of the fire, and I will wait behind the screen to hear what the guests have to say. It should be quite profitable for you and, I hope, educational for me."

Edward met Mrs. Lovell as planned, and brought her the long way around, approaching Thornfield the back way. He showed her the kitchen door and told her to present herself there and not take no for an answer.

"Give me fifteen minutes' head start, to sneak my horse and dog to the stables and bribe the stableboys into silence, then I will head in and take my place behind the screen. I will also stop in the kitchen and arrange for a lunch to be brought to us."

Edward had done just that: had hurriedly taken Mesrour into the stable, given the boys a coin each to watch the horse and Pilot and keep them out of sight. He then sneaked through a side door, and into the kitchen, pulling Mary aside to tell her he was playing a trick on his guests, and asking her to bring a basket of cold food into the library anteroom at noon precisely. He swore her to secrecy and headed down a back corridor, watching carefully to make sure he did not run into anyone and give away his presence.

He took his place behind the screen in the room outside the library, sitting down in a comfortable chair he had secreted there for this very purpose. He could see through a fold in the screen, to the seat in front of the fortune-teller. He smiled at how well everything was going so far. He was glad he had gotten such a long head start, and he had dashed behind the stable to make sure he emptied his bladder first. It might be a long, uncomfortable day of listening to fortunes if he had forgotten that little detail.

Now ready, he sat quietly to wait for Mrs. Lovell. He glanced at his pocket watch. It was a quarter past ten o'clock in the morning. A few fortunes, a quick lunch for the two of them, and then he could sneak out after she left, to ride back around the fields and come back up to the house.

He did not care about most of the fortunes. It was immaterial to him what dreams the Eshton girls and Mary Ingram cherished within their bosoms. But he had a special purpose for Blanche's presence here, if she did not consider herself too high and mighty to sit and listen to a gypsy.

And Jane... his heart beat within him to think of what Jane might say to this woman. Would she mention him? Would she speak of him as part of her dream for her future? In a moment he scoffed at himself. Jane was far too sensible to give much sway to the idea of knowing the future. But the possibility of knowing something of what was in her mind...

He heard the door open, heard Bridie speaking to his servant Sam. Poor Sam, who had been working for Thornfield since Edward's father was a boy, was probably completely befuddled by the presence of the gypsy. He was the most protective and loyal of servants, although with his advanced age and state of feebleness, he could not have defended Edward from a hostile Adèle. He sounded a bit distressed as he showed Mrs. Lovell into the room.

"Wait here, Madame." Edward heard the quaver in Sam's voice. "I tell you this is most irregular; if the Master were here he would never allow you to be present. It is only because the ladies want you here that I have let you in. If any items come up missing, you will have me to answer to, make no mistake about that."

"Rest easy in your head, old man," Bridie said, "I have no interest in making off with a speck of dust from this house. I heard of a party at this estate, that is all, and thought there might be some of the quality as wanted to know their futures. If your Master returns, I'll tell his too, and won't charge him. Now, send in any of the single women who are present; I want to talk to them."

Edward had told her to say that, and she had looked at him askance. "If you are looking for a wife, sir, there are easier ways to go about it."

He had laughed, "No, Mrs. Lovell, no wife. Actually, I am hoping to discourage at least one who is seeing herself in that position."

As if on cue while he was thinking about their exchange, in walked Blanche Ingram. With her usual haughty air she entered the room, looking over Bridie Lovell as though viewing some exhibit in a menagerie. She sniffed, her nose in the air, and sat down in the chair. Edward had given Bridie a description of Blanche, and told her what to say, and the gypsy sat erect in her chair and looked Blanche over with equal dignity.

"You are Miss Ingram, I think," she said. Edward could only see the side of her face, but she appeared to be staring intently at Blanche's face. She held out her hand, "Cross my palm, if you please."

Blanche snorted, and tossed her head, "So far this is like a scene from a very badly written novel. Can you not be more original?"

Bridie took Blanche's hand in hers, none too gently. She looked at her palm for a moment, turning her hand this way and that. She dropped it, and spoke.

"You have come to this house with ideas, and I am sorry to be the one to tell you that your ideas will never come to fruition."

Blanche blinked. "I beg your pardon?" she replied.

"You have come to this party with the hopes of snaring for yourself the owner of this home, I believe." Bridie's already heavy northern accent was growing more pronounced, she was warming to her subject. Edward leaned forward, his eyes on Blanche.

"You and your mother both, I believe, have high hopes of your being the next mistress of this home. You believe that you and Mr. ... what is his name? Rochester? ... that you and this Rochester will do very well together. And mayhap you will, if you can love a man who is going down in the world."

Blanche started suddenly, "Down in the world?" She sat up straight, her dark eyes flew open wide, and she blinked again, several times.

"Ah, yes, Miss," Bridie said, her voice dropping to a confidential whisper, "The poor man. Rich his family was, and rich was he, but a few bad investments have had their way with this fortune. Back when old Mr. Rochester died, the worth of the family was upwards of sixty thousand pounds, and in the years that followed, the fortune dwindled until now it is barely twenty. And with the bills, and the creditors baying at his feet like hounds, in a few years there will be hardly anything at all."

Blanche blinked over and over again, until Edward fancied she was nearly ready to create her own air current in the room. He put his hand over his mouth, smothering a grin as he watched her.

"You are lying," Blanche said, after a few sputtering attempts at speech, "This party – no expense has been spared; he lives well, there has been no hint of any financial problems… "

"He hides it well, poor man," Bridie shook her head, "but he knows he is on his way down, and he is spending it while he has it. And he cannot help it, but his habits do not help."

Blanche looked startled. Blink, blink. "Habits?" her voice sounded a bit high and nervous.

Bridie looked about the room, leaned closer to Blanche, "He gambles a little, but has neither skill nor luck."

Blanche could not speak. She swallowed, shook her head.

"But don't you worry," Bridie said, reaching over to pat her hand. "What with the drinking, he often cannot sober up enough to find a game in which to put his money."

"Drinking?" Blanche said. "But I have seen Mr. Rochester on many a social occasion! He holds his liquor well, in fact, only drinks a little."

"Many men have such a habit," Bridie told her. "They hold their liquor well for a while, and then in times of anxiety… " she clapped her hands together, "they drink themselves silly, completely fall apart. He is fine now, but when this party is over, it's face-down in the chamber pot he'll be."

Blanche had given up trying to speak. She looked around the room as if waiting for someone to rescue her, or tell her that this was some enormous joke.

"But if you love him… " Bridie said, "I think all will be well. There will be naught but a little cottage left to live in, but if there is love there, all will be well. Of course, the drink and the loss of his money have led to other problems, but do not worry, love. You will not be able to afford children anyhow."

"What?" Blanche said.

"Poor Mr. Rochester," Bridie shook her head. "The man cannot perform. Many women have tried, even lovelier than you. All fruitless. But that way you will not be having him bother you day and night, always after you. It is a small blessing in a life that will otherwise be very difficult. But love will light the way."

Edward was by now biting the side of his hand to keep from making any noise. The look on Blanche's face alone was worth every shilling he was paying Bridie. His shoulders shook, and as Blanche got up and swept haughtily out of the room, slamming the door behind her, he snorted with laughter behind the screen. He came out from behind it, laughing out loud.

"There," Bridie said, "I doubt you'll have much interest from that little baggage. She is probably packing her trunk even as we speak." Mrs. Lovell's face took on a mischievous air. She put her hand to her cheek. "Oh, my, she WAS the one you wanted to discourage, wasn't she?"

"Yes, thank God," Edward said, still laughing. He wiped tears from his eyes. "Although did you have to go quite so far? My lack of manhood will be common knowledge in the house by tomorrow."

"No, sir," Mrs. Lovell said, smiling herself, "she'll be too busy frantically wondering how she can extricate herself from your great love."

Mary Ingram and the two Eshton girls came in together, all holding hands as though they were going to the scaffold. Tiresome things. Edward sat behind the screen, arms folded, rigid with boredom while Bridie spent a tedious hour going over their fortunes. Edward had told her everything he knew to tell her about them, not much, but enough to make the girls wide-eyed with wonder and to leave the room exclaiming over her ability.

It was now nearly noon, and soon it would be time for lunch. There was only Jane left, and Edward knew that she would still be in the schoolroom with Adèle. They would come out for lunch at about a quarter to one, he knew from experience, and then he would have Bridie send Sam for Jane. He could not wait.

"What about you, Mr. Rochester?" Bridie broke into his thoughts. "Do you not want to know your future? I make a joke here, and have done some play-acting, but I do see some things. It is a Gift indeed, most of the time."

"What about you?" Edward said with curiosity. "Do you know what is going to happen to you? Does that not frighten you?"

"I know little things," Bridie told him. "I knew I would marry Mike, and I knew each time I was quickened with one of my children right when it happened. But I did not know if they would be boys or girls, or if they would survive, which two of them did not. And if there is someone I love, I cannot see the future for them, for good or ill. It is better that way, I could not live if I knew what would happen to them."

Edward sat down with a shrug. It could not hurt. Perhaps it would be good news. And if it were not, perhaps he might find some way to prevent it from happening.

Mrs. Lovell leaned forward and reached for his left hand. She smoothed it out, looked at it for a moment. Her breath caught and her face looked sharply up at his. Her eyes searched his face, looking sad. She held the hand for a moment longer, between her two hands, and then laid it down gently and reached for his right. She looked at it, longer than she had the left one.

She began to speak, "You are under a curse already, a great darkness."

Bertha. Edward thought. *I did not need a fortune teller to tell me that.*

"I wish I could lift it for you, but I cannot. God has willed it so. You must follow it to its conclusion, for at the end is relief and sunshine to light the darkness. But I cannot help you."

Bridie Lovell's voice had taken on a mysterious, hushed quality, different from the mocking tone she had taken with Blanche. For the first time, Edward felt a slight chill up his back.

"You have great willfulness, and you will follow a course of action from which none can dissuade you. You will give up much to gain much, and at the end your efforts will earn you nothing. You must depend upon another to give you the world and all you crave."

"There is a little girl, one who is your child and who is not your child. She is yours and yet you make her not so. She is not yours and yet you have made her so. It is not for you to know, yet you have done well by her and great blessing will be yours in consequence."

Edward swallowed. *Who cares about Adèle, damn it.* He wanted to know about Jane.

"Will I... ?" he dreaded to ask. "Will I get what I want? In the area of love."

There was a long silence. Then Bridie spoke again, "There will be a time when the dross is burned away and the gold is refined. And only then will the love you seek be brought to you."

Mrs. Lovell dropped his hand then, and seemed to come to herself, and it was at that moment that there was a knock on the door, and Mary carried in a basket covered with a white napkin. She laid it on the table and left. Edward wanted to ask Bridie about what she had said to him, about his future. But suddenly, he was afraid to know.

Edward pulled the napkin back to reveal a cold half-chicken and two tarts. The two of them sat eating quickly while Edward told her what he wanted to ask Jane.

Bridie listened carefully, then spoke, "I sense that this interview, of all of them, is important to you, sir. You know, if you want to know the girl's feelings, you don't have to do all this. You could just ask her." She shook her head, "That is a man, for you."

Edward grinned, "But if I did that, it would not be financially profitable for you, Mrs. Lovell!"

They were finishing their lunch, sitting in companionable silence, when Bridie suddenly sat up straighter, a bright and mischievous look in her eyes.

"Mr. Rochester, an idea has come to me," she said. "Instead of your governess having her fortune told by me, perhaps she should be quizzed and advised by one who knows her much better than I." She pointed to him.

Edward, in the middle of his last bite of food, frowned in puzzlement as he chewed and swallowed. He wiped his mouth with his napkin, shaking his head. "No, it wouldn't work. Miss Eyre and I can talk by the hour, but her guard is never let down. She will never really tell me how she feels, especially not now, when she feels I am as good as wed to another."

"Yes, but she will not be talking to you, sir," Bridie continued, "she will tell her thoughts to the gypsy fortune-teller, a stranger... who will be not I, but you."

"I?" Edward asked, looking startled. "How will I accomplish that, and in such a hurry? I expect her in this room in only ten minutes." He glanced at the clock.

"I remember as you sat and visited with my Mike, you talked of your enjoyment of theatricals and mimicry as a young man away at school." Bridie nodded, looking him up and down, "I may not be watching all the time, but my ears are always open. You were speaking of... "

"Of the need for artifice and showmanship when wanting people to believe the part you are playing, whether that of a wealthy gentleman or a mysterious gypsy," Edward finished for her.

"Exactly," Bridie responded, "and here is your chance to play your greatest part, and to find out yourself what you want to know."

"But my clothing, my voice... " Edward answered, pointing to himself.

"The clothing is the easy part," answered Bridie, turning to rummage in the pack she had carried with her. "As for the voice, just pitch yours higher, speak softly. Here... " She shook out several large shawls of various colours, and pulled her heavy black cloak off the chair where she had left it. She beckoned to him, "Come here, I'll have those fancy gentleman's clothes of yours disguised in the shake of a lamb's tail. Now, let me hear your best old fortune-teller's voice."

Edward moved towards her, still shaking his head even as he heard a high, reedy voice coming from him, "I'm not sure this would fool a child, to say nothing of my perceptive Jane." He chuckled as Bridie wrapped a long dark shawl around his waist, then wound another around his shoulders.

She nodded, "Speak in a bit of a whisper, so she has to lean closer to hear you," and Edward tried again, this time adding a bit of an elderly woman's quaver into his voice.

"Perfect!" Bridie said, tying a long scarf around his head and stepping back. She leaned forward to tug the kerchief forward so it hid most of his face. "You need a shave, Old Woman, so keep your head down when you speak to her. Lose yourself in these scarves and cloaks, let them do some of the work." She studied him with a frown, then peeled off her own fingerless black gloves and passed them to him. Neither of them noticed the heavy signet ring on his left little finger, and eventually that detail would give him away to an already sceptical Jane, but in every other way he could briefly pass muster as a mysterious old fortune-teller. Bridie fished her pipe out of the pocket of her own voluminous skirts, and handed it to him. "It's a prop only," she warned. "Don't get your lips all over it." Edward laughed.

Bridie smiled as well, "With your dark skin, sir, you look every inch the gypsy. Not one of us, but a gypsy from foreign lands." She handed him her cloak and gave him a gentle push towards the fortune-teller's seat nearer the fire. "But I suggest if you play the part after this, that you do it as a man. You're not very pretty." She chuckled with amusement, and headed behind the screen where he had hidden earlier.

Jane came in, moving quietly, no sign of fear upon her face. She looked so calm, so composed. And to him, so lovely. Her hair was drawn back neatly, her eyes peaceful. Edward held the scarf around his face, silently indicating the seat before him. His heart was pounding. He realized that if he had had time to think about this and rehearse, he never could have done it. Only his eagerness to speak with her himself gave him the courage to play this part. It would not be hard to keep the quaver in his voice, nervous as he was.

Jane gave him a coin, and he took her hand, gazing at it intensely. He began to speak in the voice Bridie had encouraged, telling Jane some of the facts about herself, asking how she felt about the party after all the long months alone. Jane did not look impressed.

"You might have heard all this from those who have gone before me," Jane said. Edward smiled. His sceptical, sensible darling.

He laid Jane's hand down on the table. "Your hand is smooth, there is nothing written there." He leaned forwards, hiding his face. "It is your face on which your truths are written. How do you feel, here, surrounded by the gentry. Sad? Lonely? Tired? All this work in a home that is not your own?"

Jane gave a small shrug, "I feel sleepy at times, I get tired. But sad? Very seldom."

"Then you have some secret hope that gives you strength, buoys you up in times of trial, when the future seems uncertain?"

"No, I cannot say that I do," Jane said, folding her hands neatly. "The most I can hope for is to save my money, in hopes of someday setting up a school in a house I am able to rent."

"What think you of the guests assembled here?" Edward asked her in his quavering murmur. "Are there any you feel connected to, any you feel a sympathy with?"

Jane shook her head, "They are pleasant enough to me, most of them. And those who are not, I take no notice of them. They will go home, their lives will have no impact upon mine. I find when listening to them that we do not agree on most things, and I'm sure if I were to speak, they would not agree with me either."

"Do you wish to know about a gentleman here, Miss Eyre?"

Jane frowned. "There is not a gentleman here I can think of, with whom I have exchanged more than a passing word or two."

"What about the master of the house?" Edward asked, leaning forward to hear her, his breath catching in his throat.

Jane swallowed, "He is not at home."

He made his character give a laugh, which came out as a sort of strangled cackle, "Well, what a thing to quibble over. He has not gone far, and will be back later today. If he is not here, does that mean he has ceased to exist?"

"No," Jane said quietly, "but what does Mr. Rochester have to do with me?"

"There are several young ladies here who have not ceased to speak to Mr. Rochester and to smile into his eyes."

Jane frowned, looked down at her hands, "He has a right to enjoy the society of his guests."

"And one guest in particular?" he asked. "Do you not see a love and a happiness forming between Mr. Rochester and a certain young lady?"

Jane smiled, a smile that she quickly smothered, "I cannot say that I see a love there, exactly. If you think there is, I begin to doubt your abilities." She looked down at her hands again, biting her lip as though she felt she had said too much.

"And yet," Edward went on, "Mr. Rochester is rumoured to be seeking a wife, and Miss Ingram is said to be the lady he will marry."

Jane was silent for a few moments, and then she raised her head. She looked troubled, and Edward wanted to end the charade at that moment, and hold her in his arms.

"I did not come to hear Mr. Rochester's fortune, mother," she said, her voice low and quiet, "I came to hear my own."

Edward took her hand again, "And yet your fortune depends so much upon yourself. Happiness lies within your reach, if you would just reach out and take it. I look at your face and it is so quiet and so serious, but it could be full of smiles, of softness. It could be full of love, if you chose to make it so.

"You are independent, you ask help from no one, and yet the help is there if you do not shun it out of pride. What will you do when Mr. Rochester marries Miss Ingram, where will you go? What will become of you then?"

Suddenly distressed, Jane stood up as if to go. She stood for a moment, uncertain, peering at him, trying to see beyond the cloaks and scarves, and then looked towards the door. A sudden look of comprehension came over her, and she looked down at the hand that still held hers tightly. They both saw his ring at the same moment. He dropped her hand, and stood up, saying "Off, ye lendings!" as he removed his kerchief. He could not help but laugh at the expression on Jane's face. He saw Bridie Lovell come around the screen, nodding at his performance.

Jane stared, her eyes darting from the gypsy to her employer, and she drew herself up to her full height, a look of indignation crossing her face.

Edward turned to Bridie Lovell, and reached into his pocket, drawing out a small pouch in which coins jingled.

"Thank you, Mrs. Lovell," he said. "You have done a good day's work. I was greatly entertained, and have learned the answers to some of my questions." He finished pulling off the remaining scarves and handed them to Bridie, who gathered them in her arms and moved towards the door. "Goodbye, and give my regards to your good husband."

She nodded to him, and to Jane, who looked after her in confusion. Edward closed the door behind the fortune-teller and then turned to Jane, smothering the grin that he was hardly able to hide.

"That was not fair, sir!" Jane said, crossing her arms over her breasts. "That was a trick, a trick upon us all; that was not sporting of you."

"Oh, come now, Jane," he said, laughing, "You cannot say that some of those ladies out there do not deserve it. Tell me, did Blanche look upset?"

"I do not know; I was in the schoolroom, where I belonged. Where you pay me to be. Why did you bring me here, to be tricked?"

"Oh, Jane," Edward stepped closer to her. "It was not a trick, not against you. It was just a game. I just wanted to know what you are thinking."

Jane looked down at her feet, her arms still crossed over her chest. Edward bent towards her, tried to catch her eye.

"Are you angry at me?" he asked.

"I am confused," she said, "I think you lured me here to hear me talk nonsense."

"But you did not!" Edward protested. "I do not think you could speak nonsense, not you. Now, tell me, what are they saying about all this?"

"They were not discussing the gypsy at all," Jane replied. "When I came out of the schoolroom, the guests were all assembled in the drawing room because of the weather, and they were talking to a stranger who arrived here this morning."

Edward frowned, "What stranger?"

"He is a man who said he has known you for years, and he would wait here until you returned from your business. He said he knows you from the West Indies, from Jamaica, I think. His name is Mason."

Edward felt as though he had been doused with a bucket of icy water. He stifled a gasp. A second later a hot flush moved over him, and he almost felt faint. He reached for Jane, who moved forward and grasped his hand tightly.

"Are you all right, sir?" she asked, her voice full of concern.

Edward rubbed his eyes, his vision had narrowed into blackness; he felt as though he was going to fall. He was vaguely aware of Jane holding his arm, leading him to a chair. He sank into it, gripping her hand tightly – the only solid thing in a world that was teetering around him. "Mason—the West Indies," he heard himself murmur.

Gradually his vision brightened again, he came back to himself, his hand still clasped in Jane's.

"Jane," he whispered.

She squeezed his hand in return, her face full of worry for him.

"Your face is so white," she told him, "Can I get you something?"

"Jane, if everyone out there deserted me, cursed me and spat upon me, what would you do?"

She looked puzzled, "I would stay with you, sir, try to comfort you."

"Would you? You would not leave me?"

Jane looked at him, her face soft. She placed her other hand over his, "Of course not."

Her eyes searched his intently, and she whispered, "I would do anything for you."

Chapter 32 - Mason

"Is the danger you apprehended last night gone by now, sir?"
"I cannot vouch for that till Mason is out of England: nor even then. To live, for me, Jane, is to stand on a crater-crust which may crack and spue fire any day."
"But Mason seems a man easily led. Your influence, sir, is evidently potent with him: he will never set you at defiance, or wilfully injure you."
"Oh, no! Mason will not defy me; nor, knowing it, will he hurt me—but, unintentionally, he might in a moment, by one careless word, deprive me, if not of life, yet forever of happiness."
Jane Eyre and Edward Rochester - Jane Eyre

I would do anything for you...

Edward closed his eyes, settling under the covers with Jane's words echoing in his head. He smiled to himself and rolled over, trying to find a comfortable position. He was tired and he felt that he would fall asleep quickly despite the eventful day, the shock of Mason's unexpected visit.

He grew drowsier, the words of the gypsy fortune teller drifting through his tired mind.

You are under a curse already, a great darkness...

You will give up much to gain much and at the end your efforts will bring you nothing...

When the dross is burned away and the gold is refined, only then will the love you seek be brought to you...

His brow wrinkled, pondering her mysterious words. He had not had time to think upon them, had not had time to ask Mrs. Lovell any questions. He turned again in bed, once again hearing Jane's sweet voice saying

I would do anything for you...

A scream rang out, an unearthly sound that rent the peaceful silence of the night. It was a guttural cry that rose to a panicked shriek. A few seconds later it was repeated.

The sound brought Edward straight up in bed, a frigid wave running down his spine, making his heart pound, his mind instantly awake and alert.

Another scream was heard, unmistakably a man's voice. Calling his name, asking for help.

Damn! Edward was out of his bed in an instant, stepping into his slippers, fumbling for the dressing gown at the foot of his bed. He was aware of his hands trembling as he tied the robe around his waist.

Mason surely would not have gone up to see Bertha alone. He could not be that stupid...

Edward felt a flash of the anger he had been trying to control since learning from Jane that Mason had arrived, uninvited and unannounced.

He had remained in the library, trying to regain his composure, while he sent Jane for a glass of wine to restore his spirits. She had returned to report that all seemed well in the drawing room. She told him that Mason was in the centre of a small group of guests and that all seemed relaxed, laughing and talking together. Edward breathed an inward sigh of relief. It did not appear that Richard had all his neighbours gathered around him, announcing that Rochester had been married for fifteen years to a woman who was being held prisoner on the third storey.

Edward had drunk the wine in nearly one gulp while he sent Jane to bring Mason in to see him.

Richard had entered the room hesitantly, shutting the door behind him quietly. Edward had not risen to greet him but had remained where he was, glaring at the visitor.

"Hello, Rochester," his brother-in-law said, coming to stand before him.

"Mason," Edward gave him a cold nod. "I hope you are not expecting an enthusiastic greeting?"

Mason gave him a quick sardonic smile. "I would never expect that from you, Fairfax."

"You have your nerve," Edward said, "showing up here without a by-your-leave. What are you doing here?"

"I came to see my sister," Mason answered. "You will not meet with me; you never answer my letters except to give me excuses why you cannot see me. I decided coming here was the only way to see you. I knew you would never expect me."

"What were you doing in Madeira?" Edward inquired.

"They used to produce their own sugar, but now they have need of sugar from other places," Mason told him. "I have some trade with various business owners, sugar for Madeira wine. I expect to be making regular trips back and forth in the future."

"I knew nothing of these business ventures," Edward said, frowning. "As I recall, I still have some interest in the company."

"So you do," Mason replied. "And if I could ever arrange a meeting with you face to face, we would be able to discuss it."

Edward took a deep breath, glaring at Richard. For a moment he did not speak.

"I do not know why we cannot conduct our business by letter. Or better yet, through our stewards."

"I do not care to discuss my sister with our stewards," Mason retorted. He shifted from one foot to the other, looking around the library. Then he looked back at Edward. "I just want to see Bertha, Edward. I shall not stay here above a day or two. I do not expect to be treated like an honoured guest."

Edward stared straight ahead, frowning.

"All right, I understand that," he told him, finally looking up at his brother-in-law. "But I cannot take you there tonight. I have been away from my guests all day. You and I will go up there tomorrow, when we are both well-rested. You do not want to attempt to see her without my presence, it is not safe."

Mason, shrugged, nodded. Edward stood up. "As long as you are here, you might as well have dinner with us, there is plenty. I gather you have met my neighbours. I do not have to tell you… "

Mason gave him a long, contemptuous look. "Do not worry, Rochester, your friends will hear nothing from me. I have no interest in ruining your life."

I am not entirely sure about that, Edward thought, beckoning to Mason and leading the way to the drawing room to greet his guests after being gone on his day of "business".

They had had an uneventful dinner, with Mason telling several amusing stories of Edward's time in Jamaica. As far as the assembled guests were concerned, Mr. Rochester had been there to learn the sugar business and something of importing and exporting. Nothing else was said, no hint given that Mason was anything to Edward other than a business acquaintance. But he could not relax, could not enjoy his meal.

Despite the turmoil of his mind, he could not help but notice that Blanche did not choose to take a seat by him at dinner, and kept her face turned away from him. He welcomed the relief, but did not find the amusement in it that he would have found had Mason not been there. He picked at his dinner, said very little.

There were more games in the drawing room that night; several of the ladies had come up with some amusing word puzzles, and there was great laughter and merriment. No one seemed to notice the silence of their host, or the tense posture he adopted when his friend Mason was talking to his other guests. Blanche was especially merry, tossing her head and laughing brightly, flirting gaily with Mason and all the other single men, speaking to Edward only when she had to.

No one seemed to notice the governess, watching her employer anxiously from behind the screen where she sat, a book unread upon her lap. Adèle was in great high spirits also, flitting from guest to guest, speaking French, practicing her English, having a wonderful time until Jane drew her aside and, after some firm, whispered words in her ear, led off her to the nursery.

Shortly after he saw Jane and Adèle leave, Edward noticed Mason sitting by the fire, looking exhausted, and he made an announcement to the guests that he and his friend Mason were tired from too much business and travel that day, and would see them tomorrow. He led Mason up to one of the unused guest rooms, where he had had his luggage carried earlier, telling the maid to build up the fire as large and as warm as possible for their visitor from the West Indies.

"After I see my guests occupied and entertained tomorrow, you and I will slip away and go upstairs. Wait for me, Mason, I cannot stress that enough."

The men had parted at Mason's room in a cordial enough manner, and Edward had gone on to prepare for bed.

And now the fool was upstairs, where God knows what calamity had befallen him. Edward's heart was pounding, certain that this meant the end of all his years of secrecy and careful planning.

Edward left his room quickly, trying to get upstairs before the guests began to leave their rooms to determine the source of the commotion. He took the stairs two at a time, entering the anteroom. The door to the inner room was ajar, and Edward could hear shrieks and stomping.

He rushed inside. Richard lay on the floor in the corner of the room, bleeding. Bertha stood over him, a knife held up in her hand. She was growling, cursing, muttering a stream of unintelligible words.

Edward did not think, but rushed at Bertha, grabbing her upraised arm, knocking the knife from her hand before she could attack again. The knife flew across the room, and Grace rushed over, grabbed for it.

It took several moments, but Edward and Grace got Bertha subdued. She fought them like someone possessed, which Edward seriously thought she was at times like this. At last they got her wrestled to her bed, secured with stout lengths of rope until she could be trusted to relax and lie still.

Edward rushed to Richard, who was sobbing, holding a bloodied shoulder. The next few moments were a blur as Grace and Edward helped him up, took him out to the anteroom, and laid him upon Grace's bed, after locking the door to the inner room carefully behind them. Grace had gotten some towels and some water, and she began to work on his injured shoulder.

"Richard," Edward leaned against the table, arms stiff, looking down at the bloody knife now laying on the table top, "I told you to wait for me, did I not? What in the hell has happened here?"

Mason shook his head, weeping.

"Grace?" Edward turned to look at Bertha's nurse, who looked from Mason to him.

Grace licked her lips, uncertain of how to begin, "I... there was a knock on the door, and I opened it to find this man here. Madame was sleeping. He said that she was his sister and that you had told him to come up here. He had found the room, seemed so sure of himself, I allowed him to enter... "

"It was not your fault, Grace," Edward laid his hand upon her arm. "This is indeed her brother, but I told him not to come up here alone."

"He frightened her," Grace told him. "At first she seemed happy to see him, called him by his name. She moved as if to embrace him but then... " She shook her head, looked distressed.

Edward approached Bertha's brother, heart pounding. Mason moaned, turned his head upon the pillow, "Edward... "

"Shhh," Edward told him. "Lie still, Richard, and do not fret, we will see to you."

He peeled off the makeshift dressing Grace had fashioned out of some towels. A large stab wound opened at Mason's left shoulder, resulting in a fresh trickle of blood. Mason moaned again. Edward pressed the dressing back to the wound and moved to where Grace was standing.

"I suppose she picked up the knife when she was wandering about that night, trying to set fire to me?"

Grace shrugged, looking at the floor, "I suppose so, sir."

"Well, he needs a doctor, and I need to see to my guests." He looked over at Mason, who seemed fine for the present.

"Go back inside and quiet her down, for God's sake," Edward told Grace. "I'll be back with some help and I'll go for Mr. Carter. I hope to Heaven he is not out on another case."

By the time he got back to the hall where most of the guest rooms were located, there were people milling everywhere, all talking at once. Edward caught sight of Jane, standing near the wall, her hair in a braid over her shoulder. She clutched a plaid wool shawl about her nightgown. Their eyes met, and something in his look must have alerted her to his concerned state, for she gave him a small smile and a reassuring nod.

Edward raised his voice, attempting to reassure his guests, "It was merely a servant having a nightmare." He heard his words, and marvelled at his calm tone.

Gradually the murmuring crowd dispersed. Blanche smiled at him, took his arm and allowed him to lead her back to her room. Evidently her mother had told her not to heed the gypsy's dire warnings quite yet and risk losing her prize before she could be sure all financial hope was lost.

When order was restored, Edward went to his room and dressed hurriedly. He raised his head, listening anxiously for any sounds from the rooms above. All was quiet.

When he tapped on Jane's door a few minutes later, he did so without hesitation. He knew, as he had never known anything else in his life, that he could depend on her.

When she came out she was fully dressed but wearing slippers. He felt relieved – no one would be alerted by footsteps clambering up and down the stairs. Jane's hair was pulled back in a loose knot, her eyes wide but focused on him with complete trust. Only when they began to ascend to the third floor did he sense hesitation.

"Do you want to go back?" he asked her gently. She hesitated, then shook her head. He reached out and took her hand, feeling her slender fingers grasp his firmly.

"Warm and steady," he told her. In spite of the circumstances, it still gave him a faint thrill to feel her little hand in his. She held his hand tightly and he knew, absolutely, that he could trust her with his very life.

"Do you sicken at the sight of blood?" he had asked her. She had replied that she had never been tried.

He saw her eyes widen, her cheek grow pale as she looked at Mason, lying so still and white upon the bed. But she had sat down next to him, smiled at him reassuringly as he looked from her to Edward, held her hand firmly against the wound at his shoulder. Before leaving Jane with his brother-in-law, Edward had leaned down to Mason, urgently whispering to him to keep silent. He had exhorted Jane as well, to keep silent, with the excuse that talking would tire the patient.

He went back down the steps, out the side door to the stables with a heavy dread shadowing his mind. He waved the sleepy groom back to bed, saddled Mesrour himself with a quick and steady hand and was soon racing down the road to Mr. Carter's home.

As he galloped away to fetch the surgeon, he wondered if he was insane. What had he been thinking, to leave Jane alone with Mason? His greatest fear – that Mason would betray his secret, could smash his only chance for happiness – might even now be coming to pass. What idiocy had possessed him?

He wondered at himself. Was it possible, deep within him, that he wanted Jane to find out about Bertha? To bring into the open his secret so that he would not be tempted to carry out the idea that his mind was contemplating?

Surely not. He knew Jane by now, knew her honesty, her integrity, the faith that would not allow her to share his sin. He knew that if she had any inkling of the truth of his life, she would close her heart and mind against him, would never think of him as anything but her employer. Her married employer. And suddenly he was filled with a cold fear that he was already too late.

Thank God, Carter was home and agreed to come to Thornfield at once and bring his carriage. Edward rode alongside, chafing at how long it was taking to return to his home.

Nearly two hours after he had left Jane with Mason, he and Carter entered the anteroom. Jane stood up when they came in, a look of intense relief passing over her features.

Carter leaned over Mason, exclaiming over his wounds, "He has been bitten as well as stabbed!"

"She said she would kill me, she said she would drain my heart," Mason moaned, tears trickling from his eyes.

Edward, standing next to Jane, felt a shudder run through his entire body. Jane must have felt it, because she turned to him, her grave eyes searching his face.

Edward was obliged to send her on several errands but she did them willingly, leaving and returning with speed. A clean shirt, Mason's cloak, a bottle of restorative elixir from Giacinta's quack of a physician – all were fetched quickly and soon the three of them were assisting a slightly revived Mason to Carter's carriage.

"Care for him at your home, give him all he needs," Edward told Carter. "I'll ride over in a day or two to see how he does."

He started to close the door but felt Mason's hand on his arm, holding him with surprising strength.

Mason again had tears in his eyes. "Rochester," he whispered hoarsely, "please... let her be treated tenderly, take care of her... " His voice broke.

"I will do my best, as I have done and will continue to do," Edward told him, feeling a quick flash of anger bite at his heart. He pulled his arm out of Mason's grasp, shut the door and slapped his hand on the side of the carriage to signal the driver to proceed.

He stepped away from the carriage, eyes fixed on the ground. He wanted to smash something, to fall to his knees and scream out to God, until he felt some relief from this unbearable frustration and pain.

"Did he mean Grace Poole?" he heard Jane ask. He was unsure of what to answer. He was sorry he had ever turned her suspicions to the faithful Grace, but he had never expected matters to go on as they had. He could not have anticipated the fire, could not have imagined Mason coming to his home, let alone being brutally attacked by his own sister.

Edward and Jane began to stroll in the cool softness of the late April dawn. Jane looked tired, but continued to walk with him, listening to him. It relaxed him, filled him with calm, with renewed hope.

"Were you afraid, Jane, sitting there with Mason?"

She looked thoughtful, "Yes, I was frightened. I kept hearing noises, imagining all manner of things ready to come at me from the shadows."

Edward stopped, looked at her seriously, "You were in no danger, Jane, I promise you. I would be a poor shepherd if I would leave a lamb, my pet lamb, unguarded near a wolf's den." He stopped, fearing he had said too much, given away his feelings. Jane's eyes searched his.

"What about Grace Poole, sir?" Jane looked concerned, a frown on her face. "Will she continue to work for you?"

"Oh, yes," Edward said, "Please, do not concern yourself with Grace, all is under control."

He tried to tell her how he felt about Mason, why his presence filled him with fear. It was obvious Jane did not understand and it was then that he relaxed, sure that Mason had told her nothing.

He turned to her, desperate for some sign, nearly beside himself with longing to know how she felt. He heard himself telling her of his experience. Not in detail; he could not be specific, but he wanted her to try to understand.

"Suppose that while you are away, far from your home, you happen to make a mistake. Not a crime, such as theft or murder; I am talking about making a mistake, the results of which are nearly unbearable. Are you justified in defying society's rules, in leaping over convention, to secure happiness? To gain for yourself this lovely, gracious, genial stranger that you have found, before she slips from your grasp?"

Jane looked down, her face sad and defeated. For a moment it seemed hard for her to speak.

"One's happiness should never depend upon another, Mr. Rochester. You must look higher than yourself, seek after God and His comfort, attempt to right the wrongs within yourself." She looked down again.

Edward sighed. No matter how she felt, she would say nothing to him, she would not dare to express her feelings.

He laughed, a small bitter laugh. "Well, Jane," he proceeded sarcastically, "you must have noticed my regard for Blanche Ingram. What do you think, will she regenerate me with a vengeance?"

He walked away, fists clenched. He wanted Jane so much right then, wanted to take her in his arms, kiss her, beg her to love him and to make him happy, to let him make her happy as well. He turned back to her. She was watching him from under her lowered eyelids, her face drained of colour.

"Jane," he said, his voice tender once again, "you are pale, and fatigued. Are you angry with me for interrupting your sleep?"

She shook her head, gave him a little smile, "No, sir."

He opened his mouth to speak, but then heard voices coming towards them. He recognized the voices of Dent and Lynn. He turned to Jane, quickly sending her into the house before walking over to his guests and greeting them cheerfully.

"I have just being seeing my friend Mason off. He has been up and about his business long before the rest of you, and is now well on his way."

Later that day Edward stood with Blanche, the Misses Eshton, and a few others, playing a game of billiards. He was tired from the events of the night, and irritable, stifling his yawns with difficulty.

Suddenly he realized Blanche was speaking to him.

"That person appears to want you." Her voice dripped with contempt, and as he lifted his head he saw Jane waiting across the room, watching him.

She wants me? Not as much as I want her, you miserable cow... He moved away from the table without a backwards glance at Blanche, tossing his billiard stick to the ground.

"Well, Jane?" he asked, looking down at her. She still looked so tired.

"I need to speak with you, Mr. Rochester."

He led her to the schoolroom, and it was there, with a trace of shock and dismay, that he discovered she wanted to leave for a time, to go visit a sick aunt who had, after eight years of neglect, decided she needed to see Jane.

Edward wanted to protest, to forbid her to go. But of course he could not. He made her promise to return as soon as possible, gave her the wages he owed her, so she could travel easily. He tried to give her more, but she refused. And every moment, as they stood there talking, he wanted to beg her not to go, not to leave him.

In just a few minutes she was gone, to her room to pack. In the morning she would be gone, would leave Thornfield for... ever? His heart went cold within him at the thought. He imagined never seeing her again, and it made him gasp, to think of the pain, the desolation that would again be his.

His party, initially a way to show her his wealth, to entertain his neighbours, had become a game of sorts as he had kept Blanche on his arm, had hoped she would make Jane jealous, make her fully aware of her love for him.

My move, Jane. Here is Blanche; I could easily have her. It is your play now. Love me, give me something to hold to.

Someone else could want me, if you do not.

Check.

She had made her move, more decisively than he. She had seen his plays, watched how he moved and when the chance arose, chose to leave him behind.

Checkmate.

"Then you and I must bid good-bye for a little while?"

"I suppose so, sir."

"And how do people perform the ceremony of parting, Jane? Teach me; I'm not quite up to it."

"They say farewell, or any other form they prefer."

"Then say it."

"Farewell, Mr. Rochester, for the present."

"What must I say?"

"The same, if you like, sir."

"Farewell, Miss Eyre, for the present – is that all?"

"Yes."

"...so you'll do no more than say, 'farewell,' Jane?"

"It is enough, sir... "

And then she was gone.

Chapter 33 - A Month Without Jane

Jane departed for Gateshead and outwardly the smooth operations of Thornfield Hall continued. No one seemed affected except perhaps Adèle, and she was kept busy by the careful attentions of Sophie, who had promised Jane she would keep the child occupied.

April turned over into a warm and glorious May, and the house party continued. Edward's life, so recently cleared of some of its clouds, the sun shining brightly with promise for the future, was suddenly dark and lonely again.

It had happened so quickly – Jane at the Hall one day and gone the next – that he felt a slight sense of shock when he looked around and found her gone. His sense of equilibrium was disturbed, his focus had shifted, and he found it difficult to concentrate. He could not believe that six months ago he had not known Jane Eyre even existed and now his life seemed empty without her, even more empty than it had been before he met her.

Blanche had evidently decided to bide her time until she could be sure of Edward's financial position, and her renewed attentions to him were well nigh unbearable. It was all he could do to speak to her, to be polite. The other guests were aware of a pall that had settled over the house, and it became increasingly difficult for their host to interest himself in any of the group's activities.

Edward found himself thinking, "A week, and then she will be home again." But when a week went by and there was no Jane, his spirits, which had risen a little, again plummeted.

One day as the assembled guests were beginning to pack their things and talk of moving the party on to London, Eshton pulled his host aside.

"Rochester, a word, if you please." Eshton stood before Edward, hemming and hawing, before finally coming out with it.

"Edward, I had an interesting exchange with Lady Ingram yesterday and thought you should be aware of it."

"Oh?" Edward cocked an eyebrow at his long-time neighbour.

"Er, um, yes," Eshton fidgeted, "It seems that she is making inquiries as to your financial situation."

"Is that right?" Edward responded, leaning casually against the wall, his arms crossed over his chest.

"Rochester, we have known each other long enough, God knows, as I knew your father before you, and my father knew your grandfather." Edward nodded.

"Oh, I just need to be blunt," Eshton said gruffly. "You know, all of us here, well, we all know each other's worth, give or take a few thousand pounds, and a woman with unmarried daughters knows what a man is worth better than anyone else."

"That may be true," Edward agreed. "His financial worth, at any rate."

"Er, yes. And that is all that matters to many mothers, sadly enough," Eshton said, looking thoughtful. "To the point, the Rochesters have always been rumoured to be worth a great fortune, but talk says that the fortune is dwindled to ten thousand pounds and is being so badly mishandled that even that amount is at risk."

Edward stood straight, "And who would dare malign the management of Mr. King? He has handled Thornfield's affairs for years, as did his father. Only my faith in him allowed me to travel for years without worry, and all my checking of his figures shows him to be above reproach in all he does."

"It's not the management of Mr. King that I hear questioned, it is yours," Eshton told him. "Apparently you are both a tippler and a gambler."

Edward could not help but grin, thinking of Blanche's face when Bridie Lovell had told her fortune.

"So, what did you say to Lady Ingram, Eshton?" he asked, relieved that his careless joking had not cast suspicion on his highly respected steward.

"Why, I did not know what to say!" Eshton looked genuinely distressed. "I told her I could not imagine from whence such rumours sprang and I could not comment further. And I came to you at once."

Edward leaned back against the wall, still smiling in amusement. In reality, his financial situation was the best it had ever been. His father had been a very wealthy man from the profits of Thornfield alone, not counting Ferndean and a few outside investments. John Rochester had never exerted himself greatly to increase the wealth of the Rochester estate. It had always been well-managed and had reaped a steady profit over the years once expenses were paid.

Edward had bought two properties in Paris, had invested in interests in the Caribbean, and of course still held his interest in Mason's sugar-exporting business. Those combined investments had grown to a value of nearly ten thousand pounds over the past ten or twelve years. The slow abolition of slavery in the English empire had affected it somewhat or it would have grown even more.

On top of that there was the thirty thousand pounds he had been given when he married Bertha, of which no one in England had any knowledge. Those monies still sat in the bank in Spanish Town, gathering interest, the statements sent to him personally per his instructions. He had touched none of it save for about two hundred pounds a year which he used to pay Grace and to clothe Bertha and pay for her medical care. He meticulously kept those records himself, so they would not be included in the tallies and correspondence kept track of by Mr. King's office.

By law the money was his from the day of their wedding onwards, but he felt it was tainted and could barely stand to open the quarterly statements.

Edward pulled his mind back to the present, aware that Eshton was watching him closely.

"I thank you, Eshton, for your discretion. You are indeed a true friend, but in reality, you would do me a greater service by not refuting these rumours."

"But, Rochester, surely you know that the Ingrams would never permit a marriage in which the financial outcome is unlikely to... er, um... "

Edward raised his eyebrows and smiled again, nodding.

"Oh. Um... " Eshton seemed momentarily befuddled. "I... uh, had not realized... I thought you wished for a union with the Ingrams... "

"Well, you can see that in this way, Blanche can extricate herself with dignity still intact," Edward responded. "No doubt she will still hate me, but when you are the one doing the rejecting rather than the one rejected, it is not such a bitter pill to force down."

"Well, Edward, I had no idea you were such a gentleman," Eshton said, shaking his head, still frowning in confusion.

"Do I detect a hint of sarcasm there, Eshton?"

Eshton shook his head, "I have no idea, actually." Then he laughed. "Ah, well, I believe all here present were thinking there would be a wedding, but... oh well. So, Rochester, er... financially, you, um... ?"

"I have no great complaints and will manage somehow, but I thank you for asking, and for dealing with Lady Ingram," Edward replied, clapping Eshton cheerfully on the back and leaving his neighbour more confused than he had been before the conversation started.

The house party soon dispersed, with some guests going back to their homes, but most making plans to head to London. Blanche, who had been anticipating that her time in London would include the buying of wedding clothes, departed Thornfield in sullen silence.

Edward had originally been unsure of whether to go or to stay, unwilling to be away from home should Jane return. However, in the second week of her absence, a short note had come from Gateshead for Mrs. Fairfax, sending greetings to all and notifying the housekeeper that her aunt was still alive, albeit at death's door, and that she intended to remain until all was settled.

Edward at first could barely speak for the disappointment but when Mrs. Fairfax pressed him for a reaction he could not resist saying with an edge of bitterness in his voice, "Miss Eyre is not a slave here, she may do as she pleases. It is nothing to me; I am going to London. If I am to be married, as everyone thinks, I need a new carriage."

Edward had no particular plans while in London, and although his guests had been full of excitement over this ball and that party, he had remained noncommittal at each mention of get-togethers and gatherings. He had no London home, unlike several of his neighbours, and thus he did not encounter many of them during his short stay in London, save for those few parties he felt obligated to attend.

He had hoped very much to see Robert Lathrop again while in town, but upon calling, found that he was in Brighton with his daughter's family and not expected back for several weeks. Edward left a message, thinking fondly of the long-ago summers when he had been included as a guest on the Lathrops' trips to the seashore.

Edward spent his days in London with nothing but Pilot and his brooding thoughts for company. He found he could think of nothing but Jane.

He could not live without her. These weeks of her absence had been torture for him and he could no longer deny that he did not ever want to be without her again. He had fought against the idea of marriage to her, a marriage that could not be legal or sanctioned by God, but he could no longer see any other way around his dilemma. He felt trapped, cornered, but he knew in his heart that if Jane knew the truth about his life, she would not stay.

It had always been his intention that if he found the woman with whom he wanted to share his life, if he fell in love and planned to marry, that he would lay out his problem plainly, tell the truth of his situation. He had spent his time among worldly women, those whose religious beliefs would have made allowances for certain circumstances. He had been sure that a thinking woman of sophistication and compassion would look at his marriage to Bertha and agree that, yes, he had been tricked and betrayed, and yes, he should be free to marry again.

He had no doubt that such a woman would have stood before a priest or minister and married him with a clear conscience. How was he to know that the woman he had dreamed of, the only woman he would ever want, would be a church-educated schoolgirl? A girl whose purity and innocence would refresh and rejuvenate him – yet those same traits would make it impossible for her to rationalize marriage to him.

It was so ironic, so infuriating. Part of what he loved most about her was her standards and her morals; and yet those were the very things that would keep her from him. If he were to sit her down, tell her his story, he had no doubt that her first action would be to leave him for good, and he could not bear that.

His thoughts were racing frantically. He had no choice, he decided; it was not his fault, it was God's. God had allowed the betrayal that had tied him to Bertha. God had kept Bertha alive all these years. God had allowed Jane to be led to Thornfield and God had brought him home to fall in love with her. And God would just have to understand and forgive him.

He would have Jane if it killed him.

With no great desire to continue mingling with his former house guests, and no wish to respond to all the invitations that came his way, Edward could see no point in staying in London. He had attended a party or two but found he could enjoy nothing without Jane in his life. Everything around him seemed without life and colour, and he knew that if she never came back, his life would remain like that forever.

And Blanche was there at nearly every function in London, clearly angry with him and not afraid to show it. He had made it a point to present himself to the Ingrams and had been met with nothing but coldness in return.

He didn't care. He found it amusing, in fact, but it was awkward for the other guests. When he stopped attending the gatherings and those assembled from Hay and Millcote heard that Edward Rochester had returned to Thornfield after less than two weeks, they attributed it to romantic problems, and perhaps some financial woes on Rochester's part, as rumour had it.

Several days after he returned from London, Edward took a ledger book, a pencil, and some charcoals on a walk with him through the back fields, to sit on a stile and enjoy the warmth of the early evening as summer approached. It was the first of June – summer was coming fast, and it promised to be a glorious one.

He sat for a long time, sketching aimlessly – he was no artist – and jotting down his thoughts. He had suspected that when Jane returned she would not wish to be fetched by carriage but would return on her own. But he was still caught off guard to see a small figure picking its way carefully over the grass towards him.

He sat still, pencil poised over his book, heart thudding rapidly within his breast, trying to force himself to be calm. When Jane raised her head, Edward had gotten enough mastery over himself to raise his hand and greet her cheerfully.

"Hello!" he called to her. "It is Jane Eyre, stealing her way over the back roads. I might have known she would choose this way to arrive instead of calling for a carriage to pick her up."

"It is a pleasant enough evening," Jane replied, coming to stand in front of him. "I wanted to walk."

Edward looked up at her, knowing his face was lit up with his happiness at seeing her again. "And where have you been this past month, when you have been away from me, and have quite forgotten me, I imagine?"

"I have been with my aunt, sir, who is dead."

Edward could not help but laugh at her reply.

"If that is not a true Janian answer I do not know what is!" He rested his hand upon his heart in a dramatic fashion. "Good angels be my guard, she comes to me from the abode of the dead!"

They both laughed at that, and then Edward stood and began to walk with Jane, heading towards the Hall.

"Let us get you home now, Jane," he said. "Everyone will be happy to see you back."

Jane stopped, her large eyes fixed on his face. "Thank you, sir, for your great kindness to me." She spoke solemnly, her voice full of emotion, "Where you are is my home, is my true home."

Edward stopped, a sweet pain seizing him at his heart. It was all he could do not to take her in his arms right then and there, to restrain himself from kissing her senseless. Instead he smiled at her.

She began to walk again. "I thought you were in London, sir?" she asked, with a sidelong glance at him.

He chuckled. "I suppose you found that out by second sight?"

"Not quite," she smiled at him, "I had a letter from Mrs. Fairfax."

"Did she tell you what I had gone to do in London?" Edward asked her.

Jane paused, the smile suddenly gone from her face. "Yes. She said you had gone to make preparations for your wedding."

It was nearly dark now, and Jane's face was in shadow, but Edward could feel her sorrow. He wanted to speak then, to tell her how he felt, but before he could gather his thoughts, Jane spoke again.

"Mr. Rochester, would you promise me something?" Her voice sounded subdued, somehow thick, as if she held back tears.

"I will try," he told her, his heart suddenly beating faster. Perhaps she would speak, make clear her feelings.

"Will you promise me that Adèle and I will be safely out of this house before your bride comes into it?"

Edward felt his heart clench. Obviously Jane had not missed the truth about Blanche's character either.

"Ah, so you are making a statement about my dear Miss Ingram, implying that she might walk all over the two of you?"

Jane swallowed hard before speaking. "Not at all, sir, but she appeared... annoyed... at times, with Adèle, and might perhaps be happier if she is not at the house. And she has no use for governesses; she made that quite clear."

So she had heard every word the Ingrams had spoken regarding governesses. Edward felt a new flash of anger. *Vicious bitches.*

He stood straight, looking down at her. "There is some wisdom in what you say," he told her. "Yes, I promise that Adèle will be off to school... and you, what will you do, Miss Eyre?"

Jane was silent for a moment. "I shall advertise," she said quietly, "as I did when I found this position."

"No," Edward shook his head, "I cannot let you do that. I will find you a new place. In fact, I have an idea already in my mind. Promise me you will not advertise."

He had lost his nerve about speaking to her of marriage, suddenly not ready. But he could not resist tossing out an idea he had heard Lady Ingram going on about. "What do you think about Ireland?"

"Ireland?" Jane frowned, darting a look at him before she looked away again. "It is so far away!"

Edward looked closely at her. Her face had gone dark again, and guarded. They were nearly at Thornfield now, he could hear the sounds of the household as they grew closer to the Hall – one servant calling to another, the sounds of the carriage horses from the stables.

Jane raised her eyes to his, her look intense. For a moment they stared at each other and Edward could feel the emotion between them. But he could not speak, not yet. It was such a huge step, what he was contemplating. He looked into her beautiful, innocent eyes and could not do it. He headed for the front door, getting there before her and holding it open for Jane so that she could go in first.

Chapter 34 - Marry Me

"You see now how the case stands—do you not?" he continued. "After a youth and manhood passed half in unutterable misery and half in dreary solitude, I have for the first time found what I can truly love—I have found you. You are my sympathy— my better self—my good angel. I am bound to you with a strong attachment. I think you good, gifted, lovely: a fervent, a solemn passion is conceived in my heart; it leans to you, draws you to my centre and spring of life, wraps my existence about you, and, kindling in pure, powerful flame, fuses you and me in one."

"It will atone—it will atone. Have I not found her friendless, and cold, and comfortless? Will I not guard, and cherish, and solace her? Is there not love in my heart, and constancy in my resolves? It will expiate at God's tribunal. I know my Maker sanctions what I do. For the world's judgment—I wash my hands thereof. For man's opinion—I defy it."

Edward Rochester - Jane Eyre

For a fortnight after Jane's return, life went along smoothly, at least outwardly. Long-buried feelings and deep emotions were brewing underneath calm faces and casual conversations, but on the outside, Thornfield moved along in the usual way as summer blew in on fragrant breezes.

Edward once again felt complete. Jane was back, although he still had not worked up the courage to speak to her. He knew that once he had asked her to marry him, a huge step would be taken and the deception would have to go forward. Despite his fears of discovery, and his realization that he was, in reality, tricking the person he loved most in the world, he would have to go boldly on, as if everything were normal.

Jane settled into a routine her very first day back. She and Adèle returned to the schoolroom the very morning after her return and Edward, approaching quietly, looked into the room to see two heads bent together over a book. Adèle spoke, and he saw Jane lay a hand on her arm, heard her say, "Very good, Adèle!" He smiled and moved on.

That evening, he called Jane into the library. She approached as she always did, quietly, respectfully. He indicated a chair, and watched her as she sat, smoothing her dress over her knees, folding her hands and looking at him steadily.

"So, Miss Eyre," he began with great solemnity, "tell me what subjects you covered today with my ward."

She smiled, "Well, sir, we did mathematics. I am still working on Adèle's multiplication. She does quite well up to the sixes, but tends to get confused when we reach the sevens."

"And history?" he asked her. "Which is, as you know, an interest of mine."

"I do know that, sir," she told him, a note of playfulness in her voice despite the seriousness of her facial expression. "Today we discussed the defeat of the Spanish Armada. How the Spanish fleet was beaten back as it approached the shores of our country."

"Did you tell her that hundreds of Spanish soldiers washed up on the shores of the British Isles and assumed a life here and in Ireland, which is why today many

English and Irishmen, including myself, most likely, are far darker in appearance than we otherwise would be?"

Jane laughed. "No, sir, we did not discuss that."

"And did you discuss how their defeat saved England from the yoke of bondage to the King of Spain and to the Roman church, thus keeping England from the control of the Pope and sparing us another Inquisition?" Edward went on.

"I did not go into that much detail, sir," Jane told him solemnly. "At eight years old, she is perhaps not ready for all that. And am I right in assuming that since Adèle was born in France, she might have been baptized in the Roman church?"

Edward frowned, thinking back. "Yes, she was. I had nothing to do with it; I believe Céline took her to the priest at one point. She was not given a formal christening ceremony, not being legitimate, but she was baptized by the parish priest. 'Adèle Céline Jean-Marie Varens'. I have no idea what happened to her baptism certificate, now that we are on the subject; I do not have it. I suppose that is one more thing I need to make a future job of mine. She might need it in times to come." He sighed, settling back in his chair.

For a moment he was silent, frowning. Then he recovered himself. "Well, Jane, it seems that you have settled nicely into the schoolwork routine once again. And now, I would like to hear about you. Tell me about your trip, about seeing your aunt."

"Speaking of the Roman church… " Jane replied, rolling her eyes. She began to tell him about her Reed cousins, of Eliza, who was headed to the convent; of Georgiana, who had apparently found a husband with alarming speed. Edward was familiar with Georgiana's reputation from his occasional periods of mingling with London society.

"She is said to be very handsome, but an amazing flirt. I am not surprised, from what is said about her, that she found a husband so quickly. To think that my little schoolgirl governess is related to her; I could never have imagined! And to her brother, whose name was attached to many a scandal, from the little that I heard bandied about last year." He shook his head.

"So Jane, what do you think of the life that your cousin the nun has chosen, removed from life with its earthly pain and pleasures?"

Jane smiled a little, "I am glad that the Church of England does not require that of its adherents."

"So you plan to live the opposite life, do you?" he asked. "To find a husband and live to please him, as your other cousin has?"

Jane coloured a little. "I have no plans in that direction, sir, but neither do I wish to close off all chances forever, as my cousin seems to have done. As for her sister, should I ever marry, I hope to know my partner in life longer than a week before I am committed to marriage forever."

"That certainly seems wise," Edward agreed. "But tell me, Jane – how can you be sure that you know your mate, before you are, as you say, committed, for life?"

Jane frowned a little at this. "I do not know that I have given it much thought before. But I suppose, sir, that the only way to be sure is to spend time in that person's company, to speak to them, to discuss a variety of subjects. To be honest with them and hope that they are honest with you."

Edward felt a small dart of pain at her use of the word "honest".

"Do you really think, Jane, that one person can truly know another person until they have lived with them?"

She was silent for a moment, then said, "You can only see what they choose to show you. But if you come to know someone over time, and see them in a variety of situations, you can perhaps see the kind of person they are."

Edward was quiet for a few minutes. He thought of Bertha, whom he had only seen in a favourable light before marriage, only known in a physical sense. He thought of Céline, who had lived with him but whom he had never really known. His face was dark, his eyes far away, and his voice low as he said, "I wonder that anyone finds someone with whom they can live happily."

"I think, sir," Jane began hesitantly, "if one does not look at surface features, such as beauty and wealth, but looks deeper, to see what is beneath, only then can you know someone. And if you look to God to bring you together with the person you should be with, then there can be true... compatibility."

Edward did not want to hear that. He was fairly sure that God did not want him to be with Jane in the way he intended, under the present circumstances.

Jane's eyes were on her hands, which were clenched together on her lap. Edward watched her bent head, the light from the fire making her shiny hair glow in shades of red and yellow.

"Jane..." he said quietly. She looked up quickly. Her eyes looked very bright, as if tears glistened just beneath the surface. For a few seconds they were locked on his.

"It is late," he told her, "I should perhaps let you go now. Adèle's classroom time comes quickly every morning."

"Yes, sir." She stood up, moved towards the door.

"Jane?" he heard himself ask, "do you believe that love can last forever? Real love, I mean. The kind you spoke of?"

She paused, her hand on the door frame, looking back at him. "I think that is what everyone born on this earth is hoping for, when they think of love."

He smiled. "Good night, Jane."

"Good night, sir."

Every night Edward called Jane to his side to keep him company. They talked about a variety of subjects, sometimes debating in a friendly manner, at times laughing together. He remembered the early days of their acquaintance, when Jane seldom smiled and never laughed. His heart flooded with joy to see her happy.

Yet the pressure was bearing down upon him. He knew he had to speak to her, to settle things. He wished she would speak to him, tell him how she felt, but he could not expect that. She would never make her feelings known to him, never lay her heart open. She had her pride, her independence.

One evening he was walking in the garden just as the sun was setting, when he felt a tingling along his spine. He had not seen nor heard Jane, yet he knew she was there and he knew she was watching him.

Without turning he called her over to look at a moth he had been watching. For a time they strolled along together, looking at the flowers in the gathering dusk.

Edward's heart began to pound. He knew he had to finally speak, to finally claim Jane as his own.

He drew her into a clearing where some hedges made a private spot and some benches circled a huge tree. It was quiet except for some insects and some night birds. They might have been the only two people in the whole world.

For a time all was silent as they sat there together.

Finally he spoke. "This is a very pleasant place at this time of year, is it not?"

Jane nodded, "I have found it pleasant at all times of the year."

Edward turned towards her. "I believe you have been happy here at Thornfield, Jane."

"Yes, sir."

"And you will be sorry to leave here?"

She had gone very still. "Yes, sir."

"You will even feel sorry to leave Mrs. Fairfax and Adèle, won't you?"

Jane swallowed. "Yes, sir. I have come to care for them both very much."

Whom else do you care for, Jane? Whom else would you miss?

"But," she said, squaring her small shoulders, "I will be ready to leave when I have to."

Edward felt pity for her. He knew she felt that Thornfield was her home. But he could not let her remain here, not after they were married. He remembered her words to him, "Where you are is my home, my only home."

"I believe the time has come, Jane," he told her, "I believe that you must leave Thornfield."

Her heard her sharp intake of breath. "You have found me another place, sir?"

"Yes, Jane," he replied.

Her voice was very low. "You are going to be married, sir?"

"Ex-act-ly," he said, "pre-cise-ly. And of course, when I marry, when I give up my bachelor ways, you and Adèle will need to go, as you said."

Jane's hands were clenched. "Ireland is such a long way off, sir."

"Yes, it is," he agreed. *Say something, Jane. Stand up and fight me on this.* Jane was silent. Edward continued, "It is a long way and I do not like Ireland, so we will never see each other again if you go there."

Jane was staring at the ground. Edward asked, "Are you akin to me, Jane? I feel we understand each other. For I think that if you went away, if you left me and crossed that wide expanse of land and water, some cord of communion that binds our hearts would snap, and I would bleed internally without you."

Her heard her shaky intake of breath. But still she did not look up, did not speak.

He watched her closely. "But if you did go, you would forget me... "

She looked up then and Edward saw tears in her eyes. "I would never forget you," she cried. "How can you even think that? I could never forget you as long as I live!"

Edward watched then, in wonder, as Jane stood up and finally claimed what was hers, showing him the passion he had known was there all along.

"I grieve to think of leaving Thornfield. I love Thornfield; I have lived such a full life here. I have not been abused or trampled upon. You have treated me as an equal, Mr. Rochester, and the thought of leaving you is more frightening than the thought of dying!" She could no longer hide her tears; they ran freely down her flushed cheeks.

Edward stood up, came over to her and took her by the arms. "Then do not leave me," he said, pulling her towards him, pressing his face into her hair.

For a moment she stood still, and he could feel her body against his, could feel her breathing hard, trying to control her crying. She pulled away from him, looking at him incredulously.

"Do you think I could stay here and watch you marry someone else? Stand by and see you married to someone I do not think you truly love?" She reached up, wiping the tears from her cheeks, Edward still holding on to her arms.

"Do you think I have no heart, no soul – that I am a machine? I have as much heart as you and as much soul!" She sobbed again, unable to control herself.

"Do you think that because I am poor, obscure, plain, and little, that I cannot feel or love? If only God had given me some beauty and wealth, I would make it as hard for you to leave me as it is for me to leave you!" She began to pull away from him, to struggle against the hands that held her.

"Then you must not leave me," Edward told her. "Jane, stop struggling so." He held her firmly and she stopped, standing still, her cheeks damp.

"I do not love Blanche. She does not love me. I could never marry her, never. It is you I love, Jane, only you. Since I came to know you, it has only been you. Marry me, Jane!"

She began to pull away from him again, crying harder. "You are making fun of me," she whispered furiously, struggling even as Edward pulled her into his arms. "Let me go! I am a free person with my own will and my own spirit, and I will make up my own mind."

"Yes!" Edward said, "Yes, you will. Jane, I offer you my hand, my heart, all that I have. Marry me, Jane – say you will marry me."

Jane stopped struggling, resting her head against his chest as though she were exhausted. He held her, his lips in her hair. She was like a bird who had flown for miles, against the wind. He stroked her hair, kissing her head.

"I do not believe you," she said quietly. She raised her head. "Let me look at your face."

Edward looked at her, their eyes locked together. "Do you think I would lie to you?" he whispered.

"Are you in earnest?" she asked him, her eyes searching his face. "Do you really wish to marry me?"

"Yes!" he told her, "If an oath is necessary, I swear it!"

"Mr. Rochester... " she began.

"My name is Edward. Call me Edward."

"If you are serious... " she smiled shakily, "Edward, I will marry you."

His heart swelled, and he felt that it could not be contained in his chest. He reached up and wiped her tears away, kissed her cheeks and pulled her against him.

He kissed her lips. She felt stiff and tense in his arms, but as he kissed her he felt her relax. Slowly, slowly, her arms lifted, wrapped around his neck. He kissed her wet cheeks, her eyes, came back to her mouth again, and she was kissing him back.

He was holding her tightly, and the feeling of her tiny slender body against his drove him wild. He felt her breasts against his chest, two spots of the most incredible warmth and softness. Through her voluminous skirts he could feel her thighs along his. They continued to kiss, harder and longer. He dropped his mouth to her neck. It was so warm beneath his lips, her skin the softest he had ever felt. He felt her small hands in his hair.

Tears filled his eyes; he was overcome by finally having her in his arms, his at last. "I love you," he murmured, lifting his mouth to her ear.

He felt her kiss in his hair. "I love you," she whispered in return. He felt her begin to cry again, and he swallowed down his own tears as he kissed her again, holding her tightly.

For a few minutes thunder had been rumbling in the distance, but a sudden sharp crack made them both jump and then laugh. He pulled at her hand as rain suddenly began to pour down upon them.

Holding tightly to each other, they ran back to the house. Once inside, he removed her shawl, smiling as he stroked her damp hair back from her face, squeezing the water from her hair as it began to fall from its carefully arranged knot. He took her in his arms again. He wished they were married already, so he could take her upstairs, undress her, dry her off before the fire, and then warm her body with his. He imagined them in his bed, imagined her naked beneath him, their bodies moving together as the firelight played over them... he groaned, holding her to him.

He forced himself to pull away. "Hurry and take off these wet things." He leaned over, kissed her again, and then again.

"Good night," he whispered, "Good night, my darling."

Chapter 35 - Confiding in Mr. Carter

June, 1836

Carter stood, slapping Rochester on the back. "Get dressed. We'll go to my study and crack open a fine bottle of brandy I was given as a gift." He left the room, leaving Edward to dress in privacy. He put his clothes on, lost in his own thoughts as he tucked in his shirt, fastened buttons, and put on his coat.

A few minutes later Edward sat in one of the large armchairs next to the roaring fire, welcome at night in spite of the fine weather of the lengthening summer days. He said nothing, twirled his glass, watching the amber liquid turn and rise in the goblet, reflecting glints of light from the blaze. His eyebrows were drawn together fiercely, his dark eyes shadowed and full of ire. Mr. Carter watched him closely as he lifted his own drink to his lips. At last he set his glass down and learned forward.

"Mr. Rochester, you did not suddenly wake up one day worrying about this aspect of your health. You are a worldly man, one who has always been careful in the company he keeps, not likely to yield to the dubious charms of some pox-ridden doxy. And have no fears over the spread of disease from your poor wife; from the history you gave it is very unlikely, and would have manifested itself long ere this." He smiled, leaned back in his chair. "Come, unburden yourself to your doctor, share your thoughts. What really worries you? I see no cause for it – physically you are a perfect specimen. Your emotions, now, I am not so sure about."

Rochester sighed, rubbing his eyes wearily, "It is not my health alone that concerns me – it is the health of another, one whom I would die before harming or infecting."

He raised the glass to his lips, tossed back a mouthful, and set down his glass. He turned in his chair, faced Carter. "Carter, I have long trusted your discretion and your silence, and you have been a faithful confidant. If it were known, my thoughts and plans... " He shook his head. "You could ruin me, with one careless word." Edward laughed shortly. "Tell me, how does it feel, to have such power over a man, to be able to overthrow his life with one misplaced pronouncement?"

Carter snorted, and reared back in his chair. "Sir, I hope this is merely one of your jokes. Surely you know that all that 'power', as you call it, is not what I'm about. I care nothing for such things. I despise gossip and involvement in the personal lives of others. Your secrets have always been safe with me."

He shook his head and continued. "You are mistaken, Mr. Rochester, if you think you alone have guilty secrets. All of us have our demons, our most secret sins and vices. What kind of doctor would I be if I divulged the hidden misdeeds of this town?" Rochester nodded, his face thoughtful.

"Forgive me, Carter," he sighed, "I trust you, of course I do. How could I not?"

Carter chuckled, "And you pay me well, very well, and not just in money." He raised the bottle of brandy, laughed, poured a little more into his glass. He inclined the bottle towards his guest, who shook his head, holding up his still half-full glass.

"You are not a drinker, Mr. Rochester, never have been, have you?" asked Carter.

Edward shrugged. "At some times more than others," he admitted. "I have found that the older I get, the more it behooves me to avoid over-indulgence." He smiled grimly. "I've tended to make some of my more foolish decisions while under the spell of Bacchus."

"Ah, haven't we all?" smiled Carter. "For instance, we have all found that women tend to be far more lovely when viewed from the bottom of a cup." He cleared his throat. "Mrs. Carter, now, she was lovely to me regardless of my sobriety – one of the many ways I knew she was the one I wanted."

Rochester smiled politely, thinking of Carter's plump brown hen of a wife, clucking busily over her husband and her collection of five active young sons. Carter had married late in life, after a career as a surgeon in the Navy, and was devoted to his wife and the children he still professed to be amazed to have produced. Mrs. Carter was a good woman, a kind woman; if not possessed of a swift mind, at least displaying a full and loving heart. "You are a fortunate man, Carter."

"Ah, that I am," he agreed, "That I certainly am." He gestured towards his patient. "But, back to you. Does this mood of yours, these dark thoughts you have, arise from buzzings and chatterings I hear in the town – gossip about you and a certain young belle of the county? For I hear there is to be a marriage. I dismissed the talk as foolish, told Mrs. Carter so. Said I, 'these idle reports arise each time Rochester returns to the country, and in weeks he's gone again and nothing comes of it all'."

Carter raised his eyebrows at Edward. "Of course, my wife does not know what I know, that a marriage is impossible. Ha, and the next thing we hear is of a great house party, the gentry all assembled at Thornfield. And what happens but that I am summoned there in the dead of night, to see to an injured victim of your wife's mischief, as one floor down your alleged intended sleeps the sleep of the innocent."

Carter stretched his legs out, threw Rochester a sour look. "Mind you, I'm not sure of the wisdom of a man who invites his brother-in-law to join in the festivities as he courts his sister's successor. Or rival, or what have you."

Rochester frowned, spoke indignantly. "I did not invite Mason; he dropped in, as he considers it his right to do. Taking it as his privilege, always with a copy of my marriage certificate about his person, a subtle prelude to blackmail should I not receive him, a document that drives home his right to see to his sister's interests. I had had a letter from him while abroad. I foolishly informed him that I would be in England more often this year, tending to some neglected business. I had nearly forgotten this correspondence, until his arrival.

"No, I would never invite him," Edward shook his head. "Though he was once my friend, and thinks it his due, I would not encourage him to come – that timing at the party was one of those jokes that God sees fit to spring upon us at intervals, lest we think we have control."

Edward took a long drink of his brandy, then set the glass down with a decisive sound on the tabletop. For a second his eyes stared ahead into the fire, seemingly at nothing; he nodded at something only he could see. Then he spoke: "So be it; I must tell all. I must unburden myself to one who knows all, as the one with whom I most wish to speak cannot know it."

He turned to Carter, who was pouring himself another two fingers of the fine brandy, barely listening to Rochester's musings. Carter drank, wiped his mouth. "By God, sir, you don't drink much liquor, but you can certainly choose it! I thank you again for your gift." He noticed Edward looking intently at him, laughed. "Forgive me; please speak."

Edward leaned forward earnestly, his elbows on his knees, his strong hands clasped. "You are right, Carter, there is to be a marriage. I want it; I long for it. But not with Blanche Ingram, nor any other lady at the party." He smiled, the dark, rough-cut planes of his face suddenly softening, tenderness in his eyes and upon every feature. "At least not someone at the party whom you would expect." Carter raised his eyebrows inquiringly.

Edward went on, "I have fallen in love, Carter, when I thought to have finished with all that; having dismissed it as something out of my reach. I was caught by surprise, and love has reached out and seized me. A love such as I thought I could never feel."

"Well, enlighten me!" Carter spoke. "Do not leave me in suspense, sir; tell me, which young lady has so bewitched you?"

"Bewitched indeed! It is Miss Eyre, governess to my ward," Rochester told him. "You met her: she assisted us with Mason. I could not have gotten through that night without her; in truth, do not know how I've gotten through my life thus far without her."

Carter looked startled. "My God, that child?" He thought back in surprise to the little girl who had stood quietly at Rochester's side that morning, having sat alone outside the maniac's cell nursing Mason while her employer rode through the dark to fetch him. He had a hard time remembering her clearly, for she had made no impression upon him at the time. He remembered a dark dress, a shawl, smooth hair of a lacklustre and unremarkable colour. He had had the impression of large eyes shadowed by tender blue circles beneath, a plain face that showed concern and not a little weariness. But he could remember nothing specific about her, could not have picked her out of a crowd. He did remember, however, her youth and her size.

"Good God, man, I know how you got through your life without her – for most of it she could not have possibly existed. How old is she, for Christ's sake?"

Edward laughed, with a small shrug that conceded the point. "I cannot argue with you there; she is eighteen to my thirty-seven years, so when I was her age, she did not exist, you are right. She will turn nineteen before I turn thirty-eight, but you are correct, she is very young. Young in age, but with a mind of wisdom and maturity, and blessed sanity far beyond mine."

"And a governess yet!" Carter exclaimed. "You don't care a whit for your standing in this area, do you?"

"No, I do not," Rochester said calmly, leaning back in his chair, crossing his legs at the ankles. He put his hands behind his head, looked up at the ceiling. "After spending a month in the company of the neighbouring gentry, I can honestly say I would miss few of them were I never to see them again, which I will not, have I anything to say about it.

"I plan to take Miss Eyre away, to bring her to the Continent as soon as we are married, for Wood knows nothing of my burden, and will perform the ceremony for us. I will travel with her, and remove her as far as possible from Thornfield, with all its secrets and its poisonous inmate."

Carter shook his head, "What is it you see in this girl, to contemplate such a deed?" Rochester looked at him sharply, and Carter hastened to explain himself. "Mind you, I have nothing to say against her. I spoke little to her, as I was otherwise occupied. But I ask you in all seriousness – what is it about her that leads you to risk such a step, such a huge legal and moral breach of convention?"

Rochester took a deep breath. "There is not enough time to say what I feel, what I love about her. We have connected, she and I, in a most basic and elemental way." Carter raised an eyebrow. Edward continued. "Not in the way you are thinking. It is far more intimate; it is if we are kindred, rather than employer and governess." He made a fist, pressed it to his left side, under his heart. "She is my heart, my soul, she is every breath I breathe."

"And does she share your feelings?" Carter asked.

"She loves me, I feel it, can see it in her eyes, know it in a hundred little ways. She has accepted my proposal; she loves me as I love her. It is a wondrous thing, Carter, something I thought I would never have."

"Does she love you enough to overlook your insane wife, to defy the customs and conventions of society, to marry you and lie to the parson while doing it?"

Rochester was silent then, looking into the fire, his face suddenly grim and dark, a small and sneaking fear briefly shadowing his eyes before darting away. Carter waited.

"Oh, my good God, she doesn't know, does she?" Carter asked with a stunned air. "She has no idea!"

"Mr. Rochester?" he inquired. Edward turned to him, sighed, said still not a word.

"You have not told Miss Eyre about your wife, have you, Mr. Rochester?" Carter asked, his manner suddenly serious.

Edward shook his head, looking sad and defeated. "I cannot tell her," he said hoarsely. "She would never stay at Thornfield, would never have consented to marry me, had she known." He swallowed hard, "And I cannot risk that; I cannot live without her."

Carter closed his eyes, shook his head, "Well, this beats all I have ever heard. So, you will lie to this girl, take her as your wife? And she will have no idea that she is living in sin, surrendering her virtue to someone who is only pretending to be her husband? Or have you taken that from her already; is she trapped into this situation by your actions against her so far?"

"Damn it, Carter!" Edward sat up straight in his chair, "What do you think I am? Of course I've not treated her in such a way! I love her, would never take advantage of her. I have not laid a finger on her, and will not, until Wood has pronounced her my wife, and I have her safely away from here."

"If you have to have a woman, can you not find someone else, someone older, a widow perhaps, someone more aware of the ways of the world?" Carter inquired of Rochester, who looked back at him with irritation.

"Have you ever had a virgin, Mr. Rochester?" Carter asked bluntly. "For if that is the attraction here, they are more trouble than they are worth."

"No, I have never been with a virgin, far from it," Rochester answered him. "I am not the maiden-seducing rake you seem to think I am. My experience with women is rather sparse and pitiful compared to most men of my age and station. Would you like to hear my history? It is laughable, really, quite sad when you think about it. And then you can tell me if you believe I do not deserve this long-awaited taste of happiness.

"I have had my wretched wife, as you call her (and I do not!). She was no virgin, but I was so raw and inexperienced that I thought nothing of that. She started out seducing me before the ring was on her finger, and I was not capable of resisting her. Had I sinned less, I might have been able to resist her more, and thus have avoided the marriage that was foisted upon me.

"We had a few good days, our early honeymoon days, when we feasted on each other, but soon enough I realized that we would have to get out of bed eventually, and it was then that my life was revealed for the hideous lot it was. I was her husband in the true sense for about six weeks before I was unable to tolerate her in my bed. In truth, by that time was so disgusted I could no longer even perform with her. You can imagine her ridicule of me when that happened.

"Before I knew it, I found her at a party, up against the wall with a man of our acquaintance, and there the tone was set for the rest of the time we lived in the same house. That was the physical extent of my marriage – six weeks! A year or so later, in my anger and despair, I took my pleasure, twice, with a maid who was looking after my wife. She flaunted herself before me, knowing my weakness, knowing how alone I was and how long it had been since my flesh had known a woman's touch. I was angry at myself, sickened by my weakness, but could not help succumbing to her. I forced back those feelings, and soon repented of my liaison, for in a period of lucidity, my wife had found it out and it drove her deeper into her hatred of me. I was guilty in my own eyes, and when the misdeed became known, as of course it did, I lost the already-dwindling respect of my household.

"Not counting the kisses and surreptitious touches that Bertha bestowed on me during our so-called courtship, and the stolen moments that we experienced before the wedding, when she would escape from her nursemaid and sneak across the courtyard to my room, that was all the physical pleasure I knew from the age of twenty-one until I was twenty-seven: six weeks with a madwoman and one night – two encounters – with a Jamaican servant."

He continued, his fists clenched, eyes staring unseeing into the fire. "At twenty-seven, I was in Paris, having left the lunatic at Thornfield. There I met what I thought was the greatest love I could know, a Parisian opera dancer. For two years I loved her – it was largely lust and passion, my lust, you see, and her passion for my money; but I did love her, as much as I was able to at the time, and hoped she would be mine. She professed to love me too, and for a brief time I basked in the joy of having heart and flesh satisfied together. But she betrayed me, more than once, and it wasn't until I caught her in her bedroom, watched as another man took her, that I was able to walk away from her spell.

"I cannot remember what it was like to love her; I feel only a tired amazement that I ever could have felt so deeply for such a silly, mindless, bisque-doll of a woman. But love her I must have, or it would never have hurt so badly. I was angry enough when cuckolded to shoot her lover, and although I did not kill him, my loss of control frightened me. A part of my heart was forever sealed in stone that day, never to be reached again, but Miss Eyre slowly chips away at it, with gentle, unobtrusive power and persistence, and she does not even know she does it!

"At any rate, a child was my only souvenir of those two years in Paris – my ward Adèle, who may be mine, but is just as likely the issue of any one of several others.

"I left Paris, carried my lacerated heart to St. Petersburg, where I lived for the next year. I kept to myself by day, made the rounds of parties and salons at night, and associated with women, but let none of them touch my heart. I finally allowed myself a short affair with a woman, a married woman, but detested myself for betraying a stranger as I had been betrayed.

"I was thirty years old by this time, and let us count, had had four women and no lasting love. I moved around to different capitals, still moving in society's best circles, vainly hoping to find a love I could live with.

"I returned to Thornfield from time to time, and each time was thrown into company with Blanche Ingram. I was content enough with our shallow flirtation, but she was simply one more frivolous society beauty, and I had them around me in abundance. I enjoyed her singing and her ability to ride, but knew I could never marry her, even if I had been so inclined, which I was not. I saw her at once for a vain and heartless woman of great pride, incapable of love for anything but my fortune. I could never marry anyone living close to Thornfield, for I was well aware of the gossip, you see, the speculation on the existence of the woman in my attic. No doubt Blanche had heard it too, but I'm sure she was willing to overlook the mystery if it meant she could get her hands on my money."

Edward sighed, leaned back, closed his eyes. "I digress. By this time I was thirty-three years old, and had been with four women, loved only one and been loved by none. I was lonely in spirit, and my heart longed for love, even more than my body burned for satisfaction and release. But each time I determined to leave caution behind me and lie with anyone who would have me, I thought of Bertha, of her wild, frantic, disgusting entanglements with anyone and everyone she could find, and I restrained myself. She was no longer part of me physically, but her past behaviour tainted everything I touched, influenced any joy I attempted to experience. Even in the midst of some of my greatest delight, in the very act, my mind would flash unbidden to a scene of Bertha's I had witnessed (for when she would go off on her rampages, it was I who was called for to fetch her home!), and my gratification would be spoiled a little by the memories that occupied my mind.

"I moved on to Italy, where I found a woman or two who caught my eye. One was a widow, as heartsick as I, and I am afraid I made love to her out of pity as much as for pleasure. She wept as I took her, and afterwards clung to me and did not want me to leave her. One night with her was all I could bear. I soon met Giacinta, a courtesan, a professional mistress.

"Giacinta was a woman of great beauty and allure. She did not have the frightening emotional ties of the widow, whom I left weeping in her lonely widow's bed. On the contrary, she was alarmingly free from emotion, wanted only the lusts of the flesh and my money. She led me into heights of ecstasy I had not known, but was full of mercurial moods and had an edge of violence. She drank a great deal, and took strange potions and powders that she obtained from a charlatan of a physician. He had once been her lover, and perhaps he still was; I did not care.

"It was he who had given me the philter that gave Mason such relief after his injury at his sister's hands. I had had a mild but painful injury from a fall during a mountain climb, and when I felt the total relief it afforded, I bought a quantity of it, thinking to give it to Mrs. Poole to use on my wife when she became unruly. Unfortunately, I have found that I had best keep soporifics away from poor Grace as well, but I did keep the potion, and it has been needed on more than one occasion.

"Again I stray from my subject! Back to Giacinta – she would take these medications, and at times would be violent and agitated, unable to eat or sleep or obtain enough physical satisfaction from me. Other times she would lie in a daze, drifting in and out of sleep. It was at those moments that I realized how much my time with her was beginning to resemble my time with Bertha, how I was relieved when she was at last sleeping. I never felt the same way about her again after I thought of that.

"She exhausted me with her demands, but at times I still lie awake at night, remembering the things she did to me, and know that I will never know such rapture of the body again, nor such self-disgust and remorse of my own actions, for she was like Bertha, you see. One woman was insane, and the other was not, yet I followed her, and had no more ability to resist than a pig has for a good wallow in the mud."

Rochester continued, his face sad and his voice weary. "At age thirty-five, I was tired of her demands on me physically and financially, tired of the fighting and the moods, and I left her, incidentally being struck in the face as a parting gift. I betook my split lip and bloodied tooth to Paris, where I had been summoned to rescue Adèle, who had been abandoned by her mother. This gave me the excuse to break free from Giacinta completely. Once again, my life was barren and lonely, my heart desolate, my body untouched.

"I settled Adèle at Thornfield, and as soon as I could, went back to the Continent. I lived in Vienna for a time, and communicated with my housekeeper via letter, in which I instructed her to engage a governess for the child in my absence.

"In Vienna, a chance encounter in a dress shop led me to Clara, who became my third – and please God, my last – mistress. She was older than I, but extremely handsome, widowed after an unsatisfying marriage. She was honest and quiet and housewifely, feeding me, seeing to little needs and comforts, which was a welcome change after Giacinta's whims and small cruelties."

Rochester sighed. "By this time I had much experience from learning to satisfy Céline and Giacinta. I knew the ways of a woman's body, how to please it. But I could not please Clara; she would not respond. Oh, she would allow me to do as I pleased; she never denied me my basic pleasure, but that was the extent of it. When I questioned her, she merely shrugged, said she had always been that way, had never known satisfaction when she was with a man, and so I ceased to even try, caring only for my own feelings. It was almost a relief, being so selfish, thinking only of my own body, for that is what my life had been reduced to.

"Clara would also never talk about anything interesting – she had no conversation to offer and no opinions to discuss, and soon she became only a vessel in which I sought release. I stayed with her longer than I should have, unable to bear the thought of being alone. I would not use common prostitutes; my very mind and body cringed from such a practice. I was cowardly and kept returning to Clara long after I had tired of her, for lack of other acceptable choices.

"But at last, this past winter, I gave her some money to start her own business and broke free from her, to head home to Thornfield. Right around my thirty-seventh birthday, I started for home.

"Have you been counting, Carter, all through my sordid narrative? Fifteen years, Carter, from the loss of my own virginity at twenty-one, for I was a romantic, and refused to succumb to lust while away at school. I saved myself, held back, waited for someone to love, someone to tie myself to. This virtue was rewarded with Bertha. Then Evangeline, then Céline. After Céline came Olga in St. Petersburg and my short liaison with her. That is four, are you counting? Then came the wretched widow, whose name I cannot even recall.

"Then Giacinta, who plunged me into an even deeper disgust with myself, and brought me as close as I have ever been to total degradation. That is six women, yes, such an experienced cad I am! And finally Clara, my seventh. There was a quick anonymous liaison here and there, mostly when I was at a party and drunk, but these were few and far between and I can scarcely remember them. But seven women, Carter – seven that I can tell about. Hardly a record with which to impress anyone looking for an exciting story.

"I came back to Thornfield, having given up on love entirely, and it was on the road from Hay that I met her, my darling. Remember when my horse fell, and my ankle was sprained? I teased Jane that it was she who bewitched my horse that day, but in reality it was I who was bewitched by her; I have been since we met.

"I love her, Carter, I love her so very much! I love her spirit and her passion, her honesty, her good mind and her gentle heart. Yes, she is a virgin; well, we've never talked of it, of course, but her age and her upbringing in a religious boarding school speak for themselves. I would be lying if I said her innocence and her purity were not attractions to me, but it is the knowledge that she will cleanse and purify me, rather than that I will stimulate and awaken her. Purity of body alone is not my goal, it is the innocence of her mind and her heart and soul that I want to be part of me.

"I will be gentle with her, patient, will protect her body as I plan to protect her life. I have taken her to my heart, friendless and alone and without protection, and have pledged myself to her, to never let her know a moment's want or need. Surely, that will atone at the Day of Judgment, Carter! I will give her, body and soul, all my love and fidelity. She will be married to me, will feel God's sanction on our life together, and will continue in innocence.

"She will be blameless before the God she believes in; He will not hold her accountable for my actions. She will have nothing to repent or regret as long as I can keep her innocent of all that has gone before. She will live in peace with me and I will love and succour and protect her all the days of my life.

"I feared Bertha's taint upon me, have always had that spectre lurking in the reaches of my mind, but you have reassured me, Carter, and now I can rest easy that my darling will be safe also. I will forever love her, and she will in truth be my only wife."

Carter met Rochester's eyes, looking at him intently. "Mr. Rochester, I understand your thinking, truly I do, but please, if you will, permit me to play Devil's Advocate for a few moments, at least. I ask you, what will happen when you are discovered? For you will be discovered, sir, make no mistake on that score. The very nature of truth demands it."

Edward stiffened, his eyes narrowed. He became very still, his demeanour suddenly watchful and suspicious. "Why should I be discovered? Ten years have I kept the maniac hidden, with you and Grace as my only witnesses. Why should that change now? Before God, man, if you mean to betray me now... "

Carter's hand shot up, cut off his patient's biting words in one harsh and sudden gesture. "Say nothing, Mr. Rochester, which you may later come to regret. If you think to threaten me, sir, you may as well save your breath, for I am not worth worrying over. Betrayal will not come from me, have no fear, nor from Mrs. Poole either, I'd stake my life on it. But your duplicity will be revealed just the same, and I do not say these words idly or because I wish you ill."

Edward folded his arms over his chest, clenched his fists. "And I say it will not. I have had enough, I have suffered enough, and I shall have what I want. A normal life, a wife I love and can live with as I long to. Surely even God Himself cannot deny me any longer what He has denied me so far?"

"I know nothing of God, believe nothing of God," scoffed Carter, "but I do believe in nature, and the workings of the world, the turnings of the earth, and the tides which go out and come in again. Truth is a force of nature, and it will always come to the fore. Not always immediately, but it will come.

"You will be found out, because it is not just you anymore. Of itself, keeping the existence of your wife a secret is hurting no one; you are endeavoring to protect her. But now a young woman's life and honour are at stake as well, and if you treat her thus, the lie will become a snake and will suddenly strike back at you. Keeping Miss Eyre ignorant will not change the facts – a lie is a lie whether the person being lied to knows it or not."

Rochester shook his dark head, his eyes thunderous now, and flashing. "As I said, I will take care of her... "

Once again, Carter cut in, "Yes, as you say, you will try to care for her. I have no doubt you have the best of intentions, for I know you, Mr. Rochester, and you are fundamentally a decent man, despite the tendency to deception when it suits your purposes. But this is folly and it can only be stopped by yourself! The instant you put the ring on Miss Eyre's finger, call her Mrs. Rochester, take her to your bed and know her as your wife, you will have defrauded her and she will be the one to suffer.

"You say she is a good and religious young woman. Doubtless she has strong beliefs and a rigid sense of right and wrong before God, and lying with a man outside the bonds of wedlock, and a married man at that... I tell you she will be made a sinner in her own eyes, and though she may love you now, her guilt and misery will make her despise you later. She will either stop all physical contact with you, making you hate her, or she will continue for your sake, making her hate herself. You and she will never know another moment's joy together once the truth is revealed."

Edward's face closed down, grew so dark and glowering that Carter would have feared him had he not known him. "No, Carter, that will not happen, it cannot!"

Carter went on as though he had not spoken, "And think of how she will suffer before the world. All will look at her as a loose woman, a harlot, a mistress. And those who don't despise her will pity her as a dupe and a victim."

Rochester stared ahead, his face stony now, not responding as Carter went on relentlessly, "And what of your children? Miss Eyre is eighteen years old, and you love her beyond anything, so you say, and you will make love to her again and again. Nature being what it is, you will soon fill her belly. Can you willingly bring bastards into the world, knowing that they will suffer along with their mother, for their father's deeds?"

Rochester glared at him, "I will care for my children, as I care for the Frenchwoman's bastard, who is not even my daughter. Or... or, I will not father children at all! I know now, as I did not in the early years, how to prevent it. As far as I know, I have never gotten a woman with child, save possibly Céline, and I don't know how it possibly could have happened with her, as we practiced all manner of prevention, at her insistence, which I then went on to use with other women. I do not need to have children; why should I – children who may grow up to suffer as I have suffered?"

Carter shook his head, "So you will take away Miss Eyre's honour and self-respect, and deprive her of her natural right to bear and mother children? Your pit grows ever deeper, sir."

"Many women die bearing children, and my Jane is so small, so delicate. How do I know she would even survive a birth?" asked Edward, "I would die if she came to harm, would never forgive myself if she perished bearing my child. Is it not better to avoid spilling my seed within her, if it would keep her alive?"

Carter smiled grimly, "You are playing God, Mr. Rochester. No doubt your Jane, if given the choice, would leave her life in the hands of God if it meant she could know the joys of the marriage bed and the love of children. What right have you to deprive her of the truth and of her normal birthright as a woman?"

Edward shook his head vehemently, "All this is foolish. I tell you, we will leave this place, no one the wiser, and my love will live in innocence and joy. If I get her with child, she will bear children in safety and we will rear them together in love, all bearing the Rochester name as a right. It must be, damn it! How could a loving God treat us otherwise, for a love this great must come from Him?"

"Well, I see there is no reasoning with you, man," Carter said, a hard edge to his normally kind and gentle voice. "So talk to her, tell her all – she has a right to know, to make the choice herself." Carter pointed his finger at Rochester's face, "If you love her you owe her that."

The light dimmed in Edward's brilliant eyes, his ardent glow cooled. He sat back, his broad shoulders slumping in defeat. "I cannot, Carter, she would not just refuse, she would leave me."

He swallowed hard, his mouth suddenly dry with fear at the thought. "I could not bear it if she left me. To lose her love would kill me; I would not wish to open my eyes upon another day."

"Also consider another matter, sir, if I may bring it to your attention." Carter crossed his arms, prepared to enter the fray once more.

"Can I stop you?" Rochester asked, his grim line of a mouth twisting angrily.

"Let us set aside the issue of sin for a moment; pretend God and morality and truth do not matter. Have you considered, Mr. Rochester, that bigamy (for a bigamist you will be) is not just a sin, it is a crime by the law of the land, and that you face a prison term of at least some months, and perhaps some fines as well? What say you to that? There was even a man in Nottinghamshire, and not that long ago, who was said to have been whipped, within the prison walls, for the crime of marrying one woman while still bound to another. Are you willing to risk this?"

"If I am not in England, how can I be subject to English law?" the sullen and still angry Rochester replied. "And yes, I would risk anything to be with her."

"But if discovered and punished, you cannot be with her, or you will suffer those punishments again and again. Your lands and most of what you possess are in England, two of your homes are in England, your long-trusted and faithful servants are in England. What will become of them, and your tenants, should you be thrown into prison and your lands seized for fines? People who depend upon you – and you are known in these parts as a fair and generous master – may well be turned out of their homes and made to find other lands to farm and homes to live in.

"Your servants will need to leave and seek other situations, but without the character that an un-incarcerated employer can provide. You have long striven to protect your mad wife, hate her as you will, and she could be turned out, to have to live her remaining days in an asylum, subject to those who would harm her, or at least not see to her welfare and safety as does Grace. And she could harm others, for who else would be vigilant to keep her contained save you and Grace, even if you cannot do it perfectly at all times?"

Edward's face was white, his eyes narrowed and full of rage, but Carter went on, relentlessly, "And your second wife – as wife you will call her, but truly your mistress before the law – what will she do? To whom will she turn when her protector is in prison and his riches are diminished, and she will have no matrimonial rights to those assets that remain? She will be turned out, a fallen woman, she and her bastard children."

Rochester stood abruptly, danger in his every movement and look, "You have said quite enough, sir. I thank you for your examination of me, your reassurances as to my health, your hospitality, and your advice, all your advice, which I will have no more of. I will leave now."

Carter stood, but Edward lunged past him with animal grace and an air of violence that rooted Carter to the spot. He watched as Rochester made for the door.

"Rochester!"

Edward stopped, looked back at Carter, face stony and eyes narrowed.

"You still have the scar, of course," Carter held up his own right arm, pointed to the underside, "No one can see it with your sleeve in place, but I know it is there."

Rochester shifted his weight, watched Carter warily.

"I still remember, you know, the first time we met." Carter fixed his gaze on Edward's face, "I was fairly new to Millcote, and you had just arrived from Jamaica. I knew Thornfield's master had returned, but it was the first time I had seen you. I was summoned there, late at night, to tend to a wound made by your wife's secreted knife.

"You sat in your blood-stained shirt and breeches, and took the whiskey I poured you for the pain before I stitched your arm. You took the glass, never taking your eyes from mine, and poured the entire contents over the wound. It must have hurt like the devil, but you never flinched. Do you remember what you said?"

Edward said nothing, continuing to stare at Carter. "You said, 'I'll not die of infection; if she wants me dead she will have to kill me outright.' I looked at your face, and thought, to have such rage and bitterness at the age of six-and-twenty! Soon afterwards, you sat in your chair, and barely moved as I stitched up a six-inch long bone-deep gash in your flesh.

"Later, though, after your arm was stitched and wrapped, you did take a drink, and we sat into the night as you told me your story. I saw your angry countenance soften into relief as you shared your burden. I took it on that day, felt compassion for your untenable position, meant to help you share the burden, as well as I can, and part of sharing a burden is giving wise counsel as I see it.

"You told me, sir, how your father ruined your life by arranging a marriage for you, a union based on cunning lies and silent deceptions. Is that not what you are proposing to do to Miss Eyre? To force upon your beloved exactly the same sort of trickery that your father foisted upon you?"

Rochester started, and stood for a long time, staring at Carter with narrowed eyes and a closed, set look on his dark features. Then he spoke, his voice hoarse, "I will see myself out, Carter." And he did, leaving the house with a heavy foot and a slamming of the door.

Chapter 36 - Before the Wedding

The system thus entered on, I pursued during the whole season of probation; and with the best success. He was kept, to be sure, rather cross and crusty; but on the whole I could see he was excellently entertained.

Mrs. Fairfax, I saw, approved me: her anxiety on my account vanished; therefore I was certain I did well. Meantime, Mr. Rochester affirmed I was wearing him to skin and bone, and threatened awful vengeance for my present conduct at some period fast coming.

Jane Eyre

June, 1836

In Funchal, Madeira, far removed from the cool summer warmth of England, a man sat on a sunny terrace overlooking the sea. He was an older man, in his late fifties, but rather than the still-active vigour one might expect, his face bore the marks of pain and ill health. He wore a lap robe over his knees, and a cane was propped against the table next to him.

John Eyre had for years been an ambitious businessman, well known throughout Madeira as one of its leading wine merchants. He had worked day and night to build up this business after the failure of an earlier venture in England and he should have been able to rest now, to enjoy the fruits of his labours. But just when he felt it was safe to relax a bit, to perhaps do a bit of travelling for pleasure alone and not just for business, he had begun to be seized with frequent nausea and pain in his stomach.

His doctor had examined him and found him to have an enlarged liver. Many tonics had been prescribed, some of them so revolting and noxious that they produced symptoms as severe as those they were intended to relieve. None of them helped. Although his arms and legs were wasted, his abdomen became enlarged, and his skin had begun to display a yellow tint.

His mind had been troubled for many months. He knew his time was growing short. The doctors refused to tell him so, but he could sense the spectre of death at his shoulder. His main occupation now was to settle his business affairs; he had recently sold his business to a fellow merchant looking to expand his interests.

John Eyre had no family. He had been too busy with his company and with the acquisition of money to seek a wife when he was younger, and he had assumed that eventually the opportunity would arise on its own, at which time he would slow down and have a normal family life. But that time had never come and so he had continued to work.

His brother and sister had died long ago. His sister had had three children but John Eyre had never met them, having had a falling out with their father years ago when his other business had failed. His sister's husband, Mr. Rivers, had reacted violently to the news that his money had been lost, threatening Eyre with legal action and turning against him so forcefully that Eyre had vowed never to deal with his sister's family again. His sister had written to him faithfully, once a year at Christmas, but he had never answered her letters.

Now, looking death in the face, he wept when he thought of his sister, and wished he had been softer. He had not known what it would feel like to greet death alone. He imagined he would have to leave his money to her children, for there was no one else. He had been very angry at their father, had never forgiven his harsh words, and that anger had extended to the children as well. Up to now he had seen no other way but to leave them his fortune, although the thought grated upon him. He imagined them being glad he was dead, glad to be prospering through the death of an uncle who had been a stranger to them.

He had had a brother also, who had gone into the church. William had been a gentle soul, a quiet boy who sometimes seemed overshadowed by his two more volatile siblings. When he was a curate, he had met and married a young woman of some wealth, but upon their marriage, she was disowned by her family. William had died, and his wife Jane had died shortly thereafter. They had had a daughter, but she had followed her parents to Heaven after living some years with her mother's family.

Or so John Eyre had been told.

For months now, his thoughts had turned to spiritual matters and he had prayed to God to forgive his sins, to give him a home in Heaven, and to help him settle his earthly affairs. And this morning, a letter had arrived – it appeared his prayers had been answered.

"Good morning, Mr. Eyre!" A slim, dark-haired man walked out onto the terrace, greeting his host. "Your man told me you were out here. I am glad to see you enjoying the sunshine."

"Ah, good morning to you, Mason," Eyre replied to his guest. "How are you this morning?"

"I am feeling very well today," Mason told him. "The doctor is planning to see me this afternoon and I expect to be told that I am good as new and fit for travel. I will soon be out of your way and headed back to Jamaica."

"It has been no trouble at all, I assure you, Mason," Eyre told him. "As the doctor comes every day to see me, it has been no difficulty for him to stop at the guest quarters to see you as well."

Three weeks earlier, Mason had arrived at John Eyre's villa, bearing one very deep stab wound and many superficial injuries. He had refused to divulge any details of his ordeal and Eyre had not pressed him, for his business acquaintance was obviously in deep distress. Indeed, the depression brought on by the wounds was more severe than the wounds themselves. But Mason had recovered well and Eyre realized how much he would miss the man's company when he departed to return to Jamaica.

"I cannot tell you, Eyre, how grateful I am for your help and hospitality during my convalescence," Mason told him. "I know that I cannot repay such kindness, but I wish there were some way I could show you my gratitude."

"I was glad I could help, and having you here with me at this time has been a comfort. But I imagine you are anxious to return to your home and to your wife."

"Yes," Mason told him, "I know that Evangeline has missed me and worried for me. I have tried to reassure her in my letters, but I know that she wishes me home with her. Since we have no children, she feels herself quite alone back in Jamaica."

While Mason and Eyre had for several years been business associates, it was only on this visit that they had both ventured to speak of their personal lives. Mason had not told him that Evangeline was his common-law wife and that up until the laws of abolition had passed a few years previously, she had been a slave in his household.

"Yes, you must return to her as soon as you are able," Eyre agreed. "Anyway, if you are available to aid the man to whom I have sold my business, as you have aided me, that will be repayment enough for whatever small service I have been able to provide you.

"I have taken care of my business affairs and today I received a letter with such wonderful news, I cannot contain it."

Mason sat in the chair opposite Eyre, and listened as his host spoke excitedly.

"Long ago I attempted to contact an orphaned niece with the intention of making her my daughter and the heiress to my fortune. I was told the girl was dead, but today I received a letter from her. She is alive and well, she tells me, working as a governess in England."

"Well, that is wonderful news indeed," Mason agreed. Then he frowned, "Although... not to cast a shadow over your joy, sir, but are you sure she is indeed your niece and not... well, an impostor?"

"She knows all the particulars," Eyre said. He thought for a moment.

"She merely said that her aunt had confessed upon her deathbed to having told me our niece was dead, but it was not true. This would be an aunt on her mother's side, not a blood relation of mine, you understand. I am not sure of the circumstances. I am sure there is a long story there, but I have no time for long stories, do I, Mason?"

Richard Mason shrugged uncomfortably.

"At any rate, my letter will be sent on to Briggs, my London solicitor, when I complete my will, which of course I must do soon. Briggs can verify the girl's identity when the time comes.

"There is something I want to ask you, Mason," Eyre went on, "My niece says that she is soon to be married. I believe that in the past you have mentioned your acquaintance with a family in England named 'Rochester'."

Mason replied, "I believe there are many Rochesters in England; it is a common enough name. I know an Edward Rochester of Derbyshire."

"Ah, so perhaps you do know this family, for she writes from Derbyshire. Does this Edward Rochester have a son?" Eyre asked eagerly.

Mason frowned, "The Rochester I know is a man of my age, perhaps a bit younger. I am forty; this man is about thirty-seven or thirty-eight. He has no children."

Eyre held up the letter, "Well, my niece writes that she is to marry an Edward Rochester of Thornfield Hall, and the return address of her letter is from a town called Hay, in Derbyshire."

"Let me see that letter!" Mason snatched the paper from Eyre's hand, his eyes rapidly scanning the delicate, feminine handwriting. "Oh, my God!" The letter dropped from Mason's hand and fluttered to the ground. Mason's face was white, his hands shook. He bent to pick up the letter, his mouth working soundlessly.

"Good God, man, what is it?" Eyre asked him, the blood drained from his already yellowed complexion. He looked like a dead man.

"Oh, God, he would not!" Mason moaned. "Surely he would not attempt this?"

"Damn it, Mason, you must talk to me!" Eyre reached out, grasping Mason's arm with surprising strength.

Mason took a breath. He held up the letter, smacking it with the back of his other hand. "Edward Rochester, of Thornfield Hall in Derbyshire, is my brother-in-law. He has been married to my sister Bertha for nearly sixteen years."

"Your sister, Mason?" Eyre rubbed his forehead with trembling fingers, shaking his head in puzzlement, "How... where is she?"

Mason was silent for a moment, bent over with head buried in hands, rocking with the agony of his thoughts. Finally he rubbed his face and sat up.

"My sister is insane, incurably so. Rochester keeps her confined, with a nurse, in a room on his estate. It is she who inflicted these wounds upon me, she who stabbed me and tore at my skin with her teeth."

"So, just a month ago... " Eyre muttered. "But how did Jane... "

"Six weeks ago my sister was still alive, living at Thornfield Hall," Mason said grimly.

He stopped, thinking hard. "Oh, my God – did you say your niece is named Jane?"

"Jane Eyre," his host replied. "She signs her name there, on the letter."

"There was a girl... " Mason muttered. "After dinner, Rochester's ward, a young French girl, had her governess with her, a young woman. I barely noticed her. But afterwards, when I was injured... it seemed like a dream, but of course, it was not."

He stood, pacing. "Rochester went for the doctor, but he left a young woman there with me. He called her Jane."

"So you have met my niece?" Eyre asked eagerly. "What sort of girl is she?"

"Very young, very small," Mason said, continuing to pace. "She said very little, wiped my brow, held my hand. I remember thinking that she was the only thing that stood between me and death. I think I fell a little in love with her myself, those few hours when she sat beside me. But then the doctor came, took me to his home, and the memory faded."

He came and sat back down next to Eyre, "Anyway, Rochester obviously trusted her. But to marry her... he cannot!"

Eyre shook his head, looking confused. "Mason, what sort of man is Rochester, do I dare ask?"

Mason sighed, "That would take a long time to answer. Not a bad man, not at all. He is harsh, severe, bitter. God knows, he has reason to be. But he has cared for my sister all these years. He could have left her in an asylum and been well rid of her... or left her behind with me – but he did not. He is a man of compassion, one who takes responsibility. I don't know what to think of this."

"Are you sure, Mason?" Eyre asked desperately. "Are you certain of these facts?"

"I have the copy of their marriage certificate in my trunk upstairs. I brought it with me, in case he denied my right to see my sister. I can produce it if you like."

"I believe you," Eyre said. He was now covered with a sheen of perspiration, and he looked exhausted, "God help me, I believe you. But my niece cannot know all this. Oh, God, Mason, surely she does not know?"

"I do not know, sir," Mason answered. "Perhaps she does know and it does not trouble her."

"I cannot imagine that!" Eyre cried. "Her father – my brother – was a clergyman. If he were alive…! And she is young, not yet twenty years old. Even if she knows, if this Rochester has led her astray, this must be stopped. And if she does not know… oh, God, her life will be ruined!"

Eyre's head dropped back, his face white. Mason turned to call for a servant, but Eyre's hand reached out to him.

"You must stop this marriage, Mason!" Eyre whispered desperately. "I will write to Briggs, telling him to meet you in London. Today is June 29th. The marriage is to take place at the church at Hay, near Thornfield on July 16th, at eight o'clock in the morning. My niece has invited me. It will take you two weeks to get to England, putting you in London with only a day or two until the wedding. You and Briggs must stop this folly; you must save my niece!"

Mason stood, looking around with uncertainty.

"Please, Mason," Eyre begged him. "You said, not even an hour ago, that you wished you could repay my kindness. Well, this is what you can do! Only you can keep this marriage from taking place – please, Mason!"

Thornfield Hall, June and July 1836

Edward had forgotten what it felt like to be happy. The memory of those distant days when he was first with Céline, when a contented life seemed within his reach, had been washed away by all that had transpired since. His soul seemed to have been turned into a small, crippled, useless thing, bent and paralyzed by life's blows.

Now he came awake each morning with new hope. He went about his business as he had previously, but his steps no longer felt leaden with despair. At times joy rushed over him, lightening his limbs and flooding his body with warmth. For the first time in years he did not dread waking up every day.

When he looked at Jane he saw those same feelings reflected in her eyes. He had loved her looks – her plain, sweet features that hid such a quick mind, such a loving heart. But now when he looked at her, unable to stop a smile from lighting up his whole countenance, he saw her face looking back with such love for him that her ordinary features glowed with a sort of transcendent beauty.

Yet Jane, his stubborn, independent darling, was true to her word: she continued to teach Adèle, as she had insisted she would. A visitor to the Hall would never guess that this simply dressed young woman, devoid of jewelry or cosmetics, her hair pulled back into braids and a simple knot, would in less than a month be the mistress of this great estate, the wife of its owner.

She arose at seven in the morning to wash and dress and by eight o'clock was in the schoolroom, her head bent over books and papers, diligently working with her pupil. At ten she and Adèle would stop for a time to walk out of doors, giving them a rest from their indoor labours. If Edward was at home, he would stop what he was doing to watch them: Jane walking next to her pupil, her head bent to hear Adèle's every word. Sometimes, if Edward was outside, they would walk close enough to him for them to exchange a smile, and he would give her a quick wink, making her smile again, a soft pink blush touching her cheeks.

Jane refused to eat with him, sharing a simple tea late each afternoon with Mrs. Fairfax and Adèle, while Edward conducted business in his library and then ate his solitary supper in the dining room, one eye on the ticking clock, counting the moments until seven o'clock, when he could call Jane to him and spend the evening in her presence.

He knew that Mrs. Fairfax watched them both anxiously, worried about Jane. He remembered going in to see her the morning after his proposal, telling her he had asked Jane to be his wife. She had wished him happiness, but had looked distressed and worried, and he found out later that she had spoken plainly to Jane, cautioning her.

He would have been angry at the thought that he intended any harm against Jane, but he was too happy to let anything put a negative light on his plans. He knew that he meant only good for Jane, that he would never hurt her. And Mrs. Fairfax seemed mollified by Jane's behaviour. It was only for a few weeks, and Edward was content to go along with Jane and make her happy.

And, oh, his evenings with her. He looked forward to them the way a dying man looked to the hope of Heaven. When the clock struck seven, Jane would come to the drawing room or to the library, where for a time there was no one in the world but them.

He would pull her into his arms and she would come to him, drawn as steel to a magnet. His lips would come down on hers and for a few glorious minutes their mouths were pressed together, his lips taking hers hungrily. At first she had been nervous, unsure, as his tongue moved gently against her closed lips. But each day she grew more sure of herself, more responsive, and now her mouth opened, warm and relaxed against his. Her tongue explored his, moving lightly along his lips, tasting, touching, flooding him with a desire that he did not try to hide from her. He would wrap his arms around her, pulling her against him, thrilling to the soft warmth of her small breasts on his chest, her little body on his, as she briefly fitted the length of her shape to his.

But all too soon she would break away from the embrace, stop kissing him, and withdraw herself gently from his arms. He did not know how she had the strength and discipline to pull away from him. Standing there holding her, excitement and arousal rushing through him, he could not have separated from her by himself.

He would groan, hold on to her, but she was firm and unyielding. She would move away from him and go to one of the chairs, avoiding the sofa so that he could not sit next to her and pull her into his arms.

And there they would sit and talk the evening away, discussing all subjects, from their earliest memories of their childhoods, to how the Rochesters had come to own Thornfield.

"In the time of the Civil Wars," he told her, "Damer de Rochester was a minor official in a village a short distance from here. He hid some of the king's advisors who were fleeing for their lives and later he fought alongside the Loyalists. He was killed during one of the battles of that conflict, and his property was confiscated when the Cromwells were in power. His widow and his children lived in hiding, in great hardship. I believe she died in exile.

"In 1660, when the monarchy was restored, the king rewarded some of those who had remained loyal. Through a process never quite made clear, his son was given the Hall and a purse, which he used to buy up as much land as possible, back when it truly was nothing but fields covered with thorns. The church was built, and the stone vault that honours Damer de Rochester and his wife was placed therein. They are probably not actually in there, to tell the truth, but it looks quite impressive. At any rate, there have been Rochesters at Thornfield ever since."

He leaned over and reached for Jane's hand, "And I hope someday to bequeath this land and its profits to my children – and it doesn't matter how many sons there are." For an instant, his face looked momentarily harsh and bitter, thinking of something else. Jane squeezed his hand, and deflected the conversation from the personal to the general once again. It frustrated Edward and he groaned, but she merely laughed and went on, urging him to talk to her.

Each night she kept him at arm's length, refusing subsequent embraces, rebuffing his endearments, and keeping the conversations light. It irritated him, but it also made him laugh. He understood her independence, her need to keep the relationship on her terms. He could wait. In just weeks, she would be his, body and soul, and his happiness would be permanent.

Enough of happiness would have been his now, had it not been for the continued spectre of Bertha hanging over him. Mason had been dispatched from Thornfield, and a week later Carter had released Mason to return to Madeira and from there, Edward hoped, back to Jamaica.

But Edward still felt that disaster awaited him at every turn. He was so close now, so near to realizing the love and the normal family life that had eluded him for so long. Now his only fear was that his secret would be exposed, that Jane would discover the truth of his wife, locked away in her hellish, hidden world.

He felt guilty about his deception because in every other way possible, he had been open and honest with Jane, as he knew she had been with him. But he felt no guilt at the idea of taking Jane as his wife without the legal bonds of wedlock, for he felt that they would be morally and spiritually joined. Indeed, he had felt wedded to her from the moment she came to his arms after accepting his proposal. She was his, and he was hers. His commitment to her was as complete as if they had been magically fused into the same person. He knew that he would never forsake her, never cease to love and protect her. In his mind, she was his wife already, he was her husband, and hang the law.

The month of their engagement drew to an end; only two days remained before the wedding. Jane had continued to evade Edward's passionate embraces, allowing only a few kisses each day before she left his arms and resumed their usual formality. She continued to call him Mr. Rochester, laughing when he groaned and rolled his eyes. But he delighted in her laughter, found joy in the look on her face as she followed him with her eyes.

He could read her love for him all over her countenance, knew from how she looked that her feelings matched his exactly. His heart filled, spilled over, and he knew that when she finally allowed herself to express her feelings, he would be the most beloved of husbands in every way. He could barely wait.

Two days before the wedding he was obliged to go to Ferndean. Matters at Thornfield could not be more secure and settled, but he needed to do one last inspection of his other estate and see to things with his solicitor there in the nearby town. It was a small holding – only four farms that paid a rent – but they were large, well-operated places that brought in a good sum each year and they deserved as careful a consideration as did the fifteen to twenty farms at Thornfield.

If he was going to be away from England, travelling on his honeymoon for a year or more, he needed everything taken care of before he departed.

He hated to leave Jane behind, but she had loose ends to tie up as well. She was getting papers together documenting Adèle's schooling, for Adèle would finally be going away to boarding school at the end of August. Jane had last-minute packing to do, and she had to see to her wedding dress, which would be delivered to Thornfield Hall that afternoon.

An unexpected item would be there with the dress: an elegant veil made of the material that Jane had rejected as too elaborate. Edward had sneaked off to order it after their day of shopping, picturing Jane's face glowing beneath a curtain of the beautifully worked lace. He smiled with amusement to think of her exasperation when she discovered his gift hidden beneath the wedding dress.

Edward spent most of the day talking to the farmers who rented from him, taking note of their comments and needs in preparation for his appointment with the solicitor who oversaw his affairs in this part of the country. He did not go back to Ferndean that night but instead got a room at the inn in town. He was in a cheerful, buoyant mood and did not want the dank, mildewed gloom of Ferndean to dampen his spirits. He was done forever with darkness, with loneliness and isolation. From now on his life would be filled with the warmth and cheer that only a loving wife could bring him.

He had a simple but delicious supper at the inn and then bedded down in a warm feather bed by a banked, glowing fire, for despite the mid-summer warmth, there was still a chill in the night air. He was drowsy and relaxed. Tomorrow he would settle his business in the morning and then go back to Thornfield.

And two nights from now he would sleep at another inn along the road to London, only this time Jane would sleep next to him in the bed. He lay under the covers, thinking of Jane's small, warm body lying next to his, her head on his chest, her long, shiny brown hair under his stroking fingers.

He imagined what it would be like to finally make her entirely his, to possess every inch of that sweetness, to lose himself in her at last. He trembled at the thought, his entire body flushed with heat, until he finally had to give himself some relief. It took only a short time, thinking of Jane, and then he could finally sleep, deeply and dreamlessly.

The next day, Edward spent several hours in his solicitor's office, making provision for repairs that were needed – a few new fences, some new privies, and work on all the wells, including the one at Ferndean. With some improvement of the property, it might be the answer to what to do with Bertha. To put her there now, in the dampness, could mean a death sentence, and no matter how he felt about her, he would not deliberately cause her demise before God was ready to take her. He had not fallen that low, he assured himself. He did not know how Grace would feel, taking up residence in that lonely place, but her son, caretaker of the Grimsby Retreat where Grace had once worked, lived halfway between the two estates, so she would not be any farther from him. Edward would raise her salary, give her whatever she asked for, to induce her to take Bertha and keep her safe away from Thornfield.

He imagined being able to bring Jane home to Thornfield, to live there without fear of what lived in the rooms above. He smiled to think of Jane moving through the halls, seeing to things in her quiet manner. He liked to think of her being able to roam freely in its corridors, no secrets hidden there. He thought of the large rooms at Thornfield echoing with the laughter of children and eventually grandchildren, banishing the darkness of the past with the love and happiness within its walls. He was unable to hold back his smile of eager anticipation as he turned Mesrour towards home and galloped off as fast as he could.

It was nearly dark, with clouds scudding across the surface of a large, bright moon when Edward rode along the road to Thornfield. There was someone hurrying along the lane, someone small... and as Mesrour slowed to a near walk, Edward saw that it was Jane. He took off his hat and waved it to get her attention. She stopped, raising her hand in greeting.

"Well, look who awaits me here!" Edward said, drawing alongside her. "I knew you would miss me, but I did not expect you to come out to greet me. It's a nasty night, you must be chilled. Here, come up here with me." He leaned over, directing Jane to step up onto the toe of his boot, deftly lifting her up before him.

"All this month I could not gather you into my arms for fear of being pricked by your thorns, and now it's like I am holding a lamb in my arms," he told her, as he wrapped his arms around her, feeling her warmth against him. "You did miss me; you cannot do without me, can you?"

"I did miss you, but you must stop gloating," Jane said, as she nestled against him. Edward slipped his arm around Jane's waist, pulling her to him. He could not resist bending over to kiss her neck, feeling his arm settle around her, resting beneath her breasts. He wished he could reach up and cup one in his hand, imagining its softness fitting perfectly into his palm. He knew she would never allow that, so he merely kissed her neck, and then her cheek, as she leaned against him. He wanted this ride to last longer, but all too soon they were in front of Thornfield and he was assisting her down, then climbing off the horse himself. John was at his side instantly, taking his saddlebag and handing Mesrour off to the groom.

It was not long before Jane and Edward were sitting together in the parlour, Jane watching as he ate dinner. He had not realized until he sat down how ravenous he was. There was a tiny anxious frown on Jane's face, and she looked nervous, but he could not get her to admit what was bothering her. She told him of some disturbing dreams she had had, which he laughed off, teasing her about her pre-wedding nervousness. His teasing only lasted until she brought him into her bedroom and showed him her veil – his special gift to her – ripped in two.

Edward's heart nearly stopped within him. *Bertha.* She had been in Jane's room, close enough to touch her. Close enough to kill her if she had wished. He clutched Jane to him, holding her so tightly she could scarcely breathe. Oh, God, he could not wait to get her away from this place. If only it were the next night, if only they were married already and gone from this cursed house.

"To think what might have happened," he heard himself whispering into her hair. What if he had come home to find his beloved dead at Bertha's hand? What frenzy would have seized him then? He would have gone as mad as his wife. *Wife.* Never again would he call her that. Soon, thank God, the word 'wife' would have a different, beloved meaning.

He held Jane close. He felt so much love he was overcome with it; his heart so full he could hardly contain it. He wanted to berate Grace for once again letting Bertha roam the house, but he did not want to leave Jane's side.

Let it go. Soon enough we will be gone.

He released Jane from his arms, talking to her softly, reassuring her. Once again he blamed the mischief on Grace Poole, and once again he felt guilty, treacherous. But it could not be helped. After tomorrow, he and Jane would be gone from Thornfield and Jane's path needn't cross Grace's at all.

He soothed Jane the best he could, making her promise to sleep in the nursery with Adèle that night. He kissed her sweetly. "Good night, my love," he whispered. "Go to sleep, and dream of happiness."

Shortly after sending her off to bed, he went to his own room, looking forward to the following day, when his life would truly begin.

Chapter 37 - The Wedding

There were no groomsmen, no bridesmaids, no relatives to wait for or marshal: none but Mr. Rochester and I. Mrs. Fairfax stood in the hall as we passed. I would fain have spoken to her, but my hand was held by a gasp of iron: I was hurried along by a stride I could hardly follow; and to look at Mr. Rochester's face was to feel that not a second of delay would be tolerated for any purpose. I wonder what other bridegroom ever looked as he did—so bent up to a purpose, so grimly resolute: or who, under such steadfast brows, ever revealed such flaming and flashing eyes.
Jane Eyre

16 July 1836
Edward stood in front of the full-length looking glass in his room, checking his appearance one last time before he left the room.

He looked quite forbidding in his formal suit. He tried to relax his face, tried to assume a look of smiling happiness. But he was too nervous. He held his hands out in front of him, fingers spread. He was so tense he felt he should be shaking, but his hands were steady.

He forced himself to stay calm, to coolly face the next two hours, after which Jane would be his and their life together could begin, far from Thornfield and all its secrets.

He left his chamber and headed downstairs. Pilot followed him, anxiously trailing his master. Edward's stress had communicated itself to his dog and Pilot had driven him to distraction with his nervous pacing about, as though he sensed that his master's leaving meant that he would be left behind.

Edward sighed, bending down to scratch behind the dog's ears. "What's the matter, old man? Do you think you'll be left behind? Now, when have I ever done that, eh? Six years I have had you and you have always come with me. Good thing Jane likes you too."

Jane. Edward stood for a moment, his heart swelling within him as he thought of her. His darling. Soon they would be joined forever, one flesh, and nothing would part them.

All had gone well up to now, but the fear still nagged at him, the fear that at the last moment something would happen to tear Jane from his arms.

It was past seven-thirty and Edward checked that the new carriage was waiting by the door, the luggage ready to be taken down and strapped to the top. He would give Jane a few minutes to bid farewell to Mrs. Fairfax and Adèle, and then they would depart, first to the church and from there to London. It would be a trip of several days' duration, but he and Jane would be safely wed and journeying together, that was the important part. From London they would journey to Paris, a city that had long been tainted for him by memories of betrayal and lost love. Now he looked forward to seeing it with new eyes, accompanied by one who truly loved him.

After Paris, he planned to take Jane to Italy, then back to the villa for the winter. He had already written to his caretakers to begin preparing for their arrival, to set up a new large bed in one of the other large chambers. He would not sleep with his wife in either the room or the bed in which he had slept with Céline.

Back inside, he waited for her, pacing, the tension knotting his stomach until he nearly felt ill. The sound of a soft footfall made him look up.

Jane. A beautiful bride. His beautiful bride, standing at the top of the steps, waiting for him.

Is not every bride lovely, that first moment her husband looks up and sees her? Edward had little experience with weddings, only his previous one. He remembered being struck by Bertha's beauty as well, the otherworldly aura of her coming towards him in her bridal finery.

But he had not been prepared for this. The overwhelming love that flooded his soul at the sight of her. He could not breathe. He held out his hand to her, drew her into his arms.

"Beautiful," he breathed into her hair, crowned now by the simpler veil she had wanted in the first place.

"Fair as a lily," he whispered, "the pride of my life, the desire of my eyes." She smiled at him, her eyes brimming with tears.

He released her then, granted her a few moments to swallow some breakfast. "It won't do to have your stomach rumbling in reply when Wood asks who takes this man," he teased. "It will look as though I don't intend to provide for you at all. But I will feed you sumptuously later, I promise."

He still paced, sending someone over to check that the vicar was at his place in the church. It was with relief that he was finally able to clasp Jane's hand in his and rush them up the walk to the church.

Was the weather fair or foul that day, he would later wonder? He would remember only bits and pieces of the hours that followed, in future times when he had only his mind to play back images from his life.

There were fleeting pictures through his memory – Mrs. Fairfax biting her lip, tears in her eyes as they hurried by. Adèle jumping up and down in her excitement over Jane's finery.

Jane's quick intake of breath as they advanced up the path, the brief warmth of her as she leaned up against him. The fragrance of her in his nostrils.

The church echoed with their footsteps as Wood met them at the front. Edward stood straight, his eyes on the vicar, wishing him to be done with the ceremony soon so they could be on their way. He was aware of Jane next to him, felt her steadiness, her quiet breathing. He willed himself to be calm.

"I require and charge you both, as ye shall answer at the dreadful day of judgement, when the secrets of all hearts shall be disclosed, that if either of you know any impediment why ye may not lawfully be joined together in Matrimony, ye do now confess it. For be ye well assured that so many as are coupled together otherwise than God's word doth allow, are not joined together by God; neither is their Matrimony lawful."

There was silence in the church and Wood opened his mouth to continue.

"The wedding cannot go on!"

It came as no surprise to Edward to hear the voice; it was as though he had expected it. He did not turn, did not falter. He looked straight at the vicar.

"Proceed."

He marvelled at the sound of his own voice, how clear, how cold. Now it was Jane who was restless, anxious. He could feel her eyes go from him to the man who was walking up the aisle.

Edward turned slowly, lifting his eyes to see a tall, well-dressed man. The stranger advanced steadily, eyes fixed on Edward. His thinning hair was dark, carefully arranged. His face was sombre, concerned.

"Who are you?" Edward asked, his voice low.

"My name is Briggs," came the deep voice of the man. "I am a solicitor of Doughty Street, London. I am here to report an impediment to the marriage.

"Mr. Rochester has a wife now living."

Edward reached for Jane, slipped his arm around her waist, pulling her against his side. There was a roaring in his ears. The men around him were talking, he could see their lips moving, but none of the words made sense to him.

Jane was the only reality. He clutched her to him, feeling her as the only solid thing in a hazy, wavering world. Standing there in the church, he was reminded of a long ago sermon he had heard, a fragment of which floated through his brain – something about "that which I have greatly feared has come upon me". The words repeated themselves in his head.

He heard himself talking, demanding to know what the man was talking about. He marvelled that he could speak. Part of him wanted to grab Jane's hand and run, run to anywhere, far away from what was happening around him.

He watched as Briggs removed a pair of spectacles from his pocket, putting them on and beginning to read from a document he had produced with a flourish from the pocket of his coat.

"I affirm and can prove that on the 20th of October A.D. 1820, Edward Fairfax Rochester of Thornfield Hall, in the county of Derbyshire, and of Ferndean Manor, in Yorkshire, England, was married to my sister, Bertha Antoinetta Mason, daughter of Jonas Mason, merchant, and of Antoinetta Mason his wife, a Creole, at San Benedictus Church, Spanish Town, Jamaica. The record of the marriage will be found in the register of that church – a copy of it is now in my possession. Signed, Richard Mason."

Briggs held up the paper. *He's enjoying this, the bastard.*

Edward's mouth felt dry, as though his tongue would stick to the roof of his mouth when he spoke.

"That, if a genuine document, shows that I have been married, but it does not prove that the woman mentioned therein is still living."

"She was living three months ago," said Briggs. "I have a witness to the fact."

"Produce him, or go to Hell."

Briggs turned, "Mr. Mason, will you step forward?"

Edward felt his blood run cold within him; the roaring in his ears resumed. He could see Mason step out of the shadows, his face downcast. He looked at Edward with a sort of pleading look, but all Edward felt was violence, madness. He advanced on him, hands held out. He felt he could throttle Mason with his bare hands.

"What have you to say?"

"I am sorry, Edward," whispered Mason, "but this is not right, you know it is not." He turned to those assembled, "My sister is living at Thornfield Hall."

"Impossible!" Edward heard the vicar say, "I have been here for years, and there has never been a Mrs. Rochester at Thornfield Hall."

The roaring in his ears ceased, his mind was suddenly clear. Edward looked at Jane. She was watching him, her eyes searching his face. He kept his eyes on hers as he answered, spoke the words that would confirm what he could no longer hide.

"No, I took care that none should hear of her," he said. He swallowed, took a deep breath. "Bigamy is an ugly word, but I meant to be a bigamist. But fate has outmaneuvered me, or Providence has checked me." His shoulders drooped. He reached for Jane's hand.

It was a dream. No, not like a dream, his worst nightmare come true, as he led the group up to the Hall, and up to the third storey to meet his wife. His mind was no longer in his body; he watched from a distance as a man, one who looked like him and sounded like him, brought the company into the room, where Bertha ran back and forth in an agitated fashion. The man told the people who she was, endured the attack of the maniac, fought her off, and later, stood and explained to them how he had come to be in this position. Edward watched, detached, as the play spun out before him, and came to its conclusion.

The faces before him meant nothing, all the words he spoke meant nothing. All he saw was Jane, standing before him, calm, her eyes still fixed upon his, tears sliding down her pale cheeks. Once she swiped at them with her finger, and that simple gesture tore at his heart, shook his carefully maintained shell of composure.

"Now, I must see to my wife." He was not sure he could move, but he turned, opened the door, and went inside, Jane's eyes boring into his back as he closed the door.

He stood inside the door, looking over at the bed on which Bertha lay, fighting the cords which held her. Her face was red, tendons stood out in her neck, veins pulsated at her temples. Grace sat on the bed next to her, holding her shoulders, making soothing noises. She turned at the sound of his entrance, and looked at him for a long time. Her face was sorrowful.

His feet felt heavy; he did not think he could move them. But they carried him over to the table, and he pulled out a chair and sank down into it. Grace still sat, across the room, looking over at him.

He put his hands on the table, let his breath out in a long, shaky sigh. His heart was pounding as if he had run for miles. He heard Grace's footsteps coming towards him. She said nothing, just pulled a chair next to his, and sat down. There was a pause, a hesitation, and her hands reached out and covered his. He looked at the table. Her hands were red, chapped, rough on top of his. He lifted his eyes, saw her looking at him. There was no condemnation on her face, no anger. Just sorrow.

The tears came then. He bent his head, and pulled his hands out from under Grace's, buried his face in them. His shoulders shook with the force of his sobs.

"Grace... " he faltered, "Grace... "

"Shhh," she told him, "I know."

He continued to cry, until the tears spent themselves. He reached out his hand, groped towards Grace. She reached out, took it, squeezed it. He clung to her, kept his head bowed. From the pocket of her apron, she produced a handkerchief and pressed it into his hand.

"Don't worry," she told him, "It's clean."

That struck him funny, and he gave a small laugh, shaking his head as he wiped his face.

"Grace," he whispered hoarsely, "I have made a bollocks of my whole life."

For a moment, she said nothing. Then she spoke very quietly. "Your life is not over yet," she raised her head, looked at him, "Neddie."

He stood outside Jane's door, debating whether or not to knock. He knew she was inside, he could sense her on the other side of the heavy oak door. But he could not hear her, could not tell what she was doing. He listened for a cry, a sigh, some sounds to indicate how she was, what her demeanour was now. He had expected to hear an explosion of weeping, some sounds of grief coming from the room, but there was nothing. He paced, his head inclined towards the door as he walked, but still there was nothing but a deathlike hush.

He wanted to tap on the door, to call to her, but something stopped him. There had been times when sorrow had overwhelmed him and all he had been able to do was lie down and sleep. It was an escape, but it was temporarily helpful, it was healing. If she had sought relief in that brief comfort, he did not want to disturb her.

He got a chair from the end of the hall, carried it carefully and quietly over to the door, and set it down so the seat was just inches from the doorway. If she came out, she would have to come past him. He sat down, determined to stay there until he saw her.

He could only imagine what was going through her mind, what she must be thinking. His heart ached to think of her pain, her devastation when she found out that he had lied to her, had hidden such a secret, had attempted to make her not his lawful wife, but a mistress.

Would she ever believe now that he loved her? Would she think that he merely thought of her as a plaything, a novelty? Would she think that nothing but a sensual passion for her drove him to take the steps he had taken? It nearly broke his heart to think she might believe that. He could not wait to let her know how much he loved her, how he adored her and had never meant to hurt her.

Time crept by, the shadows changed in the hall. Edward sat in the chair, leaning on his arm, the side of his index finger nervously rubbing against his lips as he stared at the door. He would wait for her. No matter how long it took her. She had to come out sometime, and when she did, he would be there.

Chapter 38 - After the Wedding

"You are going, Jane?"
"I am going, sir."
"You are leaving me?"
"Yes."
"God bless you, my dear master!" I said. "God keep you from harm and wrong—direct you, solace you—reward you well for your past kindness to me."
"Little Jane's love would have been my best reward," he answered; "without it, my heart is broken."
Jane Eyre and Edward Rochester - Jane Eyre

Edward had no idea how long he had been waiting outside Jane's door. The shadows in the hall had changed and lengthened, and the silence in her room had continued. He was starting to become frightened for her. What if she had been driven to the depths of despair and had harmed herself? Edward thought her too strong for that, but who could truly know what was in another's mind? After all, until today, Jane had believed him to be honest with her.

He had just decided to give her another few minutes when he heard the click of the latch and saw the handle of the door turn. Quickly he stood up. Jane emerged from the bedroom, her face white and drawn. Edward was standing so close to the doorway that her foot hit his, causing her to stumble. He caught her in his arms, holding her against him.

"You have come out at last," he whispered, resting his cheek on her hair. "I had told myself I would only tolerate another five minutes of that quiet before I forced the door open, I was so worried for you." Jane was silent. Edward could feel her chest under his arms, rising and falling with her quiet breathing.

"I thought that you would be heartbroken, weeping; but I was wrong. You have not wept at all." Jane shook her head, still not speaking.

Edward held her tighter, pressing his lips to her head, "Jane, forgive me. I never meant to hurt you like this." No words came from her in reply, there was only a shaky sigh.

"Jane, you know I'm a scoundrel."

She stood very still for a moment, then she nodded slowly, "Yes, sir." Her voice was nearly a whisper.

"Then tell me so, roundly and sharply."

He could bear harsh words, knew he deserved everything she could think of to say to him. But this still, white-faced heartache tore at him, made him fear for her.

She shook her head again, "I cannot. I am tired and sick. I need some water." Just then she stumbled and went limp against him. Edward turned her towards him. Her eyes were closed, her lips looked bloodless.

"Jane," he whispered. His lips trembled. He picked her up in his arms, carried her downstairs to the library, and sat her gently in the chair by the fireplace, reaching up to smooth her hair back from her face. He backed away, still watching her.

He quickly he made his way to the liquor cabinet and poured some red wine into a goblet. He leaned over and made her drink some, holding the glass to her mouth.

"Do you feel better?" he asked her. She nodded.

"Here, taste it again." Obediently she drank some more, reaching up to wipe at her lip with a shaking hand. Edward was relieved to see there was more colour in her cheek. He set the glass down, bent to kiss her. She pulled away, avoiding his lips. Her hand went up in a weak gesture, as if to ward him off, and just as quickly, it fell back to her lap.

"Jane!" he pleaded with her. She looked at him quickly, her eyes dark and inscrutable, then looked down again.

"So you will not kiss me, because I belong to another, is that it?" He crouched down next to her chair, looking pleadingly up into her face, "You think I cannot touch you, because I have a wife already?"

Jane swallowed, nodding, looking down at her hands, which were now entwined in her lap. "Yes."

Edward shook his head, standing up. "You must have a very bad opinion of me then. You must think I am very low and unprincipled, plotting to pull you into a trap and rob you of your honour and self-respect.

"I understand, Jane, you still feel weak, and I know you are afraid to speak for fear you will cry and make a scene. So instead you are sitting there, thinking how to act – I know you."

Jane's voice trembled when she spoke, "Sir, I have no wish to act against you… " She broke off abruptly.

"No, not in the way you are looking at it," Edward said bitterly, "but from where I stand, you are scheming to destroy me. You will not kiss me, you are going to stay here and be Adèle's governess only, a stranger to me, just seeing me as someone who tried to turn you into a mistress. Your heart will be hardened against me, just ice and rock."

Jane looked up at him, "Adèle must have a new governess, sir."

Edward felt the first stirrings of panic move in his chest. He was afraid he would not be able to breathe.

He began to speak rapidly. "I will send Adèle away to school, and I will take you away from here, Jane. I never should have brought you here, but I did not know what else to do. Adèle needed a governess. I never dreamed, Jane, that you would be what I had looked for all my life, that I would fall in love with you. We will go away from here."

He was thinking as he spoke. "I will close up Thornfield; board it all up and leave Grace Poole here to care for that monster, that fearful witch. Grace's son is close enough, he can help her if her patient decides to set something on fire, or stab someone, or bite them… " He could not continue. His heart was filled with such bitterness, he could barely contain it.

"Mr. Rochester, how can you speak of her that way?" Jane's distressed voice cut in. "You sound so cruel – she cannot help being mad!"

"Oh, Jane!" Edward reached up to rub his face wearily with his hands. "I do not hate her because she is mad. Did you hear the story I told upstairs, how I came to marry her, how the Masons, along with my father and brother, tricked me into marrying her? How I came to be burdened with her for fifteen years? My God, Jane, fifteen years!"

"Yes, I heard the story. I feel for you, Mr. Rochester, you cannot know how much. But it is not her fault, and to hear you speak of her like that…"

"Do you think if you were mad I would hate you?" Edward asked her.

"Yes, I think you would," Jane said firmly. For the first time, her voice showed a renewal of her spirit and energy, and Edward was glad. If only he could convince her of his love for her.

"You are wrong, my love. I know your mind, I know your love for me, and if your mind were broken, I would love you and care for you forever. If you think I would not, you have no idea of the kind of love I am capable of. The kind of love I've found with you, with you and no one else.

"That is why we have to go away, to start our lives over again away from this place," he told her desperately. "Jane, we will go away, where no one knows us. We will be married, in a church, the way we should be. I will love you with all my heart, and care for you always, and never leave you. No one will know you; you have no family to object and to worry. You will be my family and I will be yours, and no one need ever know about all this."

Jane shook her head, then looked up at him. "I will know," she told him, her voice now steady. "I would never be able to live with myself; I could never live like that."

Edward turned away from her, looking frantically about the room, then looked back at her. "Now we come to it – now the truth comes out. I knew it – I knew that eventually we would come to this." He bent over to her, his lips to her ear, "Jane, listen to me, listen to reason. If you don't, I'll try violence."

Edward felt at the edge of his control. All this day, from the time he had first heard Briggs speak in the church, he had been fighting for mastery of his emotions, and now his frayed nerves were as close to giving way as he had ever felt them. He was not sure he could stay calm. He felt frantic, almost panicking, at the thought that Jane would leave him.

He sat down near her, pulling a chair up near hers, but before he could speak, Jane had dropped her face into her hands and was crying. She had kept her composure as long as she was able, but she, too, was feeling the strain and was no longer able to stop the tears. Edward sat, watching her as she sobbed, unsure of what to say. His heart felt as if it would shatter with the pain he felt, the pain he knew he had given her. His heart ached, throbbed within his breast, at the thought of how he knew Jane was feeling right now. He would have done anything at that moment to take away her heartache.

He moved closer to her, whispering to her, entreating her to be calm, to speak to him. Eventually, her tears slowed, and she grew calmer. He passed her his handkerchief, watched as she wiped her eyes. He tried to take her in his arms, put her head on his shoulder, but once again she refused to allow his embrace.

"Oh, God, Jane, do you not love me?" he whispered with despair. "To see you shrink from my embrace, as if I were some toad, or… or… some ape… ! I cannot bear it."

Jane raised her tear-stained face to his, reaching up briefly to touch his cheek. "I do love you," she said, her voice once again unsteady, "more than ever, but this has to be the last time I ever tell you."

He reached up, held his palm against her hand, where it rested on his cheek, "Why, Jane? Why should it be the last time?"

For a moment she could not say the words. She sat, her hand against his cheek, looking at him with such anguish in her face that he nearly wept. He had felt as though all his tears had been used up earlier when he sat weeping before Grace, but now he felt his eyes fill again.

Jane pulled her hand away, settled back into the chair, "Mr. Rochester, I must leave you."

"Yes," he told her, "for a few moments, to wash your face, and comb your hair, and get ready to depart this place. And then we will leave, together!"

Jane looked at him, her green eyes searching his, and then she shook her head.

Edward felt as though he would start to scream if he sat there another minute. He stood up, began to pace. Jane stood also, moving behind the chair, her eyes fixed on him. She held onto the back of the chair, as though she could barely stand without the support.

He came over to her. "Oh, God, Jane, you cannot leave me. Please, I beg of you, tell me you will be mine; tell me you will stay with me."

He moved next to her, reaching his hands out to cup her face, turning her face up to his. "Jane, do you mean to go one way in the world and leave me to go another?"

She nodded, "Yes."

He leaned over, resting his head against hers, "Do you mean it now?"

"I do." Tears had started in her eyes, threatening to spill over.

Edward bent, kissed her forehead, then her cheek; kissed the tear that had begun to slide slowly down her cheek. He licked his lip, tasting the salt of that tear on his tongue. "Do you mean it now?" his voice was anguished. He slid his fingers up into Jane's hair, kissed her head. "Oh, Jane, this is bitter, this is wicked. It would not be wrong to love me."

Jane pulled herself free from his grasp, and moved away. He held onto the chair himself, as she told him, "It would be wicked to obey you!"

He watched her, standing there trying to keep herself strong before him. "Jane, I know you feel it would be a sin to love me, to live with me as my wife. But isn't it worse to drive a fellow human being to despair? I don't know what I would do without you – do you not think God would understand that you are not sinning, but saving me?"

She was silent for some minutes, her eyes fixed on his. Then she shook her head, "Mr. Rochester, no person can save another. You must not look to me alone for your happiness; I cannot give you what you need, not like this." Her eyes were dark, brimming with tears, pleading for his understanding.

He stood for a moment, head bowed, taking deep breaths to calm himself. Slowly, he raised his head, looking at her. "So you condemn me to live wretched, and to die accursed?"

She shook her head again, "Oh, no, Mr. Rochester, I pray you will live sinless and that you will die tranquil!"

"You are going to snatch love and innocence from me? Send me back to a life of lust and vice?" His voice rose; he was growing ever more frantic, "Oh, God, Jane, think of my life if you leave me. You will take all happiness away from me. What will I do, Jane, where will I find a companion and some hope?"

"Do as I do: trust in God, trust yourself. Believe in Heaven. We will meet again there." She looked at him, standing there with his nails digging into the upholstery of the chair. "Please, Mr. Rochester. You must look to God as your salvation, trust in Him. He loves you more than I ever could."

He was shaking all over, his heart pounding. She began to back way, her eyes fixed on him. Before he realized what he was doing, he had crossed the room, pulled her into his arms, holding her so tightly she gasped. He was barely aware of what he was doing. For the briefest moment, violent images flashed through his mind. He imagined killing her, killing himself. He imagined pushing her to the couch, pulling up her skirts, taking her by force, making her his so she could never leave him. He was horrified by his thoughts, but he was desperate to keep her here with him, where if he could only say the right combination of words, perform the right actions, she would stay with him, live with him, love him.

But they were only thoughts, just a product of his frantic grief acting on his heartbroken mind. He could no more act with violence towards her than Jane could yield and give in to his wishes. They still remained who they were... he could not harm her, and she could not obey him. She sighed and relaxed in his arms, looking up at him with such trust, such love. His arms loosened and he set her free.

"It is not just your body I want," he whispered, "it is your heart, your soul. Please, Jane, I beg you, do not leave me." She was moving away from him, leaving the room.

Edward's legs could barely support him, and his eyes were so blurred with tears he could not see. He made his way to the sofa and crumpled onto it. Sobs came over him, tore through him; he could not stop them.

From far way, he heard footsteps, felt Jane leaning over him. She knelt by him, and he felt her little hand, so soft and warm, stroking his hair. She kissed his cheek. He tried to sit up, tried to catch her hand, but she pulled it away from him, and left the room. He laid his head down again, too drained to attempt to follow her.

She went upstairs, and his tears resumed as he heard the door of Jane's room close firmly behind her.

She loves me. She will not leave me. She cannot leave me...

Chapter 39 - What Will I Do, Jane, If You Leave Me?

"There was a young lady, a governess at the hall, that Mr. Rochester fell in ... love with. The servants say they never saw anybody so much in love as he was: he was after her continually. They used to watch him—servants will, you know ... and he set store on her past everything ... Mr. Rochester was about forty, and this governess not twenty; and you see, when gentlemen of his age fall in love with girls, they are often like as if they were bewitched. Well, he would marry her."
Innkeeper, The Rochester Arms - Jane Eyre

17 July 1836

The harsh morning sunlight slanting across his bed awakened Edward with a start, and he got up quickly, fumbling for his watch, squinting at it with eyes that burned. Nearly eight o'clock. Usually he was awake by six, dressed and ready to begin his day. But the previous night had been long and restless, his periods of sleep short and troubled and dream-filled. He had tossed and turned in his bed, his mind racing as he replayed the day's events over and over in his mind.

Near daybreak he had gotten up and dressed. He wanted to go to Jane's room, speak to her further, make her listen to reason. But he knew her sleep would be as troubled as his own and he did not want to disturb her, so he kept to his room and paced back and forth in the pre-dawn dimness. His aching heart seemed too heavy for his chest and he sighed repeatedly to relieve the pressure of it.

Last night, after his unexpected explosion of tears had ceased, he lay spent and exhausted, his wet face pressed to the rough brocade of the parlour sofa. Jane had kissed him and quit the room but he knew she had gone to her chamber, and later he had stood a long while outside her door, his hand on the knob, as he listened to her restless movements within.

After walking about his room early this morning, his emotional turmoil and fatigue caught up with him and he had stretched across his bed, his arm across his face, still fully dressed. "Just a brief rest," he had promised himself, then he would go to Jane and once again present his case. They could walk together in the orchard, talk over their dilemma in the bright light of a new day, removed from yesterday's painful events. There would still be time to prepare for their journey, to leave for London in preparation for their trip to the continent. That was the answer, he felt: to remove Jane from England and all its memories and influences; to start their new life together in a place of flowers and tangy salt air and forgiving, sun-kissed breezes.

How different last night had been from what he had envisioned! In the weeks leading up to their wedding, Edward had often dreamed of their first night together, the two of them at last alone, far from the dark secrets of Thornfield Hall. He had imagined how he would caress her, make her ready for him, awaken her to all the rapture the body could give. He had thought longingly of how Jane could finally feel free to let her natural passions express themselves. He had dreamed of their joyous union, how they would sleep the night away in each other's arms after he had made love to her, gone into her and made her his own. Instead, they found themselves exiled from each other, both suffering their separate torments all night long in their own rooms.

He got up from his bed and went into his dressing room. His clothes were rumpled, his hair disheveled in some spots and flattened to his head in others. He drew near to the washstand and looked into the mirror. His eyes were red and bloodshot, his face puffy. He poured water into the basin and washed his face, shivering at the shock of the cold water on his skin. He cleaned his teeth, ran his comb through his hair and straightened his cravat before stepping into the hall.

The floor was silent. He could hear the distant bustle of the servants on the first floor but the second was quiet except for the ticking of the large clock at the stairway landing. He moved quickly to the door of Jane's room and knocked, softly at first, then more insistently.

"Jane?" he called, pushing the door open slowly. There was no answer, and he opened the door all the way and stepped inside. The room was as silent as the corridor outside. A smaller clock on Jane's wall ticked a lower echo of the clock on the landing, and from the hall he heard a muffled "bong" as it struck the half hour.

Edward's dark eyes swept the room. All was as neat and orderly as the room's occupant herself, the silver-backed brushes lined up neatly on the dressing table, the coverlet pulled up on the four-poster bed. No, a slight rumpling could be seen, as though like him, she too had merely laid on top of her bed this night past.

She must be in the schoolroom, he thought, and headed down the corridor to that chamber. It would be like her, the day after her aborted wedding and the revelations that had come to light, to resume Adèle's lessons, to soothe her battered heart with hard work and routine. But the schoolroom too was empty, neat and barren. A peek into Adèle's nursery revealed no one either, and he went to the head of the stairs and shouted impatiently for one of the maids.

"Yes, sir?" she said breathlessly, brushing her apron into place as she ran up the stairs.

"Ask Miss Eyre to come upstairs, if you please," he told her.

"Miss Eyre?" the young maid asked with some confusion. Edward was irritated with her stupid look.

"Yes, Miss Eyre," he snapped at her. "She is not upstairs, therefore she must be downstairs. Ask her to come to me at once."

The housemaid frowned, "She's not downstairs, sir."

"Well, then, where is she?" he asked her. Good God, what did it take to get a servant with some sense these days?

"I don't know, sir," the maid said, twisting her hands together. "She din't come to breakfast, and Mrs. Fairfax looked up here for her. You weren't down neither... "

"Yes," he said curtly, waiting for her to continue.

"We just thought, I mean... " A deep red blush flooded the maid's already florid complexion, and he saw her eyes dart towards the door of his bedroom. "I mean... " She stammered and her voice halted as she dropped her eyes.

Edward's face felt warm as well as he caught her meaning. He felt a flash of anger and almost lashed out at the flustered young woman, then caught himself. Wasn't that what he himself would have wanted? Would that Jane had spent the last night with him, in his arms, rather than the two of them apart, each suffering alone.

"Perhaps she is in the orchard," he murmured, more to himself than to the girl standing in front of him. "Sir?" she asked him. He looked up sharply, could see she wanted nothing more than to go back downstairs. He waved her away impatiently.

"That is all," he told her. "Thank you. If you see Miss Eyre, kindly tell her I am in the orchard."

"Yes, sir," she told him with some relief, backing away and hurrying down to the first floor.

A moment later, Edward followed her, going out through the side door that was the shortest way to the gardens and orchard. A brief inquiry to John, whom he met on the way, revealed that he had not seen Miss Eyre this morning either.

The orchard was lovely in the cool early morning. A breeze blew refreshingly across his flushed face, and he could hear birds twittering in the trees overhead. There was a sweet fragrance in the air from the blossoms on the fruit trees. He moved along the path, searching for Jane at the benches and low walls that she had loved to rest on. He expected to see her around every turn, imagined her looking up to see him approaching, the sweet smile that would light up her face.

But he did not see her anywhere and uneasiness began to work its way into his heart. He had not wanted to call for her, not wanting the servants to hear and know how frantically he was beginning to look for her. But he could stand it no longer, and finally he stopped, cupping his hands around his mouth and calling into the morning stillness, "Jane!"

The sound startled the birds in the trees around him, stopping their chirping for a moment as his voice rang through the orchard. "Jane!"

For a few minutes, Edward walked outside, calling to her as he went. Then his hands dropped to his sides as the truth finally hit him with the force of a blow. He remembered the duel he had fought with Céline's lover, nearly eight years ago now. He saw himself aim the pistol with deadly calm and coldness, pointing the weapon and coolly pulling the trigger. He saw again the man's whole body jerk, his arm twitch as his hand moved up to it, and the sudden spill of red through the clutching fingers. Was that what it had felt like? A quick painless blow that takes your breath, then a spreading pain and feeling of warmth and heaviness as your life blood flows from you. For that is what Edward felt now.

Jane was gone.

The knowledge hit him full force, and it was as though he had known it from the moment he had opened her door. He knew she wasn't in the house, nor on the grounds. She was gone and he could only admit now what he had known from the moment he had awakened this morning. He had felt her absence, had pushed away the pain of it, not willing to own up to it. She had left him, and all the searching he could do would not bring her back.

He turned then and headed for the house. His legs felt as though they could not bear his weight. His stomach felt heavy and queasy. He wanted to sit down where he was, afraid his feet could not carry him into the house.

Mrs. Fairfax met him in the foyer as he entered the house. He saw on her wrinkled kindly face a mirror of his own thoughts. He also saw her concern for him and it irritated him rather than comforted him.

"Mr. Rochester... " she began, but he curtly cut her off. He knew she had heard him calling for Jane, knew she knew that Jane was gone. He did not want to talk to her. He brushed past her and headed back up the stairs to Jane's room.

Edward entered the bedroom and shut the door firmly behind him so no one could enter. Turning the key and leaving it in the keyhole, he pivoted and looked all about him. It appeared nothing was touched. The trunks still stood against the wall, corded and locked. The cards of address that he himself had filled out were still attached to them. It had amused him that Jane was too superstitious to do them and he had pulled the cards from her hand with a laugh at her silliness. She had known. He should have known that disaster awaited them, should have snatched her then and there and spirited her away, married her on some distant shore and never let her go from him.

His heart thudded in his chest as he moved to the closet and opened the door. Her wedding dress hung there, and his shaking hand reached out and touched it, stroked the satiny texture of the sleeve. Hardly aware of what he was doing, he gathered the gown in his arms and hugged it to his chest. Had he held Jane in his arms as she wore it? He could not remember. He had been so anxious to get her to the church, to make her his own. Had he been kind to her? He remembered hurrying her to the altar, so quickly that she had had to stop for breath. Remorse flooded over him. Oh, Jane...

He buried his face in the wedding dress, breathing in the lavender scent that still clung to the fabric. He hung the dress back up, opening the closet door wider to view the clothing inside. So few dresses. He had wanted to dress her like a princess, give her something different to wear each hour! But she had refused his gifts, had continued to wear the clothes she had brought with her when she was hired. The few plain dresses he had persuaded her to accept were locked in the trunks. Her everyday black dress was gone, as was her grey dress, but the others were there.

He moved to her bureau and opened it. He did not know of course, how much linen she had had, but he ventured a guess that it was not very much. She wouldn't even consider taking gifts like that from him, although he had argued that it was perfectly appropriate to take petticoats and corset covers and chemises from him along with the dresses he bought her. But she had blushed red and shook her head, embarrassed even in front of the Millcote seamstress, so he had dropped the subject.

There was very little in the drawer, so she must have taken all her linen with her. He picked up one item that remained. It was a heavy winter nightgown, long sleeved, high-necked. He clutched it to himself also, as though he could feel her warmth inside it.

Edward stepped over to her dressing table. There were only a few items on top of it, but he saw the long, velvet-covered box that her pearl necklace had come in. Slowly, as though his arm was paralyzed, he reached for it, draping the nightgown over his arm and opening the little casket. The pearl necklace lay inside.

In one brief second, any remaining hope he retained drained away. He knew now that she was gone and gone completely. She had been embarrassed when he gave her the necklace, had been reluctant to take it, but a small smile had played around her mouth after he had put it on her, making a tiny dimple appear on her cheek. He had seen her fingers stray to it from time to time, and the necklace never left her neck from the time he had given it to her until now. If she was anywhere in the house, or even if she had gone to post a letter or to take a walk, she would have been wearing it.

For a long time he stood, one hand holding the jewelry box, the other clutching the edge of the dressing table as though it alone would hold him up. With a shaking hand he pulled the chair out, sinking into it. The box dropped from his suddenly numbed hand and he leaned over to pick up the necklace, a wave of dizziness rushing over him as he lifted his head. He caught a glimpse of his face in the mirror. It frightened him, so white and grim. He was ashen, his dark eyes huge and empty, his beard shadow even more prominent on the pale jaw. He raised his hand to his cheek, feeling the rasp of his whiskers against his palm. His eyes fell to his hand. It was shaking visibly and he became aware of the trembling of his entire body. His pain and weakness angered him and with a hoarse cry he swept everything off the top of the dressing table to crash down on the wood floor below.

He looked up again and didn't recognize the face of the frenzied stranger in the mirror before him. With a groan, he swung his fist, smashing it against the glass, shattering it, shards dropping to the table. He didn't even feel the cut on the side of his hand, nor the blood that began to run down his arm. Nor did he feel the small sliver of glass that flew against his cheek, making a tiny cut and starting a trickle of red down his face. Because now his tears had started, and he moved over to the bed, still holding the necklace in his fist and the nightgown in his arms. He lay down on the bed, laid his head in the place that had pillowed Jane's. He curled up on his side, clutching the gown. It smelled of Jane's lavender essence also, and he drew long shaking breaths, trying to keep the scent in his nostrils. He wrapped his arms around his aching middle, trying to calm his shaking, looking out at the room yet seeing nothing.

How long Edward lay on Jane's bed he did not know, but the deep cut on the side of his hand had clotted and now stung sharply. Blood dotted the white nightgown he still clutched in his hand and his head ached from panic and the effort of holding back frustrated tears. He got up slowly, dropping the nightgown on the floor with the objects he had swept off the table. He left the room, still holding the pearls, stopping in the hall as he tried to decide what to do next.

Where would she have gone? He knew she had very little money, just a few shillings at most. She had taken nothing of value with her that he could see.

He went downstairs to his library, noting the averted eyes of his staff as he passed by. He did not see Adèle at all, and she was usually eager to be near him as much as possible. He knew he should speak to her about Jane's departure, but he also knew he could not bear to.

He sat at his desk, his aching head in his hands as he tried to decide how to best begin to search for Jane. He did not think she would have gone to Hay, near as it was, but perhaps she had only gone to stay somewhere in Millcote, and he could easily find her and persuade her to come home.

Moments later he was headed outside after donning his coat. He called for John to order Mesrour saddled and soon was galloping down the road towards Millcote.

It was early evening before the Thornfield servants heard Mesrour's hoofbeats outside, and Rochester's voice calling for the stableboy.

It had been a long and anxious day for those at Thornfield, and most of the stress had fallen upon Mrs. Fairfax, who tried to keep everyone's minds upon their work, as well as to soothe the frightened and tearful Adèle. Little thought was given to the child, whose insecurity made her cling to Sophie and to Mrs. Fairfax. She had not understood the events of the previous day but it had traumatized her to see the strangers in the house, feel the tension, hear Mr. Rochester's voice raised in anger. Miss Eyre's white face and haunted eyes had terrified her.

Adèle had been as excited as the rest of the household at the master's impending marriage. She thought only that the two people she loved most in the world, now that her Maman was gone, would now be together, and she would be with them. She had not fully realized that Mr. Rochester had planned to send her off to school while he travelled with his new wife, leaving her behind. Now she knew only that Miss Eyre was gone and Mr. Rochester remained, and that the household was in an uproar.

Mr. Rochester entered the house, and it took only one glance at his white, set face to know that he had not succeeded in finding Miss Eyre. He looked for Mrs. Fairfax, and knew immediately that she did not have good news for him either.

"Any messages?" he asked her shortly, knowing if she had good news she would have met him at the door, bustling and chattering as she usually did.

"I'm afraid not, sir," she said, taking his hat from him. "Have you eaten today, Mr. Rochester? There is some cold meat and some bread, I could bring it to you in the library."

"Yes, I have eaten," he told her. "Thank you, I want nothing." He realized how much he had been counting on the idea of Jane returning in the course of the day, and greeting him herself when he returned. He was a little hungry, since he had last eaten at a pub in Millcote where he had been inquiring about occupants at the attached inn. But that small meal had not set well, and his stomach was tight and knotted. He wanted a glass of wine, wanted to relax as best he could.

"Mrs. Fairfax," he asked her as she turned to leave. She turned back. "Did you hear anything last night, or this morning... ?" He could not bring himself to say Jane's name, but she knew to whom he referred.

She looked at him for a moment, her face sad. She thought how much he resembled his mother right now, erect, proud, but with a profound sorrow in his large dark eyes. She wished with all her heart that it could be otherwise, just as she had with Elizabeth, so long ago.

"No, sir," she told him. "I'm sorry, Mr. Rochester."

His dark, wounded face closed, became cautious and aloof once again, and he nodded to her and brushed past her to the parlour.

That night, as Edward prepared for bed, he removed his coat and emptied his pockets into the brass bowl on his bureau as he always did. It was then that he found the pearl necklace that he had been clutching as he emerged from Jane's room that morning. And he found something else as well, another item of jewelry that had been dropped into his coat pocket the previous day. He pulled it out and looked at it, feeling as though a knife had been thrust into his heart. Jane's wedding ring. He had bought it weeks before, shopping carefully for the perfect ring – not too wide so as to weigh down her small finger, yet not too thin either. He had had it engraved, and had brought it home with him, filled with anticipation for the day he would finally slide it onto her finger. It had rested in the pocket of his waistcoat at the wedding, and he had taken it out in preparation for laying it on the parson's prayer book during the ceremony. But then Mason and Briggs had come in, and he had hastily dropped the ring into his pocket during the confusion. Now, holding the two pieces of jewelry, his heart contracted with pain.

These were all he had left of her. He slid the ring onto his finger, as far as it would go, which was only to his first knuckle. He held it to his lips, closing his eyes, thinking of Jane as though that would bring her to him. *Oh, God, where is she?* It was dark, growing cool, although it had been a beautiful summer day. His mind tormented him with thoughts of where she might be, what danger she might be in.

After a fitful night, broken with dreams of Jane lost, at the mercy of cruel strangers, trying to make her way back to him, Edward awakened early, bathed, and prepared to dress. He did not even call for John, knowing he would not be awake yet. It was when he had buttoned his shirt and was putting on his cravat that his eyes again fell on the necklace and ring lying on his bureau. He picked them up, unfastening the necklace and threading it through the ring. Then he took them and fastened them around his neck. Tying his cravat and arranging it at his throat, he felt the unaccustomed weight of the jewelry against his neck, and it was a strange comfort to him, to wear close to him the necklace that had rested on Jane's soft skin. He would wear it from now on, wear it until the day he found her and brought her back to him.

He finished dressing and left the room, to begin the task of finding the woman he loved and persuading her to return.

Chapter 40 - All Happiness Torn Away

"The governess had run away two months before; and for all Mr. Rochester sought her as if she had been the most precious thing he had in the world, he never could hear a word of her; and he grew savage ... on his disappointment: he never was a wild man, but he got dangerous after he lost her. He would be alone too. He sent Mrs. Fairfax, the housekeeper, away to her friends at a distance; but he did it handsomely, for he settled an annuity on her for life: and she deserved it—she was a very good woman. Miss Adèle, a ward he had, was put to school. He broke off acquaintance with all the gentry, and shut himself up like a hermit at the Hall."
Innkeeper, The Rochester Arms - Jane Eyre

July to September, 1836

Edward sat at the table in the pub next door to one of the inns in Millcote, his body drooping with exhaustion. This was the second day in a row he had been to town, and he was sure he had talked to every innkeeper in the area. If Jane was here, she was keeping herself well hidden.

He was not sure what to do now. It was growing dark, the pub owner's lady was wiping down the tables, and Edward decided that the only thing he could do was get up, mount Mesrour, and return home, his mission once again a failure. All he could hope for now was that Jane had come back to Thornfield while he was away. If she had not, he would have to start casting a larger net.

He rubbed his face wearily, then drained what was in his mug, nodding to the woman who was cleaning the tables as he stood. He glanced at a side window as he leaned over for his hat, and what he saw made his heart stop. A small, brown-haired figure wrapped in a shawl had just hurried by the window into the alley next to the pub.

Edward rushed outside, looking around quickly before darting into the alley. There, at the end of the narrow walkway between buildings, was the girl, walking quickly.

"Jane!" he cried, beginning to run, "Jane, stop, please wait." The girl glanced back and it was too dark to see her face. She turned around again, walked faster.

Edward quickly caught up with her, reached out and seized her arm, turning her around. "Jane, please don't... " He stopped. It was not her at all.

A young girl, no more than eleven or twelve, cowered back against the bricks of the building. Edward was no judge of children's ages, but this girl's face was less round than Adèle's, and she did not have the prominent permanent teeth of a child of Adèle's age. But he could see she was not much older. A plaid shawl much like Jane's was wrapped around her and she carried a small parcel from which the smell of food wafted.

"Please, sir, let me be, let me go home," the girl pleaded. Edward stepped back, put both hands up. God knows what the child thought.

"Forgive me, I mean no harm," he told the girl. "I am sorry, miss, I saw you go by and thought you were someone else." He started to back away, then stopped.

"Were you at the Golden Eagle?" he asked her. "I thought I saw you there a moment ago?"

She nodded. "Yes, sir," she told him, "I work in the kitchen. My mother used to work there but she's sick. I help out now, to keep the job open, and they give me food left over, for my mother and the young ones."

"Have you seen a young woman?" Edward asked her. "About your height, brown hair, she might be staying in one of the rooms next door?"

The girl shook her head. "No sir. Just men, in and out of the inn and the pub. We hardly ever see women staying there." She looked around, "It's not the best place, this side of town."

Edward said nothing, just nodded. "Well, be on your way," he told her. "Here, for your trouble." He reached into his pocket, took out all the coins he had. It probably was not much, he had not brought much money with him, just enough to buy food or drink at each pub he inquired at, or to give a coin or two to those from whom he sought information.

The child took the coins, "Thank you, sir." She turned to look as they heard footsteps approaching. It was a boy in his teens, advancing quickly.

"Here, Sally, is this man bothering you, girl?" he asked.

"No, Amos, no, he's not. He was just asking me about someone. I'm coming now," Sally started to move away as the boy looked at Edward suspiciously. She smiled shyly at Edward.

"He's from my street," she told him. "They look out for me."

"I see that," Edward said, nodding at her. "Good. That's good." He nodded at the boy also, backing away, as Amos took Sally's arm and led her down the alley.

Edward turned, started to walk the way he had come, back to the main street. It was dark now, and he looked around nervously. He felt alone, vulnerable.

He made his way to the stable where he had left Mesrour, and headed back towards Thornfield. He was glad he had given the little girl some money, glad she had someone to watch out for her.

Please, God, let someone help my Jane. Let someone be looking after her as well.

The next day, Edward woke to a moment of blessed forgetfulness before reality came crashing down upon him again. It was the third morning after Jane's disappearance from Thornfield, and his hope was beginning to ebb.

An idea had formed as he had ridden home in the darkness the night before. He thought of the gypsy camp gathered on his property. It was too much to hope that they were still there; most likely they were long gone, moving throughout the farmlands of England, helping in the fields. But it was something to do, some occupation for his restless body. He dressed and rode out on Mesrour, heading for the woods at the edge of his property. He came to the former campsite, and as he had suspected, there was no sign of the group. He dismounted and walked around, seeing a few bare areas with signs of long ago campfires, but other than those, there was no sign that anyone had used this spot. Edward wished for a few moments with Mrs. Lovell, for just a word of encouragement, some hope for his future.

There was nothing left for him to do. He had looked for Jane in the immediate area. It was time to turn the search over to others. Edward's anxiety was nearly unbearable, but he recognized defeat. He returned home, lost, empty, his heart hollow, cold, and fearful.

Days passed slowly by, with no word from or news of Miss Eyre. Any visitor to the door, or message sent, created an atmosphere of excitement and expectancy in the very air of Thornfield, but when nothing related to the missing governess followed, the disappointment was tangible. Edward kept himself shut in his library, and servants were dispatched almost hourly with letters to various attorneys and agents.

He had never written so many letters in his life, to anyone he could think of who might be of assistance in finding Jane. He wrote to Gateshead, to Lowood, to Jane's friend Maria Temple Nasmyth, whose address he found in the small file related to Jane's hiring as governess. He wrote to his banker, to agents suggested by his attorney and his estate manager.

He wanted desperately to take action himself, to leave Thornfield and search for her again. He wished he could get on Mesrour and ride to each place she might have gone, to inquire after her in person. But he feared to be away from Thornfield for any length of time, feared she would return and find him gone. How terrible to be away, to have her come back to him, and depart again because he was not here. So he remained, chafing at his helplessness.

Time passed, and soon Jane had been gone for two weeks. Edward awakened every morning, hoping that this would be the day that a letter would come from her, or about her. He watched anxiously, tore into each letter that came addressed to him. Most of the time it was estate business, or a short note from acquaintances in other places. Those he passed on to his agent, or discarded. He could no longer maintain pretence of any interest in any relationship outside of that with Jane.

Soon, letters began to come to answer his previous inquiries. The first was a note from someone at Lowood, briefly stating that they had no knowledge of Miss Eyre, had not heard from her, and absolving Lowood of all responsibility had she departed under circumstances involving theft or improper behaviour. Shortly after that letter came notes from Mrs. Nasmyth, and from a Mrs. Robert Leaven of Gateshead. Both denied any knowledge of Jane, both had a tone of concern over her departure and compassion for whatever had driven her to leave. They both requested that if she returned, he convey their affection and solicitude.

Letters arrived from the various agents and solicitors he had engaged. There was very little word that could be of help. An attorney in the town the opposite direction from Millcote finally talked to a carriage driver who reported conveying a lone woman in his coach in the early morning of the day in question. He stated he had taken her although she had not had the full fare, and that he had driven her to a crossroads some miles away, but he could not say where she had gone from there, as it was an area that served many coaches bound for all areas. No further news could be found of her.

Edward's moods swung wildly from despair to hope, from hope to frustration, and back again. Each day he awakened with a small kernel of anticipation that this might be the day he received good news. And each night he sat before the fire in the parlour, drinking whatever alcohol he found at hand, staring into the flames with eyes that each day grew grimmer and more bitter.

By the time Miss Eyre had been gone a month, the residents of Thornfield had realized that her disappearance was not a temporary frustration that their master would eventually come to terms with. As each day wore on and there was no word of the former governess, Mr. Rochester grew increasingly bitter and frenzied. He ate very little, and they became aware that he was drinking more than he ever had before. He had never been a drinker, just an occasional glass of port, an infrequent glass of wine with a fine cut of beef, once in awhile a brandy with company. But now he picked at his dinner, left most of it on the plate, and retired to the library with the entire bottle. He never drank it all, just poured a little and sipped it as he stood staring out the windows when it was light out, retired to his chair to stare into the fire when it grew dark outside. All in the house knew for whom he was watching as he looked out the windows, and of whom he was thinking as he gazed into the fireplace's blaze. They sympathized, but this new behaviour of his frightened them, putting them constantly on edge.

Most of what he did now was new to them. He had always been busy, in and out of the hall on business or to visit among the gentry of the area. But he began to leave only to meet with this attorney, or that agent, or to conduct a search of his own in the small areas around Thornfield, hoping against hope that she might have stayed in the area, despite the previous report from the coach driver.

He would return from these meetings more morose than before, and they noticed that within two weeks he had stopped leaving the house as often. A month after Jane's disappearance, he stopped leaving the house altogether.

He also grew unsociable towards those who would visit him. After the ill-fated wedding, word had of course spread in the area of the truth about Thornfield and its master, and it was the major topic of discussion around Hay, and eventually in Millcote. The servants who did the shopping and the errands for the Hall found that wherever they went they would interrupt an intense discussion. They would catch snatches of conversation, hearing "Thornfield", "Rochester", "lunatic" and other phrases that left them in no doubt of which subject was under examination. A silence would fall as the participants would recognize an employee of Thornfield, continuing their gossip only after the employee's errand was completed.

Members of the gentry began to call on Mr. Rochester, some with avid curiosity, some out of genuine concern and friendship, but all calls were refused, and not always politely. The caller would appear, and present a card to Mrs. Fairfax. That good lady would look distressed, cluck her tongue, and disappear into the library. The caller would then hear a raised angry voice, then Mrs. Fairfax would appear, looking even more upset, and would stammer a polite explanation of why her master could not be seen at that particular time. The caller would depart, the gossip would spread further, and finally all calls stopped.

Many members of Rochester's circle, Miss Ingram in particular, imagined how they would react if they happened to meet him in public, planning to publicly cut him for his indiscretions and the rudeness that followed, but they were never to get the satisfaction, for none of them were ever to see him in public. Now that he was solely occupied in trying to find his vanished bride, he never moved in the same circles as his former acquaintances.

None of this mattered to Edward. His focus was upon Jane – finding her and assuring himself that she was safe. He awakened in the morning with thoughts of the letters he had to write, agents he had to contact. He wrote to his banker only for the funds to pay the agents he had already enlisted. He met with his estate agent as needed to discuss the tenants and the usual estate business, but the agent would leave knowing that his client had heard only part of what they had discussed, and that he could probably drain Thornfield's funds dry and leave for the Antipodes before Rochester even realized he was gone. Fortunately, he was a reliable and honest manager, one whose family had conducted business with the Rochesters for three generations. He had dealt with Edward Rochester for over ten years now, since Edward had inherited Thornfield, and had come to like the man for his generosity and basic decency. He too, had heard the story, and was as concerned for Rochester as the rest of the members of the Thornfield household.

Edward thought of none of this. Had he been the sort to confide his worries and pain to another, he would have found many sympathetic ears, but he had always been a private man, one who was quite capable of taking care of his own affairs. He did not even talk to Mr. Carter, who had been his sounding board for many years regarding the situation with Bertha, but turned him away also the several times he had tried to call. He had not forgotten their recent discussion, and the angry manner in which he had departed Mr. Carter's house. Carter bore Rochester no ill will for his response to his advice, but he could understand why his patient would choose not to receive him.

Edward's days became quite monotonous. Get up, dress, retire to the library, correspond with those who were searching for Jane. He would occasionally lift his head from his writing with an awareness of a nauseous, lightheaded feeling that came from hunger. He would ring for a housemaid and get a small meal, which he would pick at as he sat at his desk. He had begun to eat supper with Adèle because he knew it pleased Mrs. Fairfax and because he felt guilty for how the recent events had affected his young ward, but it was almost more than he could bear to put up with the child's chatter.

Adèle was even more annoying to him now. Nervous and insecure, the little girl tried even harder to charm and beguile him, that being the only way she knew to get anyone's attention. Anyone except Miss Eyre, who had always treated her with a respectful regard she received from few others. Adèle was experiencing real emotional suffering with the disappearance of her beloved governess and friend, but no one paid her any mind, affected as they were by the pall Mr. Rochester's behaviour had cast over the household.

Mrs. Fairfax was the only one who had any idea of what Adèle was going through, and since that lady had never had children of her own, she took lightly the distress of the little girl, thinking that a child's little worries would soon pass; that Adèle would be unscarred. Adèle's nurse Sophie, who was not the brightest young woman, performed only those physical tasks that were needed to maintain Adèle, but was not willing to sit and talk to her as well. She was tired of England – the austere surroundings of the imposing hall, the cold manners of the British servants.

Sophie was weary of having no one to converse with in her own language. She had nourished high and private hopes of a relationship of sorts with her new employer, especially when she heard him converse in his fluent French. She looked at the wealthy Englishman, listened to him talk, and thought that this could be her chance to rise above her future as a plain nursemaid. She had done a little flirting, as subtle as her limited intelligence would allow, but Mr. Rochester had remained unmoved. That had irritated and embarrassed her, and she thought now only of how she could remove herself from this household as soon as possible.

One night a month after Jane's departure, Edward sat at the dinner table, his eyes never rising from the meal in front of him. His fork clinked on the china as he moved his food around on the plate. Adèle was chattering away at him, telling him some story about what she had seen on a walk with Sophie that day. The less he listened, the more she talked, a tone of desperation in her high childish voice. Finally he let the fork crash down to the plate and looked up at her.

"Adèle, will you be still, child." His voice was low, but cracked like a whip.

She looked at him, her hazel eyes wide, and then they filled with tears and she began to sob. A wail came from her, and she stood and threw her napkin down to the plate, crying loudly, "I hate you! You are the cruelest man. I hate you, I hate you." She stood at the table, crying as though her heart would break. Edward exhaled with irritation and called, "Mrs. Fairfax! Sophie! Get this child out of here now!"

Adèle continued to cry. "No wonder Mademoiselle left here. You are so mean. I will leave too, I will find Mademoiselle and will live with her."

Edward's pain and frustration spilled over and he was striding towards her before he realized what he was doing. He grabbed Adèle's arm, shook it angrily and yelled into her red face, "You hush, you hush right now."

"I want Miss Eyre!" Adèle wailed, "Miss Eyre!" She sobbed as Edward held her upper arm in a tight grip. He was seeing through a red haze, was about to shake her again and he became aware that Mrs. Fairfax was holding his arm in a surprisingly tight grasp for a woman of her age.

"Mr. Rochester!" Her angry voice cut through the fog in his brain, "Mr. Rochester, calm yourself. Let go of the child." He dropped Adèle's arm and stepped back, breathing hard, not looking at either her or Mrs. Fairfax.

Mrs. Fairfax put her arms around Adèle, and Edward heard her murmuring to her. He saw Sophie come in, and Mrs. Fairfax passed Adèle to her with an order to take her to the nursery and calm her down. He backed away from the sobbing Adèle, the accusing eyes of the two women, and left the dining room to go to the library.

He had been sitting there for several minutes, his head in his hands, when he heard a sound at the door and looked up to find Mrs. Fairfax standing there watching him. He watched her, her face set in an angry look he had never seen her display before. She was so consistently mild-mannered, so benign of demeanour that he had not realized she was capable of any kind of ire.

"I did not strike her," he said, watching her with narrowed eyes.

"No, you did not. But I saw the look on your face as you held her arm. You should not have her here anymore; it's more than you can deal with," Mrs. Fairfax told him firmly.

"You are forgetting your place," he told her. "This is my home, I will act as I like."

"Mr. Rochester, I have known you since the night you were born." Her face was suddenly gentle, her eyes concerned. "I knew and loved your mother, and watched you grow up; watched her love and care for you as she loved no one else. She is not here to help you, and I feel that I may stand in her place for just a moment. Will you listen to what I have to say?"

He didn't say anything, just looked down at the floor. But he didn't stop her, and she continued on gently. "You are about to break from the strain. I know you miss Miss Eyre, we all do. But you cannot continue in this manner. Someone will be hurt from it. Do not let it be Adèle. She does not understand what is happening here. You had made arrangements to send her to school after your marriage. Do those arrangements still stand?"

"Yes, as far as I know." Edward spoke slowly, trying to remember what he had decided, back when he was planning to marry Jane. It seemed like years since he had been vigorous and full of plans for his future.

"I would strongly urge you to go ahead with your plans to send her to the school. I do not know what the future will hold for you, Mr. Rochester. I hope it resolves itself, ends as you want it to. But you must take hold of your feelings; you must eat and sleep and try to care for yourself."

He looked up at her then, and she nearly cried at the desolation she saw in his eyes. "I will do as you recommend – I will send her to school. This is no place for her now."

Mrs. Fairfax went on, "And this is probably a good time to bring up something else to you. When Adèle leaves, I will leave too. I am tendering my resignation now. I will stay to get Adèle sent off, and then I will be going."

"Mrs. Fairfax, please, I realize I was not myself in there, but I assure you, I will not hurt Adèle, or you... " Edward was shocked at the idea of her leaving Thornfield, had considered her part and parcel of it for so long that it had never occurred to him that she would even think of going away.

She shook her head, "No, sir, it is not that. It is an idea that I have had for some time now. I had planned to arrange it while you were on your... " she caught herself before she mentioned his honeymoon, "...while you were gone. I have a friend, a childhood friend, long widowed, as I am, who has managed an inn with the help of her daughter and son-in-law. Now her daughter has been most unfortunately widowed also, and Anna wrote to ask my help. She knew of my plans to retire eventually, and wrote several months ago to ask if I would consider coming to live and work there, to help them manage the inn." She smiled. "Since I have long been the housekeeper of a large estate, they think I can manage to help with a ten-room inn and dining room. I look forward to it, in all truth. I am tired, and no longer see a need for me here."

Edward opened his mouth to protest, then thought better of it. Why would anyone want to stay on at Thornfield? This dark place with its hidden evils, its long history of pain and tears. It was a cursed place, had brought nothing but unhappiness to those unfortunate enough to live there. He nodded slowly as he spoke.

"If that is what you wish, then I in turn wish you the best. I will make arrangements for Adèle's schooling, and if you would be so good as to remain until she leaves, I will see that you are taken to your friends' inn and settled in there."

He gestured to the door. "Thank you, Mrs. Fairfax. I will bid you good night now." There was an echo of his former gentlemanly self as he gallantly waved her through the doorway, which he then closed after her. He stood for a long time, his back against the door, his eyes closed, before he moved across the room to sit in his chair by the fire.

By mid-August, all was made ready for Adèle's departure for school. Edward had written to confirm her admittance and a reply had been received with assurance of a place for young Miss Varens at the start of fall term. She was to leave on the first of September. The carriage would convey her to the academy, accompanied by Mrs. Fairfax, who would stay to see Adèle settled and would then go on to the inn owned by her friends.

Mrs. Fairfax was surprised by the good grace with which Mr. Rochester had accepted her resignation, and she was touched with the financial arrangements he had made for her. She had expected a severance payment, but not the generous annuity he had set up instead. A note had been sent to the bank in the town in which the inn was situated, and these monies, in addition to her modest savings, would ensure a comfortable retirement indeed. If it were not for Mrs. Fairfax's continued concern about Miss Eyre and about Mr. Rochester himself, her contentment would have been complete.

Miss Eyre had now been gone for six weeks. Edward's frantic searching had produced no tangible results, and his panic and frenzy had settled into a numb and sullen desperation. Every day letters arrived, none with any helpful information.

One August day a letter addressed to Jane arrived from Mr. Briggs. It was brought to Edward, who looked at Jane's name on the envelope for a long time, his eyes blurred with sudden tears. He dashed them away and opened the letter. It was a request for Miss Eyre to contact Mr. Briggs as soon as possible regarding a matter of great importance, a brief and businesslike letter that gave an address of an office in London. Edward looked at the message for some moments, then rang for Mrs. Fairfax. For some reason, he could not bear the thought of writing to Mr. Briggs himself, admitting that Jane was no longer with him.

Mrs. Fairfax entered the room in her bustling way, "Yes, sir?"

Edward held out the letter. "This is just arrived for Miss Eyre, and it needs to be answered. Would you... will you be so kind as to answer it for me? I ... " he sighed, swallowed hard. "Just inform him that Miss Eyre no longer lives here and you have no further information regarding her."

"Yes, sir." Mrs. Fairfax took the letter from his hand, watching him carefully. His face was closed and proud, but the pain still shone in his dark eyes. He turned away from her and she left the room to do as he asked.

Edward had reached the point where he never left the house now, except at night. He no longer believed that he would get any response from the correspondence that he still maintained with his trace agents, but he still wrote to each new person who was recommended. He rarely emerged from his library, even taking his infrequent meals there now.

He never left to ride Mesrour, leaving it to the groom to exercise him in the pasture instead. Pilot was at his side at all times, of course, and Edward's hand would stray to the dog's head as he sat, automatically scratching behind his ears and under his chin. The dog sensed his master's pain and sought to remain near him constantly; indeed, he seemed, to the rest of the household, to be the only tangible comfort their employer could find at this time.

Edward rarely looked in the mirror now, except to shave. He would not have done that, but he hated the feeling of being unshaven. He didn't notice the shadows under his eyes, the gaunt look of his face. He had not had any fat on his lean, muscular frame to begin with, and from his lack of exercise and his decreased appetite, he was looking pale and thinner than he had, although he still retained his athletic appearance.

Although he did not leave the house during the day, he had gotten into the habit of going outside after the sun went down. It had begun when he found the house too confining after dark, and had come to find it relaxing to walk in the late summer darkness. He would walk in the orchard and about the Thornfield grounds for hours, Pilot padding behind him faithfully. Edward found that these walks could somewhat calm his hurt and frantic soul. Only after wandering for a long time about his property, his mind on no particular subject, did he feel relaxed enough to return to the house and lie down for a few hours of restless slumber.

He thought of Jane, of course. Thoughts of her had worn such a groove in his memory that he could get no peace from his obsession for even a moment, but he made an effort to relax for the brief time he spent outside his home, and it was only these moonlight walks that helped him retain his grip on sanity. He would walk among the trees, breathing deeply of the clear air, the scent of summer fading slowly into autumn.

Sometimes when the moon afforded a clear view of the grounds with its light, he would run a little, feeling a slight uplift of his spirits with the moderate exercise. After he had spent an hour or two walking, he would go to the orchard and sit upon one of the stone benches feeling the cool air wash over him. And he thought of Jane, dreamed of her, longed for her...

September first dawned sunny and cool. The household was in a bustle of activity as the carriage, and the wagon that had been hired, were loaded with the personal effects of Adèle and Mrs. Fairfax in preparation for their departure. They breakfasted early, Adèle squirming in her seat and talking excitedly, Mrs. Fairfax attempting to calm her enough to eat something, knowing that they faced a long journey ahead. Adèle's school was a two hour trip north, and then Mrs. Fairfax faced another trip of nearly two hours beyond that.

The sound of horse's hooves and carriage wheels crunching on the drive in the front part of the house made Adèle leap up from the breakfast table and run to the window, pulling aside the lace curtain and peering out, shifting excitedly from one foot to the other as she chattered about the trip ahead. Mrs. Fairfax sighed and motioned for Leah to remove the breakfast dishes, and called Adèle over to assist her with her bonnet and cape.

"Hold still, child, you are tiring me just to watch you, wriggling about," she scolded, tying the strings of her bonnet. "Now, let me look at you."

Her gaze went over the little girl fondly, and she felt a small pang as she thought of the small child being sent away once again from all that was familiar to her. She knew very little about the school Mr. Rochester had chosen and hoped Adèle would find it an easy place to adapt to.

She donned her own bonnet and cloak and picked up her reticule and gloves. She had already bid farewell to those members of the staff who remained. For to her surprise, Mr. Rochester had begun to thin out the members of the household staff shortly after she had given her notice. He had dismissed the housemaids, with good references and a payment to tide them over until they could find other employment. He had consulted with Sophie as to her wishes, whether she preferred to return to France or to secure a position as a nursemaid with another family. She had let him know in no uncertain terms that she wished to return to France, and so he had paid her a severance settlement and bought her passage to return to her home.

All the staff that now remained in Thornfield consisted of John, Mary his wife, who had been the main cook even before she and John were married, and Leah. Of course, Grace Poole still remained to care for Mrs. Rochester, and the groom and the stableboy stayed to care for Mesrour and the carriage horses. With the departure of Adèle and Mrs. Fairfax, there would be no need for a large number of employees.

Mr. Rochester had not said so, but Mrs. Fairfax wondered if perhaps he meant to eventually quit Thornfield Hall permanently and return to live in Europe for the remainder of his life. She wondered if he had given up on ever finding Miss Eyre and would try to put distance between himself and all that reminded him of her.

She pushed her gloomy thoughts away, and turned to Adèle. "Come, Adèle, the carriage is waiting. Let us go say farewell to Mr. Rochester before we leave." She held her hand out to her but as she did so, the master himself emerged from the library and came towards them.

"Mrs. Fairfax, Adèle, you appear to be ready. Is there anything else I can do for you before you go? The coachman has directions, and he knows he is to stop if you have any needs or problems." He nodded to John, who picked up the valise that Mrs. Fairfax had placed near the door, and motioned them to the door. Mr. Rochester paused in the foyer as John stood with the door held open for them.

He held his hand out to Mrs. Fairfax and shook hers gently. He held it for a moment, looking at her. "Thank you, Mrs. Fairfax, for everything. Thornfield Hall owes you a debt. Please contact me if you are in need of anything."

Her eyes filled as she looked at her former employer. She had to swallow before she could speak.

"Thank you, Mr. Rochester." She took a deep breath, "God be with you, sir."

The words came from her before she could help herself, but instead of being annoyed he just nodded, then turned to Adèle. He laid a hand on her head for a moment as she looked up at him with her large hazel eyes, then withdrew it and ushered them to the open door.

He did not go out with them, but stood in the doorway, watching as John handed them into the carriage and shut the door, then knocked on the door so the driver could get started.

Edward watched the carriage roll down the driveway, and looked after it for some minutes after it was gone. Then he turned and went back into the house.

The harvest was well underway, and the tenant farmers could be seen in the fields from early morning until well past dusk every day. It was a bright sunny September, unseasonably warm. There had been very little precipitation, but the dryness was welcome to the farmers who were working hard to bring in the harvest before the rainfalls of early winter began.

For the residents of Thornfield Hall, it was a different autumn than they had been accustomed to previously. Mrs. Fairfax and Adèle had been gone for three weeks, Sophie had returned to France, and all the housemaids were gone save Leah, who had no difficulty keeping up with the work now that the household was so small. John had very little to do in the house except to assist Mr. Rochester, who had always required a minimum of help with his personal needs. Mary, John's wife, now had few people to cook for. Only Grace Poole's duties remained the same. She continued to watch Mrs. Rochester in the large attic rooms, the secrecy surrounding them changed, but not the circumstances.

For Edward, life had taken on a sameness and monotony. His depression was complete, his routine unvarying. Each morning he rose and dressed after a short and restless night. He tended to his correspondence faithfully, but without hope of a result. After writing such letters as to initiate a new search or to answer previous inquiries, he would move from his desk to his chair before the fire, where he would sit gazing into the blaze, usually finding himself dozing off before too long.

He would rouse himself to eat the meal that Leah would serve him, then would continue to sit before the fireplace. In the afternoon John would go to the post office for any mail that might have come but Edward had long since given up hope that there would be a useful lead in his search for Jane. He would look through the messages, fling them in frustration to his desk, and return to his chair.

By dusk his agitation would be almost more than he could bear and the members of the household would hear him pacing back and forth before the fire, pausing only to pour himself another drink, which he would sip as he moved restlessly about the room.

Finally after supper had been eaten he would slip out of the library and go outside to the orchard where he would resume his restless pacing and wandering, like a caged and dangerous tiger.

The atmosphere at Thornfield was one of anxiety. The entire household could feel Mr. Rochester's tension grow tighter and tighter, like that of a too-taut bowstring, and all feared the time when it would grow so strained that it would finally snap.

Chapter 41 - Fire at Thornfield Hall

"Then Mr. Rochester was at home when the fire broke out?"
"Yes, indeed was he; and he went up to the attics when all was burning above and below, and got the servants out of their beds and helped them down himself, and went back to get his mad wife out of her cell. And then they called out to him that she was on the roof, where she was standing, waving her arms, above the battlements, and shouting out till they could hear her a mile off: I saw her and heard her with my own eyes. She was a big woman, and had long, black hair: we could see it streaming against the flames as she stood. I witnessed, and several more witnessed Mr. Rochester ascend through the sky-light on to the roof; we heard him call 'Bertha!'"
Innkeeper, The Rochester Arms - Jane Eyre

The twentieth of September was an unusually hot day, very dry and seemingly endless to the labouring farmers. Dusk brought not only a welcome coolness, but the sweet smell of impending rain in the air, and gathering clouds occasionally obscured the brightness of the full harvest moon.

By ten that night, Edward had been walking outside for nearly two hours. He was drained and tired, not only by his pacing but by the relentless pain that was his constant companion now. He did not know when his frustration and fear and worry and longing for Jane had finally congealed into a sharp and endless hurt that seemed to settle in the region of his heart. He only knew that it could not be dislodged – not by activity, not by sleep, not by his searching. It could not be numbed by alcohol nor relieved by tears.

For he often cried now, in spite of his shame at the easy tears that he could no longer seem to control. In the first long weeks after discovering Jane's absence, he had felt moisture well in his eyes from time to time, but those tears could be easily dashed away, held at bay by a few deep breaths and a firmer set of his broad shoulders. But once he had given up hope of her return, had begun to fear that she was lost forever, he had noticed that the hot tears that welled could not be held back, not without strangling him, making him gasp for air as he tried to fight them off. The first time they had seized him, he had been sitting before the fire, suddenly overcome by deep sobs that could not be controlled. Appalled, he had sat there, one fist pressed to his lips, fearing that the gasping sounds that tore at his throat would bring the servants to his side to see what possessed him. But if anyone heard him they never let him know, and it was fire that he found himself leaving the house and walking away, where at least he could weep without fear of being overheard.

He had come to some decisions in the times he had spent walking for hours in the cool darkness. He had wasted enough time writing letters, wasted enough time waiting for someone else to find Jane. He had decided he would remain inactive no longer. There was a reason he had dismissed most of the servants once Mrs. Fairfax had made her decision to leave Thornfield, and that reason was not because he had decided to return to the Continent. Europe held no charms for him if Jane could not be with him to see its beauties. Nothing in his life held any excitement for him if Jane was not at his side. And so he had decided to go and search for her himself.

Grace Poole was still at Thornfield to care for Bertha; and John, Mary, and Leah could remain behind to care for the day-to-day aspects of the estate while he was away. With the help of his estate manager, the workings of Thornfield could continue as they always had. He was sure that Jane would have not left England; indeed, she was most likely in northern England – it was all she knew. He planned to start in Yorkshire, near Lowood, and then continue towards the vicinity of the Reeds' estate, to search each and every small town and village he came to. He would not rest until he had found her, had seen for himself that she was all right, determined if she needed anything. He did not care if it took his entire life. For what was his life without her, anyway?

"I will find you, my darling," he whispered into the darkness, leaning back with his head resting against the rough bark of a tree trunk. "No matter how long I have to search, I will find you."

He stood now in the shadow of the huge and broken tree, the one that had been struck by lightning and destroyed the night he had proposed to Jane. He pressed his clenched fist against its rough bark, hot tears coursing down his face as he stood in the cool darkness. He could smell smoke, emanating, he assumed, from a distant fire set earlier to burn brush from the harvest. He took a deep breath, his nose clogged from his crying. He reached up and impatiently brushed his palm against each cheek to dry it, then reached for his handkerchief. He dried his eyes, then blew his nose, taking a deeper breath as his nose cleared a little.

His thoughts were on Jane, of course. When were they not? He was so worried about her, wondering where she could possibly be this cool and moonlit night. Could she see the moon from where she was? Did clouds obscure its brightness there as well? Was she perhaps standing outside as he was, brushing tears from her soft cheeks as she thought of him?

At times he could not stop his frenzied imagination from leaping into the future, when Jane's memories of him might dim and another man would come into her life, one who could offer her everything that she could not take from him. It was a painful thought, to imagine her loving someone else, living as someone else's wife, but not as painful as the thought of her starving in a workhouse, begging on a pitiless city street, or dead. Dead in a hundred different ways that tormented his imagination as he tossed in his bed, trying to sleep.

As he stood there trying to drive such thoughts from his mind, he became aware that the smell of smoke was stronger, no longer with the mild scent of burning brush. It was harsh and acrid, the smell of old wood and stone and fabric. It alarmed him enough to move out from the shadow of the tree and look towards the house, and what he saw made his heart nearly stop from horror.

For several minutes he had been aware of a dancing light on the periphery of his vision, but seeing the clouds, hearing the distant rumble of thunder, he had taken the flashes for heat lightning. But now as he concentrated his gaze on the Hall, a feeling of terror washed over him, making his legs grow weak.

Thornfield Hall was on fire.

He felt his heart skip and begin to beat wildly, crazily against his ribs and he took off at a dead run for the front door. As he ran up to the entrance he could see the blaze inside now, and smell the smoke, and he cursed himself for not paying attention until now.

He flung the heavy front door open and plunged inside. He could barely see the staircase for the smoke that obscured the second level and was beginning to send spirals up to the third, where the servants' bedrooms were. The servants! They had likely gone to bed an hour before; they were always in their rooms, the hall dark save for a single lamp that John left burning to light his master's way back to his room when he came in each night. Edward snatched up this lamp now, and ran up the smoky stairway to the third level, shouting as he went.

"John! Mary!" he yelled, making his way to their room and pounding on their door. "Leah! For God's sake, wake up!" He ran to Leah's door across the hall, pounding on that as well.

He began to cough as the smoke moved up the hall towards him, and he saw that it was coming from another source as well, the anteroom outside the attic room that housed his mad wife. If Bertha and Grace were sleeping, they would not realize until it was too late the danger they were in, assuming Bertha would realize it at all.

"John, get up, man!" he shouted, again banging on the door. He had pulled his fist back to hammer on the door again when it was whipped open by John himself, night cap askew, pulling on his trousers over his nightshirt. His eyes widened at the sight of his employer yelling outside his door, lamp held up, then he noticed the smoke that was filling the hall.

He turned and shouted into the dark room behind him, "Mary, get up! It's a fire." He turned and ran to the bedside, speaking urgently to his wife, "Get up, m'girl, we need to go down now." He reached for her, but she was already out of bed, throwing her black stuff uniform on over her nightgown. Both shoved their feet into the shoes lying next to their sides of the bed and were soon out into the hall. Mr. Rochester stood across from them, pounding urgently on Leah's door. He turned as they emerged.

"John!" he said quickly. "You must run outside, rouse the groom and send him to Hay for the fire patrol... let them know so that someone can send to Millcote for the engines. Then begin ringing the bell. Get the stableboy to start fetching some buckets of water. It won't help much, but it can't hurt." John cast a desperate glance as his terrified wife, who stood still, hands pressed to the side of her head. "Go, man! I'll get the women out. Do you think I'd leave them? Go now!"

Thus galvanized to action, John moved with a swiftness that belied his age. They heard his running steps, then the slamming of the door. Edward turned back to the door, hammering on it before he threw it open and nodded to Mary to go in and shake Leah awake. However, it proved to be unnecessary. The young housemaid had heard the commotion in the hall and had also leaped up to throw on her dress and shoes. She had torn off her night-time cap and her red hair hung loose around her shoulders, falling nearly to her waist. She scraped it back from her face, tying it up as she rushed from the room.

Edward pushed both women towards the staircase, shoved them ahead of him. There were flames visible on the second floor and as they all rounded the landing, they realized that they were coming from the room that had been Jane's. The bed was on fire, the entire structure engulfed in flames. As they paused, the coverings around the canopy fell down with a large WHOOSH, and the flames grew higher. The women screamed involuntarily, and Edward pushed them again, impatiently now. They could hear the bell ringing, peal after peal in the night air.

He gestured towards the first floor staircase, "Go, now, both of you. Hurry down and out the front door." They hesitated. "Go! I need to see to Mrs. Poole. Run, you fools. Leave now, or before God I won't be held accountable!" The fierce tone of his voice roused them, and they hurried down the last flight of stairs and out the door.

Edward turned and ran back up the two flights of stairs, down the third floor hall, and up the winding stairs that led to the attic rooms, fumbling in his pocket for the key. But as he inserted it into the door, it swung open easily, letting smoke pour out into the hall. Coughing and gasping, Edward pulled back, then plunged into the room, eyes slitted against the smoke that filled the small anteroom.

"Grace!" he called, as he wrenched open the door that led to the room. He stopped, his eyes sweeping the chamber in front of him. His plan had been to pick up Bertha and carry her down, fight and resist though she might, with Grace following them.

But Bertha was nowhere to be seen and Grace lay on a pallet near the fireplace, still fully dressed, her face slack. Edward felt his heart skip a beat as he moved towards her, certain that he was too late and the smoke had overcome her. But when he approached her, touched her bony shoulder and turned her slightly, a pewter mug fell from her limp fingers with a great clatter as it hit the floor, and the heavy yeast aroma of the home-brewed beer it had contained assailed his nostrils.

"Oh, Grace," he moaned, dropping to his knees beside her and shaking her shoulder. "Grace, wake up. Come, Grace, get up." She gave no sound or movement and Edward knew there was little time to waste. He slipped his arms around her and raised her up over his shoulder, getting to his feet with a little difficulty. Shifting her higher on his shoulder, he moved from the door, and began the task of carrying her downstairs and out of the Hall. Grace was thin but heavy in her stupor, and it was hard to move quickly with his fatigue and the burden he carried.

It seemed a thousand years ago that they had stood in the woods and he had kissed her and told her he would take her away with him. They had been thirteen years old, so young and innocent. Now life had taken them both and battered them to the point where he no longer recognized her or himself. He wondered where she would end up, if she even survived this ordeal. Perhaps she would not – he could not hear her breathing, but perhaps that was because his own rasped so harshly and loudly that it obscured all sound as he moved as quickly as he could down the final flight of stairs.

Edward approached the front door, which was ajar, and through it he could see the crowd that had gathered outside. Bells were still clanging, and he glimpsed people running back and forth, carrying great buckets, calling to each other. As he burst through the door carrying Grace Poole, several onlookers approached him. He brought her down from his shoulder, passing her to another man, a massively built farmer whose name escaped him for a moment.

The man took Grace as easily as if she were a child, and Edward reached up and grasped his huge shoulder, as much for support as to thank him. He backed away then, looking up at the Hall as he did so. His heart sank completely within him. He did not have to be an expert on fires to be able to tell that it was no use at all. Flames engulfed the main part of the house, could be seen in almost every window. He stood for a long time, eyes fixed on the spectacle of the inferno that was destroying his home before his very eyes.

Out in the courtyard, Edward looked around for each member of his household. His heart pounded wildly within his chest and sweat streamed into his eyes. Swiping his forearm across his face, he moved among the milling crowd, which had nearly ceased to pass the buckets of water, so fruitless did their efforts seem now.

The courtyard seemed as light as day, the leaping flames clearly illuminating each person in the throng, with their gaping mouths and pointing fingers. He caught sight of Mary and John, Mary sobbing onto John's shoulder as he patted her back, his face glued to the spectacle of the burning manor beyond them. Leah stood several feet away from them, her eyes also fixed on the blaze as it engulfed the area in which she had been sleeping less than an hour before.

Edward ignored the shouts, the running feet, the sounds of panicked horses as the fire patrol attempted to keep each one standing near its engine. He had caught sight of Grace Poole lying in the grass, Mr. Carter and several of the village women kneeling alongside her. He started towards them and as he did, a warm weight pressed against his knees. Pilot had found him and was alternately whining and waving his tail rapidly back and forth.

Edward dropped to one knee, clutching handfuls of thick fur. "Pilot, there you are, boy," he muttered. "Thank God, thank God you stayed outside." He buried his face in the dog's neck for a moment as he tried to compose himself, then pushed himself to his feet to again make his way over to Mrs. Poole.

He mentally took note of the members of his household – John, Mary, Leah, Grace, Pilot – all safe save Bertha, whom he had not been able to find. Thankfully, the fire seemed to be confined to the house – the stables were far enough away to be safe from the conflagration.

A sudden scream from high above the crowd stopped the action briefly and faces turned up towards the battlements at the topmost part of the roof, where flames had just begun to advance. At first, Edward was as shocked as everyone else, then the blood drained from his face as he realized what he was seeing.

Bertha stood on the roof, tall and fearsome, her white nightgown flowing around her, her waist-length black hair blowing about her head. She looked like an emissary of Hell itself. She was screaming into the flame-lit night, her words unintelligible to the people below. She appeared to take no notice of the fire dancing behind her as she moved her body sinuously, coming closer to the edge.

Later, Edward would never be able to remember what his thoughts were at that instant. Surely, he mused, in the dark and silent months that followed, no one would have blamed him had he stood where he was, made the excuse that the fire was too advanced for him to go back inside. He had had the perfect opportunity to rid himself of this unspeakable burden, and without any danger to himself. Until the moment of his death, he would never remember what was in his mind, or if he had even had a thought at all, just that he stood stock-still for a heartbeat's time, then he was running, running towards the main entrance of Thornfield Hall. There were no sounds in his ears but his breathing and the pounding of his boots on the flagstones. Up to the door he raced, shaking off the restraining hands, waving aside the concerned urgings of those outside. Then he was inside the house, up the staircases to the second and third floors.

The thick smoke was choking him by the time he hit the skylight and threw himself, gasping, on to the roof to retrieve his wife. At the sound of the door, Bertha whipped her head around and saw that it was him. For a time, the couple stared at each other over the distance between them, the span so much greater than the mere width of the roof. Dark eyes met dark eyes, and the mutual hatred of over fifteen years seemed to draw an unbreakable cord between them. It was as though they had agreed to meet on a final battlefield of their hopeless union.

Bertha's dry, cracked lips drew back in a rictus of a smile, and she breathed, "Rochester, now you come for me. Is that all I had to do to bring you to me – set light to your lover's bed? I would have done it long ago. If I had, maybe she would have been in it."

"Bertha," he advanced towards her, hand outstretched. "Please, please, come away from here. It grows unsafe, we must go now. Let me help you."

"Help me?" she screamed. He flinched at the sudden sound. Both of their voices were hoarse and ragged – hers from disuse, his from smoke and exertion. "How can you help me? Would you move your whore into your house, so she can mock me in her wedding dress? Did she share your bed, while I slept alone? She will never sleep in any bed in this house."

She was backing away from him, edging ever closer to the side. Rain had begun to fall, needle sharp drops beginning to pelt them where they stood.

Edward tried to ignore her mad ravings, but he wanted to lash out at her for even the mention of Jane on her foul lips. *Oh, my little darling,* he thought, *for once I am so thankful you were not asleep in your bed tonight. Wherever you are tonight, my angel, you are at least safe from the wrath of this demon.*

He tried again, "Bertha, please let me help you down from here. You must be cold. We'll get you warm, give you some wine and you can go to sleep. Come with me."

Once again she screamed, but she turned away from him as she did so, her luxuriant hair seeming to float behind her. A memory flashed through his mind, remembering that hair brushing against his bare chest as she moved her body over his, that hair wrapped around his forearm as he pulled her head back to press his hungry mouth against the pulse that beat at her throat. He remembered how she had stolen into his room at night while he was staying in her father's house before their marriage, and had gradually swept away all of his innocence in a cloud of that inky perfumed softness.

He pushed those thoughts away, and it seemed to him that time stopped as he watched her turn, turn and lift herself to the edge of the roof. Up, and over and down, and he heard his own voice torn from him, "No!" Then he was at the edge, looking down at the body of his wife below him, sprawled horribly on the stones of the courtyard.

He backed away, shaking his head in disbelief at what he had just seen. Tears were streaming down his cheeks, tears or sweat or maybe just the rain, now falling harder. He turned then towards the skylight, aware of the sudden silence on the roof and the fact that he was now the only one who remained inside the confines of the dying hall. There was nothing he could do for Bertha any longer, no one left to save except himself.

The flames were licking at the walls of the house as he entered, and the smoke obscured his view. He dropped to his hands and knees to crawl the length of the hall, under the level of the smoke to the staircase. Groping almost blindly, he descended to the second floor, rounding the landing and starting downstairs. He was having a difficult time even drawing a full breath, and the second floor was a mass of flames, but he glanced only briefly to each side as he started towards the first floor.

He heard it then, a splintering sound that preceded a sensation of shaking that threw him to one side. He looked up as a shower of sparks from overhead fell onto the right side of his face. Crying out in pain, he backed up to avoid a further hail of ash and fragments from above him. His right hand pressed to his burning eye, he groped for the wall with his left. He had just brushed his fingertips against solid wood when another cracking and shuddering flung him out into darkness.

And the whole world collapsed around him.

Chapter 42 - Alive, but Sadly Hurt

"It was all his own courage, and a body may say, his kindness, in a way, ma'am: he wouldn't leave the house till every one else was out before him. As he came down the great staircase at last, after Mrs. Rochester had flung herself from the battlements, there was a great crash—all fell. He was taken out from under the ruins, alive, but sadly hurt: a beam had fallen in such a way as to protect him partly; but one eye was knocked out, and one hand so crushed that Mr. Carter, the surgeon, had to amputate it directly. The other eye inflamed: he lost the sight of that also."

Innkeeper, The Rochester Arms - Jane Eyre

With the fire now out, save for a few smouldering piles of wood scattered throughout the stone ruins, a handful of men picked carefully through the sad remains of the once-great Hall. The crowd had watched in helpless horror as the mysterious woman had plunged three storeys down to dash herself to death on the stone courtyard. They had rushed to surround her, but all could tell that nothing could be done. They had all seen Edward Rochester approach her with hand outstretched, attempting to coax her to safety. And they had all watched as he had disappeared into the inferno moments before it had collapsed with a great roar. John cried out in horror, and moved as though to rush in at once to save him, but some in the crowd held him back for his own safety.

The members of the fire patrol had done a cursory investigation to determine that there was no danger of further collapse before the order was given that it was safe to enter and search for Rochester. Very few among them truly believed that he could possibly be alive inside the rubble, but Mr. Carter, the surgeon, had directed a wagon to be backed as close to the wreckage as possible and had seized his bag of supplies before he and his assistant had joined John and several other men. They also took a whining Pilot, hoping that he could locate his master more quickly than they.

Holding torches aloft, they moved through the ruins. The driving rain had ceased, leaving a fine mist in the air, but the searchers shivered with more than the damp and cold of an autumn midnight. Most were certain they would find merely another battered body and that the dawning of the day would see the interment of not one corpse, but two, in the Rochester family burial ground, yet another Rochester couple to be buried together, watched over by Damer de Rochester and his wife from their narrow stone vault.

Pilot's frenzied barking and straining directed the men to the approximate area that had held the grand main staircase, and they moved to a larger pile of wood and plaster as Pilot sniffed and scratched at a certain spot. Lifting their torches high, they could see Thornfield's owner lying beneath the debris. Gathering around, they noted that the upper half of his body was entirely obscured by chunks of wood and plaster and a large beam that seemed to have fallen across him. They could see his legs, clad in worn knee length boots and fawn breeches, utterly motionless.

Carter and his assistant, a young Irishman named Padraig Lynch, moved swiftly to Rochester's side. Kneeling beside the fallen man, Carter pressed his hand to Rochester's groin to feel for a heartbeat. To his relief, a rapid pulse could be felt.

"He is alive!" he cried.

John's fervent, "Thank the Lord!" could be heard above the excited stir of the other searchers.

"He is trapped; pinned, it appears, by the weight of this beam across his arm," Carter reported. "The wood is lying on his left hand and lower arm. We cannot free him without lifting the beam." He felt inside the pile of debris, looking for a space between the wood and Rochester's pinned arm. Several inches above the wrist, he found a small spot to maneuver. "Find me something, a thick stick of wood," he said, rapidly yanking off his own cravat. "I need to make a tourniquet of sorts before we lift the beam. It alone may be staunching a flow from the arm and just lifting it could cause a great deal of blood loss before we can even get him into the wagon."

One of the men found a chunk of wood lying on the ground and Carter tied the cravat around Rochester's cold motionless arm, twisting the wood to tighten the cloth and cut off any blood flow. "Lynch, you see how I have fashioned this. Take charge of it as I assist them to lift the beam." He stood up, "Are you ready, men?"

They all assented and moved as one man to lift the huge beam. They strained it up and off of him as Lynch tightened the tourniquet around the now freed arm. As they tossed it aside and moved quickly out of the way, they could see that it had served the dual purpose of pinning him to the ground as it had protected him from other falling objects in the collapse of the house.

Rochester had fallen towards his left side, his left arm pinned just as it had been outstretched. All could now see his hand as it lay, grotesquely crushed and twisted. It had begun to swell, the fingers bent and lifeless. The little finger was nearly severed from the force of the heavy beam against the wide signet ring he had been wearing. Carter motioned for Lynch to release the tourniquet slowly, watching the hand as blood flow was restored. The hand was already a deep blue from the broken blood vessels within it and there was very little blood flow to be seen from the many wounds upon it.

Carter shook his head. "Even the vessels are crushed past their ability to bleed." He felt along the arm – from the wrist up it was sound, save for a small fracture that could be felt on the radial side. Directing a splint to be made to immobilize the extremity, he wrapped the hand in a soft cloth to cushion it.

Once the arm was thus released and protected, the group directed its attention to the rest of his upper body, gently moving aside chunks of plaster. As they moved a large piece of debris, the rest of his body was revealed and a collective gasp went up from the searchers. "Dear God in Heaven," breathed one of the men as the last of the plaster was pulled free.

Rochester's thick dark hair was matted with blood that had run from a large gash that started above his left eyebrow. It cut straight down to his cheekbone, the flesh laid open. But what riveted the group's attention was the terrible damage done to his left eye, torn from its socket. It was a gruesome sight, and more than one man had to swallow repeatedly as his gorge rose.

"Oh, Christ," Carter whispered. He tore open his supply bag, removed a stack of soft rags, and began to wipe away the blood that had flowed from the laceration. He turned the unconscious man's head gently, and saw the right side of his face. His right eye was reddened and inflamed, the skin above the eyebrow burned and blistered. Other than the devastating injuries to his eyes, he seemed to have no other serious facial wounds, just minor abrasions about the lower face and neck. Carter quickly ran his hands through Rochester's hair, relieved to find no apparent skull fractures, although several small bumps and bloodied areas could be felt where he had apparently been hit with falling debris.

Carter covered the terrible wound at Rochester's left eye and gently lifted his head to wrap bandages around it. Rochester stirred slightly and a low moan escaped his lips, then he fell silent again. Carter rapidly searched the rest of his body for serious injury, but once again could find nothing but many bruises and lacerations. He tore open Rochester's shirt and examined his abdomen and chest, noting several small misshapen areas that indicated broken ribs, but no obvious internal or spinal injuries. Still he encouraged the men to align his body carefully as they lifted him onto a large plank prior to removing him from the building. They covered him with a blanket, leaving only his head exposed, where the waiting crowd could see the bloodstained wrappings as the men slowly made their way out of the wreckage. The murmuring groups quieted and parted as Rochester's motionless body was carried over and gently lifted into the waiting wagon.

Someone had helped Grace Poole into Carter's carriage, and Leah and Mary waited for John to come to them before they too climbed into the carriage for the trip into town. The fallen body of Bertha Rochester had been mercifully covered and moved to the cellar of the church to await orders for burial.

Carter and Lynch climbed onto the back of the wagon and steadied Edward's still form as the horse was urged forward. The crowd respectfully watched as both carriage and wagon rolled slowly out of the courtyard and into the black night, leaving behind only death and ruin and the ghosts of fallen dreams.

At Mr. Carter's house and small sanitarium, the survivors of the Thornfield fire rested in various rooms that dark morning. John, Leah and Mary waited in the large anteroom outside Carter's surgery. Mrs. Carter had attempted to feed them, although none of them had been able to force down more than a few bites. Beds had been offered, but all had refused to go to sleep until they had some news of their master. They had washed up and were sitting silently, holding cups of nearly untouched tea. They listened tensely to the low murmurs on the other side of the door.

Grace Poole, still groggy from the effects of smoke and drink, was sleeping in one of the spare rooms until morning, when a message could be conveyed to her son at the Grimsby Retreat.

In the large surgery behind the door, Edward Rochester had been placed on the operating table, still on the makeshift stretcher that had carried him out of the wreckage, by Carter's strict orders to be moved and disturbed as little as possible.

As he and Lynch conferred in low tones as to what should be done for him, Mrs. Carter had used a scissors to cut away his smoke-blackened and blood-stained clothing, and had covered him with a sheet as the men prepared their instruments.

Edward was unresponsive other than a slight restlessness when his left arm was manipulated or his eye examined. Fortunately, there was as yet no sign of internal bleeding and his pulse remained steady.

As Carter and Lynch spoke softly over their tray of metal instruments, Mrs. Carter stepped out of the room, shutting the door softly behind her. She had discarded Rochester's ruined clothing, but had collected his boots and the contents of his pockets to be returned later. Holding a small object in her hand, she approached the solemn group at the table. "The poor man," she shook her head. "It looks bad for him – God knows to what extent he'll be maimed. And look at this."

She held out her hand. Leah recognized the object she held, and with a small cry, reached for it.

"It's Miss Eyre's necklace," she told them. "The one 'e gave 'er for a wedding gift. She must've left it behind when she went. Was it in 'is pocket?"

"No," Mrs. Carter replied. "When I removed his cravat and cut away his shirt, I found it secured around his neck. Look at what is on it."

Leah held up the little string of gleaming pearls. It was strung through a small, gold band.

John took it from her hand. "'Tis Miss Eyre's wedding ring," he said, his voice rough with emotion. "He never even got to put it on her finger. He's been wearing this since the day she left. We've never spoke of it, but on the mornings that I've helped him dress, I've seen him put it on."

The little ring gleamed on his work-toughened palm. Inside were engraved the letters "EFR to JER". The whole group was quiet as they took in the silent testimony to Rochester's continued despair over the vanished governess. They had all experienced the sharp side of his tongue these two months, but nothing but compassion showed on the faces that the doctor's wife saw before her.

"We will just keep this here with his other things," Mrs. Carter said, taking the ring and necklace back. "When he awakens, he will no doubt take comfort from these familiar objects."

The door opened and Mr. Carter poked his head out, motioning for John to join them. Ushering him into the room and shutting the door firmly behind him, the surgeon said, "We will need your assistance in here, if you please. There is no way to save the hand. Almost every bone in it is broken, and the blood supply is badly compromised. If we leave it, putrefaction will be the only result and it will kill him. He may die yet, although I will do everything in my power to prevent it. But the hand will need to come off, and much work must be done to the eye area. There is no chance the left eye can be saved, but there may be hope for the other one."

He instructed John to step to the end of the table and place his hands firmly on Edward's bare shoulders. "You must hold him well. He is senseless now but he many awaken and we need to keep him restrained. I have given him a little laudanum, a small amount on a spoon, which he was able to swallow, but I dare not give him more without knowing how he will fare with his blood loss and his head injuries, minor though they are. I am not really sure why he is going in and out of consciousness; the wounds themselves are not serious enough to cause this stupor. It is probably the effects of the smoke and of shock, but my fear is that he has a slow hemorrhage deep within, one I cannot detect at present. Should that be the case, he will die suddenly and there will be nothing we can do to stop it, but we must keep him as quiet and undisturbed as possible to prevent further bleeding, if present."

The women watched the door behind which John had disappeared. They sat quietly, occasionally speaking in near whispers. When John emerged over an hour later, his face was white and tears shone on his grizzled cheeks. He sat down and covered his eyes with his shaking hands.

The two doctors began to finish up the night's grim work. It had been difficult for them. Taking off the hand was a relatively simple procedure, the most complicated part involving cutting a flap of skin that would later be used to create a covering for the stump. The hand was so badly damaged there was little usable skin, but Carter chose two smaller sections and began to cut away the tissue with his scalpel. Rochester had appeared unconscious, but unfortunately had been awakened by the agony of his skin being cut in preparation for the amputation.

Unable to see, in excruciating pain, still thinking he was caught in the fire, he had fought them, crying out for help. John leaned on his shoulders, sobbing as he helped to restrain the desperately wounded man. Lynch had tied ropes around Rochester's body to restrict movement should he awaken during the procedure, and strong cloth bindings held the mutilated limb down to the board on which it lay, stretched out at a right angle to his body. A tourniquet had been firmly fastened a few inches below Rochester's left elbow to prevent excess bleeding when the hand was removed.

When Lynch was finished tying the man down, he had stepped to the head of the bed and fitted a padded stick of wood into the patient's mouth, to prevent damage to teeth and soft tissue should his jaws involuntarily clamp down in response to the pain. Rochester indeed bit hard on the wood, trying to pull his head free as Lynch held the mouth guard, his hands on Rochester's cheeks as he tried to keep the patient still. Carter restrained the lower part of the left arm as he deftly finished his task, trying to shut out the sound of his patient's muffled screams. They had taken the precaution of tying down his right arm, a wise move, they realized, as their panicked patient tried vainly to pull free from his restraints.

It was a mercifully short time before Rochester had fainted from the pain, and sawing through the bone was a quick procedure, but all three men were shaken. Even Carter, who had started his career as a surgeon with the Royal Navy and had done countless amputations, found his hands were unsteady as he put down his saw and cauterized the bleeding stump of the forearm with a hot iron. John had had to rush for the basin as the smell of burning flesh filled the surgery. Lynch loosened his tight hold on the mouth guard but still held it in Rochester's mouth and supported the head of the now silent patient as Carter folded the flaps of skin over and stitched them together to make a neat covering for the end of the stump.

As John splashed cold water on his face and rested, Carter and Lynch wrapped the arm and splinted it, both to protect the skin and to immobilize the simple fracture of the lower arm. Rochester lay still, his face white and bathed in sweat after the ordeal. Despite the mouth guard, a small trickle of blood appeared at the corner of his mouth. Carter's heart sank as he quickly assessed the spot, afraid that a gush of blood from the patient's mouth would signal a fatal internal bleed, but to his relief, he saw that it was just an area on the lower lip that was bitten into during the amputation. He gently wiped away the blood with a damp cloth, his own jaws clenched from trying to hold back his emotions. He leaned over Rochester's face, reassuring himself that he still breathed, and felt for his pulse, which still beat strongly despite everything.

Then they turned their attention to his eye, Carter shaking his head as he unwrapped the dressings and surveyed the fearsome wound. "This too is far too damaged to save. Even if we could replace the eye within the socket, we risk infection that will spread throughout his body." Silently he began to trim away the torn tissue and seal the eyelid over the empty socket, first repairing the eyelid itself, and then partially sewing the two lids together as Lynch continued to hold Rochester's head steady. Thankfully, their patient remained senseless throughout the rest of their work.

When finished with their surgery, they carefully wrapped his chest to support the broken ribs, then they washed his matted hair and clipped it close to his head, the better for Carter to determine that his head injuries were relatively minor. Lynch, who was not yet prepared to do full-fledged surgery, readied sutures in preparation for stitching up the large gash on Rochester's face. Carter had determined there was little he could do for the burned right eye except to apply a healing salve, keep it covered, and hope for the best.

They thanked John for his help and watched him slip from the room, then finished up as Carter quietly told Lynch some of the history of the man they were treating. Lynch was a small dark-haired man with nimble fingers perfectly suited to the task before him. He took a sharp, curved needle and patiently repaired Rochester's torn face with tiny, meticulous stitches as he listened to Carter's account of their patient's struggles with his insane wife. Rochester lay in his apparent stupor, with just a restless movement and an occasional slight whimper or moan each time the needle pierced his flesh.

Lynch's bright blue eyes showed great compassion as he shook his head over Rochester's dilemma. He was a strict Catholic, one of the reasons he'd had such a difficult time finding a position for further training after he had finished his medical studies in Edinburgh. He looked young, but was actually in his late twenties, and had come a long way from his parents' difficult existence as struggling tenant farmers in southwestern Ireland. As a native Irishman in England and Scotland, he knew the sting of prejudice and the grueling work it took to succeed despite great odds. His struggles had taught him empathy, and although he believed strongly in the sacrament of marriage, he had sympathy for Rochester's plight as Carter explained it.

Lynch knew Carter to be a somewhat godless man, quite agnostic in his beliefs, but it had worked to Lynch's advantage, as Carter did not care about religion and had chosen him as his assistant in spite of the urgings of others – his devout Anglican wife among them – against Lynch's Papist beliefs. Lynch also knew Carter to be kind and fair to all, and could see his compassion for the man before him.

"It was only a matter of time before his wife killed someone, and I always feared it would be him." Carter was cleaning and bandaging the rest of the burns and contusions as he spoke. "She tried to burn him in his bed once, and nearly killed her own brother when he came to visit her." He shook his head. "She could appear mad as a hatter, talking all manner of nonsense. A person might almost believe her harmless. Then she'd snap her head up and give you such a look with her dark eyes, your blood would chill. She would speak with perfect clarity, but with such spite and venom. She could make you believe in the Devil."

"What caused her madness?" asked Lynch, who had always believed in the Devil. His fingers gracefully worked the sutures; he did not raise his eyes from his task.

"A familial malady, to hear Rochester speak of it. It affected her mother and a younger brother, as I understand, but this woman was nearly grown before it manifested its true form. She apparently appeared normal enough for this poor wretch to be taken in when he was young and naive. Of course, by the time I first saw her, she was riddled with disease from the actions that accompanied her madness, and that too, had affected her mind. Sooner or later she would have died of it, although she still seemed fairly vigorous from what I was able to see."

"Disease?" Lynch frowned in distaste. "I assume you are talking about diseases of personal contact. Would her husband not be affected as well as she?"

"Rochester and I had spoken of that." Carter adjusted his spectacles and reached for another bandage roll. "It had been a worry of his, but I was able to reassure him somewhat. They apparently lived as husband and wife for only a month or so before he was unable to tolerate her further, although they did share a home for four years or more. She blamed his rejection of her, his refusal to continue their marriage in a physical sense, for her drinking and wanton behaviour. It was most likely on one of her forays out that she came home with something. Lucky for Rochester she disgusted him so, or he might have been infected by her.

"As time went on she became more uncontrollable, would disappear for days at a time. Then he would get a message to come fetch her from some disreputable place. He had to bring her home from some truly difficult situations, things he could barely talk about, things even I was unfamiliar with, Navy man that I am. It was for that reason that he brought her to England instead of just leaving her there. He was afraid of where she would end up if he left her, felt he owed it to her to keep her physically safe."

He gestured towards Rochester's still form. "And this is where his conscience took him."

He continued with a sigh, "Some three or four months ago, Rochester came to me. He has long trusted my discretion and there was a matter about which he was concerned. He had fallen in love, he said, with the governess of his ward. Loved her beyond anything he had ever known. He wanted to marry her, but was afraid. Afraid of discovery, afraid still that his wife's malady had somehow afflicted him before their marital contact was discontinued. Through questioning and examination, I was able to ease his mind on that score. It had been so long, likely any disease would have come from another source, but I saw no signs of any.

"I couldn't reassure him about the risk of discovery, though, other than to tell him that exposure wouldn't come from me. He didn't want to risk losing the governess by telling her the truth, said she was a decent young woman who would never live with him outside of marriage, so he went ahead and proposed to her, sweet young girl she was. And on their wedding day, at the very altar yet, his secret was revealed."

"And well it should have been!" Lynch frowned as he stitched carefully below Rochester's sealed eyelid. "It is wrong to marry one woman when you are already wed to another, insane or not."

"Ah, I know what they say, and the townspeople have said plenty." Carter shook his head. "But none of them have had to occupy a cold, lonely bed with no one to share it except a piteous lunatic or a series of mistresses, bought and paid for. I cannot pass judgment on a man who only wants what I have been lucky enough to have – the comfort of a decent and loving wife."

"He has been judged, if you want to call it that. His reputation is ruined in this area, not that he cares. The governess left in the dead of night, gone before first light of the next day. Rochester has searched for her like a madman ever since, but found no trace of her. She may be dead herself, a young girl like that alone in the world. He has not been the same since he lost her and now this." He looked up at Lynch until the young assistant, wondering at the sudden silence, raised his eyes also.

Carter fixed him with an intense stare. "There are worse things to be in this world than dead, young man, never forget that." He gestured at the table. "And this may be one of them."

Chapter 43 - Better to Be Dead

"Were any other lives lost?"
"No—perhaps it would have been better if there had."
"What do you mean?"
"Poor Mr. Edward! ... I little thought ever to have seen it! Some say it was a just judgment on him for keeping his first marriage secret, and wanting to take another wife while he had one living: but I pity him, for my part."
"You said he was alive?" I exclaimed.
"Yes, yes: he is alive; but many think he had better be dead."
Jane Eyre talking to Innkeeper of The Rochester Arms - Jane Eyre

September and October, 1836
Shortly before lunchtime, Alice Fairfax was out in the garden cutting the dried brown heads off the chrysanthemums, when her friend Anna called to her that she had a visitor. She wiped her hands on her apron as she headed inside, wondering who could possibly have any business with her.

In coming to live and work at the inn managed by her girlhood friend, Mrs. Fairfax had effectively cut off ties to Thornfield Hall. Mr. Rochester had given her the year's annuity payment before she had departed, with the remaining payments to be handled by his agent. She had exchanged brief notes with Mary after her arrival, but had corresponded with no one further than that, and so it was with great surprise that she entered the large main parlour to find John, Mr. Rochester's manservant from Thornfield, standing just inside the door. He looked pale and exhausted, yet agitated, with a day's growth of whiskers and dark-ringed, haunted eyes. His clothing was stained and rumpled. He turned his cap nervously in his hand.

"Mrs. Fairfax, ma'am," he blurted as she entered the room, "I've come for your help. It's terrible doin's at the Hall, a terrible business indeed."

Mrs. Fairfax hurried to his side, urging him to sit. She called to one of the housemaids, asking her to bring some tea, which John accepted with a hand that shook.

"It's Thornfield, ma'am," he told her, "burned to the ground, all in ruins. Mister Edward lies near death, his wife dead, Mrs. Poole injured." He took a long, slurping drink of the tea and set it down, the cup rattling in the saucer.

"He saved us, Mister Edward did. He was awake, walking outside as he does… did… each night. He saw the flames from the orchard, smelled the smoke. He run into the house, pounding on our doors, forcing us downstairs. Mary, me, Leah." He closed his eyes, rubbing his hand across his face.

"After he got us out, he run back up for Grace Poole. She was senseless, but he carried her down three flights of stairs, brought her outside to the air. The fire patrol was there by then, but it was pure useless. The fire spread… "

He went on to tell the former housekeeper what had transpired, Bertha's leap from the roof, the collapse of the staircase, the extent of Rochester's injuries. Mrs. Fairfax sat in horror, eyes wide, shaking her head at his account of the previous night.

"What I've come to ask you, ma'am, is would you ever help us?" His eyes beseeched her. " 'Tis just Mary and me. This morning Leah's family come for her. Said 'twas bad enough she'd kept working for a man of such sinfulness, now he was trying to kill her too. And she wouldn't be much help in nursing. She's a young girl, unmarried. 'Twouldn't be fitting for her to help care for him, the kind of care he'll be needing.

"Can you help us, even for a short time? Mr. Carter will keep him at his home, but his assistant and Mrs. Carter have all they can do with the rest of the town.

"Mary and I said we'd stay to help nurse him, but we don't know anything about the running of the business, dealing with the tenants, making the arrangements that need to be made. And if the worst happens, and Mister Edward does not live... " he swallowed, closed his eyes.

"Of course, of course I'll help." Mrs. Fairfax had thought to be free of Mr. Rochester, at least the man he seemed to have become, but at John's account her heart swelled with pity for all involved. No matter what her former employer had turned into with the departure of Miss Eyre, he had for many years been good to her, and was responsible for her comfortable manner of living now. She could not refuse him.

"I'll need to speak to my friend, and to her daughter. They manage the inn and I help them. I'll need to make arrangements here as well." She called the housemaid again, directed her to find John a room in which he could freshen up, even lie down while she packed and prepared for the trip. She directed the cook to make him up a plate of food and more tea, then went off in search of Anna.

John lay down in one of the empty rooms of the inn. He was exhausted to his very bones, but sleep would not come. He had dozed off in the carriage on the trip here, sleeping fitfully as the vehicle lurched over the rough roads. He tried to relax, to take deep breaths, to keep his eyes closed, but every time he shut them, images haunted him – the burning house; the dreadful sound of Bertha's body as it hit the ground; Rochester's still, bleeding form; his cries as his hand was amputated.

He finally gave up trying to sleep and lay awake in the bed, his mind working rapidly. Yes, he and Mary, with the help of Mrs. Fairfax, could assist the Carters and Lynch with Rochester's care. He made a mental list of tasks that would need to be taken care of when they returned, and eventually dozed a little before he was roused by Mrs. Fairfax – her bag was packed and she was wearing her travelling clothes.

It was afternoon when the two started back to Millcote. John had not slept much, but the rest had refreshed him somewhat. He and Mrs. Fairfax talked in low tones of practical things, falling silent occasionally, looking out at the sunny autumn landscape. It took about four hours to return to Mr. Carter's home, not an arduous trip, but Mrs. Fairfax found her legs felt shaky with fatigue and apprehension as she climbed down from the carriage. John carried her bag, and Mr. Carter greeted them at the door.

"John, you look fagged out," Carter told him as he entered. "You must go to your room immediately and not emerge until tomorrow. There are plenty of us to take care of things here, and now that you have brought assistance," he nodded to Mrs. Fairfax, "all will be well."

"How is he?" John asked in a low voice, gesturing towards the closed door behind which Rochester lay.

"Feverish, restless." Carter shook his head. "We have restrained his arms, fearful that he would tear off the bandages, start that arm bleeding. He has had some laudanum and that has quieted him somewhat. We have been sponging him with water to try to control the fever – a natural reaction after what he has been through. But the fever makes him restless as well. The next forty-eight hours should tell us if he will survive his injuries." He shook his head, then turned to Mrs. Fairfax, and inquired of her trip.

"It was fine, thank you," she replied to him. "I am well-rested, and would be glad to relieve someone in the sickroom."

"That would be most welcome, if you feel you are up to it," the surgeon said, leading the way to the room. "My assistant has been seeing to the regular patients from town today, and my wife and I have seen to Mr. Rochester. We have insisted that Mary rest, for she was as exhausted as John."

"How is Mrs. Poole?" Mrs. Fairfax asked. "John mentioned that she had to be rescued by Mr. Rochester as well; does she fare all right?"

"Mrs. Poole is fine, or will be," the doctor said grimly. "We received word that her son will come to fetch her in the morning. She has some minor bruises and a cough from the smoke, but she has sobered up. She took the news of Rochester's injuries badly, begged to be allowed to stay, to help nurse him herself, but we felt it would be better for her to be away from here.

"She cried quite bitterly this afternoon, over Mrs. Rochester's death and her master's injuries, asked to see him, but we persuaded her to rest. A little laudanum for her eased her pain, both mental and physical. She was sleeping the last I saw. It will do her good to be gone from the area."

Mrs. Fairfax did not reply, for they were now at Mr. Rochester's bedside, and she was too overcome by the sight of him to speak. Tears came to the elderly woman's eyes as she looked at him.

He lay completely still, his normally dark skin paled, except for the livid bruises that were now apparent over his body. Bandages covered his eyes, but she could see the stitches that had repaired his face extend down from beneath the white wrapping. His mutilated left arm was completely wrapped in dressings, and around the arm was a wooden splint-like support that was tied to the bedframe, severely restricting any movement. His right wrist had a length of white cloth around it as well, serving as a soft restraint on that side. A white sheet was pulled up over him, and Mrs. Carter was wringing out a cloth from a bowl of liquid that smelled strongly of vinegar.

The two women greeted each other, and Mrs. Carter turned to her husband with a smile, "He is finally quiet, the laudanum seems to have taken hold."

Carter reached over and felt Rochester's face, his neck. "He seems cool now, the water has helped. Mrs. Fairfax has offered to watch him for a while, so you perhaps should rest now, my dear. Let us tell her what needs to be done for him."

Mrs. Fairfax blinked in the dim light from the lamp at the side of the bed.

Someone was to relieve her at midnight, and she was ready for it, for she had been nodding off for most of the last hour. Rochester was muttering and moving restlessly in the bed, and when she reached over to feel his face, it was dry and hot with fever once again. He had been fairly quiet for most of the evening, except for occasional moments of incoherent murmurings. She had spooned some broth between his lips, and then had given him another spoonful of laudanum when he had begun to moan and pull against the restraints.

Now, as he tossed his head and cried out softly, she reached for a cloth and dipped it in the vinegar water, wringing it out and beginning to sponge his face and neck with the cool liquid. Her eyes filled as she listened to him, for it was Miss Eyre's name he uttered in his feverish delirium.

"Jane, Jane," he whispered over and over. Mrs. Fairfax's heart swelled with pity for him, and she crooned wordlessly to him as she moved the damp cloth over him. He wore nothing beneath the sheet, and she felt sadness at her proud employer's helplessness and loss of dignity. She checked the towel placed at his groin in case he needed to empty his bladder, but it was dry. Mr. Carter had told her to keep track of any urine output, and to try to keep him taking fluids during his periods of wakefulness.

But she was far more worried about his body temperature, placing cool, wrung-out cloths at his groin, under his arms, and at his neck, as she had been instructed by Mr. Carter. She adjusted the towel between his thighs to attempt to keep him modestly covered while she began to sponge his legs with the cool water, moving up to his upper body and wiping the cloth gently over his chest and arms.

The vinegar water beaded up on the thick dark hair that covered his chest above the wrappings that protected his ribs. She bathed him patiently until he began to shiver as the cool air hit him. She pulled the sheet back up over him and held his head up to give him a teaspoon of cool water. He still muttered, and Mrs. Fairfax could still make out Jane's name among the unintelligible words he spoke.

She wondered, where was Miss Eyre this night, as the man who loved her writhed in pain and cried out her name? Mrs. Fairfax had come to love the quiet little governess in the time she had been at Thornfield, and had worried so for her. She had not felt that it would be a good thing for her to marry their employer, but even she had had to acknowledge that Rochester certainly seemed to love her. And Miss Eyre had conducted herself with wisdom and good morals. Mrs. Fairfax had caught them embracing on several occasions, but she supposed that was natural for two people in love, who were shortly to marry. Miss Eyre had never given any reason to think that she was allowing any further liberties to be taken; indeed, she had seemed determined to put Rochester off, to his dismay.

Mrs. Fairfax had found herself beginning to approve of the match, seeing her master happier than she had seen him since before he had left for Jamaica all those years ago. She had always felt an affection for the younger son of her niece, had hoped for a happy life for him when he had left his native land all those years ago. It had hurt her to see him return so altered, to see the bitter, angry man he had become. His ready smile had all but disappeared from his face, and it was with joy that she had witnessed its reappearance as he waited to marry Miss Eyre.

Mrs. Fairfax had grieved over the disappearance of the young governess from Thornfield, although the quiet regret of the staff paled beside the wild and frenzied despair of their master. She had prayed daily for Miss Eyre's safety, and for Mr. Rochester's peace and reconciliation to God. She shook her head now at the calamity that had befallen her former employer, and wondered how all this could possibly fit into God's plan.

The next week was spent sharing duties in the sickroom. Rochester's fever grew higher, and his periods of frantic delirium meant he needed to be carefully watched lest he cause himself further injury. The laudanum helped, but at times it took two people to hold him in the bed for the time it took for the drug to take effect.

Mr. Carter pronounced him out of danger of dying, but that it would be a long and difficult recovery. John, Mary, and Mrs. Fairfax each kept watch at the patient's bedside, with Carter and Lynch assisting them as necessary.

All had come to appreciate Carter's young assistant. He seemed an excellent doctor already, steady and intelligent, and he did not hesitate to step in and help them when he was needed. At times it seemed his quiet, lilting voice did more to soothe their restless patient than any of their urgings.

Lynch often helped to hold Rochester in the bed, amazing them, as his small, wiry frame belied surprising physical strength. He had joked that it had come from years of farming. "My brothers had the sheep, my sisters had the chickens, and I had the cows," he had told them, smiling. "They were balky creatures."

They could all see his compassion as he laboured over his patient, watching keenly for signs of infection or other complications. Carter remained in the background, helping when asked, but for the most part leaving his assistant to manage the care. All watched anxiously, waiting to see what path Edward Rochester's physical and emotional recovery would take.

Padraig Lynch set the candle down on the table, and moved to Rochester's side to check the dressings that protected his wounds. He and Carter attempted to give those nursing the patient a brief respite from their vigilance, and used that time for their examinations and dressing changes.

In the initial days after his injuries and surgery, when Rochester had been delirious with pain and fever, he had required constant supervision to keep him still in the bed and to protect his healing wounds. But for several days now, he had been quiet, submitting silently to the various manipulations. Lynch felt that he was awake and aware, but had moved into a world of his own, retreating from fear and suffering. His body was healing as well as could be expected, given the severity of his injuries.

Rochester was relatively young and healthy; his athletic vigour had stood him in good stead against the various complications of his condition, although for the last two months he had not been eating or resting properly due to his grief over his vanished love. Lynch feared for his mind, worried over the silent compliance of the formerly combative man. He had taken to speaking to him in a quiet tone, using his name, speaking in measured tones of inconsequential things such as the weather and the latest news from London. Rochester never replied, but Lynch felt his calm voice held at bay the panic he could sense each time he dealt with the patient.

He lifted the packing around Rochester's eye, noting the decreasing swelling and discharge from the eyelid. The long gash appeared to be healing, the wound not quite so livid. The edges seemed to be well approximated; the stitches could most likely be removed in a matter of days. The right eye was still reddened, but the swelling appeared to be lessening.

Unfortunately, a slight distortion of the lens could be seen, a faint filmy covering that obscured the brilliance of the dark eye. It was very mild, and could yet heal and disappear. He applied the salve to the eyes and redressed them, the patient giving no sign of being disturbed by the treatment. But when he untied the splint from the bedside, and removed it from the mutilated arm, he felt a resistance, a tightening of the strong muscles.

"Shhh, shhh, now," he said in a soothing tone as he unwrapped the bandage from the stump, bracing himself for any signs of infection, as he did every day. But there were none, and the terrible wound at the forearm was healing quite well. This was the difficult part – the wound had to be cleaned thoroughly and salve applied to keep the stump from contracting and forming tight scar tissue as it healed. Should that occur, it would cause additional pain and prevent him from being able to fully extend the arm. He continued, "Mr. Rochester, the arm looks fine. The bone is in good shape, the skin is healing well. This will be uncomfortable, as you know; have patience with me and it will be finished before you know it."

He began to clean the arm, stretching it out as far as he could. Rochester's facial muscles tightened, his dark skin blanched, and a low moan escaped him before he pressed his lips together.

"It is all right to let me know you're hurting," he whispered to him soothingly. "I know it's not an easy thing. I have to pull on the arm and I am sorry about that."

The dry, cracked lips moved then, and Lynch heard the man speak for the first time, in a low, hoarse voice. "You have taken the hand, have you not?"

Lynch hesitated before speaking. They had all taken pains to avoid discussing the particulars of his condition in his earshot, not wanting to cause a shock to him. They had agreed that Carter would tell him the extent of his injuries when he was awake and seeking information. With both arms restrained so he could not pull off the splint and dressings, they knew he had not been able to feel anything with his remaining hand.

"Yes," he finally told him. "The left hand was too badly damaged to save. The infection would have killed you, so it was amputated. It is healing well, and your right hand was unscathed. You are dominant in the use of your right hand, if I'm correct. You will still be able to use that well."

"Yes," was the harsh reply, Rochester's voice stronger now. "I can still use the right hand. I suppose I should consider that a blessing, except for the fact that I cannot seem to see either." His voice cracked with the force of a whip.

Lynch was at a loss. "It seems, sir, that it is time I fetched Mr. Carter. He can explain in detail the injuries and their implications." It was the middle of the night, he had agreed to spend this time with their patient, but he felt that Carter would want to know Rochester was suddenly speaking to him and searching for answers. He finished drying the arm, and began to apply the salve to the stump, his hands suddenly unsteady.

Rochester pulled against the restraint on his right arm, "Damn you, untie this arm. I am awake and alert. I don't need to be tied in this manner."

"It was for your own protection, sir." Lynch wiped his hands and began to apply a clean bandage to the arm. "You fought so powerfully hard against us the first days, we feared you would damage the arm. I will finish this dressing and if you promise to lie still, will untie the right arm."

"You haven't responded to my question about my vision," was the reply. "I feel the dressings in place, feel the pain. Do not spare me from the truth."

Lynch continued what he was doing, weighing his words. When the arm was wrapped, he replaced the splints around it, then laid the arm down gently. Moving to the other side of the bed, he untied the soft wrist restraint. Rochester flexed his right arm, his face tense as he waited for Lynch to speak.

"The left eye is gone, that's the only way to say it to you. You were hit in the face, torn from here to here." With his fingers he indicated the length of the wound on Rochester's face. "The eye was torn as well. We repaired the area, but the eye was so damaged it had to be removed. The eyelid had closed naturally once the eye was gone but Mr. Carter sealed the eyelids together to protect the remaining tissue. There is a small opening but the lid is now basically shut."

Rochester swallowed audibly, his face pale and still. "And the other?" he whispered.

Lynch shook his head, then remembered the patient could not see him. He cleared his throat, "We do not know. It appears you were slightly burned on that side of your face – there is a burn above the eyebrow. Most likely some hot ash fell into the eye, causing an inflammation. It could still correct itself. You were awake minutes ago as I dressed the eyes. Could you see out of it?"

Rochester shook his head, then turned it away from Lynch. His right hand slowly moved up to his face, but Lynch did not stop him as he touched his cheeks, then his forehead, lightly feeling the dressings. After a moment, he dropped his hand, but kept his face turned away. He was silent.

Lynch felt a need to keep speaking to him, now that the connection had been made. "The rest of your injuries are very minor – a few broken ribs, bruising, scrapes here and there, a few knocks on the head. And all injuries were above the level of the waist. From there down you were unscathed." Rochester maintained his sullen silence. "You can still walk, still maintain your bodily functions, still perform as a man. These are no small things."

Rochester gave a small, bitter sound. "Walk – when I can't see where I'm going. Bodily functions – when I can't care for myself. Perform as a man – yes, a blind, helpless cripple. The desire of every woman." He laughed then, a low, harsh, black sound that chilled Lynch. Rochester clenched his jaw, turned away again. He did not speak further, and Lynch was silent too, knowing that nothing he could say would help.

The days passed in a routine. Mrs. Fairfax stayed several weeks, sharing nursing duties while Mr. Rochester was at his sickest, attempting to settle business affairs once he was out of danger. She sat down with John to assist him in putting things in order. The estate agent was contacted to apprise him of the situation and to charge him with overseeing the tenants and rents, which he assured them he would continue to do.

A letter was sent to Adèle's boarding school to continue payment and to notify the headmistress where Mr. Rochester could be contacted in the event of an emergency. A severance payment and character was provided for Leah, who remained with her family. Grace Poole, recovered physically but low in spirit, had been removed by her son and there was no further word of her.

Only John, Mary, and Mrs. Fairfax had attended the brief service Mr. Wood conducted to lay the tormented Bertha Rochester to rest. Her husband had at the time been in a haze of fever and laudanum; indeed, the risk had been very real that he would join his wife in the burial ground at any time.

Because she had been an obvious suicide, there was no official service, just a short prayer for her soul. Only her husband's money and position had enabled her to buried in the confines of the consecrated graveyard. When Rochester had later been appealed to regarding his wishes for a stone, he had merely shrugged, speaking only to give her name and birthdate before once again turning away his face. Later he spoke to Mrs. Fairfax privately, requesting that she write to Richard Mason on his behalf, informing him of his sister's death. When she brought the letter to him later and offered to read it to him before she sent it off, he refused.

Edward had lain silently as Mr. Carter had informed him of the condition of Thornfield, and the circumstances of his rescue. He had not responded as Carter had reiterated his luck in being alive, in suffering no damage to brain or spine. He had given short answers as Mrs. Fairfax had told him of the various financial arrangements she had made on his behalf. He thanked her tersely for taking the time and bother to assist John and Mary, and the Carters, and offered no further orders.

He never spoke to her of his previous efforts to find Jane, nor of the solicitors and agents he had contacted to search for her. Mrs. Fairfax had answered the letter from Mr. Briggs in August, telling him that Miss Eyre had fled from Thornfield, but it never occurred to her to tell him of Rochester's plight and where he could now be found. All seemed to feel that Miss Eyre was as lost to their employer as Thornfield was.

Edward Rochester continued to submit to their ministrations without protest. He no longer asked about his condition, and only a tautness of his muscles, a sheen of sweat on his brow, gave evidence of any pain he suffered. He now refused the laudanum they offered him, not telling them that the nightmares it gave him were even worse than the living nightmare that was now his existence. His fever never reached the point it had during the first days after his injury, but it was still present, evidence of his healing processes.

To preserve his modesty now that he was awake, only John tended to his physical needs: assisting him to use the chamber pot, bathing him, helping him to clean his teeth, shaving him and changing his linens. Edward lay, stony-faced, turning when required, following John's hesitant directions, saying nothing. His bitterness pervaded the small, sunny room in which he lay. All avoided speaking to him unless they had to.

All except Padraig Lynch. He continued to come to him in the night while Carter slept. He had taken over all wound care, and continued to treat him gently, occasionally speaking to him as he did so. Inside, he was rather angry at the rudeness of this arrogant English gentleman. Rochester cared nothing for his servants, yet they obviously cared deeply for him. He was buried so deeply in his rage and pain he could think of nothing else, and it galled Lynch to see it.

One night, after the dressings were changed and Edward assisted to sit up higher in the bed, Lynch asked him if he had given any thought to where he would go when he recovered. No mention was made of rebuilding Thornfield, and Lynch had heard John and Mary discussing their future. He knew they were willing to remain with Rochester, but they had been given no word as to his wishes.

"I will not rebuild Thornfield," was the reply. "I could never live there again." Edward rubbed his forehead with his hand. "I have a villa in the south of France. I could go there."

"And your servants?" Lynch asked, gathering the old dressings and straightening his supplies. "Where would they go?"

Edward frowned, "They will go with me if they want to keep their situations. Or I will engage others."

Lynch, irritated, snapped at him, "As easy as that, is it? Mary has children, you know. And grandchildren. John is her second husband, but he is fond of her family, and they visit them every week on their day off." He looked at the man in the bed. "Did you know that? Have you ever given a thought to their lives when they are not at your bedside? Do you think she will want to leave her family to serve a man who never has a kind word for her?"

"How dare you?" came the cold reply. "If they wish to continue their employment, they will go. What do you know of it?"

"I know that you will need help to travel to the inn down the street, to say nothing of the south of France," Lynch said, equally cold, his accent growing even stronger in his anger. "I think you are no longer in a position to treat them so lightly. I would give thought to those who would help you. I have watched John and Mary for three weeks – watched their concern for you, their willingness to perform the most odious tasks to see to your safety and comfort. They care deeply for you, though God knows why. I doubt you have given a moment of your time to think of them."

"Yes, I suppose you speak truth. I am no longer in the place I once was, am I?" Edward's face was now turned towards Lynch, his visage softened somewhat by the effect of Lynch's sharp words. "I will speak to them. I have a small estate, thirty miles from here. It is in no shape to live in, but I don't suppose it matters, for me. They could be near their family then, or at least within distance of a few hours' carriage ride."

Lynch, soft-hearted as usual, felt somewhat ashamed of his sharp words as he looked at Rochester. "I think they would appreciate word of their prospects."

"You are Irish, I believe?" Edward asked him, to his surprise. "I visited Ireland some years back, although I do not like it. I find it a sad and backwards country."

"So do I," Lynch told him. "When I am there, I feel as though I will stifle, burst from the confines of it. When I am not there, I feel as though my soul will burst with the longing for it." He gave a small laugh, embarrassed by what he had revealed. "I sound daft, but perhaps you have experienced it? The hatred for a place, the longing for it when you leave it?"

He did not expect a reply, but Rochester quietly spoke, "Yes, I know exactly what that feels like. My very home, the place my family had owned for nearly two hundred years. Now it is gone, and my life with it." "Your life, is it?" Lynch answered. "No, your life will continue. You are thirty-five, perhaps? Still young."

"Thirty-eight, this January to come," continued the sombre voice. "So many years I could still have, and what to do with them?" His jaw trembled before he clenched it, pressed his hand against his sightless eyes. His face suddenly showed fear, and he looked older than his age.

"Mr. Carter told me of your young lady, the one you attempted to marry." Lynch risked the subject. He saw Rochester wince at his words. "Do you wish for us to contact her? She would perhaps want to know of your situation. What is her name?"

"Jane." Edward's lips trembled as he whispered the name. "I don't know where she is. And I would not want her to know, would not want her to see me as I am."

"Did she not love you?" Lynch asked him. "Would she want to help, to see you?"

"She loved me," was the answer. "But she left, fled from me. She is better apart from me. She may love me still, I am sure she does, for that is like her. But our time has passed. She is better without me." A look of desperate grief crossed the dark, scarred face. "At least I hope she is, pray she is."

"How do you know your time with her has passed?" Lynch asked. "Not all love goes smooth and easy. Most goes rocky as a mountain path, with much stumbling along the way. It may not be over."

"You don't see her here with me, do you?" Edward replied. "I had my chance with her, to make things right, and I failed in it."

"You English have no passion in your souls," Lynch told him. "You have thin blood in your veins. No love is worth fighting for."

He leaned closer to the man in the bed, "The old Celtic stories of love and romance, now, they tell of real love!" He laughed softly. "They tell us that each man has one woman who belongs to him. When he finds her, she alone can redeem him, make him complete. But he must fight for it, for her."

Edward shook his head, "This is nonsense. I am tired, I have no desire to debate the nature of love with you. I think I have fought all I can fight. God knows I have no more strength left inside me."

"Aye, you have done that," Lynch's voice was gentle. "Any man can fight when he is threatened, wounded, near death. But it is later that the real fight takes place – the fight to stay alive when it seems there is no reason to. To stay alive for any lovely things that God may grant you in the future."

Edward laughed harshly, "I think God has already shown His hand. He intends to grant me nothing but evil. I wonder that I ever believed in His goodness, in any kind of mercy at all."

Lynch shook his head at the bitterness that poured out in just those few words. "My mother used to always say something to me – it came to my mind often in my attempt to study medicine. She would say, 'A Phadraig, nior dhun Dia doras riamh nar oscail Se ceann eile.'" The lyrical syllables flowed from his lips, sounding strange in this cold country, speaking to a cold man such as this.

A slight smile twisted Rochester's mouth, briefly. "Well, I must say that does not help me at all, but thank you all the same."

Lynch laughed, "It seems so much more help when my mother says it. It simply means 'God never closed one door without opening another.'" Lynch laid his hand briefly on the patient's rigid shoulder, "You are a widower now, Mr. Rochester. And your Jane may yet return."

Edward gave another bitter laugh, short and sharp. "My sight may return, my love may return. Such a bright future you paint for me, Lynch." He shook his head, turned away, his arm over his face, his fine mouth set in a harsh line. Lynch watched him for a moment, then sighed and left the room.

Later, in the quiet darkness, Edward lay awake long into the night. His face itched relentlessly beneath the dressings, a sign of healing, Carter and Lynch had assured him. He rubbed at the wrappings to try to relieve the discomfort without displacing the bandages that Lynch so painstakingly replaced each night. Now that he was lucid, his right arm was no longer restrained, the wooden splint on his left arm no longer tied to the bed. He raised the arm to try to relieve the pain that seemed a constant companion to him now. Sometimes he could count his pulse rate by the throbbing at the end of the arm. He knew that he could reach over and ring the bell, and ask for a dose of laudanum. He would drink it, and within a few minutes, the ache and torment of healing wounds would lessen, he would grow drowsy, and eventually drift off, released for a time from the physical pain.

But then would come the nightmares, the images he was more terrified of than pain. Dreams of his mother, a skeletal figure in her fine bed, reaching her arms to him, enclosing him in a bony embrace that smelled, not of the floral essence he remembered, but of rotting and death. Dreams of Bertha's screams and ravings, of the disgusting scenes he had found her in on several occasions. Dreams of Céline's taunts and insults as he stood outside, listening. And the worst, dreams of Jane. Jane wandering, alone, starving, abused. Dreams of her leaving him over and over as he begged her to stay.

And the one dream that had made him eschew the blessed relief of the laudanum forever. He had dreamed of Mari. It had been years since he had even thought of her, Bertha's old nursemaid, that old black crone who had defied him and turned the other servants against him, and who had aided Bertha for years in her mad and tortured wanderings.

Edward remembered their last conversation, there on the stairs outside the home in Jamaica. He had made preparations for their departure to England – the trunks packed, passage paid. She had stood before him, defiant as always, trying to talk him into leaving Bertha behind, returning the dowry money, and leaving Jamaica. As if he could have left easily, as if no one owed him for his nearly five years of agony, the five years that had turned him from innocence to taint and corruption, from youth to painful experience.

She had kissed the silent, unresponsive Bertha, who stood next to Edward, dressed for travelling. Bertha had been given so many calming medications she could barely stand, and he would have to practically carry her to the ship, despite how he shrank from having to touch her. Mari had cried, stroking Bertha's hair in her hands, kissing her on one cheek and then the other. "My dearest girl, my poor little one," she had whispered, before turning to Edward.

"You a blind man!" she had cried angrily. "You can't see beauty when it stands in front of you; you are blind to what you want and blind to what she needs. Go, run back to your home and your money. See if it saves you. See if it saves her." She waved her hand, turned away, raising her apron to wipe her face. "Go, you blind fool."

He had awakened now with a consciousness of what that meant. He was running sweat, yet frozen to his very marrow. What had she done to him? What evil and vicious spell had she cast back then that would reach out to seize him eleven years later? Lying here alone, pain tearing at his body, it was easy to remember her hatred of him, the numerous chickens she had slaughtered and the curses she had freely placed on any who crossed her.

Edward lay here in this bed, thousands of miles from the hot sun and ocean blue of that accursed place, one eye torn and permanently blinded, the other injured with no guarantee of sight. It had taken years, but those women had had the last victory – the bitch he had married and the bitch who had raised her.

He clenched his fist, taking deep breaths to fight the surge of panic that once again threatened to overwhelm him. At times he felt he would suffocate with it – heart pounding in his chest, throat closing off all entry of air.

He didn't know what to do, where he would go. He could not understand why he continued to live. Why had so many fought so hard to preserve his life, one that was no life at all? He tried to imagine the long vista of years that stretched in front of him. Years as a blind and helpless cripple. He could no longer read, no longer write. He could not ride – once one of his greatest pleasures.

He lay alone in the cold and silent room. How would he dress himself, do for himself the many small tasks he had once taken for granted? How would he feed himself, run two estates, meet the needs of the people who depended upon him for their very livelihoods? How could he face each day to come, each long slow hour that ticked away ahead of him, before God might choose to be merciful to him and end the life that had now become unbearable?

And who, he thought in despair, *who on earth could ever love me now?*

Chapter 44 - Tenacious of Life

"You have been resident in my house three months?"
"Yes, sir."
"And you came from ?"
"From Lowood School, in ---shire."
"Ah! a charitable concern. How long were you there?"
"Eight years."
"Eight years! you must be tenacious of life."
Edward Rochester - Jane Eyre

16 November 1836

Carter approached the half-open door of Rochester's room and lifted his hand to knock, but before he could do so, he happened to catch a glimpse of the occupant, sitting upright in a straight-backed chair next to the bed. Rochester sat quietly, looking straight ahead, his face sunken into a sadness that pulled at the surgeon's heart.

Edward was fully dressed, clean-shaven, his bandage-wrapped left arm tucked into the front of a brown wool coat. His hair, which had been clipped close to his head, the better to assess his injuries, was beginning to grow out, the short black strands just beginning to curl and wave again. The scar over his left eye was healing well and was not so discoloured and shocking at first sight. His right eye appeared nearly normal when casually viewed; it was only upon looking very closely that one could see the slight opacity of the black and formerly shining depth. Above the right eyebrow, a pink ridged scar gave mute testimony to survival of an ordeal by fire.

Mr. Carter had observed his patient closely for two months, and had seen the gamut of emotions that Rochester's injuries had forced upon him. He had awakened into a nightmare in which everything in his life had changed, and he had reacted with a quiet fury and a bitterness that was hardly surprising. The anger had actually been a good thing; it had given him an impetus to fight against the spectres of illness, infection, and depression, and the patient had recovered physically much better than most would have in his situation.

But all around him could see the change. In the past week or two, a kind of acceptance had settled upon Edward Rochester, but it was not a positive change. One thing that had always impressed Carter was the undeniable life force that Rochester exuded. He had a will and a spirit, and the life that looked out of his brilliant dark eyes was one that was constantly searching, always learning, and never still. Now that the immediate frenzy and bitterness of his initial reactions were spent, a quiet calm took its place.

But it was not the sweet calm of one who has bravely determined to face life's obstacles. This was a lifeless frame of mind, no longer one of ardor, drive, and zeal. He was like a formerly bright lamp, turned low, a mere shadow of his previous vital essence. He seemed to all who saw him to have given up.

He still talked, still responded, occasionally even managed a sardonic jest or a small chuckle, but it was lacking in conviction, the behaviour of a man who wants only to get through the immediate necessity of conversation and to be left alone once again.

Carter, aware that he was staring, was embarrassed even though the occupant of the room could not see him. He stepped back and reached up to tap on the door. "Who is it?" he heard from within.

"It's me, Carter," he answered, pushing the door open and stopping in the doorway.

"Ah, Carter, come in," Edward replied, raising his hand in greeting. Carter stepped inside and stopped a few feet from Rochester's chair. "My, look at you," he told him. "Quite a change from the usual sight we find upon entering."

"Lynch is a slave driver," grumbled Edward. "Nothing would do but a full bath, and a shave, AND I had to be fully dressed, right down to the new coat, which itches terribly, by the way." He reached up and pulled the collar away from his neck.

"You are not used to clothing, that's all," Carter told him. "Two months in nightclothes will make you unaccustomed to anything else." He pulled the other hard-backed chair closer, its feet scraping harshly on the scrubbed wood floor. "May I sit down with you for a few moments?"

"It's your house," Rochester said dismissively. "And it was not a full two months in nightclothes, as I recall you all kept me stark naked for several days at least. No doubt my entire household knows what I look like from head to toe, thank you very much."

"Your housemaid did not get to see you," Carter told him wryly. "Her family dragged her off before she got the privilege."

"Thank God for that, at least," Edward snorted. "As it is, Mrs. Fairfax could never look me in the eye again, even if I could see her."

"Mrs. Fairfax was married for years, I doubt she saw a thing she had not seen before." Carter leaned back in his chair. "We sat together one night when you were at your sickest, and she told me that she was present at your birth. I never knew that."

He gave an impish grin, and slapped Rochester's knee playfully, "So you see, it's not as though she had never seen you before."

"Matters have changed considerably since then," Edward answered, twitching his shoulders uncomfortably under the scratchy weave of the coat.

Carter laughed, "Well, I should hope so! At any rate, clothing was an encumbrance in those early days; you were battered, bloody, and feverish, and for all I knew, too much disturbance would start something bleeding within you that would finish you off. None of the women nursing you seemed concerned beyond that. And your loyal John got a pair of drawers on you as soon as I said it was safe for you to be moved. I told him it is more important to keep an injured man still than to keep his bollocks covered, but he was still eager to get you decently clothed."

He continued, "Speaking of clothes, these fit you all right then?" He tugged at the sleeve of Rochester's coat. "I know they are not what you may be accustomed to wearing. But everything you owned was burnt to a cinder. Millcote's tailors are not London or Paris quality, but I hope they're serviceable."

"They are fine, perfectly adequate," Rochester shrugged. "It doesn't signify; it's not as though I will be going out anywhere in them."

"Ferndean is isolated, John tells me, but it is situated close enough to a town," Carter said. "You will be out some in company, I hope."

"I doubt it," Edward replied shortly, his singed brows drawing together sharply.

Carter returned to the earlier subject. "I was glad to have John with me; he knew all your sizes and preferences and we made short work of our shopping. Mind you, I felt you could use a new pair of boots, and John was scandalized at the idea of you wearing anything but the Italian leather ones purchased from Milan, or wherever you are wont to purchase your shoes."

"I am not particular about most of my clothing, but I have a preference for my boots." Rochester stretched out his legs, indicated his battered black and brown footwear as though he could see them himself. "I can walk for miles in these, they are perfect for riding – not that I need worry about those two pursuits any longer – and best of all... " he held up his hand, displayed it front and back, "they are of such pliable leather that I can pull them on with only one hand. Strange, the things I never dreamed would be useful, back when I was foolish enough to assume I would always have two hands."

He sighed, "So I will continue to purchase them. I have little enough need for any luxuries, but at least I will be comfortable. I should remember to have my steward send a letter and a bank draft for a new pair. It will take months, but I can have the boots shipped to Ferndean, and should I need them again, I will have them."

Rochester turned to Carter, serious now, and very grieved. "I have a favour to ask you, Mr. Carter, an important one. It concerns something I care for immensely and have not been easy about for some time. I want you to take Mesrour."

"Your horse!" Carter exclaimed. "Are you mad? I cannot do that, Mr. Rochester! You love that animal; he is a part of you. The sight of the two of you together, you are like a centaur!"

"Yes, I do love that horse. I've cared for him since he was a colt. I trained him, and we have travelled many a weary mile together, he and I. But I can no longer properly care for him; he is not getting the attention and exercise he deserves, and if I love him, I cannot wish that for him. Over the years I've observed you when you saw us out in public, or when you came to the house. You'd inquire after the horse first, then come around to care for whatever trifling ailment you had been called out for."

Carter chuckled, "Well, he is a magnificent animal. But I cannot imagine you without him; you are kinder to him than most men are to their wives and children."

Rochester smiled then. "Well, he is more beautiful than many men's wives, and much smarter than many men's children. Present company excepted, of course, Carter."

Carter looked grieved. "But what will you do, without your friend; surely just his presence there would be a comfort to you?"

Edward shook his head, "No, it would just disturb me, to know that he is there, not being ridden, wondering where I am and why I am close but no longer come to him. It would sadden me, not to be able to ride him. You're a good rider, a careful horseman, and you are kind to your animals. I would not trust any other with him. And may I mention, you were kind to allow me to keep Pilot here, so I would have him by my side. Not everyone would allow a guest to keep a large, unruly dog."

"Ah, it was my pleasure, and my boys loved having him. In truth, they will be most bereft when he goes with you to Ferndean. They will ask why I did not refuse the horse and take the dog."

Edward sighed, "I'm sorry for your boys, but I fear I must have Pilot. I believe that now he will be my best earthly companion." He stopped then, eyebrows drawn together, and a fleeting look of pain crossed his face. He seemed to be seeing something else before him, thinking of something else, and for a moment he was silent. He swallowed hard, then he seemed to collect himself. "So you will take Mesrour, keep him as your horse, care for him all his life? He will be a faithful companion as you ride up hill and down to your cases day and night."

"If that is what you wish, I will gladly take him for you, and care for him. I thank you, sir."

"Well, it serves a dual purpose for me. I can rest easily knowing he's cared for, and can feel that in a small way, I've repaid some of your kindness and loyalty to me," Edward told him.

"Which reminds me, Carter, I hope you have prepared a detailed bill."

Edward looked over at Carter. He was trying to remember to look at the person he was talking to, even though he could not see him. It was difficult to remember how one should behave, easy to let his darkness interfere with the simplest social interaction.

Carter made a dismissive sound, and a gesture too, lost on his patient.

"I'm serious, Carter. I will be leaving here directly upon the return of John from Ferndean, and I would like to depart knowing that you have received adequate compensation for your long weeks of care and hard work."

Edward continued, "Everything, Carter – your fee, something for Lynch. I know he's your student, but he spent a vast amount of time caring for me, and I want him to be compensated. Your fees, the room and board for me and my household, all the medications and supplies. I cannot leave with an easy mind until I know you've been repaid."

"I will do so, Mr. Rochester, but it is not a concern of mine." Carter spoke earnestly, "You have always paid me well, always valued my services more highly than they rated."

"I was buying your silence, your complicity," his patient said grimly.

"Ah, you were not either!" Carter said, sounding annoyed. "You insult me, Rochester, with that statement, for you know I never said a word, nor would have. I kept silence, even when the word got out of your impending wedding, and the whole town buzzed with the talk of your marrying the governess. I never said a word afterwards, either, though the town found out I had known all along, and pressed me relentlessly for what I knew."

"I know, Carter," said Edward, heaving a sigh. "I know that you were a faithful physician and a loyal… well, you were a loyal friend to me all these years, and I do give you my thanks. I cannot thank you for saving my life, for I feel you wasted your time in that endeavour, but I do thank you for all your years of assistance to me, and if I cannot give you my gratitude for saving my worthless hide, at least I can see that you are well paid for it."

"You think we wasted our time in caring for you?" Carter asked. "Wasted our time by saving your life?" His voice was suddenly sad, and deadly serious.

"Yes, I do," Edward answered. "I wish you had not. I wish I had died under that rubble; I wish you had clubbed me to death with that cursed beam when you found me alive under it."

"The townspeople were watching," Carter said dryly. "And that beam was damned heavy; it took several men just to lift it off of you." He smiled as he said it, but Rochester was not listening for the humour in anyone's words; he was frowning now, lost in his thoughts, his words spilling forth. "Why was my life spared, to what purpose?" He took a deep breath, "Why could you not have just let me die?" He spoke quietly, in measured tones, but with unmistakable despair.

"I am a surgeon, Mr. Rochester, I had an obligation to treat you," Carter leaned forward earnestly. "It would have been impossible to let you die, a violation of my life's work."

"You took my eye, you cut off my hand!" Edward's voice was more agitated now. "You should have just left me alone. If you could not have taken your gun and shot me mercifully in the head, like a lamed horse, you should have had the decency to just let me be."

"We could not have done that and you know it," Carter said calmly. "Do you know how agonizing it would be to die from gangrene? Do you know how long it takes for the putrefaction to spread throughout the blood before it eventually kills you? You would not wish that death upon the worst of your enemies." He blew his breath out slowly, then gave a small smile. "Besides, it stinks to high heaven. You think I wanted that stench in my house?"

"I should have been dragged out into a field, shot, and left for the animals to find," Rochester retorted. "Instead my wretched life was spared and in addition to being alone, I am maimed and scarred and blinded. What sort of a life is that?"

"Most people would be happy to have survived," replied Carter. "Humans don't let go of their lives that easily."

"Tenacious of life," said Rochester, a small, bitter smile lifting the corner of his mouth. He turned his face away, and Carter saw the quick tremble of his mouth before he clamped his lips together.

"Yes!" Carter said, "Most people are, if they possibly can be."

Edward, face still turned away, reached up hastily and swiped at his cheek with the side of his hand. He was silent for a moment, then he squared his shoulders and snorted, "Well, I would gladly let go of mine, let go and float away, free of encumbrance, freed from guilt and torment and physical constraint."

"Mr. Rochester, you begin to worry me with the darkness of your thoughts..." Carter began.

"I was not worth saving!" Edward cried, his fist pounding against his thigh with frustration. "I tried, I tried to live a good and normal life, and it was snatched from me. My love fled from me and now she is flung, alone, out into the world, and I am a cripple, a blind cripple. How, Carter, how is this a life worth living? Tell me, how am I ever to live it?"

There was a silence as Carter passed a hand over his face. "I don't know, Mr. Rochester, I truly do not know. Even as I stood there making every effort to save you, I wondered in my heart if you would even want to wake up if you knew how badly you were hurt. All I know is, Lynch and I had to try to save you; we could not do less."

He thought for a moment, "I know you suffered when your marriage was halted, your wife discovered. I knew when I heard about it, how you must be feeling..."

Edward held up his hand, "Say no more about that. Why should I not have suffered? And I deserved my suffering, but my Jane... she did not deserve the pain I gave her." A spasm of agony crossed his face. "Her only crime was to love me and she was repaid with torment and exile." His unseeing eye searched for Carter's face, "I was right, in what I told you, that last conversation we had. I was right that she would not stay to become my mistress, and so she fled."

"Why did she go?" asked Carter, who had long wondered. "Why did she not stay where it was safe, at least until she could find another place to live?"

"I want to think that she fled temptation; that her love for me cried out to be fulfilled and expressed. God knows I could not have resisted, had she yielded to me." A look of such tenderness softened his face that Carter felt a catch in his own throat.

Edward's face hardened, he shook his head, "But perhaps I am just being a fool. She might only have left because she was angry and could not bear the sight of me any longer. But for whatever reason, and I think it was love, she is gone, and without protection, and if she is dead, I am responsible, as surely as if I'd shot her in the heart with my own pistol." His voice was hoarse, he spoke through a knot of grief. "How could my darling survive out there, with no help, no money? And why have I? Why am I still alive when she may not be?"

"If Miss Eyre left you to avoid the fleshly sin she felt her God abhorred," Carter told him, "then you must trust her God to keep her safe while apart from you."

Edward sat still in his chair, his body drooping, his countenance reflecting such heartbreak that Carter could scarcely bear to look at him.

"I think you should continue to search for her," Carter blurted out.

"What?" Edward looked up, roused from his dark musings of death and loss.

"Your wife is dead now, all impediments removed," Carter told him. "You need to have some hope, if you are going to find a reason to go on. I hear you searched frantically for Miss Eyre before your accident; you should keep looking still."

"No," Rochester said, his head moving decisively back and forth. "I will not. I would never let her see me like this; I am repulsive."

"You look frightening enough, at first sight," Carter agreed. "Not in yourself, but for thought of what dreadful calamity brought it about. Pity and concern, however, rather than disgust, will be the reaction of your fellows upon the sight of you, I think, sir."

"Well, I will give none the chance to feel any of that," Edward retorted. "And I'll not try to bring my Jane back to me, to see such a horrid sight, to be burdened with such a shell of a man."

Carter sighed, fell silent. An uncomfortable stillness settled over the room.

Edward sat, head bent, his fist still clenched upon his thigh, his thoughts still with his vanished love.

Carter thought of something to say. "When do you expect John and Mary to return?"

Rochester sat up, pulled from his thoughts. "It will be several days, at least. Ferndean is in terrible shape, and they will have to prepare several rooms. A room for them, one for me, the kitchen, the parlour. The house is dank and damp, the privies barely functioning before I ordered some work to be done to them. I have a caretaker who sees to the outbuildings and the security of the property, but he does not go into the house. I was there last, oh, nearly four months ago now, and after walking through the manor, chose to stay at the inn for the night."

"And yet it will be your home?" Carter asked.

"Once cleaned, it will be serviceable enough, adequate to hide me away from the world, which is all I want."

Carter sighed, "Mr. Rochester, that will not be healthy. You are strong, but this accident, these injuries, have taken their toll. You need a safe place to live. Your wounds will pain you in cold, damp air. You need to be warm and dry. Which reminds me, I keep forgetting to ask, do you still feel your hand at times?"

Edward looked startled. "The missing one?" He ran his hand through his hair, thinking. "Well, yes, I do. At times it feels as though it's still there, and I reach for something. At other times it itches, or tingles, or aches, and when I try to touch it, or move it, I remember it is gone."

Carter nodded, "Yes, that is all normal. I meant to tell you to expect it. I saw it in the Navy, over and over. Men who had lost arms, legs, other body parts. They reported still feeling them, even years after the fact."

Edward shook his head, "So I have a lifetime of that to look forward to?"

"You could take some laudanum to relieve the feeling, if it gets severe," Carter told him, "although I hesitate to tell you that, in light of our earlier conversation. However, if you were thinking of taking your own life, you would no doubt think of laudanum without my help."

"I will not take my own life," Edward told the doctor. "Unlike you, I believe in God, and as He has many reasons already to cast my soul into Hell, I'll not give Him another one." He shrugged, "And laudanum gives me nightmares."

He faced Carter, his one sightless eye narrowed. "But if Ferndean is unhealthy, so damp and dark a site that I would not even consign my poor, mad wife there, then it may take me, and soon, and I will not care, will welcome its chilling death touch. Don't worry for me, Carter, my death can only be a welcome thing. So should you hear of it, after I have left this place, know that I am finally at peace. Be glad for me."

He stood, leaning heavily on the back of his chair. He suddenly looked exhausted, as though he could barely stand.

"And now, Carter, I must rest, if you please." He let out a long, deep breath, shaking his head. "I used to be able to rush about from morn till night, but now a morning's routine exhausts me."

He moved hesitatingly towards the bed, still gripping the back of the chair, letting go only when his leg touched the bed's side. He groped for the mattress, sat down upon it with a sigh of relief.

When Carter left the room, shutting the door behind him, Edward lay down upon the bed, his back rigid, his unseeing eye fixed upon the ceiling, lost in his darkness. He had told Carter that he wished he had not survived, but lying there, he realized that it did not matter. In his heart, he was dead already.

Chapter 45 - The Road to Ferndean

"Where is he? Where does he now live?"
"At Ferndean, a manor-house on a farm he has, about thirty miles off: quite a desolate spot."
"Who is with him?"
"Old John and his wife: he would have none else. He is quite broken down, they say."
Jane Eyre and Innkeeper, The Rochester Arms - Jane Eyre

22 November 1836

Edward groped for the open door of the carriage, feeling John's firm hand on his elbow, guiding him inside in preparation for his trip to Ferndean.

He had bid good-bye to the Carters and to Lynch, thanking them for their tender care of him, and now it was time to leave this area for good. John had come to fetch him, leaving Mary behind to prepare the evening meal and to make sure the master's bedchamber was ready to be occupied.

He settled onto the cushions, leaning against the window. He could tell the light of the window from the darkness of the carriage interior, but could see nothing else, including Pilot, who had jumped in after him and was now burrowing into the seat opposite him, with great turnings and snufflings and a large yawn that ended in a high little "yip" as he laid his massive shaggy head onto his paws.

Edward smiled, glad to at least have this companionship. He breathed in the sour dog aroma that emanated from Pilot, wishing he had asked John to open the window a little, as he would never be able to manage it with his one hand.

"Pilot, you smell," he said, shaking his head at the dog. "We must see if John will give you a bath in the next day or two, and meanwhile I must put up with you for the next thirty miles."

Pilot got up upon hearing his master's voice speak his name, and took the opportunity to jump down from his seat and go to him. He tried to climb upon Edward's lap, huge though he was, and Edward laughed, pushing him down with both arms.

"No, you mad beast," he protested. "I certainly will not have you sit on me for the entire trip, get down!" He held his hand down by his knee, snapping his fingers, "Pilot!"

Pilot climbed down reluctantly, but would not go back to his seat. Instead, he sat down, and laid his head upon his master's knee. Rochester sighed, and reached to pat the dog's head, scratching behind his ears.

He leaned back, staring towards the more lighted area of the carriage interior. He gave the dog a final pat, and folded his arms over his chest, slouching down in his seat. He did not feel the need to tuck his bandaged left arm into his coat when he was alone, and it was relaxing to have a brief respite from worrying about how he must look to others.

He had planned to sleep, to while away the trip, but sleep would not come, and he soon found his mind drifting. Drifting to where it always did, to thoughts of Jane.

It was painful to think of her, but it was even more painful not to think of her, as he would sometimes attempt to do. It took great effort to try to ease his pain by forcing thoughts of her from his brain, and most of the time it did not work, so he would often give up and let his mind roam freely, trying to relive every moment he had spent with her.

He remembered the evening they had first met: how he had barely noticed her at first and how, when he had laid his arm across her shoulders, leaned on her tiny frame for support, the sensation of strength had flowed from her into him. From that moment on, she had never ceased to be in his thoughts, a very distant and minute image at first that had slowly grown into the dominant, driving force of his existence.

But what use is it now, he thought to himself, as she is far from me, miles that might as well stretch to the moon and back. She is gone, and now I am going off to Ferndean. A place where she has never been and would never think to look.

He scoffed at himself then. "As if she would look for me now; and if she did look, what would she see when she found me? A scarred and terrible wreck of a man, the sight of which would be revolting to her."

Rochester was a man much given to both superstition and philosophy, and he thought now that it was ironic that he had remained at Thornfield so long, for fear she would return and he would not be there. She had never come, and Thornfield had at last destroyed him, as he had always feared it would.

The fire, and the damage the fire had done, had drawn a kind of line across his feelings for Jane. There was what had come before, and what had come after, and he felt that he must now try to face the rest of his life, what time remained to him, without her. He wished for her, longed for her, but knew he could not look for her, and must try to go on with only the memory of her love to sustain him. At least he could die knowing that he had once been truly loved by a woman, a woman who would have been his wife had things only been different.

Strange, how fire had marked the beginning of his quest to win her, and now, he felt, marked the end of his quest to keep her.

His mind wandered back to the night she had followed sounds and smoke to his room, found him sleeping in the midst of the flames, and had saved his life. He had had no presentiments, no uneasiness of any danger that night as he had retired to his room. He was in rather good spirits. That day he had walked in the garden and talked to Jane, and had shared with her the sordid story of his time with Céline. He had felt no judgment of him, no contempt for his sinful lifestyle. Her eyes, changeable – now green, now dancing with golden glints – had followed his face, and she had spoken about his revelations with gentleness and respect for his feelings.

She had also shown a tenderness and understanding towards Adèle that had swelled his heart, knowing that if there was room for that tiresome child, there might be room for him as well. He was impressed that she, the most proper of young women, still had such compassion and love for the bastard child of an unfaithful mistress.

He had sat in front of his fire that night, sipping a drink before bed. He did not stare into the flames in his usual low and brooding spirits, but with a strange kind of hope in his heart. He got up, unbuttoning his shirt and pulling it free from his trousers, but was not quite ready to prepare for bed and retire yet. He lay down on top of the covers, hands behind his head, his mind filled with her face and the sound of her voice.

The next thing he was aware of was that voice, full of urgency, and the cold water that drenched him as he lay there. The next few moments were a blur, as he leapt out of bed to tear the bed hangings off the frame, and quench the blaze that could have killed him where he lay.

Heart pounding, he had led her to a chair, covered her with his dressing gown, gone to rouse Grace and make sure the maniac was not off setting fires in other parts of the house. He had returned to the bedroom to find Jane waiting obediently for him, but had put off her obvious questions. He felt a bit guilty, blaming Grace for the mischief, but soothed the feelings by reminding himself that if Grace would stay sober as she should, none of this would have happened.

He dismissed Jane, aware that a young woman in her nightgown should not be in her employer's bedroom in the dead of night, no matter what the circumstances. He had stood watching her as she moved towards the door, wishing he had never told her to go, wanting her to stay. Stay for what, he did not know; he only knew that he could not bear to see her walk out that door.

"Wait, you are not going to quit me in this fashion, and without taking leave!" he blurted out as she headed out of the room.

She looked back at him, her eyebrows drawing together quizzically, "But you said I should go, sir."

"Not like this, so abruptly." His mind raced as he tried to think of a way to keep her here with him. "You just saved my life!"

He moved towards her, "At least shake my hand!" He held his hand out, and after a second's hesitation, she walked back towards him, her nightgown making the faintest cottony whisper against her legs. Her hair spilled over her shoulders, and she reached her hand out. Their hands touched, slid together, her small warm palm moving against his before they clasped in a strong handshake.

Oh, God, the feel of her skin! Edward felt a warmth spread from her fingers and move down his arm, bathing him in her calm and peace. He enfolded her hand in his, holding it with gentle firmness. Her eyes widened as he tenderly pulled her towards him, then her glance darted to their joined hands. He knew she was startled, nervous, but he could not help moving his hand against her flesh, rubbing the satiny back of her hand with his fingertips.

His mouth felt dry; he was not sure his throat could bring forth words. He took a deep breath. "I knew you would do me good the first time I saw you." He didn't recognize his own voice. "I knew it when I first looked at your face, knew... " He felt himself start to stammer like a schoolboy, and he took another breath and started again.

"I knew your face, your smile, could not strike delight into my heart for nothing." His eyes were fixed on her face, and she stared back at his, her eyes drawn again and again to his. He felt her searching look, over his face, to his mouth and back up to his eyes. "I knew I wouldn't mind being under obligation to you, being in your debt."

He squeezed her hand again, his fingers still stroking lightly over the back of her hand. He felt a minute resistance, a slight reluctance to stay.

"There is no debt, sir." She continued to look up at him, her eyes wide, her lips slightly parted. He couldn't resist moving slightly closer to her, where, if he inclined his head towards her, he could just touch those lips with his. She tugged her hand back gently, but he held on. "There is no obligation, I am just glad that I happened to be awake."

As Edward stood there, he felt desire flood over him, move through his entire body, starting at their joined hands and spreading through his very veins. His breath was rapid and uneven, his heart thumping. They were standing inches apart, eyes locked together, the heat still coursing through him.

He might have been ashamed of his intense physical reaction, his growing longing for her, but as he stood there, he realized that at least some of the passion he was feeling was coming from her. He could feel her craving, her desire, radiating from her, and as it flowed back to him, he felt weak from its force and its fire. He felt its liquid warmth spread into his belly, lower, felt himself rising and hardening, an almost painful pressure against the tight trousers he was wearing. He felt the blood pounding in his ears, throbbing in his limbs.

He watched her, her dilated pupils, her parted lips, and the quick rise and fall of her small breasts under the bodice of her white nightgown. He couldn't help imagining some of the feelings she might be having, and while it fueled his desire, he also realized that she might be having all these feelings for the first time, and might be confused by them. It filled him with tenderness towards her, made him love her all the more intensely. He wanted to pull her to him, to press her body against his, but he knew he could not.

Already she was slowly, reluctantly, pulling her hand from his. "I am cold, sir," she whispered, "and I think I hear Mrs. Fairfax."

And he stepped back, let her go, watched her walk away from him, a little unsteadily, her hand touching the wall briefly for support before she disappeared from his view.

He wrapped his dressing gown about his shoulders and went to lie down upon the library sofa, his mind a welter of emotions. There was a warm steady ache between his legs, and an ebbing and flowing tide of sweet pain in his heart. His fevered brain moved back and forth between those two feelings as he tossed and turned upon the couch.

Finally he could bear it no longer. He had to have some relief, he thought, glancing at the door of the library. He got up, turned the key in the lock. He lay back down on the couch, reaching down to unfasten his trousers, pushing them down past his hips. He raised his shirt out of the way, his hand moving down...

Jane turned away from him to go back to her room, but he was at her side, lifting her into his arms. He carried her into her bedroom, laid her gently down on the bed. The covers were still turned down from where she had gotten out of bed to come and check on him. She reached her arms up to him, drew him down on the bed with her. His mouth found hers, and he rolled over on her as their lips met, first tentatively, then with growing eagerness. He ran his hands over her, slipping them up under her nightgown, her skin so soft under his searching fingers...

His hand continued to move, his breath coming hard and fast in the silent room.

"Jane, oh, yes, my darling Jane." She was touching him, she was opening for him, taking him into her, holding him tightly as he entered her...

"I love you," she breathed the words into his ear, her slender body moving in response to his slow, deep thrusts...

It happened quickly. Edward felt it building, growing within him, that sweet, hot rush of pleasure. He bit his lip, a tiny sound escaping his throat as he felt the spasms, the warm spurts across his stomach. He gave a long, shuddering sigh as he relaxed, tried to slow his breathing.

His mind cleared and he again became aware of his surroundings, the cold, still air of the library, the quiet ticking of the clock on the wall. He reached down, groping for the handkerchief in his back pocket. He wiped off his abdomen, grimacing as he folded the linen over and over onto itself and jammed it back into his pocket.

Be sure to take that out and wash it yourself, you idiot, before everything goes to the laundry...

He pulled his trousers back up, fastened the buttons and tucked his shirt back in. He looked around, feeling vaguely guilty, as though Jane could see him. He rolled over on the couch, pulling his dressing gown around himself, thinking of her.

He had known he loved her, that knowledge had been steadily growing for over two months. He had fantasized about brushing her cheek with his fingertips, perhaps even kissing her. One day they had been walking in the garden and the breeze had blown a lock of her hair free. He had gone silent, watching that small, silken strand tremble in the wind, wanting to touch it, to wrap it around his finger, imagining its softness. Only when Jane had reached up absently, casually, to tuck it behind her ear, had he been able to stop watching it, to resume his train of thought.

He was no stranger to physical desire; he had felt it nearly every day since he was thirteen years old. But he had never known it like this. With every woman he had ever known, the desire had come first, and then had come along whatever relationship could be formed afterwards. But this was the first time that he had experienced something like this – the fascination, the growing respect and feeling of kinship, the blossoming of love.

He had been so busy falling in love with her, that he had not allowed himself to acknowledge his passion for her, and certainly never dreamed that she could feel an equal desire for him.

He knew that part of the feeling was from the fire, their shared experience; knew that it was a response of the brain, a reaction to danger... such lust an age-old biological reaction to a potentially fatal situation.

But he had felt so much more than that while standing there holding, stroking her hand. Love and longing and rapture had mingled as they stood together. He had felt her ardor as well, but was it love? Love for him, as he felt for her?

His body had finally relaxed as he rested on the library sofa, but his mind did not, and two hours later he was up and preparing to leave the house.

He had to have her, had to put into motion the plan that had been forming in his fevered brain, and so he had departed Thornfield, to set up the house party that would turn Jane's eyes towards him and make her love him as much as he loved her...

And she had loved him, had loved him more than he had deserved, he thought to himself as he continued to Ferndean in the jolting carriage. But what good was it now that she was gone, and he was alone? More alone than he had been before, because now he knew what he had been searching for all those desolate years.

His heart ached, pained him far worse than his newly healed wounds. But that pain let him know he was alive, for few other feelings touched him, little else moved him. Even the brief remembrance of his intense desire for Jane had not stirred him. His soul was like a malfunctioning machine, capable only of sorrow.

His racing thoughts were interrupted by a lull in the carriage's motion as John pulled it to the side of the road and stopped. Edward sat up, rubbing his eyes. He wasn't sure if he had dozed off as his thoughts had wandered, but he blinked, vainly strained to see, as he always did. He wondered if that would ever change, if he would ever cease to try to force those sightless eyes to register images once again.

The carriage door opened, and he heard John's voice, "I beg your pardon, Mister Edward, but I was needing a short walk by the side of the road and I thought you and Pilot might need one too?"

Pilot was already at the door, tail wagging, as Rochester stretched, moved towards the sound of John's voice. "Yes, that is a good idea. I need to work my legs, thank you. And Pilot will no doubt need to chase a rabbit before we resume the journey." With John holding his arm firmly, he climbed down, thinking ruefully that he was out of the habit of travelling, or he would have remembered to limit himself to one cup of tea that morning at breakfast.

Pilot barked and eagerly bounded off to follow an elusive scent as the men walked along the road. Edward held John's arm until he was safely off the road, but then sent him away, wanting some privacy so he could relieve himself.

Later, back in the carriage after the men had walked, rounded up Pilot, and eaten a little of the lunch that Mrs. Carter had generously insisted on sending with them, Edward reflected with some satisfaction upon his progress in the past weeks.

After much practice, he was now able to fasten the buttons on his trousers with one hand, and to do it quickly enough that he was rather proud of himself. He was still not able to fasten the tie at the waist of his drawers, but he was damned if he would allow anyone else to do it. He kept it closed enough to suit him by pulling the tie as tightly as it would go, twisting it and tucking it into the waistband, then buttoning his breeches over them. It gave him a great feeling of independence. He may need John to put on his socks for him or tie his cravat, he thought, he might need Mary to cut up his food, but his trousers he would handle alone if it killed him, by God!

By God indeed. More and more his superstitious mind had drifted to thoughts of the Almighty. "From trouser buttons to God," he thought to himself, reflecting on the sometimes erratic workings of his rebellious mind.

For months now, certainly since he had awakened to the knowledge of his accident and its results, but perhaps even further back, to when he had awakened to find Jane gone from Thornfield, he had been unable to think of God without a rage, an impotent hatred arising within his breast. The thought that Jane had fled from him in response to what she felt God demanded of her, had enraged Edward.

When Briggs had stood in the echoing church to stop the wedding, Rochester had acknowledged at once that Providence had checked him. He had never been totally easy with his plans, even before Carter had strongly cautioned him, had spoken to him with words Edward had known were true even as they had driven him in anger from the doctor's house. Every time he had looked into Jane's clear eyes, seen her trusting and loving gaze upon him, a tiny twinge of guilt had plucked at his heart.

Yet when the marriage had been halted, as part of him had known it would be, his only response had been anger at God for thwarting him, for snatching away that which he had clung to as his only salvation.

Months of pain, sadness, and anguish had done their work upon him, however; and sitting here, thinking of Jane, longing for her, he had to acknowledge that God had not stopped his plans to ruin the life of Edward Rochester, but to protect Jane Eyre. To protect her from the man who was supposed to love her. As much as he tried to justify what he would have done, he had to face himself, to recognize the darkness of his soul.

He would have ruined his purest treasure. Even if he had not meant to sully her, to take away the purity and innocence that he had loved so much, he would have done it nevertheless. Admitting that hurt his soul, smote his heart, made him see himself as something small and selfish, not the noble lover he had thought himself to be.

Again he thought with agony of his words and actions before Jane had left. He had pulled her against him, held her with an iron grip. Panicked and desperate, he had spoken of violence. For the briefest, most insane moment, he had wished he could take her to himself, force her to see his love and need and longing. But he was not insane, not vicious, and in spite of how he felt at that moment, he did not lack control. He had never in his life, not even in the greatest of his extremity, raised his hand to harm a woman, and he would not have started with his dearest, his most beloved. He would never have forced her to become his mistress, but perhaps she thought he would have, and the idea tormented him.

Edward knew his brief frenzy, his apparent lack of control, had shaken her, had impressed upon her the depth of his longing, and the strength of her own temptation. And so she had gone.

There was nothing he could do; he was helpless to protect her or to care for her. For the first time since he had returned from Jamaica, he was in a situation that was out of his control. It was almost more than he could bear, to have Jane's fate out of his hands. And so he sat back, resting in the carriage that carried him to his new life, knowing that his own fate was out of his hands as well, and so angry at the One he saw as the cause of it all.

Chapter 46 - Phantom Pain

1 March 1837

In his bed at Ferndean, Edward slept fitfully. He had been in pain all day, and he was tired, longing for sleep, yet could only get a few moments of relief at a time, dropping off into a slumber that was never deep enough to take away the discomfort. He drifted in and out, dreaming of the days in Carter's house, when his wounds were fresh and the pain was constant.

Mrs. Fairfax smoothed the well worn pages of the Bible that lay open upon her lap. It was late, nearly midnight, but she had been so busy all day with nursing duties and Thornfield estate business that she had not been able to have her daily Scripture reading. Indeed, she was so busy every day that it was hard to set aside time for herself at all. She opened to the book of Psalms, thinking that perhaps hearing her read aloud might be a comfort to her patient.

"Psalm 88," she read, her voice sounding loud to her ears, in the tomb-like quiet of the sickroom.

"O Lord God of my salvation, I have cried day and night before thee:

Let my prayer come before thee: incline thine ear unto my cry;

For my soul is full of troubles; and my life draweth nigh into the grave..."

The man in the bed never said a word; gave no indication that he heard a word she said. But he was listening. He was aware, and heard all that was said around him. He had awakened to pain and darkness and fear, and for now merely lay like a stone, still part of the world, and yet removed from it.

Only once had he broken his death-like silence, when he heard the voices around his bed discussing his dose of laudanum. When the spoon touched his lips, he had turned his head, whispered, "No!" with all the force he could muster. For a moment it had felt good, to once more be in control of his life, to give an order. The medication was removed, and no one tried to administer it again. They had all waited for him to speak again, but he did not. He was so frightened, and the pain gave him no relief. He only wanted to hear one voice, and he listened in vain for it. Sometimes in his dreams, he heard Jane speak to him, but then he would wake to find her gone, and it was always dark, the pain always sharp.

"Thou hast laid me in the lowest pit, in darkness, in the deeps.

Thy wrath lieth hard upon me, and thou hast afflicted me with all thy waves.

Thou hast put away mine acquaintance far from me, thou hast made me an abomination unto them

I am shut up and cannot come forth.

Mine eye mourneth by reason of affliction..."

He knew Mrs. Fairfax watched him, and hoped he would speak. He lay motionless, listening to her voice read the words of the ancient Psalm, words that cut into his already aching heart, for every word seemed to apply to him.

"Shall thy lovingkindness be declared in the grave? Or thy faithfulness in destruction?

Shall thy wonders be known in the dark? And thy righteousness in the land of forgetfulness...

Lord, why castest thou off my soul? Why hidest thou thy face from me?"

A slight movement from the bed drew the elderly woman's attention from her readings. She looked over at the man who lay there, and saw, to her dismay, the tears that slid down from beneath the bandages around his eyes. They gleamed in the light from the lamp that sat on the table next to him, and as one slipped down his cheek, another one followed, falling steadily. He drew a shaking breath, swallowed, lay still again, no movement but for the moisture that continued to well in his ruined eyes, run down the sides of his face, onto his neck. He made no move to wipe them, and still they continued.

"I am afflicted and ready to die from my youth up: while I suffer thy terrors I am distracted.

Thy fierce wrath goeth over me; thy terrors have cut me off.

They came round about me daily like water; they compassed me about together.

Lover and friend hast thou put far from me, and mine acquaintance into darkness."

Mrs. Fairfax set the Bible aside, picked up a dry cloth from the table to dip it into the basin of cold water, and squeezed the water out. She moved to his side, bathed his face with the cool cloth.

"I'm sorry, Mr. Rochester," she whispered to him. "I am so very sorry that this has happened to you."

Edward woke from his troubled sleep and rolled over, groaning loudly at the pain that nagged endlessly at the end of his left wrist, sending a dull throbbing clear up the length of the arm itself. The March weather had changed that morning; the grey of winter sky darkening to a persistent rain that blew and pounded against the latticed windows.

The dampness seemed to sink into his bones, chilling him without relief and making his scars ache in a steady rhythm. He could feel his left hand, hurting to the ends of his fingers, but when he attempted to move them, to use his other hand to massage them free of pain, he felt the reality sink in once more as he met only empty air, gaping space where he had once been whole.

He threw the covers back, slipped out of bed, his bare feet meeting the icy floor with a slight shock. He flexed and relaxed his arm, shaking it in an attempt to ease the pain of his missing left hand.

"How?" he murmured to himself, "How can something be gone and yet hurt so badly?"

He moved across the room towards the sound of the blowing wind and pelting rain. Pushing aside the dusty, heavy curtain, he pressed his face to the glass. He could not see the rain, but with his forehead resting against the pane and the window's chill moving its frigid breath over his body, he could feel. It was some sensation, something to penetrate his constant darkness and the even darker deadness of his heart, grown cold within him.

Edward stood for some moments, listening to the pounding rain and the sound of his own breathing before the cold drove him away, made him move to another wall, where the palest orange glow signaled to him the presence of his room's fireplace. He groped for the fireplace poker that hung on the rack against the wall, but he misjudged the distance, and knocked the rack over, hearing it fall to the tiles with a harsh metallic clang.

"God damn it!" he hissed, his frustration filling him with an impotent fury.

He listened for a moment, fearing he had awakened John and Mary, who slept below him in a room off the kitchen. To his dismay, he soon heard footsteps on the stairs, and then a soft rap on his door.

"Mister Edward?" John's voice inquired at the door, "Is there something wrong?"

"Come in," Edward's voice sounded rusty and unused to his own ears. He cleared his throat, repeated, "Come in, John."

He heard the door open, heard John enter. "Are you all right, Mister Edward?"

"Yes, I'm fine." Edward thought he sounded snappish and impatient, and he tried to temper his tone towards his faithful servant, "I knocked something over; it was nothing."

"Are you sure, sir?" John sounded concerned, but wary. Well he knew that his offers of help were not always received with good grace.

Edward was silent for a moment, tempted to send John away, but his throbbing arm and chilled body overcame his pride. He folded his arms over his chest, swallowed.

"Is there any wine, John?" he asked. "I'm... I find it difficult to sleep tonight."

John thought for a moment, "There is some whiskey, sir, in the kitchen. An old bottle, but it might be fit to drink."

"That will do," his employer shrugged. "Anything that will help me sleep. And build the fire up before you go back to bed."

John left the room and returned a few minutes later with a cup, which he put into Edward's hand before crossing the room to pick up the toppled rack and straighten the fireplace implements. He stirred up the fire, and laid several logs upon it.

Edward sniffed the contents of the cup, grimaced, and took a drink.

"God Almighty!" he gasped, as the burning liquid went down, outlining his gullet with its fire.

John chuckled, "'Tis is a mite strong, but it will cure what ails you."

Edward thanked him, dismissed him back to his room, and sat back down on his bed, drinking again from the cup that he held. He drank deeply, feeling the heat spread through his stomach, creating a warmth and tingle in his thighs, a welcome heaviness in his legs. He set the glass on the bedstand and lay back, waiting for the blessed relief to move upwards, to lull him into numbness and rest.

He had deliberately avoided drinking alcohol since his arrival at Ferndean, knowing it would not take much persuasion to convince his tortured mind to give over to anything that would give him forgetfulness and relief, respite from his physical and mental torment. His life was a daily misery, an endless cycle of loneliness and tedium with no expectation of anything better to come. And yet his life was his own, and as long as he controlled it, he could keep the illusion of strength, could claim some mastery of it. To escape into the tempting haze of drunken oblivion would be, he sensed, the end of him.

A warmth, a calm, stole into his upper limbs, easing his discomfort. He slipped into a kind of sleep, and it seemed to him much later that he felt it, a soft pressure at the edge of the bed, heard Jane's voice.

"Mr. Rochester," she said softly, leaning over him, "are you awake?"

He opened his eyes. It was not possible, one was sealed and both were sightless, and yet they opened, and they saw her. He smiled, moved his eyes over her face, drank in the sight of her.

She smiled too, spoke again, "How are you, sir? I worry for you so, have you slept at all?"

He lay motionless, only his eyes moving, following her. He watched her, afraid to blink, afraid to move, for fear of making her flee from him.

"It hurts, Jane," he told her, "it all hurts so much." He held out his left hand, so recently throbbing with phantom pain, and saw it was whole again.

Jane caught it, laced her small fingers through his, held his hand in both of hers. She looked as she had the night she had saved him from the fire. Her chestnut hair hung around her shoulders, her white nightgown glowed in the darkness. He could almost believe that it was that night once again, that he could go back and do it all differently. That he could have another chance.

She pressed her lips to his hand, laid it against her soft cheek. "I'm sorry you are troubled, Mr. Rochester," she said gently. "I wish I could be of help to you."

"Come back," he whispered, "return to me, for I am lost without you."

She smiled, but did not reply. She held his hand, and he clung to her as one who was drowning.

"Where else does it hurt?" she asked him, her eyes searching his face.

"Here," he responded, taking her left hand and laying it against his heart, "here most of all." He pressed her hand against his ribs. "My hand hurts sometimes, my heart constantly."

She pulled her hand free gently, drew her legs up and lay down next to him, laid her head against his chest. "I hear your heart beating," she told him, pressing her ear to his breast.

He reached up with his right hand, stroked her hair back from her cheek. "It is broken, shattered, and somehow it still beats," he murmured.

"Shhh," she told him, "sleep now."

His eyelids were so heavy, they closed against his will, and he lay back, sinking into sleep, still feeling her warmth against his side, the weight of her head against his chest. "I love you," he whispered.

No reply. He was cold, alone once more. He sighed, opened his darkened right eye. Blackness all around him, blackness deep inside him. Pain again, this time squeezing his heart.

At times he longed for night to come, hoping she might come to him, however briefly. Her touch, her kisses, the fleeting feeling of being loved, if only for a few moments, fed his starving spirit.

But oh, the pain when he had to wake up.

Edward felt the tears welling, the hard knot constricting his throat. But he swallowed hard, forced the tears back into the recesses of his empty soul. He knew that if he let the crying start, he might never be able to stop.

"I love you," he spoke softly into the darkness, "I love you."

How can something be gone, and yet hurt me so badly?

He let out a long breath, "God, help me."

He thought of Mrs. Fairfax, bidding him farewell from Thornfield, that long ago September morning, "God be with you, sir."

"Are you?" his heart cried out. "Are you with me?"

He had blamed God, named Him as the author of his torment, and yet, as each endless day slid into lonely night, and back into day again, Rochester slowly grew more humbled. He acknowledged that God had checked him, stopped him, halted him in his headlong rush through a life of pride and arrogance and control over others.

"God bless you, my dear master," he remembered Jane saying, *"God keep you from harm and wrong, direct you, solace you, reward you well for your past kindness to me."*

"Bless me?" he spoke aloud. "I no longer expect any blessing. Reward me? For a life of pride and of toying with the feelings of others?"

Edward had not truly prayed since he was eight years old and his mother lay dying. He had spent years being angry at God, angry at Him for his mother's death, angry at Him for allowing him to marry Bertha, angry at Him for allowing him to love Céline, allowing her to hurt him so greatly; and above all, angry at Him for letting him have Jane for a short time, for giving him a brief glimpse of what it was like to be truly loved, and then snatching it all away again. But his heart was empty now, cold and dark, and he no longer was angry with the Almighty; he had not the energy. He could see his own folly and mistakes, could see and admit the hand of God in his doom.

He rolled over, wrapped his arms around his pillow. His missing hand had ceased to pain him, but he still felt it – heavy, useless, lost. Like himself.

"Help me," he begged a God he barely knew. "Help me."

"Please, God, help me."

Chapter 47 - Voices in the Night

31 May 1837

Jane moved towards him, her grey silk dress whispering around her. She was smiling, walking faster as she approached until she was running to throw herself into his outstretched arms. He wrapped them around her, closing his eyes as he laid his cheek atop her head.

"My love, oh, my love," he was weeping, "I have missed you so." He held her at arm's length, looking at her beloved face. "Please, please, do not ever go away from me again."

She was laughing and crying at once, "No, no, my Edward. Nothing can ever take me away from you; I will never again leave you."

They embraced again and he kissed her – kissed her forehead, her tear-filled eyes, her damp cheeks. Then her lips, sweet and warm against his; and his arms tightened around her until it seemed their bodies would meld into one, never to be separated.

For endless moments, his mouth took hers, her lips opening hesitantly against his. Then he pulled away from her, heart pounding, legs trembling, and steadied himself with his hands on her shoulders. He reached to touch her cheek, feeling his hand shake with the overwhelming love she brought forth in him – and it was then he saw it. Not a hand at all, just a stump. Ugly, shocking, useless. And as his eyes met hers, he knew she saw it too. Her sweet smile vanished, her gentle look twisted with disgust, and she pulled free from his desperate grasp with revulsion for his scarred body showing plainly on her face. As he reached for her she backed away, shaking her head, turning from him.

"Jane, please!" he cried out, "Please don't leave me here alone..."

Edward sat up with a start, jolted awake by his dream and the knowledge that he was indeed alone. It took him a moment to remember that he was sitting in a chair in his bedroom, near the open window. It had been a warm, refreshing May evening when he had sat down to enjoy the night air, and he had gradually been lulled to sleep by the singing of the night insects, and by the hazy glow of the moon that was all he could see as he faced the open window tonight. He ran his hand over his face, surprised to feel the traces of tears against his cheeks. His heart thudded wildly against his chest, his panting breaths roaring in his ears.

The air had felt perfect, but now it chilled his sweat-dampened skin. He knew he should get up and go to bed but he remained in the chair, his body leaden with hopelessness. He lacked the energy to even lean over and close the casement.

His neck and back hurt from sleeping upright and as he shifted in the chair he was aware of a now unfamiliar heat and hardness; he felt an ache of desire deep within him, the remnant of his dream of Jane's sweet embrace. He had once been a man of strong passions, of frequent needs that burned to be met, but the physical pain and depression of the past months had driven such feelings far from his mind. When he had thought about these sensations at all, it was with doubt that he would ever have them again. He took no pleasure in their return. It was just one more vivid reminder of all he had lost.

All he had lost... *Jane, my little love,* he thought with despair. All his losses – his home, his hand, his sight – all paled in comparison with the emptiness in his soul at her absence. The past ten months had not dulled the pain of her departure – it only grew sharper each day.

Her face filled his mind: her soft, pale skin, the pink blush beneath when she was delighted, or embarrassed or moved. Her huge green eyes that seemed a different shade with each emotion. The thick, shiny brown hair he had loved to feel beneath his hand. The sound of her voice – the sweetest he had ever heard, unusual in one so young. Low, a little husky, melodic: well-modulated tones with her northern accent still detectable underneath.

He longed for her, and sitting there near the window he felt the constant pain in his heart become so great he grew breathless with it.

He longed for her in every way – not just to lie with her, although once he had dreamed of it and had imagined nothing sweeter. Not just for her touch – although he thought that if his last sensation on earth would be her arms about him and her kiss upon him, he could die content. He did not just long for her company and her conversation, although he wished for both every moment. No, his very soul longed for her and would not be satisfied without her; longed for her love and her presence in his life.

He had felt for a long time that she must be dead. How could his darling survive alone in such a harsh world? Of course, he reminded himself, her world had been harsh from the moment she had entered it. Not like his, which had been easy in many ways. Hers had been difficult until he had given her a glimpse of ease and riches, only to snatch it away from her and send her off into a dangerous world. Not meaning to, oh God, no! He had wanted nothing more than to hold her and protect her and never let her know any further hardship. Instead he had hurt her more cruelly than she had been hurt before, and that knowledge tore into his soul, cutting deeper than any surgeon's knife.

He had searched so hard for her in the short time that he was able to. He wanted to help her if he could; to let her know that he required nothing of her but to let him protect her. But he had found no trace of her.

He thought of how connected he had felt to her, how that cord of communion had seemed to join their hearts together. He had never had that with another person. It was there still.

No, she could not be dead. If she were, he would know it. He would know because he would have died with her, would have disappeared from the earth without that strong bond to hold him here.

But he felt as though he were bleeding to death. Slowly and painfully, each day of her absence leached more of his life from him. Like a plant deprived of sunshine and water, his soul was withering within him.

His fist clenched on the arm of the chair, so tightly his nails dug into the palm of his hand, and then he thought to pray, to ask comfort from the God he was only beginning to seek again.

"Heavenly Father," he whispered, "look upon me tonight and grant me some small measure of your mercy. I know I have no right to ask it. I am in despair. I have suffered, although I know it to be by my own actions. Have I not suffered enough, Lord, for my many sins? I do not know how much more I can endure." He was weeping now, the hesitant words coming more boldly to his lips.

"I pray for my Jane tonight. Oh, God, have her in your keeping. Take care of my darling. If it be your will, take me from this life, admit me to your life to come.

If Jane is already there, I will be with her and my suffering will be ended. If she is not yet there, I will wait for her, for all eternity if need be. She is both the beginning and the ending of my life... "

He was unable to go on as the sobs came harder now and the only words he could manage became a prayer in themselves as they burst from his lips, "Jane! Jane, Jane... " His voice started as a cry and then became a whisper; her name both a sweet balm to his soul and a continued sorrow.

With only the sound of his weeping in the room, the forest noises all around seemed to fade away, and he was aware of an almost sweeping grandeur to the silence, like that atop a great mountain.

Then it came to his ears, as clearly as though she stood in the room with him, "I am coming, wait for me!" He sat bolt upright, his heart nearly stopped within him as he listened. "My love, I am coming."

"Jane!" He stood, his hand reaching out into the darkness. He groped, but felt nothing but air. A soft cry of frustration escaped him, and then he heard her voice again, "Where are you?" This time the voice echoed in that mountain-like stillness, and died gently away.

He stood for a long while, listening for the voice to be repeated. A soft hilltop breeze blew across him, slowly drying the tears that still glistened on his cheeks. Gradually, the quiet again grew into the oppressive closeness of the Ferndean wood.

His heart still hurt within him, but for a few moments her presence had seemed near enough to give him a small measure of comfort. Moving slowly, he closed the window and went to the bed. Pulling off his cravat and kicking off his boots, he lay down fully dressed.

His hand reached up to close around the necklace and ring that he still wore around his neck, and eventually, still hearing her voice in his mind, he slept.

Chapter 48 - Sweet Madness

"Who can tell what a dark, dreary, hopeless life I have dragged on for months past? Doing nothing, expecting nothing; merging night in day; feeling but the sensation of cold when I let the fire go out, of hunger when I forgot to eat: and then a ceaseless sorrow, and, at times, a very delirium of desire to behold my Jane again. Yes: for her restoration I longed far more than for that of my lost sight."
Edward Rochester - Jane Eyre

3 June 1837

Edward groped for the armrest as he lowered himself into his chair near the parlour fire. He felt chilled from the rain that had fallen upon him as he walked outdoors. Or attempted to walk, he thought, his face growing hot at the memory of his clumsy, faltering steps outside the front door of his home, John coming to fetch him in from the rain as if he were a child.

He had grown so weary of sitting in that chair. The fire had died down as he sat, lost in his thoughts, and before he knew it he was shivering, the room noticeably gloomier even to his vision. It did not seem that he had sat there long, but with a start he realized that the afternoon must have passed on as he sat there unaware. The huge gaps of time that slipped by unnoticed frightened him more than anything else in his life these days.

He felt he was going mad. He had prayed to God to release him from his torment, but instead of the death he craved, it appeared his freedom would come from insanity. It would be a fitting way to end his days, he laughed bitterly to himself, shut up in his own attic rooms.

The loss of hours at a time as he sat alone, the loss of all desire to live as he was, the darkness of his thoughts, made him fear for his already-tenuous grip on the world. It seemed that he truly was doomed, as he had once told Jane, to live wretched and to die accursed.

Yet as he reflected on the events of three nights ago, sitting in his room with Jane's sweet voice all around him, madness did not seem so dreadful. At least he could hear her again, if not see or touch her. The sensation of her, the feeling of her nearness, had lulled him to sleep that night, and remained to warm him the next day. But it had begun to fade, and his pain was even greater.

He knew he could not take much more, that the anguish would begin to swallow him, until all his heart and mind and soul were devoured, leaving only a scarred and hideous shell that would live on until released by the mercy of physical death.

These thoughts had disturbed him, driven him from the chair to attempt to warm himself out of doors. But it was even later than he thought, near dusk; he wore no hat or overcoat, and rain was beginning to fall lightly. He attempted to walk a little, judging his position by the crunch of the stones beneath his boots.

But he could not go far, and no matter how he strained with his right eye, could discern no light. He had reached out his hand to feel something, anything, but it seemed he was alone in the black void. And then John had come for him. "It begins to rain, sir," he had said, taking his arm gently. "Hadn't you better go in now? Mary will bring you your supper."

"Let me alone," he spat out, and after hesitating, John had done just that. Edward stood outside for a few more minutes, arms folded across his chest, wishing he could disappear from the earth, willing his life to be wiped out, as though he had never been. But then he had turned, making his way back into the house, into the parlour where he spent most of his waking hours.

He had sat back down, cold and thirsty, the darkness growing oppressive. He heard a muffled knock from the kitchen, then John's and Mary's voices raised in conversation with another person. Someone from one of the neighbouring farms dropping by, or the parson with another fruitless attempt to minister to the soul of this bitter, reclusive parishioner, he thought to himself.

Edward groped for the bell on the table near his elbow and rang it impatiently. A moment later he heard Mary enter the room. "Yes, sir?" she responded. She sounded anxious and flustered.

"I would like a glass of water," he told her, "and a candle for the table, if you please."

"Yes, sir." He felt her hesitate near his chair, then heard her speak, "Ah... Mr. Rochester, there is a... a person here who wishes to see you."

"Who?" he asked sharply. Damn these villagers hereabouts. He had curtly turned away all who had tried to visit when he had moved in, and still they disturbed him. He wanted no one, no one!

"This... person did not leave a name," Mary stammered.

"Blast it, why should I have a household staff at all if they cannot manage to take a simple message and convey one in return – that I wish to be left alone." He slapped his hand down on the arm of the chair, and then wished he had not, as a jolt of pain shot up his arm. That would be a fine thing indeed, he thought, to bugger up his one remaining hand. Mary would have to feed him herself until the last day of his life, not to mention all the other things she would have to do for him.

He grimaced at the thought, and exhaled with irritation. "If this visitor wishes to see me, let him send in his name and business first." He waved his hand at her, "Just go, get me what I ask."

He heard her footsteps, then the click of the door as it shut. He rose and went to the fireplace, nearly tripping over Pilot, who whined and moved out of the way. Edward stood near the dying fire, straining to see the slight glow that still remained. He leaned his arm against the high mantle, rested his forehead against it.

He was so lonely, painfully lonely, yet could not bear the thought of meeting anyone who would gawk and gossip and pity his condition, however kind they might sound as they sat before him.

John and Mary were eager to do whatever they could to help him, but he could not stand to be dependent on servants, although he now paid them as much as he had paid Grace Poole. He knew he had only to ask and they would take him outside, lead him willingly, help him with any task, until every last ounce of his manhood and independence was drained from him.

Yet deep in his heart he hungered for the presence of another person, the touch of a hand in friendship or in love.

It had been so long since someone had laid a hand on him other than to perform a task for which he paid them, to help him with something that he would rather have been doing himself. He was back to where he had been on the Continent, paying for someone to touch him, to care for him; and now not even as a man, for his pleasure, but as a pathetic, helpless cripple. He sometimes felt that his death or madness would be far preferable to the prospect of living the rest of his life without the loving touch of another human being.

He heard the door open and Mary entered, a glass clinking on the tray. She approached and placed the glass into his outstretched hand. Pilot growled, then gave a low bark.

"What's the matter?" Edward turned towards Mary, straining to catch the glow of the candle she was to have brought him. He could see it but dimly – all else was smothering blackness.

But then his attention was distracted by the soft voice from the darkness, "Down, Pilot." Edward listened for a moment, his head turned towards the sound. Then he sighed and took a long drink of the water.

As he set the glass down, he grew more aware of the person standing nearby. The months of blindness had gradually sharpened his other senses. He was aware of steady breathing, a scent in the air, a general presence. And he did not think it was Mary.

Edward felt his heartbeat quicken, "This is you, Mary, is it not?"

"Mary is in the kitchen," the quiet voice replied.

No, it could not be. Monday night, halfway between sleeping and waking, in a grieving state, he could understand hearing her voice. But not now, just after sunset, wide awake. It was a trick of his frantic mind; madness was indeed overtaking him.

"Who is this?" he whispered desperately. "Who is speaking?"

"Will you have some more water, sir?" the soft voice went on, "I'm sorry, I spilt half of it out onto the tray."

"Who is it?" he whispered again. "Oh, God, I am going mad! A sweet delusion has seized me."

"No, you are not mad!" she told him. "You are still healthy and strong, your mind too sound for madness."

His breath came fast, and fear clutched at his throat. He swallowed convulsively against it – the fear and the tiny flame of excitement that had inexplicably begun to flicker in his belly.

He held out his hand, "Oh, what is it? Who is it?" He was trembling now.

"Pilot knows who I am," her voice continued from the darkness. "John and Mary know I am here. I have just now arrived at Ferndean."

Odd, how the voice calmly replied to each word he spoke. Monday night, brief phrases had seemed to be borne on the breeze, but now this unseen apparition stood near and conversed in such a normal way.

Tears prickled his eyelids, and he took several deep breaths to gain control. He feared he would break down, fall to his knees begging this phantom to be real, not just a mockery of his most fervent desire.

He groped towards the speaker, "Let me touch you." He felt that his teeth would start to chatter, and he clenched them against the fine tremor that he felt throughout his entire body. "If I cannot feel you, if you are only a voice, then I cannot live."

For a brief second there was nothing but the rustling of cloth as the presence came nearer. Then he felt it: the gentle touch of a hand on his.

He clutched at the fingers – so small, yet so strong. And so warm.

Oh, dear God. Surely this cannot be so. Do not let this be another dream.

"Her very fingers, so small and slight," he whispered in a cracked, husky voice. "Jane, is it you?"

The fingers in his gave way to two warm little hands clasping his cold trembling one between them. He moved towards her, sliding his hand up her arm.

Oh, God; oh, God...

He felt her shoulder, slipped his hand behind her neck. And then she was in his arms, his left arm around her tiny waist, his right arm across her back as he pulled her tightly against him. His Jane, his Jane. It could not be possible, yet she was in his arms; her silky, sweet-smelling hair beneath his flushed cheek, her arms around him.

"Oh, it is Jane," he breathed, "I can feel her size, her shape. Tell me that it is you, Jane."

Chapter 49 - I Am Come Back to You

Jane Eyre stood in Edward Rochester's embrace for the first time in nearly a year. She could feel the trembling of his body against hers, could feel his heart pounding so fast, so hard, that she could count its beats where she stood. She held him tightly in return, feeling his frame, thinner than it had been, less powerful, yet still strong and vital. Her cheek was pressed against the rough wool of his coat. His smell, his feel – all the same as she remembered. She looked up at him, at his ravaged face – scarred, haggard, brooding, yet so familiar, so beloved, so beautiful to her.

She felt his lips in her hair, on her forehead as he whispered, "You cannot know how many nights I have dreamed of holding you like this, kissing you." His lips brushed against hers gently. "I could feel that you loved me, felt that you would never leave me... "

"I will not leave you," she told him fiercely, her hands reaching up to touch his cheeks. "I never will, from this day."

"Never," he said, "but my dreams always ended, and I awoke without you. I am afraid that this is a dream also, that I will come to myself and find that you have vanished again, just a phantom, like the other Janes of my imagination. Just kiss me before you go, touch me... "

She stroked his face, "I am not a dream, Mr. Rochester. It is Jane Eyre, and I am come back to you." He felt her come up on her toes, felt her soft lips caress his face. He closed his eyes, leaned into her embrace.

He let her hold him for a few moments, soothed and quieted by the feel of her hands on him. Then he pulled back, suddenly conscious of how he must look to her.

Disheveled and disfigured. He could do some things with minimal assistance – he could bathe, and did so regularly, awkwardly, but mostly by himself. He could put on most of his clothing, and, in truth, did not mind John's help with most of the tying and buttoning and fastening he required, for John had assisted him for years, as any gentleman's valet would.

But for the tasks he used to do himself, or had once hired someone to do for him, he needed to force himself to ask for help. He could no longer see to shave, nor manage the razor with one hand, so days would go by before he asked John to do it for him. And his hair, though clean enough, hung long and tangled because he could not mount a horse and ride off to the barber, and did not like to ask John to cut it for him either.

So he saw himself as she must see him, and felt ashamed. He had never seen his scars, of course, but many nights he had lain awake in his bed, his fingers tracing the damage the fire had done to his body. He could feel the roughness of the small burn scar above his right eyebrow; could feel the thin tight ridge of scar tissue that cut through his left eyebrow, down through his eyelid, and on to his high cheekbone. His right eye felt normal, but nothing but the brightest light would penetrate his darkness.

And his arm – how dreadful it must look, stopping abruptly where his finely shaped and muscular hand should have started; the rough and twisted scar marking the place where Carter's saw had done its grim work.

He thought of these deformities and was suddenly glad he could not see. Glad he did not have to see in her eyes the pity and disgust he knew would be reflected there as she looked on the wreckage of his once proud and athletic body.

Despite all this, he continued to hold her against him, kept her tightly within the circle of his arms, because she was his life, his breath, his very soul, and he could not bear to let her go.

"Have you really come back to me, Jane?" he whispered. "You do not lie dead in a ditch, as I have feared? You are not a pining outcast among strangers?"

She leaned back against his restraining arms. He knew she was looking up into his face, but he had not the energy to turn his face away.

All of a sudden he was so tired, so overcome with weariness of his life. Her presence left him drained, just wanting to rest in her arms, to have her hold him and make the rest of the world go away. He felt a hope he had not felt in months and yet he was too afraid to hope.

"No sir. I am an independent woman now!" she spoke brightly.

"What do you mean, Jane?" In the back of his mind was the thought that she had married someone else in the past year, and had just come to let him know how her life had changed. Or maybe it was still a dream. He could still feel his arms tightly around her, but perhaps the whole feeling was a continued delusion.

"I had an uncle, who lived in Madeira," she told him. "The one who – well, he knew Richard Mason... " her voice trailed off. "He died several months ago and left me five thousand pounds."

The words hit his ears like a welcome splash of cold water. No dream, even that of a completely deluded man, would include a detail like that. "That is practical, that is real," he heard his voice speak excitedly. "I would never dream that! And your voice, it is still the same. So animated, so piquant. It makes my heart swell to hear it. Are you really rich, Janet? Really independent?"

"I am quite rich, sir," she spoke reassuringly. "You may not want me to live with you, but I can build a house nearby, close enough so you can come to see me if you want company of an evening."

Once again, he tried to squash the hope that kept rising within him despite his efforts to quell it. "Well, Jane, if you are rich, you no doubt have friends who would object if you came here to devote yourself to a blind cripple like myself."

"Well, sir," she said, "I told you I am an independent woman. Therefore I would care not if friends, as you call them, tried to prevent me from doing as I pleased."

His lips felt stiff, his throat tight. "And you will stay with me?" he heard himself whisper.

"Certainly!" her hands tightened on his arms. "I will be your companion, your nurse, your housekeeper. I will read to you, walk with you, wait on you, be eyes and hands to you. I will not leave you desolate; please do not be so melancholy, my dear master."

He started to speak, then thought better of it. All goodness, all charity, but no love. Not a word about being his wife, his lover, his other half. Just a friend, a nurse, someone to care for the needs of the poor wounded man whose life was over. He expected that of her – she was the most charitable person he had ever known.

But he was no case for charity. He was no longer much of a man in his own eyes, but there was enough of his old self left that he could not bear her to look upon him as anything else. He wanted her as a woman, to love him, to be a wife to him. If he couldn't have her that way, he did not want her at all. The only thing he could think that would be worse than never having her at all, would be to have her because she pitied him. He did not want her to be with him out of mercy, because she felt sorry for him. He only wanted her there out of love and passion.

Yet, even as he thought these things, was prepared to send her away if she did not love him, he felt her start to withdraw from his arms, to pull away. His arms tightened around her. Oh, God, how could he bear to give her up? What would he do if she left him again? And how could he stand to have her live here and care for him, knowing it was mere pity that drove her?

"No, Jane, you must not go," he told her urgently. "Please do not leave. I have nothing left, nothing in myself. I must have you. I have held you in my arms again, kissed you, heard your voice. I cannot give up those joys." He drew a shaking breath, his heart hammering against his chest once again. "The world would think me selfish, but it does not matter. My soul must have you if it would be satisfied, or it will destroy me."

He let go of her then, and groped for his chair. He sat down in it, no longer trusting his legs to support him. He felt her nearby, standing near him. He rubbed his eyes, feeling them burn with suppressed tears, and then gripped the arm of the chair tightly, breathing deeply to attempt to calm himself.

"Well, sir, I have told you," he heard her speak softly, "I will stay with you."

He exhaled, needing to make his thoughts clear to her. "Yes, you will stay with me. You are a kind person, and for someone you pity, you would make the sacrifice of caring for him, to linger by my chair and do for me what needs to be done." He uttered a short, bitter laugh. "That should suffice for me, should it not? I am old enough to be your father; I suppose I should just entertain fatherly feelings for you now?"

She stood next to him, so close he could feel the warmth of her hip against his shoulder. The feeling of it flooded through him in a decidedly unfatherly manner.

She remained silent. He spoke harshly, "Come, tell me what you think."

She spoke quietly, "I do not know, sir. I will think what you like. I am content to be your nurse, or whatever you think best."

"You cannot always be my nurse, Janet. You are young – someday you must marry." He could barely bring himself to say the words.

She answered him, her voice heated, "I don't care about being married."

"You should care, Janet." He clenched his teeth. "If I were what I once was, I would try my best to make you care, but what can I do now? A sightless block."

His frustration overwhelmed him, and he could speak no longer. He leaned over, resting his eyes on his hand. He felt as though he had run a long way, or been in a pitched battle. He was drained of all energy.

For several moments neither of them spoke. He could still feel her at his side, hear their breathing in the quiet room, hers soft and measured, his loud and uneven.

Then he felt her soft hands on his lowered head, her fingers brushing through his long, tangled hair. He heard her chuckle softly. "It is time someone tried to rehumanize you, sir. You look like you are changing into a lion. Do you remember the story of Nebuchadnezzar out in the field? That is what you remind me of, with your hair like eagle feathers. I have not noticed whether your nails have grown like bird claws."

He wanted to sit here forever, feeling her hands stroking his hair, but at the mention of nails, he thought of his amputated hand, the disgusting stump that remained. She had looked upon his face, but he had kept his arm hidden from her. He felt a flash of anger and despair as he pulled it from his coat and held it up to her. There, let her look upon that and still be able to treat him with tenderness. He spoke fiercely, "On this arm I have neither hand nor nails. It is just a stump – a ghastly sight, don't you agree, Jane?"

There was a sudden silence which for moments hung in the room, his rage palpable around them. She said nothing, and for what seemed like an eternity he sat with his arm held out to her. Then he felt it, her soft hand upon his arm, gently stroking it with the tips of her fingers, brushing it with the back of her hand.

Her voice was low and moved with emotion, "It is a pity to see it. It's a pity to see your eyes, the scar on your forehead. But you are still you." He heard her deep breath. "The problem is, it makes me love you even more and I am afraid I will make much of you over it."

For the rest of his life, those words would live in his mind; this moment would rest in his memory. He felt as though he had been holding his breath for months and could finally breathe the air.

His voice was unrecognizable to him as he answered her, "I thought you would be revolted, Jane, once you saw my arm and my scarred face."

She laughed, a quiet, sad sound, but a laugh just the same, "Did you? Well, don't tell me that unless you want me to insult your judgment."

She drew back from him, "Now, you must excuse me for a moment while I build up this fire and ring for Mary. Will you take supper, sir?"

He shook his head. He wanted nothing but for her to come back to his arms again. "I never take supper."

"Well, you shall have some now. You must be hungry, you just forget." Jane went over to the table and rang the bell. "I know I am hungry."

Edward felt embarrassed. He had given no thought to how far she must have travelled, what she must have endured to get here. He had not asked her anything about herself. He reached his hand out to her, "Jane, please tell me some of what you have been doing, where you have been. How far have you travelled today to be here with me?"

He could hear her moving furniture, bringing a small table over between his chair and the chair she had placed beside his, then they were interrupted by Mary's entrance. Jane went over to speak to her, ordering supper for the two of them. She returned and sat down near him.

"Let us not discuss weighty matters tonight," she said cheerfully. "I am feeling too lighthearted to go into such details. Tell me of yourself, how you ended up here at Ferndean... "

Over the next two hours they ate the meal that Mary had prepared, and they talked together of many subjects. Whenever a topic came up that threatened to become too burdensome, Jane gracefully steered the talk to a lighter vein.

She sounded happy, her voice bright, and with the fire and the conversation, the room seemed warmer, more comfortable to him. He actually found himself laughing several times at what Jane had to say to him.

After supper he tried again to draw her out as to where she had been for the past year, but she put him off. "It is late, Mr. Rochester, and we are both too tired. I will tell you tomorrow."

He was tired, the events of the day draining him more than he had realized. He still could not believe that she was truly here next to him. He found himself feeling nervous whenever she fell silent for even a moment, afraid he had dreamed the whole evening. He would reach out for her, touch her hand, feel the material of her sleeve, say her name. She did not appear to mind it, but would reassure him of her presence each time.

"Are you truly a real person, Jane?" he asked her once.

He heard the smile in her voice, "I conscientiously believe so, Mr. Rochester."

"But I cannot understand how you came to be here tonight." He shook his head. "I rang for Mary, expecting her to come and bring me what I asked for, and you appeared."

"Because I took the tray out of Mary's hands and came myself," Jane answered. "She tried to discourage me, told me that you refused all company. I feared that unless I just came in to you, you would refuse me."

"Oh, Jane, you cannot imagine how these last months have been for me. My life has been so dark, so lonely and hopeless. The same day after day, doing nothing, expecting nothing. Day would change over into night almost without my realizing it. I was aware of nothing except the feeling of hunger when I forgot to eat, or of feeling cold when I let the fire go out." He swallowed past the lump in his throat. "And all the time a constant sorrow, a frantic desire to see my Jane again. I wanted you, more than I wanted my lost sight. For months I longed for you. How can you be here all of a sudden, saying you love me? I'm afraid I will awaken tomorrow and you will be gone."

He felt her approach him, felt her fingers on his face again. They traced his eyebrows, she placed a gentle kiss between them. "Your eyebrows are scorched, they are no longer as heavy as they were. I have something to put on them. It will make them as broad and black as ever."

"What is the use of doing anything good for me, when at any time you can break my heart by going away, never to be found again?"

He felt her hand reach out to him. "Have you a pocket comb about you, sir?"

"What for, Jane?" he asked her, puzzled.

"Just to comb out this shaggy black mane of yours," she told him. "You know, when I look closely at you, you do look rather alarming."

"Am I hideous, Jane?" He could hardly bring himself to ask her, but he wanted to hear what she would say, if she would lie to him.

She laughed, "Yes, sir, very; you always were, you know."

He laughed a little in spite of himself, feeling the tension in the room decrease somewhat. "Well, the wickedness hasn't been taken out of you, wherever it is you have spent your time."

"Yet I have been with good people," she told him airily, as she began to work the comb through his hair, "Far better people than you, full of ideas and views you have never entertained in your life."

He turned quickly towards her, almost forgetting he could not see her, then drew in his breath sharply as the comb hit a snarl. He asked with irritation, "Well, who the deuce have you been with?"

"If you twist around in that way, I'll end up pulling the hair right out of your head, and then you will know for certain that I am real. Now turn around and sit still." She tapped his head gently with the comb, and continued to work on the tangles.

He reached up and caught her wrist. "Jane, whom have you been with?"

She laughed again, "You are not going to get it out of me tonight. If you will just wait, I promise that I will tell you tomorrow. If I leave my tale untold, it will guarantee that I must appear in the morning to finish the story. And I'll bring you more than a glass of water then – I must bring you a full breakfast instead."

She handed him the comb. "There, I have made you look decent. Now I'm going to leave you, sir. I have been travelling these last three days and I too am tired. Good night, Mr. Rochester."

He heard the rustle of her skirts as she started to walk away from him. "Wait, Jane, just one word. Were there only ladies in the house where you have been?"

That question brought even more laughter from her, and he heard her run lightly from the room and firmly shut the door.

It was a short and restless night for Edward. Long after John had left the room after assisting him to prepare for bed, he lay tossing and turning with the turmoil of his heart. His mind travelled back and forth from disbelief to joy.

Could he have actually spent the entire evening with Jane? The thing he had most wanted and yet had never expected to happen, could it have come about after all? He remembered to thank God for answering his prayer, for at least bringing Jane back to him, for letting him know she was alive and well.

Early in the morning, he called impatiently for John, who came hastily to his room, still buttoning his own coat. Edward had washed up and was anxious to get ready for the day ahead. He asked John to help him shave, then dressed hastily, eager to make his way downstairs.

He went to the kitchen before Mary had even come in to start breakfast. John had laid the fire and Edward paced in front of it, accosting Mary as soon as she entered the room.

"Is Miss Eyre here?" he demanded of her.

"Well, sir, I imagine she is," she told him, shaking her head as she looked over at her husband.

"Which room did you put her into?" he asked her. "Was it dry? Do you know if she's up yet?"

Exasperated and wanting to start breakfast, Mary answered him as best she could, before assuring him that she would go upstairs and check on Miss Eyre. She rolled her eyes at John as she left the room.

Edward knew they felt he was being foolish, but he didn't care. All that mattered to him was having Jane near him again.

He left the kitchen and went to sit in the parlour, in his usual lonely spot. He sat for a while in the silent room, lost in thought, until Jane's voice came to him from the doorway, informing him of the beautiful sunshine that had followed the previous day's rain and promising him a walk in the open air.

Chapter 50 - Jane, Will You Marry Me?

4 June 1837

After breakfast they went outside, walking hand in hand through the still-damp grass, listening to the chirp and twitter of the birds as they swooped and soared in the summer air. Jane described it all to him – the way the drops of water still glittered on the fluttering leaves, the flowers that dipped and waved in the light breeze.

Edward himself could sense the change from sunlight to shadow as they passed beneath the trees of the woods near the house.

At last, when he was somewhat fatigued by the unaccustomed exertion, they came to a small clearing where the stump of a fallen tree made a natural seat hidden among the other trees and bushes. It was private and lovely, and Jane helped him to make his way over to it and to be seated comfortably.

He then tugged gently at her hand, bidding her to sit as well – not next to him, but upon his knee. She hesitated but a moment before doing so, and before she could change her mind he clasped her tightly in his arms.

"Cruel deserter!" he exclaimed. "Jane, you cannot imagine how it felt to enter your room that day, to go fetch you and find that you had left me. And then to see that you had left everything behind but the clothes you had brought with you." He shook his head.

"I saw you had left the trunks, still locked and tied, prepared to be taken on our wedding trip. And I found the pearl necklace I had given you, in its box.

"I knew you could have no money, nothing you could use to trade for food or shelter. I thought, what can my darling do, with no money, no family, no help in the world? I was nearly insane with worry. Tell me, love, what did you do?"

"I will tell you the whole story, sir," she said reassuringly, "It is a long and amazing narrative – I still cannot believe it myself."

"Jane, you must understand – I never would have forced you to become my mistress," Edward told her. "I have suffered with such remorse, knowing what you must have thought, what you feared." He took a deep breath. "You could have had half my fortune, without even a kiss in return, rather than cast yourself helpless and alone upon the world. I should have known, should have guessed what you would do..."

She hushed him, and began to tell him how she had walked, weeping, through the summer dawn to catch the coach. How she had looked for a town she had never heard him mention, searching for a place to live and work, before coming to the home where a young clergyman and his sisters had cared for her so lovingly.

His heart ached within him. "Jane, you make light of your three days wandering, but you must have suffered so. You must have been so hungry, so exhausted. Are you telling me all?"

"Oh, Edward, whatever I suffered, as you call it, it was very short; please have no worries," she told him, touching his cheek briefly.

She went on to tell him how she had taken a job as school mistress, how she had come to discover that the minister, St. John Rivers, and his sisters, Mary and

Diana, were her cousins, and finally, how Mr. Briggs had tracked her down to notify her of her inheritance.

Throughout her narrative, he noticed the recurrence of the name of St. John Rivers, and pleased as he was by her good fortune, he began to feel a nagging, unpleasant sensation of jealousy start below his breastbone, forcing its way up until he could no longer contain his feelings.

"This St. John, he is your cousin?" The question burst from him. "It is quite a coincidence, is it not, that you came to be rescued by people who happened to be your cousins?"

She answered softly, remembering that his beliefs and her beliefs had never been totally in agreement, "Not if you believe, as I do, sir, that God led me to them, as He has led me in other situations."

Edward thought for a moment, went on, "And this St. John, did you like him?"

"Well, yes, I liked him," Jane told him, "I could not help but like him." There was a smile in her tone as she answered him, but he was suddenly too worried to notice it.

With a gradual sinking of his buoyant spirits, Edward listened as Jane told him of her twenty-nine-year-old cousin in glowing terms – his height, his fair hair and blue eyes, his handsome features and classic profile, and his fine mind and great accomplishments.

He could not – could never – compete with a man such as that, he realized with a bitter pain that cut through him. He was nearly ten years older, shorter, darker, less handsome, and on top of it all, blind, maimed, scarred and hideous.

Why had she returned to him? What could she hope to accomplish by comparing him to such a paragon?

Did she just want to hurt him as he had hurt her, to twist the knife a little within him before she pulled it free, leaving him stunned and bleeding and completely drained of hope?

He thought he would choke with the pain that grew in his chest until it wrapped its icy fingers about his throat.

He began to ask her questions – what they had done together, how often they had met and talked and spent time together.

She told him how Rivers had taught her Hindustani; how he planned to marry her and take her off to India, never to see the shores of England again.

He clenched his teeth and stiffened, pulling back from her, "Perhaps you had better not sit any longer on my knee, Miss Eyre." The words seemed to drop, heavy, from his numb lips.

He felt her shift upon his knee, felt her gaze upon him, "And why not, Mr. Rochester?"

"You must go your own way, with the husband you have chosen."

He heard her soft laugh. "He is not my husband; never could be. He does not love me. I do not love him!"

She sounded vehement now. "He is cold, he is distant. What little love he has is for another woman, sweet and lovely, but totally unsuitable as a missionary's wife. That is why he wanted me – he thought of me as a useful tool to him."

"No, Jane," Edward shook his head. "You have formed a new tie. All this time, grief has torn at me, but I knew you loved me even as you left me. That made it a little less unbearable." He swallowed past the lump in his throat. "I had no idea that as I mourned for you, you loved another."

His voice dropped to a hoarse whisper, "Leave me, Jane, go and marry Rivers."

Her voice replied firmly, "If you want me to leave you, you must stand and put me off your knee, for I'll not leave you of my own accord." He felt her arms tighten around him, felt her cling closer. "How could I leave you, to marry him? I am not happy with him, the way I am with you."

He felt his heart rise, felt as though someone had lifted a huge burden from him. "Are you in earnest, Jane?" he asked desperately. "Is this really how matters rest with you and Rivers?"

"Yes," she told him firmly. "Oh, you need not be jealous, sir. I only wanted to tease you a little. You are so despondent; I thought anger would be better for you than grief. If you want my love, you have it. If you could know how much I love you, you would never worry. My whole heart is yours, will be yours even if I were exiled from you forever. You are all I want, all I could ever want."

His heart rose, but he had no way to tell her how her words made him feel.

He hugged her tightly to him, kissed her mouth passionately. Oh, how he wanted her, to make her his wife, to never be apart from her. But how could he tie her to someone like himself – how could he ever think he was good enough for her?

He whispered, "My seared vision. My crippled strength." He felt the tears well, the tears he had fought to suppress for two days now. One spilled over and ran down his cheek, and he hastily brushed it away with his knuckles as he turned his face away from her, embarrassed to have her see him cry.

But she had seen. He felt her reach up, brush away the tear track that still glistened on his cheek. She laid her palm against his face, kissed him softly, but said nothing. She sat quietly, as if she sensed his internal battle.

When he could trust his voice, he spoke, his voice low, "I am no better than the lightning-struck tree at Thornfield. What right would that tree have to expect a young vigorous vine to grow around it, to cover its rot and decay with sweetness?"

"You are no lightning-struck tree, sir. You are also young, and vigorous, and a young plant would want to grow around you because of your strength and shelter, your feeling of safety."

He smiled as he understood what each of them was saying to the other. He felt comforted, and drew fresh courage to speak to her of what was in his heart. He knew that this was the time to speak, to settle what they wanted.

"Jane, I don't need a nurse, I don't want just a friend. I want a wife." He spoke the words firmly, determined to leave nothing unsaid now. "Is this news to you?"

"Well, yes," she told him, "you've said nothing of it so far."

"Is it unwelcome news?" he asked her.

"That depends, sir," she replied seriously. "It depends on which wife you choose."

He took a deep, shaky breath, then let it out. "I will let you choose, Jane, and will abide by what you decide."

"Then choose, sir, her who loves you best."

"I will choose her I love best," he told her, then he forced himself to ask her what he had wanted to ask her since she had come to Ferndean. "Jane, will you marry me?"

"Yes, sir," her soft voice replied immediately.

"A blind man, one you will have to lead about by the hand?"

"Yes, sir."

"A crippled man, nearly twenty years older than you, whom you will have to help and wait on?"

"Yes, sir."

He let out the breath he hadn't even been aware he was holding, and his hand found hers, closed around it, "Truly, Jane?"

She held his hand in both of hers. "Most truly, sir."

They talked for a long time after, some about when and where they would be married, but about other things as well.

He tried to tell her all he felt for her, what it meant to him – to have her return to him, to have her overlook his scars and injuries, and to continue to see him as the man she had fallen in love with more than a year ago.

She brushed aside his gratitude, telling him in turn how much she loved him as well, how all her dreams were coming true now that she would be his wife.

They held each other closely; she rested her head upon his shoulder, as his lips found her forehead, her cheeks, and came back again and again to her sweet, responsive mouth. They both knew what they had and how good God had been to them.

Edward told her more, told her how he was trying to know God again, to be forgiven and reconciled to Him. He told her of his experience of Monday night, how he had heard her voice and how it had comforted him. She seemed very interested, making him tell her everything, but he could not tell whether or not she believed him.

Finally, when the sun showed them how late it was and how long they had sat there, they rose, and headed back to the house, arms around each other, all things settled between them, the pain of each lacerated heart now ready to be healed.

Chapter 51 - Reader, She Married Me

"The third day from this must be our wedding-day, Jane. Never mind fine clothes and jewels, now: all that is not worth a fillip."
A quiet wedding we had: he and I, the parson and clerk, were alone present..
Jane Eyre and Edward Rochester - Jane Eyre

7 June 1837

Edward emerged from his bedroom and made his way downstairs to the parlour where he was to meet Jane. He felt alive in anticipation of the coming day, alive in a way he had not felt since their previous wedding day nearly a year before. He tried to push that thought from his mind, the thought of his last happy day before his life had changed so irrevocably. He had been happy that day, but fearful too, afraid that something would happen to wrench Jane from him before he could make her his wife. That something had happened just as he had thought it would, and he could not help fearing that again.

The previous three days had gone by in a blur of joy for him. Spending his days with Jane, walking with her, talking with her, never wanting each day to end. It had been painful for him to bid her good-night each evening, to have her leave his side to go to her own room.

His mind almost could not grasp the fact that after today she would not leave him to retire alone to his cold, lonely chamber, but would instead come to it with him. To sleep all night with her in his arms seemed a thought too heavenly to be achieved.

It was Friday afternoon that she had accepted his proposal, agreed to become his wife. His legal wife now, his only wife. He supposed it was inevitable that their thoughts should stray backwards to their previous wedding day, but he hoped her thoughts today were happy ones, not clouded by earlier fears and memories.

He had so little to offer her and wanted everything to be perfect in her life. He hated that all he could give her was a blind, crippled, scarred excuse for a man. She was so young and lovely – she should be marrying a handsome youth who would care for her and require nothing. Yet she wanted him, loved him; him alone, she said, and his heart, so long hardened and cold within him, swelled with the wonder of it.

He entered the parlour but before he could decide whether to be seated or to pace the floor while waiting, Jane entered behind him.

"Good morning, sir," he heard, and he turned to reach for her. He took her outstretched hand in his, kissed it, then took her in his arms and kissed her forehead.

"Oh, good morning, my sweet Janet," he responded, continuing to hold her close to him.

"Have you been waiting long?" she asked. "I was hoping to arrive before you, for surely you have paced a furrow in the carpet by now." He heard the teasing note in her voice and it made him smile.

"I preceded you by only a moment, and if you will notice, the carpet is quite unmarred," he answered her. "You gave me no time at all to enjoy my last moments as a single man."

Jane laughed, "I will be glad to give you some time to reflect on the gravity of your situation. I will take a leisurely breakfast and return later to claim you if you have not changed your mind."

Edward caught her to him again with a pang in his heart. "Change my mind, she says. It would never happen if she were to take the time to eat a hundred meals! My heart has been filled with fear that you would in some way change yours."

"Never," she whispered, "I will never change my mind about marrying you, have no fear." They clung tighter together for a moment, then he put her from him gently.

"It feels so good to hold you in my arms," he told her. "Tell me what you are wearing."

"I'm wearing my old grey silk dress, the one I wear for every special occasion, such as house parties with the gentry." Edward sighed, hung his head. Jane laughed softly, touching his cheek with her fingers. "I have bought some new dresses since I received my inheritance, but this is still the finest I own, although completely inappropriate to the time of day. If John and Mary see us leaving, they will know that something is afoot."

"I do not care what colour you wear and I do not care if John and Mary know," he said. "When you are safely mine, I wish to shout it from the rooftops."

Edward stepped back, reaching into inner pocket of his waistcoat and drawing out a small object which he held out to her. "Jane, I have worn these for nearly a year, since I found the necklace lying on your dressing table the day you left Thornfield. Will you give me the ring and wear the necklace again, my angel?" He gave her the little string of pearls.

She could not speak for the lump in her throat, but took it from him.

She thought of the day he had given it to her, only days before their first wedding. He had stood behind her and fastened the necklace around her neck, his warm fingers making her shiver as they brushed against her skin. Then he had grasped her shoulders and gently laid his lips to the spot where her neck and her shoulder met. His mouth moving softly on her flesh had sent a flame down to her lower belly and she had pulled away from him, afraid she would turn, go into his arms and lose herself in the fire he had ignited within her.

Now he could not fasten it around her neck, so she undid the clasp and slid the gold band off it, closing her fist around it briefly before she handed it back to him. Then she put the necklace around her neck as he stood, listening for her next words. She straightened the pearls, then reached for his hand, gently placing the tips of his fingers against her throat, where the necklace rested against her soft skin. His fingers lingered on the pearls, and she saw him swallow.

Before he could speak again, she picked up his hand, kissed it and whispered, "Should we not leave now, sir? We told the parson nine in the morning, and it is a quarter of now."

They entered the church hand in hand, their footsteps echoing in the empty building. They had chosen not to bring John and Mary with them, their unspoken thought being that it should be just the two of them. Since Edward had been so publicly exposed at their previous ceremony, they both were reluctant to make any obvious display. The parson had been accommodating when they had appeared to request his services. He had done what was necessary to get them their license, and had made no requirements of them.

The parson had heard the whispered gossip about the reclusive owner of Ferndean, had attempted to visit him repeatedly, but had been turned away each time, and not always politely. The manor house at Ferndean was not a huge one, and as he had stood in the doorway on his visits, hat in hand, he had been able to hear Rochester's raised voice, snapping at the servant who had gone to announce the minister's arrival. The parson had eventually given up, and he had been most amazed when Rochester and his bride had entered the church Saturday morning to request his help.

His old faithful housekeeper, who knew all the parish business, snorted that he should have rebuffed Rochester as Rochester had repeatedly rebuffed him, and sent the couple off to visit Gretna Green to be married by a blacksmith. But the elderly minister had cordially received them, listened at length to their story, and found he could not refuse them. Not when this nearly broken man sat before him, his awe at the miracle of this woman's love shining upon his scarred face. Not when this tiny, ordinary girl turned her face towards this man with her fierce adoration of him showing in her every look and gesture.

The parson had been young and now was old, and he knew that often the Lord best showed His love through the love of a man and a woman. Why else would God use the illustration of the marriage relationship to show the beautiful love Christ had for His people? He sensed that this man's only chance for redemption rested in the small hands of this plain young woman.

He told them that he would bring the church clerk and meet them Monday morning at nine. When they came in at promptly that time, the couple was waiting for them. Rochester was freshly shaven, thick black hair cut and combed, dressed in a dark suit, looking joyous and younger than he had only two days before. His young bride stood in her drab coloured silk, a small string of pearls at her creamy throat. Her brown hair was neatly braided and coiled, her pretty green eyes large and luminous.

And the parson felt that what he was about to do was one of the holiest endeavours he had undertaken in his long ministry.

When Rochester and his bride had taken their places, she to the left of him, the parson began:

"Dearly beloved, we are gathered together in the sight of God, to join together this Man and this Woman in holy Matrimony; which is an honourable estate, instituted of God in the time of man's innocency, signifying unto us the mystical union which is betwixt Christ and his Church..."

Edward took a deep breath. Part of him still believed that he was trapped in a long, long dream and that at any time he would awaken and be alone again. How had he ever deserved to be standing here in a church, once again taking this beloved woman as his wife? He listened carefully as the parson recited the reasons for marriage, then began the part that made the couple catch their breath, remembering the previous time such an admonition had been given to them.

"I require and charge you both, as ye will answer at the dreadful day of judgement when the secrets of all hearts shall be disclosed, that if either of you know any impediment, why ye may not be lawfully joined together in Matrimony, ye do now confess it." The parson went on, unaware of the significance of what he was saying in the lives of the two people who stood before him.

"Edward Rochester, wilt thou have this Woman to thy wedded wife, to live together after God's ordinance in the holy estate of Matrimony? Wilt thou love her, comfort her, honour, and keep her in sickness and in health; and, forsaking all other, keep thee only unto her, so long as ye both shall live?"

He did not know if he would be able to reply, so great seemed the obstruction in his throat, but he heard his voice come forth, strong in the quiet church, "I will."

"Jane Eyre, wilt thou have this Man to thy wedded husband, to live together after God's ordinance in the holy estate of Matrimony? Wilt thou obey him and serve him, love, honour, and keep him in sickness and in health; and, forsaking all other, keep thee only unto him, so long as ye both shall live?"

Edward heard her voice next to him, so soft and sweet to his ear, "I will."

The parson directed them to join their right hands, to repeat after him the words that would join them together.

"I, Edward Rochester, take thee Jane Eyre, to my wedded wife, to have and to hold from this day forward, for better, for worse, for richer, for poorer, in sickness and in health, to love and to cherish, till death do us part, according to God's holy ordinance; and thereto I plight thee my troth."

Jane held Edward's hand tightly in hers, feeling a slight tremble. She could not tell whether it came from his hand or from hers.

She blinked her tears back and repeated the words "I, Jane Eyre, take thee, Edward Rochester, to my wedded husband, to have and to hold from this day forward, for better, for worse, for richer, for poorer, in sickness and in health, to love, cherish, and to obey, till death us do part, according to God's holy ordinance, and thereto I give thee my troth."

They let go of each other's hands, and Edward reached into his coat pocket for the small gold band that had not been off his person since it had been returned to him by Mrs. Carter those long months ago. Holding the ring carefully between his thumb and forefinger, he turned to Jane, who carefully slipped her fourth finger into the ring to assist him in putting it on her.

Edward recited with a shaking voice, "With this ring I thee wed, with my body I thee worship, and with all my worldly goods I thee endow: In the name of the Father, and of the Son, and of the Holy Ghost. Amen." He slid the ring the rest of the way onto Jane's finger, and gently squeezed her hand, then turned as they knelt down for the parson's prayer. After he was finished, they stood, and he joined their right hands again. "Those whom God hath joined together, let no man put asunder."

He smiled at the couple, and continued, "Forasmuch as Edward Rochester and Jane Eyre have consented together in holy wedlock, and have witnessed the same before God and this company, and thereto have given and pledged their troth each to the other, and have declared the same by giving and receiving of a Ring and by joining of hands; I pronounce that they be Man and Wife together, In the name of the Father, and of the Son, and of the Holy Ghost. Amen."

"God the Father, God the Son, God the Holy Ghost, bless, preserve, and keep you; the Lord mercifully with His favour look upon you; and so fill you with all spiritual benediction and grace, that ye may so live together in this life, that in the world to come ye may have life everlasting. Amen."

Jane and Edward moved together almost before the words were out of the minister's mouth. Their arms about each other, their lips meeting and holding, they celebrated the joining of their lives together. The only thing each could say was, "I love you." It was all either of them wanted to hear.

After the ceremony, they proceeded to the vestry to sign the register in the presence of the clerk, affirming that on the seventh day of June in the year eighteen hundred and thirty-seven, Edward Fairfax Rochester of Ferndean, son of John Rowland Rochester and his wife Elizabeth Fairfax, was married to Miss Jane Eyre, daughter of William Eyre and his wife Jane Reed. Edward signed the book in a sprawling hand, unable to see his own signature, then he handed the pen to his bride. She carefully wrote "Jane Eyre Rochester", her hand suddenly shaky as she wrote her new name for the first time.

The Rochesters returned to their home, somewhat fatigued with the tension and excitement of the morning's events. They went into the parlour and as soon as the door was shut, Edward drew Jane into his arms, embracing her with joy and gratitude, overcome with relief. She was his now, and the idea was wondrous to him.

"My little Jane, my wife," he whispered to her, holding her to him. The reality of it struck him afresh as he repeated the words, "My wife."

She held him tightly in return, unable to speak herself. He kissed her, then reluctantly let her go. He moved to the chair, reaching into his coat for his pocketbook. Handing it to her, he asked her to remove a five-pound note.

"I will ask you to perform your first task as mistress of Ferndean," he told her.

"The custom is to provide a week's salary to household employees and a week's free rent to all tenants to celebrate the master's marriage. We can notify the tenants later, but for now, would you kindly notify John and Mary of our wedding and give them this note with my compliments? Then perhaps we can take a walk after dinner." His hand lingered gently on hers as she agreed to his request.

As he heard her leave the room he sat down, stretched his legs and relaxed back with a sigh. For the first time in days he felt able to release the tension he had carried within him since Jane's return. Such joy, such fear, had fought for mastery within him, but their wedding ceremony had laid his fears to rest. She had chosen him, blind and crippled though he was.

A short time later Jane returned to the parlour. Lost in his thoughts, nearly drowsy, he became aware of her as she drew near to him and kissed his forehead tenderly, smoothing his hair.

He caught her hand and raised it to his lips. "And how did you find the household, Mrs. Rochester, as you broke the news of our marriage?"

"Mary nearly set herself afire, and as John was sharpening the knives, I feared I would be a party to his inadvertent blood-letting, but I feel that in general they approved." She laughed as he pulled her down to sit upon his knee. "I heard them talking between themselves after I had left the room, agreeing that although I was not as grand as other women of your previous acquaintance, that we should suit quite well!"

"You are grand enough for me, and as for you suiting me, they are certainly correct in that," her husband said, reaching up to cup her chin in his hand and draw her mouth to his.

Chapter 52 - With My Body, I Thee Worship...

7 June 1837

After dinner, the couple went for a long afternoon walk in their beloved woods. They strolled slowly, his arm around her shoulders, sometimes talking animatedly, but just as often lapsing into a comfortable silence.

They sat on the stump of the tree as they had each day, Jane on Edward's knee, and it was there that he brought up the subject that was on his mind.

"Janet, later we will retire to my bedroom, well, now our bedroom, and there enter a new aspect of our life together... " He stopped, not sure of how to continue.

She sat quietly, waiting for him to go on. Her heart began to beat faster, her breath caught in her throat. She knew it was not decent to dwell on such thoughts, but she had wondered when they would reach this point. It was a source of both anticipation and anxiety to her.

"I find myself wondering if you are frightened, or... hesitant to approach this part of our marriage," he finished, his hand finding hers, linking his fingers gently through hers.

She was silent for a moment, then whispered, "No." She cleared her throat and continued, her voice stronger, "No, I am not afraid. Perhaps a little bit nervous, as one would expect, but not at all frightened. You are probably not aware that Mrs. Fairfax spoke to me on this subject the day before our previous wedding."

"Mrs. Fairfax?" he frowned. "I almost wish I could have been privy to that discussion. What the deuce did she say to you? It could not have been too dire, for you still agreed to marry me in spite of it."

Jane smiled, remembering that talk one year ago. "You were away from home and I was anxiously awaiting your return. Mrs. Fairfax felt, given my sheltered life and lack of maternal upbringing, that she should caution me as to the expectations of a husband and the role of a new wife."

The conversation had made her intensely uncomfortable at the time. Worried as she was regarding other matters, such as who had torn her wedding veil in half, the thought of going to her new husband's bed gave her no particular fears. In fact, she felt a shivery sort of excitement about it. But while the subject had sent a deep red blush to her cheeks in the Thornfield library, it felt natural now to be sitting on her husband's knee and confiding to him the contents of the discussion.

She sighed, "She assured me that while it would be painful and humiliating, if I submitted humbly to the will of God, I would grow accustomed to it in time; that while I might not like it, I would at least grow used to it and fulfil my duty as God intended."

Edward reached up, brushing his fingers against one soft cheek, then the other. "And did you believe her?"

Jane spoke so softly he had to listen carefully to hear her, "I fear Mrs. Fairfax thought me quite a wanton for the scepticism with which I greeted her instruction. I did not feel as though I would not like it – your kisses and embraces had only made me look forward to more and I could not pretend otherwise. I feel she was quite sure that I was already far too accustomed to being in your arms."

She felt her cheeks grow warm as she remembered how had it felt, his long-ago kisses and embraces. Remembered the mysterious feelings that had swept over her, the hot rush of sensation between her legs, the ache and wetness. She did not know everything at the time, but in her bed at night she would close her eyes, longing for him to touch her. Craving something she could not name and could scarcely imagine.

Edward chuckled at the image in his mind, "I can nearly hear her. But in reality, my fairy, it must make you apprehensive, and... " He paused, and took a deep breath. "I have been... alone... for quite some time, with no hope for... " He exhaled. "I barely dared to dream of the blessing of your return, and I know this has all come very suddenly for you. If it is your wish, I can wait until you are comfortable."

Jane protested, "No! I would not dream of asking you to wait. I knew what marriage would mean in its entirety when I accepted your proposal. I did it gladly and I do not fear it."

She saw him smile.

"I am afraid then, that the fear is all on my part."

"You, afraid?" she replied incredulously. "You are teasing me now."

"No, it appears that I bear the apprehension." He sighed, "Fear that I will frighten you, disgust you, hurt you in some way. You see, I have never been with one who is... innocent."

She was silent a moment, unsure of what to ask, then risked a question. "Your wife? She was not... " She stopped. He grimaced, shaking his head, "Oh, no. Not her, by no means. Her knowledge far exceeded any of mine. I'm afraid that it was I who was the innocent then." He swallowed hard, shook his head again.

She brought both hands up to his face, a gesture of comfort, a caress he had come to love. "As you had to learn, so shall I." She leaned forward, kissing his cheek, "Then I will be your wife in every way. I could never fear that. And you would never hurt me."

He leaned towards her as well, resting his head against hers for a moment. Then he did something he had long wanted to do, and now could, as Jane's husband. He rested his head gently against her breast as he slipped his arms around her. She stiffened slightly and he felt her inhale quickly, then she relaxed. He felt her kiss against his head, her small hands stroking his hair, his cheek, the back of his neck.

They sat together, holding each other close, in the soft, sunny warmth of that glorious June day.

Edward stood near the fire, waiting for Jane to emerge from the dressing room. He wore only his nightshirt, his dressing gown tossed to the foot of the bed. He had washed himself again even though he had had a bath that morning, and brushed his teeth, wanting to be pleasing to her.

He was very hot and chose to believe it was from the low fire and the June night rather than his nerves and excitement. He felt as he had when he was an untouched youth of one-and-twenty, just as if the intervening seventeen years had never happened, as if he had known no women in the meantime. His mind was a knot of fear and desire, joy and anxiety. He could not believe how his life had changed in just a week's time.

It was not possible that only a week ago this very night, he had sat by the window in this room and heard Jane's voice calling to him in what had seemed a dream of madness. And now he stood here, waiting for her to come to his arms. He feared once again that he was mad, that he was lost in a dream. His fingers went to his neck. No pearl necklace. He had given it to Jane. He focused on the day's activities, trying to remember the voice of the parson, some of the scenes Jane had described on their walk.

"It's not a dream, Rochester," he told himself fiercely. "God has granted you this blessing; get control of yourself and be ready for it."

It had been so long since he had been with a woman. He thought of the last time, with Clara. He had taken her, used her for his pleasure, knowing that he would soon return to England and never return to her. It had been December and less than a month later he had departed for Thornfield, leaving Europe and all its memories behind. Clara had reacted little when he had told her he was leaving, watching him with narrowed eyes that were suddenly hard and cold. She accepted the money he gave her, and said nothing as he took his leave with only relief in his heart.

He had not thought what would come next, how long he would be alone. He had felt he was quite finished with women, their games and wiles. Finished with the madness of lust, burning to be satisfied, that once spent left him with painful emptiness and shame.

Then had come his love for Jane, and his desire had taken a different form. A longing for her, to awaken her, to give her pleasure and delight. To love her with soul and body, to be loved so in return. Then he had lost her and his passions and desires had seemed destroyed, abolished forever.

Now she was his wife – their love consecrated, holy before God. Tonight would be her first time, but he felt in his heart that it was his too. He had never before joined himself to one who had his heart, his love, and his devotion in a sanctified union. He wanted to make the night beautiful for her, to show her with every touch and embrace and caress how he loved her.

He heard the door open, and turned towards the sound of her soft footfalls on the carpet. He felt his heart quicken as she moved towards him. She came and stood before him, not touching him. He could hear her soft, rapid breathing, feel her anxiety. It filled him with tenderness.

He reached for her and they came together, holding each other as closely as they could. His arms went around her and he could feel that she had taken down her hair. It flowed down her back, spilling over his arms as they wrapped around her. He heard a soft sigh escape from her as he embraced her, his right hand coming up to touch the delicious, satiny fall of hair. He held it in his fist, let it go, slid his fingers through it with a moan that he could not hold back...

Jane Rochester opened her eyes, rolled over and squinted at the window, where she could see an expanse of pearly grey sky, the soft light of very early morning beginning to come in through the windows. Edward slept next to her, his skin so warm against hers that she could hardly bear the thought of getting up.

She reached for her wrapper, easing it around her shoulders as she slipped carefully from the bed. She put the robe on, tying the sash around her waist, pulling her hair free and letting it cascade down her back. She reached down and picked up her discarded nightgown from the floor, where she had dropped it after taking it off, at Edward's request, the night before. She could still hear his whisper, feel his breath warm against her ear.

"Jane, will you take this off for me? I want to feel your skin against mine."

She made her way into the dressing room next to the bedroom, and approached the washstand with its large mirror. Her hairbrushes and sponges had been moved to the top of the stand; an assortment of wash rags and towels were folded on top. She reached for one of the hairbrushes, and began to brush her tousled hair as she watched herself in the mirror.

She worked the brush through the tangles, remembering how Edward had run his fingers through her hair, buried his face in it, pushed it aside to run his hand over her back and kiss his way down her spine as she lay on her stomach, half asleep.

Her eyes were wide, her normally pale skin flushed. She drew near to the mirror, unable to tear her eyes away from the image of the woman she saw before her.

She was a woman now, felt it in every pore of her skin and with every beat of her heart. She had never felt like one until now. She untied her robe, slipped it off her shoulders, and gazed at herself in wonder.

She felt powerful, powerful and beautiful.

In nineteen years, she had never seen herself completely without clothes. She had been trained from earliest childhood to bathe while still in her nightclothes, to dress for bed while still half-dressed from the day. At Lowood, even for their customary full bath on Saturday night, they had stood in their nightgowns as their hair was scrubbed, and had washed while mostly covered. After leaving Gateshead, she had not bathed immersed in a tub until she came to Thornfield, and then she had done so while dressed in a linen bath shift.

She could hardly believe that she had spent the night held closely in her husband's arms, his bare skin pressed against hers. She thought of how she had sat up to peel off her nightgown, suddenly so anxious to do as he wished. She had dropped it to the floor, slid back down under the covers, her breath catching at the sudden shock of feeling the cold sheets against her bare body. Edward had moved over to take her in his arms, murmuring, "Oh, dear God," as he laid his naked body along hers and his mouth came down upon hers again. Her heart thudded in her chest, her heartbeat echoing in her ears, face flushed with heat. She could feel the cold of the muslin sheet against her back, and the warmth and firmness of Edward's muscled skin against her front, could hear his whispered gasp, "Oh, Jane, oh, Jane," as he kissed her cheeks, her eyes, and came back to her mouth again. It was the most delicious sensation she had ever known. At one time it would have embarrassed her to even think about it, and yet it had been the most beautiful and natural feeling she had ever experienced, to give herself completely to Edward, to be swept along on a tide of passion more wonderful than she could ever have dreamed of.

She drew closer to the mirror, watching herself as colour flooded her cheeks, fascinated by the sight of her body, remembering what effect her touch and her embraces had had on her husband. He had clung to her, and she felt him touch her with a hand that at first had trembled and then grown steady as he felt her respond to his caresses.

He had whispered to her, murmured things that had made her go hot all over, made her glad she was already lying down, since she knew her shaking legs could not have supported her. He had moaned, said her name over and over as his lips and hand had moved over her, and their deep, panting breaths mingled together.

Her heart thumped at the memory of him touching her, caressing her, those strange, wonderful feelings sweeping over her.

And the feeling of him on top of her, and then within her. Feelings she could never have imagined until he was finally there, covering her, opening her, filling her...

At the end he had gone still and rigid in her arms as he cried out into the darkness of the candle-lit room.

Then he had slowly relaxed in her embrace, his head dropping to her shoulder as he wept a little. She thought of the words he had whispered against her skin.

"Jane, I thought I was dead inside," he had told her softly, "I thought my soul had died within me."

He had recovered his composure, wiping his cheeks with the heel of his hand, laughing at himself for crying on the happiest day of his life, but she reminded him that they had both shed tears that day. She held him close to her, his head cradled on her bare breast, kissing him and stroking his hair. He had dropped off into sleep, and she finally slept as well, still holding him against her.

In the wee hours of the morning, they had both awakened, to change from their cramped positions, to stretch out in each other's arms. They had talked, whispering to each other in the darkness, laughing together, sharing kisses and gentle touches and embraces, until they had come together again in the barely visible light of the dying fire. Then they had slept again.

Jane thought of Edward, how the brooding, severe lines of his face had softened as he joined himself to her, how he had seemed to be soothed and comforted by her embraces. She looked at herself closely in the mirror, noticing several small blue marks over her neck and chest. She ran her fingers over them, smiling, thinking of her husband's hungry, searching lips upon her skin.

She was beginning to grow cold as she stood there, thinking these lovely thoughts. Silly, she thought, to stand here imagining when she could be back in her warm bed pressed up against him in reality.

She poured water into the basin, and began to wash, shivering a little in the cold. She hadn't gotten any warm water from the kettle near the fire, but she had grown used to bathing in cold water at Lowood. It wasn't until she came to Thornfield that she once again had all the hot water she could ever want. She didn't mind using cold, it seemed natural to her, and she could warm up in the bed in a very few minutes.

Once finished, she put her nightgown back on, and came back to the bedside, standing there for a moment to look at her sleeping husband. Love for him flooded her heart, and she felt tears come to her eyes as she watched him. The light in the room was brighter now, and she could see him clearly, lying on his stomach, his beautiful, muscular back exposed, his face in the crook of his arm as he slept soundly, his breathing deep and even. He had told her that he hadn't had a full night's sleep since he came to Ferndean, and she was glad to see him sleeping so well now.

She eased into the bed, not wanting to disturb him. She pulled the sheet and blankets up over herself, pulling them over him as well.

As she lay down on her side, she felt him moving over to her, reaching for her even while half asleep. He put his arm over her, pressed against her back, brought his legs up to nestle them behind her bent knees. They lay like that for awhile, his heat slowly warming her as he gradually grew more alert. She felt him lean up, sightless eyes in her direction, and she turned her head to look at him and to reach up to kiss him. He looked exhausted, but he smiled and tightened his arm over her.

"My darling," he hugged her tighter, pressing his lips to her cheek. "How are you this morning, my little wife?"

She was unable to keep the smile out of her voice, "I am just fine this morning, how are you?"

He moaned, burying his face in the curve of her neck. "I haven't been so well in a long, long time," he answered her.

"So... it was fine, then?" He heard her quiet, faltering words. "Did I please you?"

His arm tightened around her, "You were... " He stopped, kissed her neck, ran his warm lips up near her ear, "You were lovely, perfect. My perfect little wife."

"But are you sure, are you positive you are all right?" he continued. "Are you in pain at all? You told me early this morning that I hadn't hurt you, but I worry so that I have."

She smiled, brought his hand up to her mouth and kissed it. "No, Edward, you didn't hurt me."

She was telling the truth, he had not hurt her, not really. Her body's momentary resistance, the few seconds of burning, stretching pain as he slid himself into her, were eclipsed by the countless moments of pleasure before and after. His every touch upon her felt exciting, made her want even more. In spite of the slight discomfort, his hardness within her had felt more wonderful than she had ever imagined. His obvious enjoyment at being inside her had added to her excitement. He had given her wave after wave of delicious feeling as he pushed himself deeply into her, and she had not wanted him to stop. The second time had felt even better, ending in the same delicious rush of heat and release as when he had been touching her. She did not want him to have any lingering fears of harming her, as the reality of their coming together had been better than she had dared to hope for.

He hugged her close to him again, pressed his face to her back. "You were lying here in bed, but I could tell from your breathing that you weren't sleeping. What were you thinking about?"

She hesitated, then spoke, "I am not sure if I should speak of him, but you asked, and I want no constraints between us. I was thinking that St. John was wrong."

"St John!" he exclaimed, lifting his head. "What could possibly have made you think of St. John on this morning of all times?"

Jane rolled onto her back, and looked towards him. "When he asked me to marry him, he told me... " She stopped, unsure of what to say.

"He told you what?" Edward asked indignantly, already prepared to be offended on her behalf.

"He said that I was made for labour, not for love," she told him, looking at her hand, which was still holding Edward's hand tightly.

She stroked his fingers with her other hand, and sighed. "I thought of those words often, wondered from time to time if he was right." She looked over at him again, smiled even though she knew he couldn't see her. "But after last night, I think he was wrong. I think that maybe I was made for love after all."

Her husband groaned, dropped back onto his pillow, shaking his head. "Oh, God, Jane, what would possess a man to say that to any woman, and especially to you?" He sighed, "I have to say it, he may be a servant of God, but the man is an idiot."

Jane laughed softly, hugged his hand to her breast, "So you don't agree with him?" she asked.

"Oh, Jane, my dearest love," Edward wrapped himself around her again, his head against hers, "never was there anyone so made for love as you."

She rolled on her side, put her arms around him and pulled him to her. She said nothing, just clutched him tightly. He lay back, pulling her to lie against him, her head against his chest. He stroked her hair, ran his fingers over her cheek.

He spoke softly, "I want to be with you again, but I don't think I can just now. This night has taken much out of me, and it might be a few hours before I'll be ready again." She nodded against his chest.

He hugged her, "But it has nothing to do with you, you know that, don't you? It's not because you are made for labour and not love." There was a teasing note in his voice.

"I know that, Edward," she assured him, hugging him back.

"Oh, I love to hear you say my name," he whispered, kissing the top of her head.

She smiled, "I'll say it as often as you want me to, now."

"I'm glad to hear it," he answered her. He covered his mouth, trying to suppress a deep yawn. "What time is it?"

Jane sat up, reaching over to the bedstand for his watch, squinting at it, "It's nearly six."

He pulled her back down to him. "We don't have to get up yet, do we? Let's just sleep here a while longer."

She nodded again, sinking back down on his chest, listening to the slow, steady beat of his heart under her ear as the sound lulled her back to sleep.

This, then, is how it is supposed to be. This is what I have been searching for and have never had with another. It is not a joining of bodies for mere pleasure, it is a merging of souls, the bodies merely a picture of what the hearts have done already. Now I will not have to leave this world never having had this perfect communion.

Edward lay quietly, his arms wrapped around Jane as she drifted back off to sleep. Her head rested against his chest, and his hand lay upon her hair, loving the feel of its softness against his skin.

It was hard for him to sleep now. He was very tired, his whole body relaxed after the night they had spent. But part of him still feared to sleep, afraid she would not be there when he woke up.

It was so wondrous to him, that now they were married in every sense of the word, truly one flesh. His mind could not take it in, still felt that she was a phantom who could slip from his grasp without warning.

He smiled, bending down to place a kiss to her head as it lay against him. She felt so tiny in his arms, so fragile, so easily lost.

She had been naive, so unschooled, as they had come together. She had not known what to do, how to touch him, how to move with him. But that had excited him, had filled him with both tenderness and ardor. He loved it that she was his alone, that she would be with no one but him.

For all her lack of knowledge, she had not lacked passion. Her reactions were natural, spontaneous, unstudied. Her body had responded to his, he had felt it, both physically and emotionally.

When she had asked, he had told her the truth. It had been perfect.

Yes, this was how it was meant to be. When it was over, when their bodies had come together and then separated afterwards, for the first time in his life there had been no emptiness, no loneliness. Only peace, contentment, joy. And security.

Belonging. Jane was his, but even more miraculous, he was hers. Never again would he know the particular isolation of having no one. From his singular position of solitary, cloistered desolation, he had gone to being one half of a greater whole. Together they were so much more than either could be alone.

He took a deep breath, sighing with contentment as he thought of the night that had just passed. He had been afraid, he had admitted it. Jane had been innocent, awkward, but not frightened, as he was. When he held her close, he felt no fear from her. She was merely nervous, afraid of her lack of experience, afraid of disappointing him, although he had assured her that there was nothing she could do to displease him.

He had kissed her for a long time, caressing the skin of her face and neck with his fingertips, which had grown much more sensitive in the months since he had lost his sight. His heart was full, as his fingers traced and adored what his eyes could not. Jane kissed him back, pressing herself against him, seemingly comfortable with the feeling of his body next to hers, not shying away from his obvious arousal. His hand moved down from her face, and gently traced the contours of her body in long sweeping strokes, sliding down over one breast and over the curve of her hip and then back up again. His fingers found the buttons of her nightgown, and one by one he slowly worked them free. He opened the front of her nightgown a little, first one side and then the other, and lightly ran his fingers down the middle of her chest, hearing her quiet gasp. He kissed her forehead.

"Are you all right, my Janet?" he whispered. "Shall I stop for a while?" He felt the shake of her head against his lips.

"No," she whispered. Her hand came up to where his hand rested, covered it, held it down to her chest, over her pounding heart. "I am fine, Edward – please, don't stop."

He kissed her again. "My darling, how lovely you are." He moved his hand from beneath hers, slipping his fingers under the edge of her nightgown. His fingertips brushed her breast, feeling the little tip tighten, and he moved to her other breast, his touch still feather light upon her skin. "So very lovely." He felt the sting of tears behind his eyelids. To have her in his arms, to feel her sweet, soft flesh at last, after all his misery and loneliness. How had he come to deserve this bliss?

Jane gave a tiny whimper deep in her throat as his fingers caressed her. He could tell she was not distressed, but aroused by his touch. He moved his hand up to her face again, cradling her cheek as he kissed her again and again, stroking her hair. "My Jane, how I love you."

He had sat up, impatient with the nightshirt that kept tangling around him. He had tugged it up, pulling it over his head and tossing it aside, going back to kissing her again before he was overcome by his longing to feel her warm, delicate body against his. When she had removed her nightgown, and he had felt her skin on his, he thought for a moment he might faint. He felt her arms around him, her hands caressing his back and shoulders as she kissed him, heard her little moans as she tilted her head back to let his lips move slowly over the silky flesh of her throat. But it was a few moments before he worked up the courage to reach out and lay his hand over her breast again, cupping it in his hand, caressing her, hearing her sharp little intakes of breath as he ran his thumb slowly back and forth over the nipple. First one, then the other, as he felt her breathing quicken in his ear. Her small soft breasts, fitting perfectly into his palm, as he had imagined they would. Never had he wished so hard for his lost sight, thinking he would give anything for just a glimpse of her body.

He finally got the nerve to kiss more than her mouth, her face and her neck; he moved down to run his mouth over her breasts, kissing them, tenderly brushing his lips over each nipple, lightly running his tongue over each hard little tip as she shivered in his arms. When he finally sucked them gently, moving back and forth between each breast, she was breathing in tiny gasps, her fingers gripping and releasing his skin.

He kept this up as he moved his hand over her body, making her writhe against him. He pulled her close, moved his mouth to her ear as he softly whispered to her what to do, what to expect. He took her hand, guided it to him to show her what he felt like, although he soon had to stop her, because the feel of her little fingers stroking him was more than he could bear and he did not want things to end before they even began.

He could feel his hand quiver a little, as he ran it over her flat belly, moved his fingertips over her thighs. He could feel her muscles, taut as she pressed her legs together, her breathing quick and audible in the quiet room. She shivered a little as he touched her, her skin so satiny and warm as he stroked one thigh, then the other. He did not think he had ever been this nervous.

"Open for me, my love," he whispered, running his hand higher, moving it gently between her legs and then back to her thighs again as she nervously separated them. When he laid his hand lightly upon her and slid a finger against her, felt that she was already warm and wet and ready for him, his hard-won control nearly deserted him. But he kept touching her, spent time caressing her, starting with a gentle stroking up and down, then changing to a soft, circular pressure in one spot. By now his hand was steady, for he was no longer nervous. She was responding, growing more and more prepared for him, unable to keep her body completely still as she opened her legs even wider, moaned softly. He was doing well, he was succeeding in pleasing her.

"Do you like this?" he asked her, never stopping the easy movement of his fingers against her, sliding easily into the wet warmth of her tender flesh. She was writhing, her breathing hard and fast, tiny whimpers sounding in her throat as she fought to stay silent.

"Yes," she whispered hoarsely, "oh, yes."

He pressed his lips against her hair, moved his mouth to her ear. "Then let me hear you, my darling," he breathed, "I cannot see your passion, please, I need to hear you."

When her end came, the tiny spasms he could feel beneath his fingers, he could hear the cries that she was trying to stifle. He smiled, listening to the little sounds she made against his skin, her lips pressed to his shoulder as he cradled her against him, his hand slowing now, barely touching her. She was quiet, afraid of losing control. He smiled, holding her tightly, feeling the shudders that ran through her whole body before she relaxed in his arms, still breathing fast.

He kissed her, and they laughed softly together, pleased with her pleasure. "How are you, Jane, are you all right?" He reached up to touch her head, felt that she had covered her face with her hands. "You had never felt that before, had you?"

She shook her head, laughing a little, but embarrassed, "I cannot believe I was so... so... I felt I could not control myself."

Edward pulled her to him. "No, my love, no," he whispered. "You were perfect, you were beautiful. I love your pleasure, your passion. I want to feel it, to hear it. I want to give you those feelings over and over, all the time."

Jane said, "I'm afraid John and Mary will hear us."

Edward laughed softly, "I hate to tell you, my love, but they must know what we are doing – it is expected the night of one's wedding. But I have never heard them, so I do not think they can hear us."

Jane gave a small gasp. "Hear them? But they are... " she stopped.

Her husband laughed again, "Old? Jane, I think John is perhaps, oh, sixty. And Mary is younger than he. Do you think people of their age do not do this also?"

"I don't know," Jane whispered, "I had never thought about it."

"Well, I must tell you," Edward told her, rolling over on her, kissing her again, lightly, and then more deeply, "I hope that we will still want each other when I am long past John's age." He had reached down, touched her again, stroking his finger slowly up and down as he positioned himself over her.

A few minutes later, he had finally taken her for his own, put himself inside her. He could wait no longer, and she would not make him wait. "I want it too, Edward," she had told him, when he had hesitated above her and worried aloud that he would hurt her. "I am not afraid."

She lay trustingly in his arms, responding to his whispered instructions. He had guided her legs up and around him, felt her slick and eager for him, but he still felt something he had never before felt as he entered, his breath coming in short gasps as he tried to control himself.

Tightness, resistance. A feeling that he could go no farther. He stopped, supporting himself on his elbows, his hand lightly stroking her forehead. He paused, kissed her. He felt like a brute, but he pushed harder, feeling the slight stricture give way before him. He heard her sharp intake of breath hiss next to his ear, felt her fingers tighten on his shoulders for a moment. But that was all, and then he was joined to her, slowly moving deeper as she relaxed beneath him.

He paused for a moment, just wanting to feel the sensation of resting inside her, being part of her. He swallowed, dropping his head to run his lips over her forehead.

"Oh, Jane," he breathed against her skin, "oh, my love."

When he finally moved, trying to hold his full weight off her with his right hand held to the mattress, it was all he could do to control himself. It had been so long, and he was so overwhelmed, both by the physical feelings and by his love for her and his joy at finally being with her.

It took very little time, just a few moments of slow thrusts into her, his heart pounding hard within his chest, unable to believe he was really with her. He stopped, no longer able to move as the incredible sensations swept over him in wave after wave. Jane's arms held him tightly, and he heard his voice, crying out, beyond all reason or control. "Jane, oh, yes, my Jane..."

He stopped then, shaking, overcome by his emotions. He laid his head down on her shoulder and began to weep, and she held him, rocking him in her arms, a wordless soothing sound in her throat. He was embarrassed, but she understood his tears and cradled him, pressing her cheek against his wet one. They laughed at themselves, before he lay down against her, dropping off to sleep, the release of tension so great that he could not stay awake.

Later he awoke, his head still pillowed against Jane's chest. He got up slowly, easing himself away. She rolled over with a tiny sigh. He reached out to touch her, just to feel where she was. She lay on her stomach, but as he repositioned himself in the bed, she murmured to him, her voice muffled in the sheet. He moved over to her, his hand stroking her hair, pushing it tenderly aside to stroke the soft, warm skin of her back.

"Ummmm," she murmured, stretching out like a cat, remaining on her stomach, and he moved his hand over her back as he edged closer to her, laid his body along hers, kissing her as he ran his fingertips over her satiny skin. He moved down, down, his lips travelling over the delicate bones of her back, stroking the tips of his fingers over her bottom, and down to her thighs. She moaned, opened her legs to his searching hand.

She had finally turned over, and once again they kissed and caressed each other, their passion growing, their excitement increasing. He moved his mouth over her neck and chest, she grew bolder, her stroking hands touching him all over. Once again he pleasured her, and this time she did not hide her feelings, but moaned softly as he touched her. He had not intended to go into her again, afraid of hurting her, wanting to give her some time, but it was she who pulled him to her, urging him to take her once more.

"Please, Edward," she whispered, "please." Once again they were joined, once again he felt that bliss. This time there was no hesitation, no stopping. His head fell back, an expression of total delight on his face, and she told him she thrilled to see it, to know she was pleasing him. He thrilled to her every movement, how she arched her back and gave a tiny cry when he pushed himself gently into her, how quickly she seemed to adjust to his rhythm and to move hesitantly with him.

This time he could wait, this time there was no haste, just an easy, growing rapture as he moved inside her slowly and deeply. She was feeling it too, he could hear her soft sounds in his ear, feel her urgency. He had not expected it, but was happy to feel her climax when it came, and this time she did not stay silent, but cried out his name, clung to him, gasping with the sensations as they washed over her. He was so excited by her that soon he was finishing too, their breathing fast and harsh in the silent room.

They had both fallen asleep then, pressed together, warming each other, to wake again at dawning of the day. Once again he had slept and then awakened to find her still here, no longer a futile dream that disappeared when he reached for her. Now, as he held her in his arms and heard her soft, even breaths as she rested there, he fought his weariness.

My impossible desire, now come true; my darling love, my wife. I do not want to sleep. I do not want to miss this...

His one open eyelid grew heavy and he slipped into slumber, trusting that when he once again awoke, she would still be at his side.

End of Part Two

Chapter 53 - Lost Without You

You have not forgotten little Adèle, have you, reader? I had not; I soon asked and obtained leave of Mr. Rochester, to go and see her at the school where he had placed her. Her frantic joy at beholding me moved me much. ...I took her home with me. I meant to become her governess once more, but I soon found this impracticable; my time and cares were now required by another—my husband needed them all.
Jane Rochester - Jane Eyre

August, 1837
Jane finished tying Edward's cravat, reaching up to kiss him afterwards, as she did every morning.

"Edward, I do wish you would change your mind and come with me today," she said quietly. "It's not too late for me to pack your things; the coach will not be leaving until one o'clock."

Edward shook his head, sitting back down on the bed and groping for his socks. He found them, and sat waiting for Jane to come and sit down next to him.

"I'm sorry, Jane, I'm not quite ready for that. I am growing more comfortable attending church services on Sunday morning, and I'm looking forward to Mary's and Diana's visit at Christmas, but anything more right now... " He sighed, left his thoughts unspoken.

Jane took the socks from his hand and leaned over to put them on for him as he automatically lifted each foot, resting each in turn upon his opposite knee to make it easier for her. "I do understand, darling," she said, giving one leg a pat as she finished, "but I hate to be separated from you, even for a short time. And I know Adèle would be thrilled to have us both there."

It was August, and they had been married for just over two months. They had fallen into a comfortable rhythm and routine that had begun the very morning after their wedding. They had awakened at about nine that morning, still in each other's arms, suddenly self-conscious that, for a pair of early risers, they had slept so late. They had gotten up, sharing the large dressing room and rushing somewhat to get dressed and ready for their day, as though to pretend that they hadn't just spent the entire night together when they went downstairs to have a late breakfast served by a very deliberately straight-faced and casual Mary.

Edward's clothing had been laid out the afternoon before, as was John's habit, and when Jane saw her new husband sitting quietly, socks and cravat at his side on the bed, she moved quickly to assist him. He accepted her help without feeling strange or awkward. After the wonderful night they had spent together, nothing unsaid or unshared between them, it felt a natural extension of their intimacy for her to help with whatever he needed. And this had continued, freeing Edward from his dependence upon servants.

Jane was matter-of-fact in her help, with no shyness or awkwardness in her care of him. Over the weeks, she had become adept at shaving him, at tying his neckcloths, and when her husband bathed in the large tub John set up for them, she was there to wash his back or help him lather and rinse his hair.

Her help was not unreciprocated. Edward too would sit near Jane as she bathed, washing her back as well, or dangling his hand in the water, to caress her knee or rub the foot that she would prop on the edge of the tub as she leaned back to relax, eyes closed, luxuriating in the feel of the water and the presence of her husband close by. Sometimes he would chuckle and slide his hand up even further, caressing her in other places as she lay there.

She would laugh and slap his hand away playfully, but she enjoyed his attentions. His love for her was evident in a hundred little ways, and for the first time in her life, Jane felt the constant affections of another person in a way that others took for granted their whole lives.

Their physical love for each other thrived, as each day Jane grew more comfortable with its expression. Edward was slow and patient with her, gradually introducing her to its many joys, and she was an enthusiastic learner, turning to him eagerly when he reached for her at night. She very rarely refused him, the only time being when her menstrual flow arrived, to her surprise, only a few weeks after their marriage.

She had been hesitant to discuss the subject with her husband, but wanted to tell him why she did not feel like walking out that afternoon. When she brought up the subject, feeling a hot blush wash over her face, Edward had been so kind and understanding, so totally comfortable with the discussion, that she felt silly for being embarrassed. He proposed that they retire to their bedroom for the afternoon, to catch up on the sleep that they sometimes found scarce at night.

"I was older than most girls when this started, or so I am told," Jane had told Edward. "I was seventeen, and most girls are somewhat younger. But Miss Temple told me that all the Lowood girls seemed to start later; the doctor said it was probably because we did not eat as much as other girls. I was never regular, although when I came to Thornfield, I began to eat more, and gained a bit of weight. Then it came more often, but still not every month as it is supposed to be. When I... left Thornfield, and was... not well at first, I stopped having my cycles at all for a while. They returned, but I had not had one since this past April, so this has caught me by surprise."

"Well, do not worry, my love, I will care for you, and when you are ready again, we will walk as much as you choose," Edward assured her as they undressed down to their undergarments and lay down upon the bed, Jane moving into his arms, "And at night, when you are ready for me, of course I will be there."

They had laughed a little, kissing each other for a while as they lay together, and then Edward had asked Jane if he could brush her hair. She had been surprised, but had fetched her hairbrush, and sat cross-legged with her back to him as he leaned back against the headboard of the bed, his muscular legs on either side of hers. He worked the brush slowly through her long brown hair with his right hand, smoothing it down after each stroke with his left wrist as she sat, her hands resting on him, fingers gently stroking his kneecaps and the soft, dark hair of his legs. They didn't talk, just rested there for a long time as he brushed her locks into shiny brilliance, and when he was finished and laid the brush aside, she had leaned back onto his chest as he wrapped his arms around her, kissing her neck and cradling her against him. She felt so loved, so absolutely cherished, that she could hardly speak.

She had never had anyone to tend to her so lovingly; when Bessie had fixed her hair when she was a child at the Reeds', she had done so quickly, pulling impatiently at the knots in her haste to get the job done and move on to other tasks.

The only other people who had paid attention to her hair were the teachers at Lowood, who would come around occasionally on Brocklehurst's orders, to shear off everyone's hair to ward off both lice and vanity. Jane's reaction to Edward's attentions was so positive, so thrilling to him, that his brushing of her hair became a regular ritual in their marriage, one more little activity that bound them firmly and closely to one another.

Now, on this sunny Tuesday morning, they were facing the first separation of their union. They had only been married a week when Jane's anxiety over Adèle had led her to broach the subject of a visit to the boarding school where Adèle was a student. Edward, who had long been suppressing a niggling guilt over his neglect of his ward, could not deny that something needed to be done.

His reluctance to be parted from his new bride had warred with his anxiety over travelling and facing the harsh scrutiny of a group of strangers, and he had finally decided that the best course of action was for Jane to take a short trip to see to Adèle's welfare.

He had dictated a letter to the headmistress, advising her that his wife would be coming for a short visit to see to his ward's needs, and asking her to keep it a secret from Adèle, in case something should happen to prevent it. He had received an answer informing him of a date appropriate for her to come, and Jane planned to spend a day at the school, checking over the work Adèle was doing, and making sure that Adèle was happy.

The school was a four-hour trip from Ferndean. Jane would get to the town on Tuesday evening, spend the next day at Adèle's school, and return on Thursday, arriving at Ferndean sometime Thursday afternoon.

John was to take her to the nearby village inn to catch the coach, and Jane still hoped Edward would reconsider and accompany her. Jane knew that Edward's presence would command the respect and attention of the boarding school's personnel, far more than she felt she could on her own. She wanted the headmistress to take her seriously because, as she had already informed her husband, if Adèle was not happy there, she would be bringing her back to Ferndean when she returned.

Edward sincerely hoped Adèle was happy, because he was the one who had sent her to that school without having visited it for himself beforehand. He felt guilty for his feelings, but in his own private soul, he'd been somewhat glad to have her away, where he could feel he was meeting her needs without having to see her mother's likeness every time he looked at her. Not that he could see her any longer, he thought ruefully. He was not looking forward to having her permanently at Ferndean, where her presence would make demands on Jane's time and stamina. But Jane loved her former student, worried over her, and he would have done anything to make his wife happy, so he was resigned to the possibility of having Adèle back in his household if necessary.

Jane waited until they were in the dining room, eating their breakfast, before she sighed, and murmured, shaking her head, "I still cannot believe that no one remembered Adèle at Christmas time. What must she be thinking?"

Edward frowned, feeling defensive and guilty, "I had made arrangements for payments to be sent to the school, and they have my address here, to let me know if there is a problem..."

"But Christmas, Edward!"

"I'm sorry, I truly am!" he insisted. "I was not myself at Christmas. I know that's no excuse, but we had only arrived at Ferndean in late November, and I was still in a great deal of pain and sleeping a lot." He sighed, "I did think of her later, and in February had Mary buy some sweets and send them off to her."

There was a silence, and he sighed again. "I know, there is no excuse." He put down his fork, wiped his mouth and sat thoughtfully in his chair.

Jane stopped eating also. "I thought of you so often at Christmas time. Everything I did, in the midst of all the festivities, you were constantly on my mind. I pictured you, Mrs. Fairfax, and Adèle, all eating Christmas dinner together. I hoped that was what was happening.

"My deepest fears had you drinking bottle after bottle in some hotel on the continent, trying vainly to drown your anger and bitterness at me." And in the arms of some strange woman, she thought privately, though she did not say it. "If I had only known what the truth was, my heart would have broken for you."

She reached over and covered his hand with hers. "What did you do, on Christmas Day?"

Edward frowned, "I slept, I believe." He thought a moment. "I gave John and Mary leave to visit their family. It was to be a quick trip, like yours of today. There on Christmas Eve, spend the day, back on the day after Christmas." He smiled, "Poor John and Mary, a five- or six-hour trip one day, to spend a day and make the same trip back. I should have been more generous."

Jane squeezed his hand, "But who was caring for you?"

"I had a caretaker who has long watched over Ferndean," Edward answered. "A farmer, a grim and taciturn man, who has lived for so long with his goats and his cows that he has very little facility for conversation left in him. Not that I was good company myself, or given much to talking at the time. Mary had left two loaves of sliced bread and some cold meat, and Silas was to come several times a day to see that I was not unconscious at the foot of the stairs, and to leave me some food where I sat in the parlour."

He laughed a little, remembering. "For some reason, I was not hungry, but I was extremely thirsty. I ate a few pieces of bread, a few slivers of meat, but mostly I drank water. I requested a pitcher whenever he came, and drank and drank. So most of what he did for two days was fetch water and empty chamber pots. Poor man, I hope I paid him extra.

"As I recall, I felt no need to dress, just sat for three days in my nightshirt and dressing gown, and I also felt no need to bathe or brush my teeth. I mostly slept, in the chair during the day, dragging myself up to bed at night. I don't think bathing has ever been a great priority with Silas either, so by the end of the three days, I'm not sure which of us smelled worse.

"John and Mary came home and John had me in a tub before their bags were unloaded. I heard them outside my door, saying that they would not be going away again anytime soon, that I was not fit to be left alone. I listened to them talking, and bellowed out to them that I was blind, not deaf. Since then they have taken care to discuss me out of my hearing." He smiled, thinking that the pain of those days seemed a more distant memory with Jane by his side.

Jane was silent.

"Oh, my darling," she whispered, squeezing his hand. He felt her sorrow. "I wish I had known… "

He gripped her hand tightly. "I didn't mean to make you sad, my sweetheart. It's funny, looking back on it; I was so useless. This story was supposed to make you laugh."

"It is not funny," Jane said. "It breaks my heart. I think of my own happy Christmas, happy as I could be without you, and all the time you were here, suffering, and I didn't know it…"

"Oh, Jane," Edward drew her out of her seat, pulled her down upon his lap. "Don't. All is well now. I remember, one of the times you came to me in my dreams when I was alone here, I told you that you must return, that I was lost without you.

"And so I was, but now you are here, and my Christmases will be happy ones. And I will smell much better." He hugged her, kissed her forehead and her mouth, flicked her chin with his finger. "Are you smiling? Hmmm?"

She did smile then, kissing him back, "Lost without me, are you? Then how am I to go away today, thinking of you here alone? Well, not alone, thank God for Mary and John. But here without me."

She leaned back, looking at him, and reached up to hold his face in her hands. "I know how you will be. The coach will carry me away, and you will become most unpleasant. You will forget to eat, you will sleep all day and prowl the house all night, and you will be surly to John and Mary."

He frowned at her, opened his mouth. She put her hand over his lips, "Shhh." He was silent. "You think I have not talked to Mary? She told me how things were with you."

"Mary called me 'surly'?" he asked indignantly.

Jane laughed, "No, that is my word. Mary is your employee; she has to be diplomatic in her descriptions of you. I no longer work for you; as your wife, I can say what I wish about you. You have been known to be surly in days past, and I imagine you being so again. So you must promise me, on your honour, that while I am gone you will behave yourself. You will eat what Mary prepares, you will sleep in our bed, at the time appointed, and you will be polite."

Edward snorted, and Jane shook his face gently between her hands.

"I'm serious! Promise me that you will behave as a gentleman in my absence."

He could hear the laughter in her voice, and he smiled. "I promise. Now finish your breakfast, you'll miss your coach." He patted her bottom as she slid off his lap, but both were smiling.

Later, Edward stood at the end of the long road leading to the house, holding Jane tightly. She was dressed in her travelling clothes, and he hated them, hated them without even seeing them, because she was wearing them to go away from him.

He wanted to tell her not to go; suddenly wanted to have her get his things so he could go with her. But he knew he could do neither of those things, so he held her tightly, kissed her, and smiled at her so her last sight of him today would be a happy one.

He hugged her again, whispered to her, "Safe journey, my love." He rested his forehead against hers for a moment. She kissed him in return, and left his arms. He heard her footsteps, heard the creaking of the carriage steps as John helped her inside, heard the closing of the door. He turned towards Mary, who waited to take his arm to help him make his way back down the path to the house.

Edward sat in his chair in the parlour, his right eye dimly perceiving the changes in the light as the flames leapt high in the fireplace. It was an August night, and although it was not at all cold outside, the added warmth of the fire was welcome in the chilly room, which was unaffected by the warm sun of the mild summer days.

It was Wednesday evening, and he should have been heading up to his bedroom to prepare to sleep, but he enjoyed watching the fire, light and flames being the only things he could see. His bed was cold and lonely; Jane was not due to return until the next afternoon, and so he put off going upstairs.

He felt that he had done quite well in his wife's absence. He had followed a schedule of sorts, going to bed when it was time, getting up early as was his habit, eating the meals that Mary prepared. Jane had asked him to do what they would ordinarily do, and to be pleasant to John and Mary while doing it, and so he did.

It was only in between all these tasks that he wasn't sure what to do with himself. He realized that the added activities of his life were all due to Jane, and now that she was gone, he found himself at loose ends.

Every day he and Jane would take a long walk, and now he was deprived of that, although he did go out to the front of the house to pace on the stones close to the front entrance – he was familiar enough with that area to navigate it now. But that took very little time, and he was soon back indoors, where he sat down again with nothing but his own thoughts to occupy him.

He had not expected to sleep well the night before, but after tossing and turning a little, he finally had. He missed Jane's warmth in the bed next to him, her soft breathing and the little sighs and murmurs she made as she slept up against him.

He had taken her pillow, and hugged it to him, resting his face against it, breathing in her scent; that had helped him to relax while making him miss her all the more. He tried not to worry about her, but he couldn't help imagining carriage accidents, robbers along the coach route, and drivers who took wrong turns and weren't sure where to go. He had worked hard to banish such thoughts from his mind so that he could assure Jane that he had done as she had requested and slept well.

Edward sighed, shifting in the chair. He missed his wife dreadfully, and sitting here in the parlour with nothing to occupy him felt too close to the memory of his nightmarish solitary months before Jane had returned to him. If he imagined hard enough, he could almost convince himself that nothing had changed and that he was still alone. *Abhorrent thought,* he told himself, shuddering.

He made himself dwell upon more pleasant musings. Their nightly reading, for example. Right now, had Jane been here with him, they would be reading together before they went to bed, or rather, Jane would read aloud while he listened raptly, loving the sound of her voice as much as he loved the stories. This had become a ritual they looked forward to as much as their daily walks together.

They had decided to plumb the depths of the Ferndean library before sending for any other books, and Jane had laughingly told him that that would not take long, as there were few books to be found. An old Bible, the presence of which puzzled Edward, who knew his father had visited Ferndean for two reasons, neither of which involved the word of God. There were some old hunting and field dressing manuals

("Ugh!" Jane had remarked, pushing them aside), and a huge volume of the plays of William Shakespeare.

So they had spent the last two months reading that, for while both were familiar with some of the author's works, neither had read all of the plays. They had started with *Romeo and Juliet*, and although they had enjoyed it very much, found it depressing enough to want to move on to something more lighthearted. Next they had read *Much Ado about Nothing*, which was a favourite of both. They had laughed together night after night, and were disappointed to see it come to an end. They had decided to alternate tragedy with comedy, and had just finished *Othello* a few nights before; that was rather a strange selection for a pair of newlyweds to share, they had decided once it was finished.

Edward smiled, remembering the night before Jane had left. They lay in each other's arms, after passion shared and spent. As the weeks of their marriage had progressed, he had gradually introduced other ways to make love, and Jane was always eager for him, as passionate as he had always thought she would be. This time he moved his hand and lips over her body, working his way downwards until he had her trembling beneath his searching mouth, loving her slowly, taking his time until her soft moans became cries that even Edward thought John and Mary might hear.

She was nearly sobbing with her need, and he could feel her fingers digging into his shoulders as she arched her back and cried out his name. He was hardly able to control himself as he felt the contractions that signaled her climax, felt her grow even more slippery and eager for him. He moved up over her, rolling her over on top of him and positioning her, helping her to take him in. She moved over him, sitting up straight as he ran his hand over her.

"Oh, Jane," he gasped, his hips rising to meet her, "how I wish I could see you right now." Their delicious finish came together, Jane leaning over to kiss him so that their shared moans nearly became one, breathing into each other as she braced herself above him, moving her body on him, gripping him tightly inside her.

Afterwards, Jane lay atop him, soft and warm and feather light upon him, all their senses heightened by the thought that this was their last night together for several days. She rested against him, her breasts pressed against his strong chest. He was still joined to her, both of them hating the moment when he would slide from her, separated again.

He had lifted his head, threaded his fingers through the soft hair at the back of her neck, and pressed his cheek hard against hers to whisper hoarsely in her ear a quote from their most recent reading, *"Perdition catch my soul, But I do love thee! and when I love thee not, Chaos is come again!"* She had laughed softly, and whispered "Oh, yes!", hugging him and burying her face against the damp skin of his neck. She had remained on top of him for a while, even after he had slipped out of her, pressing gentle kisses over his face and neck. He had relaxed, delighting in the feel of her caresses, remembering when he had lain alone in this bed night after night and would have sold his soul for just one touch of her sweet lips upon his skin.

Edward sat quietly, thinking of the play. He felt for the character of Othello, an older man, surely battle-scarred, married to a young woman he feared he did not deserve. He wished he was not of such a melancholy frame of mind, for he could not stop his thoughts turning towards the dark and the disastrous. Jane's absence had turned him into his own Iago, for his very heart turned traitor against him and whispered to his mind that such perfect happiness as he had known for two months was not meant to last. He closed his eyes, leaned his head back. His whole adult life had felt to him cursed and unlucky, certainly he could not expect that to change now? And truly, if Jane ceased to love him, or was no longer with him, his life would indeed be chaos, a dark and empty existence not worth living.

His mind went back to coach accidents. They happened, one heard of them. He wondered how long it would take to get word. Thursday would come and go, Jane would not appear when John went at mid-day to pick her up. He wondered what happened in such cases – would he get a letter, perhaps from a doctor or a minister? Or would they notify the keeper of the inn from which the coach departed, so when John went to inquire, they would receive the news?

His mind moved to the next scenario, robbers and bandits along the way. He imagined Jane with a pistol pointed at her, removing her pearl necklace and wedding ring, handing over her purse, the robber nervous, looking over his shoulder, worried of discovery, his finger accidentally squeezing the trigger…

Enough! He remembered the long nights after Jane had vanished from Thornfield, when he had lain awake in his bed, thinking such thoughts, seeing her in one perilous situation after another, frantic with worry for her. It had not done any good then; it would do him no good now. He opened his eye, looking once again at the fire.

What if she just did not return? What if it was too much for her, the care of this blind, crippled man to whom she was now bound for life? She could take a coach headed for anywhere, just keep going. She had enough money, she did not have to return if she did not want to. He would never hear from her; he would just stay like this, alone forever…

Edward realized he was annoying himself immensely. He shook his head, and said aloud, "If she knew what a fool you are, she might think twice about returning." If he went to bed now and slept as he was supposed to, then tomorrow would be the day of her return, and he would see her sooner than if he continued to sit here in this chair, borrowing trouble and putting disturbing thoughts into his own head.

He thought of her last words to him, after she had kissed him, there at the end of the path. "I'll see you on Thursday, dear Edward," she had said softly, her hand resting on his cheek.

He smiled, got up from his chair, and headed upstairs, where he pulled off his clothes, got into bed, and slept the night away, holding Jane's pillow tightly in his arms.

Jane sat in the rocking coach, staring out the window as her fingers absently rubbed back and forth over her pearl necklace. Adèle was sleeping, her head pillowed in Jane's lap.

Jane thought of Edward, wishing there was some way to make the coach go faster. She missed her husband greatly, felt that three days away from him was far too long.

She stroked Adèle's dark curls gently, thinking of her last two nights at the inn, sleeping alone. It was too close to her months of long and lonely nights, back in her cold narrow bed in Morton. She had thought of Edward then with a pain born of hopelessness, dreamed of his kiss and his warm embraces. Now it was hard to lie alone, knowing that such embraces awaited her at home, knowing that he was lying alone as well, missing her, and no doubt thinking dark thoughts that only her presence next to him could banish.

She smiled, looking down at Adèle. She hadn't actually been alone in her bed last night, she thought ruefully, thinking of Adèle's thin little body next to hers. Adèle was a restless sleeper, tossing and turning, and more than once Jane had awakened to feel herself poked in the side by a small knee or elbow.

She had longed for her husband's solid warmth against her. In addition to the other benefits of their being in bed together, he was simply very nice to sleep with. He was warm and he was quiet, curling against her and sleeping soundly in one position for hours at a time. Occasionally he would snore if he rolled over on his back, but a gentle nudge from her would make him move, and once more he would be still. And always, she felt his love for her, in the arm that he slid around her waist as he moved closer to her, the hand that rested on her hip or her back, or the feel of his whole body spooned against hers; a strong, steady comfort to her the whole night through.

As sometimes happened, although she did not share these thoughts with Edward, her mind went to St. John. Now that she knew the reality of being loved so deeply by a devoted husband, she occasionally thought of St. John with a brief flash of anger. She loved him as a cousin and respected him as a man, but she knew if he had gotten his way, she would be living in India now, married to him, working hard by day and sleeping at night in a lonely bed. Oh, St. John might have come to her from time to time, out of a sense of duty, or to keep under control his own fleshly desires. But she would have been a mere tool, useful but unloved.

St. John would have been incapable of loving her as Edward loved her. Her body was her husband's shrine and his place of peace and happiness; her pleasure was his pleasure. St. John would never have been moved to tears, nor felt such joy, nor been suffused with contentment, simply by being in Jane's presence. He never would have touched her with such adoration. Jane smiled as she thought of Edward's little caresses on her – his warm fingers stroking the soft skin behind her knees, or his lips moving gently on her throat and around her ears. Little things, perhaps, to anyone else, but to Jane, each little touch and gesture confirmed how very much she was adored, how every inch of her was precious to him.

Her mind now returned to the present, and Jane wondered how displeased Edward would be when she arrived with Adèle. He had "Hmmph'd" a little when she informed him that she would bring Adèle home with her if the school was not to her liking, but had said nothing beyond that. But if he had only seen the place…

Jane thought back to her first sight of Adèle, a little taller than she remembered, very thin, her hazel eyes enormous in her pale little face. Her whole countenance had lit up with a wild, frantic joy and she had hurled herself against her former governess, crying "Mademoiselle!!!" She had clung to Jane, arms tightly around her waist, and Jane had seen the thin lips and disapproving scowl of the headmistress, who stood nearby watching them.

Jane had leaned over and kissed the top of Adèle's head, hugging her in return, and then had gently disengaged her, still keeping her hand on Adèle's shoulder. She stood as straight and tall as possible as she requested permission to take Adèle to a private place to speak with her. The woman reminded her of Miss Scatcherd, and it made her stomach squeeze painfully to have to deal with her. The woman had grudgingly allowed them to walk outside on the grounds, and when she had Adèle alone, she held her hand and talked to her seriously.

"Adèle, have you received any word on Thornfield, or of Mr. Rochester since you have been here?"

"No, Miss Eyre, no one has spoken to me of them, and I have had no word and no letter from anyone." The words were spoken plainly, her accent much less pronounced, and with none of the plaintive drama that might have accompanied them just over a year ago. She was quiet, defeated, no longer the little Parisian coquette that her guardian had once portrayed her as.

Jane took her hand in both of hers, and began to tell her of all the changes that had taken place since Adèle had seen her last.

"Adèle, I am Miss Eyre no longer; I am Mrs. Rochester now." Adèle's eyes lit up with happiness, but before she could speak, Jane continued, "I want you to know that Mr. Rochester has been very ill for some time, and was not able to see you or write to you, but now he and I are married, and I wanted to see you and make sure you are well and happy."

Adèle watched her solemnly as Jane squeezed her hand and they resumed walking. "Thornfield had a fire, and it burned completely, so Mr. Rochester and I live at a place called Ferndean now. Mr. Rochester tells me that you visited there once, long ago?"

Adèle shrugged, looking puzzled, and Jane continued, "Well, I had not been there before, but it is my home now, and you will come there too, on school holidays. Or I will take you back with me now, if you tell me that you are not happy and that they are not good to you here."

Jane could already tell that the school was harsh and severe – she could see it in the surroundings, could see it on the faces of the students, and could tell from looking at Adèle. So she wasn't surprised when Adèle started to cry, and told her how miserable she was, how she was always hungry, how she had been punished for speaking French, for laughing, and for not knowing all she was supposed to know.

Jane questioned her closely on what she was learning, and was surprised to hear that the pupils were expected to know things far too advanced for their ages. She also learned that their contact from home was restricted, and that they were not allowed treats that were sent for them.

"So you did not receive the sweets that Mr. Rochester sent you at Christmas time?" she asked. If the children were not allowed gifts, and the package for Adèle had never arrived, it would not hurt her to think that she had been remembered at Christmas, not forgotten until February.

"No, Mademois… I mean, Madame," Adèle said awkwardly. She had had a miserable Christmas, but as she had been unhappy since her arrival, the date had made little difference. Certainly, some of the other girls who had had to stay over the holidays were miserable too, so she had been in good company.

It had not taken Jane long to go back into the school and inform the headmistress that she would be leaving, and would be taking her ward with her. The woman had replied that she would have to wait for permission from Mr. Rochester, who was her student's true guardian. Jane had taken a deep breath to calm the churning of her stomach, and had once again risen to her full height and tried to assume a position of dignity that, as a very small nineteen year-old, she did not always feel she fully possessed.

"Very well," she informed the woman calmly, "You may dispatch a message to Mr. Rochester. It will take four hours to get there, and then my husband, who is a very busy man, will have to answer the letter. It will interrupt his work, and perhaps his meal, and he will be displeased. The message will have to return, which will take another four hours by coach." She sat down in a chair by the woman's desk. "I will wait. Or perhaps you will be sending the message by mail, in which case I will require accommodations until return post, and you can explain to Mr. Rochester why I will not arrive tomorrow afternoon, when he expects me."

She folded her gloved hands demurely, and looked at the woman with a calm expression that belied her pounding heart. As she expected, the headmistress soon gave her leave, and she departed within the hour, bearing Adèle and her pitifully small collection of possessions away from that place forever.

That day was the first happy one Adèle had known in months. They were too late for the return coach by this time, and so retired to the inn for the night. They had eaten a good meal, and had taken a walk in the lovely little town, before going to sleep in the small, comfortable room. Adèle, used to having to hold her tongue, was slow to warm up and feel comfortable, but soon was talking to her beloved friend as though they had never been apart, reveling in the warm fire, the soft sheets, and the presence of her adored teacher beside her.

Now they were headed back to her new home, and Jane had spoken seriously to Adèle about Mr. Rochester's injuries and altered appearance. She did not want her to be frightened by her first sight of him. Adèle had nodded solemnly, but was so excited to be away from her school, and back with the people she loved, that she did not think anything could upset her.

At long last, the coach had arrived in town, and there was John, waiting to meet them and convey them back to Ferndean. He greeted Adèle warmly, and informed Jane quietly that he had been waiting for quite a while, as his employer had insisted on sending him to fetch her an hour before the coach was due to arrive.

"I left him pacing like a tiger, back and forth outside the door, so anxious is he to see this carriage bring you home," John told her, as she smiled widely, picturing Edward in her mind.

John left the carriage on the road that led to the woods near Ferndean and carried the bags as Jane and Adèle made their way up the path to the estate. Jane was trying not to hurry, mindful of the older man and his burden, but she wanted to fly down the road and back into Edward's arms. As she drew nearer the house, she saw Edward pacing restlessly on the gravel walk, just as he had been doing the first time she had come to Ferndean. Then, he had had no hope; now, he waited eagerly for his love to return to him. His keen ears heard the three of them making their way to the house, and he turned towards the sound of their voices.

"Edward!" Jane called, suddenly heedless of John and Adèle. She lifted her skirts and ran lightly to him, and he held his arms out, his hand still gripping his cane as he wrapped his arms about her. John smiled as he walked past them, bringing their baggage indoors. Adèle paused for a moment, looking at her guardians, and when they appeared to take no notice of her, she hesitantly moved past them as well, and went on into the house, where she was welcomed wholeheartedly by Mary. Jane and Edward remained standing outside, clasped in each other's arms.

"How are you, my darling?" she asked him, hugging him hard. "Did you fare well in my absence?"

"Oh, everything was fine," he shrugged, as though to dismiss any negative feelings he had allowed himself in her absence. He held her tighter and kissed her enthusiastically.

Jane leaned back and looked up at him, "Really? Everything went well?"

"No," Edward admitted, hugging her again, "just as I predicted, I was lost without you."

She laughed then, and linked her arm through his as they turned to enter the house.

---

20 September 1837

In the stillness of the autumn night, Edward lay awake, holding his wife close to him as she slept.

Her quiet breathing soothed him, the gentle rise and fall of her chest under his arm lulled him into relaxation. His fingers rested on her cheek, drifted over to trace the delicate curve of her lips. She slept soundly, worn out by her busy day of teaching Adèle, and assisting her husband.

After a great deal of discussion, and with some guilt on Jane's part, they had decided to send Adèle back to school after Christmas. Teaching her was a huge undertaking, and for Jane, whose husband still needed her time and her assistance in nearly everything, being Adèle's governess again had been far too difficult. And Ferndean, deep in its lonely wood, far from the neighbouring farms, was too isolated for Adèle to be able to have playmates and other children to be with. Their only neighbours were the old farmer Silas, and the elderly parson of the nearby church, whose homes were each half a mile away on either side of Ferndean.

The parson had recommended a good girls' school less than an hour away by carriage. But for now Jane taught her here at Ferndean, and her long days made her fall into bed exhausted each night.

Even after nearly four months of marriage, Edward still found it difficult at times to believe that he was no longer alone in this bed. He had spent so long tossing and turning as the sole occupant in large beds, stretching out to find only empty space, that it amazed him to reach out his arm and find Jane lying close beside him.

While they had fallen into a comfortable daily routine, he had not ceased to awaken in the night, pull her gently against him and thank the God whose mercy had brought her safely back to him. He had thought that he had shed so many tears during their separation that their reunion would dry them forever. But he found himself many times swallowing a lump in his throat, blinking back tears, over the sheer joy of having her back in his life, forever his.

Tonight after retiring to their room they had rested on the rug in front of a roaring fire, greatly welcome these first crisp nights of autumn. During the day they had walked, Adèle in tow, several miles through crunching leaves as Jane had described the beautiful colours of the turning trees and the way each leaf fell in a gentle spiral to the damp ground. They had inhaled the pungent air with its spicy scent of bonfires from neighbouring farms.

Adèle had run along, kicking exuberantly through fallen leaves, calling to Pilot, who had barked and run back and forth from Adèle to Jane and Edward.

Tired but content, they had returned for supper, Jane and Edward sending Adèle off to bed before going to their bedroom for the night. They sat, leaning against each other as they talked of the previous autumn and the pain that they had separately endured, each thinking almost constantly of the other.

For it was one year ago this very night that Thornfield had burned, almost one year ago that Rochester had awakened to a nightmare of searing pain and darkness and fear. Jane sat with her arms about his shoulders as he described what he could remember of that night and of the days that followed.

Edward stared into the fire. When he spoke, his voice was husky, and there was a slight quaver in his speech as his mind went back to those fearsome days.

"The last thing I remember is looking over the edge of the roof, seeing Bertha lying below. The blood, her body sprawled there... " he broke off, swallowing hard. Jane tightened her arms around him.

"The doctors say my injuries must have given me some loss of memory, as I remember nothing else until I woke up several days later. They say I was delirious, fighting them, talking out of my head, but I remember none of that. I just remember waking, as from a long sleep after too much wine, because my head hurt, inside and out. I lay there, trying to figure out what was happening, but my brain felt slow, as though I could not form a complete thought.

"I could hardly move, everything felt heavy, as though I was tied down. Later I found out my arms were restrained, for fear I would tear off the dressings, do myself more injury, but at the time of my awakening, I was panicked, fearful I was trapped somewhere terrible. Deep in my mind I must have had a memory of lying in the ruins of Thornfield, under the rubble, for I was afraid I was lost and no one would ever find me.

"I lay quietly, trying to make sense of what was happening. I was naked, bound, unable to see, and every part of my body hurt. I concluded that I was dead, and that this must be Hell. Certainly I felt that I was burning. I lay, terrified, knowing that if I opened my eyes, I would surely see the Devil, and then I would go mad.

"Then, from the darkness, I heard it, the voice that made me realize that wherever I was, it was not in the pits of Hades, ready to face my eternal punishment."

Jane rested her cheek against his shoulder, "The voice?"

Edward smiled. "Mrs. Fairfax. I heard her speaking, heard her call me 'Mr. Rochester'. I did not know if I was dreaming, but I knew that no matter what, Mrs. Fairfax would not be in Hell with me." He laughed, "And I knew I could not be dead and by some miracle in Heaven, for if we were in Heaven, surely Mrs. Fairfax would not still be working for me and having to call me 'Mr. Rochester', for the Lord would not lay so heavy a penance upon such a good woman as she. Then I knew that at least I still lived, and it remained for me to lie quietly, to figure out as best I could what had happened to me, for I was far too afraid to ask.

"Later I was told how they found me, how I was trapped under a huge beam that robbed me of my hand while it protected me from whatever else was falling around me. They did not know what floor I was on when I fell, only that I was coming down the staircase, trying to make my way out of the building. At some point, something caught me in the face, tore it deeply enough to take the eye with it." He heard Jane's intake of breath at those words.

"Some sort of burning befell the right side of my face, hence the scar and the eye injury. I will probably never recall that night completely, and as Carter says, it is better that way."

Jane kissed him as though she could banish all bad memories forever. Then she drew his head down to her lap, stroking his dark hair as she told him of her autumn in Morton.

"I used to work hard all day, and try to stay busy into the evening," she said. "But in the dead of night, the dreams would come.

"Over and over you came to me, held me in your arms, kissed me and begged me to stay with you. You told me how you loved me, asked me to love you forever. We would embrace, talk together, love each other.

"I would begin to awaken, and for moments after I would squeeze my eyes shut, hoping to be drawn back into that dream world, where we could be together always. Each time I realized that the dream was over and I was awake, I burst into tears and sat on the edge of the bed, rocking with the force of my sobs, holding my arms tightly over my broken heart. I would lie back under the covers of my narrow, frigid bed, try to go back to sleep, and in the daylight I would rise, go to my classroom, and pretend to be a decent, hard-working school-mistress instead of a broken-hearted outcast clinging vainly to a dream that had long ended.

Her soft fingers traced his eyes, his lips; stroked the wavy black hair from his brow. He lay quietly, thinking of how different his life was now that Jane was with him, than when he had been alone, desolate, without hope of love and of a real life.

Never did she shy from him in any way, never did he feel that she could not bear the sight of him. If his right arm was nearest her, she would take it, but if he faced her with his left arm, with its missing hand, its terrible imperfection, she freely took that also.

Her kisses were spontaneous, her lips making no distinction between the scarred and the unscarred upon his face. In their bed he had placed her on his left side so he could easily reach over and touch her with his hand, yet he had worried to have her there where she had only to raise her eyes and have to look fully upon his ruined face. But she did not seem to mind.

She loved him, and he could feel it. Every moment of his life now, her love enveloped him, warmed him.

He took her hand, brought it to his cheek as he tried to tell her how he felt. "In your arms I am reborn, cleansed of all yesterday's pain and sorrow and loneliness. I feel as though I'm free now, freed by your trust and innocence from all the sordid burdens of my past."

He reached up to her, embraced her, drew her down to lie beside him. She did not pull away, but turned to him with her arms, her lips, her entire heart.

"It's taken me so long to be able to say this, but I feel complete for the first time in my life. You, Jane, you and your love, have finally made me whole."

Chapter 54 - Sight Restored

"Mr. Rochester continued blind the first two years of our union: perhaps it was that circumstance that drew us so very near—that knit us so very close: for I was then his vision, as I am still his right hand. Literally, I was (what he often called me) the apple of his eye. He saw nature—he saw books through me; and never did I weary of gazing for his behalf ... impressing by sound on his ear what light could no longer stamp on his eye."

Jane Rochester - Jane Eyre

April, 1839

The bright sunshine of the mid-April day streamed through the freshly-washed windows of the Ferndean parlour. Edward paced back and forth across the carpet in front of them, his fingers massaging his furrowed brow as he thought how to best word the letter he was dictating to Jane.

"Therefore, in light of this situation, I feel that it is only right to offer you..." He broke off and looked in the direction of the small writing desk where his wife did her daily correspondence. "Am I talking too fast, my Janet?"

"No, Edward, you are fine," she said, and he could hear her murmuring, "I feel that it is only..."

"If you are too tired, we can stop for a while," he told her, concern rather than deep thought now making him pause.

"No, Edward, I am fine," she said, and he could hear the smile in her voice as she answered him. He smiled back at her, but of course could not see what she saw, how the warm and genuine smile lit up his dark, scarred face and made it younger and almost handsome, despite the flaws that cut across it.

He looked in her direction, almost as though he could see her, and his smile was disturbed for a moment by an almost imperceptible frown which flickered across his face, but he turned away from her before she could ask him what was wrong.

He resumed his pacing, trying to remember where he had been. His train of thought had been distracted by all the things that were crowding his mind.

Jane was first and foremost on his mind, as always.

She had entered the fourth month of her pregnancy, and for nearly a week now had been free of the nausea and fatigue that had plagued her so badly. She was filled with new energy, and Edward almost could not keep up with her in her eagerness to walk and resume their regular activities.

She laughed over bodices that would barely button, and waistlines that were becoming too tight, and he had insisted on taking her to town to buy her some new dresses more suitable to her changing figure.

The dressmaker had enthusiastically measured for several designs that could be worn with a girdle before and after, and left loose "in the latter months" as she had delicately worded it. The dresses had arrived yesterday, and Jane was wearing one of them. He had forgotten to ask her to describe it for him in his eagerness to get this letter written and posted.

"...only fair to offer you a sum in keeping with the market value of said item," he finished, and turned again in the direction of the window as he paced.

He knew he faced the window, because as he approached it, there was a definite change in the brightness that he could perceive in his remaining eye. But as he turned, the light hit him with such force that he flinched and stepped back. He felt his eye water, and involuntarily pressed his hand against it.

"Edward?" He heard Jane's questioning voice, "Are you all right?"

He pulled his hand away, blinking. "I'm fine," he reassured her. "It was just that I looked fully into the light, and it was so bright for a moment." He swiped beneath his left eye with his thumb, where it had also watered with the sudden irritation to the other eye.

He could not say anything definite to her because he was not sure what to say. For several weeks now, he had been able to discern flashes of light, colour, and movement with his right eye.

For two years he had been able to "see" only the brightest of lights, and he feared he was mad now, but he felt that the film that obscured the eye was lessening. He was aware of being able to perceive light more readily, and as for the other flashes, he did not fully trust his impressions, and was afraid to mention it to Jane for fear he was deluding himself.

Still blinking rapidly, he raised his head and looked over in her direction again. And then he moved quickly towards her, his breath fast, his heart pounding.

"Jane, have you a glittering ornament around your neck?" he asked her, bending over her as she sat at the desk.

"Yes, it is a gold watch chain, holding the watch you gave me," she told him, her hand moving up to the chain as she spoke.

"And have you a pale blue dress on?" he asked, his anxiety evident to his own ears.

"Why – yes. Yes!" He heard the puzzled tone of her voice, and then a second later, as comprehension seized her, a low gasp. She stood then, nearly hitting his head with her own as he bent towards her.

She flung her arms around his neck. "Edward... Edward?" He heard the question in her voice.

He held her tightly. "I don't know, Jane. I have felt for some time that the obscurity clouding this eye was lessening. But I felt I may be mad, felt I was imagining things in my eagerness to see again. But now I am sure of it."

His arms squeezed her. "I could see it, Janet. For a moment, earlier, and then just now – I could see the chain glittering, see a flash of light blue. I could see it."

"Oh, Edward," she buried her face in his shoulder, and he could hear tears in her voice. They clung together, unable to fully absorb the enormity of what might be happening.

With John's help, Edward climbed into the carriage and took his place beside Jane. She reached over to hold his hand, which was clenched into a fist on his knee. She knew how nervous he was. He smiled in her direction, but his smile felt forced and artificial. They were on their way to London, to keep their appointment with Mr. Smythe, the oculist recommended to them by Mr. Carter.

Two weeks ago, they had returned to the area near Thornfield, to visit the Carters. Over the years, Edward had come to think of Carter as a friend, as well as a trusted physician. And during his grueling recovery, he had come to appreciate the devoted care provided by Carter's assistant Lynch, and the kindness of Mrs. Carter.

None of them had seen him since they had put him into the carriage over two years ago to send him to Ferndean, although he had dictated a brief note for Mary to send off at the time, informing them of his safe arrival and expressing again his thanks for their excellent care.

Since marrying Jane, Edward had dictated a few notes to the Carters, informing them of his marriage and sending his good wishes to their family. They had responded in turn with short, friendly letters. But this was the first time they had all met in person, and they discussed many subjects not covered in their brief correspondence.

Carter was speechless at the sight of him, standing for a moment with his hand on Edward's shoulder, shaking his head. He then turned to Jane with a broad smile, reaching to take her extended hand. "Young lady," he said, his eyes moving over her, nodding his approval, "it is indeed a pleasure to see you, to see the both of you."

He ushered them into the parlour, receiving them as honoured company now, not as he would patients. The maid brought tea, and Carter sat, listening to Edward's account of the recent changes in his eyesight. Mrs. Carter joined them when the tea was served; she was happy to see the Rochesters and to hear of the improvement in Edward's sight. She beamed at Jane, holding Jane's hand in both of hers.

When there was a pause in the conversation, Edward asked after Lynch. Carter started to answer, but then with a smile he deferred to his wife, who broke in with an exclamation.

"Why, Lynch is gone, that rascal," she told them. "He finished his training right enough, and instead of going back to his home, he headed for America. He went with his parents and such family members as would go with him. New York, it was, and then on to Boston.

"He writes that there are so many poor Irish immigrants there, that he is of more use there than even in his own town back home. He has married a girl he met on the ship, and they are busy morning, noon, and night. He writes to us from time to time. May I mention that I have seen you, when next I write to him?"

"Yes, please do," Edward smiled at her. "And please, will you tell him that he was right, that my Jane did return." He reached over and took his wife's hand, and neither of the Carters missed what passed between them as she placed her hand over his and smiled.

"I will indeed," Mrs. Carter said. "He'll be most pleased to hear of it, I've no doubt."

After the exchange of pleasantries, Carter took the Rochesters back to his one of his examination rooms. He looked at Edward's eye carefully, and agreed that the clouding in his eye had not worsened, and in fact did look much improved from what he remembered.

"But beyond that, I cannot tell you," he said ruefully. "I am afraid that conditions of the eye are not my specialty, and as far as further surgery or treatment, I would not be able to provide it. But I think I know just the man to see you. He is in London; I would be glad to contact him on your behalf."

Edward agreed readily, sitting quietly as Carter washed and dried his hands, lost in thought.

Edward assumed Carter was thinking deep ophthalmic thoughts, but then he spoke, laughter in his voice. "We've gotten the mundane part of your visit over with; now for the really crucial part. You'll want to see your horse."

Edward smiled. He had been thinking of Mesrour since their carriage had pulled in, and intended to ask after him, as a casual aside, when they were ready to go. He felt he had forfeited any rights to him, and didn't want to appear presumptuous, or to make Carter think he was thinking of taking Mesrour back.

Carter patted him on the back, "Come now, you've been wanting to know about him, haven't you?"

"Yes," his patient admitted, "I just didn't want to appear as though I had any right to him. I was trying to have some dignity about the exchange."

"It's a horse, man, it's not like he's an old sweetheart that I moved in on and married under your nose. You've every right to see him." Carter led the way out of the room and through the house.

Edward held Jane's hand tightly as they headed out to the stables. She knew that one of the hardest things he had ever done was to give up his beloved horse, and she wondered if it would be painful to him to see Mesrour now. But he followed Carter eagerly, and when they drew near to the horse's stall, he dropped Jane's hand and walked closer on his own. It was too dim in the stable to see much, but he advanced, hand out.

Mesrour nickered in recognition, his mouth nuzzling his former master's outstretched palm. Edward smiled, swallowed hard, his hand reaching up to stroke the horse's soft nose. His left arm came up, wrapped around the horse's neck, and he leaned his head against Mesrour's. Jane felt tears well up in her eyes, and Carter pressed his lips together, visibly moved.

Carter turned to Jane. "Where are you staying tonight?"

Jane answered, her eyes upon Edward, "We were planning to stay at The Rochester Arms. Mr. Rochester has plans to visit with his estate manager tomorrow. He has been conducting all his communications by letter, and thought it might be best to meet with him in person, since we were going to be in this area anyway."

"Why don't you have your driver take you to the inn in your carriage, and I'll see that your husband joins you safely later?" Carter asked, winking at her.

"What... " Jane asked him, then broke off as she watched her husband, seemingly lost in conversation with the beautiful black horse. She smiled, but looked concerned.

"Mr. Rochester has been riding for years; I don't think he needs eyes or a hand if someone else is with him, riding such a horse as Mesrour. This horse will not let him come to any harm." Jane smiled gratefully at him, and moved over to kiss her husband.

"I'll meet you at the inn, Edward. I believe Mr. Carter has plans for you."

A short time later, Edward stood next to Mesrour, his heart beating quickly. It had been nearly three years since he had sat a horse, when he had been searching for Jane after her disappearance from Thornfield. He stood near the horse's head, his hand moving over Mesrour's face and neck to familiarize himself with the tack that Carter had used when he saddled the horse.

Carter watched him, "I ride him with a plain hackamore and leather rein, you have him that well nose trained. But I've a good gag snaffle there, felt you might feel more secure with a bit on him."

Edward stroked the horse's neck, patted him affectionately, "Thank you, Carter. But I would feel confident on Mesrour with just a rope halter. I had stopped jumping, you know, after my brother's accident. I felt it was better to take the long way round than to risk my neck. The plainest of equipment always served us well. We trusted each other, didn't we, my friend?" he asked Mesrour, leaning his forehead against the horse's head again. Mesrour blew his breath out, stomped his hoof.

Edward smiled, taking a deep breath to calm his pounding heart. He felt anxious, but as Carter held the stirrup steady, assisting him to climb the short stool and sit on the horse's back, all time seemed to melt away.

He gathered the reins in his hand, straightened himself in the saddle, the heels of his boots automatically pointing downward and his thighs tightening against the horse as though he had never been off his back.

As Carter mounted the other horse he owned, Mesrour seemed anxious, stomping and turning to watch his new owner, confused by the presence of his old owner upon his back. Edward pulled the reins slightly, turning Mesrour in a circle in case he decided to suddenly bolt in his nervousness.

He spoke firmly to the horse, and Mesrour calmed somewhat, his memory dredging up the by-gone days when he and his master had moved together as one, and had communicated together with and without words.

The two horses moved out of the yard, headed for the road, Mesrour following Carter's horse. Edward's heart was pounding, his breathing fast, but he felt his body automatically assume the correct movements, posting easily as the horses began to move faster, hips to ribcage moving with the horse's motion, the rest of him straight and still.

Carter spoke to him, "I don't suppose you've spent much time on a horse, since last I saw you."

"You suppose correctly. Who would there be to assist me? My wife does not ride, nor do my servants," Edward told him. "I walk miles in a day, but riding? No, not at all. I know I will pay for it with many sore muscles tomorrow."

"You and Mrs. Rochester appear so happy together," Carter said. "I think she has been good for you. I cannot tell you how glad I was to see her step down from the carriage, holding your hand."

"She has saved me," Edward said simply. "I'm not sure how much more I could have endured, there alone. My life has started again, with Jane."

"I'm relieved to see it," Carter said soberly. "My wife and I have thought about you, wondered how you fared. Word filtered back to us, you know, probably from those with whom you communicate on business. They said you lived as a hermit, refused all callers, were very broken down."

"That I was," Edward said. "But her coming changed that. I did not look for her, as you said I should. Instead she came to me, when I thought all hope was lost. She is helping me to face the world again, and I find that despite my worries, people have other things to do than watch and judge someone who is scarred and blind."

"That is true," Carter said. "We always fear to have more of a negative impact on the world than we really do." He then changed the subject. "Your wife is expecting a child, I notice. That must make you both happy."

"Yes," Edward said, looking serious. "Time had gone by, and nothing happened, although every month I expected it to, Jane being so young. I was just as happy to go on as we were, was almost relieved to not have to face the situation. But then God decided it should happen, that we should be blessed. The child should be here in October, the midwife says." A frown crossed his face. "I cannot help but wish we were here with you available to attend her."

"Well, a midwife should do adequately, as long as there are no complications, and there should be a surgeon or doctor nearby, surely?" Carter asked.

"Yes, there is a doctor, who assists Mrs. Collins when needed. Believe me, I have inquired," Edward assured him. He hesitated, then ventured a question.

"Carter, you have assisted with many births, have you not?"

"Well, as a Navy surgeon I did not see many, but since I've settled in this area, I have done my fair share. I would be most happy to assist Mrs. Rochester, were you to be in this area, but the trip to Ferndean might be a long way for me to travel."

"Oh, I know that," Edward told him. "And I am trying to remember that the midwife has had many years of experience in this matter. My wife likes her, trusts her. But I... " He stopped, his face troubled.

Carter turned to look at him as the horses continued to walk along the roadway. "You are frightened for her." It was not a question.

Edward took a deep breath. "I am terrified. I've been frightened since Jane told me she was with child. I have tried to share her happiness, have tried to trust God and be content, for it should be a happy time, but I cannot help but fear for her. I cannot tell her of my fears; I don't want to worry her. She is so joyful, Carter, not frightened at all. She wants to give me a son."

"And so she may!" Carter told him. "All has gone well up to now; there is no reason to think it will not continue to go well. You might have a daughter, of course, but that's not so bad, is it?"

"Oh, God, no," Edward exclaimed. "I have assured Jane that I will be happy either way, and I will – I care nothing for that. A will can be amended to provide for a daughter as well as a son. I care only for Jane's safety." He was silent for a moment, then the words came forth, expressing his weeks of worry.

"I hold her in my arms, feel her tiny, delicate form, and I cannot help but think that she will never survive such an ordeal! It is too much to expect, for God to bless me in such a way, to have my Jane and to have children with her also. If I lose her, I cannot go on; the very thought fills me with terror. I wish I had been more careful, I wish she did not have to face this upcoming pain and misery."

"Mr. Rochester, you must try to think of hopeful outcomes!" Carter shook his head. "I know how fearful a thing it is; I have seen my wife endure it five times now. But they are amazingly strong, these women. They can face it time after time, and when it is over and they hold your child in their arms, they act like it was all nothing."

He went on, trying to assume a soothing tone of voice. "More women survive than not, I assure you." This was not entirely true; Carter knew that in poorer districts, half of the women did not survive childbirth. But he would not tell Rochester that. "And it is 1839, not medieval days. Our medical knowledge is far more advanced than it was. I have seen girls of twelve and thirteen birth infants as easily as anything. Your wife is small, but she is fully mature and healthy, she has as good a chance as any I've seen. Please tell me you will not let a time that should be joyful be overshadowed by your dark and melancholy spirit."

Carter smiled, "I know you from years back; it is your nature. But you must think of what blessings you have been given, and surely you are entitled to more."

Edward shook his head, "I know, I know I should think only of good things, and I do try to change my ways. Surely I have to be happy for my Jane's sake."

He was quiet a moment, thinking. "Carter, I once told you I could not thank you for saving my life, but I have since changed my mind. I have been given more of a life than I ever thought I would have, and I owe much of that to you, to Lynch, and to Mrs. Carter."

He continued, "When I left your home after my recovery, the only thing that kept me sane was the thought that surely I would die soon. I thought my life was over, that there was no possible reason for it to continue. I could have gone anywhere, but I chose Ferndean, knowing it was not a healthy place to live. I knew it would be but a short time and I would be released from my torment."

Carter nodded, suddenly serious, "I feared for your life, at that time. I knew I could not keep you at my home, but I was afraid what you might do."

"Well, as I told you, I feared suicide and would not have done it," Edward told him, adjusting his position in the saddle with a grimace. He was not used to this, he knew he would feel it tomorrow. "But I thought I would not have to, that God would take me soon. He had other plans for me, however. He wanted me to acknowledge Him, to give Him the place He should have had long before. And he wanted to bless me, at long last. Bless me with Jane, with love and a new life."

Carter asked him, truly curious, "You feel that God allowed this to happen to you, took your sight, took your hand, and yet you bow to Him at last?"

Edward smiled, "I was exceptionally stubborn. I needed something to get my attention, and perhaps God knew this was the only way. I used to think of it as a punishment, Carter. But now I am not so sure. When I was whole, I was miserable. Now I am blind, and in the world's eyes, crippled. But at last, I am happy. And had you allowed me to die, as I first wished you had, I would never have known this peace, so I do thank you, all of you."

Carter laughed, "Oh, we knew that you appreciated us, deep within your heart, and that someday you would admit it. Now show your appreciation in a definite fashion by looking forward to a healthy wife and a fine infant, be it male or female."

Edward laughed also. "I shall try with all my heart." He was sober then, "But in all earnest, I do thank you, for my life, for once again listening to my worries, and for this… " He gestured towards Mesrour's head. "I needed this, and no one but you would have known that… "

He felt the horses leave the roadway, head onto turf. "Where are we going?"

Carter chuckled. "Well, you still own Thornfield, don't you? I think this field is as good a place as any to let these horses run. Hey!!" He kicked his horse, started a canter, which Mesrour followed. "Don't worry, it's nothing but clean, open field," Carter yelled. "I confess to taking shortcuts through Thornfield land often; I assume the owner won't mind."

Edward laughed, a firm hand on the reins. "Be my guest!"

"Be ready now, master your rein," Carter told him. "Enough of this ladies' riding; we might as well be on side-saddles as continue like this." He urged his horse to a gallop, and Rochester, his heart pounding wildly, did likewise. He trusted Mesrour, and felt that between Carter and this wonderful horse, they would watch over him.

He felt as though he were flying, his legs gripping the horse's sides, the warm air whipping his face. He felt more alive than he had in nearly three years, bound as he had been by the constraints of blindness and injury. It had been difficult to assume a more sedentary life, accustomed as he had once been to sport and physical activity.

Even Jane's love, precious as it was, couldn't restore his independence, could not give him back some aspects of his manhood that he felt were lacking now. For the first time since his injury, he felt as though all things were again possible. He lifted his face, felt the warm sunshine, exulted in the brief and thrilling freedom.

Later, back at the inn, bathed and dressed in nightclothes, snuggled in the narrow bed next to Jane, he admitted that perhaps galloping along had not been the wisest thing he had ever done, considering his blindness and that he had a pregnant wife waiting patiently for him to return to her.

But he was exhilarated, thrilled, and Jane wisely did not upbraid him. He had survived the experience, and been brought back to the inn safe and sound, and she recognized that some small part of his soul had been restored by being able to ride that day.

She just laughed, reaching over to pat his leg. "Well, your thighs will be sore tomorrow, and it will serve you right!"

He laughed, slapping his abdomen. "My thighs and my stomach muscles. But you can rub them for me." He leaned over to kiss her, and lay down with a sigh. It had been an eventful day, and he drifted off to sleep quickly, still smiling a little. Jane watched him with a light and happy heart.

The estate business completed the next day, the Rochesters headed back to Ferndean. Messages were exchanged with the office of the oculist, and just a few weeks after Edward had first seen Jane's blue dress and her watch chain, they left for London to see what Mr. Smythe would recommend.

May, 1839

It was a trip of nearly two days to London, and by the time they arrived, both Rochesters were exhausted, but Edward was anxious to stop in and pay his respects to Robert Lathrop before they moved on to their hotel. Knowing what it meant to him, Jane put aside her own fatigue; she had to admit she was curious to meet this man of whom her husband had spoken with such fond regard.

Edward had last seen Mr. Lathrop in January of 1836, and for a time after that, occupied with Jane, and then with his injuries, he had lost touch with Hugh's father. Before the aborted first wedding, he had planned to take Jane to visit Mr. Lathrop on their way to Europe, eager to show off his new bride. He had not contacted Robert Lathrop until months after he and Jane were actually married, when he sat down and dictated a letter for her to write telling of his accident, the extent of his handicaps, and the good news of his marriage.

He had not been sure of a reply, not even positive Lathrop was still alive and well. But a month after his letter was posted, he had received a letter in return, a kind and gracious note congratulating him upon his happy marriage and expressing concern over his blindness and the loss of his hand. The two men had kept up a fairly regular correspondence since then, and when the plans were made to come to London, he had written Hugh's father to tell him so, following it with a note letting him know when he would attempt to call.

A maid ushered them into the Grosvenor Square townhouse, and soon Edward heard the deep voice of Robert Lathrop greeting them. He was warm and gracious when meeting Jane, but when he turned to Edward, his handshake lingered as he reached up and grasped Edward's shoulder.

"Oh, Edward," the old man murmured in a suddenly shaky voice, as he looked upon his late son's friend. The sight of Edward's scars and unfocused gaze, as well as his empty sleeve, stood out in such stark contrast with his last sight of him – a healthy man in the prime of his life, brimming with restless energy.

He drew near to Edward, his unsteady hand squeezing his arm, "I would never have dreamed, long ago, of the fates that would befall you and my Hugh. Such pain, such sorrow. Oh, Edward, these lives of ours can be so terribly difficult."

Edward found himself trying to comfort Mr. Lathrop, reaching up to pat his shoulder in consolation, speaking enthusiastically of his high hopes for a restoration of his sight. In truth he had no such hopes, but he could not bear to bring sorrow to this kind man, who seemed to see in him a connection with his much-loved and mourned-for son.

Hugh's father made a determined effort to control his emotions, taking a deep breath and letting go of Edward with one last squeeze of his arm. He smiled as he turned to Jane. He was about to offer her his arm in a courtly gesture, but realized that her help would be needed to guide her husband into the drawing room. Instead he ushered them into the room and spoke with a teasing note in his voice.

"Mrs. Rochester, I do not know how much you have been told, but the first time your husband entered this house, he was a spotty youth of fifteen years, brought here by my son on a school holiday."

Edward laughed as they moved into the room and Jane guided him to a sofa, sitting down beside him, "Now, Mr. Lathrop, I was never a spotty youth, I am glad to say. I had my afflictions, but spotty skin was not one of them. As I recall, my main trouble was a voice that went up and down several octaves in each sentence, increasing in range especially in the presence of Mrs. Lathrop and Alice. Alice, I remember, seemed to find that highly amusing; she nearly made me afraid to open my mouth."

The three sat together for several hours, as a maid served tea and the two men caught up with each other's lives. Lathrop asked after Pilot, who had been left behind at Ferndean with John and Mary, and told them that Butterfly had finally died the year before, mercifully in her sleep one afternoon lying before a warm fire.

There was laughter and conversation, and Mr. Lathrop told several amusing stories, directing them at Jane, who enjoyed this glimpse of her husband's younger years. She loved the idea of him as a young boy, joyful and free. She laughed over the story of Hugh's breaking Edward's nose with the cricket bat, with the accounts of the pranks all the boys played upon each other. It gave her a picture of her husband that she had never imagined.

Late in the afternoon the Rochesters departed, having had a wonderful time but eager to get to the hotel to rest. They had not talked openly of Jane's pregnancy with Mr. Lathrop as it was not a subject for mixed company, but Jane had noticed him glance at her waistline and then look delicately away. He exhorted them to keep him informed of the results of the oculist's visit and "any other happy news you are able to impart to me."

Edward kept up his appearance of lightheartedness while he was with Lathrop, but by the time they settled into their hotel room, he was a bit tense and snappish, worried about Jane and feeling the stress of anxiety over his appointment in the morning. They spoke little as they ate a light supper, and then retired to their bed in the hotel. It was still somewhat light outside, and they could hear the evening bustle of travellers outside their window as they bedded down for the night.

Edward lay on his side, trying without success to relax, and then he felt the bed shift, felt the warmth of Jane's small frame as she pressed herself against him. Her arm stole around him, she drew him close to her, and he felt her lips against his upper arm, his back. He reached around, wrapped his left arm around her hips, leaned back against her.

"It doesn't matter, Edward," she whispered to him. "Whatever he tells you tomorrow, it will not change our love for each other. Things can only change for the better. If your sight is restored, to whatever degree, it will be a blessing. If it cannot be restored, nothing will change. I will still love you just as much, I will still be there with you, to be your eyes, as long as we live."

Edward sighed deeply. He tried to answer her, but his voice came out in a whisper, thick with emotion. "I know. I know, my dearest. But I want so much to see you, want so much to give you a husband whom you do not have to wait on. I want to take care of you."

He heard her soft laugh behind him. "You no longer want my services?"

She moved even closer to him, kissed his neck, stroked his hair. "I'll have you know, I still intend to wait on you, regardless. For what would I do with myself, if I could not care for you? I would be so bored all day, with nothing to do."

He laughed in spite of himself, rolled over to face her. He slipped his arm around her, pulled her against him, "Well, if this man Smythe can suggest treatments that succeed, then you can have some leisure time, and I can watch over you part of that time. We can care for each other, rather than you always caring for me."

She nodded her agreement, and pressed closer to him as his lips found hers. They kissed deeply, passionately, moving together as they sought comfort and solace in each other. It had been awhile since they had made love, as the nausea and fatigue of early pregnancy had so affected Jane. Edward, ever solicitous of her comfort and safety, had been content to wait. When Jane turned to him now, kissing him with sudden passion and eagerness, he felt a flood of desire that overwhelmed him. They did not linger, as they often did, with long slow kisses and caresses of each other's bodies, but moved together with the fierceness of longing. They did not even undress, just pulled up their nightclothes as he rolled over upon her, both of them panting; low moans sounding in their throats as they kissed frantically.

Jane pulled him down, her arms and legs wrapped around him. She lifted herself for him, gasping out her pleasure as he entered her in one quick motion. He stopped for a moment, his breaths rapid and shaky with nearly uncontrollable need. Her warmth, her comfort, was exactly what he needed at this time, and he pushed his hard, aching fullness inside her, groaning loudly as he finished after just a few deep thrusts into her.

She held him tightly to her, as he shuddered and let out a strangled cry of relief. It was a moment before he could speak, letting his head drop to her shoulder.

"I'm sorry, Jane," he whispered, "I know you need this release also, give me a little time and I will... "

"Shhh," she murmured to him, hugging him, "it's all right, Edward. Sleep now, let yourself rest, you need it. We have plenty of time; I am fine."

Edward soon fell asleep, weeks of hidden fear and anxiety somewhat relieved by their coming together. Jane left the bed briefly to wash, but soon returned, snuggling up to him. A few hours later she woke with a start as she felt him stiffen against her with a loud gasp. She turned, reaching for him in the dark.

"Dear Lord, Edward, what is the matter?" she said, as he pressed himself against her, groping for her, clutching a handful of her nightgown as would a frightened child. She could feel his heart pounding as he tightened his arm around her.

His whisper was hoarse in her ear, "I was dreaming. I was at Thornfield, and I could suddenly see again. My eyesight was perfect, but you were gone. I looked everywhere, and you were nowhere to be found. I ran and ran and found myself at Ferndean, but it was deserted as well. You were gone, I could not find you." His head rested upon her shoulder, he was breathing as if he had, indeed, run a long way. His hand moved up her body, once again clutching at her nightgown.

"Oh, God, Jane, if I did not have you... " he murmured, his voice shaking, "If you were to leave me... "

"Hush, darling, it was only a dream," she told him, kissing his head, reaching up to tangle her fingers in his thick hair.

He lifted his head, "Tell me that you love me, Jane. Please. I need to hear it."

"Shhh," she whispered, lying back and pulling his head down to her, stroking his hair, moving her body against his, "I love you. You know I love you. I will never leave you, not of my own volition, never. I love you, my dearest husband."

He relaxed against her with a long shuddering sigh, listening to her voice as she whispered to him, "I love you, Edward. It's all right, I am here. I love you... "

The next day, Edward sat stiffly in the oculist's chair as the man probed and poked at his eye.

Jane sat upright in a chair over to the side, wincing at the sight of Mr. Smythe's instruments. The man was brusque and businesslike, making no wasted motions as he worked, saying little. He had listened to Edward's account of the fire and of the injuries that had resulted from it, interjecting the occasional question, and then had proceeded to his examination.

When he was done examining the eye, he pushed his chair back and stood, moving to a washstand. He poured water into a basin, washed his hands and dried them on a towel. Then he resumed his seat.

"Mr. Rochester," he said, his voice seeming loud in the quiet room, where the ticking clock provided the only constant sound, "what do you know of the nature of your injury?"

Edward frowned. "The surgeon's assistant called it 'traumatic cataract'. He had trained in Edinburgh, had seen industrial accidents involving the eye. He said it was a filmy covering over the eye, resulting from injury."

"Quite so," the oculist agreed. "Tell me, what do you see when you look at me, can you see all of me, or are there patchy areas in which you can see nothing?"

Edward considered for a moment. "I can see in a circle, as though the outside of the eye can form a picture, but the centre is all greyness and obscurity. I have to be in a good light and move my head to be able to see anything, and what I see is not clear."

The oculist nodded. "What you report is consistent with what I see. You have an area of scar tissue in the centre of the eye, quite thick in the middle and thinning out as you get to the edges of the iris. My guess is that the eye is healing slowly from the edges out, but the patchy scarring in the middle is thick enough that I believe it will never improve without intervention."

Edward nodded. "I understand."

Mr. Smythe looked at him. "And do you know the only treatment for it?"

"Surgery, I would imagine," said his patient in a low voice. Jane leaned forward, her eyes on the two men.

"Yes!" the oculist exclaimed, bringing his hand down to slap against his knee. "I believe that with just a simple operation, there is a good chance to restore your sight. What would you think of that?"

Edward took a deep breath, looked over at Jane instinctively. "As simple as that? I would be glad to do it, glad to take the chance."

"Good," Dr. Smythe rubbed his hands together. "It is a very good chance. I'm not a gambling man, and if I felt there was little chance of restoring your sight, I would not recommend the surgery. At worst it will remain the same; the chance of at least some of your sight returning is fair to excellent.

"But there is a decision that must be made. The surgery is rather simple, but after it is completed, you must spend several days in bed, utterly motionless. You must eat, bathe, perform all your tasks in bed, flat, with your head immobilized. Usually that will only need to be for a few days, but it may be up to a week.

"Then it could be longer until you are fit to return to your home in a carriage, bouncing and jouncing as carriages will do. Can you do what is needed? Can you remain in London for the time that is required?"

Once again Edward looked over at Jane. To the watching oculist, it appeared that the man could actually see his wife, so strong was the connection he could feel between them.

"It is your decision, Edward," she said, so softly Mr. Smythe had to lean forward to hear her. "I will help you, will do whatever is required. We will do what needs to be done."

Her husband bent his head, moving it from side to side. Jane knew he was testing his eyesight, trying to determine what he could see with the small areas of his eye that still worked. She sat silently, awaiting what he had to say.

When he finally spoke, his voice was quiet also.

"I want to see my wife. I want to see my child, when it arrives," he said firmly, lifting his head and looking towards Mr. Smythe. "I want to have the surgery."

That night they returned to the hotel room, having made arrangements for the surgery to take place the next day. They made love again, but this time it was not a desperate frantic union, clothing pulled up, under the covers, clinging together for comfort. They undressed each other, taking a long sweet time, knowing it would be weeks before they could come together again. Edward rubbed Jane's belly, resting his head against her. There was only a subtle change there; her abdomen had once been a flat expanse that he could span with spread fingers from hipbone to hipbone. Now his hand lightly traced a gentle rise from bone to bone, kissing her there before he moved his mouth over the rest of her body. They merged in a slow, loving dance of mutual desire and excitement, nothing held back. Edward knew that the next time they were able to do this, she would be big with his child, and his heart overflowed with tenderness towards her. He so loved the bodily excitement mingled with the love and the emotional connection that made him feel they were two halves of one person. How had he ever been satisfied with less?

When they were finished, and they lay together, her head on his chest, he held her close to his heart, drained, exhausted, but at peace, and as always, so very much in love with Jane. Sometimes his heart was so full… he loved her so much it hurt him. He felt he could not possibly love her more. And he was always wrong. His love for her grew every day. He rested his cheek against her head, thinking that even if the surgery did not work, even if he was blind until he drew his last breath, it did not matter. He had everything there in the circle of his arms.

Jane walked back and forth across the carpet in the sitting room of their hotel suite.

It was warm in the room, the late May sunshine streaming in through the high, velvet-curtained windows. Her dark skirts swished back and forth over the toes of her shoes as she paced across the room. Her arms were folded across her chest and she clutched her elbows, hugging herself, trying to comfort herself as best she could.

She wished Edward were there to hold her in his arms, but he was lying on the bed behind the securely closed door, enduring God-knows-what from the oculist and his assistants. She had not been allowed to stay, for fear that the trauma of the surgery would cause her to lose the child she carried. She had tried to tell them that was nonsense, that she could endure anything if she could be with Edward, but even he had insisted she wait outside.

So now she paced outside the bedroom, her ears straining to hear even the smallest sound from behind the closed door. She could hear the murmuring of male voices, but could not tell if any of them were Edward's.

She knew some of what was happening, knew that they could give him no laudanum, that they needed him awake and aware of his surroundings. She knew one of those men would be holding his head still to prevent any movement as Mr. Smythe operated. She imagined that it would be painful, but she heard no outcry from him.

She continued to walk, her hands instinctively sliding down her abdomen, to cradle the small swelling that was now evident beneath her skirts.

She held her hands over it, rubbing her belly gently. She remembered Edward's quiet words, the day before, "I want to see my child." Remembered his tender stroking of her abdomen, his sweet kiss upon it. She sent a prayer to Heaven, that her husband's wish would be granted; that the child would come into the world whole and healthy, and that he would be able to see it.

The bedroom door opened then, and she turned rapidly to see Mr. Smythe emerging, drying his hands on a towel that was tucked into his waistband. He was smiling at her.

"I believe the surgery went well, Mrs. Rochester," he said, moving towards her.

He put out his hand to prevent her from entering the room. "My assistants are bandaging his eye now, and cleaning up the room, but I knew you would be worried, and I wanted to come out and tell you. Only time will tell the degree of our success, but the operation itself went without difficulty.

"Your husband is a strong man, Mrs. Rochester. Much depended on his ability to remain still, and he did so, in spite of the fact that it was painful to him. He took a little brandy before the surgery, to numb the pain, but it only made him drowsy, it did not put him to sleep or block all sensation. His cooperation made our job a great deal easier."

Jane nodded, her eyes filled with tears. The oculist patted her on the shoulder. "In a few minutes you will be able to see him very briefly. I will call you."

Her knees feeling weak, Jane moved towards the sofa and sat down. She leaned back, her eyes closed, tears sliding down her face as she sighed with relief.

As she sat there, she felt something she had never felt before. There was a strange sensation in the middle of her belly, right below her navel. A soft fluttering, a gentle bumping motion.

Jane's eyes flew open, and her hands moved to her abdomen as she realized what she was feeling. Laughter bubbled up beneath her tears, as joy and relief banished the fear and worry inside her.

A short time later, Mr. Smythe stuck his head out the door and beckoned to her to come in.

The room had been cleaned, the surgical implements removed by Dr. Smythe's assistants, one of whom sat in a chair by the bedside. Edward lay on the side of the bed nearest the bedstand, a thick dressing over his eye and a large bandage wrapped around that. His head lay on one pillow, two other pillows lay on either side of him, and on either side of those a small sack rested.

"Sandbags," Mr. Smythe told her, as she poked one with curiosity. "Small, not too heavy, but there as a reminder for him to keep his head still."

He raised his voice, "Mr. Rochester, I have brought your wife in to see you. She may see you briefly, but then it is important that you go to sleep for a time."

Edward murmured her name sleepily, raised his hand a couple of inches, seeking hers. She moved over, grasping it in her hand, bending over to kiss him. Then she remembered herself, and glanced at Mr. Smythe first. He nodded, smiling.

Jane bent over to kiss his forehead gently, then squeezed his hand.

"The doctor tells me you were very brave, darling, and that all went well," she told him. "I want you to sleep now, and I'll be waiting right outside."

She turned towards the assistant. "I'll be right outside the door, should he need me." The man nodded at her, and as she took one last reluctant look at her husband lying so still in the bed, Mr. Smythe escorted her back out to the sitting room, and closed the door behind her.

Late May and June, 1839

The days passed by slowly for the Rochesters. Edward lay in almost total darkness and quiet for several days, his head immobilized by the two firm pillows wedged in next to him. His entire eye area was swathed in bandages to protect the delicate right eye from light as it healed following the removal of the scar tissue.

He was quiet and thoughtful, saying very little. He thought a great deal about his earlier recuperation back at the Carters' home, how much his life had changed, how much it could still change.

A nurse came daily to help care for him – to do the bathing and linen changes that neither Edward nor Mr. Smythe would permit Jane to do in her condition.

The nurse was a coarse, unwashed woman who smelled strongly of the drink that made up part of a nurse's pay. But she was strong and efficient, and strangely gentle in her gruff way. She, too, refused to let Jane do any of the work that she deemed too strenuous for her, even though Jane ended up performing many of the same tasks later after the woman had gone home.

There was not much to do in the quiet room. The dim lighting made reading to Edward impossible, but it was not permitted anyway, according to Mr. Smythe. He wanted a minimum of stimulation to his patient, not even wanting him to do much talking. It was far more important that he lie still and rest, he told them sternly.

Jane was willing to sit at his bedside, holding his hand, talking quietly if he so desired, or just being near him. Edward would whisper to her, trying to keep his head completely still, telling her to go outside, to see London, a city she had never seen before.

If the truth were told, Edward longed for her presence, wanting nothing more than for her to sit near him and hold his hand. At times, he would drift off and dream that he was back in the small room at Mr. Carter's, alone, wounded, without hope, without love, without a future.

He would wake suddenly, heart pounding, frightened that the past two years had been only a beautiful, protracted dream. Was it true, could it possibly be? Was he married to Jane, had they spent a lovely two years together, was she carrying his child? Or was it just a cruel figment of a crippled man's desperate imagination?

With the bandages wrapped around his head, and the dull and nagging pain he still felt from the oculist's sharp knife, it was easy to believe that no time had passed, that he was still trapped in that bed at Carter's sanitarium.

At times he would slowly inch his arms together, take his hand, and reach for the stump of his forearm, to reassure himself that it was long healed, no longer dressed and wrapped in layers of bandages, that enough time had passed. He was too embarrassed to confide all this to Jane. Oh, he knew she would be sympathetic and understanding; she probably knew how he felt without him even explaining it to her.

But he was tired of his weakness, tired of depending on his wife. He was the husband, a man forty years old. She was a mere one-and-twenty, delicate, pregnant. He wanted to be the strong one, wanted to take care of her for a change. So he would bring her hand to his lips, kiss it gently, wave her away from his bedside and urge her to take Kitty, the young maid assigned to their room, and go out walking in Hyde Park, go shopping, go carriage riding.

Kitty was more than happy to earn a few extra shillings by accompanying the young Mrs. Rochester out in public, released by the head housekeeper who was happy to earn a small fee herself for allowing Kitty to do so.

And everyone was happy, except Jane, who really wanted to remain with her husband, but would do what she believed he wanted; and Edward, who desperately wanted her beside him, but would do what he believed she needed.

Yet in spite of all this, London was a fascinating city for Jane, for whom Millcote had seemed a large place.

She watched with wide green eyes all the sights this splendid city afforded. Kitty had lived within a few miles of the hotel all her life and knew exactly where to go – which greengrocer carried the freshest fruits, which shop would not cheat a visitor, which street corner would provide a moment's entertainment by a roving performer or by an agitator hoping to make a quick speech before being chased away by a constable.

Yes, if not for her anxiety over Edward, Jane would have enjoyed herself completely. Kitty was only a few years younger than Jane, and had a ready wit and sly sense of humour, and Jane found herself laughing freely at some of Kitty's often cruel but clever observations of the people around them.

Three days after the surgery, Mr. Smythe checked beneath the dressings, and gave permission for Edward to rise from his bed and renew some of his activities. But he still could not ride in a carriage, so the Rochesters were not able to return home.

Jane and Edward were able to resume their normal conversation, which was a great relief to them both. Their first chance to really talk to each other was almost comical, as both nearly tripped over their own tongues in their eagerness to share their thoughts with the other. Jane sat with him by the hour, excited to relate what she had seen in London.

She told him about the people passing by, made him laugh with some of Kitty's keener observations. She shared with him the news on the street – unrest in various factories throughout the country, rumours that a marriage was being planned for the young Queen Victoria. He held her hand, happy to hear that she was enjoying herself. At times he felt guilty for keeping her in the isolation of Ferndean. She seemed happy there, but sometimes he regretted for her sake the lack of a larger society.

Several days after he was able to be up, Edward received permission to be outside, so they were able to resume their daily walks. They stepped out into the early June sunshine for an hour at a time, revelling in the warm air and their togetherness, at all the new possibilities in their lives. Edward still wore a bandage around his eyes, still held his cane when he walked, but Jane ignored the curious glances of passers-by as they strolled. She had grown accustomed to the sidelong glances they attracted when they went out in public in the town close to Ferndean, but found that most people, after evincing a brief initial discomfort, treated Edward normally despite his blindness and despite the scars, fading but still evident, on his face.

Their second anniversary came and went during their London interlude, and that day was especially wonderful for them, with the added promise of Edward's restored eyesight, and of their first child. That night, Edward had a bottle of champagne sent to their room, and they toasted each other and the future, which looked even brighter now than it had a few months ago.

Most importantly, Jane, who had been sleeping on the sofa in the sitting room, was allowed to sleep back in the bed with Edward, and it was there that they held each other in the quiet darkness, talking softly into the night. She would hold his hand against her abdomen, trying to let him feel what she could feel, but to no avail. He chuckled, kissing her head as she lay next to him. "It's a little too soon, dearest. A few more weeks and I'll be able to feel these little movements, have no worries."

This trip seemed almost like the honeymoon they had never taken, and they were almost reluctant to return to Ferndean on the day, four weeks after their arrival, when Mr. Smythe finally said that it would be safe to take the carriage ride back home. They had orders to return in July so the large dressings could be removed, and the success of the operation could be determined.

Mr. Smythe was quite hopeful, he told them. He had been gratified to find that the scarring was quite firm and it separated easily from the eye's surface, and that he was able to remove a great deal of it. He warned Rochester that his sight would be dim, that he would never again have full use of his eye. He also told him that reading and writing, while possible in small amounts, would likely always require assistance. But Mr. Smythe was confident that enough sight had been preserved that his patient would be able to regain some degree of independence.

It was the middle of June when they arrived at Ferndean. John and Mary greeted them eagerly, and it was gratifying to realize how much they had been missed. Mary exclaimed over the change in her mistress's shape in just four weeks, making Jane blush scarlet, before Mary set to work preparing a sumptuous meal to celebrate their return home. All Jane and Edward wanted to do was to rest, and take up their lives where they had left off a month before.

July, 1839

Edward approached his side of the bed, holding the candle aloft. He had prepared for bed entirely by himself, now able to find and see every item on his table.

Pleased by his success, he had come to bed, only to find Jane stretched out, fast asleep. He looked at her tenderly, his angel. These last two months had been difficult for her, he knew. His surgery, his recuperation in darkness and quiet, his needs, and all the travel that accompanied the situation, had to have taken its toll at a time when she needed rest and security herself. His heart filled at the sight of her, and he vowed that from now on, he would care for her as she had cared for him.

He set the candle on the bedstand, and carefully eased himself into bed, still watching her, not wanting to disturb her.

She lay slightly tilted towards him, in her white cotton nightgown. Her left hand lay upon her stomach, protectively cupping it; her right hand was up near her face, her fingers curled. Her hair was spread out over her pillow. She usually caught it back in a neat braid, but she must have been too tired to even do that. He reached his hand towards her, but pulled it back, loath to risk waking her no matter how much he wanted to feel the softness of her shining hair sliding through his fingers. Her lashes cast tiny shadows on her cheeks in the light of the candle.

The most wonderful thing about regaining his sight, he thought, was being able to see her again. He had come to terms with his blindness, and as long as he had Jane with him, he had felt he could face a lifetime of never being able to see, if that was God's will for him. But God had again tempered His judgment with great mercy, and allowed Edward the blessing of being able to see his wife's face.

He would never forget his first sight of her, last week in the oculist's office. When the final dressings had come off, he had blinked rapidly in the sudden light of the room, and looked up past the doctor's shoulder to see her, smiling through her tears, the anxious look on her face replaced by joy.

He could still see her in his mind's eye: the same face he remembered, the same Jane. She was wearing a green dress that had darkened her shining eyes to emeralds. Her hair was arranged differently than he remembered – instead of the severity of her pulled-back braids, she had a lustrous heavy chignon at the back of her neck, with soft curls at the temples. Her hair was entwined with a green ribbon that matched her dress. She looked older, more elegant than he could have imagined, but her face… it was still his darling, and he drank in the sight of her.

And almost as wonderful as the sight of her face was the soft curve of her belly under the fabric of her dress. She appeared so lovely, her straight little body with its new look to it, no longer slight and thin, but full and blooming. It was one of the most joyous moments of his life.

His eyesight had been blurred, and a new bandage was put on to replace the large dressing, but that brief sight of her had sent his heart soaring. And when the bandage had finally come off for good, this evening, he could see her even more clearly.

He had not been able to stop looking at her, his gaze returning to her again and again throughout their dinner and the hours that followed. She had laughed at him, a blush coming to her cheeks, and finally had admonished him.

"Edward, please, you are embarrassing me. Your gaze is relentless upon me!" She was smiling, pleased, but self-conscious.

She continued, "I am overjoyed at the return of your vision, but almost wish it could have happened a little sooner, when I looked more as you remember me. Surely you are wondering at the presence of this little milk cow in your parlour." She had passed her hand over her abdomen, blushing again. He was enchanted by the entire picture of her.

"You are the most beautiful sight I could ever imagine." He spoke seriously, for it was absolutely true, and she shook her head, but he could see the soft smile touch her lips again.

Tonight, she had gone to the dressing room to wash up before bed and to put on her nightgown, and Edward had sat in the chair by the fire, smiling as he watched the orange flames leap and dance. For so long, light had been all he had been able to see, and to see the fire was like looking into the face of a reassuring old friend. Jane had come out of the dressing room, barefoot, dressed in her thin cotton nightgown. Her long hair was hanging down over her shoulder, held in her left hand, a hairbrush held in her right hand as she worked it through her shiny tresses. She came over to stand near him, and as she passed in front of the fire, he could see her body, backlit by the flames, through the fabric of her gown. A rush of desire moved over him, surprising him with its intensity.

For two years he had made love with only his hand to determine how her body looked – with none of the stimulation that a man's eyes provide at the sight of a woman. It had certainly been adequate arousal, but his first sight of her through her gown made him reel with longing for her. She felt the change in his demeanour, saw it in his eyes, and she suddenly felt the tingle of her own desire. He did not need to speak; she knew right away what he wanted. She came over to him, stood in front of his chair, her eyes fixed upon his.

"Jane" he said, a catch in his voice, "you have seen me many times, but I have never seen you. Please, I need to see you now. Will you allow me that?"

She nodded, suddenly feeling as nervous as she had on her wedding night. While she and Edward had spent night after night in each other's arms, no one had ever seen her entire body. She felt shy, embarrassed. But at the same time, she could not wait for him to see her. She felt silly for her mixed emotions. This was her husband. By touch alone he knew her body better than she did, as intimately as she knew his. And she had seen him completely naked countless times in their two years together. She lifted her hands, feeling them tremble as they went to the ties of her nightgown, slowly pulling each one free, opening her gown before letting it fall off her shoulders, slide down her body. She stepped out of it, watching him.

He gave a little gasp as he took in the sight of her for the first time. He reached up, stroked the softness of her hair, pushing it aside so he could see her without anything covering her. He took her hand, pulling her towards him.

He had felt the new fullness of her breasts, the roundness of her belly, but now he saw them, and he ran his gaze over her, looked up to her face, back down to her body. He couldn't see her perfectly, but he could see her. For two years he would nearly have sold his soul for just a brief glimpse of her naked before him, and now she stood in front of his chair. His heart beat faster as he gazed at her lovely breasts, and at the darkness of her hair where her slender legs met. He reached up, lightly touching one nipple with his index finger, circling it slowly before stroking the tip again. He heard her sharp intake of breath, and he did the same with the other side. She moved closer, slid her fingers into his hair as he leaned forward and touched her breasts with his mouth, kissing first one nipple, then the other; soft, light kisses that made deliberate circles around each one. His tongue flicked over each tip, teasing them into tight, hard little points. He could feel her fingers travelling down to grip his shoulders, heard her soft moans.

Jane was breathing hard now, leaning on him. His warm mouth travelled over each breast, drawing each centre into his mouth, making her gasp each time. His hand stroked down to caress her belly. He pulled her against him, laying his face on her abdomen, resting his head against her.

"My Jane," he whispered, "you are so lovely, so perfect." She could not speak, could only stroke his neck and his face, bend to kiss him. Tears stood in her eyes as she watched him take in the sight of her naked body, watched his awe and wonder at finally seeing her. It was the greatest moment of her life thus far, to see his sight restored, and to see him adoring her, thrilled by what he saw.

At the same time, she could not remember when she had been so aroused, and she moaned, moving so that she stood between his legs, his face resting against the soft skin of her belly. His warm breath against her drove her wild. When he stood up, took her into his arms and kissed her, she pressed herself against him, feeling his erection against her bare stomach. She reached down, touched him through his trousers. Her fingers traced the shape of his hardness, rubbing her hand against him, feeling his body shudder against hers as she touched him.

He took her to the bed, laid her down on the edge, and knelt before her, sliding his palm along her right thigh and opening her legs. For several minutes he just watched her, the rapid rise and fall of her breasts, her fingers digging into the cover of their bed in anticipation of his touch as he ran his fingertips over one inner thigh, then the other. Her skin felt like silk. He leaned over and began to kiss her.

"Oh, God, Jane," he whispered, as he dropped gentle kisses over her thighs, moving between them, running his lips over the soft hair, "oh, Jane, you're so beautiful, just so beautiful."

She twined her fingers into his hair, moaning as his lips continued to caress her with soft gentle kisses between her legs. From all the walking they did, her thighs were slender, but muscular, and he took in the sight of them, spread for him, as he reached up with his arms and pushed her legs farther apart. With his fingers, he opened her gently, just taking in the sight of her, the part of her that had brought him so much pleasure. He touched her lightly, running his fingers over the soft, wet skin, sliding a finger into her, feeling how much she wanted him. He felt a surge of heat in his loins, nearly lost control himself.

She cried out, reached for him, sitting up to pull him up to her, "Edward, please, now, please." He felt her hands on his trousers, unfastening them, and he gave a soft groan as she pushed them down his legs, untied the drawers she had tied that morning and pushed them down as well. She lay back, drawing her legs up, and he moved over her, bracing himself over her on his arms to keep his weight off her belly. The bed was just the right height, and he entered her slowly, feeling her grip him, so tight, so warm; hearing her cry out, "Oh, Edward, yes."

He moved the way she liked him to, slow and deep into her, and felt her grasping his hips, rising up to meet him. They were ready, both so ready, and their voices rose in unison with the sounds of their pleasure.

And they looked into each other's eyes.

Jane lay beneath him, her eyes fixed upon his face as they moved in their gentle rhythm. Her gaze was intense, her eyes never leaving his even as her face changed with her escalating sensations. He fixed his eye on hers, trying to tell her with every breath and every heartbeat how very much he needed her.

He fell into her gaze, lost himself within her eyes.

"I love you," he whispered, "oh, Jane, how I love you."

"And I love you," she told him. She smiled, but once again she was weeping. Tears slid from the corners of her eyes, as she watched him watching her. Finally she could bear it no longer, and her head fell back, her back arched, giving a cry as the rapture grew and spread within her. Edward thrilled to the sight of her as he felt her gentle pulsations grip him, buried his face in her neck as he gave himself up to her at last, spilling himself deep within her. For a long time they clung together, unable to speak for fear of shattering the magic of what had just taken place between them.

When they had separated, each wiping tears from the cheeks of the other, they lay together on the bed, as Edward leaned up on his elbow and stroked her soft skin. She relaxed beneath his hand as he moved his fingertips over her, her eyes blinking sleepily as she dozed off and awakened again. He just wanted to look at her, and his gaze searched her, as though to memorize her form should his eyesight be taken again. She finally forced herself to move, got up and went back to the dressing room to put her nightgown on, coming out ready to help him prepare for bed. But he had declined, kissing her with thanks, but eager to try to do what he could by himself. When he came back out, ready for bed, she was already asleep, and he now stood looking down at her, his heart full as he watched her.

She took no pleasure in her looks, having been compared all her life to those who were taller, more pleasing, more vivacious than herself. Edward could not convince her how much her appearance pleased him, because she had never believed herself attractive in any way. He watched her now in the candle-light, free to fix his gaze completely upon her. He loved everything about her.

If he looked at her objectively, he could see no great beauty in any individual feature. Her face was very ordinary in every way. Her eyes were lovely, large and green, but her brows and lashes were not distinctive enough to help them stand out in particular against the rest of her features. But Edward Rochester could not look at her objectively, and had not been able to look at her so since the second day of their acquaintance. To him she was perfection and always had been, and the fulfillment and satisfaction of their life together had only enhanced her loveliness in the three years since he had last seen her face.

A woman who is loved and cherished carries a special kind of beauty with her, and this beauty was evident in Jane Rochester, no matter the plainness of outward appearance with which she had been endowed by God.

He could still remember, with great pain in his heart, his last sight of her before she had kissed him and walked out of the Thornfield parlour and out of his life on that terrible day three years earlier. Her image had been fixed in his mind, to torment him all his lonely days and nights before her return. Her face had been as white as the collar on her dress, her lips equally bloodless. Her green eyes were like the stormy ocean depths, dark and haunted and far away. Gone was the bridal radiance she had displayed earlier in the day. She was pale, ghostly, struggling to keep herself upright and focused on her goal – to leave him and save what was left of herself. He had known just looking at her that she was already gone, had already slipped through his hands, had been gone from him from the moment Mr. Briggs had begun to speak in the echoing church.

But now that fearful image could be banished from his mind, replaced by the sight of his lovely wife, glowing with health and happiness, secure in his love and devotion.

Edward Rochester had known many women, some intimately, most as acquaintances. He had previously preferred women who were tall, well-built, dark and exotic. Jane was none of these – yet any other woman he had known paled in comparison to her.

He thought of the kind of women he had previously known. Their elaborately arranged hair, their fine gowns, their cosmetic trickery, all meant to enhance fine features and disguise those that were less than perfect. He thought of how they had dropped their eyes before his piercing gaze, disguising their calculations and appraisals, hiding behind the long-practiced skills of flattery and falseness. He thought of the vapidity, even the viciousness, which could be hidden behind the most startling beauty. He had returned to Thornfield having had his fill of that kind of feminine society.

And then, just when he had thought there would never be another woman who could move him, he had met Jane. Tiny, thin, pale, quaintly dressed. Not one trick, absolutely no skills of false flattery or allurement. She had met him squarely, looked him in his eyes, matched his intellect, not retreated from his rudeness or his arrogance. And he had fallen, down, down, into a love he had long felt he would never find.

She was totally pure, completely honest. What he saw when he looked at her was what she was. She did nothing to tempt or beguile him, there was no snake hidden in a bouquet of roses; there was just Jane. Simple, plain – and yet to him, the most beautiful woman he had ever seen in his life. He wished he could convey to her exactly what he saw when he looked at her.

He needed to sleep and wanted to let her continue her rest without disturbance. But before he blew out the candle and lay down beside his sleeping wife, he moved closer to her for a moment, listening to her quiet breathing, resting his face against her satiny hair. He leaned over her hand, touched his lips to the spot where her pulse beat against the delicate bones of her wrist.

"My beauty," he whispered, "I love you so."

Chapter 55 - His Father's Eyes

When his first-born was put into his arms, he could see that the boy had inherited his own eyes, as they once were—large, brilliant, and black. On that occasion, he again, with a full heart, acknowledged that God had tempered judgment with mercy.
Jane Rochester - Jane Eyre

October, 1839

Jane lay still, stretched out on the parlour sofa, her stockinged feet in her husband's lap. He rubbed them absently, his face fixed on the fire, lost in thought.

For days, ever since the small guest bedroom off the kitchen had been prepared for the upcoming birth, the single bed layered with sheets of newspaper and covered over with several cotton sheets, Jane had felt unable to reach Edward. He was quiet, walking in silence when they stepped out in the afternoons, sitting motionless staring into the fire, and when Jane read aloud in the evenings, she knew he could not have repeated back a single word.

He was not ill-tempered or morose; his actions were, if possible, even more loving and gentle than they always were. But he was quiet, still, his dark eye deep and unreachable. Jane knew what troubled him. She knew he was frightened for her, knew that he was afraid of losing her as a result of the events to come. He would not tell her so, of course, not wanting to burden her. But she felt his fear, understood what it was about.

"What are you thinking of?" she asked him softly. "Your face is so far away."

He smiled at her, his hand circling one of her ankles, his long fingers caressing her gently. Her feet were a little swollen, but for the most part, she was well. Other than feeling ungainly, and unable to get a full night's sleep due to the demands of her bladder and the nearly constant movement of the child within her, she felt wonderful.

"I was thinking of my mother," he said. "Both of my parents, really." He sighed, "You know, it has been thirty-two years since my mother's death, and about fourteen since my father's. I don't think of either of them often, in the course of the day. But I've been thinking of them frequently now."

"I suppose that's natural," Jane said, nodding. "I find myself thinking of my mother also, wondering how she felt, as close to my birth as I am to this one. I know nothing about her, really, and there has never been anyone to tell me of her."

Edward watched her, her sweet face calm and serene in the flickering firelight. He smiled, reached for her hand, and assisted her to sit up. He put his arm around her, feeling her snuggle up against him.

"We really haven't talked about what we will name this child," he said. "But if it should be a girl, I wonder if we could name her for my mother."

"Elizabeth," Jane said. "I have always liked that name. If it would make you happy, then of course we can." She reached over to hold his hand. It was one of the only times he had really initiated a discussion about the baby. He would respond when she spoke of the subject, and seemed to enjoy it when she reached for his hand, holding it against her belly as they lay in their bed at night, but at times he seemed afraid to even acknowledge the child's coming.

One night they had been lying together, holding each other in the dim light from the fire, and he had rested his hand against her stomach. They didn't talk, just enjoyed their closeness as they lay in each other's arms, feeling the occasional kicks and rolls of their child, who always became more active as night approached. Suddenly, both of them noticed the swell of a small movement across the side of Jane's belly, a tiny lump poking up from beneath her nightgown and gliding from one side to the other. They had broken out into laughter at the sight, and Jane covered Edward's hand, moving it to the spot where the lump had been seen.

"A foot," she told him, turning to him with a huge smile, "or a knee or elbow, Mrs. Collins tells me." She pressed down on his hand with hers, reaching up to kiss his cheek.

Edward had moved down in the bed, pushing her nightgown up and laying his head against her abdomen. "Oh, Jane," he whispered, overcome with emotion. She had stroked his hair, urged him to talk to her, but he had shaken his head, his cheek against her stomach, jaw clenched. Eventually he had moved back up to his pillow, where he seemed to come back to himself, smiled at her, and pulled her against him gently. He was obviously moved at this thought of their baby. Other times he seemed to ignore the fact of her pregnancy, other than his solicitous worry over how she felt. But she felt his gaze upon her, watching her often when he thought she was not observing him, his eye following her as she moved through her day.

For a few weeks after his sight had returned, he had been happy, animated with a new-found joy. But as he looked upon Jane, watched her grow larger, her pregnancy more evident each passing week, he seemed to become freshly aware of her condition, his previous worries returning. Now that the birth was imminent, he felt as though some ominous clock was ticking behind him, signaling that his love was in danger, that his darling's very life was in peril.

He had joined in the bustle of activity at Ferndean, as Jane, John, and Mary prepared one of the empty rooms as a nursery. He had even helped, his sleeve rolled up, carefully brushing paint around the windows in small, neat strokes, before John had come in with a larger brush to do the actual walls. He and John had pulled ivy away from the stone walls outside the baby's room, Edward standing on the ground and pulling the clinging vines away close to the ground, while John stood on a ladder and pulled at the higher growth. From the grass, Jane walked back and forth, watching them with a smile on her face, her hand resting upon the bulge of her belly, sometimes reaching back to stretch, her hands held to the small of her back. She looked beautiful, her figure round, the autumn winds blowing her soft shiny hair free from its restraints. At times Edward would stop, just wanting to fill his gaze with the sight of her, always rewarded with her beautiful smile.

This work could have been hired, of course, but Edward, with some sight freshly restored and plenty of time on his hands, had insisted on doing as much as he could do himself, thrilled to have an occupation after three years of a more sedentary life. Jane helped get things organized, exclaiming over the fabrics that Mary brought from town, helping to sew linens and tiny garments. She was so happy, Edward could not believe how joyful she was. He remembered her when she had first come to Thornfield, how serious she had been, how little there had been in her short life to make her truly happy. To see her so radiant now tugged at his heart. He wished he could be as happy as she was, wished he was not so afraid for her.

"I wanted her to be named for you, of course," Edward continued now. "But lately I have thought so much of my mother – wished she were still alive, to be able to know you. She would have loved you, you know."

Jane smiled. "Only because I love you so much. Anyway, Elizabeth is a good choice. I would not like her to have the same name I do, for then we would never know who was being called. She could avoid all manner of responsibility simply by saying, 'But I thought it was Mother you were calling!'"

He laughed. "We could call her by Elizabeth, but give her 'Jane' for a first name. Then she would be named for you, and for both our mothers."

"Jane Elizabeth... " Jane considered for a moment, then nodded. "If you like that, then Jane Elizabeth she shall be."

"And should it be a boy, he will have to be Edward, for his father," Jane continued. "There has never been any other thought on the matter, for me."

Her husband groaned. "Oh, no, I don't like that. Surely there are countless other names that would do much better."

"No!" Jane said firmly. "Nothing else has ever crossed my mind. 'Edward Rochester', that is all there is to it. How did you get your name, by the way? Are you named after someone in the family?"

Edward shook his head. "My brother was named after our father. But I was named for a king."

"That is fitting," his wife said, kissing his hand.

Edward shook his head. "No, it's not. But my mother loved history, loved to read about royalty. My parents really wanted a girl... that's what they were hoping for; my brother made sure to tell me. But I was foisted upon them rather than the desired daughter, and so I am named after one of England's kings. My father never listened to a word my mother said, so he didn't even know which king. Hopefully not someone too evil and despotic."

"It is a lovely name," Jane said loyally, "and I shall be proud to give it to our son."

"Edward Eyre Rochester," Edward said, as she frowned, thinking, then nodded. He smiled. "But then we will run into the same dilemma, you calling me, and me replying that I thought it was our son you were calling."

"We shall have to think of a nickname for him," she told him.

Edward tilted his head back on the sofa. "When I was a little boy, my nurse used to call me 'Neddie'." Jane smiled. "Only in private, of course. One time, my father heard her call me that; she had no idea he was nearby, listening. He was furious, 'That is Master Edward, to you!'" He imitated his father's angry tones. "She was wonderful, Nellie; she cared for me deeply. It was more than just a job to her." He shook his head, looked over at Jane.

"She was Grace Poole's mother, did I ever tell you that?" His face grew soft, his mind far back in time. "Nellie Carey. She nursed me, for my mother was too ill, and it was not done, then, anyway, for the lady of the house to feed her infants. Grace and I nursed side by side, like siblings, really, for over a year. Then my mother hired Nellie to care for me during the day. It was she who came to me in the night, to tell me my mother had died. It was her shoulder I cried upon, her hand I held when I was brought to my mother's bedside to kiss her good-bye.

Jane touched his face. "What happened to Nellie?"

Edward sighed. "My father had engaged a tutor by then, to teach me. He dismissed Nellie, afraid too many women would turn me into a milksop. His word. I was tutored during the day, and John, who was newly hired, was to assist me with my personal needs. My father had hired a man to replace our aging and doddering old butler, but the new butler soon departed to be the proprietor of the nearby inn, and so John was brought in to be trained. He was kind to me, but for the most part, I was left alone. Indulged in some ways, ignored in others. I still played with Grace, and sneaked over to visit Nellie.

"Mrs. Fairfax was kind, and wanted to watch over me, but she was very busy with parish activities. Her first duty was to her husband, the incumbent pastor of Hay. She wasn't hired as housekeeper until I was ready to return from Jamaica. So Nellie remained the closest thing to a mother I had. Father did not like me to be with her; as I said, I had to be sneaky to visit her, and at times weeks went by without my seeing her. She was quite ill by the time I was twelve or thirteen, and while I was away at school, she died."

Edward seemed to remember himself, shook his head. "So this child can be 'Ned', in memory of Nellie's name for me. What do you think of that?"

Jane smiled, "I think that will be lovely." She cocked her head, thinking, and asked, "Edward, whatever did become of Grace?"

Edward shook his head, "She was taken away while I was still unconscious, and it was a long time before I thought to inquire. Carter said his questions had been turned away by her son, during my recovery. Before I was brought to Ferndean, I established an account for her at a Millcote bank, not an annuity, but a generous payment. The estate manager says it is still there, in its entirety, although Grace has been apprised of it. She is still alive, I'm told, but answers no inquiries and responds to no messages." He shrugged. "Someday, I must try to contact her. I am nearly afraid to. I imagine she and I are both afraid to see each other."

Jane sat for a few moments, watching him stare at the fire, then leaned upon his shoulder, pushing herself up off the sofa. "I'm very tired, shall we go upstairs to bed?"

Edward, still frowning, looked up at her, all his fear and love for her written on his face. She knew that this discussion – his speaking of the women who had loved him in his childhood, and whom he had loved – had not distracted him from thinking about her. Perhaps it had reminded him of the love he could lose. Jane stopped, bent to him, her hand against his cheek. She looked at him intently.

"Edward, I know you are afraid for me, but everything will be fine, I know it will." She put her hand under his chin, made him meet her eyes. "Please try not to be frightened."

He looked up at her, trying to smile, then he stood up and reached for her hand, following her upstairs to their room. In the past, when he had been upset and troubled, she had offered him the comfort of her body, knowing that her warmth and closeness could soothe him better than any words. But for weeks, he had refused to touch her in that way, afraid of hurting her, and so she could only embrace him and tell him how much she loved him. Her sweet words did not help, as it was their love that made him so afraid to lose her.

21 October 1839

Edward lay awake for several moments, blinking in disorientation at the change in the brightness of the room. Squinting in the midnight gloom he realized that the fire in the hearth, usually banked and reduced to glowing embers at this hour, was burning brightly, the flames leaping and crackling. He rolled over and reached for Jane, but her side of the bed was empty. Sitting up, he saw her standing close to the fire, her shawl wrapped around her, looking into the blaze.

He reached for his dressing gown and got out of bed. "Dearest, are you well?" He wrapped the gown around him against the late October chill of the room and moved towards her.

She turned at his approach. "Oh, Edward, forgive me. I did not mean to disturb you."

She turned back to the fire, "I just cannot seem to rest easily in bed and I cannot get warm. I thought I would put more wood on the fire and stand in front of it until the discomfort in my back and legs eases a bit."

He stepped behind her, encircling her with his arms, wrapping his gown around her also. "Are you in pain? Shall I send John for Mrs. Collins?"

"No, I don't need the midwife yet." She sighed and leaned back against him. "At least, I don't believe I do. I thought that it would be more obvious and dramatic than this, but I'm just uncomfortable. I thought that if it continued I would go speak to Mary. She has had children, she can advise me. Perhaps I just need to move around." Her fingers found his hand, stroked it gently, tracing his knuckles.

Edward felt the growing fear inside him. He knew this was a natural thing, had known it was coming, but he was not ready for the reality of it. He clasped her closer to him, burying his face in her loosened hair. She smelled of wood-smoke and lavender. He breathed in her scent and kissed her head. She felt so small, so vulnerable in his arms. His hand moved down her front, over the curve of her rounded belly, and rested there. The child inside her stirred, rolling against his palm. A sweet pain seized him and he knew he would give anything – his newly restored sight, his life, his very soul – to keep them safe.

Such fear – that he could lose her, that his beloved wife could die delivering this child. Other men lost wives and children both; it happened every day… as his father had eventually lost his mother. He had grown up with his brother's accusations in his ears – that his mother would have lived a long and healthy life had she not given birth to him. He did not think he could survive if he lost Jane.

But he did not want to frighten her. He kissed her hair again, bent and pressed his lips to her neck, spoke in spite of himself.

"I wish we were at Thornfield, " he murmured. "I wish Carter were here to care for you. I would rest easier."

"Mrs. Collins is an able woman," Jane responded. "Some of the first infants she delivered have grandchildren now. She will care for me well, she and Mary." Jane turned around and looked up at her husband, grasping the lapels of his robe. "You have been through this before, when Adèle was born. You should not be afraid."

"Céline had an accoucheur to attend her, not just an untrained midwife." He shook his head. "And I was out shooting when Adèle was born, and didn't return until it was all over. She came earlier than I expected." A shadow passed over his face briefly as he stared over her shoulder at the leaping fire. He did not tell her the truth: that not once had he ever feared for the lives of Céline and Adèle. It had never occurred to him that one or both might not survive the birth process.

Jane took his hand in both of hers, "Mrs. Collins is not untrained – she has delivered babies for over forty years. We settled this matter months ago, or so I thought. You know if there is a problem, she will send for the doctor." She kissed his hand. "And I would not want a man with me, unless it is you. I wish you could be there with me." She smiled, "Not that Mrs. Collins would ever allow that!"

"I would if I could," he answered her, reaching up to push back the loose strands of hair from her face. "If it were allowed, I would stay with you. I would do it all for you, take the pain for you, if I could."

"I know you would." She leaned her head against his chest, feeling selfish for worrying. He had suffered such physical pain already. If he could lose an eye, have his hand amputated, suffer the surgery he had undergone to restore his sight, she had no right to fear a little pain with such a great reward at the end.

He felt her small fingers tighten on his arms, heard her breath hiss between her teeth as she inhaled sharply. Before he could say anything, she bent her head harder against his chest, "Edward, please get Mary for me, will you?"

The night had worn on endlessly for Edward. After dressing quickly and knocking on their door to awaken Mary and John, he had remained with Jane, rubbing her back, giving her sips of water, supporting her as she walked endlessly back and forth across the kitchen floor while they waited for John to return with the midwife. When Mrs. Collins had arrived with her young assistant, she and Mary had whisked Jane into the small bedroom off the kitchen, which had been made ready for the birth two weeks before. There the women had remained.

"She's made fair progress, I think she is more than halfway there, from the signs I see," the grey-haired midwife told him, coming out to answer his questions and let him know what was happening. "But it's her first, and she'll be at it awhile." She was a stout, large-breasted woman who no doubt made free to tell God Himself where to sit and stand. "She's a wee little thing, but young and strong, and quite capable of doing this without problems, like most young women. Now you run along – you've other things you could be doing. I believe you're the cause of all this commotion to begin with." She chuckled as she waved him away from the door.

Edward had retired to the dressing room to wash up and get himself in order, but then had resumed his spot in the kitchen. He wore no coat or cravat, just a white shirt, which was open at the neck, and despite this, he was still sweating. The kitchen fire was kept blazing, water on the boil, and the room was very warm.

He sat stiffly at the kitchen table, hand balled into a fist in front of him, resisting all of John's attempts to offer him comfort. John had placed a cup of tea before him, but it had grown cold, and he flatly refused all offers of food. He found himself holding his breath for long periods, and had to remind himself to breathe. He stared straight ahead, his thoughts in turmoil. He could feel his heart thudding painfully within his breast, with Fear his closest companion in these long hours.

The time passed slowly, and when the silence in the house gave way to Jane's low moans, and then her cries, he stationed himself once more outside the heavy oak door, locked securely against the risk of his panicked entrance, pacing desperately. Once, long before, at Thornfield, he had paced and waited outside her bolted door, frantic to know what was going on inside. The door had finally opened, and she had come out, only to leave him.

God, please don't take her from me. I cannot live without her.

Jane lay in a haze of pain. By the time one wave ended, another was beginning, and she started to feel that her life would be reduced to this – struggling to get through each red-hot, gripping agony, only to catch her breath in time for the next one. During her early labour she had tried to stay silent, knowing that Edward would hear and be frightened for her, but finally she could no longer control what she did as each contraction overtook her, shook her in its powerful clutches, completely overpowered her mind and body.

"Mrs. Rochester! Jane!" She heard Mrs. Collins' commanding voice. "You are almost finished, love. You have done beautifully. Open your eyes, lamb, look at me."

Jane forced her eyes open. They felt like two burning coals in her head. She was hot, then cold. She shivered uncontrollably, feeling as though her body was trying to separate itself from her very soul. She lay on her side, burying her face in the pillow each time a contraction started, trying to bite down on it to control the sounds she heard herself making.

Mrs. Collins looked into her eyes. "Your waters have not yet broken. I am going to break them for you with the next pain. Then I want you to roll to your back and bear down, and it will not be long, I promise."

Jane felt the next wave start, and felt herself push down without even meaning to. A hot gush flooded the linen shift she wore, her legs, and the bottom of the bed. The women helped her roll to her back, supporting her head and her legs. She heard Mary's voice in her ear as the woman used a cold damp rag to stroke her hair back from her sweating face. "Nearly there, Mrs. Rochester, do not stop now... " She felt Mary's arm supporting her back, assisting her to lean up. Mrs. Collins and her assistant held her legs apart as they encouraged her to bear down.

She pressed her hands into the damp bed, her fingernails scratching desperately at the sheets beneath her, and although she heard the women urging her to grasp her knees to help steady herself, she could not let go of the bed, her fingers digging into the mattress.

She took a deep breath, bent her head and pushed down again, feeling that she was being torn in two. The world was going black around her, and she heard her own screaming come from somewhere far away...

Edward stood near the door, his forehead against the rough wood. His breath came fast, his fist was clenched tightly as he heard Jane's scream. He pressed his hand flat to the door as if he could shove it open by sheer will.

He was thinking of his marriage, of the warm, sweet nights in Jane's arms. He had felt himself so fortunate in his tender and passionate wife, and he had loved her freely with all the pent up desire of his long and barren years alone. She rarely refused him, and he thought of her arms and legs around him, her soft cries of pleasure in his ear as he moved within her, thought of the total delight and enjoyment each had found in the other.

He was surprised, standing outside her door, to realize how much the sounds of pain resembled the sounds of pleasure. He listened to her moan, and remembered other moans, he heard her cry and thought of other cries. It was almost more than he could bear. He expressed his heart and soul during their lovemaking, tried to take the strength of his love and passion and leave it deep within her each time he took her to their marriage bed, and he could not believe that this was the result. He could not think of the miracle of it, his seed taken hold within her, his child grown inside Jane and about to be born. He could only think of what she was enduring now. To hear her on the other side of that door, crying out in pain because of what he had done to her... His heart smote him, guilt came to share the space in his heart that fear had so lately occupied.

Jane, Jane... He wished he had never laid a hand upon her. At this moment he would have traded all the joy and rapture he had known with her, if he could just spare her this.

He heard her scream again, and then, rising above the sound, an infant's loud and furious wail.

Jane felt the sudden, blessed release of pain and pressure as the baby was delivered. With a cry she fell back, breathing hard, then leaned up on her elbows, lifting her head to watch as Mrs. Collins placed the infant on the towels that the assistant had laid between her legs.

The baby was silent – blue and motionless. Something froze inside her, her breath caught. She could not speak.

For one heart-stopping moment she watched as the midwife began to rub the baby with a cloth. Then, to her overwhelming relief, she saw the infant's limbs move, saw it squirm, and heard the glorious cry ring out.

She cried out again, with joy, her head falling back, her heart too full to speak. Mrs. Collins smiled up at her, as Mary placed pillows behind her so she could sit up more easily.

"It's a boy, Mrs. Rochester," the midwife told her, still drying the baby vigorously. "They often take a second or two to start up, but he's a fine one, and looks very well." She lifted him off the wet towels, then laid him on some dry ones. Her assistant handed her two strings, which she used to tie the infant's cord off in two different places. She was then handed a knife, and deftly cut the cord between the two ties. She wrapped the baby in a blanket, lifted the squalling child and reached up to place him in Jane's arms. Jane took him from her, and all sense of time and place narrowed to the one fact of her son there before her. She scarcely noticed as the women delivered the afterbirth, and examined her, determining that no stitches were needed and that all was well.

Jane clutched the baby to her, laughing and crying at once as she looked at him. He was still a little blue, but grew steadily pinker as she watched him draw a breath and cry, then draw another and cry again. His fists were balled close to his face, his tiny mouth opened wide, his eyes squeezed shut as he shrieked with indignation. His little chin quivered with his exertions.

His mother lifted a corner of the blanket that covered him, took in the sight of him, his little arms and legs, his tiny male sex, the dark hair plastered to his fragile skull. She kissed him and whispered, "Oh, my little darling, hello!" She looked up as Mrs. Collins came to her side, and glanced over at Mary, who was sniffling, a handkerchief clutched to her face.

"Please, would you tell my husband that we are well?" she asked Mrs. Collins. "I know he is waiting outside; he is probably so frightened." She turned to Mary, "You know how he will be, he has been so afraid for me." Mary nodded, her eyes full of tears.

"Aye, the master's thought of nought but what could go wrong;" Mary agreed, "that's just his way."

Mrs. Collins directed Mary to take the baby and get him ready for his bath, and told her young assistant to fetch the kettle of hot water, then she headed for the door.

"Mr. Rochester, you have a son," the midwife told him. "And your wife is fine, she did a lovely job. An easy birth, although I know it never sounds like it to those who wait and pace outside."

Edward registered the news, nodding as his entire body relaxed and he slumped back against the wall. He wanted only to see Jane, to see for himself that she was well. As he opened his mouth to ask for her, Mrs. Collins said, "We've some things to set to rights, then you can see your wife and son. Go have a brandy, you look like Hell."

And now Mary stood at the door, beckoning to him. With knees shaking, he crossed the threshold, going straight to Jane as she lay on the narrow bed. He heard water splashing, heard the angry crying of the child as he suffered the indignity of his first bath. But he saw only Jane. She looked so small under the blankets, her hair freshly combed and braided, her face white, dark shadows beneath her emerald eyes. Her face bore the temporary look of broken blood vessels from vigorous pushing. Her lips were dry and cracked – but she smiled at him, smiled radiantly as he came towards her. He sank down beside her on the bed, laid his head on her breast. His voice was muffled, "My darling, I will never put you through this again."

She was laughing. Laughing! Her warm hands came up to cradle his head, her fingers twining in his thick hair. She kissed him over and over. "Oh, Edward! My Edward, I am fine; it was not so very bad. And he is so beautiful!"

Mrs. Collins came over to them. "Will you get off that bed and give the girl a moment's peace! Sit down in the chair and I'll hand you this child." She shook her head – what fools men were. As if a one of them remembered their promises the moment their wives recovered. This one would be no better and more likely worse, besotted as he was with his young wife.

He moved to the chair next to the bed and Mrs. Collins laid the child in his arms, first pulling the blankets aside to show him that it was indeed a boy. Tucking them back around the baby, she urged him to hold the infant closer. "Don't be so afraid of him; he's not got a tooth in his head, he'll not bite you!"

Edward barely heard her as he looked at the face of his son. He was so tiny and yet so perfect. He had silky black hair, and his long, finely-shaped fingers were a miniature of Edward's own. The baby opened his eyes, blinking in the light, and Edward saw his own eyes looking back at him. His eyes as they had once been, large and dark, with the promise of brilliance to come. They were framed by dark lashes, sparse yet, but long. The baby waved his tiny clenched fists, his eyes fixed upon his father's face. Edward felt his heart swell within his breast, and he squeezed his eyelids tightly shut as he felt the tears well. He sent a prayer to Heaven, "Thank you, God, you who have once again tempered judgment with great mercy."

He looked down at the little boy, feeling the tears beginning to spill over. He bent his head and pressed his lips to the baby's soft forehead. He reached out to his wife, who grasped his hand tightly. "Thank you, my love," he said. "Thank you for my son."

He looked up at the midwife, "We all thank you, Mrs. Collins." She nodded at him.

He looked at his son again, shaking his head in wonder, "He's so very tiny."

Mrs. Collins smiled, "Yes, but look at his mother! We'd have had some work getting him out, if he took after you." She gestured at the infant in his arms. "Now he's out, you can work on getting him as big as his father."

His father! Edward shook his head in disbelief, looking at the child. *Oh my God, I am this child's father. He is truly my son, how can it be, after all this time? I never thought I would have all this.* His heart was overwhelmed, he could not believe it. He started to laugh, but the tears still came. Jane watched them both, her face full of joy and tenderness.

Suddenly she was so tired, her eyes were growing heavy. Mrs. Collins felt her abdomen, smiled. "All is well. Would you like some food?"

Jane shook her head, blinking. "I just want to sleep; I'm so tired all of a sudden." The midwife nodded. "That's fine, it's what you need, but first try to feed this youngster a little. It'll get him well started, and keep you from bleeding too much. Then you can sleep the day away."

Mrs. Collins leaned over to take the baby from his father. Then, smiling, she jerked her chin towards Edward as she said to Mary, "Take this one and feed him. And liquor him up a little, I think he could use it."

Edward shifted in the chair and stretched his legs. He sat up and looked over at Jane, then at the wooden cradle positioned between his chair and the bed. There was a soft light coming from a lamp on a table nearby, and he reached for the pocket watch that Jane had given back to him when he had regained his sight. It was nearly four o'clock in the morning.

Jane lay on her back, sleeping deeply, a little more colour in her face than she had had earlier in the evening. In the cradle, the baby slept on his back as well. Edward leaned over to check that the blankets were tucked around him, that he breathed easily. As Edward had dozed fitfully in the chair, he had been aware of the tiny baby noises the child made, and he found the sounds reassuring. He made a minute adjustment to the blankets, and his index finger strayed to the baby's cheek, softly touching its satiny roundness.

His son was nearly fourteen hours old. Earlier in the evening, Jane had fed the baby for the second time, her awkwardness bringing a lump to the throat of her watching husband. Such a strength of feeling rose within him, such a great protectiveness as he watched the two people he most loved. They both seemed so vulnerable.

Jane had laughed at herself as she had leaned back against the pillows, putting the hungry baby to her breast as she had been instructed. For the first feeding, Mrs. Collins had hovered over her, helping her to position the infant correctly, fussing over her two patients as she assisted Jane to move the tiny boy from one breast to the other. But the second time, Mrs. Collins had not been present, and Jane's wide eyes had met Edward's gaze with sudden alarm, as both parents realized that they were responsible for this fragile little life.

Jane had succeeded in feeding little Ned, and then had relaxed against the pillows as she cradled him in the crook of her arm, wincing at the cramping that the feeding had intensified in her abdomen. Edward had moved tentatively from his chair to the side of the bed, looking furtively about him as he did so.

"Is it safe to sit here now?" he asked, sliding up near his wife to peer at the red, wrinkled face of his son in her arms.

Jane had laughed softly, "Yes," she whispered, "There's only Lily, Mrs. Collins' assistant, and she is supposed to be sleeping on a pallet by the kitchen fire. I'll not tell her if you sit by us, I promise."

Together they had peered at the face of their child, and had laughed at the idea of the name "Edward" for such a tiny mite. They agreed that he would have to grow into his imposing name.

"We can always start by calling him 'Neddie' – as his father used to be known," Jane had suggested.

Edward thought for a second, then shook his head. "No, not 'Neddie'. Someday he'll wish to grow out of it, and by then no one will let him. Let us go on with our previous plan and call him 'Ned' right from the first. It's a simple, strong name, although he looks far too little for a strong name at the moment."

"You're right," Jane agreed, "and it certainly is not so ponderous as 'Edward Eyre Rochester'." She leaned over, handing the baby to his father. "Now, could you please place little Master Ned in his cradle, for I fear I will fall asleep while he is still in my arms."

Edward had awkwardly rewrapped him, and placed him in his cradle, but before they were able to resume any conversation, Lily had come in, roused by the sounds of their voices.

She nodded with approval at Jane's account of the feeding, and picked up the baby to carry him over to a low table and change his diapers. She paid no attention to his kicking and the howling that had ensued as he was unwrapped and disturbed. She deftly stripped off his old diapers, dropping them into a covered bucket and tying on several new ones. She then wrapped him in his blankets far more efficiently than Edward had been able to, and laid him back in his cradle.

Lily then moved over to Jane, palpating her abdomen and looking over at Edward with a pointed glance. He knew she wanted him to leave the room, but he feigned ignorance, instead getting up from his chair to move to the other side of the room, his gaze rising upward to the one small, high window in the room. Nothing but darkness met his eye, the window a black rectangle in the flickering lamplight of the room. The midwife's assistant sighed, then got warm water and rags from a table near the fireplace. She helped Jane to wash up, replacing the soiled linens with clean ones. She picked up the bucket of dirty laundry, leaving the room with one last reproachful glance at Edward.

He returned to Jane, a frown on his face. "It appears she does not want me here as she tends to your needs."

Jane smiled, then reached out to her husband, who took her hand and lifted it to his lips. His unshaven face felt scratchy against her skin, and she laid her hand against his jaw, rubbing her thumb across his whiskered cheek. "Really, my love, I wish you would go upstairs to our bed. I don't want to think of your sleeping in that hard chair. I'm fine, truly. If I can sleep I will be even stronger, and Lily and Mary are here to assist me should I need it."

Edward shook his head. "No, I could not sleep if I were apart from you, and I find now, from the child. It's a strange thing – he has not been here a full day and already he seems part of what I need near me to keep me content." He raised Jane's hand back to his lips and kissed it again, "Sleep, my darling, and let me stay near both of you."

She smiled at her husband and then squeezed his hand, leaning back on the pillows, a deep, contented sigh escaping her as she relaxed.

He watched her now in the soft lamplight. Her face was relaxed, her breathing even and unlaboured. He sighed, thinking of his fear yesterday, his panic at the thought of the ordeal she faced. He had not ceased to thank God for His mercy in allowing Jane to emerge alive and healthy from the childbirth experience.

He knew that things could still go wrong, that women sometimes had complications even after a safe delivery. He thought again of how fragile she seemed, how he sometimes felt that she could slip away from him so easily. Yet she had laughed over what she had gone through, had held the tiny creature and kissed him with such love and adoration, with seemingly no thought of the pain she had endured to bring him into the world. Edward marvelled at her strength, her courage.

His love seemed too great for his heart to hold, too vast to be contained in this small room. His eye was fixed on Jane's face as he leaned back in his chair, folding his arms across his chest. He did not notice the discomfort of the hard chair, for next to him was his entire world.

November, 1839

At one month of age, Edward Eyre Rochester was christened in the Ferndean church by the same parson who had joined his parents in marriage. His godmother was Diana Rivers, who had come to visit and also to share the exciting news of her recent engagement to Captain Fitzjames. Her sister Mary was unable to travel, due to her lying-in with her daughter Diana, born two weeks after little Ned Rochester.

But Mary Rivers Wharton, her husband, and their newborn daughter would see them all in the spring, when the Rochesters travelled there for yet another wedding. Last December had seen the wedding of the Whartons; this coming April would see the wedding of Diana and her Captain. Ordinarily, there would have been visitors to Ferndean this past summer, but with the pregnancies of each wife, and Edward's surgery and recovery, plans had been changed. But they all looked forward to seeing each other again.

Following the baptism, the group headed back to the house, where Mary had prepared a lovely luncheon, presided over by their host, who accepted everyone's toasts to his new son and heir.

Edward finally was relieved of the fear he had carried since the news of his wife's pregnancy months ago. In his dreams he had lost her over and over, but the reality was as Carter and the midwife had said – all had gone well. She had recovered in a very short time, looked the same as she always had, and felt, she said, "better than ever".

In a few short days, she was sneaking out of her bed to pick up her son and attend to his cries, although she always hastily laid him back down in his cradle and got back into bed when she heard the knock that heralded Mrs. Collins' daily visit. The whole household was afraid of Mrs. Collins, and no one wanted to go against her. Mary privately felt that Jane was fine, sniffing "I had my first in the morning, and that night was up cooking for my man and all his friends that were out haying that day!" But when the midwife was in the house, they all did as she said, even the master.

Edward loved his wife more than ever, although he could hardly believe that he could love her more than he had. He almost felt she'd been given back to him once again. And his love for his son was enormous, more than his heart could hold.

He had been afraid he would not know what to do, as he had had no loving and nurturing father from whom to take an example, but he realized that when he followed his natural instincts, his fears were unfounded. His love for his son came as naturally as his own breath and heartbeat, and he daily grew more adept at handling the infant, at knowing what he needed when he cried.

At times Edward would hold the baby, his fingers tracing the softness of his son's skin and his tiny features, and he would think of his own father. He had come to realize that if John Rochester had not loved him, it was due to some lack in the father, and not to any failings of the son. That conviction settled something in him, healing a long-time injury within him that he had not even realized was there.

The baby was content with him, and would grow quiet in his father's arms as well as he did in his mother's. On the day before his christening, when his great dark eyes had fastened on to his father's face, and he had given his first real, wide-awake smile, Edward felt he'd been given the world. He would lay a finger in the baby's palm, feeling his son's tiny hand close around it, and know there was no greater contentment to be had upon this earth. In all his years of travelling, no place he'd ever visited – nothing he had experienced – could compare to this.

Jane was nursing their son, on the advice of Mrs. Collins, who had said, "That's why royalty can't seem to keep their legal issue alive, and why the farmers are breeding all over; those that nurse their own do better. And I don't think you could pay enough money to lure a wet nurse out to this place, lost in the woods. So you'd best just do it yourself."

She had leaned close to Jane then, and said, "And you've got a better chance of not having to go through this again anytime soon, if you keep him to the breast. Mind you, it won't work till he's ten years old, but it should buy you a year or two, if you're lucky." While Jane wouldn't have minded going through it again, she did not think her husband could stand the strain of another pregnancy, at least not any time in the near future.

Now, on the day of their son's baptism, Jane looked at Edward, standing at the table, holding his glass aloft and looking as happy as she had ever seen him. She raised their son to her shoulder, rubbed his back, his downy little fragrant head bobbing against her cheek. She looked around at the assembled friends and family, thinking how blessed they were, and how far they all had come.

Christmas of 1839 was in every way a world of difference from his first Christmas here three years before, Edward thought, looking around at the Ferndean parlour. He still remembered sitting in his chair before the fire, utterly alone, his body still plagued by the pain and fatigue of his recent injuries, his heart a cold stone within his breast. There was no hope at all in him, and he wanted only to sleep; sought only the blessed relief of a few hours' oblivion from the nightmare of his life.

Now he wanted to laugh, as he looked around. The walls were hung with pine garlands that exuded the crisp scent of a winter forest all about the room. The garlands were decorated with red velvet ribbons, and candles burned everywhere. Pilot lay on the rug before the roaring fire, his paws moving occasionally as he chased rabbits over the lush green of long-remembered meadows. The dog's belly was full of remnants of greasy Christmas goose, which he would tomorrow morning leave by the front door, to his relief and Mary's annoyance. But today he slept, content.

Edward watched his servants, John and Mary. He was so grateful for their faithfulness, their loyal devotion to him and his. He had given them a large bonus, and tomorrow they would take his carriage and go for several days' holiday with their family. Today they stood in the parlour for a few moments, accepting their gift and lifting a glass of wine in a toast to the coming year.

Adèle, home from school for a few weeks, sat on the sofa, Jane next to her, assisting her to hold little Ned in her arms. She was thrilled with the baby, holding him close and playing with him, no sign of jealousy evident in her at all. Ned watched her, from time to time breaking out in a large, gummy grin as Adèle made faces and talked to him. Edward watched the two children.

One was his without a doubt; the other... well, how could he ever know? One he loved with every fibre of his nature, and as for the other, his feelings were a little more complicated. He knew he did not feel a father's love for Adèle. Not when he thought of the pure adoration he felt every time he thought of his son. He would have given his life for Ned without a moment's hesitation, and he felt a tiny shame in his breast that he could not say he felt that way about Adèle. But he cared for her and would always see to her welfare. He would never turn her out to make her own way in the world, even if he did not truly love her.

Surely it was not just her parentage. He knew that many men stepped in and reared other men's children with the love and devotion they would have for their own seed. John, he knew, was as fond of Mary's children as he could be, considering her grandchildren his own. Edward knew his feelings for Adèle were much more confused, and at times he hated himself for it. He knew it was all tied to how he had felt about Céline, how his pride had been so wounded, his heart so lacerated by her. He had grown up knowing his father did not love him, feeling himself to be inherently unlovable. Céline's actions had only strengthened that certainty. And every time he saw her daughter, he was reminded of that nagging feeling of unworthiness.

But Jane loved him. His gaze turned from the children to his wife. She adored him, and had made him feel for the first time in his life like a man worth loving. He watched her now, laughing with Adèle, leaning over to kiss the girl's cheek before taking her son into her own arms. She saw him watching her, and smiled at him.

He smiled back, his largest, most unreserved smile, given only to her, and now to his son. Oh, she loved him, he had no doubt. She was the most loving woman he knew, and this house was filled with it, overflowing with the warmth that she had brought to it. Everyone there felt it. She was truly the heart of his home.

He thought of the sweet nights they had spent the last two months. Ned slept in a cradle by their bed, and when he cried to be fed at night, Edward would get up, scooping him up and bringing him to Jane. She would roll over sleepily, take Ned in her arms, and arrange herself to feed him. She would unfasten the front of her nightgown, lay the baby down with his head at her breast.

His parents would laugh to see him, bellowing with indignation, his little head whipping back and forth, rooting frantically as he caught the scent of his mother's milk. Jane would guide her nipple to his open mouth, and they would laugh again to see him begin to nurse, his tiny fists working against her breast, gulping loudly at first, then settling down to a steady contented sucking. Edward would reach over, stroke his son's silky head with his fingers, leaning up on his elbow to watch his wife and baby, never tiring of the sight of them together. He would reach up, stroke Jane's cheek as well, feeling her lips brush against his hand, her eyes moving from her husband to their son.

He watched them now, his family.

My life is perfect. I have everything I could ever want. How can I thank you, Lord? I do not deserve all this, but I truly thank You...

Chapter 56 - The Rochesters

1839 - 1842

Ferndean, once such a dark, dank, and forbidding place, now echoed with the sounds of a family's life. The birth of Ned Rochester had given a new pulse to the rather sedate rhythms of the manor, and everyone responded to it.

John and Mary, who had known Edward Rochester since he was young, had been surprised and gratified to see their once stern and forbidding employer go from a broken and wounded shell of a man to a smiling, quietly satisfied husband. Now they looked at each other in amazement to hear him laughing, talking in animated tones to his wife and son, once again an active and involved employer and master of two estates.

Despite his father's own description of Ferndean's damp inclement air, Ned thrived and prospered as he grew older there. He was chubby and healthy on his mother's milk, and grew from a bright-eyed infant to an active toddler. His parents, busy with the operations of their estates and investments, knew that he would need a nursemaid, and were able to engage Mary's granddaughter Molly.

Molly was only sixteen years old, but was the eldest of a family of seven, and had been working for a Millcote family since she was thirteen, giving her plenty of experience with children. She was happy to leave her present situation to be with her grandmother, and to work for Jane, whom she had met on previous visits.

Ned began to walk shortly after his first birthday, and soon showed a great interest in climbing, which brought moments of anxiety to his father. Jane tended to be relaxed in her reaction to the normal minor injuries of the growing child, letting Ned experience the usual bumps and scrapes of any active baby, while Edward watched him nervously, wanting to follow him around to prevent any little accident from occurring.

"Edward, you must let him take his little bumps, darling," she told him, watching him castigate himself for his carelessness when he was a bit too slow to prevent Ned from falling while running out on the lawn. She kissed Ned's chubby hands, which she had examined for abrasions, and after determining that there was no real injury, she set him back down. He was soon running again, attempting to chase poor Pilot, who had grown old and found no amusement in the attentions of this young interloper.

"I know," Edward sighed, "but I cannot stand to hear him cry, and don't want him to ever be hurt. I believe I am too old for all this!"

"Well, it's a bit late now to think of that," Jane said, kissing him and moving off to rescue Pilot. "You had best get used to this, for it will not get any better from now on!"

And indeed it did not, for in early summer, when Ned was twenty months old, they found out Jane was once again expecting. She had continued to nurse Ned as long as he would take the breast, but after his first birthday, he had begun to wean himself, taking his milk from a cup and messily picking his way through the cut-up food placed before him. True to Mrs. Collins' prediction, little changed in the Rochester marriage. Edward and Jane still craved each other as much as they always had, and so another child was inevitable.

With the progression of Jane's second pregnancy, Edward began to realize that Ferndean was not going to be adequate for a growing family. He had been surprisingly happy there, much more so than he had ever thought when first he was brought there to live.

The dark rooms that had once smelled of mildew and mouse-droppings had improved greatly with all the changes that had come about with constant habitation. Edward had finally found married happiness within these walls, his son had been conceived and born here, and soon they would welcome another child. But decisions would have to be made. Should rooms be added on to the existing building? Should another home be built, or should he take his family and move to a new home?

It was Jane who requested that they move back to Thornfield, and rebuild there. She had an attachment to that place that Edward could not fathom, as the thought of it still made him shudder, with all its dark and hateful memories.

"Think of it, Edward," she told him one autumn night as they discussed the subject. They were lying in bed, a warm fire blazing, Ned sleeping in the bed between them with his thumb in his mouth, his little index finger curled around his nose. Molly had brought him in after his bath, his curly hair damp, dressed in his long nightshirt. He had crawled in with them, chattering endlessly to them both, and then had finally grown sleepy and drifted off. His parents, whose patience could be sorely tried by the constant activity and talk of their two-year-old son, found that when he was asleep they could not bear to stop looking at his angelic countenance, and so neither of them had moved him back to the nursery. Jane rolled over awkwardly, shifting her weight to accommodate her growing belly, and faced her husband, who was lying on his side, his fingers absently toying with his son's dark curls.

He smiled at her as she continued, "We don't have to build on the exact site of the old Hall. We can move the new house over somewhat – there is still a large grassy expanse next to it. We can put new gardens in the site where the Hall was. The old stones would make a lovely wall around a garden, or a very nice terrace."

Edward raised his eyebrows. "You've been doing a lot of thinking on this subject, haven't you?"

"Thinking, yes, and sketching too!" she said, beginning to gesture excitedly. "I can just see it: no turrets or rookeries or dark mysterious rooms, just a large, airy home for a family, big rooms, plenty of windows. I have jotted down ideas, and would show them to you, except it would involve my getting out of bed, and I find that just rolling over is more effort than I want to expend right now."

"Is this your way of telling me that I will be the one to take Ned back to the nursery?" Edward asked her with a laugh.

"Would you?" she asked him, smiling at him, reaching over to trail her fingertips over his cheek. She stretched, "I feel much less inclined to move this time; this child is making me positively lazy." She watched as her husband stood, leaning over to lift Ned up to his shoulder. Ned wiggled and murmured, turning his head restlessly. His father shushed him and patted his back, turning towards the door.

"Will you think about it?" Jane asked him. "And then if you are inclined, I can show you my ideas later?"

Edward paused in the doorway, looking at her over their son's head. "You know how just the thought of Thornfield chills my heart," he told her. "But I will think about it. Perhaps we can banish enough ghosts and demons to render the place less terrifying."

In December 1841, when Ned was a little over two years old, Jane gave birth to Jane Elizabeth Rochester in the same small room off the kitchen where her son had been born.

Her labour progressed quickly, the contractions starting shortly after breakfast and growing strong in just a couple of hours. John left to get Mrs. Collins, and Jane's water broke as she was changing into her nightgown with Mary's assistance.

Ned, frightened by the tense atmosphere of the house, had followed his mother into the room, clinging to her legs and crying as she sat on the side of the bed, trying to cope with her pains as well as comforting her little boy. Edward lifted him as Ned screamed and kicked, and carried him out of the room to the kitchen, too distracted by his son to be as anxious as he had been the last time Jane had disappeared into that bedroom.

Molly offered to take him, but Edward said he would take charge of Ned, freeing her to fetch and carry for Mary, who was tending to Jane. By the time Edward had Ned settled at the table and was feeding him a hastily prepared lunch, Mrs. Collins had arrived, and less than an hour later, the vigorous cry of his daughter was heard throughout the house.

Edward was relieved that things had progressed so quickly, and thrilled with his little girl. He held her closely, marveling at her tiny fingers and sweet little face, while Ned huddled possessively in the bed next to his mother, scowling at the newcomer with a face so like his father's when angry, that it made his mother laugh gaily and point out the similarity.

Unlike her brother, Elizabeth did not strongly resemble her father. She was a pretty baby, but her light brown hair and bluish eyes were ordinary and did not point to any particular parentage. Ned looked more like Edward with each passing day. He had his father's sturdy frame and his strong limbs. Their eyes were exactly alike, large and dark and brilliant as jewels. His skin was darker than his mother's, but lighter than his father's; his hair was the darkest brown rather than true black, but it was as thick and curly as his father's, falling across his brow just as Edward's did.

Edward felt as happy and content as he could be. He loved his wife and was loved in return, and felt blessed by their two healthy children.

As Edward's eyesight had returned and he could finally look at himself in the mirror, he was relieved to see that he did not look as frightening as he had privately feared he might. His left eyelid was permanently sealed, the faint scar running through it, and there was still a shiny patch of scar tissue above his right eyebrow. His right eye looked nearly normal, but tended to get bloodshot when he overtaxed it or was tired. He had grown quite skilled in using his left arm despite the lack of hand, and as he kept it covered with his sleeve at all times, the empty cuff attracted very little attention.

But he had worried that as his children grew, they would notice his handicaps, and perhaps even be frightened of him. He need not have feared. His son and daughter adored him, and his appearance was as normal to them as their mother's was.

Edward had looked over Jane's sketches and ideas for the new Thornfield, and had finally agreed that they would rebuild on the site. But long months passed, and during this time, Ned went from an active toddler to a quiet, well-behaved little boy who showed an early aptitude for reading. Elizabeth grew active and healthy also, looking more like her mother and toddling endlessly after her adored older brother. Edward agreed to consult with a builder, and using Jane's ideas, blueprints were drawn up for a new home to be built near the site of Thornfield Hall. But for the time being, the family remained at Ferndean.

May, 1843

"I hope you don't mind, Jane, that we are taking a detour on our trip," Edward said, shifting his daughter from one knee to the other, and looking over at his wife.

Jane shook her head, still puzzling over her husband's odd behaviour.

They were on their way up to Morton, for their yearly visit to Mary and Diana. Jane was not looking forward to the trip of two days, as it was difficult to keep three-year-old Ned occupied, and even more difficult now with Elizabeth, who had turned one in December. She was an active baby, not calm as her brother had been, and her father was finding it a challenge to keep her settled on his lap.

"Here, Mr. Rochester, I will take her." Adèle reached out for Elizabeth, and with relief, Edward handed her over.

Adèle, at age fifteen, had recently finished her course of study at the small boarding school near Ferndean, and had come home to live permanently with her guardian and his family. She was good with the children, offering her help to Molly, and Jane was grateful for her presence.

Jane smiled at Adèle appreciatively, and then craned her neck to look out of the carriage window. "No, I don't mind that we're not going straight to Morton, but I still don't understand why you would want to go to Lowood, of all places."

Edward smiled, and beckoned for her to come over to his side of the carriage. Jane glanced at the children: Elizabeth was squirming on Adèle's lap, and Ned was frowning seriously at a picture book.

Jane moved over next to her husband, who shifted in his seat and took her hand. "I want to see where you spent your early years, my darling. I want to know you completely, and thought it would be nice to see places that made you what you are."

Jane grimaced, "I grew to be content enough there, once conditions changed for the better, but I'm not sure I want to linger on the memories. Why you want to see it, I cannot imagine. It looks quite like a setting from the most frightening novel."

Edward smiled, and squeezed her hand, letting go of it to put his arm around her. He was a little restless with anticipatory excitement, as he had a surprise for her.

Some months before, Jane had been thoughtful, sighing as she went about the house. When he had asked what was wrong, she had told him, with suppressed tears in her eyes, that it was the anniversary of her friend Helen's death, and she could not stop thinking of her. She wondered if anyone else, anywhere, even remembered Helen, and said quietly, "She has no grave marker, just a mound to show where she is buried."

She had smiled and wiped her eyes, trying to lighten her mood, and had said no more about it, but it had gotten her husband thinking. He doubted she even remembered now, but he hoped that what he had done would make her happy.

Jane leaned up against him, nestling into his warmth, watching her children. For a short time, the carriage was calm, Ned looking at his book, Adèle dangling

Jane's watch in front of Elizabeth, making her reach for it and giggle, and Edward sitting quietly with his wife's head on his shoulder, while Molly sat next to Jane and Edward, keeping one eye on the children and one eye out the window at the passing scenery.

But travelling with children can never go completely smoothly, and within a few short miles, the calm of the trip was interrupted as Ned, quiet and serious as always, looked up at his parents, said, "Mama, I don't feel well," and promptly vomited down the front of himself.

The carriage was in an uproar as Jane and Molly gathered diapers and rags together to clean up Ned, Adèle sat looking faintly sick herself, and Edward retreated to a corner of the carriage to hold Elizabeth and stay out of the way. By the time all was cleaned up – the rags having been deposited into a bag to be seen to later, and Jane returning to her husband's side – they were approaching the inn in the town near Lowood.

Jane sighed, "I should have stopped him reading his book; I can never read in a moving carriage… I should have known it would lead to trouble." She gathered Elizabeth into her arms as they all climbed down from the carriage. Edward took his son's hand, "Feeling better now, my boy?"

Ned nodded, "Yes, Papa." Edward smiled, lifting his son out of the carriage, "Well, you smell like a bad night in a pub alley. You and I will have a bath, eh, son, and let the ladies rest up."

"Edward!" Jane laughed, shaking her head as she supervised the unloading of their luggage and led them inside to find their rooms.

The next day, Edward and Jane left the children with Adèle and Molly, and took the newly cleaned carriage out to Brocklebridge Church, after Edward had casually mentioned his wish to see Helen's grave. Edward had paid the owner of the inn handsomely to have the carriage's interior cleaned, but it still smelled faintly of sick inside, and they rode with the window open. Edward could not resist making the observation that he had never had to tolerate this sort of thing before he had had children.

As they passed Lowood, on the way to the church, Jane pointed it out to him. She fell silent, looking out of the coach window. "It's sunny today, but the night I arrived, it was cold, snowing hard." Her eyes looked very dark and far away. "I was so cold, I didn't think I would ever be warm again." She shivered as though she could feel the long-ago chill of those days.

Edward put his arm around her, wanting her to feel his warmth, and they sat like that for the two miles that it took to get to the churchyard. They stopped in front of the stone building with its high steeple, and Jane looked around. "I'll be just a moment," Edward told Jane, touching her shoulder. He stepped back to speak to the coachman they had hired so that John would not have to leave Mary alone at Ferndean.

Jane watched as the man nodded and handed Edward a small parcel, which he then handed to Jane. She looked puzzled, and unwrapped the paper, to find a small bouquet of wildflowers within. "For me?" she asked him.

"Well, not really." He put his arm around her again, and they began to walk. "I thought you might like something to place upon the grave of your friend Helen while we are here."

Jane felt her eyes fill with tears. "Oh, Edward!" She hugged his arm, buried her nose in the fragrant wildflowers. They began to walk towards the cemetery in the churchyard. "You are so thoughtful! I confess I did not even think of it, busy as I was with the children."

"Oh, you would have thought of it once we came, and we could have made another trip out here, it's not far." She smiled at him gratefully, and dropped his hand as they approached, "Now, it is just over... "

She stopped, approaching the familiar spot where she had come so many times to read, to draw, to sit and think of Helen, and stared at the handsome stone marker that now sat at the head of the small mound. Her eyes widened as she read:

RESURGAM
Helen Burns

"What... ?" she turned to look at her husband, who was smiling widely at her. She shook her head, looked again at the stone, and then back at him.

"Do you like it, Jane?" he asked her. "Do you think it fitting for her?"

She looked again, from the stone to him.

"I didn't know her, of course, but I hoped that would suit."

"You?" she asked incredulously.

He smiled at her tenderly, reached for her hand. She laughed a little, suddenly remembering – they had talked of Helen, once, a few months ago, and while Edward had been sympathetic, he had said nothing more of the subject. But she recalled now, catching him at her writing desk, seeing him squint at the paper as he laboriously wrote a letter by candlelight, waving away her offers of help. He had finished, asking her help only to affix his seal to the other side of the letter, but not letting her see to whom it was addressed. She had forgotten about it, and now it came back to her. She burst into tears, hugging him fiercely.

"Oh, my darling Edward, thank you, thank you so much!" She sobbed against his coat, clutching it with her free hand, the other hand holding the bouquet. "How good you are, I don't deserve it."

"Of course you do," he told her, taking the flowers from her, "Come, you're going to crush them, let me hold them." He put his arm around her and held her against him while she wept into his chest.

When she was done, she gave him a watery smile and took the flowers back. "How did you ever accomplish this?" she asked him.

He grinned, pleased with himself. "I wrote a letter to the Lowood administrator, and told them what I wanted, sending the payment later. It was no trouble to have John post my letters, and in turn watch for the Lowood address when he picked up the post every time. He was my accomplice."

Jane wiped her face with her hand, and moved to place the flowers upon the small grave. She crouched down by the stone, head bowed, while Edward stood watching her. She reached out and touched the lettering on the grave, traced Helen's name with her fingers, and looked over at her husband. She smiled at him radiantly, and he lost his breath for a moment, looking at her. There was such love on her face, and after nearly six years of marriage, it still struck him with awe, to be the recipient of such feelings, emotions he still did not believe he fully deserved.

She stood up, hand on the stone to brace herself, then moved over to her husband, hugging him again. "It is so lovely, Edward, thank you."

"I'm glad to see where your friend lies, at last. She will never be forgotten, not as long as we live, and as long as this marker lasts." He held her tightly, leaned over to kiss her cheek, shaded by her bonnet. Her skin was soft and warm and fragrant, and he kissed her again, brushing his lips against the still damp tracks of her tears.

Her voice was soft, "Perhaps we can name a child for her."

"Yes, perhaps," he said absently, his fingers reaching up to stroke her cheek. She reached up for his hand, moved it from her cheek down to her abdomen.

"In December?" Jane asked him. He looked at her in surprise, his eyebrows raised.

"I'm not completely sure, but I think so," Jane told him.

He smiled, hugging her again, and she took his hand, to lead him back to the carriage that would take them to their visit at Lowood.

September, 1843

Jane drew her legs up, wrapping her arms around them and resting her cheek on her knees as she stared out at the ocean. The sun had risen gloriously and the sea glittered as though diamonds floated on top of the dark blue water.

The sand felt cold beneath her, not yet warmed by the day's sun, and her white cotton dress fluttered around her. The breeze felt cool against her skin, which was exposed by the lower neckline and shorter sleeves that were appropriate here in the south of France.

Edward and the children were back in the villa, still deep in slumber. She had looked at each of them, trying to let her love for them warm her heart, before she took her customary sunrise walk down to the beach. All around her was perfection and calm.

She wished she could say the same for her aching heart. She laid her hand against the spot where the pain throbbed within her breast. Tears gathered behind her closed eyelids where the light of the sun and the sea still penetrated the darkness. But it could not break through the night that had fallen upon her soul.

It was two weeks now since the burial of their baby, their tiny, precious son whose beating heart had slowed and stilled within her, who had then been delivered into the world lifeless.

Lifeless – that was how she felt. Her mind felt guilty that she could not look on her healthy, living children and let that be enough to ease her pain. But her heart yearned for her lost baby. She found herself waking early each morning, long before Edward did; and rather than disturb him with her sighs and tears, she would slip quietly from the bed, put on her simple dress without corset or petticoats, and walk down the stone steps of the small villa, across the stepping stones in the yard, and down to the beach. There the surf, beating and pounding like a huge, patient heart, drowned out the sounds of her sobs.

In May, she had told Edward that she suspected another child was coming, and by June, when their visit to Mary's and Diana's families was drawing to a close, she was sure of it. She had sat outside with her cousins, watching Ned romp with Diana Wharton as Elizabeth toddled after them trying to keep up.

Mary held her infant daughter Jane, and cast anxious glances at her sister Diana. Diana tried to be cheerful, but the women could see the sadness on her face as she watched the children. It had been three years since her marriage to Captain Fitzjames, and she had not yet had a child.

Jane, who had been married for nearly two years before becoming pregnant with Ned, could remember the anxiety and the longing she had felt, and her heart ached for Diana. She kept silent the news of her third pregnancy, speaking of it only to Edward.

By the time the Rochesters had returned to Ferndean and then departed for France, Jane had loosened her waistbands, raised the top hoop of her petticoat to hide her growing abdomen, and had begun to feel the first fluttering movements of the tiny new life within her.

Edward had worried about Jane being able to travel, but Mrs. Collins had assured them that their plans to winter in the south of France could be achieved if they headed straight there and remained until the birth.

"I will miss attending this birth, Mrs. Rochester, as I have your two others, but I wish you well," she told Jane. She sniffed disapprovingly, "I would rather not trust a French midwife if I were you, but no doubt they are fit to bring Frenchmen into the world alive, for God knows there are far too many of them."

Jane had laughed and hugged the elderly midwife, bidding her a fond farewell and telling her that she, too, would miss her kind attentions with this birth. She also worried about being under the care of French doctors, far from her home, but Edward had spent much time at his villa, and was familiar with the village. She trusted that he would not take her there unless he felt confident of her safety.

Edward had originally planned to take his family to Paris and spend the summer, then head south in time for the winter, but with Jane's pregnancy, he decided they would go straight to the villa.

"It will be hot, but we shall have the sea outside our door, and there will be time enough for travel after we greet this new child. He or she will have many adventures long before most children do."

Edward had been making arrangements all summer, contacting the couple who had always worked for him. They were caretakers of the villa when he was not there, and he requested that they make it ready for his family's occupancy.

John and Mary had been invited along, but they had declined. They would remain at Ferndean and care for it as the Rochesters wintered in France and then toured several European capitals. In a year's time, when the new Thornfield was due to be finished, John and Mary would travel there to take up their positions, engage more staff, and prepare for the return of the family.

They set out for the continent in July – Edward and Jane, Ned and Elizabeth, with Adèle, and the children's nurse, Molly. It was an easy trip, but a long one, and as it progressed Jane felt more tired and more sick. She had begun to bleed, not a large amount, just occasional tiny spots of blood on her undergarments, but felt no other symptoms. She rested, hid her fears, and did not tell Edward, even when she had to rebuff his tender advances to her. They had always continued to make love during the first half of her pregnancies, with Edward loving every sight and touch of her slowly changing body. Even on the occasions throughout their marriage when she had not been able to return his attentions, she had always made sure that she saw to his needs with her soft stroking hands and warm mouth. Through the years he had lovingly shown her how to please him, and she was eager to do so whenever she could.

Now, not feeling well and experiencing problems in pregnancy for the first time, she was not able to return his feelings, and so turned him away, although she did it gently. He was patient and very understanding, and she felt guilty, both for refusing him and for concealing the reason. But he was under stress with the burden of conveying his entire family abroad, and she did not wish to add to his worries. She was greatly relieved when they finally arrived at their destination.

They had only been settled for a day or two in the lovely villa she had heard so much about, when she suffered a bleeding episode that was heavy enough to send Edward into a panic. He awakened Luc and Marie, their servants, and sent them for a doctor. They returned with a Doctor Neveu, who examined Jane and gave her reassuring news.

"No doubt your travels have strained you, Madame," he told Jane, who had to listen carefully to his unfamiliar accent, accustomed as she was to Parisian French, "But you tell me the child still moves?"

"Yes," Jane answered, pressing a hand to the tiny curve of her abdomen.

"Then all should be well," the doctor assured her. "Rest with your feet up, and when the bleeding stops, you may cautiously be up and about again. Send for me if my help is needed." He picked up his bag and his hat and left the room, pausing to speak to Edward, who waited in the doorway with folded arms and an anxious face.

After answering the few questions Edward had for him, the doctor leaned his head towards his patient's husband, "I am afraid, sir, that there can be no marital relations for the duration of the pregnancy."

"I am not an idiot;" Edward answered him tersely, "I knew that without you having to tell me." The doctor raised his eyebrows at the curt tone, but nodded to him, and left the room.

Jane remained in bed, for no sooner did the bleeding stop than it would start up again. Dr. Neveu came and went, shrugging his shoulders as he tried to reassure her that if the baby continued to move and grow, the bleeding might mean nothing. Marie cared for Jane and the household, while Molly and Adèle saw to the children.

Edward was torn – he wanted to stay with Jane, but he was afraid to let the women take the children down to the ocean. He knew the fearsome power of the sea and, although he trusted Molly's care, he did not feel that she could protect Ned and Elizabeth the way he could.

So each day he took turns taking the children to the water. After breakfast he would take Ned's hand and they would go down to the beach. The two would strip to their drawers and would run into the ocean, chasing each other up and down the sand, their laughter echoing over the beach and coming into the open window of Jane's bedroom, where she smiled to hear them and longed to be there with them. When Edward had played with his son for an hour, he would take him to the small shower that was set up at the bottom of the lawn, where buckets of fresh water were pumped and hanging to warm in the sun. He would shower and dress Ned, re-dress himself, and come to the house for Elizabeth.

Molly would hand his daughter over, dressed in her little cotton slip, and Edward would carry her down to the beach as well, spending an hour sitting in the sand with her as she giggled and splashed in the water that washed up on the shore. Edward would carry her, laughing, to the water's edge, and dangle her over the surf, swooping her up again into his arms, and then back down towards the water. Elizabeth never tired of this game, shrieking gleefully. When he was done with the children, and was decently dressed again, he would come back to the house, and then Adèle and Molly could put on their bathing dresses and splash in the sea without any men around to see them.

Jane loved seeing them come to her room, freshly showered and dressed. Both Adèle's and Elizabeth's brown hair were filled with glints of sunlight, their pale skin turned to honey from their time in the sun. Edward and Ned both grew as dark as Indians in the sunshine, and Edward began to grow a rakish moustache, which Jane said was acceptable for holiday, but would most definitely have to be shaved off before they left for the city.

"You don't like my moustache?" he asked her, stroking one side of his whiskers and smiling at her. "I used to have one, years ago, when I lived in Paris. I was quite striking."

Jane frowned at him, "With your skin so dark, and this moustache, you look like a pirate. I could almost be afraid of you." She smiled then, and he came over and kissed her, brushing his newly grown facial hair against her cheek. She waved him away, laughing.

Their lovely times were marred only by their worry, and as Jane rested in bed, she soon grew aware that there was much to worry about. The bleeding was not heavy, but it was constant, and she began to realize that this baby was not growing larger. The tiny fluttering movements that had started in July grew more feeble, and finally ceased altogether. Although Jane and Edward knew what was coming, they both wept when Dr. Neveu told them regretfully that he feared their baby was no longer alive.

"I could give you some medicine to start the pains, but it is hard on a woman and very painful. We will wait, and see if Nature begins things for you."

Thankfully, Nature mercifully did her work, and only a few days after Dr. Neveu's visit, the contractions started up. The labour was very hard, but very quick, and before the doctor could be summoned from the village, Jane delivered her tiny son, attended by Marie and Molly. Marie picked up the baby, ready to wrap him and carry him away, but Jane cried out:

"No, please! Let me see the baby!"

Marie looked uncertainly at her mistress, "Are you sure, Madame?"

"Yes," Jane whispered, tears sliding down her pale cheeks. She took the little bundle from Marie, holding him closely as she wept over him. When Marie had taken the baby away, and Edward came in, she turned to him, still crying bitterly.

"Edward, I'm sorry."

He felt a pain that was nearly physical. That she should think this was her fault! He held her against him, "Shhh, my love, you have nothing to be sorry for." She curled into herself, weeping as he stroked her hair and kissed her.

Dr. Neveu, arriving soon after, gave her a powerful sleeping draught, and then came out to talk to Edward.

"This was tragic, but I see no flaw in the child. It was just Nature's way, and as you have had healthy children already, I see no reason that this would be repeated."

Edward looked at the baby, who had been carried into the next bedroom by Molly, and wrapped in a blanket. He wept as he held his son, who was tiny enough to fit into the doctor's two cupped hands, surprised by the depth of his pain over this child he had not yet known. The baby was very small, but perfectly formed, and as Edward cradled him in the crook of his arm and looked at him, he fancied he could see features of his brother and his sister.

The grief in his heart was great, and he was anxious that Jane should be spared further pain. He called the priest, who came and blessed the child even though the Rochesters were not Catholics, and took the baby away in the heartbreakingly tiny casket that Luc had built. The priest assured him he would see to the baby's burial, and Edward thanked him gratefully, telling him he would provide a stone marker later, and promising a generous donation to the church's orphanage.

When Jane awoke, she discovered that the baby was gone, and was told what had been done while she slept.

"Edward, how could you do all that while I was sleeping?" she cried. "I didn't even get to tell him good-bye!" She rolled over and wept into the pillow.

Edward sat on the edge of her bed, stroking her hair. "My darling," he murmured, "I felt it would be easier on you, and the priest agreed."

"The priest?" Jane leaned up on her elbows. "What did the priest have to do with it – we are not Papists! Why would you call a priest?"

"No, but we are in France, Jane," Edward said, his hand still reaching out to her. He lowered it. "There is no Church of England here in the south of France, and I am not familiar with the other Protestant churches in the area. I know the priests of this parish; I sometimes stopped for comfort in the church when I would stay here. They are kind and have always been understanding."

"I don't know them, or anything about them," Jane whispered. "Now they have taken my baby, and he will be buried with God-knows-what rituals and prayers said over him, and I have nothing to say about it."

Edward sighed. "The priest prayed with us all, and took the baby away. There will be a simple burial, and when you are well, we will go to the grave and have a stone placed. It would be the same if we were home."

Jane shook her head, and lay down again with her back to her husband, crying bitterly. Her womb cramped painfully, but it was not as painful as the ache of her heart.

Edward put his hand on her head again, and leaned over to her. "Forgive me, my darling," he whispered, laying his head against hers. "I held him, and the pain in my heart was so great. I didn't want you to have to feel the same way; I tried to spare you by seeing to the burial. I thought it might ease your burden."

Jane spoke, her voice muffled, "The pain is great either way – at least I could have seen him one more time." Her tears continued, and Edward lay down next to her, a knot in his throat, unable to say anything of comfort to her.

Jane was not angry with Edward; she understood that he had been trying to keep her from suffering. But there was a wall between them, despite their loving words and actions, a wall neither of them could breach at the moment. It did not in any way alter their love or their communion, but it placed an unaccustomed tension upon their marriage.

Jane's grief felt boundless, and her husband did not know how to relieve it, as he longed to do. It was not that he did not grieve himself, but he was thankful for Ned and Elizabeth, and hopeful for the future. He did not think it was productive to linger on past pain, but tried to understand Jane's need to mourn.

And mourn she did. Her womb ached, her arms felt empty, and when she lay still she fancied she still felt the baby move within her. At night she turned restlessly in the bed, half waking to hear the faraway sound of a baby's wail. They had not named the baby, and she would sit on the beach with thoughts of names floating through her head.

So she sat, this September morning, on the beach below her husband's villa, a place she now associated with pain and loss. She wondered how long it would take for her heart to stop hurting and for new associations to replace the old ones, for the villa she had so longed to see now felt like a place of tears and heartache, and for the first time she saw why the thought of moving back to Thornfield had so distressed her husband.

A shadow fell over her, and she looked up to see Edward standing there. He was barefoot and dressed in light cotton trousers and a white shirt that was open halfway down the front. His skin was deeply tanned, his moustache dark and luxuriant, but he no longer looked dashing and rakish to her, just sorrowful and lonely. He looked down at her, taking in her long hair escaping from its plait and her tear-stained face, his expression showing both love and heartbreak. Their eyes met in a long look, and they both smiled at the same time – small, tentative smiles. She reached up for his hand, but rather than pulling her up to him, he squatted down on the sand next to her, bringing her hand to his lips.

"How long have you been here?" he asked her.

"Since sunrise," she said. "I come here every morning now."

He sat down next to her, putting his arms around her. She leaned up against him, and he sighed long and deep, his hand reaching up to press her head against him.

"I love you," he murmured into her hair. "And I am so sorry, my love, that I upset you."

He took a deep breath, "The day of his birth, after you went to sleep, I held our son for a long time. The grief in my heart was so great, I was overcome with it. I've felt such joy when I held Ned and Elizabeth for the first time; only you have brought me greater happiness. And the pain I felt as I looked upon this baby made me want to spare you."

His arms clasped her tighter. She heard him swallow hard before he continued, "Jane, the night before our wedding, I could not sleep for many hours. I knelt by the side of the bed, praying. It was new to me, talking to God, and I am afraid I kept Him occupied for a long time that night. I told Him that if you changed your mind, felt you could not take the burden of marriage to me, that I would still thank Him for at least bringing you to me, showing me you were alive and safe.

"And I made Him some promises that night. I promised that if He did allow me the joy of making you my wife, that I would first of all never lie to you again. No matter what it cost, I would tell you only the truth. And the second promise I made was that I would never hurt you. Not by my actions, and not by my words. God gave me my greatest blessing when He gave you to me, and I have tried to honour those promises.

"I just wanted to make everything right again for you, keep you from pain. I did not mean to hurt you more."

"I know," she said, rubbing her face against his shirt. "And I'm sorry I have been so distant and so… " She could not find the word she wanted to use. "I love you too, you and the children. You are my life, the very beat of my heart. I will be myself again, I promise. But I didn't expect it to hurt like this." She kept her face pressed against him, and the tears began again.

"I know," he said, his hand moving through her loosened hair. "It will take some time, but we will be happy again."

She nodded, and they sat for a long time, holding each other while the surf pounded, washing its white foam across the beach until it nearly reached them where they sat, before it rushed out to sea again.

Chapter 57 - Grace Restored

May, 1847

Abe Poole dug his spade into the soft earth of the garden, moving it back and forth to loosen the soil. He was so occupied in his work that he was not aware of the man's approach until he heard the footsteps behind him.

He turned to see a dark-haired, strongly-built man standing nearby, a man of medium height, with dark features. Abe guessed that he was in his mid to late forties.

"Are you Abel Poole?" the man asked. His voice was deep.

Abe leaned on his spade, straightening slowly as he surveyed the man. He noticed that the man had only one eye, a very dark eye that was fixed upon him appraisingly. His other eyelid was closed, a faint scar visible through it from forehead to cheekbone.

"I am," he answered in response to the man's question. "I do not know you, sir."

"Edward Rochester," the man responded, holding his hand out. Abel wiped his hand on his trousers, then reached out to shake the hand of the stranger.

He knew the name, of course. He had heard it often enough from his mother. His eyes swept over the man, sizing him up in a short time. Abe was used to checking out a situation quickly, determining what was needed. He had been caretaker of this retreat for many years, since he was in his late teens. He could make quick judgments, solve a problem quickly.

He did not know what to make of this man, however. He had been aware of him since his childhood, as his mother's employer. He had visited his mother in this man's home on a number of occasions, although he had never met Rochester himself. And he had witnessed his mother's guilt and torment, had had to live with the aftermath of her turmoil after she had left this man's employ.

In his mind he knew it was not this man's fault that his mother had had such troubles. But he could not help feeling a slight resentment all the same.

Rochester had been surveying him as thoroughly as Abe had been examining Rochester, and then he smiled.

"You look like your grandfather," he told Abe.

Abe raised his eyebrows. "I wouldn't know about that," he answered, "I never met the man. Never met either grandfather; I am lucky to be able to remember my father."

"Your mother's father was quite big, like you," Rochester told him, "but his eyes were very blue. Yours are darker, yet you are like your mother in colouring."

"So what can I do for you, Mr. Rochester?" Abe asked, weary of small talk. He had many tasks to complete in the two weeks that the retreat would be closed, and he wanted to get to them.

"I was hoping to hear some word of your mother, or even to see her myself," Rochester answered.

"Why?" Abe asked, suddenly wary. He was not sure he wanted her past stirred up before her. He had to admit he would never entirely trust her to be able to handle her adversities well.

"I have worried for her," Rochester told him. "I was not…" he paused, "not aware of my surroundings when she was removed from the Thornfield area. When I recovered from my injuries, I learned that you had taken her away shortly after the fire, but no one had any other information. I set up a fund for her and was told she had been notified by my steward, but the funds lay untouched for years. Now, I am told that the account was closed, the monies withdrawn. I was afraid she was dead, but the steward informs me she still lives, yet he knows nothing else of her; she will not respond to his letters of inquiry. I had hoped that perhaps I could see her, or hear of her."

"I am not sure that is a good idea," Abe told him, "My mother is finally at peace; she has a settled life. I am afraid that to stir up her past may disturb or upset her."

Rochester nodded, looking around at the carefully tended grounds. "I understand," he told Grace's son, looking back at him.

"I have no wish to upset her. I just wanted to have news of her, to assure myself that she has no needs, that she is cared for."

Abe looked surprised. "I did not expect that reaction," he said with a shrug. "My mother's actions resulted in the loss of your wife, your home. You were permanently injured. I had not imagined that you would ever wish to see her again, to say nothing of wishing to see her cared for."

The man before him shook his head. "No, no," he told Abe, holding up his hand, "Grace meant no ill will against me. She would never have hurt me deliberately."

"Well, she blamed herself," Abe told him, "Blames herself. There was considerable mending of her mind and heart to do after the fire. Not, of course," he hastened to say, "that it can compare with what you suffered. But she has enormous guilt, that her problems, her carelessness, led to your great misfortunes."

Rochester shook his head again, "It was Grace's carelessness that allowed my poor mad wife to roam free, but it was my wife's actions that resulted in the catastrophe. And it was my doing that led to my wife's actions, in many ways. At the end, it is I who am responsible. And it was God's will, it was He who allowed it all. I blame no one, now. There is no purpose to it."

"You did save my mother's life, I am told," Abe said, "and for that I thank you."

"I could have done no less," Rochester answered, "You know, of course, that your mother was my best friend from my earliest memory. She was as a sister to me, at the start of my life."

"Yes, she has told me," Abe said. He beckoned to him, "Come inside, if you will. We may as well have a cup of tea while we talk."

Abe led him into a large, high-ceilinged kitchen, gestured to him to sit at a long wood table, its top nicked and scarred but scrubbed clean.

"What is this place, exactly?" his guest asked, looking about the room.

"At one time it was a monastery," Abe told him, from the fireplace where he was preparing the tea. "After the dissolution of the monasteries it was destroyed inside, the monks forced to depart. It eventually became the property of a family – the Grimsby family, hence the name, of course." Rochester nodded.

"Money was spent freely on the place," Abe said, coming over with two cups of tea, one of which he handed to Rochester, who thanked him. "It has served as a place for nuns and priests to come if they leave the church. It has been a place for people to come as they recover from accident or illness; for wives to flee from abusive husbands; for some to escape their lives for a short time to pray and meditate. A parson employed by the Grimsby family runs it now, with women here who serve as nurses, of a sort. Several local doctors refer people here and are available to treat those who need it."

He sipped his tea, "My mother did some nursing here herself before going to work for you, as did the sister who reared me. I have worked here since I was a boy, and now have been the caretaker for years. The retreat is now closed for two weeks, to give the workers a chance to rest and be with their families."

"Do you live nearby?" Rochester asked him.

"I have a small house on the grounds," Abe told him. "I live here with my wife, who does some work in the kitchen here, and keeps the herb garden. We have three small children, and they keep her busy now."

"And your mother?" asked Rochester, "Does she do any nursing anymore?"

Abe gave a small smile, shook his head, "No. She has never nursed again, after the fire."

Rochester drank his tea, set the cup down. "Mr. Poole, I did not come to disrupt your mother's life, or to hurt her," he said, "I have built a new home on the Thornfield grounds, and my family has taken up permanent residence there. Now that I am back in the area, I felt I could not be here without at least trying to hear of your mother."

Abe nodded, "I understand." He took a deep breath, set his cup down and leaned back.

"I picked my mother up from Mr. Carter's house two days after the fire. She was not hurt, other than having a cough which took awhile to go away. She was distraught, crying. She wanted to see you before she left, to apologize. No one would let her see you. It was explained to her that you were not conscious, and that you might not even survive your injuries. She was devastated at the thought that you would die, as your wife had died, and all due to her.

"I took her away, and brought her here. She could not get any drink here, and she grew very ill from not having it. I had no idea she drank that much; she'd hidden it from me. I had visited her occasionally, but she always knew I was coming, and was sober. I had no idea she was a drinker until after the fire."

Abe continued, watching Rochester, who sat quietly, listening. "Word came to us that you were alive, but blinded and had lost a hand. As soon as my mother was able, she moved from this place to a small house in a town not too far from Millcote. She had saved a good amount of money from her salary from you, and could afford to go for a time without working. It was a small house, one she could easily afford, and for a while she did nothing but sit in the house and drink. She blamed herself, hated herself, for what she had allowed to happen to you. I didn't know what to do. After six months she was ill from drinking, from not eating right. All messages from your steward were passed on through me, and she received the one saying you had left her some monies for her long years of care, but that made her feel even more guilty. She refused to touch it, refused to even allow me to answer his messages. Mrs. Fairfax kindly wrote as well, to ask after her, but she would not answer those letters either."

"So what happened?" Rochester asked. "How is she now?"

"A man had been coming to visit her," Abe said, "a farmer, a tenant of yours. David Walker. Do you know him?"

Rochester shook his head, "The name is familiar, from the rent rolls as I have gone over them, but I do not recall the face. I was away so much, my estate manager handled most of the business."

"Mr. Walker was there at the fire; he helped the fire patrol as they worked to put the fire out. When you came out, carrying my mother, he took her from you."

Rochester nodded, "I remember... I remember handing her to someone, a big man."

Abe smiled, "Yes. He carried her to the grass, laid her down, and remained nearby as the doctor saw to her. He did not know her; he'd only ever seen her at church, but he was concerned for her. When we got her to the Grimsby retreat, he came to visit, to see how she was. After she moved to her own house, he continued to visit her. He's a good man. He had never married, just farmed, and cared for his mother. She had died, and he was lonely. He kept coming to see my mother, even though she was quite rude to him at times. He's a quiet man, keeps to himself, with no inclination to gossip, and so your steward wouldn't even have known he was in contact with her.

"He's a little younger than Mother, just a few years. But he's a hard-working man, kind, quite religious, but not intolerant about it. My mother says he is very like my father in actions – very gentle, very decent.

"Anyway, he was her friend, and would come a good distance to visit her of an evening," Abe said. "She began to look forward to him coming to see her. He talked to her for hours, in the evening after his work was done. Eventually, they fell in love. But he would not marry her while she was drinking, said he could not bear to see her kill herself as he watched. She stopped drinking and regained her health. They were married eight years ago. She would not return to Thornfield with him, so he found work farming on another estate.

"She still felt guilty about you. She would not touch the money – she let it sit there and collect interest. But it was Mr. Walker's dream to have a farm, to own his own land. Only that, the fulfillment of his dream, convinced her to take the money out and use it. They bought a farm, not too far from here. They have a good life. My mother is happy, and I had never thought to see that." Poole drummed his fingers on the table thoughtfully, "We have had our troubles, my mother and I. But I love her, and would not like to see her upset."

"I am glad she is safe and cared for," Edward said. "Glad to hear it." He drained his cup, set it down. "Would you greet her for me, Mr. Poole? Tell her I am glad of her good fortune."

"Where are you staying, Mr. Rochester?" Abe asked, "This area is not too far from Thornfield, but it's still over an hour's trip here. Did you ride all this way?"

Rochester smiled. "I cannot easily ride now, not for long distances," he held up his left arm. The stump was wrapped, but Abe could see the empty sleeve. He nodded, trying to imagine the difficulties of adapting to only one hand. "My wife and I came in the carriage, and took a room at the inn near here. It's a lovely area; many beautiful fields and rivers. We left our three children behind with their nurse, and came for a night or two of peace and tranquillity."

Abe nodded. "I will talk to my mother," he told Rochester. "I will tell her I saw you, and ask her if she would consent to see you. You can be reached at the inn?"

Rochester nodded, "Yes, the Bird and the Barley, in town. If she will agree to see me, I will meet her at her convenience. If she does not want to see me, I understand. But please tell her I asked after her, and that I wish her well."

Edward stepped down from the carriage, then turned and offered Jane his hand as she came down after him, one hand lifting her full skirts. They stood in the drive, looking at the small, neat farmhouse in front of them. There were sweeping green fields on all sides, and they could hear the lowing of cattle from a distance.

John got down from the carriage, moving up to see to the horses while watching his employer out of the corner of his eye. He could not help but be curious about this visit, how it would go. He had promised Mary he would tell her everything when he got home.

Edward and Jane had just decided to go up and knock on the farmhouse door, when they saw a small girl come running around the side of the house, running up to them. She had brown hair, with a sprinkling of freckles across her nose, and large hazel eyes.

Edward knew those eyes. He had seen them from his earliest memories.

"Mother, they are here," the little girl yelled over her shoulder towards the house. She turned to them, waving excitedly.

"Hello!" she called, coming closer. She was smiling, bouncing on the toes of her brown lace-up shoes.

"Hello," Edward answered. "May I ask to whom I have the honour of speaking?"

The little girl shook back her brown hair, "I am Ellen Walker. Are you Mr. and Mrs. Rochester?"

"We are indeed," Edward said solemnly. "I am a friend of your mother's, from long ago. I met your brother yesterday. He did not tell me about you."

"Abe is coming tonight, to eat dinner with us," the little girl said, "He said you have children. Did you bring them? How old are they?"

Jane laughed, then answered her, "No, I'm sorry, they did not come with us today. They are back at home with their nurse. Ned is nearly eight years old, and Elizabeth will be six. Helen is just a year old. We have another girl also, but Adèle is nearly grown up, she is nineteen. How old are you, Ellen?"

Ellen gave a pout, "I'm seven. I was hoping you would bring your children; it is so boring here! Abe brings Abie and Gracie and Rachel, but they're just babies. I wanted someone to play with."

Edward was about to answer her, but he stopped at the sight of someone approaching from the side of the farmhouse from which Ellen had just come. He straightened up, squinting at the figure coming towards him.

The afternoon of Edward's meeting with Abe Poole, the Rochesters had received a message at the inn. It was from Grace. The message was short, inviting them for dinner tonight at their home. Edward had sent a short message in return, saying they would be delighted to come. He only now realized how nervous he was. His heart was thudding in his chest as he watched Grace walk towards them. She stopped, a few feet from them, and they stared at each other.

Grace reached a hand out, her face crumpling, "Mr. Rochester." It was all she could say. She looked at him, taking in his missing eye, the scars on his face, faded now but still visible. She noted his empty sleeve, which was hanging down by his side. He kept that arm wrapped in a bandage under the sleeve, not to protect it, as it was long healed, but to keep others from having to look at the scarred stump, which was still red and shocking at first sight, even after all this time.

Edward caught Grace's hand, squeezing it. She was crying silently, the tears rolling down her face, her lips trembling. He impulsively held her hand to his cheek, gazing into her eyes. It had been ten years since he had seen her, but she actually looked better at forty-eight than she had at thirty-eight. Her thin frame was filled out, and her face had healthy colour. She no longer showed the rough skin and broken blood vessels of the heavy drinker; the signs of hard living had faded. Her reddish hair had no grey in it, unlike Edward's, which had begun to show the occasional white hair, and which was greying along the temples.

"Don't, Grace," he said quietly. "Please do not cry. It's all right. I look fearsome, I know, but all is well. I am fine."

She looked down, her head bent before him, trying to compose herself. She fumbled for a handkerchief in the pocket of her apron. Finding it, she pulled gently away from Edward, wiped her eyes and her nose. She looked back up at her former employer, tried to speak, "I have to tell you, Mr. Rochester, please, let me say what I need to say... "

"Grace, there is no need," Edward said gently, looking down at her. "I know what you want to say, but do you think I don't know how you feel? I am not angry. I have never been angry, not at you. It is not your fault. I cared only that you were alive and well; that someone was taking care of you. Now I find that you are better than I could have dreamed, and that makes me content."

He held out his hand, drawing Jane forward. "Now, let us renew old friendships," he said, looking from one woman to the other. "Darling, you remember Grace Poole. Well, she is Grace Walker now, I am told."

Jane held out her hand to Grace, as Edward continued, "And Mrs. Walker, I am sure you remember Miss Eyre, now Mrs. Rochester for these ten years." The two women shook hands.

Edward turned to Ellen, who was standing nearby, watching the adults, upset by the sight of her mother in tears. Edward gestured in her direction, "I made the acquaintance of your son Abe a day or so ago, but he did not tell me about this young lady. I am assuming she is your daughter, for I would know those eyes anywhere."

"Yes, my daughter Ellen," Grace said, putting her arm around the child. "We called her Nellie at first, but she got herself into a snit about that a year or so back, insisting on being called Ellen instead." She smiled fondly down at her child. Edward felt the sting of tears, as he thought of Nellie Carey, seeing this little girl in front of him.

"Nellie would have loved her," he said, feeling ridiculously sentimental and having to reach for his own handkerchief.

He addressed the little girl, "I knew your grandmother, did you know that?" Ellen shook her head, looked up at her mother. "She was a wonderful woman, she loved me like a mother. I still miss her." He looked into Grace's eyes. "And I have known your mother since we were babies. She was very like you, once, to look at. And she could run faster than I could, and throw a ball farther." Ellen laughed, looking from her mother to their visitor.

The initial awkwardness of their meeting began to dissipate as Grace led them into her comfortable home, where a haunch of beef was being turned over a fire by a red-faced woman, and the delicious smell of baking bread filled the kitchen. Grace nodded to the woman.

"This is Rachel, my stepdaughter. She lost her husband a few years back and her children are grown and living elsewhere. She lives with us now, helps me out with the place. She's a good cook, thank God, for I was never blessed in that area." She led them to a long wood table, where fresh flowers were set in several pottery vases. The kitchen was large, light and airy, and Edward and Jane settled into the seats that Grace indicated, breathing in the lovely smells and the warmth of the place.

A scuffling noise was heard at the side door, and everyone turned to see a huge man enter the kitchen, wiping his boots on the mat by the door. Edward and Jane stood, and he came over to them. Edward recognized him instantly, remembered him from the estate years ago. His mind flashed back to the night of the fire, when he had handed Grace into this man's arms with great relief.

"David Walker," the man said in his deep voice. "I would offer you my hand, but I need to wash up; we've been in the fields all day." He smiled at them, kissed Ellen, who was bouncing up and down next to him, then turned to Grace, his smile widening, "Hello, love! Have I got a minute to clean up?"

She smiled back at him, "Take what you need, Davy, Abe isn't here yet. We're just catching up now."

The kitchen began to bustle with activity, as Rachel and Grace began to set out plates and utensils, and the beef was placed on the end of the table. Jane offered to help, but both women looked scandalized, and told her to stay where she was. Pitchers of cold water were placed on the table, napkins neatly folded and laid out by Ellen, who grinned at them as she worked. In the midst of the tumult, Abe arrived with his three children and his wife, a quiet woman who barely met their eyes as she greeted them shyly. Abe kissed his mother, reaching over to shake Edward's hand and nod at Jane as they were introduced.

Walker returned to the kitchen then, freshly scrubbed, his brown hair still wet. He greeted his stepson's family, taking the littlest child from her mother's arms and lifting her high, making her chortle. He handed her back, and took his place.

When everyone was seated, he bowed his head, to Edward's surprise. The room grew still.

"Lord," he prayed, "we thank you for your provision for us, for allowing us to live another day. Thank you for your bounty, and for old friends who have been brought to be with us again. Bless this food and bless us to your service. Amen."

"Amen," all around the table repeated, and then the kitchen fairly exploded with noise, with everyone talking at once, all the happy sounds of a family meal. Jane and Edward would later agree that their dining room, with only them and their older children, was fairly cold and austere compared to this noisy brood, laughing and enjoying each other's company.

The meal was delicious, and no one spoke of the past. There was talk of farming, of cows and planting. Then someone asked Jane a question about her children's schooling, and an animated discussion of learning followed.

Edward said little, but watched the happy group around the table. Since they had been adults, Grace had treated him with a respectful distance, the deference due him as her employer and the master of his estate. He had not seen her in such high spirits since they were children. He watched as she laughed, talked, corrected children, and passed plates. From time to time he caught her watching him, and he would smile at her.

He had long become used to dealing with his handicaps – to altered vision and to the inconvenience of having only one hand. Those with whom he dined noticed very little trouble as he deftly maneuvered fork, napkin, and glass. But he saw Grace bite her lip and look away as Jane quietly cut up his meat and made sure his food was in manageable portions. His wife did this so quickly and unobtrusively that it was barely noticeable, but he realized that to Grace it was a fresh stab in her heart as she watched him, to know how much his life had changed due to his injuries.

Edward's initial good impression of David Walker grew. He seemed to be a reserved man, but was a good host. He spoke to all those around his table, teasing the children, asking intelligent questions of his guests. There was a quiet strength about him, and as he watched the glances Walker exchanged with Grace, Edward could see that they were happy, that the marriage was a good one. It calmed Edward's fears, and relieved the unease he had felt each time he had thought about Grace. After supper, as Jane was speaking to Rachel and to Abe's wife, Edward turned to Walker.

"I wonder if I might have a brief word alone with your wife, Mr. Walker?" Edward asked him. "Just to catch up with an old friend."

Walker's eyes darted to his wife, who smiled at him. "It's all right, Davy," she said softly, patting his arm. She wrapped her shawl around her shoulders and led the way out of the kitchen and into the cool evening air. The two walked a few feet, towards a large expanse of yard in which chickens were clucking and scratching, some of them heading inside a large chicken coop at the side of the yard.

Edward spoke first, "I enjoyed meeting your family, Grace, and I thank you for allowing us to come to visit. It was a wonderful meal."

Grace glanced at him, reaching up to brush a stray hair away from her face. "I was quite surprised when Abe told me you had come to see him. I had not thought we would ever meet again."

There was a silence that lasted some minutes, then Grace spoke again. Her voice was low. "I thought you would hate me."

"No, Grace," Edward shook his head, "I never hated you. I was angry, afterwards. Angry at God. Angry at myself. But never at you. We had some settling to do, God and myself. The fight was always with Him. Not with you."

Grace let out a long, shaking breath. "Well, I hated myself enough for both of us. I was so... " she sighed, "so guilty. I know you probably don't understand it, but I cared deeply for Mrs. Rochester. I know she was a sick woman, and at times she drove me to my limit. But other times... I believe she grew to care for me a bit; knew I wanted the best for her. She would talk to me sometimes. She did not always make sense, but sometimes I knew there was still a woman deep inside, one who longed for a normal life. And at times she would speak clearly. Twice she reached for my hand and looked into my eyes. She said, 'Thank you, Grace,' and I believe she meant it. When I knew she was dead, because of my carelessness... I wanted to die myself. And you... when I heard what I had caused to happen to you... " Her voice broke.

Edward touched her arm lightly, shaking his head again, "I have thought about it all, over and over. That year after the fire, all I could do was think. I tried to see how I could have done it all differently.

"Would she have been better off in an asylum? Who can know? But I believe she always meant to kill herself, eventually. And me with her, if she possibly could. You allowed her more time, and she was watched over, she was safe. She had someone to care for her. You made her miserable life a somewhat happier one, Grace, with your affection. That is worth more than anything. Sooner or later, whatever nurse she had would have turned her back, let down her guard. And then she would have been gone. It was only a matter of time. The drinking... well, it really was only part of the problem."

"I don't drink anymore," Grace told him, "Not for eight years. I realized I could not. I had never thought it was a problem, but when I realized that it stood between me and having a normal life, I had to stop. I realized that I had become like my father was, and I didn't want to live like that."

"I asked you once, many years ago, Grace, if you were happy," Edward said, his face serious. "You couldn't really answer me back then. Now I'm asking you again. I believe you are, but I need to hear it."

Grace looked up at him, a wide smile shining through the sadness of her face, "Yes, Mr. Rochester, I am happy. I never believed I could be so happy, but I am. I do not deserve it, but my life is good." Her smile vanished then, "They told me later that it was you who saved my life, carried me out of the fire. At the time I wished you had just left me there. Now, every day I am glad you did not."

Edward smiled back at her, "I do not believe any of us deserve anything we have been given, but I'm glad we have it. So Walker is good for you; I had thought he was. Tell me about him."

Grace heard herself beginning to talk, trying to put into words how she felt. "When you came to see me, when I was expecting Abe, I couldn't talk about how I felt. I was so confused. I did not love my husband, and I had not wanted a child. I was sixteen, and felt unready for all that. Then Abe was born and for the first time since my mother, I loved someone with all my heart. For three years we were happy; Abel, and the baby and I.

"Abel loved me, and I tried to treat him as lovingly as I could, but sometimes I was not good at hiding what I felt, although I tried. But we had a good life; he was good to me and to his son. Then he got sick. He had a disease of the lungs, and the doctor said it went to his brain. He was not himself, and he got difficult and even violent. I sent young Abe to live with Rachel, to keep him away from the house.

"Abel died, and it was then that I realized how I had grown to love him. I held him in my arms as he died and told him I loved him, but I don't think he knew me or heard my words... I felt so guilty. I never forgave myself, that he got sick and died not knowing how I loved him.

"When David began to come around, I was so angry. I was angry with myself for not being a good wife to Abel, for having to send Abe away to be raised by someone else while I had to work. I was guilty for what had happened at Thornfield. I did not trust that a gentle, decent man could care for me, and that I was worthy of being cared for. I was a nasty, ugly person to David, and I was still drinking part of the time. But he never gave up on me.

"I finally grew to trust him and told him everything. He was so kind, so understanding. He said he knew that Abel understood and forgave me, and convinced me that I had not been as bad a wife or mother as I had believed. I began to trust that. But he could not make me stop feeling guilty about you. Some gossip filtered back this way; I heard that you married, that you had children. But I was still wracked with guilt. When I got the message from the bank saying you had set up some money for me, I could not imagine why, even when the steward told me you had asked after my welfare. I could not believe you didn't hate me.

"David and I fell in love, and we married. Then we were blessed with Ellen. I couldn't believe that either; I thought I was going through the change, could not believe I was young enough to have another child.

"When she was born, I could hardly look at her, convinced I would be punished through her for Mrs. Rochester's death and for your injuries. I even dreamed that she was born blind and missing a hand. When I saw her for the first time, saw she was healthy and perfect, I couldn't believe I could be so blessed."

Edward laughed, "I know, I felt the same way when my son was born. I still felt I did not deserve such a blessing. I could not believe he was whole and healthy. But I have come to realize now that while God chastens and judges, He also shows mercy. He has shown it to us both, has He not?"

Grace nodded. The two of them stared at each other for a moment, then Edward looked around. "This is a wonderful farm. I am glad you accepted the money at last."

Grace smiled, "Only the knowledge that David wanted land of his own induced me to take it. I thank you, Mr. Rochester, for without you we could not have had this. My husband is happy, content to farm his own ground. The farm will be paid off in just a few more years, if things continue the way they are."

Edward felt embarrassed, but was also relieved to hear her words. He made a dismissive gesture. "You did a difficult job for me for many years, you deserve the money. I hope that you and David will have many good years here." He held out his hand, "I thank you for seeing me, Grace, and setting my mind at ease after all this time."

Grace shook his hand, her grip strong. "And you, Mr. Rochester; I thank you also. You have eased my mind as well. To know that you bear me no ill will... " She pressed her lips together, looked away for a moment.

"Be happy in your life, Grace. Be thankful for it," Edward told her. "I am happy in mine. We have both been given so much, Grace, at long last." He squeezed her hand tightly.

"You were my best friend, Grace. I have not forgotten that. Will not forget that. There was a time, after your mother's death, when you were the only person at Thornfield who really cared for me, the only one to whom I genuinely mattered." Grace pressed his hand between both of hers, before she let go and turned away, reaching up to wipe her eyes with the corner of her shawl.

They headed back into the house, the two old friends, reconciled at last and blessed beyond either of their expectations.

That night, Edward and Jane rested on the sofa before the fire. His head lay in her lap, and she stroked his hair back from his forehead with her left hand as her right hand held his tightly. They were quiet, no words needed between them.

The night before, Edward had been tense and nervous. The message from Grace had come in the late afternoon, after they had come in from a long walk, and he had been anxious about what would pass between them. He had sat with Jane, brushing her hair as they talked about how the visit might go. After they were done, Edward had lain face down on the bed while Jane rubbed his back and shoulders, his muscles knotted with his tension. Long after Jane had gone to sleep, he had found himself lying awake, thinking of the past, and as he still sometimes did, wondering how he could have done everything differently.

Now he felt relaxed, his worries relieved. He was freed from the nagging guilt that had haunted him whenever he thought of Grace, which was more often now that they had returned to Thornfield and taken up residence in the large, newly-constructed manor. He had worried for her: afraid that she was still drinking, ill, alone, poor.

Jane spoke, her soft voice breaking in on his thoughts, "So, darling, do you feel relieved of your anxiety regarding Grace? I know you have worried for her and now you can rest easy, I hope."

He smiled up at her. Jane was sitting in her white cotton nightgown, with her long hair flowing over her shoulders. "Yes, I feel much better. I don't have to wonder any more. And of course, as often happens, I am once again humbled."

"Humbled?" Jane asked him, still stroking his thick hair, pulling it a little between her fingers and watching the curls snap back to their original shape.

"Yes," he answered. "I had worried for her, in the back of my mind thinking that Edward Rochester had such power over someone that his attention or lack thereof could make a difference. Then I find that Grace has long been well, and has a fine life through nothing I did or did not do. I'm glad, though, that at least I was able to benefit her materially, that eventually she overcame her guilt enough to accept the money that I certainly felt was due her. It is no small thing, to own one's own land, and I'm glad I could have a hand in that."

Jane said softly, "Your friendship had to mean much to Grace, as hers did to you when you were children. She will never forget that. I'm so happy that you could be of some financial blessing to this family, and surely, to know that you have never borne her ill will has to ease her mind. She had blamed herself for so long; such a burden that must have been to her."

"Yes," Edward said quietly, "And my mind was eased as well. I know I did not do completely right by her, in a number of ways. There are many things I should have done differently, but did not. And I am relieved to know she does not see it that way."

He sighed, bringing her hand to his lips, brushing them over her soft skin. "David Walker is a good man. She says she is happy with him. I told Grace I was happy as well."

"Good," Jane answered, her tone light and teasing, "I would have hated to hear that you are not!"

Edward smiled, "I am amazed at times, how happy I have been. Ten years, Jane, do you believe it? In a few weeks it will be ten years that you married me, made my life one worth living at last. I told Grace I was happy, but I wondered, when was the last time I said it to you? Told you again how happy you make me?"

Jane leaned over him, kissed him full on the lips, "You don't need to tell me, I know it. You make me happy too."

"And do I still please you, an old man whose hair is turning grey?" he asked, reaching up to where she was still stroking his black curls.

"Oh, you are not that old," Jane replied. "You need a haircut, though."

"I am old," Edward insisted. "I feel it, and when I see myself in the mirror, I look it."

Jane gave a little snort, ruffling his hair. She sat up, pushing him gently to make him move off her lap. "You are not old, and I suggest we retire now and I will prove my continued attraction to you."

Her husband laughed, and sat up at those words. They stood up together, and she came into his arms for a long, hard kiss, before she laughed again and took his hand, pulling him towards the bed. They made the sort of slow, deep love known to long-married couples, nothing amazing, nothing different; just the rich pleasure and soul connection to be found with the one person known and loved like no other.

Later, the room dark but for the glow of the moon coming in through the window, Jane leaned up on her elbow, watching her sleeping husband. He lay on his back, his face relaxed and free of all care. He still looked young, and was still vigorous. She reached out, lightly stroking the skin of his arm. All these years and she still loved the feel of his skin. If she were to be blinded, she could recognize it by her touch alone. Jane smiled to herself, and leaned over to kiss his brow before lying back on her pillow and closing her eyes.

I have now been married ten years. I know what it is to live entirely for and with what I love best on earth. I hold myself supremely blest—blest beyond what language can express; because I am my husband's life as fully as he is mine. No woman was ever nearer to her mate than I am: ever more absolutely bone of his bone, and flesh of his flesh. I know no weariness of my Edward's society: he knows none of mine, any more than we each do of the pulsation of the heart that beats in our separate bosoms....

Jane Rochester - Jane Eyre

Chapter 58 - Adèle Demands the Truth

Paris, April 1851

Edward reached into the pocket of his waistcoat and drew out his watch, holding it up close to his face to check the time. He frowned, tucked it away, and folded the newspaper he had been reading. He could not read unaided for long and he rubbed his eyes, feeling the slight headache that always let him know when he had attempted too much.

He and his family had been on holiday in Paris for nearly a week, after spending several weeks at the villa. He no longer enjoyed Paris, the city he had once loved, and had only agreed to come because Jane and Adèle had requested to make a visit.

He had been waiting for Jane so that they and the children could take a walk through the Bois de Boulogne that afternoon. They had been in the sitting room of their hotel suite, as the children were given their lunch in the large sunny room that served as their nursery. And they were also anxiously awaiting the return of Adèle, who had gone out that morning without informing anyone of her destination, and had now been absent for several hours. Jane had just opened her mouth to speak when Adèle burst in. Her hair was in disarray, her face flushed.

"Adèle, where have you been? We have been concerned," Jane said, rising to her feet. She noticed Adèle's face, moved towards her. "Adèle, what is it?"

"Jane, may I speak with you?" Adèle spoke quietly, glancing at Rochester before again looking at Jane. She looked quite agitated, and Jane put her arm around her, also looking over at Edward.

"Edward, I will be a few minutes, then we can leave when the children are ready. Would you check on them, please?"

He nodded, watching Adèle and his wife as they left the room. Adèle was much taller than Jane, but she seemed a child again as Jane led her away.

Edward had waited a few moments and then headed to the nursery to find the children still eating, chattering and clattering their silverware, all three in animated conversation with Molly, who had been their nursemaid since Ned was still in dresses. She was still young but very competent and the children loved her.

He watched them, unnoticed by the children. Molly deftly controlled the luncheon. "Master Ned, one mouthful at a time, please, and do not talk, you'll choke yourself, you will. Miss Elizabeth, mind your cup, love, you nearly knocked it over when you reached for the bread."

She clucked with loving impatience as she stood, moving towards his youngest, "Miss Helen, let me wipe your mouth; you've more food on your face than you have in your gullet." She wiped Helen's face with her napkin, holding her head firmly despite her squirming.

"I declare, I have my hands full with the lot of you. Your parents expect three children who can eat out in company some day, and what they have are three heathens not fit to dine with the crew of a merchant ship."

Edward grinned, watching the little group. He sometimes felt overwhelmed with his children, thinking that at the age of fifty-two years he was far too old to be coping with such an active young family.

He well remembered Mr. Carter shaking his head as he looked at all his own boys, saying, "Who are these children and how did they come to be here?" At times Edward felt like saying the same thing, but he never lost sight of his long lonely time before Jane and his family had come along, and never ceased to thank God for what he had been given.

He looked at Ned, his pride, the eleven-year-old who was still the image of him, but with the loving and open demeanour of a boy who has been loved and cherished by both parents since infancy. Nine-year-old Elizabeth was very like her mother, but without the robust health that Jane had enjoyed despite her difficult early start. Elizabeth caught every little illness that came along, and her health was a worry to her parents, but her bright, inquisitive mind and her sweet nature made her especially precious to her father.

Edward watched them, thinking of their births, the fear that had gnawed at him each time Jane was brought to bed with another of his children, and the happiness each time when he saw that God had once again spared his Treasure, and blessed them with another child.

He thought of their precious second son, gone to God before he had ever drawn a breath, and of the losses Jane had suffered early in her next two pregnancies. And then there was Helen. He looked at his four-year-old daughter, their darling, their blessing when they did not think they would have any more. He watched her, her black curls so like his, her wide green eyes just like her mother's.

After the heartbreaking death of their baby boy, both had been afraid of future pregnancies, and Edward had taken steps to prevent Jane from having to carry another child. But those fears had been overcome, and she had become pregnant again a year after the stillbirth of their son. But that pregnancy had ended after only three months, as had another one six months later. This saddened the Rochesters greatly, but they both believed that perhaps another child was not in God's plan for them, and they tried to focus upon Ned and Elizabeth, whom Jane was schooling a few hours a day as they travelled on the continent.

In 1844, the large modern manor home that replaced Thornfield Hall was finally finished, and the family moved in. They were welcomed back to the area with great enthusiasm, and were soon settling in. One advantage of being back at Thornfield was once again having Carter as their doctor, and he had listened to Jane's account of her pregnancy losses with great sympathy.

"This is very common, Mrs. Rochester," he told her. "One never speaks of them in public, but it is a common feature of the childbearing years. It is rare to have a lifetime of having children without losing some of them before birth. The chances are good that you have had your bad luck and that no more losses will follow."

Jane tried to keep that in mind when she found out she was once again pregnant, shortly after Christmas of 1845. She and Edward were nervous, but her third month passed without the tell-tale cramping and bleeding, and the pregnancy progressed normally. In the middle of a close, humid night, in an August that had been unusually hot for England, Jane's labour began.

Perhaps it was the fact that she had not given birth to a living child in nearly five years, or perhaps it was the memory of all the other pain that had led only to heartbreak and emptiness, but she had clung to Edward during her contractions, and begged him to stay with her. When Carter had arrived for the delivery, he had shrugged with nonchalance at the idea of Edward staying for the birth, telling him only to roll up his sleeves and stay out of the way.

And so it was Edward who had sat behind Jane on the bed, supporting her as she leaned up against him, labouring with great effort to bring their child into the world. He was too absorbed in her needs to dwell on his own fear as he held her hand, whispered encouragingly to her, wiped her face with a damp cloth, and braced himself as she pushed back against him each time she strained. She had to work hard; her body was unaccustomed to such labour, and this baby was bigger than her others. At the end, Carter had her lie on her side, her head resting on Edward's lap. Edward's head had bent to hers, whispering words of love and encouragement as he stroked her damp hair with a none-too-steady hand. Mary stood behind Jane, supporting her leg as Carter frowned, concentrating hard.

"This is a bigger child than a little woman like you is used to delivering," he muttered. "He can probably sit and have his dinner at the table with the rest of the family tonight."

But all had gone well, and Edward had watched over Jane's shoulder as she lay still, fighting hard to control her cries of pain as Carter did the last of the work to ease their daughter into the world with as little trauma to Jane as possible. Carter had wrapped Helen, screaming and red, in a towel, and put her up on her mother's chest. Edward had cradled Jane while she had cradled Helen, and had taken in the sight of his newest child, looked at her sleek black hair and the deep pink of her soft skin. He recalled vividly his joy and wonder at the whole amazing process, watching his daughter enter the world bellowing loudly with her indignation at having to leave her comfortable nest to come into this strange new place. In spite of the few stitches Jane had had to have because of Helen's birth, she felt wonderful, and the whole household had been excited over the birth of the newest Rochester child. Helen was a happy child, but a stubborn one. Edward and Jane found their child-rearing skills tested, realizing that Ned and Elizabeth were very easy children, while their little sister was more of a challenge.

Now he stood in the doorway of the nursery, as Elizabeth looked up.

"Papa!" she waved in greeting. He moved towards the table, tousled Ned's dark curls, leaning over to kiss the top of Elizabeth's head. Helen bounced up and down in her chair, happy to see him, waving her spoon, from which a collection of English peas fell and scattered over the floor.

Edward went over to her. "Molly is right, a pack of uncivilized children you are!" He grimaced as he accidentally ground peas into the carpet, and lifted his foot, frowning at the crushed green pieces on the bottom of his shoe.

"Helen, get up and pick up those peas. Molly should not have to do that for you." Helen giggled, sliding off her chair to begin picking up the peas, and her sister, ever obliging, moved to help her.

Ned cleared his throat, "She hates peas, Papa. She thinks we don't see her, picking them off the spoon and dropping them on the floor. I told her to pick them up, but she kicked me."

His father shook his head, "Helen, do not kick your brother. He is trying to help Molly, who doubtless needs no help, but sees all your tricks."

Molly nodded firmly, "Indeed I do, sir. The children protest loudly over their nightly dose of cod liver oil, Miss Helen most of all, but perhaps it would not be necessary if they would eat their vegetables." These last three words were directed at Helen with special emphasis, but Helen merely giggled again, coming to deposit a handful of crushed peas on her plate. Elizabeth also dropped a handful of peas on Helen's plate, pulling a face at her father as she wiped her hand on her napkin and resumed her seat. He winked at her, mouthing "thank you'", as he turned towards their nursemaid.

With a smile on his face, Edward informed Molly that he would be in the sitting room waiting for his family to be ready. The children had all come to join him, dressed to go out, but as the time passed Ned and Elizabeth grew bored and returned to the nursery to play. Molly had entertained Helen in the corner with some paper dolls so that her employer could get out his reading glass and look over some of the newspaper.

Now he sighed, drumming his fingers on the arm of the chair. "Helen, do something for me: run to Mama and ask her when she will be ready. Tell her we are all waiting."

Helen, who was at the age where she loved to be useful, ran off and in a few minutes returned.

"Mama says you and Molly should take us and go without them." She drew near to her father's chair, leaned towards him and spoke in a loud whisper, her little hands cupped around her mouth, "Papa, Adèle is crying!"

"Oh, for the love of God," Edward muttered, reaching for his daughter, who climbed upon his lap. He sat for a few moments, bouncing Helen on his knee, listening to her prattle, then he stood up.

"Molly, I have here a chattering monkey who needs to be returned to the zoo," he said, turning Helen upside down. His left arm was wrapped around her legs, to keep her skirts decently arranged, his right arm held her carefully as he dangled her in front of him. Her black curls nearly swept the floor and she shrieked with glee.

"Papa!" she chortled, "I am not a chattering monkey!"

"What are you then?" he asked, swinging her gently back and forth.

"I am Helen Maria Rochester!" she cried, giggling.

"You are?" Edward stopped, then quickly turned her upright, "Oh, my, so you are. My apologies, Miss Rochester." He set her on her feet. She laughed, jumping up and down with arms raised to him, and he reached out and rubbed the top of her head with his fingertips.

"Molly, would you be so kind as to take this young lady to the nursery, while I go see what is keeping her Mama?" Molly reached for Helen's hand as Edward headed for Adèle's room.

He paused, fist raised to knock, then hesitated. He was not sure whether or not to intrude. Adèle was set to marry Thomas Cooper upon their return to Thornfield and it occurred to him that she may have received some unpleasant news.

Cooper, the curate of the Hay church, appeared to adore Adèle, but perhaps something had happened to change his mind. Adèle's position as the ward of the Rochesters was well known, although not her illegitimacy. Edward had presented her in public as the daughter of friends no longer able to care for her. Cooper, orphaned himself and reared by a now-deceased uncle, had seemed to find nothing but perfection in her, and Edward could not imagine that anything might have occurred to alter his opinion.

Edward was hosting her wedding. He planned to walk her to the church and give her away, and to gift the couple with two thousand pounds, thereby fulfilling his long-time role as Adèle's guardian.

Despite his years of care of her, relations were still strained between Adèle and Edward. He knew that he had been somewhat harsh to her in her early years, and his treatment of her had been inconsistent, ranging from material indulgence to benign neglect.

Adèle had sometimes borne the brunt of his pain and disappointment, especially when he saw in her the woman who had broken his foolish heart so many years ago. Her brown hair was darker than her mother's had been, but in every other way she was the image of Céline Varens. To Edward, her appearance gave no clue of who her father was.

Adèle was quiet and respectful, still calling him Mr. Rochester, although she had long been calling Jane by her first name. They were more like sisters than ward and guardian, and Edward appreciated Adèle's loving friendship to his wife and her patient assistance with their children. But he didn't know how to bridge the gap between himself and her, and he suspected it was far too late.

He recalled a day, shortly before their move from Ferndean. He had been talking to Elizabeth and was suddenly overcome with his love for her. He swept her into his arms and asked her, "Are you Papa's girl?" He had turned to see Adèle standing in the doorway, watching them. Her hazel eyes had narrowed, her face full of such sorrow that for a moment his heart had smote him with guilt. He had stood holding his daughter, while Adèle's eyes had locked on to his, before she lowered her face and turned away.

Now he tapped on the door to her room, entering as he heard Adèle's quiet, "Come in." He stood inside the door, seeing his wife and Adèle sitting side by side on the sofa before the room's fireplace. Jane was turned towards Adèle, her arm on the back of the couch behind the girl. Adèle's face was so red and swollen that Edward knew there had been a storm of weeping since she had returned to the room.

"Edward, I'm sorry, I am not going to be able to go this afternoon; Adèle needs my help. You go and take Molly and the children, I'll see you when you return," Jane told him, her free hand holding Adèle's tightly.

"But something is very wrong, of course," Edward said. "Adèle, is it Thomas? Has something happened?" Adèle shook her lowered head.

"Edward, dear, please, just go and take the children... " Jane began, but Adèle raised her head and said firmly, "No."

Jane and Edward looked at her, and she looked in turn to each of them. "No, let him stay." Her voice was hoarse, but steely, and she took a deep breath.

"Let him stay, and let him talk to me. He alone can give me the answers I need."

Her eyes looked deeply into Edward's, and he had never before seen quite the look of anger that he now saw on her face. His eye still fixed on hers, Edward came closer, and stood in front of the two women.

For a long time, no one spoke. Edward folded his arms across his chest, raising his chin and narrowing his eye as he met Adèle's hostile gaze. For years she had been so docile, so quiet and polite and respectful, that he was shocked to see this passion, this depth of feeling upon her face.

Jane looked from her husband to Adèle, anxiety on her face, and Edward was suddenly irritated with Adèle for upsetting his wife.

"Well?" he asked. His voice sounded harsh to his own ears, and he tried to modify his tone. He felt defensive, and was not even sure why; nothing had yet been said.

"You said I was to stay and talk to you," he said to Adèle, his tone gentler now. "I am here; what is it you want to know?"

"I... I have... " Adèle bent her head again, pressed a large white handkerchief against her face, and began to cry softly. Edward felt guilty, and once again a small flash of anger went through him. He looked towards his wife.

Jane spoke softly, "Today, Adèle went to her old home, where she lived with her mother. She met, and spoke with, a Madame de Simone."

Edward felt a shock run through him, at the name he had nearly forgotten after all those years. He looked over at Adèle, who was wiping her eyes.

"How... ?" He shook his head in confusion, "How on earth... ? You were six when you were left with Madame Frédéric, seven when I came and took you to England. How did you even remember where you used to live?"

Adèle shrugged, "When you are suddenly separated from your mother, when all you cared about is gone, you never forget the last place you saw her." She pressed her lips together suddenly as they trembled. "I got the address from your steward; he has all the old financial records, they were housed in his office, outside of the Hall, and were not lost in the fire."

Edward felt her words go straight to his heart. Had he not been nearly that age when his mother had taken to her bed for the last time? Those days were a frightening blur, but some things were as clear to his mind as though they had happened yesterday.

Edward, my darling boy. He could still hear her weak, beloved voice. *God bless you, my little son. Do not forget, your mama loves you so very much...*

He took a deep breath, shook those thoughts away. He marvelled at her ingenuity in being able to ferret out the address.

"But de Simone, how did she come to be there?" he asked, suddenly picturing the woman in his mind. He saw her rouged cheeks, her dyed hair, the long nose like a witch's. A look of distaste came over his face. He had hated her, Céline's foster mother, if indeed such a title could be given to someone so evil. But de Simone had hated him as well...

Adèle couldn't speak, her lips again quivering. Jane spoke up, quietly, "Madame de Simone still owns the house."

Edward nodded. He had forgotten who owned the home that Céline and Adèle had lived in after he had broken with her. Part of the money he gave Céline was intended to allow her to break free of the old witch, but de Simone's influence on his former lover had been very strong.

Adèle seemed to gain control, sitting up straighter. "I stood out on the sidewalk in front of the house; I had only intended to look. But this woman, this old woman, was in the courtyard, and she saw me. She called me Céline. She said I looked just like her, and when I said Céline was my mother's name, she knew me. She called me Adèle, and invited me in. We sat in her garden, and she gave me coffee, and was so kind." She smiled a little. "As we were talking, I thought that perhaps she might be my grandmother."

Edward swore, under his breath, the blunt, harsh Anglo-Saxon term that he had not used since before he had married Jane, and that he certainly never used in the presence of women. Jane and Adèle looked at him in surprise. "Edward!" Jane said.

"Forgive me, I could not help it." He dropped his face to his hand for a moment, rubbed his eyes, "Agnès de Simone your grandmother! No, she most certainly is not, and you should thank God for that."

Adèle looked at him gravely, "Why did you tell me my mother was dead? I mean, she is dead, now, but she was not dead back when I came to England. Why did no one ever tell me the truth?"

"Céline is dead?" Edward could not help asking, "How do you know this?"

"Madame de Simone told me," Adèle said, her eyes shining with tears again. "Three years ago. My... Céline... wrote to her. She was in Italy, in Rome, I think, and had been deserted once again by a man. She was penniless, alone and sick. Madame went to her, brought her back to Paris. She had consumption, and soon afterwards she died."

"Madame?" Edward asked, trying not to think of Céline, and how terrible her life must have been. He did not look at Jane; he hated even talking of all this in front of his wife.

"That is what she said to call her: Madame," Adèle said. "She said she hoped I would come again to see her." In her distress, she once again slipped into the phrasing that she would have used to translate French into English. For years she had spoken English, and had even lost her accent, but suddenly she seemed to sound more French than she had since her childhood.

"You will absolutely not go to see her!" Edward said loudly. "I brought you to England to get you away from that woman, and you will never see her again, not if I have to carry you bodily to the ship and put you on it myself."

Adèle looked at him, puzzled, and looked at Jane, who gave a little shake of her head.

Adèle spoke again, "You did not answer my question: Why was I led to believe that my mother was dead? Even now, when I am an adult, I had to hear from a stranger that my mother had deserted me, and died later."

Edward shrugged, "For that I am sorry, Adèle. When I got you from Madame Frédéric's house, I found you had been told that your mother had died. I felt it easier, and kinder, to carry on with that falsehood, and over the years, it became as though it were true. I didn't know what had become of Céline as time went on. I never thought to correct the impression – it seemed better to let you believe that your mother was dead than that she had run away with a man and left you behind."

"And then," Adèle continued, as though he had not spoken, "Madame said that my mother, in her last days, asked for me continuously. Madame didn't know what to tell her. But she did say that I was with my father."

She raised her eyes to Edward's face, and stared at him. "With my father, she said. Was it easier to carry on with that falsehood as well? You presented yourself as a friend to my maman, someone who took me in out of the kindness of his heart." Her voice rose, a note of hysteria entered. "You did not think to mention in all these years that you are my father?"

Edward paused, his mouth open. He looked over at Jane, who gave him a small smile, and a shrug. He came over to a chair near the sofa and sank down into it, watching Adèle, who had resumed her weeping.

"Adèle," he began. He stopped, his arms slack at his sides. He was not sure what to say.

She raised her head, looked at him again with eyes narrowed and piercing. "Are you? Are you my father?"

Edward shook his head, "No, Adèle, I am not." Adèle closed her eyes, opened them, looked over in Jane's direction, before she looked back at him.

"Madame said you are," Adèle told him. "She talked as though I knew this, as though I had been part of your family, your eldest daughter, for years and years. Why would she say I am your daughter?"

"Because that is what your mother told her," Edward said. "At least I assume she did. I imagine your mother went to de Simone when she found out she was with child by one of her lovers, and since I was her richest suitor... "

"Edward, don't," Jane said quietly.

"No, Jane," Adèle said quietly, but with unmistakable anger. "I want to hear all he has to say, no matter what, or how hurtful. He owes me that." Jane looked down at her lap with a sigh.

Adèle looked at Edward again, "So Céline told Madame that you are my father. Is that what my mother told you?"

Edward was quiet for a moment, thinking before he spoke. "Adèle, Jane is right, I do not want to say things that will hurt you, and if we continue in this vein, I will say things that are harsh, things that you will never forget. Can you not just remember your mother as she was, a woman who loved you as much as she was able?"

"No!" Adèle's voice was strident, and she suddenly stood up, her fists clenched. She paced over to the fireplace, and then turned back to Edward, "I have to hear, I have to know whatever it is that you have to say, no matter what, and I would like to have some answers now."

Edward sighed, then he spoke again. "I do not care to speak of these matters before my wife. It is not respectful to her to speak of such things."

Adèle laughed bitterly, "I could not tell Jane the part about you being my father, I stumbled over the words. It was she who said it first, asked me what I could not put into words, if Madame had said anything about my parentage. She guessed, from my fumbling, stumbling words, what I was trying not to say."

Jane spoke up, "That is true, Edward. I don't mind if you speak the truth before me. Or I can leave the room, and you can speak frankly together."

"No!" Both Edward and Adèle spoke together, which lent the scene the first tiny thread of humour to be found. Neither wanted to be alone in the room with the other, without Jane's steadying influence. Adèle continued, "Please, Jane, stay here. And Mr. Rochester, I want to hear whatever it is you have to say."

He sighed, rubbed his eyes wearily, and looked up at Adèle. "Yes, Céline said I was your father. She continued to say so, up until our relationship ended. As years went on, and I would come to visit, to see you and to look after your welfare, she ceased to refer to me as your father. She never introduced me as such to her other visitors, but it was understood that I continued to give her money on the pretext that you were my daughter. But I knew you were not; I am sorry."

How did you know?" Adèle asked him. He shook his head, would not speak.

"How?" she asked him again. "I did not come from the womb with a letter of introduction in my hand. 'Dear Edward Rochester, this child is not your daughter.' How did you know, if you were with my mother, that I was not your child?"

Edward spoke, "I just knew. I suspected it when your mother was... carrying you. And when you were born, I still suspected, but tried to bury the thought, because I wanted... " He sighed, "I wanted a home, and a family, and hoped against hope that my suspicions were wrong. But then when we separated, I knew it. And I've always known it."

"Why?" Adèle persisted, "Because I look like Céline and not like you? How is that proof?" Adèle gestured wildly towards his wife, "Elizabeth looks exactly like Jane, yet you have no doubt she is your daughter."

Edward frowned, "A man knows his children, that is all."

"No, that is not all," Adèle said, frustration in her voice. "I repeat, you have a daughter who looks just like her mother, and nothing like you, and yet you have no doubt in your mind that she is your daughter. I know the situations are not the same, but if it is looks alone that make you think I am not yours... "

"I have no doubt because I know my wife!" Edward said angrily. "And I know you are not my daughter, because I knew your mother. She pretended to love me, but in truth she despised me. She would never have had a child by me if she could help it.

"I know you are upset, and I will pass over anything you have said that could be taken as a slur against Mrs. Rochester, who has been nothing but kind to you, and who deserves better... "

Jane spoke up. "Edward, she did not mean anything by her questions; I am not offended. She means no disrespect."

"No!" Adèle turned a stricken face to Jane, "Indeed I do not!"

She came back over to the sofa, and knelt down beside Jane, her face raised to her, the tears starting again. "Jane, I would die before maligning you, please, I meant nothing... "

Jane reached over to stroke Adèle's disheveled hair, "Oh, dearest, I know that." She patted the sofa beside her, "Come, sit back down here with me."

Adèle sat, not meeting Edward's eye. Jane held her hand. For a moment, there was silence.

Edward spoke. "Adèle, I know I have not been to you as I should have. But can you accept that I meant only your good and your safety, and have done the best I could for you – cared for you even though you had no natural right to expect it? Can we not just leave it at that?"

Adèle shook her head, "No. Because I have hated being a dependent. Since I was a little girl, and you brought me to England, I pretended you were my father. I prayed you were my father, and hoped that that was why you took me to England. But once we were there... " She swallowed, "you left me behind, went back to your travels, and I was more alone than ever. I hated being beholden to you, hated the idea that you were just taking care of me as a... a good deed. It makes me nothing, a nobody. Just a rare fortunate girl. If I was really your daughter, as I once pretended to be, I would be somebody."

Edward stared at her, "I never knew you felt that way. I never knew you thought about it at all."

"No, you never asked me anything at all," Adèle said, "I was just an annoyance to you, and the fact that you took me in just makes me luckier than most. It is not fair, that I was cared for while others are not."

Jane spoke up. "Adèle, life is not fair. And we are all dependents, in one way or another. We must just thank God for whatever good fortune we have, and use it to help others. Someday you might save a life as well, as a result of just being, as you said, a rare fortunate girl. As many of us are."

Adèle turned to Edward, "Why did you not just leave me at Madame Frédéric's? Perhaps my mother might have returned for me... Madame Frédéric knew how to contact my mother, I'm sure. Perhaps my mother and her lover meant to return for me.

"You did not have to come and take me to England. Maybe my mother did not return for me because she knew I'd been taken away. Or Madame de Simone would have taken me, and she would have contacted my mother..."

Edward folded his arms, shook his head. "Adèle, there is much you don't know. As I said, can we not just leave it at this? I'm sorry you were led to believe your mother was dead, but she is dead now. And I'm sorry you had to find out this way that I am thought to be your father. I never thought to say anything, as I knew I was not.

"I cared for you because you were a helpless child, and because of what your mother was to me at one time. Because I was around when you were born, I have seen to all your needs, and have tried to keep you safe. I felt it was a good deed, one that God would consider against all the bad deeds of my life. And He did. You were safe and cared for. And because of you, I met Jane, without whom my life would be worth nothing. Indirectly, you gave my life back to me, and I have cared for yours. Is that not a bond nearly worth that of father and daughter?"

Adèle spoke quietly, "I don't know if it is or not. I only know what I have learned today. My whole life seems to me to be a lie. And you said there is more I don't know. Well, I want to know everything. Everything you know, and everything you have to tell me."

"Adèle..." Edward spoke the word wearily.

"Everything, Mr. Rochester."

Edward frowned. "Adèle, to tell you of de Simone, of your mother... so much of the story is..." He rubbed his fingertips over his forehead as though it would help him think of the proper words. "It is not fit for your ears..."

Adèle was shaking her head before the sentence was out of his mouth, "No. No. I am not a child any longer. I have read many books. Jane and I have talked as she has helped me prepare for my wedding. I know what passes between a man and a woman."

Edward stood, pacing, his hand thrust down into his pocket as Adèle continued speaking.

"You must help me understand." Her tears welled up again. "Why was I taken from Paris, from what was familiar? Why was I taken from those who might have loved me? Instead I was uprooted, brought to a strange, cold country to live among strangers, to be reared by someone who has never really cared for me. I am in this family because of your sufferance. Jane and the children love me, but you never have." Her eyes met his.

Edward turned to her, "Adèle, you think I did not care for you..."

He stopped. Did he? Could he honestly say he loved her? He cared for her welfare, for her future. But a fatherly love? He thought of the vast, overpowering love he had for his children, and knew it could not compare. He had started out, he felt, loving Adèle, love as his heart had understood it back then. But when her mother's coldness and treachery had broken that heart, he had closed his mind against them both.

He sat, facing Adèle with a sigh, "I could talk to Jane, and she could tell you what you want to hear."

"No," Adèle whispered, "I need to hear this from you."

Edward leaned back in the chair, silent for some moments, his eyes far away. Then he began to speak.

"Agnès de Simone was once a dancer in the famed Opéra Fantaisie. She was said to be a great beauty, although I could never see it. She had had many suitors. She was called Madame, but if she had ever been married, I did not know about it.

"As she grew older she found it more difficult to dance, so she was given a position overseeing the young girls in the ballet dormitories of the Opéra. They trained to dance, and to sing, but also did much of the work around the opera house.

"De Simone trained them and saw to their futures, keeping the dancers and singers who were promising and getting rid of those who were less talented or not as pretty as she felt they should be. The Opéra Fantaisie was known throughout Paris for the beauty and talent of its dancers and young chorus singers."

Adèle held Jane's hand, the eyes of the two women fixed upon Edward. He took a deep breath and continued the story.

"Your mother, Céline, was an orphan. She told me she remembered little of her early life, that she felt she was born knowing how to dance. She never remembered learning, but someone must have taught her back in her earliest days.

"She travelled with a pack of other children, moving through the streets of Paris by day, hiding in the shadows by night. The children kept themselves alive, banded together to steal, to beg, to pick pockets. Céline was a beautiful child and found that by singing and dancing she could collect enough coins to buy some food for her little band of friends.

"De Simone saw her on the street one day, dancing, and told me later she was struck by her incredible beauty and her grace. How old was she? Perhaps seven or eight. She was taken off the streets by de Simone, to live at the Opéra Fantaisie, to train as a dancer. It seems like an act of kindness, does it not?

"There was a mix of girls at the Opéra – some had parents who wanted to see them succeed in the opera world, but some were orphans, at the mercy of strangers who would protect them or betray them at a whim.

"Céline became a protegée of de Simone, a favourite. She gave her choice roles, favoured her over the others, even spared her share of the chores all girls were expected to do. Céline was talented, and more beautiful than the other girls, and this, along with her favoured treatment, earned her no friends among them. De Simone was all she had. She had rescued her from hunger, from the streets, had given her the only affection she could remember. She grew devoted to her rescuer.

"But de Simone had a dark and evil aspect. She had another line of work, as a procurer. She seemed to know everyone in Paris. She knew what people wanted and how to get it. If there was a young woman in the Opéra who wished to advance herself by a liaison with a wealthy man, de Simone knew how to bring this about.

"As she was responsible for developing the talents in the Opéra, she had to get rid of the dancers who were not the best. The girls with families could simply go back to them, or to one of the smaller and less prestigious opera houses.

"But the orphans, the ones with no protection, well... de Simone had a place for them too, for she had contacts within the brothels around the city, and she profited handsomely from the ruin and disgrace of these girls."

Adèle and Jane looked horrified.

Edward said, "You see why I did not want to tell you all this. It is ugly; a part of the world I wish I had never known, and that I did not want you to see."

Adèle's voice was deadly calm, "Is the story complete?"

"No," her guardian told her, his voice equally quiet.

"Then please do not stop there."

He continued, his jaw set grimly, "I was so naive once, so ignorant of the world. As a young man, I assumed that every other man wanted what I wanted: a woman who was his equal. I did not realize, until I was with Céline, that there are men who only want children. Not young women, you understand, but children. Little girls."

Adèle frowned but he saw comprehension and horror cross his wife's face. "Edward... " she began.

"Children." Adèle said, "Little girls as... " She could not continue.

"Yes," Edward said. "There was a man de Simone knew, a very wealthy Englishman. He had been forced to leave England as a result of his actions and the censure of his countrymen. He came to France and lived in a chateau outside Paris. He was rich beyond de Simone's wildest dreams."

"He came to the opera, and there his eyes fell upon Céline."

Adèle's eyes were closed, her face still. Jane held her hand in both of hers, squeezing. Tears stood out in her green eyes.

"I am not sure how old she was then, but she thought perhaps she was about nine or ten." His jaw clenched painfully, "Around the same age as our little Jane Elizabeth."

He swallowed and went on, "Who knows how much de Simone was paid to allow this, but he had unlimited wealth and for nearly three years Céline was... at his mercy. But believe me, he showed her no mercy. Anything that a man might... demand... of an adult woman, was forced upon Céline. She was his toy, his plaything, and what she endured at his hands... " His face was dark and far away. Jane watched him closely. She had not seen him look so grim in many years.

"She would dance every night and do two shows on Saturday, and after the show on Saturday night she was taken to his villa. De Simone was given her money, and she left Céline there with him. So, every Sunday, while the church bells pealed all over Paris... " He stopped, rubbed his eyes wearily.

"I was with Céline for two years and never knew why every Sunday when the church bells rang out, she was in a foul temper and would act distant and unreachable. Most of the time she doted on me, and acted her part towards me, but on those days... Only later did I understand. For there I was, just another wealthy Englishman... "

Adèle was crying now, silent tears rolling down her cheeks.

Edward went on, "When Céline became a woman, this man lost interest and discarded her like trash thrown out onto the street, no doubt to move on to another child. Céline had only de Simone. They never talked about the Englishman and what he had done to her – what de Simone had allowed him to do to her. Céline continued to dance, and de Simone was her foster mother, her mentor, her source of income, the only one who appeared to care for her. Is it any wonder Céline still clung to her despite the monstrous betrayal?

"I came along when Céline was in her mid-twenties. She had long graduated from the corps de ballet and was now a principal dancer. She had grown quite celebrated and I was dazzled by her.

"De Simone encouraged Céline to allow my attentions, as she quickly determined how rich I was. De Simone and I hated each other from the first, as I saw her for the opportunist she was, but that did not stop her from urging Céline to stay in my good graces for the money. Only later did I know how truly wicked she was."

"I was deluded enough to dream that Céline would truly love me, after you were born. I knew, deep down, that she had other lovers, but I denied it for so long. Céline was desperate to keep her independence. After your birth, she was frantic to return to the stage. She bound herself, and you were fed by a wet nurse. She starved herself to lose any weight she had gained, so anxious was she to get back to dancing. She refused to wait any longer than she had to, to get back to the stage.

"But for two or three weeks after your birth she could not dance and she fell deeply into depression and despair. One Sunday, as the church bells rang, she broke down, holding you in her arms, and told me the story. I was in a rage, I wanted to kill the English monster, and to kill de Simone, but Céline would not hear a word against her."

Adèle wiped her face with both hands, visibly trying to control her shaking as Edward continued, "Céline made me promise that I would protect you. And although she never said a word against de Simone, still Céline made me promise that de Simone would never be permitted to raise you. I could do so little then to make Céline happy, but I promised her that."

Edward ran his hand through his hair, thinking back to those days. "We were separated months later, although I continued to send money and to visit you. I had reconciled myself to the knowledge that you were not my daughter as I had once believed, but I was still concerned for your welfare. De Simone did not live with you and your mother, but she was a presence in your lives and although I hated that, there was nothing I could do."

"I don't remember Madame," Adèle said, shaking her head. "I feel as though I had never known her."

"I believe your mother still had contact with de Simone, still considered her a close friend. But she apparently kept her away from you. She was a good enough mother to you to do that."

Edward said, "Years later, I was in Rome and had not seen you or your mother for well over a year, although I sent money. I received a message from a Madame Frédéric, who kept children in her home for a fee. You had been left there by Céline, when she ran off with her lover.

"Madame Frédéric said that Céline had left her some money, and information on how to contact me, but had provided a false address for herself. When she could not contact your mother, Madame Frédéric wrote to tell me that the money was nearly gone, and that a Madame de Simone had called at the home twice and had offered to take you off her hands. Madame Frédéric said that your mother had left strict orders that you were to be released only to me, but she did not know what to do and Madame de Simone had seemed so kind, so concerned. How de Simone found you at the Frédérics, I do not know. Perhaps she had someone watching you and Céline all along.

"I sent Madame Frédéric a message from my hotel in Rome, telling her to keep you there, and that I was on my way. I returned to Paris and eventually took you from that home. There was nowhere in Paris, I felt, where de Simone could not find you, and so I brought you to England where I knew you would be safe.

"I know I have not been as I should to you, Adèle, but I hope you will understand that I acted to protect you from the evil that had so blighted your mother's life. I think of her to this day, crying as she held you tightly and worried for your future, and despite all that transpired, I cannot hate her. She hurt me deeply, but knowing all she had endured, I felt I should treat her charitably, partly for your sake, but partly for hers as well.

"I don't know why she left with another man and left you behind. I am not sure now whether she herself knew why she did the things she did.

"She had no chance of a normal life, but she begged that for you, and both of us, in our feeble and faulty ways, tried to give it to you."

Adèle nodded, her face grave, before she once again began to cry softly and turned to Jane, who gathered the girl in her arms and held her closely, her eyes meeting Edward's over Adèle's bowed head. He stood for a long time, watching Adèle and his wife, but his thoughts were elsewhere. And then he turned and left the room.

Chapter 59 - Adèle's Engagement

Thornfield Manor, June 1851

Edward looked up as he heard the knock on the door of the library, and put down his reading glass as John announced the arrival of Thomas Cooper, the curate of Hay's church. Edward stood to shake his hand, then offered him a seat. Cooper refused the drink Edward offered him, watching solemnly as his host resumed his seat.

"I thank you for seeing me, Mr. Rochester," Thomas told him.

"Not at all," Edward said.

Cooper sighed, "I suppose you have heard by now that Miss Varens has released me from our engagement?"

"Yes," Edward answered, his dark eye fixed upon Thomas.

The Rochester family had arrived back at Thornfield from France only days before. Adèle, whose sadness and silence had remained after she had confronted Edward about her past, had apparently written to Cooper during their trip, telling him that she wished to discontinue their relationship. Several letters had subsequently arrived at the hotel addressed to her, which she accepted silently, and never referred to.

Upon their arrival back in Derbyshire, Thomas had come to the house almost as soon as the family had left the coach, but Adèle refused to see him, and it was then that she informed her guardians that she had broken off the engagement. Jane had attempted to discuss matters with her, but Adèle had politely yet insistently refused to talk about it.

Edward looked at Cooper, a tall young man of pale colouring, who had always seemed the most phlegmatic and unflappable of men. He was a quiet fellow, one who thought before speaking, seemingly the opposite of Adèle with her vivacious personality and love of laughter. But Edward had realized that they were suited to each other, that Cooper could have a steadying effect upon Adèle, whom he had never ceased to view in light of the flightiness of her mother. At the same time, she could make Thomas loosen up a bit, make him laugh.

Edward noted Cooper's pallor, the red rims of his light blue eyes. He had always enjoyed a joke or two at the curate's expense, referring to him as "The Vicar" and teasing Adèle about the serious demeanour of her intended. But he felt a flash of pity for the man now, realizing that for all his silence, he was suffering the loss of his love and was taking this with the utmost gravity.

He leaned forward to speak to Cooper, "I think you should know that Mrs. Rochester has attempted to speak to Adèle a number of times regarding your situation. She refuses to discuss it. I am afraid that I myself do not know what she is about. May I inquire as to the reason she gave for her change of mind?"

Thomas cleared his throat, "She tells me that she is unworthy. That her blood is tainted, that she is not fit to be the wife of a decent man, or the wife of a minister. She fears she will bring me embarrassment in the future; that her parentage will cast a shadow over our entire lives."

Edward frowned, his brow furrowed as he pondered Cooper's words.

"And what do you think of this, Cooper?"

The curate shook his head, frustrated. Then his voice burst out, "I think it is nonsense. I wrote her over and over, telling her so."

"And did she answer your letters?" Edward asked. "We saw the mail arrive for her. She would take the letters and go to her room. She never discussed them with us."

Cooper looked defeated. "She never answered them. I received the note from her, notifying me that she was breaking our engagement and then laying out the reasons why. I sent her several letters, in which I begged her to reconsider and assured her that I had no such worries about her background. But she did not reply. Finally I resigned myself to waiting until her return. I did not imagine that she would refuse to see me. I had thought we could discuss things face to face, that I could convince her in person." His shoulders slumped, as though this statement had exhausted him.

Edward tossed out a thought, knowing in advance what Thomas would say. "You had a formal agreement, the date was set. Breaking the tie is a breach of her promise. You could bring action against her, force a confrontation. Men very rarely do, but you would be within your rights."

Cooper looked horrified. "No, sir! I would never do that. This is a private matter, between Miss Varens and myself. I would never force her to explain her actions publicly. If she no longer loves me, I can accept that, in time. But if she thinks she is not worthy of me, that she would taint me by association, that I cannot accept, not without a chance to refute her ideas."

Edward nodded, satisfied. He had suspected that that would be the curate's answer, but he had wanted to be sure.

"So, Mr. Cooper," Edward asked him, "what do you want of me?"

Thomas swallowed, "You are the guardian of Miss Varens. She considers you a father. She would listen to you if you insisted she speak to me face to face."

Edward looked up at the ceiling, frowning, before looking back at Cooper. "Adèle is still under my protection, but she is of age. At twenty-three, she is responsible for her own decisions. I can no longer compel her to do anything."

Thomas flushed. "I realize that, sir, but you and Mrs. Rochester carry great weight in her opinion. She looks up to you, loves you both. She has told me as much. If you told her to speak to me... " He broke off, his face now flaming. Edward realized what it cost him to plead his case to his fiancée's guardian.

Edward leaned forward, his face softened with sympathy, "Mr. Cooper, I must speak to you plainly, man to man." Thomas flinched at these words, fearing the worst.

Edward went on, "There has been a change in Adèle, since this summer. And I am afraid that change was brought about by revelations about her past. Several painful ones. She was told that I am not her natural father, which apparently she secretly hoped I was. Why, I do not know, as I have never been very good to her. I should think she would consider it a relief that I had nothing to do with fathering her, but it pains her. And she fears that her natural father is... well, someone she would not care to be associated with."

Thomas frowned, a look of sadness crossing his face, which had paled again.

Edward continued, "She also came to know something ill of her mother, whom she remembers fondly, as a child will. She learned that the woman abandoned her, rather than dying, as she had been told. She also learned of her mother's tendency towards promiscuity. These tendencies were not the mother's fault; I have come to believe her mother had a dreadful life. But all these revelations have greatly disturbed Adèle. I think they have affected her mind."

Cooper clenched his hands until his knuckles were white. He stared at the ground for a long time, before looking up. There were tears standing in his eyes.

"Mr. Rochester, I decided a long time ago that I love Adèle no matter what might be in her past. I knew that there was more to it than just two parents who had died – there were too many unanswered questions. I would never have asked her to marry me if I thought there was any chance I would worry over her past. I put those fears to rest before I ever let the friendship deepen. For her to think now that she is unworthy..." He stopped, looking miserable.

Edward was irritated at himself for how touched he was. He was becoming soft in his old age.

"I believe that of you, Mr. Cooper," he said, annoyed at the lump in his throat. "I do not think anyone could ever accuse you of being frivolous, of acting without thought."

Thomas Cooper pondered those words for a moment, and then his lips twitched. "You are right about that, Mr. Rochester," he answered. He was silent for a moment, then went on.

"I have always been serious, even as a child. I found it hard to laugh and play like other boys. There were too many thoughts going through my head. I know I am sombre." He sighed, "Let us be frank – I can be boring at times. There is much going on in my mind, but it is hard for me to express it. But in Adèle, I have found something I did not know I could be. She made me laugh. I had fun. For the first time in my life, I had real fun. With her.

"I cannot go back to how I used to be, Mr. Rochester. With her, I enjoy my life, and can see how happy I could be. I do not want to be without that again."

Edward nodded, becoming increasingly disgusted with himself, as he felt tears sting behind his eyelids. "I will talk to my wife, Mr. Cooper. We will see what we can do."

That night, Edward brought up the subject as he and Jane sat in their room before bed. He told her about Cooper's visit, and how the young curate had asked for Edward's assistance. Jane shook her head sadly, looking into the fire.

"I was afraid of this," she said quietly. "Her whole demeanour has changed; she is so quiet and sad now. I have tried to talk to her, but she simply will not discuss it. She says it is her problem to work out and will not trouble me with it."

"She is young," Edward said, looking frustrated. "Young women like a certain drama in their lives. Those of us who've lived a little while know that when love presents itself to you, take it as what it is – a gift from God, who has decided to give you a great blessing in an otherwise difficult life."

"It's more than that, Edward," Jane answered. "She is really not given to displays of drama any longer. It's true she was a child who was given to frivolity and who lacked discipline, but she has become quite sensible as she has grown." She playfully squeezed her husband's chin with her fingers and smiled at him, "Just as I told you she would, remember?"

She sighed, growing serious again. "I truly believe that she feels unworthy of Thomas, that she feels she is tainted. She learned a great deal about her mother, and has had to face many unpleasant truths."

Edward was silent. Jane leaned her elbow on the back of the sofa, watching Edward's face as he stared at the leaping fire.

"Edward," she started, her voice hesitant, "how certain are you that you are not Adèle's father?"

He frowned, looking over at her. "What?" he asked.

"You seemed quite positive that you are not Adèle's father," Jane told him. "How can you be sure of that?"

Edward shrugged, thinking. "I am nearly as sure as I can be in that case," he told Jane, turning to her. "I have thought about it a great deal through the years, believe me. Everything, all the circumstances point to her not being mine. I can't even go into it all, but from the time Céline told me she was expecting, I doubted it. There are many reasons, but now I'm more sure of it than ever, since being married."

"Oh?" Jane looked surprised.

"Yes," Edward said, "I didn't know much about childbearing then, and so could not base my suspicions on anything certain. But now I have seen you – six times you have carried my child, and I've seen the changes brought about by pregnancy. I saw those changes in Céline, before she ever told me she was with child, before it was... possible, had the child been mine. And Adèle was born over a month earlier than the date Céline told me she was expected. She was large, vigorous, healthy. I saw Ned and Elizabeth, carried a full nine months, born smaller than Adèle was."

"Not our Helen, though," said Jane with a smile.

Edward grinned, "No, not our baby girl. She was a healthy bundle." The two laughed together, remembering.

"Anyway," said Edward, his smile fading, "I have never thought of Adèle as my daughter; only as I would a friend's child, left in my hands. I suppose it is possible that all my suspicions were wrong and that I am Adèle's father. But I've never felt in my mind that I was; in fact, quite the opposite. All my instincts tell me I am not.

"There are other reasons I am fairly sure Adèle is not mine. I made inquiries, after Céline and I were parted. People who knew Céline told me of a serious relationship she had while I was out of the country for a few months. It was with a man who was married, and Céline was apparently quite enamoured of him. My thought is that he deserted her, and she was desperate to have a 'father' for the child she then found herself expecting. I believe he is Adèle's natural father."

"I had an idea," Jane ventured. "I doubt you would like it, though, if you are that certain of Adèle's parentage. I thought, perhaps, if you acknowledged Adèle as your daughter, that she might feel better, more inclined to keep to the engagement."

"I can hardly do that, since I was so insistent about not being her father," Edward frowned.

"No, I suppose you cannot," Jane agreed. "But I thought it might ease her mind, make her more able to hold up her head as Mr. Cooper's wife."

"And meanwhile, it would reflect badly on you, my love," Edward said, reaching for her hand.

"Why?" Jane asked. "Everything happened long before I met you. One thing I have realized, now that I move with the gentry, is that this is not a new story. And I can honestly say it does not matter to me if she is or is not. I learned the possibility so long ago, when I was still her governess, that it is an idea I am completely accustomed to. I love her as my own daughter; knowing she is your daughter could only make her feel more mine. Nor do I mind if she is not, but I do believe that many of our acquaintance assume that she is."

"Many people have wards, children for whom they are responsible," Edward protested. "And Adèle looks nothing like me."

"As Adèle pointed out, Elizabeth doesn't look much like you either," Jane told him. "The poor girl looks like me."

"Poor girl!" Edward said, "She is quite fortunate to look like you, Jane."

Jane rolled her eyes, laughing, "Well, I'm glad you think so."

"Besides," Edward continued, "she looks like you on the surface, with her brown hair and serious face, but when she begins to speak, or holds her head in a certain way, she looks like my mother. The older she gets, the more I see her grandmother in her. And when she stands in the sunlight, and I see the red glints in her hair, then I see my father in her as well.

"No, I cannot make Adèle my daughter, not now. She is my ward, she will have to accept that. Look at you – you had little family, and the family you did have cast you out. It was not until you were grown that you found our dear cousins Mary and Diana; found your family."

"And St. John, do not forget him," Jane said, her voice teasing.

Now it was Edward's turn to cast his eye Heavenward, shake his head with a smile, "And St. John, of course. At any rate, your lack of family did not ruin your life; you went forward bravely and forged a life for yourself."

"I don't remember my parents," Jane told him. "And my parents died; they would have remained with me if they could have. Adèle remembers her mother, remembers being loved by her. Now she finds out that her mother did not love her enough to stay with her – and that the man she hoped was her father is not her father. It's no wonder she's confused."

"Well, she needs to get over her confusion," Edward said with irritation. "They're supposed to be married at Michaelmas. They can keep it hidden for a while, but when the day comes and the marriage does not go through, it will become a scandal in the town, and Mr. Cooper will bear the brunt. He does not deserve that."

"No, he does not," Jane agreed.

"I still plan to walk her down the aisle, in a father's place, if she chooses it," Edward told her. "But that is all I can do. I'm not her father, much as she might wish it, and I cannot make myself so. I am sorry, Jane… I have tried to care for her the best I can."

Jane reached over to kiss him, before standing up, "I know you have, Edward. Come, we had better go to bed. Are you going to talk to Adèle tomorrow?"

Edward sighed, "Yes. But will she listen to me, that is the question?"

Chapter 60 - Nothing Without You

Adèle tapped on the open doorframe of Edward's study, craning her neck to look into the room. He looked up, smiling at her as he beckoned her in.

"You wanted to talk to me, Mr. Rochester?" Adèle said, entering the room.

"Yes, Adèle; please sit down." Edward indicated a chair in front of his desk, and came around the desk to shut the door after her. Adèle's eyes followed him as he walked back and took a chair near her. She folded her hands, her hazel eyes fixed on her guardian.

"I hope you do not think that Mrs. Rochester and I are prying into your private concerns, but I think you should know that Mr. Cooper has come to me, regarding your engagement. Or former engagement, if I understand him correctly." Edward leaned back in his chair, trying to look friendly and concerned rather than intimidating, as he feared he would.

Adèle sighed, looking down at her folded hands.

"Am I right, you have broken off your engagement?" Edward persisted.

Adèle nodded, still looking down at her lap. "Yes," she said quietly.

"And may I ask why?" Edward went on. "I know what Mr. Cooper said, but I would like to hear what you have to say."

"Because I do not feel worthy to be his wife," Adèle said, a slight catch in her throat. "He can do better than the illegitimate daughter of... well, whatever my parents were."

"Now this is where Mrs. Rochester and I begin to overstep things and interfere," Edward told her. "She and I have discussed the situation, and she tells me you refuse to talk to her. Therefore, she asked me to speak to you."

Adèle looked up. Her eyes looked very shiny, as though tears swam upon the surface. "There is really nothing to discuss," she said, her voice low. "I have made my decision. Thomas... Mr. Cooper... he may be upset now, but in time I believe he will thank me."

"He is not thanking you now," Edward told her. "He is terribly upset. I spoke to him at length yesterday, and the man is distraught. He is heartbroken. And he cannot believe you would make such a decision without consulting him."

"I knew if we discussed it that he would try to dissuade me," Adèle told Edward. "I knew I would not be strong enough to keep my resolve. And so I wrote to him, and have refused to see him. It is better this way."

"Do you not think that that course of action was rather cruel?" her guardian asked her. "You had time to think of it all; Mr. Cooper had no time to consider it, and now he can think of nothing else."

"I'm sorry," Adèle said softly, "I did not want to hurt him, but I think in the future his being married to someone like me would hurt him more."

"Are you afraid you will do wrong in your life, Adèle, that you will follow the wrong path and disgrace Thomas?"

Adèle shook her head, "I do not know. I don't think I would purposely choose a life of sin, but I do not know myself. I just feel dirty... unworthy. I feel my blood is tainted; that I would sully Thomas by my very presence. That our children would be people I would not recognize or care for."

She quickly swiped at her cheek with her hand. "What if I loved my child at first, and then did not want to care for it, what if I deserted it? What if I thought I loved Thomas, and decided later I did not?" She continued with difficulty, "I feel I cannot trust myself. I feel evil, in here." She laid a palm against her breast.

"Oh, Adèle," Edward sighed, "we are all the children of Adam. We are all tainted. We do the best we can – we try to live well, to live the best life we can. Some people do not, they follow their evil impulses. But you are not one of those people."

"How can I ever know?" Adèle shrugged. She looked away, her full lips trembling.

"Do you love Thomas Cooper?" Edward asked his ward.

"Yes," Adèle said without hesitation, "but love is never enough, and he is too good for me. Somewhere in the world is a good woman, one who is worthy of Thomas."

Edward laughed then, he could not help it. "Adèle, if we let the people we love slip through our fingers so they can marry one worthy of them, I would never have married Jane. Do you know about St. John Rivers?"

Adèle frowned, "Jane's cousin? The brother of Mary and Diana?"

"Yes," Edward said. "He is a missionary in India, and writes to Mrs. Rochester several times a year."

"Yes, I know of him. I have heard him spoken of; when we have visited Moor House I have seen his portrait," Adèle answered.

"Ah, yes, the painting," Edward nodded. "I have never seen the man in person, but my wife tells me it is a good likeness. It is a portrait made from a drawing Mrs. Rochester did while she lived with them for a year. You can see he was a very handsome man."

Adèle wagged her head back and forth, thinking. "I suppose so," she said.

"Well, what you might not know, is that he wanted to marry my wife, and take her to India with him," Edward told her.

"No, I did not know that," Adèle said, a spark of interest lighting her eyes.

"Oh, yes," Edward said, "We don't talk much about it; it's as though he is only her cousin, nothing more. He did not love Jane, as a wife, and she merely loved him as a cousin. But he was most put out that she would not marry him. He never even mentions my existence or that of our children, in his letters. He just wishes Mrs. Rochester well and then goes on to tell her everything he has been doing. I believe that he thinks her life as a wife and mother is a step down in the world from becoming a dried-up husk along the Ganges preaching to the heathen."

Adèle said nothing, just sat with her eyes upon her guardian.

"At any rate, I have to say that he is a better man than I. I have never willingly sacrificed anything. I went my own way through life, never thinking of others, until it took God Himself to stop me. And stop me He did, but even then I was unwilling to give up the one I loved." Edward leaned back, resting his chin upon his hand as he thought back.

"If I were a better man, I would have refused to marry Jane, and sent her off back to Yorkshire to marry Rivers just as fast as the carriage could convey her. Because, you see, I was not worthy of her. I was tainted – truly tainted, in years of action, not just in theory. I should no more have married her than married the

Queen, but I was not willing to give her up. I was not noble enough, because, you see, I loved her with all my heart. St. John Rivers may have been a more worthy man, is probably still a more worthy man than I, but he could not have loved my Jane the way that I could. No one could have loved her the way I could, and so I clung to her with all my might."

Adèle swallowed hard, looked down. A small bead of a teardrop trembled on her lowered lashes.

"Now, fourteen years later, Mrs. Rochester is happy, and so am I. She has never had the joy of tending to souls in India, nor has she had the particular privilege of laying down her life for God. She has lived a most mundane existence as the wife of an old, ugly, crippled gentleman in the most sedate county in England." He grinned at Adèle, his brilliant smile making him look anything but old and ugly. "But she has the life she was meant for, with me. And happy does not begin to describe how I have been with her.

"Now, if you were happier with the idea of being without Thomas, I would say nothing, Adèle," Edward told her. "But I have seen you on a regular basis since you were seven years old, and I know when you are happy and when you are not. And you have not been happy without Thomas, am I correct?"

"Yes," Adèle whispered. "But I am afraid I will ruin his life."

"You might ruin it more if you leave him," Edward told her. "The man I saw before me yesterday is miserable without you. He told me that you have brought laughter and fun into his life. He says he is boring and joyless and that you alone bring sunshine to his lonely soul."

"He's not boring," Adèle said, wiping her cheeks with her hands. "He is very quiet. The first time he asked me to go walking with him, I went because I felt sorry for him. I had seen him watching me, in church. But once he started to talk, I realized that just because he was quiet did not mean he was dull. He is very funny, has the most wonderful thoughts and ideas. He makes up the most exciting, fantastical stories, he makes me laugh... " Adèle broke off, and looked up at Edward, her cheeks pinkening.

"Adèle, if you stay on the course you are starting out on, you will not be happy, and neither will Mr. Cooper. What do you propose to do, anyway, if you do not marry?"

Adèle looked startled. "I don't know… I had not thought about it. I suppose I should leave this house. I am of age, I should make my own way."

Edward held up his hand. "I did not say that because I wish you to leave if you do not marry. You have a home with Mrs. Rochester and me as long as you want it. If you never marry at all, you are as welcome here as Elizabeth and Helen." At these words, Adèle's mouth once again betrayed her emotions with a quiver, her hazel eyes gleamed with fresh tears. "I just wondered if you have given any thought to your future, if you have thought one month beyond today."

Adèle shook her head, looking miserable.

"Adèle, you are in pain. You found out many difficult truths this past spring, and it is causing such upheaval in your heart that you are trying to give yourself some real pain, something truly tragic to hold to. You are punishing yourself for things that are not your fault." Edward stopped, secretly rather proud of his philosophical little turn of mind. *If only I had been so good at working out my own problems, years ago.*

"But you are not alone in this," Edward went on. "Mr. Cooper will suffer also. Not just in his heart, but in the eyes of the church and of the town. I reminded him that he has a right to make this issue public, to accuse you, as you have broken a promise." Adèle looked startled, then her eyebrows came together in a glowering frown.

"You hadn't thought of that, had you?" Edward asked. "And before you get yourself too upset, Cooper refused to even give that a second's consideration. He will act as a gentleman, never saying a word against you. But in the eyes of everyone around him, he will suffer. People always assume it is the fault of the man if an engagement is broken. He might even have to leave the parish, because he will feel himself the object of pity and gossip. And I would not like that. It's the first time Wood has gotten a curate with any common sense whatsoever.

"Now, if you want to be free of Mr. Cooper, because you have decided that you no longer love him, or were mistaken in your feelings for him to begin with, then I urge you to sit down with the man and tell him to his face, as an honourable woman should," Edward told her. "But if you are acting to save him from some bad behaviour that you think you might be subject to in the future, I beg you, do not be so foolish. We can none of us trust ourselves; we can only do what is right and proper each moment of our lives.

"You are not your mother, Adèle," Edward said. "I know that there are times I have been unkind; I have not been to you what I should have been. I admit this freely, and I must bear the blame for your present turmoil. But do not confuse me with Thomas Cooper. He is a good man. Blame me, hate me if you must, but do not punish him."

Adèle sat quietly, tears running down her pale cheeks. Edward felt a flash of pity. He could see, watching her, how thin she had grown, how her colour and life had faded. Suddenly, her resemblance to her mother did not trouble him. He could separate the two women. A longing swept over him, an urge to make things right for her before it was too late.

"You are not your mother," Edward repeated. "Her life was terrible, tragic. But you do not have to pay for it. Her heart had been twisted within her; her natural feelings stunted by the cruelty she suffered. But your heart is a loving one. I have seen it, in your tender friendship with Jane, in your affection for my children. You will love your own children, you will never leave them desolate and bereft of a mother's love."

He stood, coming back around to where Adèle sat. "Now, after I brought you in here, Mrs. Rochester brought Mr. Cooper in for tea. Will you speak to him?"

Adèle looked up, an agony of pain and indecision on her face. She reached up to wipe off her cheeks, fumbling in her pocket for a handkerchief. She realized she did not have one, just as Edward reached into his pocket for his.

"Yes," she whispered, reaching for the handkerchief, "I will see him." Edward handed her the white cotton square, startled for a moment to feel Adèle's hand grasp his in a hard grip.

"I will talk to Thomas," she said, her voice louder.

"And, Mr. Rochester... I do not hate you."

30 September 1851

The church at Hay was filled to overflowing on this sunny, cool day when Adèle Varens walked down the aisle on the arm of her guardian, to meet her betrothed at the altar. She was dressed in a simple pale blue dress with a matching jacket over it, and a white, veiled bonnet decorated with a sprig of violets. She carried a matching nosegay of violets and a small white Bible in her hands, a gift from her husband-to-be.

Edward walked her down the aisle, feeling the slight tremble of Adèle's hand where it rested lightly upon his arm. He tried to smile reassuringly at her, but her gaze was upon Thomas, who stood at the altar, his eyes fixed on his approaching bride. Edward caught the eye of his wife, sitting in one of the front pews with Ned at her side. She looked as though she wanted to cry, but she returned his smile. Edward brought Adèle to stand beside her groom, giving Thomas a slight nod as he stepped back and joined his wife and son in the pew.

Jane clasped his arm tightly as both of them turned their eyes to the front to watch their ward as she left their care and was given to her new husband. Edward did not even hear the first words of the ceremony. He was struck by an air of unreality as he watched this young woman, nearly the image of his long-ago lover, marrying this kind, gentle, country clergyman. He forced his mind to the present.

God, let her be happy, as her mother never was. Let her live a calm and happy life, as it took me so long to do. Do not let the sins of this generation infect the next. Undo the damage in her heart that I have done.

Adèle's outfit was to double as a travelling suit, for as soon as the wedding breakfast was over, she and her husband would be leaving, first for London, then for a trip across France to the villa owned by the Rochesters. They would be gone a month, and then would return for Thomas to resume his work as curate, living with his new bride in the small cottage he had occupied for the past two years. The trip was a gift from her guardians, who had also been most generous with her trousseau, bearing in mind that she would now be a curate's wife and would have no need for fancy dresses or lavish household appointments.

Mr. Cooper was attended by his cousin, the son of his childhood guardian, and Adèle was attended by the Rochester daughters, Elizabeth and Helen. They were dressed in matching blue dresses, with flowers in their hair. Elizabeth was solemn as a judge, awed by her responsibility, while five-year-old Helen was too excited to stand still, bouncing on her toes and waving to people in the congregation. She was avoiding her mother's eyes, knowing Jane would be looking firmly at her trying to calm her down, but she settled down at an equally stern look from her father, and faced her eyes forward, earning her an approving pat from her older sister.

Adèle looked beautiful and very happy as she took her place beside Thomas, who was radiant with the joy of finally taking this woman for his wife. His hands were damp and his voice shook as he said his vows, and Adèle squeezed his hand to reassure him, a loving glance passing between them.

The service was short and simple, and the newly married couple soon retired to the study next door with the parson and the clerk to sign the register while the congregants filed out. The new Mr. and Mrs. Cooper emerged hand in hand to a shower of flower petals and shouted good wishes, before heading back up to

Thornfield Manor for the small wedding breakfast that the Rochesters were hosting for the happy couple and some invited guests.

Ned, who was attending the village school until his parents were ready to send him away to school, had spotted some of his friends in the crowd and wanted to go play with them, and he was a bit sullen as his mother told him that he needed to keep his new suit on awhile longer and sit at the wedding breakfast with his family. Elizabeth was trying hard to maintain her dignity, and Helen was just happy to be free of the church, and ran around getting in the way of those serving the breakfast until Jane finally sent for Molly and asked her to take Helen and let her eat in the nursery.

Later, when the breakfast was over and the guests had departed, Ned was at last allowed to put on his play clothes and go fishing with his school companions, and Edward looked towards the upstairs where Molly had Elizabeth and Helen tidying the nursery before they went out to play. He pulled Jane, still dressed in her finest, into his study, pinning her against the closed door and kissing her until they were both breathless.

She was laughing as she finally was allowed to come up for air.

"Edward, what on earth has gotten into you?" she said, pushing on his shoulders in mock disapproval.

"I was just thinking of our own wedding day; how nervous I was, and how beautiful you were."

"You could not see back then, have you forgotten?" Jane asked him, reaching up to take his face in her hands and kiss him again.

"I could see you with my heart, and you were the most beautiful bride who ever stood at the altar," Edward told her.

"You have had too much champagne this morning," Jane answered, laughing again as he pulled her hips against his.

"I had only one glass, and it was well diluted with punch," he told her. "Helen could have had some, it was that mild."

"We should have given her some, then perhaps she would finally take a nap," Jane said thoughtfully, before grinning at her husband.

"Perhaps we should take a nap," Edward suggested.

"Ha!" Jane told him. "Nap indeed! I am worn out from this wedding business and I know how much sleep I will get if I retire with you." She evaded his reaching hand, and circled him, a teasing smile dancing across her face, "It's only noon; the household will be scandalized."

"I hope so," Edward said, following her, turning to watch her as she moved. "Did I tell you that you look beautiful this morning, even more beautiful than you did when we married?"

"How do you know?" Jane teased. She moved into his arms again, kissed him hard, pressing her thighs against his. He groaned, melting into her as they stood clinging to each other, kissing with passionate abandon. Then, Edward stopped the kiss.

"Jane, do you regret not having all that?" he asked. "No wedding breakfast, no bridesmaids, no wedding trip?"

Jane shook her head, "No, not at all," she said seriously. "I was sitting there in the church, watching them, holding your hand and thinking how much better I liked it the way we did it."

"Are you sure?" Edward asked. "Looking back, I realize I was probably a bit selfish, rushing you to the altar. I should have given you time, time for Mary and Diana to come to stand up with you."

"No, it was lovely, and just right, the way it went for us," Jane told him, kissing him on the mouth, her lips sliding down his neck, then up to the slight indentation below his ear. She kissed him there, reached up to whisper in his ear.

"I would not change a thing, not about the wedding, nor about the wedding night either." She planted a series of small, soft kisses along his jawline, then kissed his mouth again as he gave a little moan.

He pulled her against him again, "I think you are very tired, Jane, after all your hard work. I'm afraid I am going to have to insist that I take you up for a long rest in our bed."

Jane rolled her eyes teasingly, "Well, if you think I look that exhausted... " She took his hand, and let him lead her upstairs to their bedroom, the two of them pretending to sneak upstairs, watching out for servants and laughing like guilty children.

Later, Edward lay naked and relaxed, sprawled upon the rumpled sheets of the turned-down bed. Jane rested on top of him, still straddling him, their sweat-dampened skin making them stick to each other. Jane peeled her breast away from his chest, and he opened his eye, blowing on her hot chest to cool her off, making her giggle. The September air, warmer as the day progressed, blew in through the slightly opened window.

Edward reached up and stroked Jane's hair from her shoulders, tugging at it gently where it adhered to her skin. His eye was fixed on his wife, and he smiled a little, his gaze moving over her.

"What?" she asked him softly, moving off him with a graceful motion of her body, shifting to press herself alongside him, her head resting on his chest. His arms clasped her in a tight grasp.

"I meant what I said, you know," he told her.

"What is that?" she asked him, teasingly. She dropped a kiss on his chest, raised her head to look at him.

"How beautiful you are," he told her solemnly.

"Yes, well, I will excuse you for that," she told him. "The wedding spirit has overtaken you and your romantic flights of fancy can be easily excused."

He laughed, a comforting rumble under her head. Then he bent and kissed her.

"I am serious," he said, his voice suddenly sombre. "Today I was reminded anew of how blessed and fortunate I am, that you stood at that altar with me fourteen years ago."

His arms held her tighter. "My dearest love," he murmured. Her arms hugged him in return.

"When I am with you like this... when you are in my arms... " He stopped, his voice grown rough with emotion. "When we are joined... together... I cannot describe what is in my heart." Jane nodded her head, watching him.

His hand stroked her hair, "I feel as if I am you, and you are me."

Jane nodded again. "I know," she whispered. She thought of how it had been, just minutes before. Their bodies joined, floating together in a perfect rhythm. She had leaned over him, supporting herself with her hands on either side of his head, leaning forward to tease his lips with hers. He had raised his head, buried his face in her neck, groaning as her warmth took him in and he began to meet her every movement. He lay back then, watching her the way he loved to do, their positions giving him the perfect view of her still slender form, her lovely breasts, her shiny hair spilling over her shoulders. Her soft sounds urged him on, each delicious motion bringing them closer to what they both craved, yet neither of them wanting it to end. They had been one, perfectly together. One of just many times together, yet each time unique and lovely.

I am you, and you are me.

He pressed his lips into her hair. "I am nothing without you."

Chapter 61 - Through the Valley of the Shadow

Thornfield Manor, September 1855

Jane stood at the nursery window staring out into the darkness. Behind her, in their narrow beds, her daughters slept restlessly, their fevers not allowing them to sink into the escape of a deep and healing slumber. Down the hall, Edward was trying to sleep as well. He was not as sick as Elizabeth and Helen, but he was uncomfortable – his throat raw and aching, his fever never completely leaving him.

Jane could not remember the last time her husband had been ill. He occasionally caught a mild cold, one that left him coughing and cranky, snoring at night through a congested nose. But his high fever, the aching of his bones, the fine rash over his dark skin, frightened Jane. Adding to his distress was his worry over his girls, and his sorrow at the grief that had suddenly overtaken Thornfield.

A week ago, Henry, the younger son of Adèle and Thomas, had died after a short and sudden illness. Both he and his elder brother Tom had fallen ill with what at first seemed to be one of the numerous complaints of early childhood. Tom had been mildly sick, feverish and fretful, but Henry had rapidly grown more ill. His mother had fetched Mr. Carter, who came and examined both boys.

"Scarlet fever," was his solemn pronouncement. "There are several cases in Hay and a number in Millcote. The warm, dry spring and summer does it every time. Everyone is happy with the unseasonable warmth, but people have fewer crops, do not eat as well, and invariably sicken."

Molly fell ill next. Since the Rochesters' daughters had grown older and no longer had need of a nurse, Molly had begun to work for the Coopers, helping Adèle with little Thomas, born ten months after her marriage to the curate, and then with Henry, born a year after his brother. She had worked tirelessly to help nurse the two little boys, but finally had had to take to her bed.

Jane and Mary had come each day to help care for the two children and their nurse, and had watched helplessly as little Henry lapsed into a stupor and then died in his father's arms, as his mother looked on, sobbing uncontrollably.

"Please, dear Lord, do not let this be true," the young mother wailed, fighting against Jane's arms, which encircled her shoulders in an embrace meant both to comfort and restrain, "Do not take my baby from me!"

Sorrow descended upon the little home near the church that housed the curate and his young family, and scarcely less upon Thornfield Manor. Elizabeth and Helen, who had adored the two little boys and saw them almost daily, were grief-stricken. Edward was terribly upset, although he tried to be strong for his wife and daughters. Jane cried, thinking of the night she had gone to help Carter bring Henry into the world. She had given Henry his first bath, and had been the one to carry him over to Adèle and place him in her arms. She had loved Adèle's little boys from the day they born.

Jane continued to care for Tom, who Mr. Carter said would most likely make a full recovery. But now she was caring for Adèle as well, who had taken to her bed with grief over her two-year-old son. Mary cared for Molly. And when Jane and Mary looked at each other, fear was evident on both their faces.

And then the sickness had come to Thornfield.

Elizabeth showed the signs first. By now the symptoms were familiar, and Jane did not even need to see the brilliant strawberry rash on her tongue before she knew her daughter had caught the scarlet fever. Elizabeth had never been terribly strong, tending to get sick easily. When Mr. Carter checked her, and nodded over her head at her parents, they had smiled at their daughter reassuringly and kept their composure, but had both cried with fear once they were out of Elizabeth's sight.

They stood in their bedroom, clinging to each other, the thought of Henry's still little body fresh in their minds.

"Jane, I cannot bear to see her ill or in pain," Edward whispered. "What if something..." He stopped, unable to go on.

"Shhh, Edward," Jane told him, swallowing back the fear that seemed caught in her throat, fighting its way upwards. "Don't say it. We have to be strong in all this. We must write to Ned, tell him not to come home as planned."

My dear son-

I am afraid this letter brings ill tidings, although we hope for the best. There is some sickness at Thornfield, scarlet fever, the doctor says. Your mother will write soon with the details, but for now I must dash off this quick note to tell you not to come home under any circumstances. Elizabeth is sick, but seems to be doing well. We are hoping Helen will be spared. Please remain at school until you hear otherwise. Keep your family in your prayers, and pray also for those around Hay and Millcote who have fallen to this sickness. Your mother and I long to see you, but even more we desire your safety. I remain your loving

Father

Carter talked to Jane, who assured him that she had had scarlet fever as a child. "I was about seven, I believe. I caught it, as did my three cousins. The household had their hands full, with four children ill at once. My oldest cousin was the sickest. Or perhaps he just made the most noise."

Jane grew silent, her mind going back to Gateshead and that winter when all the children had been ill. She could still remember John Reed's fretful wailing and complaints, and the way the whole household had rushed around to tend to his and his sisters' needs.

She remembered Bessie, coming to her as often as she was able, to bathe her hot face, or to wrap another cloth around her neck to protect it from cold. But she was always summoned back, to take care of Eliza or Georgiana, or to fetch something else for John.

Jane remembered the fruit ices. Her aunt had made such a fuss; ordered all the children to be given bowl after bowl of fruit ices, to ease the pain of their sore, raw throats.

Except for Jane, of course. She had been given one fruit ice, and had longed for more, but was given only porridge, thinned with warm milk to help her swallow past her painful throat. She had sipped her cold water and thought enviously of the delicacies that she was sure her cousins were enjoying.

For some reason, perhaps to take her mind off her fear for Elizabeth, she found herself telling the story to Mr. Carter.

"Hmmph," he grunted. "Although they might have done you a favour. Plain food is best for a sick child. Fancy meals just upset the constitution, raise the risk for more problems. Did your cousins live through the illness?"

"Yes," Jane answered, "My cousin John is dead now, but not from scarlet fever." *Why am I telling him all this?* she thought to herself. She caught the doctor's arm, her hand shaking, "Mr. Carter, will Helen catch it as well?"

"I cannot lie to you, Mrs. Rochester," he told her, "she most likely will. But we will do our best for her."

And Helen had indeed caught the dreaded fever, falling ill four days after her sister. Jane tucked the feverish girl into bed, and tried to stay calm.

And then Edward got sick.

He had not been able to remember if he had had scarlet fever or not, but assumed he had, until he felt the start of the mild fever, the sore throat, the relentless aching of his bones. Jane felt immobilized with sudden terror when she realized her husband had been stricken as well, but she assisted him to take to his bed, letting him lean on her while he changed into a nightshirt, unsteady with fever and weakness. She moved from Edward's bedside to that of her daughters, depending upon John's help with her husband as she cared for her girls. Poor John, in his seventies, was very worried over Molly, the granddaughter of his wife, but his devotion to Edward was so great that he worked tirelessly beside Jane to see to his employer's comfort.

Edward was fretful, turning in bed and unable to sleep, as much from anxiety as from discomfort.

"Jane," he rasped hoarsely from a sore and swollen throat, grasping her arm. "Elizabeth and Helen… how are they?" His head moved restlessly upon his pillow. She smoothed his damp hair back from his hot forehead.

"They are coming along well," she told him in a low voice, trying to keep her constant fear from affecting him. "They have fevers and they are fretful, but Mr. Carter does not seem unduly worried. Two of the downstairs girls have had the fever as children, and they have stayed to help me."

She tried to keep her voice light, "Helen is cranky, and keeping Elizabeth from resting, but when I tried to move her to another room, Elizabeth would not let me. They are company for each other." Edward smiled, and his eyes closed as his fears were temporarily eased, but each time he woke, he asked about his daughters, unable to rest easy in his mind.

"My girls," he whispered, moving restlessly in bed with his pain and fever, "My babies."

Carter came every day, only able to stay a few moments at a time. He was exhausted. His oldest son had completed his training and was now in practice with his father, and that lightened Carter's load, but he was tiring fast. He was nearly seventy years old and had been a doctor for over forty of those years. He was ready to retire. But he had seen the Rochester family through so much, and felt he could not abandon them now. He sent his son to various homes and farms, seeing to their patients, but came to Thornfield himself.

Like Jane, John and Mary had previously had scarlet fever. So had Thomas Cooper. Adèle had not had it, to the best of her recollection, but she did not fall ill, which was surprising as she could neither rest nor eat in her grief over Henry and her fear for Tom. Carter stopped in there as well, to see to Molly, and to Tom, who was slowly getting better. He did not talk of the cases among his patients, nor of the occasional deaths.

And then Molly died. She had not seemed extremely ill, but just when it seemed she might recover, she had begun to have difficulty breathing.

"Pneumonia," Mr. Carter said, privately holding out little hope. When scarlet fever progressed into another illness, it was serious indeed. And so Molly died, two weeks after her little charge.

She was only thirty-one years old, and had been with the Rochesters since she was sixteen. Jane did not tell Edward or the girls, but she wept as she went from one room to the next, pausing only to catch a few moments of sleep on a cot in the nursery. Even then her sleep was broken by frequent dreams in which she lost Edward, or one of the girls.

Or all three of them.

In her dreams she was ten years old again, looking at the body of her dearest friend. The friend who bore the same name as Jane's younger daughter. Who had been fourteen, the age of Jane's elder daughter.

Jane stood, watching her sleeping girls, begging God to spare their lives. And then felt guilty, thinking of Adèle, who had just buried her tiny son. And thinking of Mary, who would shortly bury her beloved granddaughter.

And she begged God to spare her husband.

She could not imagine losing Edward. He had always seemed so strong, so invincible. Even with the long-faded scars of his injuries, the loss of his eye, and the lack of his hand, he had seemed to Jane to be untouchable. She sat by him, leaning her elbow on the bed, her eyes fixed on his face as he slept. In repose, the harsh lines of his rugged features and stern brow seemed relaxed, making him seem younger.

He was fifty-six years old, his hair going grey, lines etched around his eyes. But when he smiled at her, all the years seemed to fall away. She had loved him since she was eighteen, and she was thirty-seven now. For more than half her life, this man had been her centre, the linchpin of her existence. When they had met, Edward had been the age she was now. It seemed a million years ago, and yet it seemed yesterday. He had been young and had seemed to her so dashing, miles above her in life. She had fallen deeply in love with him, and that feeling had not diminished in nearly nineteen years. The attachment between them had only grown stronger with each day and each trial they had faced together. Their hearts were entwined, he was as her own soul. Her husband, her lover, her friend.

She leaned her head against his arm, still so strong, so capable. He was not so large and muscular as he had once been, now that he was not running and riding and engaging in the sports of a younger man. He had kept his shape by careful living, and by the long walks they still took nearly every day. He was still vigorous, still the virile lover he had always been. When they came together in the night, it was as though no time had passed. But he was growing older, and when she took his hand and held it to her lips, she realized that he could die, leaving her desolate and longing for him, as she had been once before.

Please, merciful Lord, let me keep him a while longer. How could I ever live without my Edward?

She would sit for a time, taking a break from the girls, watching Edward sleep. His dark face showed a sheen of perspiration, his skin was so hot. She would bathe his face with a damp cloth, and once again he would wake, grab for Jane's hand, begging her in a hoarse whisper for the truth about his daughters.

"They are fine, Edward," she would whisper, clutching his fingers in hers. "They are sleeping. And you must sleep too, my darling." She would kiss him, go back to the nursery, to gaze in turn upon Helen and Elizabeth, to look closely at their chests until she saw the rise and fall, just as she had when they were babies.

She would lean over them, listening for the faint sounds they made as they slept, their breaths foul with the smell of sickness. She stroked their hair, sweat-soaked and clinging to their heads, as they grew feverish, broke their fevers in a rush of chills and perspiration, and then grew hot again.

She covered them when they were cold, uncovered them when they were hot. She fetched bedpans when they were needed, stripped wet nightgowns from hot bodies, bathed her girls over and over again, and in her frantic mind, she buried them a hundred times.

Then she would return to her husband, bending to press her lips to his damp hair, stroking his hot cheek. "I love you, Edward," she breathed into his skin. "You must get better soon."

I cannot live without you. I cannot live without any of you.

She had heard that deaths come in threes. Her sensible and intelligent mind told her that was nonsense, but she could not stop her heart's fear. Could not stop worrying that Death's next stopping place would be her own household. She could not shake the morbid thought that death had touched their family twice in this illness, and that one more would be required. Who? Edward? Elizabeth? Helen? The thought of any one of them dying made her cold with terror.

Her thoughts were irrational. She prayed for each one in turn, an endless litany of pleas for their safe recoveries. Worn down by lack of food and sleep, she could not stop morbid thoughts from intruding, and dropped off into a shallow sleep in which she had bizarre dreams of having to choose which of her loved ones would live and which must die.

They had not been untouched by death, of course. She thought back, to the loss of her baby son, of her other unborn babies. Heartbreaking, but she had been able to endure it, especially with Edward by her side and sharing her pain.

There had been other losses. Shortly after their tenth anniversary, they had been saddened to receive a note telling them of the death of Mrs. Fairfax. Edward's faithful housekeeper had written them often in her last years – long, rambling letters, which Jane answered. Mrs. Fairfax never visited the Rochesters, despite being invited. She was tired, content to remain with her friends at the inn. But she had requested to be buried at Thornfield, near the church where her husband had served so faithfully for so many years. Edward had brought home the body of his mother's aunt by marriage, and had seen to it that she was buried next to her beloved husband.

Then several years ago, they had received news of the death of their friend Robert Lathrop. He had lived to be past eighty, long enough to have seen the birth of several great-grandchildren. Edward had sat quietly for a long time upon receiving the letter from Lathrop's daughter. He had brushed tears from his eyes, but had smiled at Jane as he told her the news.

"I can see him now, walking with his dear Charlotte," he said thoughtfully. "And he is with Hugh again. I am glad of that."

Jane even smiled a little as she thought of Pilot. Edward's faithful old dog had finally died at the age of thirteen, while the family was at the villa on the

Mediterranean. He had been frail, his eyes filmed over with cataracts, his hearing no longer keen. But he still tried to follow his master through the house, rising slowly, moving stiffly as he tried to keep up with Edward. Edward, remembering his own recent days of blindness, had been patient with him, and he had insisted that Pilot's food dish stay in the same place, and requested that anyone approach the old dog slowly so as not to frighten him.

One sad day Pilot had suffered what appeared to be a stroke, and could not move his limbs or control his functions. Yet he remained alive, feebly raising his head to swipe his tongue against Edward's hand. Luc had offered to do what needed to be done, but Edward had refused.

"He has been my friend all these years," Edward said, his voice rough with unshed tears. "I raised him from a puppy. He ran alongside my horse mile after mile; such loneliness I would have had at times if not for him. When I was blind and alone, he rarely left my side. No, I will do for him what needs to be done. My voice should be the last he hears on this earth."

Luc dug a grave in a lovely and shady spot in the gardens, and helped Edward to move Pilot onto a patch of lush green grass in the warm sunshine. Jane and Molly had taken Adèle and the children to the village for the day, and Jane had walked with them through the sunny streets, laughing and talking, but her heart was back at the villa, heavy with sorrow for her husband and the sad task he had to perform.

While they were gone, Edward had sat for a long time, his head bent down against Pilot's, stroking his heavy fur and talking to his faithful pet, before he picked up his pistol and gave his old friend the relief that all good animals should have at the end of their lives. He was stoic as he helped Luc to wrap Pilot in a sheet and lay his huge body to rest. But that night he had turned to Jane in the dark, his tears wetting her shoulder as she stroked his hair and comforted him as best she could. Jane hugged herself now as she thought of how she had held him closely that night, not even speaking, as she knew no words could suffice. She had just stayed close to him, bending to kiss his head and his damp cheek.

And now Jane needed comfort, but it was not to be found. Worn from the endless cycle from sickbed to sickbed, she sat awake long into the night, alone with her fears.

October, 1855

As the days went on, the disease spread through the hamlets near Hay and Millcote, touching many homes. Most victims recovered; some died; some never fell ill at all. The hardest hit were the poorer families, the very young, and the old. But the dark hand of Death was not discriminating. It took whom it wished.

A letter had come from Eton. Shortly after receiving his father's note, Ned had written to his parents. Jane had not been able to bring herself to write all that had befallen those around Thornfield, but she had sent a short note telling Ned that his father and sisters were ill, and asking him to pray for his family.

Ned wrote in his sprawling hand, with the appalling spelling that years of Jane's and Adèle's efforts had not been able to remedy.

Dearest Mama,

Do not worry, I shall defenitly NOT come home. I am sorry to hear Papa and the girls have gotten sick but I do not fear for them. Papa is feirce and tough and will fight his way to health, I do not think I remember him being sick!!!!

Helen is far to wild a child to stay ill for long, she will be up and back to mischef soon. And Elizabeth will be fine you will see.

I hope you are fine and getting enough rest Mama, and I am eger to see you all again. My love to all my family and tell Molly she shall see her boy soon!

Ned

Jane dashed tears from her eyes, both from his mention of Molly and from missing her son so very much. Yet she could not help but smile at his once again calling his father "Papa" just as he had as a child. At about age twelve he had begun to treat his mother more formally, dodging her caresses when others were around, and addressing Edward as "Father." Edward had been a bit hurt, Jane thought, but she had urged him to honour his son's attempts to be an adult, and to let him be.

"I shall have to read this to Edward," Jane murmured to herself, slipping the note into her skirt pocket.

For Jane, the fever meant several weeks of worry and waiting, but at last things began to get better. Edward and the girls showed some improvement after a week or ten days. Their fevers began to abate, rising in the evenings but no longer as high as they had been the first few days. Their throats gradually returned to normal, the soreness receding every day. The rashes disappeared, leaving all three with peeling skin across their palms and their cheeks, but this was a minor complaint. Mr. Carter pronounced himself satisfied with their progress. He declared Edward out of danger completely, but instructed him to remain in bed.

Elizabeth and Helen gave him greater concern because of their age, but he was carefully optimistic about them as well. He was most worried about Elizabeth, who did not enjoy the robust good health of the rest of her family. She tended to catch many respiratory illnesses and they took longer to leave her. Even after he had declared Helen out of danger, he continued to come every day for Elizabeth.

Jane was still worried. She was reassured by Mr. Carter's confidence in the recoveries of Edward and Helen, but when she saw Elizabeth, looked at her thin, white face and listened to her wracking cough, she could not help having a cold feeling of fear deep in her chest. She was frightened for Elizabeth's sake, praying to God to spare her elder daughter. But she was concerned for Edward's sake as well.

Jane knew that her husband played no favourites among his children. He had felt the sting of rejection by his father, and knew the terrible damage that partiality caused among siblings. He had also felt the warm glow of being his mother's favourite, but wondered now if that had been part of the reason his brother Rowland had been so willing to betray him all those years ago.

Edward loved his children equally, treated them the same. But Jane knew in her heart of hearts that Edward had a tiny, special little corner of his heart that belonged only to Elizabeth. He was extremely close to his son, and they got on well. It was partly Ned's physical appearance, so like his father's, and his position as heir to the Rochester name, but it was also Ned's personality. He was a relaxed and affable young man, and father and son genuinely liked each other and enjoyed spending time in each other's company. Edward also adored his younger daughter – enjoyed her humour, her boundless energy, and her stubbornness, seeing in her a reflection of himself. But Elizabeth, who looked like his beloved wife, who also had some features of his long-dead mother, and who was intelligent and sweet, was a bit special to him, and tugged at his heart even more than his others.

Jane knew that to lose Elizabeth would kill a little part of her husband.

By the time all three were convalescing, the toll was beginning to tell on Jane. She was thin and pale, having had no appetite during the time she had worried over her family. She had gained a little weight after having her children, and, while still slim, had a lovely roundness to her figure that her husband delighted in. But the strain of illness had whittled away at her until she began to resemble the tiny, elfin girl she had first been when she met Edward. She had dark circles under her eyes, her clothing appeared loose on her, and she drooped with fatigue, but could not sleep easily, accustomed to only catching an hour or two here and there.

Edward was very concerned for her. He was feeling much better, though still quite tired, and was chafing at Mr. Carter's insistence that he remain in bed. He had defied these orders once his fever was gone, getting up and shakily going down the hall to the nursery, to see for himself that his daughters were well. He had moved from one bed to the other, bending over them and kissing them in turn, saying a silent prayer of thanks over each of them. Only when he had seen them were his fears relieved.

Once he was better, Jane sat down and told him of the death of Molly. He shook his head sadly, at the news of her death and of the deaths of others in the area. In the end, twenty-two people in Hay and the surrounding countryside would die of the scarlet fever; many more had died in the closer quarters found in Millcote.

Jane still feared that death would swoop down and carry one of her loved ones away. But she tried to hope and to trust. Once the worst of her nursing duties were over, she resumed her visits to Adèle, who was white and thin herself, from grief. She sat by her son Tom's bed by the hour, even though Mr. Carter had reassured her that the danger was past. Jane and Thomas urged her to sleep, to eat something, but she was afraid to close her eyes. She dreamed of Henry, still awoke with the sounds of his voice in her ears, and Jane's heart ached for her. She knew that only time would heal Adèle's pain, and that of Thomas, who was having to go off by himself and grieve in private, trying to stay strong for the sake of his heartbroken wife.

She sat by the hour with her foster daughter, still as dear to her as her own girls were. Adèle clutched Jane's hands, sobbing as she spoke of her little boy.

"Jane," she cried from the depths of her misery, "how will we go on? How can we live now, Thomas and little Tom and me? We cannot do without our Henry. How can I bear it? Thomas tries to be a comfort to me, but he is hurting too. We cannot even talk about it, he and I. When he speaks, I cry, and he stops speaking because he does not want to make me cry. But I need to cry, and I need to cry to him. How shall we live through this?"

Jane held Adèle close, letting her pour out her pain. She longed to speak comforting words, but knew no words could help, and so she just listened, sometimes crying herself.

The parish had come forth with an outpouring of love for their curate and his little family, and Mr. Wood visited daily, but Adèle could not bear the sound of people talking of "God's Will" and Henry as their "Angel in Heaven."

"How can they speak so?" she sobbed to Jane after a particularly trying visit, "I cannot stand their talk, it is unbearable."

Jane had been so happy with how well things had gone for Adèle. She and Thomas had settled down nicely in their little home, happy with their two sturdy little sons, both of whom had been the picture of health until this illness. Everything seemed so perfect, and now this. Jane wiped away tears, grieving for the pain of Adèle and her husband, and thinking of Henry, so dear to her whole family and now lost to them.

She thought back to the day, four years ago, when the Coopers had returned from their honeymoon, radiant and happy with each other. One had only to look at their shining faces to know all had gone well, and when Adèle came to Jane only a few months after the wedding to confide that she was already pregnant, their joy seemed to overflow. Thomas was thrilled and proud. Jane was pleased with his treatment of Adèle. He was no St. John Rivers, saving his passion for God alone. Thomas was devoted to the work to which he had been called, but he was also deeply in love with his wife, and Adèle bloomed under his affections, knowing at last the joy of being first in someone's heart.

Adèle had been a great asset to her husband in his work as curate. Wood, the vicar, was growing old and feeble, and Thomas took over many of the duties of the parish. Until Adèle grew so big with her pregnancy that it was no longer considered decent for her to be in public, she and Thomas would go visiting nearly every day. Thomas cared deeply for the people of his parish, but was not always able to express that with his shy personality. Adèle's vivacity and wit helped him immensely, and her memory for the details of their parishioners' lives was a tremendous asset.

"Mrs. Taylor has a son in London," Adèle would murmur to Thomas as they stood at a door, awaiting an answer to their knock. "He could not pay his debts and they were threatening him with prison. Her grandson had to leave school to get a job. Mrs. Taylor is quite worried." They would hear footsteps on the other side of the door, and Adèle would hurriedly add, "Oh, and Thomas, ask her how her rheumatism has been."

With the curate of the parish visiting with his young and pretty wife, the parishioners felt noticed and cared for, and they tended to come to church more often. Church attendance grew, and so did the popularity of the curate.

Thomas had also had an unexpected success in another area. He had long enjoyed making up little stories, and had shared some of them with his wife, the first person he had entrusted with the knowledge of his little hobby. He had looked forward to telling these little stories to his expected child, and Adèle convinced him to write them down. He refused to consider sending them off for anyone else to read, so Adèle had secretly copied several in her free time, and sent them off to a literary magazine in London. The editor of the magazine had written to Thomas, who had agreed to their publication, but only under a pseudonym. Under the name "Henry Thomas", he saw three of his stories printed in the magazine and its editors wished for more. They were fanciful tales, aimed at young boys, but grew quite popular with girls as well, and Thomas was as surprised as anyone.

Thomas and Adèle had been so happy in the safe arrival of little Thomas, and Edward and Jane felt almost like grandparents. Edward, so irritated in the past with Adèle and her silly ways, was ridiculously happy with Adèle's little son. It was he who insisted that Thomas call him Uncle Edward, and his wife Aunt Jane, and he often walked over to see the little boy. He was equally fond of Tom's little brother, who arrived almost exactly a year later and was named after Mr. Cooper's uncle Henry, who had reared him lovingly after the death of his parents.

And now their happiness was shattered. Jane wished with all her heart that she could magically make their pain disappear, but she knew that only time could work its healing on the Coopers.

A month after the initial outbreak, the scarlet fever had seemed to release its hold on the area, and had moved on to wreak its havoc in other counties. All began to go back to normal, except for the families of the dead, for whom life would never be the same again.

Jane was getting more rest, as her husband and girls recovered from their illnesses. She no longer spent all of her time going between the two sickrooms, and began to resume her duties in the rest of the house, noticing how slack things had become. Many of the servants had gone home, afraid of the fever, and John and Mary had tried to see to things, despite their sorrow over Molly's loss, and their fear for their employer and his children.

Jane had been working hard to re-engage the servants and return the house to its normal working order. She had written to Ned, telling him that it was at last safe to come home, that she could not wait to see him.

She was sitting in the parlour, having a rare moment to herself and a quick cup of tea, when Mary brought in the post. Jane looked through it quickly, happy to see an envelope with the familiar handwriting of her cousin Diana. She set the other mail aside and opened the letter, settling back to read what Diana had to say.

Some time later, Jane entered her bedroom and sat down on the bed next to Edward. He blinked in the light and turned towards her, his smile turning to concern as he noted her swollen face and the redness of her eyes.

"Dearest, what is it?" he asked as he reached for her. Wordlessly she handed him the letter.

He scanned the note that she handed him, squinting in the dim light, and she took it back from him with a quick kiss of apology, so distraught that she had not even thought how difficult it would be for him to read without his eyeglass.

"It is from Mary and Diana," she told him, her voice low.

She read aloud:

Our dearest Jane,

This letter bears tidings that we can scarcely bear to write, let alone to convey to you, although we know we must.

We received news today in a letter from the mission society, that our brother has died on the field. The letter was several months in coming to us, but we are told it was the middle of February when St. John was taken.

We know few of the details, only that there was a cholera epidemic in the region that St. John was known to be serving. He was urged by some fellow missionaries to leave; indeed, all of them sent their wives and children to the cities or even out of the country. Many of the men fled as well, but St. John and one or two others refused to leave. One of those who survived wrote that St. John said he had long ago laid down his life to God's service, and it was up to God whether or not his time here on this earth was to continue. It is said that he remained, tirelessly caring for those who were ill and that he had to be persuaded to take to his bed when he began to feel the symptoms himself.

We are devastated at this news, but must take comfort in the fact that our brother died doing what he felt was asked of him. Those who remain must go on with the tasks that God has given us. We wanted to share this news with you as soon as possible, knowing that you also loved St. John as a brother and have prayed for his safety and happiness. We like to think that he died as he would have chosen to. And he has been buried there, in the graveyard near the orphanage that he helped found. That was his final wish.

Before he lost consciousness, St. John recited a poem of his to the person caring for him. It was enclosed with the letter. I have written the verse at the bottom of the letter, as well as enclosing part of the lock of hair that was so kindly sent on to us.

Your affectionate cousins,
Diana Rivers Fitzjames
and
Mary Rivers Wharton

At My Life's End
The moment I shall finally see my King
The day that I at last lay down my sword
No earthly pleasures life could bring
Compare with seeing Him, my risen Lord
St. John Rivers

Edward rested his hand over Jane's as she put the letter down. Her eyes were tear-filled, but she smiled a shaky smile at her husband. He reached his hand to her cheek, brushing at her tears with the backs of his fingers.

"I am so very sorry, my darling," he told her. "I teased you about him, I know, but I know what he meant to you; how happy you were that you had family. I am sorry he has been taken. How old was he?"

Jane thought a moment. "I recall he was ten years older than I am. I am thirty-seven now, so St. John was forty-seven."

Edward sighed, "That is still young. For his life to end, I mean."

Jane shook her head, "In all truth, I expected that he would die before this. I am amazed that he lasted eighteen years on the mission field. He has not been in the best of health for some years, according to Mary and Diana. I think they have been preparing themselves to hear of his death for a long time."

"Well, I am sorry," Edward said. "Is that his hair that you are holding?"

Jane opened her hand, to show him a small lock of golden hair, shot through with silver strands, mute testimony to the hand of time upon St. John's body. The hair was tied with a small black ribbon. "Yes, it was kind of them to send me some. I shall keep it always. I tend to think of it as all that he left behind, but that is not the case. He started the school and the orphanage, and others joined him in the work, others who are still there to carry on, so there is something left. He served God long and faithfully, and helped so many children. In a way, his legacy shall last forever."

"Yes," Edward said. He reached out his arm, "Come here to me, my love."

Jane curled up against him, and he felt her begin to cry again, softly. He reached up to stroke her hair, making soothing noises.

"I'm sorry," she whispered, "I am a little overwrought right now. I have been walking around, terrified that someone else would die. I knew someone would die; I had the certainty. It went around and around in my head: you, Elizabeth, Helen. I begged God for each of you in turn, pleaded with Him to save your lives. And all the time I never remembered St. John, never gave him a thought. I feel guilty, but I am so relieved. He was ready to die, but I was so fearful that God would take you or one of the girls. I feel so selfish."

"Oh, Jane," Edward bent and kissed her head, "it's natural to feel a little selfish. This fever has made the whole town worry; it has certainly taken its toll. It is expected that we would feel a little occupied with ourselves. But Carter has been here, he has seen us all, and we are all safe, he says. Life will be back to normal."

"No," Jane said, shaking her head, "it will never be normal again. Not for Adèle and Thomas. Not for Mary. You and the girls have been spared, but Molly is gone, and little Henry. How fragile life is, how easily it can be taken away!"

"Yes." Edward shifted a little in the bed so Jane could lie next to him more easily. He wrapped his arms around her, kissing her again. He could not wait to be stronger, could not wait for his girls to be healthy again, but for now, he was content to hold Jane to him tightly, selfishly glad that their family had been passed by and left intact for now.

"For now," he thought, resting his head against Jane's.

Chapter 62 - From Mrs. Rochester to Mrs. Fitzjames

Mrs. Arthur Fitzjames
25 Watt Road
Hebden Bridge
West Yorkshire

Mrs. Edward Rochester
Thornfield Manor
Hay, Derbyshire
18 May 1860

My dear Diana!

How happy I was to receive your letter in the mail yesterday! I finally have a moment to myself and promised that it would be spent in writing to you. To finally be settled in your new home after returning safe and sound from the East Indies, how relieved you must be! Imagine, a whole year travelling there and back!

As you would think, Mary and I have spent the last year writing letters back and forth to each other, most of them containing great concern about your safety. But of course, there was a bit of envy also as we imagined the fabulous sights you were able to see as you travelled with your Captain. As you say, there are compensations to not having been blessed with children, and you have faced that situation so bravely. So many sights you have seen! How lucky you are that you have been able to accompany Captain Fitzjames on some of his journeys – but we are glad to have you safely home.

No, I do not blame you for not living at Moor House; why should you not want to be settled near your dear sister? How good Captain Fitzjames is to understand the bond between you and Mary, and I am glad you were able to find a good situation not too far from Mary and Mr. Wharton. I'm sure Moor House is in capable hands with the agent you have employed, and as you say, the rent does bring in a little sum for you and for your sister. We are looking forward to being with you all this summer – the children are already talking about it.

You have urged me to tell you all about the children, and my dear Cousin, I am afraid I might bore you senseless with the mundanity of our life here at Thornfield. I do not believe that I have engaged in one activity that could be seen as an adventure! Even our reading is dull. We have been reading a lot of poetry lately, some of it is quite unique. Well, that is what I call it; I will not even tell you what Edward calls it.

I must proceed. Ned has come home from his third year at Oxford and I am sorry to say that all is strain and tension in the house. He came to his father and informed him that he would like to quit his university studies and marry Miss Ellis this autumn instead of next summer as had been previously discussed. My dear Diana, I was very distressed as I always am when I saw the vein begin to protrude on my husband's forehead. I absented myself from the room and let Edward proceed with the discussion. I remember being warned by our friend Mr. Eshton back when our son was younger, that the years of youth are difficult ones for men and their sons.

He spoke at some length about male deer and antler formation and young stags versus old ones, but I quite lost the train of his thought, and remember musing that my son and husband had always been the closest of friends and was smug in my surety that they would remain so.

It seems strange that at the age of nineteen, my son should begin to clash with his father, but I suppose it could be worse. I have told you, Diana, that Ned is not the most inspired of scholars. He is intelligent enough, but only cares to do that which he is interested in, and I fear that knowing he is the heir to Thornfield has not induced him to further study. He says he knows his future and is quite content with it, and why should he be a meticulous speller and well-versed in grammar when he shall not need it?

He enjoys history and he and Edward have numerous discussions, and I am amazed to see him do his sums. His father has had him helping with the household accounts for several years and he can add a column of figures in his head with amazing rapidity. He reads a great deal, for enjoyment, but takes very little seriously. Edward and I have repeatedly spoken to him about his need to do things well simply for his own satisfaction, and he agrees with us but then proceeds to do as he wishes. At times we wonder if we did the right thing in allowing him to remain home until he was fifteen before sending him away to school, but at the time we simply did not want to part with him, and his education at the village school was deemed adequate enough.

He does well enough to keep his place at Oxford, but has only distinguished himself in mathematics, which annoys his father, who prided himself on his good marks in college. And, of course, since Miss Mary Ellis arrived in the area three years ago, there has been little else on Ned's mind. From the moment the two set eyes on each other, it seems to have been destined. Oh, we have no great objection – she is a very sweet girl. But I do worry about the fact that she is flighty and cares little for study herself.

Her father, who owns a glassware factory, has paid for a good enough education at a small girls' academy in Sheffield, and now that Miss Ellis is finished, she and Ned seem determined to proceed with their marriage. Of course, Edward flatly refused to consider Ned's quitting college, and the atmosphere has been grim and dark in the home, with much romantic angst in the air.

As I have told you in the past, my Edward did not enjoy pleasant dealings with his own father, and he has been determined to get along with his own son, perhaps to the detriment of his effective discipline. But this time I was pleased to see that he held fast, although I feel he is worried that his relations with his son will be forever altered. I reassured him on this point. To young lovers a year might seem a lifetime, but Ned will come to see that it is not so long until next spring.

One happy note is that Elizabeth arrives home from Miss Cheltenham's for good next week. It seems the years have flown by; it feels as though no time at all has passed since we tearfully sent her off to London to attend to her higher education. When she has come home for her holidays, it has never seemed long enough, but now she will be back home with us. You know, dear Diana, that I would have happily gone on teaching my girls for years, but as difficult as it was, Edward and I had to concede that Elizabeth did need some time at a formal school.

We worried for her health, as she has never been entirely strong, but she shrugged off our fussing and concerns and headed off to school quite cheerfully. She has done well in her studies and we wish that a bit of her scholarly diligence could magically be transferred to her brother. She also has a great interest in history and current events, which pleases her father, because he enjoys discussion of those subjects himself. On her visits home, I have nearly fallen asleep several times during their long discussions on the recent war, with which Elizabeth has become fascinated. She has especially become interested in the return to London of Miss Florence Nightingale, and has read with great attention all the newspaper accounts of that lady's works during the war in the Crimea.

We are not sure of any definite plans Elizabeth has when she returns home. There is no young man in whom she takes an interest; in fact, she seems quite unconcerned with the subject. We have discussed plans for a small party in which to bring her out into society, but she flatly refused to do so in London and shows no great interest here either. I shall not press her. Goodness knows that for all my years as Mrs. Rochester, I am no great society matron. I know for a fact that I am still referred to as "the governess" by certain long-established families in the area.

One woman told another that I taught my own girls and refused to engage a governess because I was afraid Mr. Rochester would fall in love with her. It took my Edward an entire evening to stop laughing over that, and finally I saw the humour in it as well. Those who wish to gossip would never believe the truth, that I taught my own children not because I worried about losing my husband, but because I did not want to lose the society of my own daughters. They would think me foolish, but I would not trade that precious time for anything.

Helen continues to be a fresh springtime breeze blowing delightfully through Thornfield. If only she could hear that sentence, how her eyes would roll in her head! We have many times told her that if she continues to cast her eyes to the ceiling with every statement her father and I make, eventually they will stick there. I cannot believe that my dear little girl is now thirteen, and that very soon she must finally go off to Miss Cheltenham's too.

She insists that she is not going, and that we cannot make her, and keeps referring to the school as "Miss Salted Ham's Academy for Well-Preserved Young Ladies." Elizabeth says she's terribly afraid she herself is going to slip one day and say that at school and repeatedly threatened to stop writing to Helen unless she mends her ways. Helen rolls her eyes at her sister also. And she has Ned furious at her because she can do an imitation of Miss Ellis that is unfortunately so accurate that we cannot help but have difficulty keeping our composure.

Helen does well in her studies; she can make good grades with very little effort, unlike Elizabeth, who works hard to maintain her marks. But Helen cares for nothing but her horse, and the moment her work is done, she is down at the stables. She says that the only way she will go to London to school is if her mare Daisy can go with her. I did check into the cost of having Daisy sent with her and boarded, and it is a ridiculous expense. I am afraid, though, that Edward will pay it. He is so pleased that one of his children shares his love for horses, that I daresay he would not object to Daisy being Helen's actual roommate at Miss Cheltenham's.

Ned rides well, but does not have the deep love and understanding for horses that his father has, and Elizabeth shares my ambivalence towards the animals. She and I are content to ride in a carriage, thank you. But Helen would be on her horse from morning until night. She and her father have clashed a little, in that Helen wants to learn to jump and to take part in the hunt and her father is adamant that she shall not jump.

Helen has told him that she does not care what happened to Uncle Rowland, that she suspects he was a poor rider anyway. Edward informed her that Rowland was an excellent rider, that accidents happen to anyone, and that even he stopped jumping after his brother broke his neck, but Helen argues still. Edward has gotten to the point where he is afraid to let her go riding alone for fear she will jump just to prove him wrong. He has made her promise not to jump for now until he can think about it, but I know the idea terrifies him.

Helen can be a trial at times, but at other times she is so sweet. All the children are affectionate and loving, but she has remained the sweetest of our little brood, cuddling with us past the age when the others were more "dignified". I confess I love it and hope she remains so for a long time to come.

You asked about Adèle, and I am happy to report that she is well. I feared greatly for her after Henry was taken, but she still had little Tom, thankfully, and had to remain well for him. She and Thomas gradually coped with their heartache, and they emerged stronger, I believe, from the experience. Tom is now seven and an active and vigorous boy, and their little daughter Emma is nearly four. Adèle would like more, but so far it is only Tom and Emma. The children are quite wonderful and are like grandchildren to Edward and myself.

Mr. Cooper is now the incumbent at Hay, as our Mr. Wood died this past autumn and the parish voted without dissent to put Thomas in his place if he wished. He and Adèle were quite happy to remain here, and so they have moved into the larger rectory. The bishop engaged a new curate a few months later, and perhaps the less said about him the better. Edward is not pleased.

For a year or so Thomas refused to do any more writing. He said it broke his heart to think of telling the same stories which he had told to Henry, but at last he gave in and wrote some more, and now Emma sits raptly and listens to her father's tales as her older brothers did. Thomas's little stories for children are becoming more popular, and a publisher wants to put them together in a book, as up to now they have all been published in story form, some of them in weekly serials. They have been read here in Hay and over in Millcote, and Thomas is uneasy, believing that it is only a matter of time before his true identity is revealed. Adèle and I feel that the parish could not object, as they are very wholesome stories, but some people still think of writers as a dissolute breed and might have a poor opinion of Mr. Cooper's hobby. It remains to be seen how things will develop in that respect.

Finally, you asked of my Edward. I conveyed your greetings to him and he wished me to assure you of his affection for you and your good husband, and his envy as well regarding your travels. He wants us to take a journey of some sort in the next year, and while I feel I had quite enough travel when the children were small, I know I should consider it.

I am happy to be able to tell you that my husband continues in good health and spirits. He says that sixty-one feels little different from fifty-one, and that he prays to remain in good form. He is increasingly busy with the estate business, and looks forward to Ned's assistance next year. Ferndean needs some attention and he is beginning to fret over that, so I suppose that he might need to stop there for business. He suggested that he and I go there for a week or two to have time to ourselves and for him to see to things, and I like the idea of that. He lost his long-time caretaker some years ago, and has had to employ a series of agents to see to the place, and it is becoming quite an irritation to him. Both of us would sometimes like to sell it, but we both have such an attachment to the place, it having been our first home. Anytime you and Arthur would like to come and stay there for a long rest in quiet and solitude, please tell us and you are more than welcome.

We are going through an upheaval here at home as we are trying to adjust to a new housekeeper and cook, as well as to a new butler. Mary is quite lonely since her John died last year, and indeed, we feel that we have lost a member of the family. Mary is not up to much cooking any longer, but it was hard to bring in someone new. We had hoped to get a couple, but have been unable to find one, and so have three fairly new employees, which is always an adjustment. Mary is making her home with us, although her family urged her to come to them. She says she will visit often if they will come to fetch her, but will remain where she is accustomed to living, and this is certainly fine with us. We have plenty of room here, and Mary remains as sharp in her mind as always.

Please tell your sister Mary that she must write to me soon. (Goodness, how many Marys I shall have in my family if Miss Ellis becomes my daughter-in-law!) I have not heard from her in well over a week and am getting lonely for her familiar writing appearing in our post. I must close this very long letter now, my dearest Diana, but please know how happy I am to have you back on England's shores. How eager I am to see your face again!

Your affectionate cousin,

Jane

Chapter 63 - The Rochester Children

June, 1860

"You cannot be serious," Edward said incredulously, as Elizabeth sat watching him. She was still, her folded hands in her lap, but her face was anxious as she watched her parents.

"I am serious, Papa," she replied quietly. She turned to her mother, "Mama, I know this is a bit of a shock, as I have said nothing about an interest in nursing before. Papa and I discussed Miss Nightingale's work at length and he seemed to admire her..."

Edward broke in, "Admiring the work of a great woman is an enormous difference from wanting your seventeen-year-old daughter to pursue the same course of study. A woman who nurses is not seen as quite so base and common since Miss Nightingale went to the Crimea, and I am aware that there is a growing sympathy for the cause of better medical care for everyone, but it is still a career mostly suited to women of low breeding and education. It is not for women of good family, with a promising life ahead of them." He stopped, shaking his head.

"Papa, that is so old-fashioned an argument!" Elizabeth said passionately. "Miss Nightingale comes from a very wealthy and well-established family, and Miss Cheltenham has been a friend of hers since they were girls. She is a great supporter of Miss Nightingale's work in improving military medical care. Not only is she a friend of Miss Nightingale's, but she lost her brother to an infection he got after being wounded while serving in the Royal Navy."

"So Miss Cheltenham is a supporter of your interest in nursing?" Jane asked her. As was usual in matters concerning their children, Jane would sit quietly, musing on the subject while her husband was more vocal. She never failed to make her opinion known, usually remaining silent and thinking the matter through thoroughly as her husband expressed his thoughts, and then speaking once her thoughts were more organized.

Elizabeth nodded, "I have spoken of my interest to her, and she feels I would make an excellent nurse. She says I am intelligent and compassionate. She has mentioned me in a note to Miss Nightingale, and has said that she will speak up for me if you and Papa allow me to enter this training school."

She indicated the letter in her hand, notifying her of the prospective establishment of the Nightingale Training School at St. Thomas Hospital in London. A group of interested women was set to enter training in a matter of weeks, and Elizabeth had postponed notifying her parents until she had received the letter assuring her that she had a place among them.

"I have been chosen to be part of this group, Papa, and it is an honour. They are not taking everyone, and some of the women are already experienced – they have been nursing informally for a long while."

"To be in London, studying for such a profession, on your own," Edward frowned, "I cannot see it; it is not feasible, Elizabeth. You are too young to live in London alone, so far from your parents."

"I will not be on my own, Papa," Elizabeth protested. "There is a dormitory in the training area; I will be living with other girls. We will have classes, and work in the hospital. It will be strictly chaperoned. Miss Cheltenham has written to you and

Mama, explaining how it will be set up. She is one of the sponsors. There is a fund that has been set up to establish this school, and she has been instrumental in collecting the monies. But I cannot do it without your support, as there is limited money in the fund. They can subsidize only a few students, those who have no family support. I will need a living allowance and your permission, as I am not of age."

Elizabeth appealed to her mother, "Mama, you understand, don't you? You were not much older than I am when you set out, entirely alone, for a new life. You left Lowood, came here to work for Papa, all on your own. You hungered for a new life and you made one for yourself. Surely you know how I feel."

Jane reached a hand to her older daughter, who came over and sat by her mother. "Dearest, I do understand a need to change your life, to better yourself. But I had no choice – I was entirely on my own. If I did not support myself, I could not live. But you have parents, a family that supports you. You do not have to make your own way in the world. You are free to seek out what you wish at your leisure. There are sufficient funds to make a good marriage if you choose, to do good works without the hard work and degradation of nursing."

Elizabeth pulled her hand away from her mother's gentle grasp, balling her fists in frustration upon her lap, "That is precisely what I am talking about, Mama, Papa." She looked from one parent to the other.

"I do not wish to 'make a good marriage' – if love should come my way, I shall embrace it, but I do not wish to seek it out. If I meet a man I can respect and love, I will be glad of it, but if I do not, then I would rather live without the ties of matrimony. Marriage for the sake of marriage... that is an old notion. A woman need not tie herself down just to make a life for herself."

Jane understood that, and secretly was glad to see her daughter bear that opinion. She herself had been blessed beyond all her imaginings, with a husband who was her true love, who respected her and treated her as his equal in every way. He had refused to even take her money, as a husband was entitled to do, but instead had established a separate account for her funds alone. It was in his name, of course, but he had made it clear many times that it was her money, to spend or save as she wished.

"Those funds are yours, my Janet, left to you by your uncle," Edward had told her shortly after their wedding. "The law may say they are now mine, but I do not choose to take possession of them. That money is yours, to ensure that never again will you be thrust penniless upon the world, at the mercy of strangers. When you have need of it, talk to Mr. King, and he will see that you have what you want, as I have instructed him."

Edward saw to her every need, and so the money from her Uncle John had remained essentially untouched for years, slowly building up interest in the bank. Occasionally she had taken from it to buy gifts for various members of her family – beautiful monogrammed gold cuff links and a cigar case for Edward, to replace those lost in the fire, some tokens of her affection for the families of Mary, Diana, and Adèle, and donations to the orphanage started by St. John in India. She had also purchased fine gold lockets for her daughters when each had turned thirteen and cuff links of similar value for Ned when he had left Eton for Oxford. But for the most part the money had been left to accumulate, and she knew how lucky she was to have a husband who allowed this. In financial ways, as in all others, she was blessed beyond measure in her kind and loving husband.

Jane's thoughts came abruptly back to Edward's library, where they sat, having been summoned by Elizabeth, who had come to them solemnly asking to speak to them about an important matter. Now Edward was pacing across the floor, frustrated, unable to stop his mental picture of a nurse being a working class woman drinking gin in an attic watching over a lunatic. Jane was torn between wanting to support her daughter's natural feelings of independence and selfishly wanting to keep the girl safe at home with her family.

She turned to Elizabeth, "My darling, I do understand your need to break free from the confines of your life; many women have that desire. But I speak practically. You are not terribly strong, you contract every illness that comes your way. How will you cope with the rigours of this life? Nursing has never been easy for a woman, and I'm sure it is not easy now."

Elizabeth answered her earnestly, "I know, Mama. But I am fine, most of the time. A few trifling illnesses from time to time shall not dampen my resolve. I feel well, and... " She paused to gather her thoughts, "I feel strongly that it is better to die while you are really living, doing what you feel drawn to, than to die a little at a time in an elegant drawing room, living a life that is boring and confining."

Jane felt a start of recognition at these words. Where had she heard similar words, in whom had she seen this glow of passion for a longed-for future? It came to her: St. John. He had stood before her, his face alight as he spoke of his hope to bring God's word to the far-away Hindus. Elizabeth was not acting with religious fervour, but her face was equally alight as she described a longing to do something different from the predetermined path of the other girls of her age and station.

Jane knew that the other girls of the area near Elizabeth's age were coming out into society, looking for husbands. Some were going off to stay with relatives in other cities, in the hopes of meeting men of money and property. She could not help a small glimmer of pride as she looked at her daughter, seeing Elizabeth's longing to live a different life, to make a positive difference in the world.

Elizabeth was never going to be beautiful. But she was an impressive young woman, her back ramrod straight, her gaze direct, a sharp intelligence gleaming in her brown eyes. They were clear eyes, not as dark as her father's and grandmother's while showing glints of her mother's green, and they gleamed with vitality and a desire to break out of the life for which she seemed destined. Although she was not a woman of great height, she was taller than her mother, and carried herself with her mother's quiet dignity.

Edward voice broke into the women's discussion. "What on earth will you possibly do when you finish this training?" he asked. "Go off to some distant country to care for soldiers? Slave away in hospitals and institutions all your life? Why should you work your fingers to the bone when we can give you everything you want right here?"

"Papa," Elizabeth sighed, "Miss Nightingale fought the disapproval of her family, of society, and look at all she has accomplished. Her family eventually supported her, and she has done wonders, in England and in the world. How wonderful it would be, to change the world like that!"

She went on. "She is not strong; she is confined to her bed and sees very few people, but she still is working to improve medical care for people all over the world. As to where I would work, there are many hospitals all over, or there is private nursing care. I don't know what will happen in the future; I only know how very much I wish to pursue this now. I will not change my mind, Papa. If I cannot do this at this time, I will find a way to do it when I am older. If you will not allow this now, I will wait until I am of age. But I will study to be a nurse. I feel it is my destiny."

"I will not hear of it," Edward said, standing up straight. His dark eye swept over his daughter, his face set in lines of frustration. He had missed Elizabeth dreadfully while she had studied in London for three years, and he had looked forward to the day when she would return to his home. With his son entering his last year of college and already eager for the day that he would marry, and the time fast approaching when Helen would also leave for school, his only comfort was the thought that at least his older daughter would remain home with her parents.

He knew that she must someday leave him, to marry and set up a home of her own, but as she had shown no great interest in boys and had no young man with whom she was keeping company, he had anticipated having her around for a time. He had not expected this interest in nursing, and his first impulse was to flatly refuse, as he had refused Ned's request to leave Oxford a year early.

"This is completely ridiculous. You're only seventeen – you have no idea of your own mind. I will never permit it."

Elizabeth, usually so good-natured and quiet, folded her arms and leaned back in the chair, looking at her father. She adored him, and had never defied him in her life; indeed, there had never been any cause to.

She had been surprised, after being away from home in the months since the Christmas holidays, to see her father's hair a little greyer and his eyes a little more lined. His back was still straight, and his form still strong, but looking at him she could see the subtle hand of time as it worked upon Edward. He looked younger than his years, and could be mistaken for his early fifties, she thought, rather than sixty-one. But she felt a sudden dart of cold fear at her heart. Her father would not live forever. The thought of Edward Rochester no longer being there shocked her, frightened her. She closed her mouth upon the hot words she had nearly said, and just looked at her father in silence, her face set in a stubborn line he rarely saw in her.

He felt a sudden tightness in his throat, watching her, this beloved daughter of his. She was such a mixture of the two women he had loved most in his life, his wife and his mother, and he did not think he could refuse her anything.

But it was unthinkable, what she was contemplating. He did not want to discuss it further, and with one last stern look at his wife and daughter, he turned and left the room.

Elizabeth turned to her mother, "Mama... "

Jane sighed, "He loves you so much, Elizabeth."

"I know that, Mama. And I love him too, so very much. But if he loves me, why won't he want me to be happy?"

Jane smiled, "He does. He just wants you to be happy here with him."

"You understand, don't you, Mama?" Elizabeth asked her mother.

Jane put her arm around her daughter, "Yes, I do, my love. We won't discuss it for a day or so. Then I will talk to him." She hugged Elizabeth, and leaned over to press a kiss to her soft hair.

Elizabeth stood at her dressing table. Her long hair was unbound, and she was brushing it vigorously, trying to work out her frustrations before she climbed into her bed. She turned at the sound of her door being opened.

Helen came into the room, her feet bare, her curly black hair pulled back into a severe braid. She was in her nightgown, and she tiptoed across the room in an exaggerated fashion that made her sister laugh.

"So, how did the talk with Papa go?" she asked. "I was sitting outside the library, but then Ned came home from seeing Miss Ellis and caught me listening outside the door. He said he was going to tell Papa, but I don't think he will."

Both girls smiled, thinking of their lovelorn brother. He spent every moment he could at Ellis Wood, the stately old home that Mr. Ellis had bought from an impoverished neighbour when he had moved his factory to the area three years ago. He had promptly named the home after himself, and Elizabeth and Helen had laughed privately over Mr. Ellis's attempts to appear a long-established landowner. The more serious Rochester girls, who loved to read and discuss deeper subjects at times, were puzzled by their brother's infatuation with Mary Ellis. She was beautiful, to be sure, with her porcelain skin and her blonde curls, but she was a silly creature. This was a subject they could only discuss with each other, as their brother refused to hear a word against his beloved. They knew their parents privately held the same view they did, but were anxious to appear supportive of their son. And, too, they were both aware of the fact that nothing makes a loved one more attractive than parental disapproval.

Elizabeth sighed, but couldn't help a small laugh, "Ned might tell Papa. He is in such a horrible temper since he's been home that he might do anything just to cause trouble. I wish he weren't in such bad spirits."

"And over that silly girl he likes so much," Helen said, pulling a face. She sat on the end of Elizabeth's bed, crossing her legs, "Lizzie, what shall I do if you go off to London to study nursing, and in your place I have only that idiotic Mary? Ned will marry her, and she will come to live at Thornfield. She giggles so much I want to stick something in her mouth. How can Ned listen to that all the time?"

Elizabeth sat down next to her sister, slumping back on the bed. "What are you worried about?" she asked. "You're going to Miss Cheltenham's in August and I'll be the one stuck here listening to Mary giggle. Papa has flatly refused to allow me to go to Miss Nightingale's school. Mama is my only hope, and if she can't persuade Papa to let me go, I will be here forever. I shall have to start going to parties and choose a husband from among the very slim pickings here at Hay. I am doomed." She rested her head on one hand, and smiled at Helen.

Helen, about to turn fourteen, was already taller than Elizabeth and had the makings of a beauty. She was awkward and gangly, but her fine bones and clear green eyes showed that in a few years she would be someone to be reckoned with. But Elizabeth was not jealous. She loved her younger sister, was proud of her beauty and her quick wit. She hated to think of being separated from her when Helen went off to school. She had been hoping to at least be able to see her if she was in London studying nursing.

"Want to sleep with me tonight?" Elizabeth asked Helen. "I haven't had a chance to hear all the latest gossip in the neighbourhood, and I need you to make me laugh a little."

Helen scrambled up and pulled the blankets back, fighting for most of the pillows as she did every time she slept with her sister, grabbing for them as Elizabeth made a futile attempt to snatch them from her.

"You can't do that at Miss Cheltenham's you know," she told Helen, taking the one pillow Helen had left her and swinging it at Helen's head. They started laughing, hitting each other and giggling louder and louder until they heard their mother's footsteps outside the door. Jane had heard their rowdy behaviour and she attempted to settle them down as if they were seven and four instead of seventeen and nearly fourteen. Chastened, the two girls settled into Elizabeth's bed and huddled together, giggling and talking for a while before sleep finally overtook them.

Jane came into the bedroom she shared with her husband. Edward was already in his nightshirt, sitting and staring glumly into the fire. He looked at her as she came over and stood by his chair, looking down at him.

"I don't want to talk about it," he said crossly, looking back at the fire.

Jane held up both hands and smiled. "I wasn't going to say anything," she told him. She leaned over to kiss the top of his head, and headed to her dressing room. When she came out a few minutes later, having prepared for bed, her hair was down and she was wearing a filmy nightgown of fine French batiste. She came directly over to Edward and sat on his lap, her knees on either side of his legs. She wrapped her arms around his neck.

"Come here, you cranky old thing," she whispered, kissing his forehead. He chuckled, and shifted in the chair, pushing himself against her. They kissed for few minutes, and it soon became obvious that Edward's thoughts were no longer on his children.

"Is the door locked?" he whispered, as they got up and moved to the bed.

Jane pulled the covers back, "Yes. But even if it were not, Ned is busy sulking in his room, brooding soulfully. He has informed me that you have no idea what it is like to burn inside and not to be able to be with the one you love." Edward snorted. "And the girls are giggling in Elizabeth's room; it's so good to have them here together." She climbed into bed, moving down under the covers.

"I don't want to talk about the children," Edward said, frowning again. He reached down for the hem of his nightshirt, pulling it over his head. "Come here. I'll show you a thing or two about burning inside."

Jane laughed, and slid over to her husband's side of the bed, her nightgown very soon joining his upon the floor. They clung together, all outside thoughts forgotten as hands and fingers and soft lips caressed warm skin, as quiet whispers became moans and murmured words of love and desire.

Jane lay back, taking her husband's weight upon her, feeling him slip into her as he had a thousand times before, and yet each time new. She arched up to meet him, giving a moan of pleasure as his body came down upon hers, as he filled her and made her complete. Sighing with contentment and anticipation she wrapped her arms around him, kissing him, urging him on as their bodies began to rise and fall together.

Never, never did they tire of this lovely meeting of bodies and souls. It was sweet and mellow, like a great old wine growing better with age. Edward's hair was greying and his body changing as the years went on, and hers was changing as well, but in each other's arms there was no age, no time, only the reality of warm skin on skin, lips meeting lips, each as familiar to the other as their own. They did not come together as often, and they both took a little longer to be ready than they previously had, but each time was still magic, a blessed refuge from all their stresses and worries.

"Edward," Jane whispered, her pleasure spiraling within her as he moved slowly inside her, their eyes meeting in a long tender look before his closed and he bent his head to her, his mouth caressing her warm, soft body. He was groaning as she moved up to meet him, her fingernails digging into his skin with just enough pressure for him to know how much she loved this, needed his touch and his desire and his flesh on hers, in hers. Their feelings rose, sensations peaked together, cries of desire and release mingling into the cool air around their bed. The world fell away, all cares vanished, and for a short blessed time, there was no one in the world but them.

Chapter 64 - Off to School

Hay Vicarage, July 1860

Adèle handed Jane a cup of tea, and then sat on a nearby chair. As she sank into it, she paused to dislodge her daughter Emma's doll, which was lying on the seat.

"So, all is now solved?" she asked Jane. "And Mr. Rochester is allowing Elizabeth to study nursing at last?" Adèle was aware of the present drama at Thornfield, as Elizabeth had come to talk to her on several occasions. She had listened sympathetically to the girl she regarded as a younger sister, but could not help thinking of her own children, and feeling for Jane and Edward.

Jane sighed, her cup poised at her lips. "Well, I would not say all is solved, exactly," she began. "Edward has agreed because Elizabeth so obviously longs to do this, and because I offered to finance it. He will never allow me to pay for Elizabeth's upkeep; he would consider himself a poor father not to support his child. But he is not happy about it. One would think Elizabeth were going to live among heathens in foreign lands rather than merely being two days away in London."

"Is he afraid for her safety?" Adèle asked.

"I don't believe so," Jane replied. "He just doesn't want to be without her. My goodness, I feel no harm could befall Elizabeth at that school! They have classes all morning, and work in the hospital all afternoon. After dinner they have schoolwork, including keeping a journal of all they see and do, for Miss Nightingale's perusal. They are permitted only an hour for relaxing and socializing, before they are expected to retire to bed to begin the whole ordeal again the next day. This goes on Monday through Saturday.

"They are permitted no visitors during the week, and only on Sundays after church may they have the afternoon off to visit with family. They are not allowed to leave the hospital grounds unless they are accompanied by family members, and if they are caught corresponding with or talking to men who are not family members, it is grounds for dismissal. If Elizabeth were entering a convent, she would not be more closely watched."

Adèle smiled in amusement, "Surely a father must not worry for his daughter under those conditions. But it is only for a short time, isn't it?"

Jane blew on her tea in an attempt to cool it, and put down her cup. She laced her fingers together in her lap and sat back in her chair with a sigh of relief, for the last weeks had been stressful ones.

"Elizabeth will be considered a probationer, doing basic study to determine her intelligence and fitness to learn, while helping with the most basic tasks in the hospital – cleaning, laundry and kitchen service. This will last four to six months, and if she is deemed suitable, she gets to put the white cap and apron on over her blue uniform and begin actual nursing study and care of people in the hospital. She cannot wait."

She continued, "Elizabeth's interest in nursing is beyond me, I confess. Between the typhus epidemic at Lowood and nursing the children through their illnesses, I have no desire to do further care of the sick. But Elizabeth is longing for it. I found her reading a book she had gotten Ned to borrow for her from the lending library in Millcote. There were all manner of anatomical drawings, some things I had never seen.

"I had seen art books when I was Elizabeth's age, drawings of men and women from life, prints of great works of art, so I was not totally ignorant of the human body. But those figures at least had skin on them. These were drawings of flayed skin, with muscle and bone clearly visible, and organs in plain view. It was enough to make my stomach feel quite uneasy. Yet Elizabeth sat quietly, reading the book while she ate her sandwich." Jane shook her head.

"And yet you were such a comfort to me when I had the children," Adèle said, reaching over to place her hand on Jane's arm. "You never gave me the idea that you were distressed or upset by the process."

"That was different," Jane said, remembering. "Those were happy occasions. I was in too much pain when my own were born to be revolted, and too excited when your children were born. It was an altogether different thing. Where are the children, by the way?"

"They're out with Thomas," Adèle answered. "Mr. and Mrs. Walton, that sweet elderly couple from church, so enjoy Tom and Emma. And since they have no children, they shower mine with attention. Thomas likes to take the children with him when he visits them. He has finally relaxed, after all the recent uproar, and as it's such a beautiful day, they are walking there and back. That is why I have some time to myself, and it was much needed!"

Jane nodded, thinking of the events of the past months. At long last, Thomas's identity as an author had been made public. A young would-be reporter, anxious to prove himself to a newspaper that had recently hired him as a copy boy, had ferreted out the identity of the author of the popular children's book "The Magic Caverns" and revealed him to be Thomas Cooper. "The Magic Caverns" was a compilation of Thomas's previously-published children's stories, adventure stories involving two young brothers who had stumbled into a mysterious cave and discovered all manner of wonders. Following the birth of his daughter Emma, Thomas had been led to add the character of a younger sister. The fact that the book – equally popular with girls and boys – was now revealed to be the work of a young vicar in Derbyshire had caused quite a sensation.

It was no great surprise to the Rochesters that after a week or so of buzzing and gossip, the parishioners of the Hay congregation had reacted to the news of their minister's secret life with great delight and pride. The stories were amusing and wholesome, and as their author's obvious love for children shone through on every page, there were very few who could find fault with the news of their much-loved parson's hobby.

Among the very few who could find fault was the curate, a thin, severe young man with strict views on the correct behaviour of everyone from the youngest child of the parish to Thomas himself. Mr. Chadwick was only twenty-five to Thomas's thirty-five, but he was an ascetic, used to doing without the vain pleasures of this earth. He rarely failed to hold an opposing view to that of his superior, and his few loyal supporters in the parish constituted a tiny but vocal minority.

Jane disliked the curate, who reminded her of a younger Brocklehurst. Edward, with all the power afforded a wealthy, established landowner, detested the man.

"I do not know how a man of Chadwick's personality was ever judged to be fit as a curate," he ranted one day to Jane as they sat in the library. "I would almost think he has caught the Bishop in a compromising position and has blackmailed him into giving him a parish. He has certainly blackmailed someone into speaking for him; the man is worthless!"

"Edward!" Jane had hissed, looking towards the adjoining drawing room where Ned, Mary Ellis, Elizabeth and Helen were having an afternoon of games and music with some of the other young people from the neighbourhood. "Keep your voice down, someone is going to hear you!"

"I don't care if they do," he grumbled, but lowered his voice as he continued to complain. Mr. Chadwick had clashed with Thomas Cooper in the first month of his duties as curate, when a young woman of the parish was found to be with child out of wedlock. Chadwick was all for tossing the young woman out of the church membership, as well as out of her home without a penny, and was angry that her parents would not do so. Her parents, heartbroken, but determined to support their daughter, had found comfort in Thomas's gentle assurance that the parish would help in every way.

Chadwick took great exception to what he looked at as a liberal view of sin.

"The young woman is repentant and humble," Thomas argued in a meeting of the parish board that Chadwick had insisted upon. "She believed herself in love and would have married the child's father had he not deserted her and left the area. She is determined to rear her infant in the church and needs our help more than ever. If ever she would turn her back on God, it would be because the people of the parish turned their backs upon her."

Edward, the present head of the parish board, agreed, and the board voted not to expel the young girl from the church rolls.

Chadwick had listened to the vote, and then had told Edward, "This permissive attitude is only what I would expect of you, sir."

The other board members had watched with interest, knowing of Rochester's pride and lack of patience with those who annoyed him. But Rochester surprised them by smiling at the angry curate and saying calmly:

"Those to whom God has shown great mercy must wish for mercy for others in need." He gave Chadwick a bow of the head, and took up his hat. "The day may come, Chadwick, when you may wish mercy to be shown to you. Good day, sir."

Privately, Chadwick was heard to mutter to his allies in the church that the liberal vote was what he expected would happen, for Cooper himself had married Rochester's bastard daughter, no doubt for the financial benefit of it, and everyone knew it.

The matter was dropped, and the young girl had borne her child, was living with her parents, and never missed a Sunday, bringing her young son with her to every service. Her presence had not led to a rash of out-of-wedlock births, as Chadwick had predicted, and Cooper was looked upon as a man whom people trusted to be merciful in times of need. But he had not ceased to clash with his curate. Thomas, a quiet, peace-loving man, had not complained to his superiors, choosing to handle the problems himself. But other men had complained, although to date they had been unsuccessful in ousting Chadwick from the parish.

Jane now laughed, as she and Adèle talked over the newest "scandal" to catch Chadwick's attention. "I wish I could have been in the parish meeting when the Bishop himself revealed that 'The Magic Caverns' is now his own children's favourite book and that he and his family read from it before he tucks his children in at night. Edward laughed heartily at the look on Chadwick's face – I do believe that has been his happiest moment so far this summer. With Ned longing to marry, Elizabeth eager to go to nursing school, and Helen leaving for Miss Cheltenham's, my dear husband has been in a grim mood. He needs all the amusements he can get, and this latest set-to with Chadwick has amused him greatly!"

"And what is the current state of Ned's life?" Adèle asked, lowering her voice as though Ned himself were in the room to hear her.

"That is the funniest thing of all," Jane told her. "After all Ned's anguish, and Edward's solemn pronouncements, it is Miss Ellis herself who has become the voice of reason. Upon hearing that Ned and his father were having difficulties, she said that she could not live with herself if her wedding were the cause of any pain to us. She has refused any further talk of moving up the wedding, and is now determined that Ned return to Oxford this autumn. The wedding is set for next July, towards the end of that month, most likely. Who would have thought that our flighty Miss Ellis should be our greatest ally in this fight?"

Ned Rochester was happy enough to remain behind at Thornfield Manor that August, as his parents and sisters travelled to London for the girls to begin school. He had gotten his fill of larger cities in his time at Eton and Oxford, and was content to remain in the country, seeing to the estate that would one day be his.

He had kissed his sisters good-bye with regret, for he loved them dearly despite their mutual teasing. But in another month he would return to Oxford to finish his final year and he had much to occupy himself with until then. He and Miss Ellis had reached an agreement when she had refused to clash with his family, and she was adamant that Ned should return to Oxford and finish out his schooling.

Miss Ellis was not terribly scholarly herself. Having completed her education at a mediocre girls' finishing school, she now looked forward to her future life as a wife and a mother. Her own father had had little formal education, learning only to read, write, and cipher before he was obliged to give up school forever and go to work to help support his mother and siblings. He was proud of a future son-in-law with a good education, and Mary recognized that Ned's Oxford education would reflect well on her after they were married.

She was reluctant to cause a problem, no matter how Ned might insist that he did not need to finish out his final year. Upon hearing that the intimidating Mr. Rochester had refused to consider Ned's quitting, Mary supported Edward's decision. As eager as she was to be Ned's wife, she knew that she would be living with the Rochesters at Thornfield after her marriage, and that it behooved her to keep the peace. Her own father looked upon her as only a silly, pretty burden who must marry well, but Mary knew that her dear Ned enjoyed an uncharacteristically good relationship with his parents and she was wise enough not to wish to disrupt that bond.

Ned knew that some day his father would be gone and Thornfield would be his, but he dreaded that day. He had a deep respect for his father, whom he regarded as his closest friend. He had good companions from school as well as ties of friendship in the area, but in his father's company he had found a close comfort and communion that he knew was rare among men his age. Certainly few men at Oxford enjoyed such relations with their parents.

Despite the fact that he would be a very wealthy man upon Edward Rochester's death, Ned hoped that his father would live for many years yet. He was active and vigorous and Ned knew quite a few men who were hale and healthy into their eighties. He fervently hoped his father would be one of them. He did not worry for his mother. At only forty-two, Jane Rochester looked younger than her age, and Ned felt confident that he would have his mother in his life for many years to come.

Ned Rochester, at nearly twenty-one, was a young man of simple desires and no great ambitions. He was intelligent enough, although he lacked both his mother's diligent study habits and his father's sharp wit. Ned, despite his great physical resemblance to his father, was in personality a blend of both his parents – Edward's active, restless nature perfectly diluted with the quiet and resolute calm of Jane Eyre. But Ned possessed one quality that both his parents had lacked in their youth: contentment in himself.

His mother had developed a great yearning for a larger life, a need that had propelled her forth from Lowood to new adventures at a mere eighteen years of age. And Edward Rochester had lived a peripatetic existence from age twenty-one to age thirty-seven, when he was brought to a forceful halt by circumstances. In each other, Ned's parents had found a happiness that had given them a calm and peaceful life. Their two daughters inherited their parents' restlessness; not so Ned.

Elizabeth, longing for higher education and service to others, was poised on the brink of a new and growing profession. And Helen was active, her wit constantly in search of a new target, while her body sought the thrill of riding fast and of jumping her horse (for she did jump small hedges and obstacles at times, despite being forbidden to do so by her anxious father).

In Ned, these traits were all but absent. Within his family, he was well aware of a history of longing for excitement and change: a cousin who had died on the mission fields of India, a great-uncle who had taken his energy to Madeira to start a new business, a grandmother who had defied her wealthy family and turned her back on riches for the sake of love. But Ned was uncomplicated. He loved to read and could have excelled greatly in mathematics, but he was happy to settle for a good education without distinction. He knew that as the sole male heir to the property at Thornfield, his future lay in managing two estates. Unlike many young men, he was content with his destiny.

He loved to hunt and fish but was happy just to be out in nature, revelling in the beauty of the countryside even if he caught nothing. He liked to ride, but did not need to win races or excel in the hunt, unlike his younger sister. He could have, with his family's wealth, courted and won any London society beauty but he was happy with the daughter of a Millcote manufacturer. Mr. Ellis would never be counted among the gentry because of his background in trade, despite wealth that rivalled or exceeded that of his neighbours. But Ned, son of a former governess, minded not at all his future wife's lack of family background.

Ned also had a quiet religious faith, but he felt no need for deep philosophical thoughts or great theological understanding. He was content to attend most services, to listen to Thomas, whom he admired greatly, and to Chadwick, whom he found more amusing than annoying. Internally, Ned enjoyed a private relationship with a God who seemed to him quite benign and fatherly.

No one realized it, but Ned was in fact very like his grandfather John Rochester would have been, had John Rochester not been raised in a cocoon of privilege and entitlement. They were both simple country men who loved their ancestral home and wished only for an uncomplicated life upon it.

But where John had been spoiled, Ned had been disciplined. Where John had been arrogant, Ned was humble. Where John had had a streak of cruelty, Ned had compassion. Where John had wanted no controls put on his life and no master but himself, Ned was content to look up to his father.

And where John had burned with a strong sexual need and had taken his pleasures where he found them, Ned, like his own father, longed only for a loving wife and a lifetime of fidelity to the right woman. Ned could hardly wait to marry Mary. He had shown restraint with her, knowing she was a proper young woman. Their increasingly passionate embraces had gone no further than an occasional brief touch of her breast on the outside of her clothing, but he longed for the day when he would bring her to Thornfield as his bride, when he would take her to his bed as his wife.

"Son, do not, I beg you, make the mistakes I made," Edward had told Ned in their private talks together. "Your body will burn with need; all men know what that is like. But exercising those passions will blind you to what is truly important; will lead you into a snare from which it may be hard to escape. A long life of loving happiness with a good wife is better than the temporary relief of your body's urges."

Ned believed that, seeing the happiness of his parents. But he wondered at times how he could wait this one more year. His impulsive wish to quit college had been born of desperation, and had been the one real time he had clashed with his father. But he was now persuaded that he should wait. Now that he and Mary had set a date for their wedding, Ned felt it would be better for him to be away from Mary as they waited, for at times he did not know how he could keep his hands off her if they were together.

He loved Mary Ellis, loved her with a true and abiding passion found in those lucky few who find their great loves in childhood or youth. And she adored him in return.

Mary was not entirely the silly creature Ned's family thought she was. At only nineteen, she lacked maturity. And as the daughter of a newly-rich tradesman who had started as a shop-boy many years ago, she lacked confidence among the Hay and Millcote gentry – the old families such as the Dents, the Eshtons, the Ingrams. And the Rochesters.

But she was a decent girl, bright enough if not intellectual. She was the perfect counterpart to Ned, content to be the wife of a landowner and the mother of his children. In time, her loving devotion to her husband and her children would earn her the respect of her in-laws. But that would come later.

At one time Ned and Mary would have been perfectly suited to the life of their peasant ancestors, living quietly and asking for very little. Not for them the intense and life-changing experiences of their families. Only fate had made them wealthy, only chance had placed them in a position of prominence.

Ned and Mary were the stuff of which many of our forebears were made – simple people, asking little of life – and for now they waited for the next summer to arrive, so they could finally have what they wanted: a quiet life with each other.

So it was that in early August, Ned remained behind to watch over Thornfield, as Jane and Edward reluctantly set out for London to take their two daughters to school. Helen, with good-natured resignation, was set to enter Miss Cheltenham's Academy, where Elizabeth had just completed three happy years. She had the added promise of being reunited with her mare Daisy, which Edward had promised to board at a stable near the school if Helen did well in her first semester.

Helen also had the comfort of knowing that her sister would be only a few miles away, although the two girls would not see each other often due to the demands of Elizabeth's nursing school schedule.

Elizabeth, so eager to begin the new phase of her life, looked out of the carriage window happily, willing the horses to go faster while feeling a tug at her heart as she looked at her parents. She knew it would be a long while before she was with them again – and when she was, it would never again be with the childish dependence and feeling of protection she had enjoyed while home with her family.

Helen was feeling a bit sulky, as she had wished to take the train to London rather than the carriage. The closest place to catch the train was Sheffield, as the tracks had not yet been extended into Millcote. Sheffield was a trip of nearly two hours by carriage and Edward, who still harbored a slight scepticism about travelling by rail despite nearly ten years of occasionally taking that route, had refused.

"Why should we travel to crowded, dirty, smoky Sheffield, wait for the train, and endure a packed, filthy day-long journey by rail when we can travel quietly in our private carriage, stopping when we wish and enjoying pleasant dinners and nights at a good inn?" he had asked Jane.

Jane, who had quite enjoyed their occasional train rides, did not mind either way. She knew, as did Elizabeth, that Edward wanted to stretch this trip out to remain with his girls as long as possible. But this was no comfort to Helen, who viewed her parents as hopelessly old-fashioned and entirely provincial.

The family travelled on, stopping occasionally to rest. Sometimes the sisters sat together, talking or teasing, while their parents listened, delighting in their daughters. Occasionally Jane reached over to give a comforting pat to her husband's knee. Sometimes Edward and Elizabeth sat together, talking quietly about the countryside as Edward remembered it in days gone by, as Helen lay with her head in Jane's lap, dozing fitfully.

Later Elizabeth sat next to Jane, her head resting on her mother's shoulder as Edward and Helen bantered back and forth about exactly how well Helen would have to do at school to earn a trip to London for her horse.

"Top grades and excellent deportment, nothing less!" Edward teased, as Helen pulled a face and groaned, "Papa!"

The carriage rolled on, each turn of the wheels bringing Edward Rochester closer to what he dreaded – the time when he would leave his much-loved daughters behind in London, and return to a home that was emptier, quieter, and much more lonely.

Chapter 65 - Letters to Loved Ones

Thornfield Manor, Autumn 1860

All three children were gone, dispersed to their respective schools. Edward and Jane were finding it hard to adapt to the large, empty house; and where Edward had less than a year ago been urging Jane to agree to take a trip with him, he now was finding it hard to leave the house, as letters from his children were the only ties he had with them at this time.

Every day he waited eagerly for the post to arrive, and if the mail came without a message from one of his children, Jane noticed that he was a bit morose for the rest of the day. Eventually, their daily walks all seemed to end up at the Hay post office.

Jane tried to lift Edward's spirits by reminding him that by next summer, Ned would be finished at Oxford and if all went according to plan, would be back at Thornfield with Miss Ellis also living there as his bride. But he reminded her in a gloomy tone that the girls would still be away at school except for holidays, and that nothing would be the same again with Ned.

"He will belong to his wife now, Jane, never again to us," he said, in a tone of such tragedy that one would think Edward was contemplating his son's imminent demise rather than his marriage.

"But that is the way of things, my darling!" Jane told him, taking his arm in hers and hugging it against her. She gave a sudden laugh. "I cannot believe that this is the same man who once stood at a party for the assembled gentry and made the statement that he did not like children!"

"I never said that!" Edward protested, frowning at her.

Jane sighed, her lips twitching with suppressed laughter. "Why don't you take those sweets we picked up in Hay and deliver them to Tom and Emma yourself instead of waiting until they come to supper tomorrow night?" she suggested to Edward. "You can check on how Adèle is feeling."

After waiting and hoping for several years, Adèle was once again with child, and unfortunately feeling much more tired and nauseated than she had in her previous pregnancies. Jane was concerned about her, but hoped for the best. Adèle was happy, even between bouts of vomiting that left her weak and exhausted.

"I'm too old for this," she would sigh to Jane and to Thomas. "I'll be thirty-three when this child is born, imagine that!"

Now Jane watched her husband fondly as he left the house, his shoulders hunched against the November chill and his arms stuck deeply into his coat pockets. She shook her head a little as she reached for the newspaper, which she had been reading to Edward earlier that day, and settled back into a comfortable armchair. As deeply as she loved her children, she was coping with their absence better than Edward was. The work of running a large household, as well as the letters she wrote every day to her children and to her cousins, kept her busy. She sometimes felt a lump in her throat as she thought of one or another of her children, but all in all she was handling the emptier household quite well.

It was August when they had taken the girls to London, arriving first at Miss Cheltenham's where they stayed for a day to get Helen settled. They met her teachers, who were delighted to see the family again and informed Helen that they were thrilled to be able to teach a sister of Elizabeth Rochester.

"Uh-oh," Edward had murmured to Jane, bending his head to whisper into her ear. "Give them a week or two with our Helen and they will be singing a different tune." She had laughed softly and pushed playfully at his arm, but had to admit she agreed with him.

They met Helen's roommate, Emily Broderick, a chubby, vacant-eyed girl to whom Helen took an immediate dislike, hissing to her parents that she would die if she had to spend a whole year sharing a room with that bovine creature. But Edward and Jane had informed Helen sternly that the world was full of people and that she must learn to get along with them. Kissing her good-bye, and hiding their tears behind forced smiles and artificial cheer, they had taken their leave of their youngest daughter.

From Miss Cheltenham's, they had taken Elizabeth to St. Thomas Hospital, where Miss Nightingale's training school had begun classes back in July. They looked with trepidation at the large hospital with its dour nurses walking the halls in their starched uniforms, and its grim row of cots in the dormitory of the student wing. They had met Mrs. Wardroper, a former matron, or one in charge of a hospital ward, who had now been placed in charge of the new nursing trainees.

Edward and Jane were nervous for Elizabeth, but she appeared happy and excited, her demeanour only briefly changing when she was told to tell her parents goodbye before she was shown to her assigned area. All three shed tears when they kissed goodbye, and their last sight of Elizabeth was of her being led away by Mrs. Wardroper, her carpetbag clutched in one hand.

Both parents were silent and depressed on the trip back to Thornfield, where they began the wait for the letters that were their only link with their daughters.

In September, Ned left for Oxford to prepare for the Michaelmas term of his last year of school. Shortly after his departure, Jane and Edward went to Ferndean for a few days so Edward could see to his other estate. It was a nice change for the couple, bringing back memories of their early married days. They took long walks in the woods, visited their tenants, and did some work in the house, laughing and talking freely without worrying about being overheard by children or servants.

They made love more often than they had at home, mostly in their old bed, but also once on the slightly dusty parlour rug in front of a roaring fire (overcome by their passion beforehand, they found themselves sneezing afterwards, making both of them laugh in a most undignified fashion), once in the kitchen when Edward had sneaked in on Jane as she was inspecting the woodwork for needed repairs, and once, on a memorable afternoon that was unseasonably warm, outside on a blanket in the woods, their picnic basket forgotten beside them. It was a wonderful holiday for the couple, and they went home to Thornfield refreshed and happy.

At Christmas, the children had all come home to Thornfield, and Edward and Jane hosted a large house party, including Mary Ellis and her parents, Diana and Arthur Fitzjames, and Mary and William Wharton, who brought with them their younger daughter Jane.

In early January, Jane remained home to help care for Adèle, who was confined to bed with her pregnancy, while Edward took the girls back to London. This time he and Elizabeth rode in the carriage while Helen rode Daisy alongside. Occasionally, Edward traded with Helen, riding the mare while Helen rode in the carriage with her sister. Edward was tired out and his backside was extremely sore by the time they reached London, but he would never admit it.

Letters arrived from all the children. In the past, when notes had arrived addressed to both of them, Jane would sit with Edward, reading them aloud. But she noticed now that her husband was eager to read them himself. Seeing how he hastily opened each letter, holding it to the table with his left arm while eagerly slitting it open with the letter opener held firmly in his right hand, grabbing up his eye-glass to peer closely at the handwriting, she was patient. She realized that just being able to hold the paper in his hand, absorbing its contents, was his way of keeping a connection with his children, and so she said nothing and waited for him to hand each letter over.

Miss Helen Rochester
care of Miss Cheltenham's
Academy for Young Ladies
25 Clapham Close
Kensington, London

Mr. and Mrs. Edward Rochester
Thornfield Manor
Hay, Derbyshire
19 January 1861

Dearest Mama and Papa,
Happy birthday Papa!! I hope you are having a wonderful day and that Mama is serving you a special meal, with a nice dessert of course! I wish I could be there to give you a birthday kiss.
I miss you both so much, for after being home at Christmas it feels strange to be back at school. But I am SO happy to have Daisy here and I cannot thank you enough, my darling Papa.
There are five of us here who ride and four of us have our horses boarded here at the stable. The other girl, Sarah, rides the horses at the stable and she is the best rider I have ever seen! She and I have become friends and she is already helping me to ride even better than I already do. We cannot share a room as the assignments are already made for the year but we have put in a request for next year. Emily is not so very bad as I thought, but she is still a lazy spoilt creature and I will be glad to be free of her next year.
I do like school, mostly, and do you know, Mama, that you have already had me read many of the things that we are reading in literature. I can already speak French, thanks to your teaching, but Miss Cheltenham has decided that next year I must study Latin. She says that Elizabeth worked very hard at Latin and did well.

As much as I love my sister, I think the teachers here are disappointed that I am not like her. I know that she is much sweeter and kinder than I am but I cannot help that, I must just be Helen!

I miss Lizzie so very much and wish I could see her here. Last semester Miss Cheltenham took me to visit her one Sunday afternoon and I hope she will do that again soon. I would like to take some of my allowance and visit Lizzie every Sunday. I could take a hansom cab to the hospital, but Miss C says it is not done for a young lady to take a public conveyance alone. There are a lot of things that Miss C says are "not done" and I do not like that!

I need to close this letter now my sweet Papa and Mama but I will write again soon. Know that your Helen misses you very much. Much love from your daughter

Helen Maria Rochester

PS. Do you see the little daisy I drew over the "i" in my second name? That is a thank you from my little mare who is so happy to be here with me!

Edward smiled as he read his daughter's letter with its large looping letters and its elaborate flourishes. He passed the note to his wife, then took out his handkerchief and blew his nose loudly.

Letters came from Elizabeth, written in her small, neat hand:

Miss Jane Elizabeth Rochester
Student Dormitories
St. Thomas Hospital
St. Thomas Street
Southwark, London

Mr. and Mrs. Edward Rochester
Thornfield Manor
Hay, Derbyshire
16 March 1861

My dear parents,
The weather in London continues to be wet and cold. But do not worry, Mama and Papa, I am keeping warm. Please thank Adèle for the lovely warm woolen stockings she has knitted for me; I wear them constantly beneath my uniform. I am sorry to hear that she has to continue in bed, but I know that she is eager to do what Dr. Carter says. Or "Doctors Carter", that is. How wonderful that Mr. Carter has three sons back in Hay to take over his practice since he has retired, or will have now that the youngest has finished school and will be training with his brothers. I do not know Dr. Ephraim Carter – he has always been away at school and I do not remember him. Funny how the two eldest Carter sons, and the very youngest, have become doctors but the other two have gone in completely different directions, one to the Navy and one off to Manchester to the cotton mills.

Anyway, I laughed to read that Adèle is knitting yards and yards of wool in an attempt to keep busy. How funny, Papa, what you said, "Only old men wear mufflers." You must not hurt Adèle's feelings, and must wear the muffler anyway. I'm sure it is cold there in Derbyshire also and you must keep warm and care for yourself.

You asked how I am now that I am off probationary status and have started my nurse's training. I am happy to say that I find it interesting and wonderful and every day is full and busy.

Now, Mama and Papa, do not be upset when I tell you that I have seen my first surgery! I was quite nervous, not that I would be sick but that I would drop my journal, or miss writing some of the details as Miss Nightingale has instructed us. But I do not believe I did anything wrong, although I found it so absorbing that at times I forgot to write. It was quite a tragic case, a young girl of only twelve who had to have an amputation up to her forearm after she caught her hand in some machinery at her factory job. Fortunately they were able to give her chloroform and so she was not conscious during the operation.

I was assigned to her ward afterwards and was able to talk to her a little. I told her about you, Papa, how you had lost your hand years ago and how there are very few things you cannot do now. Poor little thing, she seemed so young and frightened there in the ward. Her entire family works in the factory and so she never has any visitors, as they are all working during visiting hours. I am sorry that she has lost her dominant hand, and do not know how this bodes for her future.

I am glad to hear that there is a movement calling for the reform of laws regarding child labour. I know that life is very hard for some of the families, but children her age should be in school, not working all day in a factory. It humbles me to realize how fortunate I am not to have had to work ten and twelve hours a day, and makes me even more eager to be of use in society. Many people go their whole lives never knowing that children are spending their entire childhoods working in factories, in mines, in foundries. Oh, I know that children work hard in Derbyshire also, but those are mainly on farms, out in the fresh air. But even in Millcote, children work in the factories there. It does not seem right and there are so many things I wish I could help to change.

I must finish this letter, my dear Mama and Papa. I miss you both and wish I were there to kiss you and tell you of my love in person. Please be assured that I am well and quite happy to be here. If only I could be in two places at one time – here fulfilling my dream, and there with you, my loving parents. I remain your devoted daughter

Elizabeth

"It's you she takes after," Edward muttered, laying down his eye-glass and passing the letter to Jane. She said nothing, just taking the paper from his hand and settling back to read it with a small, satisfied smile playing about her lips.

Occasional letters came from Ned, still in the same careless scrawl but with the spelling much improved from years before:

Edward Eyre Rochester
Magdalen College
University of Oxford
Oxford

Mr. and Mrs. Edward F. Rochester
Thornfield Manor
Hay, Derbyshire
England
31 May 1861

Dear Mother and Father,

I hope you are both well and healthy now that summer is starting to come to England once again. I am busy as my college days are coming to an end (Thank God!) and of course, hardly a day goes by that I do not receive a note from Mary asking my opinion about something else regarding the wedding. Truthfully I would not care if the tables for the wedding luncheon were set with damask or burlap, but Mary is sweet to want to include me. It seems hardly possible that in exactly two months she and I will be married and heading to Ireland for our honeymoon.

Dear Mama, it would be wonderful if you could have a word with Helen. She is driving Mary to distraction saying she will not wear the bridesmaid's dress that Mary has chosen. I keep telling Mary that Helen is teasing her, but her nerves are a bit on edge right now and it would be better if Helen left her alone.

At any rate, what news from home!!! Twin boys for Adèle and Thomas, who would have thought it! Thomas writes that they are alike as two peas in a pod, and that they are gaining weight now. I did not think that month early sounds like much but apparently it is, and I am glad to hear that little Jacob and Joseph are doing well now. Poor Emma is quite outnumbered and I can just imagine the pout on her little face. Mary writes that Emma is quite excited to be part of the wedding party and that it will do her good to get some attention now that her little brothers are here taking up everyone's time.

All is well here at Oxford, although of course everyone is buzzing with the news of the newly declared war in America. I have paid little attention to the gathering storm over that country, and when I did think of it I wondered why they are in such a stir over slavery when we went through abolition years ago with little trouble. There is a great deal of discussion on the concept of "States' Rights" and the implications of separate countries breaking off from their established government. I look forward to discussing it with you, Father, as I know that you have been absorbed in your newspaper on a daily basis. I had not thought that a war there would affect us, but one of the fellows here is the son of a Leeds cotton mill owner and he buys all his cotton from the States. Already there is fear over what a war there will mean for the textile mills here in England.

Back to my studies now. I look forward to seeing both of you in just a little more than a month. I send you congratulations in advance for in just a week you will be married twenty-four years! I hope that Mary and I will enjoy the happiness you both have had. My love to you both-

Ned

Edward passed the note to Jane, saying, "Hmmph, I'd wager that Miss Ellis gets five letters for every one he sends to us."

Jane nodded. "You would probably be right, darling," she agreed, taking the letter from him with a small sigh.

And indeed, Edward and Jane were not the only ones who received letters through the long months:

Edward Eyre Rochester
Magdalen College
University of Oxford
Oxford

Miss Mary Ellis
Ellis Wood
Millcote, Derbyshire
20 June 1861

My love-
I sit here by the light of the single candle, looking up at the moon and wondering if you are doing the same. Or perhaps you are deep in slumber? I can see you there, your lovely hair spread like silk over your pillow. Do you dream of me, my beloved, as I dream constantly of you?

You write that I must surely be too busy to think of my Mary, but I assure you that could never be the case! You are my only love, and my greatest thoughts are there with you. My schooling here at Oxford is just something I must get through until my real life can begin, with you, my darling girl.

I cannot believe that in just three weeks I will be there with you, and in a little more than a month we will be joined forever as man and wife. My breath catches in my throat and my heart jumps to think of it. How happy you make me, my darling, and how happy I will strive to make you, forever.

I do not have any preference for which hymns I wish to be sung at the wedding. I know some hymns of the Church of England, but do not know any of the Methodist hymns which are surely familiar to you and your family. I will leave that to you and to your parents.

My heart aches for your presence, my love, and I cannot wait to hold you in my arms again. Until then I hold your handkerchief to my face, breathing in your scent and longing for the moment I will see your beautiful face again. I love you with all my heart, and I am and forever will be
Your Ned

Chapter 66 - A Wedding in the Family

31 July 1861

The day of Ned and Mary's wedding dawned bright and clear, the sun shining brightly from the moment it rose. Edward and Jane had been awake long before sunrise, pulled from their sleep by the sound of the birds that had begun to stir and chirp long before the sun came up.

Each had sensed the other was awake, and Edward reached over and took his wife's hand. For a while there were no words spoken, and then Jane heard her husband's voice in the darkness.

"I awoke this morning remembering the day he was born," Edward said quietly. "It was right about this time of morning I saw you disappear into that tiny bedroom next to the kitchen. I was beside myself with fear for you. I knew I could lose you, and knew I could not survive that."

"But you didn't lose me," Jane replied, "and by two in the afternoon we had our little son."

"And now he is leaving us, making a home of his own, even though he will still be here at Thornfield," Edward sighed. "And someday there will be grandchildren. I have never felt old, Jane, until right now. I am sixty-two... I never dreamed, back when I was young, that I would ever see the day when I would be this age."

"You're not old," Jane protested loyally. "You have always appeared younger than your age, and you still do. To see you, no one would think you much past fifty!"

Edward chuckled softly, "I thought I was the one who is half-blind."

Jane laughed in return, "Well, all right, much past fifty-five." She rolled over and kissed her husband, snuggling into the warmth of his still-strong arms. "There is so much to do today and yet I cannot imagine getting up. Eleven o'clock will be here before we know it, but I just want to lie here with you, remembering Ned when we could still control him." She felt the low rumble of her husband's laughter, felt him kiss the top of her head.

She smiled as she spoke quietly, "Edward, you know that Ned thinks so highly of you. He respects you, and will always listen to what you tell him." She heard her husband sigh wistfully, felt his hug around her again.

Thornfield was full today, as house guests filled the spare rooms: Diana and Captain Fitzjames, Mary and Mr. Wharton, their younger daughter Jane, and their older daughter Diana with her husband and small son. Friends of Ned's from Oxford, and Helen's best friend Sarah from Miss Cheltenham's, who had been invited for this occasion and who would stay a few weeks before the girls returned to Sarah's home in London and then back to school.

And Elizabeth had been allowed to come, given a few days' holiday from school. She had arrived by train the day before, travelling with a small party that included some of the other guests. It had taken all Jane's organizational skills to arrange for the group to travel together, but in the end it had worked well, and she and Edward rejoiced to have their whole family under their roof again.

The wedding would take place in the small Methodist chapel in Millcote, and then everyone would return to Ellis Wood for the wedding luncheon. Mary Ellis was the family's only daughter and the oldest child, with three younger brothers, and no expense had been spared on the wedding and the entertainment afterwards.

After the wedding, Ned and Mary would set out towards the west, to Wales and then over the channel to Ireland, where they would travel that country for a month before returning to Thornfield. A small suite of rooms was already being prepared for them at the other end of the long hall from Jane and Edward's own.

The entire household was in a bustle of activity, doors opening and closing, voices calling to each other, maids dashing hither and yon on all manner of errands. Edward looked in the mirror at himself, clad in his new morning suit, before leaving his room to walk down the hall to the room that Ned had occupied since they had moved into this house so many years ago.

He could hear Helen's voice raised in protest as he passed her door, and stopped as he heard Jane's voice over hers, quiet but extremely firm.

"Helen Maria Rochester, I am not going to discuss this with you again. That brooch is what Mary chose for the bridesmaids to wear on their dresses and you are going to wear it. I am losing my patience with you and if you have any intention of going to stay with Sarah in a few weeks, you will not test me today of all days."

Edward grinned as he moved on past Helen's door, listening for any further tumult. Jane was usually totally capable of handling any fractious behaviour on any of the children's part; in fact, at times she could be much firmer than he. He heard no further sound from his daughter, and he reached out to tap on Ned's door. Hearing his son invite him in, he opened the door and went inside. Ned was standing by the long pier glass, with Simon, their butler and valet, helping him into his coat.

A sudden obstruction in Edward's throat stopped him and for a moment he stood still, staring at his son. He saw a young man, one who looked remarkably as he had on the day of his own first wedding. A sudden memory flashed through his mind, of Richard Mason standing near him as he made a last-minute adjustment to his cravat before turning to take the top hat that Mason held out to him.

He could see himself so clearly, his black hair curling over his high formal collar, his brilliant black eyes so full of hope and light. He could see his hands – his two hands, beautifully shaped, strong and steady – reaching up to straighten his tie, reaching out for his hat as he and Mason turned away from the mirror...

He blinked, and the picture in front of him wavered, faded away, replaced by the sight of his son. Simon gave a little bow to them as he moved away, and Ned gave Simon a quick smile and nod before he turned back to his father.

Edward stared at him, taking in Ned's dark skin, his nearly black hair, his brilliant black eyes framed by thick lashes. They were of a height, eye-to-eye, his son's shoulders as broad and strong as his had been in youth. Superimposed upon this was another flash of memory, that day long ago when a tiny infant had been placed in his arms, had suddenly blinked and looked up at him with the very eyes into which Edward looked today.

He reached for his son, unable to speak, and Ned smiled, his own lips none too steady. He reached for his father's hand and clasped it in both of his and for a moment the two men stood together, emotion flowing between them in waves that left the two of them locked in silence.

Ned spoke then. "Father," he said, his voice husky. He squeezed his hand, then released it, for he had seen a tear start in his father's eye. Edward reached up and hastily brushed it away, before he attempted to dispel the heavy emotion in the room with a chuckle.

"No doubt you have heard your sister complaining away; something about a piece of jewelry," he said, shaking his head. "I hastened in here where I felt I would be safe from feminine displays of temper."

"Oh, that child," Ned said with exasperation. "And she is acting like a child, and has been for days. Even longer, really. I'd like to slap her, my hand has been itching to since I came home!"

"Oh, your mother is handling her quite well, son, don't worry!" Edward's eyes were dry now, the great emotion lessening as they laughed over Helen's histrionics. "She's threatening not to let Helen go to Sarah's home to visit, and Helen doesn't want to look like a child in front of her good friend. Your mother means what she says, and I think we'll have decent behaviour from your sister for the rest of the day at least."

Ned laughed, shaking his head, "It's all so stupid anyway. Helen doesn't like the bridesmaids' dresses and complained about them until Mama made her stop. Then Mary decided to have the bridesmaids wear the brooches. Mrs. Ellis had six heirloom pins handed down from her family; she is very proud of their antiquity.

"Even she agrees they are not terribly pretty, but they have sentimental value. Mary was going to wear one as her 'something old' and then she decided 'one bride, five bridesmaids' – each girl could wear one to hold the lace collar of her dress in place. Everyone was agreeable to that except Helen. She's acting like a fool. The pins are small, barely noticeable, but the way Helen carries on, you'd think they were enormous.

"You know, Father, there are times I'm not sure Helen is really related to us. I think she was left on our doorstep, the daughter of some... some Greek, or Italian. She's so emotional."

Edward laughed, "Unfortunately, your theory is faulty, son, as she is the only one of you children at whose birth I was present. I watched Helen come into the world, and she's hardly been out of our sight since, until recently. We cannot even claim the fairies left a changeling in her place – she looks too much like your mother and me."

"Well, she is some sort of throwback," Ned grumbled. "Adèle is French, but she is calm and sensible. Helen is English, but she acts like an orphaned gypsy."

Edward smiled, "My father used to call my mother a 'Spaniard'. Mother didn't know where she got her dark looks, but you and I inherited them. Perhaps there is Spanish blood in the family, and it's coming out in Helen."

The two men laughed, then their laughter died away, and they were silent for a few minutes. Ned's eyes had grown serious.

Ned hesitated, "Father... " He took a deep breath, exhaled, "Forgive me. We've never really discussed it, but of course you know the gossip of the area, what everyone has always said. For some reason, I have to ask it, today."

Edward waited, his breath held for a moment. The children knew he had been married before, they had seen Bertha's headstone. It was not a subject for discussion; it had only been mentioned in passing. They knew little else of his background; nothing had ever been asked. He looked at his son, wondering which difficult question he would be called upon to answer.

Ned bit his lip, brushed his fingers across his lips in a nervous gesture. Then he spoke.

"Speaking of Adèle," he said nervously, "you must know the talk, Father."

Edward nodded, "That Adèle is my daughter."

Ned nodded, "Is it true?"

Edward looked intently at his son. "No, Ned, I do not believe it is true." He shrugged his shoulders, "But I do have to be honest. The possibility is there. I was told she was, by her mother. But no, I do not think she is, not at all."

Ned swallowed, "You were... involved. With her mother."

Edward said, "Yes. But for many reasons – reasons I cannot go into – I am fairly sure Adèle is not my child."

"You have warned me, through the years, of the problems of... involvement with women," Ned said awkwardly. "But you never really said... "

Edward waited.

"Have you had many lovers, Father?" Ned asked.

Edward hesitated. "What is it you wish to hear, Ned?" he asked quietly. "Will it change the way you think of me, will you hate me, to hear of past liaisons? I've told you there were things I was ashamed of; I tried to use myself as an example, without saying too much. Would you think less of me if I said there were many? Or would you think even less of me if I said there were not many?"

Ned frowned, "No, Father, no." He reached out a hand, dropped it. "I only ask... " He sighed.

"I'm not sure why I asked," Ned said, then turned back to the mirror.

"Father, we have talked a little, you and I," Ned said to his reflection in the mirror. "Of women, of... marital relations." He stopped, touching the tie that was already straight. "But you asked me no questions. You gave me that book, told me a few things. But you never asked about how much I knew."

Edward nodded, "That was just a few weeks ago, Ned. You are twenty-one, a grown man. I felt you deserved your privacy. We have talked, through the years, and I advised against entanglements, for the sake of avoiding disease and pregnancy. I hoped you would heed my advice, back then. And then I hoped you would be careful, once you were grown."

Ned nodded, "I did listen to you, Father. I was too scared, back at Eton. We hardly saw women, let alone had time with them. Then at Oxford – well, there was a girl. She worked in a shop; we saw each other for a while, just friendly. She would never let me... you know. She was afraid of getting in trouble. But we – well, we did a few things." His cheeks were red. Edward nodded, trying to appear understanding.

"Then I came home from school, and that Christmas I met Mary. I knew right away she was special, that I liked her and she liked me. When I went back, the other fellows were beginning to – well, they had things to talk about, and I didn't." He gave a little laugh, "Of course, I talked anyway. But I wouldn't do the things they did; I just wanted Mary."

His words came out in a rush then, "I'm afraid now. I am wondering if I did the right thing, in waiting. What if I cannot make Mary happy? What if... tonight... I don't know what to do? All I know is from that other girl, and from what you and I talked about. What if it's not enough? And I never... you know. I was waiting for Mary." He swallowed, his throat making a nervous sound.

A wave of relief came over Edward. "Is that what you're worrying about?" he asked Ned. "That you have no, well, little experience?" Ned nodded, his face flushing again.

"You read the book, correct?" Edward asked. Ned nodded again. "And I talked to you, some, about the marriage bed." Ned nodded, remembering the frank talk he and Edward had shared just a few weeks ago.

Edward smiled, "I didn't know if you were experienced, and asking at this late date what you had been doing wrong."

"No," Ned said, "I know very little, really. And I guess I wish to know if your experience helped or... well, did not help. Whatever experience you had."

"I had many experiences," Edward told him. "But not before I was... first married. I had almost no experience then. You know, of course, that I was thirty-eight when your mother and I married.

"I had had women, but Ned, I was never in love, never really in love, until I met your mother. And that, my son, is what makes the difference. The love you have for your bride, the desire to please her, to make her happy. That is what will determine things between you. All the experience in the world does not matter, for when you lie down with the woman who is meant for you, it is all brand new.

"Be patient with her, and with yourself. You will learn together." He cleared his throat, "And use an... easy touch, light, gentle." He ran his thumb over his lips, wondering why he felt suddenly embarrassed to speak so, "A woman does not need such a firm touch, as we men do." Ned's cheeks looked a bit flushed also; the men were silent.

Ned nodded. There were a million questions he wished to ask. He guessed, from his father's words, that he had not loved his first wife. But he knew nothing about it, and knew not to ask. He did not know what had happened with Adèle's mother. There were so many things he did not know, and not enough time to ask about them. They were due at the church soon and it was time to leave.

He looked at his father, their eyes meeting again, and this time it was Ned's voice that broke. "Father," he said, reaching out his hand, "Papa... "

Edward nodded, the two moved close to each other in a manly embrace, their hands clasping each other's shoulders. Then Edward grabbed his son fiercely, his arms tightening around him and Ned hugged him in return.

"You have all my love, son," he whispered. "You always have, from the moment I first saw you."

"And you mine," Ned told him softly. "I could not have a better father."

And then it was time to go...

Jane reached over and clasped Edward's hand as they saw Ned emerge from the side door, accompanied by the minister and his friend George, who had been his roommate at Oxford for the past four years. She brought her lace handkerchief up to her trembling lips as she watched their son turn to watch his bride, his eyes widening as Mary started down the aisle on her father's arm. Mary's fair complexion was flushed, her blonde hair styled beautifully beneath a gauzy veil, her blue eyes shining. Her slender form was shown to perfection in a white satin gown.

The congregation was standing, packed into the small church, and they all turned to see Miss Ellis as she made her slow way down the narrow aisle. But

Edward did not turn to see the bride. He watched his son, saw Ned's face light up from within, awed by the sight of his bride as she came towards him. He saw Ned's eyes begin to gleam with tears, saw the love that was written plainly on his face.

And Edward relaxed, freed from a fear that he had not even truly known he had. His son was happy. His son was in love. Not for Ned the pain and emptiness of a loveless union. Oh, marriage was risky, he knew that. One took a chance on opening one's heart to the whims and inconsistencies of another. But if there was love...

He had been hearing of the manifold charms of Mary Ellis for three years now; at times he'd wished she had never moved to the area so he would not have to hear of her yet again. But he had never been confident that the relationship had a chance of succeeding, had not been entirely sure that his son's feelings were not all based on the mindless passion of youth – until now.

He felt a lump in his throat, squeezed his wife's hand, and turned towards the front as they all prepared to sing the opening hymn. He smiled at the sight of his two daughters, both looking lovely as they held their flowers and stood in their bright dresses, watching their brother marry his longtime sweetheart. Adèle's little daughter Emma stood there as well, solemn on this occasion. Edward smiled to see her. She looked just like Adèle had at that age, but was a quiet and serious child, not given to the constant singing and dancing her mother had displayed when young.

The hymn began, the members of the Methodist congregation singing loudly, the Anglican guests singing a little more uncertainly,

Love divine all loves excelling, Joy of heaven to earth come down;
Fix in us thy humble dwelling, All thy faithful mercies crown...

Edward caught sight of Chadwick, peering distastefully at the plain paper hymnal in his hand, not singing, his cold blue eyes looking disdainfully around at the unadorned building with its plain wooden pews and simple altar. Edward turned back to the hymnal he shared with Jane, raising his voice to praise the Lord in song even though he was not totally familiar with the hymn.

"If Chadwick disapproves, then I shall make up in approval what I may lack in knowledge," he laughed to himself, his strong voice booming out with a rich sound that drew a smile from his wife.

The congregation finished the hymn and then sat down for the simple ceremony. In just a few minutes, Mary Ellis became Mary Rochester, and her lovely face glowed as the happy couple went back up the aisle past a sea of smiling faces. Except for Mr. Chadwick.

The guests followed the couple to their flower-bedecked carriage, tossing flower petals and cheering them as they began the three-mile trip down the road to Ellis Wood, where a splendid luncheon awaited the guests.

Edward and Jane did not join the carriage's boisterous followers, but hung back, watching the throng, at times stopping to accept the congratulations of various members of the crowd.

Edward raised Jane's hand to his lips, his eye meeting hers. "You look beautiful, my dear Janet," he told her, "but are you all right?"

She raised her eyebrows.

"I heard you crying during the ceremony," he told her, squeezing her hand.

"Oh, you did?" she asked, her voice teasing. "I'm surprised you could hear me, over all the sniffling you were doing."

"Oh, nonsense," he told her. He put his arm around her shoulders, and they began to move towards the road, where the rows of carriages stood in a neat line, their coachmen waiting patiently for the assembled guests.

Jane rolled her eyes at him, and then stopped, reaching up to kiss his cheek before they continued on. His cheek was still a little damp beneath her lips, but she said nothing as they headed for their carriage.

The party spirit continued beyond the wedding luncheon at the Ellises' home, as Jane and Edward's house guests returned to Thornfield Manor. After they'd all had their fill of the fine food and drink that was offered by the Rochesters and had retired to their rooms, Helen knocked on her parents' door and slipped into their bedroom.

Jane and Edward were relaxing on the sofa, Edward stretched out with his head on Jane's lap. They had hardly had a chance to respond to Helen's knock before she had come in. Her face was red and tear-stained.

"Why, Helen!" Jane exclaimed, while Edward sat up hastily. Helen, clad in her white nightgown and wrapper, quickly crossed the room to her parents, and knelt by the sofa with her head against Jane's leg. Jane reached out a hand to stroke her daughter's black curls, raising her eyebrows at Edward.

"Mama, Papa," Helen wept, "I'm sorry I'm such a horrible child. I have behaved so badly."

Jane's lips twitched with amusement at Helen's dramatic behaviour. Edward smothered a smile as well, and assumed a more serious face as Helen looked up.

"I just couldn't bear the thought of Ned marrying and... and... not belonging to us anymore," Helen said tearfully. "I know I was horrible to Mary, and I know that Ned is angry with me. And now he's gone and I cannot tell him."

"Helen, really!" Jane told her. "Ned has gone on his honeymoon, it's not like he will not be back. You can apologize to both of them when they return. But I would venture to guess that neither of them is thinking of you and how you have acted."

"You were a dreadful brat," Edward said to her, folding his arms over his chest and leaning back on the sofa, watching Helen with a mirth he did not try to hide.

Helen cried again, putting her head down on her mother's lap and sobbing pitifully. "I miss Ned," she wept, "and things will never be the same now that he's married. Lizzie is busy at school and has to go back in a few days. I just want things to be the way they used to be."

"Oh, Helen, darling," her mother told her, leaning over to kiss her daughter's bent head, "I'm sorry, but that is how life goes. Everyone grows up, they must get on with their lives. Nothing can stay the same. Ned will come here to live with Mary, and we must all get used to living together. Surely now that Mary is part of the family, we will come to love her as Ned does."

Edward reached over, patting his daughter's shoulder. "Come here, you silly girl," he said with a laugh. She got up, sitting down between her parents and leaning her head on her father's shoulder as he put his arm around her. She sniffled into the handkerchief Edward handed her and he put his palm against her cheek, leaning over to kiss her head the way Jane had.

He could still remember holding her, sitting in this very room, feeling her drift off to sleep on his shoulder. Her little head would bob against his hand as he reached up to steady it. He could still feel the weight of her tiny body against his chest, hear the quiet snuffling breaths she took as she slept. When had she grown up like this? When had all his children grown up?

"Now," he asked her, "where is Sarah?"

Helen sniffled, "She's asleep. I was talking to Elizabeth, but she got tired too, and went to her room. I started feeling so guilty for being so horrid, not just today, but all the time. I didn't want this wedding to take place. But I should not have acted so badly."

Her mother laughed again, reaching over to pat Helen's knee, "You weren't that bad, child, my goodness! Now, you must go to bed as well – it's late. If you and Sarah wish to take the long ride that Papa was talking about earlier, you must get some rest now."

"You're a good girl," her father told her, kissing her again. "A little wild, but what can I expect? You are my daughter. You will improve with age."

Helen smiled a little, wiping her eyes. She kissed both her parents, and headed off to bed. Edward watched her go, shaking his head.

"My, my, these changes in mood are very tiring. I used to think sons were a worry, but they are very easy compared to daughters. Although I don't remember Elizabeth being so volatile!"

Jane laughed incredulously, "You don't remember her locking herself in her room and sobbing because John and Mary had gone to a hog slaughter and brought back two suckling pigs for us and for Adèle's family? She wouldn't eat a bite of it, and called us murderers. And you don't remember her reading that novel – I can't even remember the name of it – and crying for two days because someone in it died?"

Edward shook his head, "I must have blocked it out of my mind – mercifully, it sounds like."

"All young girls are emotional," Jane sighed. "Their bodies are changing, their minds are in a turmoil. Elizabeth grew calmer, and I imagine Helen will as well."

Edward frowned uncomfortably. He had not minded Ned growing older, didn't mind the thought of him marrying. But he did not want to think of his girls grown into women, getting married someday.

Jane laughed at the look on his face. She reached over to kiss him, then stood up with a groan.

"Oh, dear, did you hear my knees crack?" she asked him. "I'm getting old as well. I think it's time we went to bed; this has been a long hard day." She bent to kiss him again, and headed for her dressing room, leaving her husband frowning at the fire, wondering where on earth the time had gone.

Chapter 67 - The Rochester Line Goes On

Late November, 1862

Jane and Edward sat in their parlour, listening in vain for some noise from upstairs. The house was large, and the parlour was at the opposite end from Ned and Mary's suite of rooms, and so – strain their ears as they might – they could hear no noise. From time to time, they heard muffled voices from the hall, or footsteps directly overhead as servants rushed back and forth, but that was the only evident sound to disturb the peace of the household this evening.

Upstairs in her bedroom, Mary was labouring to deliver her first child. In the next room, which had been set up as a sitting room for the couple, Ned paced anxiously in front of the windows, where he could now see nothing but his reflection in the glass against the darkness outside.

Dr. John, the eldest of Mr. Carter's three sons, had been the one to respond to the servant's summons, and he attended Mary, assisted by Adèle, who had become a trusted friend to Mary.

Jane had chosen to remain out of the room, not wanting to add any stress to her daughter-in-law's experience, and Mary had flatly forbidden her own mother, who was somewhat excitable, to be on the premises while the birth was taking place.

"Ned will send you a message, Mama," Mary had told her firmly during their previous visit, kissing her mother on the cheek. "And when I am feeling better you and Papa will come to see us, but not before."

Two of the maids fetched and carried for Dr. Carter, and Adèle sat next to Mary, speaking softly to her and encouraging her as the pains grew stronger, while Ned waited outside. He knew he should go give a report to his parents, but he remained in the sitting room, looking out the window and thinking of all that had happened into him in less than two years.

Ned and Mary had begun their married life with a lovely trip around Ireland. Neither of them had ever travelled there previously. They enjoyed their travels and returned to Thornfield a month later, relaxed and refreshed, to set up housekeeping in the three large rooms set aside for them. They were happy, but before they were totally comfortable in their new relationship, they found they had had to make adjustments to each other on a deeply personal level.

Their wedding night had been particularly stressful. Ned had eagerly awaited the night, anxious to express his love to his new wife. From his reading and his private conversations with his father, he had looked upon their union as a way to please his wife, and he hoped he could give her what she needed. However, like most couples of their day, they had not talked together about the physical side of marriage. Ned assumed that Mary felt the way he did, and was surprised to learn that she had been taught differently.

While Ned had grown up seeing the happiness of his parents and learning from his father that there was a mutual pleasure to be had in the marriage bed, Mary had been reared in a household where the man ruled and the wife and children did his bidding. She had very little education in the human body, had been terrified when she had begun to menstruate, having to find out from a maid what was happening, and was only told the night before the wedding what was expected of her as Ned's wife. Her mother had whispered that she must allow Ned to do what he wished, that it would hurt but it would soon be over and that women must bear such things if they wanted to have children eventually.

Mary, who had never felt that her mother derived much pleasure from her children, saw nothing to look forward to at all in this process. She loved Ned and was determined to please him, but she was quite frightened, and that night in their hotel suite, Ned found not the eager loving bride he had anticipated, but a terrified girl prepared to endure the coming ordeal just to make him happy.

There were many tears shed and many long serious talks between the couple during their honeymoon. Ned tried to be patient, but was disappointed and bewildered by his wife's attitude. Mary expected him to do what he needed to do and to get it over with, and was irritated when Ned was too nervous to proceed unless she was going to enjoy herself, which she was not prepared to do.

The marriage was not actually consummated until they were finally in Ireland, but each night there was a great deal of kissing and caressing, and gradually each became more accustomed to the other. Mary began to relax and enjoy Ned's touch, while Ned was finally sure enough of Mary's enthusiasm to be able to proceed without being totally intimidated.

By the time they returned from their honeymoon, Ned was happy enough with the state of his marriage, and Mary, while not completely enjoying their physical union, was at least no longer afraid. It had taken her nearly three months after their wedding day to begin to like it and six months to finally reach a climax. Less than two months later, she was pregnant.

Edward stared into the fire, his face dark with worry. Jane was knitting the sleeve of a tiny sweater, although later she would see so many poorly worked stitches that she would tear it out and redo it. Only the clock on the wall made noise, ticking on and on until it chimed the half-hour, and eventually the hour.

"Why is there nothing happening?" he finally burst out with frustration.

"Oh, I'm sure there is plenty happening; we just are not there to see it," Jane said, trying to appear calm when in reality her stomach churned with anxiety.

The Rochesters, while still thinking their daughter-in-law quite silly and frivolous, had nevertheless grown fond enough of her to be quite worried for her now. She had been surprisingly easy to live with, nearly always cheerful and happy. She chattered a bit too much for Edward's taste, but she was polite and respectful of him, and he was grateful to her for her sweet and loving treatment of his son. She was also kind and deferential to her mother-in-law, and if she had any complaints about her husband's parents, she made them privately to Ned.

She had even won a grudging friendship from Helen, asking her all about her horse and showing an interest in her school activities. Helen no longer made fun of her cruelly behind her back, now teasing her in fun to her face, as she did her own family, and Mary realized that this meant she was now considered to be a true Rochester.

The family did not often see Elizabeth, who had finished her nurse's training and was now working in a ward at St. Thomas Hospital, but she always included Mary in her greetings when she wrote letters to her family.

It was with Adèle, however, that Mary formed the deepest friendship. Adèle, with the kindness that made her so popular with her husband's parishioners, had shown special attention to Mary, and Mary had responded eagerly. Adèle knew what it was like to feel oneself an outsider. Despite the love shown to her by Jane, the years of care given to her by Mr. Rochester, and the sisterly relationship she'd had with the Rochester children, Adèle had grown up never really feeling herself part of the family. She took Mary under her wing, and Mary grew to love her like the sister she had never had. She visited often and Adèle appreciated having Mary's help with her active twin boys, who were now eighteen months old.

When Mary suspected she was with child, it was Adèle she confided in, and the two women had grown closer as Mary's pregnancy progressed. Mary had a tendency to magnify the symptoms of pregnancy and to want to be pampered, and Ned was grateful for Adèle's gentle chiding of Mary, which caused her to act a little more mature about the experience.

"Mary, darling," Adèle would say in her gentle way, "I know you don't feel well. But women have done this for thousands of years, and they have survived. You are not the only one to go through this, you know."

Mary's pregnancy had gone well, and she had also grown closer to Jane as the months progressed. Jane enjoyed knitting, but did not like to sew, while Mary did not knit well, but could spend hours patiently stitching tiny garments. Adèle, who had sworn that she would never knit another stitch after having to rest in bed with her twins, would sit with them, all engaged in lively conversation as Jane and Mary worked. By the time Mary entered her confinement, the three women had formed a close bond and the baby had a lovely layette waiting.

Jane and Edward both looked towards the parlour door as they heard a sound outside. They rose to their feet as Ned entered the room, looking anxious and frightened.

"Nothing yet," Ned said, shaking his head at the eager looks his parents cast his way. "She is crying and moaning; I can hear her, but I don't know what's going on. Adèle comes out every so often to tell me all is well, but I'm afraid it isn't." He looked miserable and suddenly, to his worried parents, still very young.

Edward forced himself to appear calm and unruffled. "I'm sure everything is fine, son. I remember worrying and pacing a trench in the floor waiting for you to be born, and look at you now." He patted his son's arm. Jane came over and kissed her son's cheek, giving his arm a squeeze.

"First babies take a very long time, Ned," she told him. "I'm sure all is well, and you will hear some good news soon."

Ned nodded, but his face was still set in anxious lines. "I need to go back up to her," he told them. "I just wanted to let you know that nothing has happened yet. But I will send Adèle for you when it is time. Stay here and try not to worry."

He left the room and his parents heard his footsteps hurrying away. Edward sighed, and turned to Jane.

"You look far too young to be a grandmother, my Janet," he told her, putting his arms around her.

She rested against him, feeling the reassuring beat of his heart. "Well, today I feel far too old. This is so worrisome. But at least we get to be here. The poor Ellises – they are probably quite worried, and Mary has strictly forbidden them to be here."

"Margaret would be flitting around here like a bat," Edward said. "And Ellis would be blustering about, acting like a factory master and ordering the servants around. It's better that they are not here. I'd sooner sit here with Chadwick for company as with either of them."

"I could have him fetched for you," Jane said, her face muffled in Edward's coat but her tone mischievous. Her arms tightened around him.

"Thank you, no, my helpful little wife!" Edward said. "But where is Thomas? I thought perhaps he would be here, sharing our worries."

"He has worries of his own, two of them," Jane said, lifting her face from her husband's chest. "The twins are getting some new teeth and are acting like little demons. He didn't want to leave the nurse alone with them. But he'll come when the baby gets here, to visit and to walk Adèle back home."

"He needs whiskey," Edward told her.

"Thomas does?" Jane raised her eyebrows.

"Well, probably Thomas too, by now," Edward replied. "No, for the twins. He could rub a little whiskey on their gums, they'd go right to sleep."

"Edward, you are terrible," Jane laughed. "Thank God our three never had bad nights from teething; you might have actually done that to them!"

"I did," Edward said. "That's why they never had bad nights from teething."

They were laughing, and Jane had just raised her hand to slap him playfully, when they heard the sound, the tiny, far-away wail from upstairs. Both of them stopped with a gasp, their eyes locking together, standing completely still. The sound went on for a few minutes as they stood there, unsure of whether to stay there or head upstairs – then it stopped and there was silence.

"Should we... " Jane whispered, just as Edward reached for her hand and said, "Come, I cannot wait here, even if Ned said we should."

They started upstairs, just as Adèle came to the top of the steps, her hair in disarray, her face moist with perspiration. She was taking off a damp, stained apron, but she was beaming and she beckoned to Edward and Jane. They hurried up the stairs and followed Adèle down the hall. When they reached the sitting room, it was empty, but they could hear voices rising and falling in the next room.

They stood there for a few moments, looking at each other, as Adèle waited, watching them excitedly. They turned at the sound of the door opening, and saw Ned walking out of the room, his face red and his eyes swollen. Their breaths caught in their throats, for in his arms was a tiny bundle, wrapped tightly against the chill of the room. Ned walked towards his father, his eyes fixed on Edward's face.

Edward looked at his son, and his firm mouth suddenly trembled as Ned reached out and laid the baby in his arms.

"Father," Ned whispered, "this is Edward Ellis Rochester. I wanted you to be the first to meet him."

Edward stared down at the tiny boy, and an unexpected gasp caught in his throat. The baby seemed so tiny and frail in his arms, and he suddenly feared he would drop him. He held the child against him, seeing the damp dark hair that covered his little head, his fragile closed eyelids, the tiny clenched fist poking out of the blanket.

He shook his head wordlessly, looked over at his wife, who had her arms around Ned, who held her tightly in return. They were both crying, but smiling at the same time.

"Mary is fine," Ned choked out, reaching for his handkerchief. "Dr. Carter is seeing to her now. Mary wanted me to show him to you as soon as I could, since he is a Rochester." He stopped, overcome with emotion, and hugged his mother again, who laughed and kissed him.

"My Ned, you are a father!" she marvelled, and their tears began again.

Edward looked down at his grandson. "Edward," he told him, a smile beginning to creep across his face, "your father and grandmother are a little overcome at the moment, so you must just deal with me."

The baby made a tiny grimace, and squirmed in his grandfather's arms, letting out a tiny cry.

"Edward Rochester," Edward whispered. "It's not a bad name, all things considered." He shifted the baby in his arms, and leaned down to kiss him softly on his tiny forehead. "Shhh... I know you don't think so right now, but this is really quite a lovely world you have come into, I promise."

Chapter 68 - I Shall But Love Thee Better After Death

Millcote, February 1870

Dr. Ephraim Carter stepped through the door of his office and spoke to the young woman who was seated outside.

"I am so sorry to have kept you waiting, Miss Rochester;" he said as he ushered her into the office, "please, won't you come in?"

He could not help staring at her as she sat down in the chair across from his desk, and before he could stop himself, he blurted out what he was thinking.

"You are nothing like your brother and sister," he heard himself saying.

Elizabeth Rochester looked up at him as he spoke. They gazed at each other for a moment – the doctor blushing with sudden embarrassment, Elizabeth meeting his eyes with a level, measuring look that she drew out a moment longer than was perhaps polite.

"I'm glad that you included my brother in that statement, Dr. Carter, for if you compared me to my sister alone I would believe you were casting aspersions upon my appearance."

Carter felt totally flustered, and at thirty-five years of age, he was not used to feeling that way. He had meant no disrespect to the young woman sitting across from him. Indeed, if he were to be totally honest, he would have said that he had never seen anyone like her before. But he knew he could never say that and have it come out the way he intended, so he just stood behind his desk staring at her.

It sounded ridiculous when he thought about it later, but the first emotion he had felt upon greeting Miss Rochester was a strange sort of peaceful happiness. The feeling of her gaze, her eyes both bright and dark upon him, the gentle smile she had given him as she had first risen to her feet, had made him feel comfortable and warm all over.

He felt anything but comfortable now. "I'm sorry, I meant nothing disrespectful by that remark," he stammered, feeling like a raw schoolboy.

Elizabeth took pity upon the young doctor. "I know the Rochester children do not much resemble each other," she told Carter. "My brother favours our father, while I look more like my mother. My younger sister tends to resemble them both, although we all say she inherited the best that both sides of the family had to offer."

Carter, still staring at her, could only think how much he preferred her to her younger sister. Helen was a beauty, to be sure, but despite the loveliness of her white skin and her flashing green eyes, which were such a contrast to her thick black hair and lush eyelashes, her looks did not appeal to him. It was this woman, with her rather serviceable travelling outfit and her ordinary appearance, whom he wished he could keep looking at.

Ephraim Carter, who spent his spare time rambling in the hills and woods, watching birds and being alone with his thoughts, looked into the eyes of Miss Rochester. They reminded him of something, but he was not going to compound his initial error of speech by describing them to their owner.

Carter loved to walk in the autumn, when the ground was covered with newly-fallen leaves, leaves which were in the process of turning a pale brown while still retaining a vestige of summer's green. When rain glistened on a carpet of such leaves he thought them one of the loveliest sights in the world. And he saw that sight now, in coldest winter, in the eyes of this young woman he knew only by reputation. She had shining eyes of a luminous pale brown shot through with emerald green.

Ephraim Carter, a man of science, who yet retained a small amount of poetry in his heart, and whose busy loneliness was eased by the faint hope of someday having the happy family life that his older brothers enjoyed, took one look at Elizabeth Rochester and knew he wanted to see those eyes for the rest of his life.

Love had been the furthest thing from Elizabeth's mind as she alighted from the carriage in front of the large house in which the Carter brothers practiced. She stared at the sign in front of the house:

John Carter — Andrew Carter — Ephraim Carter

Physicians — General Surgery

Taking a deep breath, she had gone up the walk and knocked on the door, presenting herself without prior warning. The older Carters were out on calls and it was Ephraim's turn to mind the office. She had to wait a good while to see him, but she was willing to wait. She had not yet been home, having taken the train into Millcote, then hiring a carriage to bring her to her parents' house. They didn't even know she was coming.

Elizabeth now was face-to-face with the doctor who was so highly spoken of by her mother. She looked at Ephraim Carter. He very much resembled his father, or what she remembered of him. Mr. Carter, the surgeon who had cared for her father for years, had died while she was working in London. His sons, however, were carrying on their father's work and were apparently busy, as Millcote steadily expanded, and Hay grew from a tiny village into a busy town. Unlike their father, who had received his training as a surgeon in the Navy, the younger Carters had all been to medical school and each had various areas of expertise that they shared with the others. It was a good and thriving partnership.

Carter was tall, with clear blue eyes and wavy light brown hair that was thinning a bit at the temples. He towered over his brothers Andrew and John, who were shorter and plumper, as their mother was. Elizabeth asked after his mother, and about his two brothers who had not gone to medical school.

"My mother is in good health, thank you for asking," answered Ephraim, sitting down wearily in his chair with a relieved sigh. "She misses my father, of course, but she stays busy with the grandchildren – my two brothers here have five children between them."

"My brother Jeremiah is still in the Navy; my mother despairs of him ever coming to rest on land. But he loves the life and his wife does not appear to mind. She occasionally comes to stay, bringing their three children. And my brother Ezra is still in Manchester, still managing a cotton mill. They had quite a time the last decade with the war in the States, but things are looking up and the mills are doing better again. He is married with four children."

Elizabeth told him, "I remember your oldest brothers, but I do not remember you and the younger ones – I don't know why... I suppose it's because you were also away at school when I was."

Ephraim smiled, "Well, your father remembered me. Did he tell you what he said when I first came out to the house to care for your family?"

Elizabeth shook her head, already smiling.

"He pointed at me as I stood there, having come in and introduced myself," Ephraim grinned. "He shook his finger at me a couple of times and said, 'Young man, the first time I saw you was when I came to your father's surgery to be examined. You were about this high,'" – Carter indicated a spot down near his knee – "'and you were wearing a white lace dress. And now I'm supposed to allow you to treat me for an illness?'"

They laughed together. "That sounds like Papa!" Elizabeth told him. "Did he let you treat him?"

"Oh yes," Ephraim answered. "He asked me many questions, but he allowed me to proceed. It was for his angina, and I said the same things my brothers had said, so I suppose he felt I was safe."

"Well, my mother certainly likes you; she has spoken often of you in her letters." Elizabeth was suddenly solemn, her eyes darkened. "And so I have come to ask you many questions too," she told the doctor.

"I received a letter from my sister which was most distressing; I had no idea things had become so serious. I haven't even been home yet; I came here first. And I need you to tell me, Dr. Carter, how my mother really is."

A darkness had fallen across Thornfield. Despite the muted, rain-washed glimpses of sun that occasionally brightened the late winter gloom, all seemed dim within the once-cheerful household.

Dr. Ephraim Carter, whose area of interest was conditions of the heart, had examined Jane at length, confirming what was already known but long-denied by all. There would be no recovery now. Death was a soaring hawk and she the prey that waited beneath its looming shadow.

The previous June had seen the wedding of Helen Rochester to Sir Rodney Davies-Lamb. Twelve years her senior and widowed after a brief marriage years before, Sir Rodney had become enchanted by Helen at a neighbouring hunt. Her excellent seat, her keen hunting skill, and her enthusiasm for the sport all attracted him. Years of dodging husband-hunting women and matrons homing in on eligible matches for their daughters had left Sir Rodney as gun-shy as any skittish horse.

Ironically, Sir Rodney was a relative of Blanche Ingram's by her marriage. A nephew of her husband's, Davies-Lamb had visited the area many times and stayed with the Ingrams, and it was through the casual association of the two families that his attention had been drawn to the beautiful daughter of Edward Rochester.

Helen Rochester, who was as passionate about riding and hunting as Sir Rodney himself, and as yet unmindful of men save her father and brother, caught his eye as no woman had in years. At twenty, only three years from her schoolgirl days and bored with the immature boys of her age in the area, Helen welcomed the attentions of the sophisticated older man.

First as a diversion, then with growing interest and finally love, Helen allowed Davies-Lamb to court her. He did so under the watchful eyes of her amused brother and her father, whose glowering protectiveness grew increasingly annoying to her as time went on.

By the time a solemn Edward Rochester had walked his daughter down the aisle to give her in marriage to Sir Rodney, the entire household had watched with growing hilarity the interplay between Rochester and the child he could not bear to give up. Day by day the jesting escalated, culminating in a wedding gift Ned had had made and delivered to Helen one morning. It was a tall wooden ladder, on whose top step was carved in ornate lettering "Helen's Only Hope".

In the merriment that followed, Jane had promised solemnly, lips twitching with a suppressed smile, to lock her husband in the water closet the day of the wedding until the couple was safely on their way. Edward had harrumphed and retreated with theatrically wounded dignity to the library with his newspaper, choosing to take his eye-glass and painstakingly read it himself rather than give his wife the satisfaction. This had led to another round of jokes and laughter until Helen, nearly as tall as her father, had deposited herself unceremoniously in his lap, rumpling his paper and teasing a grudging smile to his face.

Still, both Rochesters were gloomy at the prospect of their youngest child's departure, and they busied themselves with plans for further renovations to Ferndean. Improvements had been made over the years and the formerly drafty old manor was now a snug and comfortable home which would be used often as a hunting retreat for Helen and her husband, who, it was said, only dismounted to eat and sleep. It would also be available as a holiday home for Ned and his wife, or for Jane and Edward themselves, who still stayed there occasionally, drawn by their happy memories of their early married years when Ferndean had been their first home together.

Edward Rochester had turned seventy in January of 1869 and, despite his vigorous health, was finding it a strain to oversee Ferndean alone, small though it was, from his home thirty miles away at Thornfield Manor. His joints kept him abreast of even the slightest weather changes and in the cold of winter his scars and old injuries pained him so badly that occasionally his old sarcasm and harsh demeanour reared their head. Jane spent many patient hours rubbing his arm and his back to ease his discomfort.

He had suffered from the pain of angina for several years and his wife had come to know Ephraim Carter well in her worry over her husband's heart. Edward shrugged off her concerns and went about his daily routines, although he depended more and more upon Ned to see to the day-to-day workings of both homes. Ned was now the father of two boys and a girl, and he and Mary raised their own family while Ned increasingly helped his father run the estates. He was careful not to injure his father's pride by taking over completely, but as time went on, more and more responsibilities fell to him.

Notwithstanding her father's grumpiness, Helen's wedding had brought joy to the family. Thornfield Manor was the site of many parties and gatherings to celebrate the couple. Distant family and close neighbours alike came to witness the happy event, which was presided over by Thomas Cooper, who still held his position as vicar of the Hay church, although Mr. Chadwick had long ago left the parish for "greater things", as he had put it. No one cared what had become of him, but Edward Rochester's hearty "Good riddance!" expressed the opinion of the vast majority of the parishioners.

Elizabeth, who was still in London helping to oversee the infirmary of a workhouse in the East End, travelled to Thornfield for the wedding and for a much-needed holiday with her family. She attended her sister as bridesmaid and tearfully saw her off afterwards, realizing with a pang in her heart how the demands of her work had deprived her of the company of her beloved sister all these years. Elizabeth was tired, worn out from a long period of hard work, and although she loved nursing, she was feeling the strain. It was with reluctance that she once again left her family to return to London after the wedding festivities

Only days after Elizabeth's departure from Thornfield, Jane had fallen ill. A nagging sniffle had turned into a sore throat, which increased in severity. Soon she was turning restlessly in bed due to fever and joint pain. By the time the family was alarmed enough to send for the doctor, she was delirious, her temperature dangerously high.

Edward barely left her side, spending his waking hours sponging her hot face and body with cool water, spooning sips of liquid between her parched lips. When he slept, it was in a chair beside her bed. She had rarely been ill during their marriage other than with the fairly normal physical complaints related to pregnancy and childbirth, and it terrified him to see her thus.

For days she alternated between feverish delirium and restless stupor. The doctor had recommended the removal of Mary and the children, so Ned dispatched his family to Ferndean. Jane was diagnosed with an infection from which recovery was uncertain, but Ned chose not to alarm Helen on her wedding trip – a riding and shooting expedition through Scotland. There would be time enough to notify her and fetch them back should it become necessary.

One night, after Jane's fever had risen extremely high and her husband had prayed desperately on his knees beside her bed, she was suddenly silent. His heart in his throat, Edward had reached for her, finding her soaked with perspiration, but sleeping deeply and peacefully for the first time in days. He had summoned two maids, one to bathe Jane and change her gown, and the other to draw a bath for him. He had locked the dressing-room door, submerged himself in the scalding water, and released his fear and relief in great sobs.

Jane was still in some danger, but although she continued to be ill, her fever never again rose as high as it had. By the time the doctor had allowed Ned and his family to return, she was sitting up in bed, thin and pale, but smiling and eager to regain her strength. When Helen and Rodney returned from Scotland, all health and exuberance, laden with gifts, Jane was rising from bed to take brief walks about the room and to sit up in a chair for short intervals.

By autumn she was up and around the house. Though even brief periods of activity tired her, she felt that by gradually increasing her walks and duties she would regain her strength. But she was never again to resume her daily walks with her husband, and by Christmas time, when even sitting up to wrap gifts left her dizzy and breathless, she knew that more was wrong than merely a slow recovery.

Jane spent Christmas Day reclining on a sofa, wrapped in a bright shawl brought from Scotland by Helen. Jane's large eyes, still bright, watched her happy family as they sat around the candle-lit tree. Elizabeth had not been able to come for the few days off she was allowed, and instead remained at the workhouse. The nurses there had thrown a party for the children of that neighbourhood, financed by the elegant ladies who donated some of their money for charity. Elizabeth had written to her family, promising to come home for a period of several weeks in the spring.

But the rest of the family had a good time that Christmas. Sir Rodney and Helen had stayed for several days and they all enjoyed the antics of Ned's children.

Eddie was now nine, his younger brother James was nearly seven, and their little sister Margaret was five. Only days before, Ned had confided to his father that his wife expected another child, to be born in the summer if all went well, and this happy news had brightened Edward's spirits, subdued as they were with worry over his wife.

Edward adored his grandchildren and spent happy hours in their company. It had become the custom for their grandchildren to accompany Jane and Edward on their daily walks once they had become old enough to walk for any distance, and although Jane could no longer go, she urged her husband to continue that little custom. It was common to see them now, the white-haired but still-active older man, taking his cane but only occasionally leaning upon it, accompanied by three active children, and sometimes five when Adèle's twins, Jacob and Joseph, came with them.

He would walk along, listening to their endless chatter and constant laughter, patiently answering their many questions. His pockets were always full of sweets, and he treated their childish concerns with a kindly seriousness that they did not always get from their busier parents. His granddaughter Margaret especially loved him, and often she would remain behind, holding his arm while the boys ran and tumbled on ahead.

"Grandpapa," she would say eagerly, once the boys had left them in some peace and quiet and her grandfather would lean on his cane, navigating carefully along the root-strewn paths in the woods of Thornfield, "tell me again how you and Grace went fishing and got lost in the woods."

"You've heard that story a hundred times," Edward would say, his face crinkled into lines of patient amusement as he looked into Margaret's eager little face.

"I know, but it's my favourite!" And off Edward would go, spinning tales, always adding a new outrageous detail which Margaret would correct amidst gales of laughter.

So this Christmas was a happy one, despite Jane's illness, which she refused to dwell upon or talk about. Her cousins Mary and Diana exchanged worried looks with each other and with their husbands, and Helen had many anxious conversations with her father and her brother, but Jane ignored all their concerns and from her position on the sofa, she joined in the activities as best she could. Her husband's great dark eye never left her. Even as he joined in the carols around the piano, or watched the children play games in the evenings, his gaze returned to his wife – as though he could imprint her image permanently in his sight should she be removed from it.

By January she was in bed. The doctor had come and listened to her heart for a long time, his face still and serious as he worked. Afterwards, he joined his patient's worried son and husband in the library.

The heart had been damaged, he informed them, most likely by her recent bout of infection. It was enlarged, the muscle working inefficiently. This happened sometimes with certain types of infectious fevers, he told them. Sore throat, joint pain, high body temperature – the symptoms eventually went away but left heart damage of varying severity. There was no cure. They could, if they wished, convey her to London to consult a specialist, but in her weakened state he did not advise it.

"So," Elizabeth asked Ephraim now, her handkerchief knotted into a damp ball in her clenched hands, "my sister was not exaggerating? My mother's condition truly is going to be fatal in the weeks ahead?" She took a deep breath, "I had hoped that Helen was just being dramatic, trying to make me feel guilty for not being here."

"I am sorry, Miss Rochester;" Ephraim told her solemnly, "I wish I had better news for you."

"How did my father take the news of my mother's prognosis?" Elizabeth asked, her tear-filled eyes meeting the doctor's.

Ephraim frowned, remembering. His heart had caught at the grief and sorrow that had fallen across Mr. Rochester's face. Edward's countenance had been so full of hope, and Carter had not taken lightly his role in dashing those hopes.

"He was... devastated," Ephraim said finally, with a sigh. "But he only wanted to know one thing – would it be painful, will she suffer?"

"And what did you tell him?" Elizabeth said, his eyes fixed on him. Her fingernails were digging into the hard wood of the straight chair beneath her.

"I told him the truth, that there would be no pain as such," Carter said, meeting her gaze. "I explained to him that people in this condition often find it progressively harder to breathe. But I feel, and I'm sure you have seen it, that there is often a stupor at the end, which makes it easier. And we can give her medications to ease her last days, something to draw off some of the fluids and to help her sleep."

Elizabeth was silent, thinking of the patients she had seen with these conditions. There had been so many of them, worn out by years of hard work and worry and never enough food, their lungs ruined from the smoke and grime and pollutants of their various livelihoods. They died alone, in the hard narrow beds of infirmaries, or in the tiny crowded rooms of their mean little homes, rarely with any opium to ease their way out of this world, and with their families often too busy scraping together a living to see to the last days of their dying family members. At least that would not be the case with her mother. She would rest in a comfortable bed, surrounded by her family, medications given to ease her way.

Elizabeth burst out, "Why did they not send for me?" She felt close to tears of frustration. "I would have come. The last letter from my father said she'd had a minor illness. I had no idea... "

Ephraim broke in gently, "Your mother would not allow you to be fetched. She is so proud of you, Miss Rochester! She feels your work is so valuable, and she did not want to take you from that. She often talked to me about your efforts in workhouse reform. Is that what you have done all this time?"

Elizabeth was silent for a moment, then forced herself to give a polite answer.

"Yes; in the last decade, there were so many workhouse scandals, so much corruption. Miss Nightingale felt that nurses could play a valuable role in reform. In 1865 she sent twelve nurses who had been trained at St. Thomas's to the Liverpool Workhouse infirmary, with detailed plans for how to improve care. I was one of that number. In just a few years we had made a difference, and since then, we have been dispatched to other cities to institute those same changes in additional locations. Now some of the workhouse infirmaries are giving excellent care; in some cases, superior care to the hospitals in those areas. I have the charge of a workhouse clinic in the East End, among some of London's poorest citizens. There is no end of work to be done."

Very valuable indeed," Ephraim said, looking at the young woman before him with even greater respect than before.

"But tiring," Elizabeth said. "It has taken its toll." For a moment her sweet, plain features were hardened, a little bitter, the sheen of suppressed tears once again in her eyes.

Ephraim stood, holding his hand out to assist her to her feet. "I must keep you no longer, Miss Rochester," he told her. "You are tired, you've had a long trip. I must let you get home to your family." She nodded, and stood up slowly as she thought about going to Thornfield and facing the days and weeks ahead.

It was with great reluctance that Ephraim Carter let go of her hand, as he ushered her out and helped her into the waiting carriage.

Elizabeth returned home to a household under a pall, a household waiting for the end.

Her mother was happy to see her, although Elizabeth was nervous about suddenly appearing after Helen's summons, not sure of how much her mother knew. But she found that Jane knew what was coming, although the doctor had left her with many cheerful assurances that they would do what they could to ease her symptoms and make her comfortable. When Jane had pressed her husband for the truth, he looked into her eyes and gave it to her, gently, as she had known he would. He had never lied to her after the failure of their first wedding, having vowed to God to speak only the truth to her. He held her in his arms as he told her what Dr. Ephraim Carter had told him. They held each other, their tears mingling together on their faces as they kissed and comforted each other.

She lay propped on pillows to make breathing easier, her husband near her side. She could not speak easily, but their eyes spoke for them. Thirty-four years fell away as they sat together, Edward telling her of his love for her. He spoke of the early years of their marriage – how she had been his eyes, his hope, his life, as she would always be.

He barely left her side once again, just as he had not left her during her original illness.

In the mornings, Elizabeth or Helen, or Ned's Mary would come in to help Jane get cleaned up, to change her gown, fix her hair. Edward would take that time to attend to his personal needs, to bathe and change, to eat a hasty meal. Then he would return to his wife. He sat with her by the hour, telling her stories; he sang to her, and read to her briefly as he was able. He would recite her favourite passages from the Bible, or poetry they had learned together.

One poem brought a smile to her face, remembering how once she had sat upon his knee and read it to him, as excited as a child to discover the works of Mrs. Browning, whose words so mirrored Jane's own feelings for her husband:

How do I love thee? Let me count the ways.

I love thee to the depth and breadth and height
My soul can reach, when feeling out of sight
For the ends of Being and ideal Grace.
I love thee to the level of every day's
Most quiet need, by sun and candle-light.
I love thee freely, as men strive for Right;
I love thee purely, as they turn from Praise.
I love thee with the passion put to use
In my old griefs, and with my childhood's faith.
I love thee with a love I seemed to lose
With my lost saints,—I love thee with the breath,
Smiles, tears, of all my life!—and, if God choose,
I shall but love thee better after death.

Elizabeth, having come home to nurse her mother, found herself at times unneeded, as her father refused to leave his wife's side. She did what she could, helped as she was able, administering the medications that Dr. Carter prescribed and brought with him when he came to see her mother. Ephraim – as she increasingly called him in her mind – looked in on Jane every day, pleased with the excellent care she was receiving.

There was nothing further her could do for her, but he would do an examination, listen to her poor heart as it laboured, trying to do its job despite being enlarged and weakened. Often he would sit and talk to her, and she shared bits of her early life with him: her unhappiness in her Aunt Reed's house, her time of starvation at Lowood, her happiness once she had come to Thornfield.

"Do you think, Dr. Carter, that my time at Lowood damaged my constitution?" she asked him in a weak voice one day.

"I am sure it did not help you, Mrs. Rochester," he told her. "But you received good physical care previous to that, and you have been in good health since then. If we could only do something for your heart, your body would remain strong for years." He felt a slight sting at his eyes. He would never get used to this part of being a doctor – seeing a patient come to the end of life.

"You have feelings for my daughter, don't you, Dr. Carter?" Jane asked suddenly. He looked at her sharply, and she smiled at him. "My heart may be failing, but my eyes still work well."

He was silent for a moment, but then he nodded. "I do not believe she returns the sentiment," he told her.

She smiled again, leaning back on her pillow. "You must tell her, and you may have to tell her more than once. She is stubborn, like her father. I'm not sure she always knows how she feels."

Carter wished to tell her, but when he would come upon Elizabeth, her face tired, pinched with worry and care, he felt small and unworthy to speak of love when she was facing such heartache.

One day, after a visit with her mother, he had come upon Elizabeth sitting in the garden. He sat down beside her, both of them now comfortable with saying nothing for a while. Carter could feel that her heart was heavy and her mood was dark.

Finally he spoke. "I am very sorry that your family is having to go through this; that you are having to go through this."

She shrugged, "I should be used to dealing with illness by now."

"Yes, but you are not used to dealing with the illnesses of your loved ones," Carter told her. "That is an entirely different thing. You need to care for yourself." He paused, then hesitantly spoke the words he was thinking, "Or have someone to care for you."

Elizabeth looked over at him, but said nothing.

Once again they were silent, and then he worked up the courage to ask her something.

"Did you never give any thought to marrying, Miss Rochester?"

"I did consider it," she answered. She looked down at her folded hands. "There was a man, a few years ago. He was a doctor. He came from a rather wealthy family, but they were interested in more wealth, I suppose. He paid no attention to me until he found out who my father was. Of course I didn't know this at the time; someone told me later."

"What happened?" Carter asked her.

"His family wanted me to give up nursing, in favour of leading the useless society life of his mother and sisters, and I was not willing to do that – at the time, anyway." She spoke lightly, but there was still a little pain there, for at the time giving up the first man she had ever loved had broken her heart.

"I'm afraid I took it all more deeply than he did, for he married someone else within six months. Yet something must have held me back, for had I truly loved him and been comfortable with the match, I would have given up the nursing and been happy with him. So I must have made the right decision back then."

"It sounds like you are sorry, at times," Carter said, feeling a small dart of jealousy bite at his heart.

"Not about him," Elizabeth shook her head. "But there are many days, getting up at the crack of dawn, working all day, nearly every day, coming back to my room just to write letters to those I love... well, I think my life would be easier had I married him."

"I know you work hard." Carter wanted to reach over and take Elizabeth's hand, but something stopped him. He felt like an idiot schoolboy. Why did he not just say how he felt?

"I love my work, or at least I did," Elizabeth told him. "For a time I could want nothing more than to work hard, to refurbish the infirmaries and to do what I could to make the lives of the people better. But I am tired. I used to think I was being useful and making a difference in the world, and now I am not so sure anymore. Those who can make their way will eventually do it, with or without us. Those who cannot never will, no matter who helps them."

He did put his hand over hers then, and he heard her swift intake of breath, as if she were shocked at his touch. She looked over at him and he smiled at her. She squeezed his hand for a moment and then pulled hers away as she asked him, "And what about you, Dr. Carter? Why have you reached the age and position you have without finding a wife?"

I was waiting for someone like you, he nearly said, but instead he just shook his head. "I don't know, really. There were one or two girls I was interested in and perhaps might have married back when I was in medical school, but I had no money. One girl would not wait, and the other... well, it just didn't last. They were nice girls, but it was not meant to be, I suppose."

"We had both better be careful," Elizabeth said, standing and smoothing her skirts, "Life is going to pass both of us by. Now I must go back to my mother, if you'll excuse me."

March, 1870

One night after dinner, Ned went to his mother's room to sit with her. He often did this of an evening, talking to her or reading to her of current events, so his father could have a brief respite from the sickroom. Edward would spend some time visiting with Elizabeth, or taking a few moments with his grandchildren, who were quiet and sombre at the depressed mood of the household. They visited their grandmother every morning, remaining subdued and silent despite her urging them to tell her of all their activities. They could not help but be affected by her illness, and by the long absences of their normally attentive grandfather.

The room was dim, lit only by several candles and a low fire in the grate. On the table sat a bowl of beef broth, barely touched. Ned knew how his father would sit, patiently spooning it to her mouth in between her pauses for breath.

Ned stopped outside the door. His father sat by his mother's bed, holding her hand. In his deep voice, merry but with barely disguised anguish beneath, he was telling her of his first sight of her – his falling horse, his sprained ankle, his first careless appraisal of her small childish form, the life that had flowed into him with the touch of his hand on her thin shoulder. Ned stood in the shadows, barely daring to breathe for fear of shattering the spell in the room. His mother said something in her weak, breathless voice. He couldn't hear her, but it made his father throw back his head and laugh softly, then pick up her hand and kiss it.

As Ned watched, Edward plumped Jane's pillows, helping her to sit up against them. She leaned back, bracing herself on her thin arms, closing her eyes, those beautiful green eyes, now sunken into the dark shadows around them. His father sat on the edge of the bed, stroking her greying brown hair back from her pale face, then he kissed her forehead. He dropped tender kisses across her face, his lips caressing her eyes, her cheeks, her mouth, her chin.

Then he moved lower, kissing her neck, the hollows where her collarbones met her shoulders, across the soft white skin above the ruffle of her nightgown, before he laid his head against her chest, lightly, so as not to burden her. He saw his mother's thin hand come up to stroke his father's thick white hair. Ned backed away, tears stinging his eyes.

He thought of the legend of Orpheus, who had descended to the nether-world to retrieve his beloved wife. Orpheus had failed, because he had looked back to reassure himself that she was following him, and so had lost her forever. Ned knew that if Edward Rochester could, he would descend to whatever fearsome depths were required to save the wife he loved beyond anyone – and would never look back, would never waver in his resolve to do whatever was needed to rescue her.

Several nights later, Edward sat on the bed with Jane in his arms. She could now only breathe when she was completely upright, so he sat on the bed, his back against the headboard, propped against a number of pillows, as he held her in his arms like a child, up against his chest, feeling each breath as she took it in and let it out. Unconsciously, he breathed along with her, much as they had always done, those nights as they slept in each other's arms, breathing as one person. He slept in small snatches here and there, dozing off with his head back against the pillows, but always waking with a start to look down at her and see that she still breathed. He was afraid that she would slip away from him as he slept.

Her hand clutched his, her grasp so feeble. He thought of the children, remembered holding them as newborns. He would sit, touching his finger to a tiny palm, feeling the baby's hand close around it with surprising strength. Jane's whole hand held his with less power than those long-ago babies' fingers had. Her once-strong hands – so small, yet so steady – had for all those years led him where he needed to go, and had done for him whatever needed to be done.

He thought of her hands caressing his body as they made love, comforting him when he was in despair. Of her hand outstretched as he slipped the wedding ring on the finger he could not even see. He thought of her hands doing all the small tasks for him: combing his hair, shaving him, tying his cravat every morning for years. Washing his back as he bathed, wiping away his tears the times he had shed them in joy or in grief. All the thousands of times those hands had touched him, and soon he would never feel them again. He felt as though it were his own life that was slipping away, sliding through those weakened fingers.

She could no longer speak, but her eyes fastened on his face, searching his. He could read the love in her eyes. A few hours earlier, she had told him how she loved him. "My darling, my Vulcan," she had whispered, "I love you so."

She had told him she did not fear death, felt Christ's victory over the grave grow stronger even as she grew weaker. But she ached at the thought of leaving him, even for a short while. She had said good-bye to her children, assuring them of her love for them, her pride in them, encouraging them to lead good and happy lives.

"But you, my husband, you I do not want to leave," she murmured. "Our bond will break, it will cause you pain. I do not want to be apart from you even for a moment."

He had held her close, tears slipping from the corners of his eyes as he assured her that they would never be apart, not truly, "I will join you soon, my dearest love, my heart." He kissed her, "Being Jane Eyre's husband has been my joy. You have been the best part of my life."

Now, as he cradled her, her head resting on his shoulder, he felt her laboured breaths grow farther apart, until they ceased and she relaxed in his arms. He held her tightly against him now, closing his eye and resting his head against hers as his hand stroked her face and he rocked her back and forth.

Deep inside him, at his heart, the cord of communion broke free. He felt the great tearing within himself, gasped with the pain of it. And slowly, slowly, the bleeding began.

Ephraim Carter never got the chance to be alone with Elizabeth after Jane died. He had come to Thornfield as soon as he heard of Mrs. Rochester's death, to offer his condolences, to see if Edward Rochester had any needs. Upon his arrival, he found Mr. Rochester sitting near his wife's body, and the children all occupied making funeral arrangements; to speak of his love seemed somehow wrong.

He had attended the funeral, where he was warmly welcomed by the entire family as the person who had made Mrs. Rochester so comfortable in her final weeks. But he got no chance to talk at any length to Miss Rochester, and did not want to intrude upon the family's grief.

Ephraim and his brothers were very busy, and so he did not call at Thornfield Manor again until nearly a week after the funeral. He felt that although that was still not a long period, perhaps enough time had gone by that he might be forgiven for speaking to her of his feelings so soon after her mother's death. He asked for Miss Rochester and was shown into the library. A few minutes later, he was joined by Ned Rochester.

"Oh, I'm so sorry," Carter told him. "There's some mistake. I had wanted to see Miss Elizabeth Rochester; I'm sorry you were disturbed."

"I'm sorry, Dr. Carter," Ned told him. "I was sure you knew, but when I was told you wished to see my sister, I realized you were not aware: my sister left for London this morning.

"She wanted to stay to look after my father, but my father insisted he was fine and that she should return to her work. My mother had been so proud of Elizabeth's work, and it made her happy to think of all the good that she was doing. We took her this morning to catch the train from Millcote." He pulled his watch from his pocket and took a look. "She should be back in London by now."

Epilogue

Jane! Jane, Jane...
Where are you?
Wait for me, I am coming...

The man rode on, spurring his black horse onwards as he recognized that he was getting closer to home. His strong, finely shaped hands held tightly to the reins as he sat up straight, his heart thumping with anticipation, for it would not be much longer.

He scanned the horizon, his brilliant black eyes as dark as midnight and as bright as jewels beneath his heavy brow. And a smile lit up his stern face, for he saw what he was searching for.

A small young woman stood by the side of the road, watching anxiously for his arrival. She heard the hoofbeats as they grew closer, and her wide green eyes were fixed on the road. The man slowed his horse to a walk, and came closer. Their eyes were fixed on each other's as he drew alongside her. He reached down, and she reached up, and their hands met and held.

"I waited for you," she said softly, looking up into his face.

"I came as soon as I could," he told her, his dark eyes searching her face as though to memorize every feature. "I was lost without you."

She smiled then, still staring into his eyes, and he reached down for her. She stepped up onto his boot toe, and he pulled her up in front of him. His arms enfolded her as she melted into his strong chest. Their lips met, and they clung together, fitting to each other as though they were made as two halves of a complete whole.

"Let's go now," she whispered, and he smiled, kissing her again before he reached around her to pick up the reins with one hand, holding her tightly against him with the other as they turned towards home.

Edward Eyre Rochester
Thornfield Manor
Hay, Derbyshire

Miss Jane E. Rochester
care of Whitechapel Workhouse Infirmary
Whitechapel, London
25 April 1870

My dear sister-
This message brings news difficult to write and even more difficult for you to read, I am sure. We have lost Father. I feel terrible that you have returned to London and settled back into your work, only to have to be called away again within such a short span of time.
Helen was at Ferndean and has just arrived, and we expect Rodney will be arriving at Thornfield within a day or two, after he settles some business. We will hold the

burial as soon as the family can be assembled. Safe journey, Elizabeth, and we will see you very soon. Your affectionate brother
Ned

Elizabeth had known what the message would contain the moment she came down to the front desk of the infirmary to find the Thornfield coachman standing there, still in his trappings of mourning from the death of Jane Rochester less than one month before.

Following her mother's funeral, Elizabeth had planned to stay on to look after her father while she decided what she should do with her life. She had seen Ephraim Carter once before the funeral, and he had stood with his brothers and their wives the day of the burial. But she'd had no time to speak to him, and while she half expected him to come to see her after the funeral, he never had. After a few days of starting whenever someone came to the door, and inquiring hopefully after the post each day, she'd begun to feel silly.

She had sat by the hour with her father, thinking he might want to talk about his wife, but Edward Rochester had been silent, looking inward, and he had finally turned to Elizabeth and laid a gentle hand on her arm.

"My darling girl, why do you not go back to London? There is nothing for you here. I am fine, and am not good company for you right now. Your work is so valuable, and your mother was so proud of her daughter. That is how you can best honour Mama."

Edward was right, there was not much for her to do at Thornfield Manor. Ned's wife Mary ran an efficient house, there in the big, modern home that had been built to replace Thornfield Hall those years ago. Unlike Jane, who had preferred to run her home with a minimum of servants, as Mary Rochester had gradually taken over the Manor, she had hired more help. The house had every new convenience, so different from the cold drafty halls of the workhouse, but when Elizabeth looked around, she much preferred the workhouse to Mary's household.

She missed her mother, missed her quiet voice and the scent of her lavender sachet. When five days had passed after the funeral and Dr. Carter had neither written nor sent a message, Elizabeth had let her brother take her to the train station and she had returned to London.

But back in London, she felt as lost as when she had been home. This had been the work of her entire adult life, and under her supervision the workhouse infirmary had been transformed, as the Nightingale Nurses, as they were known, had done with infirmaries all throughout England. The monies were properly handled, the patients were thriving under the good care of nurses and aides, watched over by earnest young doctors from the nearby medical schools. But Elizabeth looked at it all in a fog, and now that she was here, she realized how much she missed what she had left behind – her father, her brother and sister, and her niece and nephews. Adèle and Thomas, and their children.

And Ephraim.

How could she not have realized, while she had been at home, that she had grown to love him? She had seen what she thought were the beginnings of a tender feeling on his part but, worn out as she was by work and worry over her mother, she had set that aside to be dealt with later. Surely, if he had feelings for her, he would have said something. But he had not.

And now, tearful and heavy-hearted, she prepared to pack her clothes and leave with the driver her brother had thoughtfully sent for her, heading back to Thornfield.

Adèle Cooper looked around what had once been Jane's bedroom. She missed Jane very much and just being in her room brought her to tears.

Within days after Jane's funeral, Mary had conferred with Ned and had proceeded to pack up Jane's effects and distribute them among the family members with what Adèle privately felt was a disgraceful haste. Despite having three young children, and being heavily pregnant, Mary moved rapidly when she felt she had a mission to perform.

"I so wish to spare Father any further pain and trouble, and Helen is so busy, back and forth between London and Ferndean," she had confided to Adèle in a conspiratorial tone one afternoon at tea.

She continued, "You know, he barely left Mother's side that last month when she was so ill, and the doctor had said the end could come at any time. So many nights he sat up with her in his arms so she could sleep more easily, since she could not breathe when she was lying down." She set down her half-eaten biscuit and wiped crumbs briskly from her fingertips before standing to lead the way to the bedroom that had been Jane's.

"I was so impressed with Ned's father when I came here as a bride. He did not look almost twenty years older than Mother. He was so vigorous, despite his handicaps."

Her voice dropped to a whisper, "But I fear these last months have quite aged him. He has always been so kind to me, so charming. And I could not have asked for a more devoted grandfather – he spends hours at a time with the boys and with Margaret. But now he is so quiet, so subdued. He is kind to the children, but does not spend time with them the way he used to. I have told them to be patient and to give their grandpapa some time to himself."

"Did anyone ask Mr. Rochester how he felt about someone disposing of his wife's possessions so soon after her death?" Adèle realized her voice sounded somewhat sharp and she tried to modify her tone. She was not sure what annoyed her the most – Mary's proprietary attitude towards the situation, or the fact that she called the Rochesters "Mother" and "Father". After thirty-five years of involvement with the family, Adèle still called him "Mr. Rochester", although "Miss Eyre" had become "Mrs. Rochester", and finally just "Jane" after Adèle had left school and had come to live with them before her marriage.

She was being petty, she knew. Jane could not have been dearer to her, no matter what she called her. Sometimes a mother to her, sometimes a sister, always her dearest friend. Their relationship had become more equal after Adèle had had her children, and she knew Jane had looked on Mary's take-charge attitude with some amusement, fond though she had been of her exuberant daughter-in-law.

And Edward Rochester was not Adèle's natural father, no matter what she had been told in Paris – he had made that abundantly clear. But he was Mary's father-in-law, so it was natural for her to call him Father, as Ned did.

If Mary noted Adèle's sharp tone, she did not appear to mind.

"Oh, I believe he was only too happy to have me take the chore off his hands," she went on brightly as she and Adèle entered Jane's room. "He told me most calmly to do as I thought best, and dear Ned agreed with me. We are both so relieved by how well Father is coping with Mother's loss."

"I'm sure 'dear Ned' agreed," thought Adèle, still feeling angry, yet confused by her own emotions. She had always loved Ned so for his sweetness and easy manner, but now she felt that if he stood near her, she would have tweaked his ear as she had so often done when he was eight and would not attend to his lessons.

Adèle could see plainly that Edward Rochester's demeanour was not that of a man who was "coping well". It was the look of a man who had come to the end of himself and was merely biding his time here among them. She was basically nothing to Rochester, so why was she the only one who looked into his one good eye and saw its light dimming a little more every day?

The others spoke brightly of his calm acceptance, his ability to go on because of his children and grandchildren. Adèle knew he loved his son and daughters, doted upon his young grandchildren, and indeed, had doted on Adèle's children as well, but it was Jane who had been the centre of his world since she had been Adèle's governess. He would not last long without her.

Adèle had taken little from among Jane's things: a shawl, a large ribbon-tied packet of letters that Adèle had written to Jane from boarding school on – fancy Jane saving them all those years! She had taken a book of poetry they had both read and enjoyed discussing together, and finally a gold bracelet. She had not chosen it, but Mary had insisted.

"She would want you to have something valuable of hers, she cared so for you. And it's not like there will be provision for you in the will, being only a ward of the Rochesters, and that so long ago." Mary faced the mirror over the dressing table, frowning at her shape in her black mourning dress, patting her perfect blonde hair into place.

"Elizabeth will get the pearl necklace that Mother wore every day, and I have no use for the bracelet. Ned buys me jewelry for every occasion. We bought her that bracelet for her fiftieth birthday, but she never seemed to care about jewelry. Ned presented me with a lovely collection of jewelry handed down from the Rochester women and Mother had never really worn any of it. Only those pearls and her wedding ring." She turned to Adèle and pecked her on the cheek, adding "Besides, December was your birth month, and as Mother was so sick, you got no gift from us. Ned looks on you as his sister, as do I. Take the bracelet, please."

Adèle had sighed and accepted the bracelet. Mary was really very good-hearted, just young and heedless. But Adèle could not bring herself to wear the bracelet, feeling that Edward Rochester might perhaps see it on her wrist and wonder why it had been given to her.

She had spoken to Mr. Rochester privately after Jane's funeral, to tell him how sorry she was that he had lost his beloved wife. She told him how she had loved Jane too; how she would always feel her loss. If only she could cry in his arms the way Elizabeth and Helen had; but they were his daughters – his and Jane's – and Adèle was merely the bastard child of his cast-off mistress and one of her lovers.

Mr. Rochester had listened to her halting, tear-choked sentiments and had laid his hand briefly on her shoulder as he replied. "I thank you, Adèle, for your kind words," he had responded. "God was very good to all of us, to allow her to be a part of our lives. And yet I cannot wish her back again, back to the pain she had experienced. I can only look forward to the time when I will join her. She is with her parents now, and with our little son, and in due time I will be with her as well."

"A short, formal, and correct response," Adèle had thought sadly. "One you would use when speaking with any well-meaning stranger."

Adèle had spent time at Thornfield assisting Ned, Mary, and Helen in making funeral arrangements for Mr. Rochester. When Elizabeth arrived, the actual time of the service would be planned.

Thomas was worried for Adèle – she had spent so much of her time the past month weeping, and now that Edward Rochester was gone, her grief seemed doubled.

Thomas and the children were a comfort to her, but even they could not combat the melancholy that she faced. She was once again a lost and parentless child, uprooted from the familiar, and these feelings frightened her, disturbing her usual calm and gentle personality.

Her older children were away: Tom at his first year at Oxford and Emma at Miss Cheltenham's, both under the sponsorship of Edward Rochester, at his insistence. Her younger sons, Jacob and Joseph, at ten years old, did not need as much of her attention, and for the first time in years, Adèle was feeling a depression she could not shake off.

"And will you be all right, my dear?" Thomas had asked her. Only Thomas knew the jumble of emotions she felt concerning Edward Rochester – the love, the gratitude, the resentment, all living restlessly together within her breast for decades.

"I will be fine," she assured him, hoping it was true. She was no longer the eight-year-old French orphan who had crossed the channel so many years ago to live under Mr. Rochester's sufferance. She was forty-three years old, a respectable Englishwoman, a vicar's wife. No one in the parish knew her shameful history – only that she had been the ward of an English gentleman and his wife. She could hold her head up in their village, liked and well-thought-of by all.

So why did she feel like a guilty child where Mr. Rochester was concerned? She had often turned suddenly to see him watching her, and had wanted to shout at him, "I am not Céline. I may look like her, but I am not her. Perhaps my mother never loved you, but I do!" But words that should have been spoken never were, and eventually the chance to say them seemed to have passed. She appreciated Mr. Rochester's loving and gentle relationship with her children, appreciated as well that he had been the only grandfather they had known, and tried not to dwell on what he had never been to her.

I should have told him I love him, and now it is too late.

It occurred to her now that she no longer had to worry under his judgmental gaze, and it was that thought that left her weeping as she sat with Edward Rochester's children at Thornfield.

The following day Elizabeth arrived at Thornfield, and the family sat around the dining room table, speaking of the funeral plans over a mid-day meal. Ned was silent and serious, the women occasionally tearful. Helen talked at length, for when she was silent, she invariably cried.

"I wanted to come to Thornfield for a visit last week, but Rodney was so eager to try out our new hunters. We'd had them shipped from Ireland and they had just arrived. I let him persuade me to go to Ferndean instead... " she trailed off, looking out the dining room window, her lips quivering in an effort to control her emotions.

Elizabeth was amused in spite of herself. Helen, the beauty of the Rochester family, was still the tomboyish hoyden she had always been. With her pale skin, delicate features, flashing green eyes, and the elegant upsweep of her black hair, she looked as though she should be presiding over a grand drawing room. No one would guess that the lovely wife of Sir Rodney Davies-Lamb could out-ride and out-shoot any man in these parts save Sir Rodney himself.

"Will your husband be able to be here for the funeral?" Adèle asked her.

"I hope so," Helen dabbed at her eyes with her lace handkerchief. "I sent a telegram to him at our home in London. He had planned to bring some friends and join me at Ferndean later this week. He will have to see to our guests and then come to Thornfield afterwards."

In less than a year of marriage, the Davies-Lambs had turned Ferndean from a rather run-down old estate to a veritable hunter's paradise. Thomas had jested that he feared to attend one of the many huge parties at Ferndean for fear someone would set the hounds upon him.

Adèle reached for Helen's hand, "I am sorry, Helen, that you have lost both parents now, in such a short time." She looked around the table. "I'm sorry for you all. "

Helen smiled weakly and squeezed Adèle's hand in return. "Thank you, Adèle. Papa seemed so well, but I know he would not have been happy without Mama, and now they are together once more. That is a great comfort to me." Ned and Elizabeth nodded in agreement.

And they sat in silence, each lost in thought.

It was a small and solemn family group that stood around the grave site in the Rochester burial ground three days later. Adèle stood alone, a little apart, one hand resting on the shoulder of each of her twin boys. They had not sent for Tom or Emma, who had just been to Thornfield the month before to attend the funeral of Jane Rochester.

Ned stood with Mary and their three solemn children. Helen stood next to them, her black-gloved hand on her husband's arm. Elizabeth stood nearby, feeling as alone as she had ever felt. She was acutely aware of Ephraim Carter standing a few rows back, and she'd made sure she had caught his eye. He had smiled at her, and she wondered now how she could ever have missed the light on his face when he looked at her. God willing, she would not miss the chance to speak to him soon.

The beautiful day belied the sorrow of the occasion.

Because Edward Rochester had only marginally joined the members of the gentry upon his return to Thornfield, Ned had not expected a large crowd to gather for the burial service. Yet a goodly number of people had gathered outside the fence around the family area, having come to pay their respects to the long-time master of Thornfield. Townspeople, the tenants who had appreciated their fair and generous landlord, past and present servants. Even Mrs. Carter, widow of Rochester's doctor, stood at the front of the crowd, clutching the arm of Dr. John, her eldest, as Andrew and Ephraim Carter stood nearby.

"...In the midst of life we are in death..."

Ned Rochester watched the casket as it was gently lowered into the grave. He felt once again the air of unreality. He could scarcely believe his father was gone, that vital man whom he had loved and admired so much. He could not fathom that he was now the owner of Thornfield and Ferndean, the landlord of all these tenants. He had assisted his father for years; had all but run the family concerns as his father was occupied with his mother's illness. But as he stood there clutching his wife's hand, he did not feel equal to the task.

"I am also Edward Rochester," he thought to himself, "but I am not the man my father was."

He thought back to his mother's burial service. They had left the church, walking behind the casket to the graveyard, his father's arm through his. Edward had always seemed so powerful, despite his seventy-one years – still erect and strong, his white hair only adding to his air of authority. But he thought of how his father's body had trembled as his mother's casket was lowered into the ground, how he had pressed his hand to his heart and moaned softly as the dirt was shoveled into the grave. Ned had looked at him in alarm, had seen his father shake his head and gesture for him not to be worried. He thought of the long talks they had shared this last month, and he realized anew the source of Edward Rochester's strength for all these years.

"...Lord, have mercy on us..."

Ned looked around at the stones and vaults in the cemetery. His mother's grave with its brand new stone reading:

Jane Eyre Rochester

Beloved Wife

Loving Mother

1817-1870

Nearby was a stone honouring his lost infant brother, whose body really lay in a Catholic cemetery in the south of France.

There were the graves of the grandparents he had never known, John Rochester and Elizabeth Fairfax – they were just names on stone. Similarly, his uncle Rowland, and all the previous Rochesters, clear back to Damer de Rochester and his wife in their secure marble vault. So many Elizabeths in this graveyard. If the child his wife carried was a girl, they had planned to name her Jane Elizabeth after his mother and sister.

He remembered too the grave his father had shown him, in a far corner of the burial ground. The simple stone – "Bertha Antoinetta Mason Rochester, 1794-1836" – and the astounding story his father had told him. He had seen the stone as a boy, when he'd explored the graveyard with the avid curiosity about death that any child has. But something had always prevented his asking. Now he knew the story, and yet another mystery of his father's past was made clear.

His father had stood for a long time, looking at Bertha's grave stone after he had finished telling Ned of his insane first wife. Then he had spoken in a low, defeated voice. "For so long I wished to be made a widower. Now I must pay the price for wishing a wife dead. God finally released me from my wretched vows, but has decreed that I must be separated from my darling Jane as well. Always, He has tempered His judgment with mercy, but the judgment still remains." He looked over at Jane's resting place, the earth so newly in place, the grave stone not yet laid. "Forgive me, my beloved."

Protests rose to Ned's lips, but died away. His father would not believe him. He would never cease to believe he still paid for his long-ago sins.

"...Christ have mercy on us..."

Helen looked down at the grave as the workers began to shovel the dirt over the casket. Her vision was blurred from tears and by the black veil over her face. "Papa, you are truly gone from me now," she thought, "and Mama too." She had spent her whole life chafing at any restrictions upon her, wanting to grow up, and now, she thought, I have to. She had never realized that the very boundaries she fought against were her safe haven; that she had been able to fight because of the love and security her parents had always provided for her. Now, despite her husband's presence, she had never felt so lonely.

Elizabeth, too, felt the tears well in her eyes and spill over onto her cheeks. She wiped her eyes with the small lace handkerchief she clutched in her black-gloved hand.

"Papa, I loved you so," she thought. "I never saw enough of you and of Mama for all these years. I know I had to live my life, but how will I ever forgive myself for being away from you both for so long?"

Adèle bent her head and let her tears fall on the grass as she said good-bye to the only father she had ever known. Her time at Thornfield was truly over now. She loved Ned and Helen and Elizabeth, but her future lay with her own family now, not with this one, where she had never been a part, not in reality.

The next day, Ned walked down the road, arm in arm with Helen. He had asked her to accompany him on a walk so that he could speak privately with her, and they strolled in companionable silence for a while. Neither of them was able to find Elizabeth, who had inexplicably disappeared, saying only that she had someone to see.

"Well, I shall speak to her when she returns," Ned said. "If I'm any judge of people at all, I can guess where she has gone."

Ned turned to Helen.

"It seems strange to see you walk on two legs!" he said teasingly. "I'm so used to seeing you with four extra legs beneath you."

"Perhaps we should be riding today," she teased in return. "It's the one place I know I can get the better of you."

"Don't be too sure of yourself, Lady Whatever-you-are now," Ned told her. "My riding grows more accomplished every day."

Helen gave a yelp of laughter, "I can trounce you any day of the week, Edward Rochester, and don't forget it!" For a moment they were both silent, as the name "Edward Rochester" hung in the air, making them think of their father, the first man to bear the name that his son and grandson now carried.

Ned reached over and gave her hair a yank, just as he had when she was younger. "Yes, I have to admit defeat when it comes to any riding, shooting or hunting in which you are involved."

They laughed easily together, then he gave her hand a squeeze. "I asked you out here, away from listening ears. I have something of great importance to discuss with you. The solicitor will be here from Millcote this afternoon, and we have something unexpected to settle."

He sighed, then went on, "I told all of you that Father died easily in his own bed, in his sleep, but that was not quite the truth. Father and I had taken many walks this past month, and he talked to me a great deal – about his youth, his travels, and his life before Mother. It was incredible, and I will share it all with you as you desire. But I had the impression, from his manner of speaking, that he felt the end of his life was near.

"Occasionally I would come upon him to find him sitting with his hand over his heart, and a look of pain on his face. I urged him to have the doctor summoned, but he dismissed my concerns."

He continued, "I awakened quite early the morning he died, with a feeling that something was amiss. I got up and looked for him. It was still dark outside. I searched his room, the dressing rooms, all through the house, and found no trace of him. Then I went outside. I felt I knew where he would be, and he was. He was lying on Mother's grave. He had cut some roses from the hothouse, as he often had when she was alive, and had placed them near her stone. It appeared he had just lain down there, perhaps as his final pain and weakness came upon him. He looked very peaceful, very content. I knew at once he was dead. I called Simon, and he and I moved him back to his bed."

"And no one else knows that I found something, sitting on his bedstand." Ned reached into his coat pocket and withdrew a white envelope. Helen could see writing on the outside but could not make it out.

"He had written this himself," Ned said, his voice thick with emotion. "It's a new will, and a letter explaining it. His writing is hard to read, but he made his wishes known. But ultimately he left it up to us. I feel honour-bound to abide by his wishes, but it does not just affect me – it concerns you and Elizabeth too. If you do not agree, I will throw this into the fire and we will never speak of it again."

He reached out and placed the envelope into her hand, "Read it and tell me what you think."

He turned away from her, and looked out at the vast expanse of rolling lawn around the house. "You know, we are fortunate to have received a legacy, and a secure future, but our legacy is more than just money and property."

He went on at her puzzled look, "When I was away at school we read all the great literature. I read the stories of all the great lovers – Tristan and Isolde, Heloise and Abelard, Romeo and Juliet. But from the time I was a child, I saw the way our parents looked at each other. As I grew older, I vowed I would not marry until I had what they had."

"And have you?" Helen asked frankly. It seemed a time to talk plainly.

He smiled, "I'm older now, and wiser. I know very few couples have what Mother and Father had. They were one soul. Mary is a good woman, and will get better. I will get better too. I will always love her, always be a faithful husband, as Father was. But what Edward and Jane Rochester had..." He shook his head, thinking of them. "I wish the whole world could read about our parents. Theirs is the real love story. It takes very little to die together. It takes much to live together."

Helen impulsively hugged her brother. His tender heart had always amazed her. "Does Mary know you have such a romantic bent?"

He laughed. "No, and I would appreciate it if you don't tell her. She may expect demonstrations of it every day. Read what Father has written, and tell me your wishes on the matter." He kissed her forehead, pushed her shoulder teasingly, and walked away, leaving her looking at the envelope in her hand. On the outside, in her father's sprawling handwriting, were written the words, *My Jane, I do this because you wished it.* Puzzled, she opened the envelope and began to read.

Miles away, in Millcote, Elizabeth stood outside the Carter brothers' surgery, gathering her thoughts and marshalling her courage. She looked for a long time at the names of the brothers on the sign, before she walked up to the door and prepared to knock. As she raised her hand to tap on the door, the door was opened from the inside, and Ephraim stood there.

He was in his shirtsleeves, his eyes tired-looking and bloodshot. Elizabeth stood with her hand raised, before she slowly lowered it.

Ephraim spoke first, "I've been walking the floor since I came home from the cemetery yesterday, trying to work up the nerve to intrude on your family's grief by going to speak to you. I vowed I would not let the opportunity go this time, would not let convention interfere with my speaking my mind. If you knew how many letters I started to you this past month, how many times I was tempted to get on the train and come to see you... "

"Well, now I have come to see you," Elizabeth said, talking past the lump in her throat.

"Miss Rochester... Elizabeth." Carter took a deep breath.

Elizabeth stared into his eyes, and he looked steadily back at her.

"Please don't go back to London," he asked her.

She shook her head, whispering, "I have no plans to," and stepped forward. Carter met her in the doorway, and then they were in each other's arms.

"I love you so, my darling Elizabeth," Ephraim whispered. "You must marry me, you know. Your mother wished for it."

"My mother!" Elizabeth exclaimed, drawing back to look at Ephraim. "She never said anything to me about it."

"No," Ephraim said. "She told me to tell you, and like an idiot, I waited, not wanting to intrude upon your grief. But now I am intruding, and I'm telling you that if I do not have you, I cannot stand my life. You must ease my suffering." They laughed together.

"Well, all right," Elizabeth said, smiling, as she stepped back into his arms. "But only because I'm a nurse, and that is my job, to ease the suffering of others." They clung to each other, tears and laughter mingling together.

That afternoon, a small group gathered in the Thornfield Manor library as the solicitor prepared to read the will left by Edward Rochester. They had requested Adèle's presence, and she sat at the table, wishing she did not have to be a part of this. The solicitor read through the terms, explaining its content, reporting gifts and bequests to some of the servants, then he began to list the assets now owned by Ned Rochester and his sisters.

As expected, Ned was now the owner of Thornfield and of Ferndean, with provision made for both sisters to use Ferndean as a holiday home as long as it was agreeable to Ned. The villa in France had been sold a few years after Adèle and Thomas had honeymooned there, as the family found it inconvenient to travel that far.

Elizabeth and Helen were each left an annual percentage of the profits from the estates, from the money of Jane's that still remained, and from Edward Rochester's many investments. The amounts were not large but would furnish each sister with a comfortable if not lavish income each year.

It was all routine and expected, until the solicitor read the last item.

" ...and a percentage equal to that of my younger daughters, from the profits of the estates of Thornfield and Ferndean, and from my investments, for the rest of her natural life, to Adèle Varens Rochester Cooper, my eldest daughter."

The End

Author's Note

This book has been a long time in the making. I did not read *Jane Eyre* until well into my adulthood and once I did I was captivated. Over time and with repeated re-readings of the book, I grew fascinated with the main male character, Edward Rochester – I wanted to know all about him. I watched the various filmed adaptations; it didn't take me long to realize that Edward Rochester as played by an actor is not exactly the Rochester of the book. And while I feel that each actor who has performed the role has captured at least some facets of Rochester's personality, it was the Edward Rochester of the book who fascinated me. Can one have a crush on a literary character? If one can, I did.

I've always written stories for myself, and so I began to write about Edward Rochester. There were many questions in my mind, and in my writing I could work out the answers. I wondered how I could reconcile the things I liked about Rochester (his passion, his deep capacity for love, his humor, his intelligence) with the things one naturally dislikes about him (his deceptions, his self-absorption, his pride). This book is my attempt at that reconciliation.

Within *Jane Eyre*, in the details of the story, myriad unanswered questions are lurking. Thus my interest extended to some other characters connected to Rochester in the story – for instance, Grace Poole. She is portrayed in some of the adaptations as an older woman, not too much younger than Mrs. Fairfax is. But Charlotte Brontë wrote Grace Poole as a contemporary of Mr. Rochester. Jane Eyre, despite seeming to be one of the most sheltered young women in literary fiction, nevertheless ruminates about Grace Poole in one of Brontë's chapters – and makes some rather frank assumptions regarding the possible nature of the relationship between Grace and her employer. Grace is extremely loyal to Rochester, and although she is said to like money, it seems to me that something more than money underlies her willingness to work at such a difficult job and to keep Rochester's secret for over ten years – therefore I decided on the possibility of a different and more tender tie between the two of them.

Another fascinating character is Adèle Varens, the very catalyst for the meeting of Edward and Jane. Why did Rochester bring Adèle to Thornfield when he apparently didn't find her an easy child to love? Obviously, Charlotte Brontë had to get Jane Eyre to Thornfield somehow, but I wanted to understand the "why?" of it, and by exploring Rochester's earlier life in my own writing, I could address that question.

I could have done nothing with this character unless Charlotte Brontë had created him, and I freely acknowledge that I owe every bit of what I have written to her. Brontë surely would not have imagined a 21st-century woman making a hobby of creating a backstory for one of her characters. I hope she would accept this effort for what it is: a tribute to the genius that could create a male character who has captivated women for over 150 years.

Tara Bradley
January 2011

Acknowledgements

In addition to the huge debt I owe to Charlotte Brontë for all the enjoyment I have gotten from her book, and the pleasure of writing my own because of loving hers, I must acknowledge what others have done for me.

My father, for his great love of books.

My mother, for her great love of me.

My husband and my children – you are my reasons for everything.

Along with giving the world the book that has become my favorite classic novel, Charlotte Brontë indirectly led me to many other people I would never have known otherwise, and I would like to dedicate this book to them:

In 1999, while looking for literary criticism and articles about *Jane Eyre*, I went searching the Internet. I found an online Brontë discussion group and began a casual relationship with some of the most gifted and intelligent people I'd never actually met. In 2000, I struck up a friendship with one of them, a woman from the Netherlands about my age, and with a similar sense of humor, God help her. In more than ten years' worth of emails about not only the Brontës, but also about family, work, and everything else, she has become one of my dearest friends. We have taken a Brontë-related tour in England; I have visited her family, she has visited mine, and I can't imagine my life without her. Had I never read *Jane Eyre*, I would never have met her, and so would not only have missed a wonderful novel but a wonderful friend. Monika, thank you for your friendship.

In the course of writing *Jane Eyre's Husband*, I shared my fledgling scribblings with some like-minded *Jane Eyre* fans. Afterward, I got an email from someone who basically said, "Hey, great writing, but could you break up your paragraphs a little?" I'd been writing and re-writing this for so long that I couldn't see the forest for the trees. The woman who sent me that email has become a combination editor and encourager. Further, she and her husband have provided ongoing advice and help with the technical issues involved in the world of electronic publishing. Deep in my heart, I'm a writer who could conceivably write an entire book longhand, using only a pencil and an old notebook. Sarah and Albert, I'm not sure I could have done this without you. With all my heart, I thank you.

I shared my initial manuscript on an Invision site writing forum, and would like to thank the many wonderful readers there who took their time to go over what I had written and offer their opinions, their criticisms, and their wonderful encouragements. I would like to list you all, but know I would miss someone. I'd especially like to thank Cynthia, who was the first to call my attention to Kindle publishing. Thanks to all of you who cheered me on.

And to you, Reader, I thank you for the time you put into reading this book.

Tara Bradley
January 2011

3319995R00284

Printed in Great Britain
by Amazon.co.uk, Ltd.,
Marston Gate.